DARE

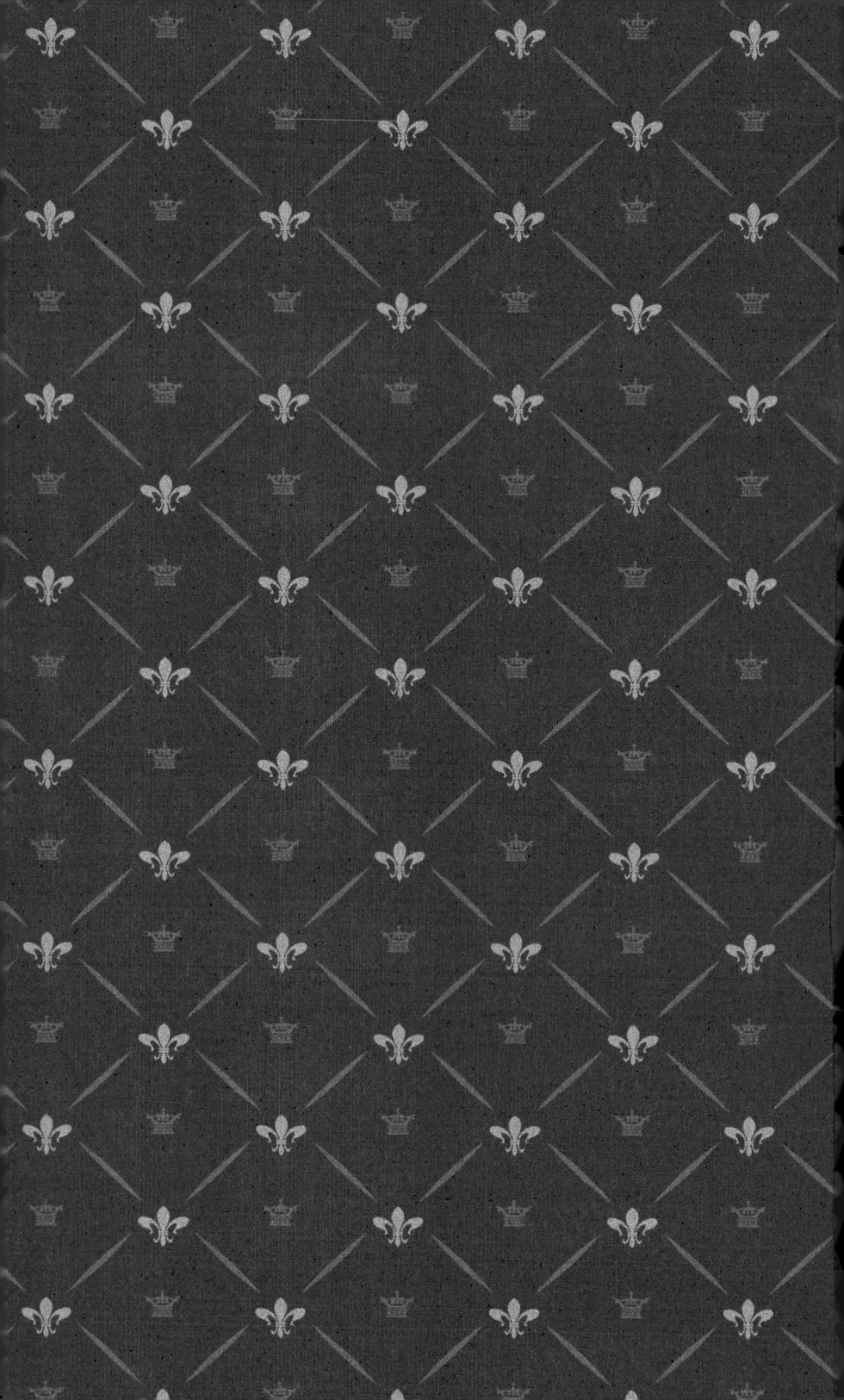

FOOLISH KINGDOMS
DARK SEASONS WORLD
4

NATALIA JASTER

Books by Natalia Jaster

FOOLISH KINGDOMS SERIES
Trick (Book 1)
Ruin (Book 2)
Burn (Book 3)
Dare (Book 4)
Lie (Book 5)
Dream (Book 6)

SELFISH MYTHS SERIES
Touch (Book 1)
Torn (Book 2)
Tempt (Book 3)
Transcend (Book 4)

VICIOUS FAERIES SERIES
Kiss the Fae (Book 1)
Hunt the Fae (Book 2)
Curse the Fae (Book 3)
Defy the Fae (Book 4)

Second edition copyright 2024 Natalia Jaster
First edition copyright 2017 Natalia Jaster

All rights reserved
ISBN: 978-1-957824-10-9

Cover design by AC Graphics
Chapter headings & scene breaks by Noverantale
Jeryn character art by Mageonduty
Jeryn & Flare character art by Covers by Juan
Typesetting by Roman Jaster
Body text set in Filosofia by Zuzana Licko

Content and trigger warnings can be found at nataliajaster.com/dare

This is a work of fiction. Names, characters, places, and incidents either are the product of the author's imagination or are used fictitiously, and any resemblance to any actual persons, living or dead, events, or locales is entirely coincidental.

This book may not be reproduced, scanned, or distributed in any form, or by any means, without written permission from the author.

For the ones who like their villains cold as ice.
Jeryn won't apologize for what's about to happen.
I *dare* you not to love him anyway.

You are everything I want and nothing I deserve.

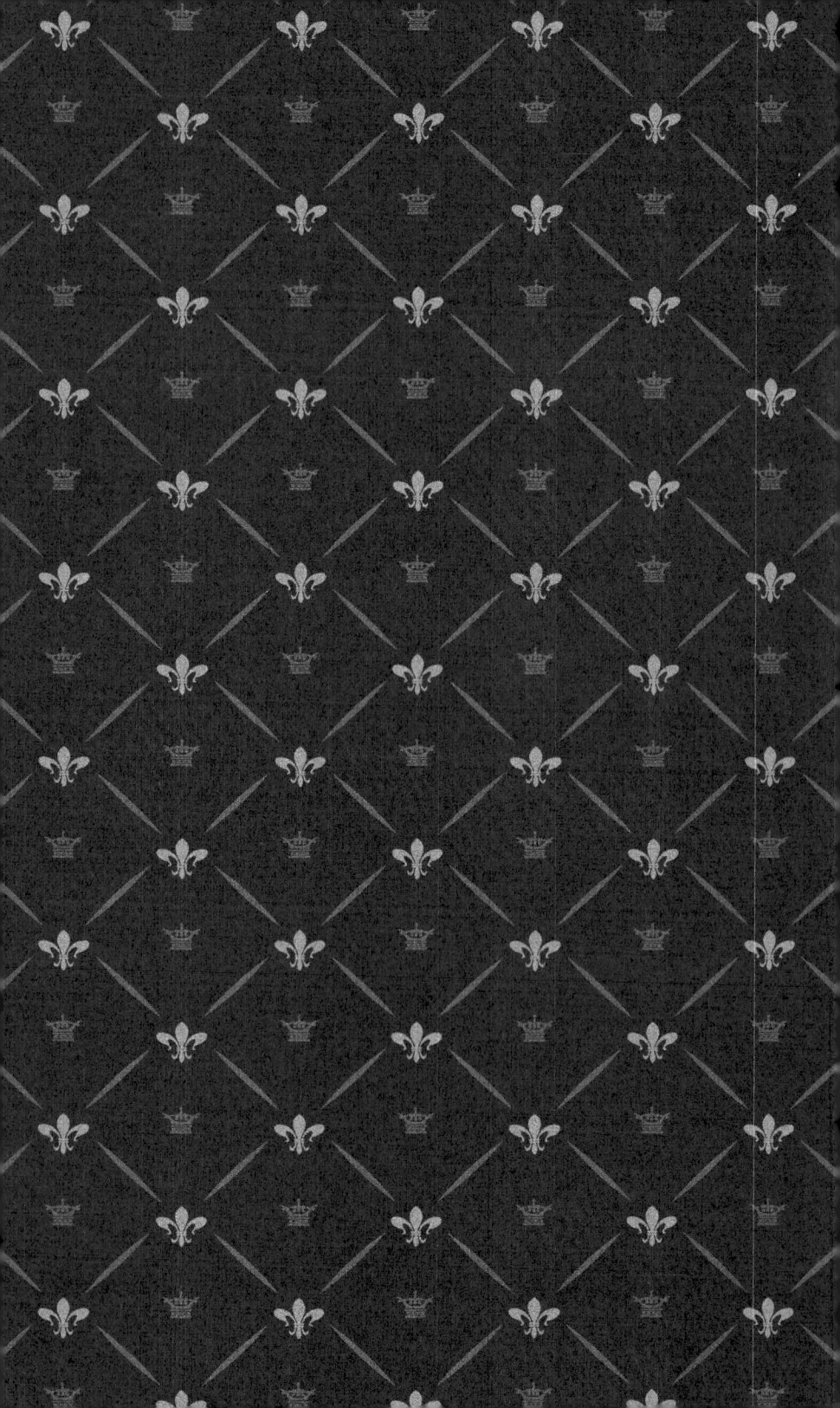

I

Flare

Kingdom of Autumn. On the night of the Reaper's Fest riot.

In most stories, the villain wore a black cloak and lived in the shadows like a ghost. But in my story, the villain wore a crown and ruled the world.

Tucked behind an overturned wagon sizzling with smoke, I grasped the wheel and peeked into the market square, my gaze searching for him. Yet blessedly, the enemy was nowhere in sight amid the chaos.

Pitched roofs crackled with flames, the blazes chewing on merchant shops, forges and smithies, and homes decorated with glowing pumpkins. Scattered amidst the cobbled streets, bonfires spat embers, which danced like fireflies across an eventide sky.

Tonight, the Autumn Court burned. Its annual revels had turned into a nightmare, a riot of blood and rage in what used to be the most peaceful of kingdoms. The people had lashed out, turning against one another—because of people like me.

Because they called us fools. Because they wanted to keep us as their property, their entertainment, and their slaves. Because this world hated our kind. Because they believed us to be cursed errors of nature. Most thought so, but not all. Some defended us.

I riveted my gaze on two figures rising from the ashes like phoenixes. The woman's red locks shone brighter than an inferno, with a rose planted in her hair and her singed black dress fluttering in the wind. Beside her stood a man with the greenest eyes I'd ever beheld, the wicked irises as verdant as clovers. The jester's pupils darkened with intent, protectiveness and fury flashing in those kohl-lined eyes.

Poet. Briar.

Jester. Princess.

Together, the continent's most notorious pair strode from the largest bonfire. As one, they stepped from the womb of a blaze that had been constructed to roast the princess alive, in protest of her compassion for born souls, her crusade for their freedom, and her love for the man beside her. But like an indestructible force, the couple materialized, untouched by the flames.

Gasps erupted from the crowd, and the same awed breath fell from my lips. My voice had died long ago, but while I couldn't speak, I had the enchanting ability to hear myself privately. In my mind, every sound and tone of voice—a whisper, a scream, a laugh, a growl, a sigh—resounded clearly, as if they came out aloud. Somehow, it had always been this way.

Though, no one else could hear these noises. I didn't know why. But at least, that would make it easier to flee, to escape before someone caught me.

Hidden from view, I watched the princess and jester make history. Surrounded by bruised nobles, battered tradesfolk, and bloody soldiers, Poet and Briar knelt. They spoke to the crowd, inspiring their rapt audience to bow in remorse and chant in reverence. And so, the duo won back their nation.

That was also how they toppled a king. I watched that too. Saw Poet run his knife across Rhys's body, saw Briar restrain her lover, saw them force the fiendish king to his knees, and saw them shackle him to the same timbers where Briar had been ensnared. They didn't burn the

Summer King, but they did break him.

At the sight of his humiliation, a stone's weight dropped from my chest. Nine years of sorrow and fear buckled my limbs. Finally, that monarch learned how it felt to be scorned, to be treated like he was worthless.

To be treated like me.

My fingers traced the collar tattoo branded around my neck. I tilted my head, marveling at the scene, at the rioters who joined the jester and princess, everyone uniting to staunch the flames and sweep up the debris. The Royals of Spring, the Queen of Summer, and the reigning pair of Autumn worked among their subjects.

But one Season was missing.

Dread chilled my stomach. I scanned the crowd for a towering masculine frame outfitted in a fur coat and steel-tipped boots. It would be easy to spot his long, cold blue hair and those glacial irises. Yet I failed to locate that murky silhouette.

He would be looking for me. If not now, then soon. But if he knew I was here, I didn't feel it. My skin would have prickled the moment his eyes seized on me. It happened every time, like an ominous sixth sense.

Three ladies rushed to the princess's side, snatching her in a hug while tears sprang to their eyes. Next, a man with blond stubble hauled Briar against his broad frame. After that, a knight with eyes the shade of a twilit sky embraced her, then clasped Poet's hand in a gesture of relief. As one, the group formed a circle and crushed themselves together.

My heart squeezed, longing swelled in my throat, and a hundred wishes flooded my soul. How I wished to be a member of their clan, to be a part of their mission, to be one of them, to be included. To have that same freedom.

Their fight was my fight, but my fate wasn't their fate. I'd have to carve a path forward on my own. And I would have to do it now, far from here.

If not, *he* would find me.

Beyond the town, Autumn's castle rose like a snuffed candle. Among soaring maple trees, the fortress's unlit windows reflected the constellations. An hour ago, I'd been locked in there, trapped in a cage and awaiting a gruesome fate. Now I stood on the threshold of escape. Yet I could not move, would not move.

Poet and Briar had saved me from that cage. So even after they'd let me go, even after we had parted ways, I'd stayed behind to untie Briar from the bonfire, to rescue her the way she'd rescued me, to make sure she and Poet were safe.

The jester and princess grabbed one another. Their arms entwined, their gazes fused, and their mouths collided in a feverish kiss.

My lips curved into a smile. Finally, it was time to save myself.

I gazed at the pair through watery eyes. "Friends," I whispered, the word as light as a feather.

My friends. Someday, I would see them again.

Creeping from my hiding spot, I darted into the shadows. My bare feet slapped the cobblestones, skirting around toasted chunks of wood, smoldering ale barrels, and chips of broken glass. I sprinted faster, heeding Briar's urgent words.

He will find you.
If you stay, he will find you.

The Summer King wasn't the monarch I needed to worry about. He wasn't the ruler I needed to flee from. He wasn't the enemy I needed to fear.

Not anymore. Because he wasn't the predator hunting for me.

Dashing around market stalls, I swiped an apple and a blackened loaf of bread from the ground. Rounding a corner, I skidded in place, my gaze tripping across a shop window. Golden eyes shone in its reflection, and a picture of shocked features gazed back. Sweat and soot coated the woman's deep olive face, starvation hollowed her cheeks, and dryness chapped her lips as if they were made of bark.

Me. That was me.

My shaky fingers traced every facet. I hadn't seen my reflection in nine years. Banked in the firelight, the vision knocked me off balance. A bereft cry slipped across my tongue, as raw as a wound, the noise inaudible to anyone else but me.

Next, my gaze stumbled to the neck tattoo. The collar of black sunbursts wrapped around my throat, the ink permanent and the punishment eternal.

Outrage sparked like cinders across my fingers. The fragile noise I had unleashed now hardened into a growl.

No one owned me. Especially not *him*.

I veered from my reflection and bolted out of town. Whereas pacing from one end of a space to the other had become second nature, moving this far without hitting a barrier—no jail bars or four solid walls to block my progress—felt like walking toward the edge of the world. Soon, I might fall off.

I might, were it not for Briar's directions. Her voice played in my head, propelling me forward.

Take the adjacent alley until you reach the beech forest, then head northwest. Eventually, you'll reach a creek. It will split into four directions and take you wherever on the continent you wish to go.

The dagger Poet had given me thumped against my waist, its fancy hilt tethered with a length of rope. I would find a sheath later. But for now, the cord would hold. My callused fingers knew plenty about tying hearty knots, and flames had never scared me, which was why I'd been able to release the princess from the blaze. With Summer flowing through my blood, I could handle fire.

Ice was a different matter. A different monster.

Run, I told myself. Fast, I urged myself.

Never look back.

Briar's whisper swept through my mind as I vaulted from the lower town, then down the brick road between the harvest fields. With the castle suffering a blackout but the riot coming to an end, the night watch and parapet sentinels had resumed their posts. Nonetheless, my small frame helped to avoid detection. And blessedly, I had grown used to the darkness long ago. Living in a dungeon had gifted my sight with a nocturnal sharpness, like a sea creature at the bottom of an abyss.

Pumping my arms and legs, I sprinted up the hill and into a woodland laced with gilded leaves. I smashed through the bushes, threads of air sawing through my lungs, my side wincing in pain.

Amid the exposed roots of a tree trunk, I hunkered to the ground and sucked in blasts of oxygen. Dirt caked my feet, and one of my ankles leaked crimson from a tumbleweed that had scraped my flesh. My chest heaved as I waited for the stitches to ebb.

Once they did, I fished out the apple and bread loaf, the succulent aromas weakening my knees. My teeth ripped into the booty, the sweet and yeasty flavors overpowering my senses. Poet and Briar had fed me well, but still. The hunger never waned.

Juice from the apple wetted my tongue. The taste wrought a grateful sob from me, and I gobbled those treasures to the last bite. With a sigh, I wiped my arm across my mouth and dragged myself off the ground.

The hectic flight from the castle with Poet and Briar had distracted me. Then the lower town's riot overwhelmed me. But with no one around, I stumbled forward in a daze. Craning my head, I blinked—and saw the sky.

So much sky. Beyond the branches, a crescent moon slashed through the heavens like a scythe, its brightness hurting my eyes, agonizing yet blissful. Celestials sparkled like divinities, their brilliance another shock to my vision. It had been eons since I'd seen the firmament this way; I feared it might be a mirage or a cruel trick of light.

Ravenous to see color, color, color, I stretched my trembling arm toward the mural of stars, my quaking fingers sketching them like one of my drawings. My chin wobbled, my lips peeled back into a grin, and two droplets leaked from the corners of my eyes.

Beneath the constellations, tree silhouettes reminded me of …

They looked so much like …

A place I'd never been. A place I longed to find someday. A place out there, waiting for me.

An icy breeze cut short my joy. I lowered my hand and rubbed my arms while contemplating the journey ahead. My moth-eaten shirt and grain-sack hose cut off at the thighs did little to combat the chill. Hellfire, I should have stolen a cloak and looted the cobbler's shop on my way from town.

Strange fragrances wafted from the soil. The earthen aromas smelled nothing like Summer, where one could taste salt in the air. Foreign sounds pushed through the foliage. Hoots. Snorts. My gaze leaped around, unable to soak up a single noise for too long. I twisted toward every crunch of dry leaves and each fauna call, whirling this way and that while grasping Poet's dagger. Half-fearful, half-enchanted, I consumed this world with famished eyes.

Briar had said to go northwest. Gauging this without a compass might be rough for some fugitives, but once upon a time, I'd led a seafaring life. At least, until the monarchy had chained me.

Pretending to stand on the deck of a boat, I contemplated the stars' locations, then forged ahead. Seconds passed. Countless minutes passed. I alternated between jogging and picking around uneven terrain, my unshod toes freezing. At last, a babble of water flowed through my ears. I hastened toward the sound, clouds of air steaming from my lips.

The creek Briar had mentioned snaked through the undergrowth, flowing between toadstools and hedges. My steps slowed. As trenches of glistening water split into four directions, I understood what she meant. This intersection must lead to each Season, which explained why one of the rivulets trickled back the way I'd come. As for the other three ...

Spring. Summer. Winter.

I grimaced. Anything was better than Winter. Imprisoned or not, everyone knew the gruesome things scientists did to born souls there.

The gruesome things *he* did to them.

Leaves the color of brass gleamed. Some rained from the branches and bobbed on the creek's surface like a fleet of ships. My gaze landed in one direction, the flux pouring toward freedom. With hope fluttering its wings inside me, I moved toward my path.

Then I stalled. The nape of my neck heated like a bad omen. And then came the telltale prickle across my scalp.

I knew one other thing about the darkness. I knew when someone else occupied it. And now I understood why I hadn't seen him among the other Royals.

He'd already been searching for me.

My lashes lowered. I skated my gaze across the undergrowth, where a spider wove its net through a bramble. Feigning preoccupation with the creature, I strolled forward—then whirled with my dagger braced.

On a growl, I twisted his way. At the same time, his hand snatched my hip like an iron band and hauled me forward. My breasts slammed into a male torso hewn from stone, my blade's tip thrust in his direction, and his own knife sliced forward, our weapons stabbing the air between us. Like that, we froze.

And then my eyes collided with a pair of icy irises.

Flare

Cold. So cold.

The mercenary chill stung my veins as I peered into those vicious eyes. Streaks of blue lined his lower lashes like frost, territorial hatred sharpening his orbs. That, and repugnance.

His mythical height and muscled body dwarfed my own. Velvet pants encased his towering limbs, and an ebony coat accentuated his frame, the garment trimmed in fur.

Like the first time I beheld him, I didn't need an introduction. This man wore his Season as clearly as his title.

Prince of Winter.

My enemy. The monster who'd stalked into the dungeon a week ago and haunted my every waking hour since.

His skin was a deadpan pale, contrasted by a set of raven black brows and slate blue hair tied at the nape of his neck. And that brutal face. Hellfire, the severe angles could hone granite. The temperature of his gaze reached bone deep, draining the breath from my lungs.

"What have we here?" he murmured in a penetrating baritone. "A little beast set loose from its cage?"

The frigidness I felt seconds ago thawed. In its place, anger blazed across my skin.

I was no beast.

The edge of my weapon aimed at the tip of his own knife. Our exhales collided like fists. With my breasts mashed against the solid plate of his chest, it would be easy to stab him through the jugular, to silence him the way this continent had tried to silence me.

I put my whole body into motion. Jolting forward, I pitched the dagger at his throat.

The prince saw it coming. Dodging my attack with a calm twist of his head, he lifted one powerful arm and blocked the weapon, the muscled plank of his shoulder inflating like a mountain.

Good. I'd seen that countermove coming too. With his forearm staying the dagger's hilt, he'd been forced to release my waist. I swerved, spinning out of reach and thrusting my weapon again.

Once more, the prince reacted quickly. With a series of clicks, his knife's blade retracted into the hilt. At the same instant, a larger one appeared from a different slot, flicking open as mine struck, stopping the momentum.

I spied a collection of grooves in the prince's handle. It must contain more than one deadly option, allowing him to cherry pick between murder weapons.

We paused. The prince's irises glittered like crystals—bleak and numb and hiding nothing.

Yet his pupils were another story, the wells dark and fathomless. I focused there, searching for a chink. The instant my stare made those orbs twitch with suspicion, I flung myself at him.

Expression tapering, the prince met me halfway. Whereas battle training must occupy chunks of his spare time, I'd earned my fair share of skills. Captives didn't grow up in a prison supervised by baiting guards without learning how to defend themselves.

Our weapons clanged. I ducked and swung. He slipped out of reach, his movements akin to liquid metal, the steel toes of his boots flashing.

A twig cracked under my foot, pain shooting up my calf. As I stumbled, the prince seized the upper hand. Clamping his free palm around my nape, he wrenched me into his torso like a rag doll.

The impact knocked the wind from me. I wheezed as he fisted my hair, our mouths hovering inches from one another, my hot pants firing against his arctic breaths. The prince's fur collar bristled against the ledge of his jaw, and his gaze bore into mine with rancor.

At that moment, I guessed what he must see. An olive-skinned woman with a body thinner than fish bones, a jungle of shoulder-length waves, and sand clotting her fingernails. In his eyes, he saw a prisoner with a mind as frayed as the roughspun rags she wore.

This monster thought he saw a fool.

"If I were you," the villain prince cautioned, "I would not do that again."

Being pampered must be nice, to have such pearly teeth, to have those canines filed on a daily basis. Except I had canines too. Even better, the fur sleeve had slid up his forearm like an invitation. Veering my head sideways, I fastened onto his arm and bit. Blood squirted, the tang of him drizzling across my tongue.

With a growl, the prince released me. I bolted to the left, jetted across several leagues, then yelped when his arm slung around my waist. He spun me with such force that the beech trees whirled, the forest cycling in my vision.

My back hit one of the trunks as the prince rammed me into its surface, while vines dangled around us like dead serpents. He dug his fingers into my palm until my lips parted on a scream, the sound audible only to me, and the dagger toppled from my fingers. Jammed between the column and his heaving chest, I squirmed, my thighs splitting around his narrow waist, my bare flesh chafing against his hips.

"Much better," the prince rasped, the control in his voice slipping a notch. "Now then. Where are you headed in such a rush?" His eyes diced toward the four-way creek, then back to me. "Who told you about this crossing?"

Based on his caustic tone, the man had a hunch.

On instinct, my attention cut to Poet's dagger, abandoned in the grass. Following my gaze, the prince's chiseled profile examined the weapon's ornate handle, from its fine curve to the embedded scarlet gems.

Recognition darkened his pupils. "Those fucking anarchists."

Remorse boiled in my veins. He could retaliate against Poet and Briar for helping me. If something happened to them, I would never forgive myself.

No, I wouldn't let this fiend hurt them. Not my friends!

Taking advantage of his distraction, I used the only means of defense left. My right knee catapulted like a slingshot. I aimed where it hurt, hammering his Royal cock and nailing his balls so hard I hoped they got stuck up his asshole.

On a furious hiss, the prince buckled and dropped his weapon. I swiveled while grabbing one of the vines and ripping it from the branch. Barreling toward the creek, I splashed into the waterway, hightailing to the intersection.

A shout popped from my mouth as the prince snared my waist yet again and flipped me toward him. One hand trapped my lower half, and the other shackled my jaw, angling my gaze to his. Like this, he backed me through the water, his boots cleaving through the surface.

"Learn this lesson, fool," he said in a lethal timbre. "Winter does not take kindly to its possessions being tampered with."

An invasive scent emanated from his clothes, something masculine and crisp. In the V of his shirt, a fang-shaped glass vial swung from a low chain around his neck, the keepsake's surface cracked. I'd damaged that pendant by throwing it at the bars of my cage. That was how we met.

In the dungeon, I had guessed the talisman was special to him, if he kept it close to his frozen heart. I'd broken the trinket to hurt him, to destroy that precious item like he'd wanted to destroy my drawing. The one I'd sketched in a dirt pile of my cell, my only refuge from the nightmare of that place.

For my uprising, I had become his target. On that score, he must have caught sight of me after the riot ended. While everyone united to douse the flames and clean up the town, the prince must have seen me run.

"You have a debt to pay, Little Beast," he seethed, his lips in danger of scraping across mine.

My mouth sizzled. I owed nothing to this villain. If he thought I was some inanimate possession like that necklace, then fuck him to hell and back. It didn't matter that Queen Avalea had traded me in a bargain with Winter. She'd done it to save her poisoned daughter, because the prince was the only man who could heal Briar. But while I would have gladly offered myself, if it meant curing the princess, I belonged to no one. And I would never belong to him.

The prince halted, his voice narrowing, burrowing in. "Still no peep from you?" But when I refused to answer, he shook me by the jaw. "Speak."

Rage detonated inside me. I waited, my gaze incinerating him.

Realization struck, his eyebrows crimping. Because this man was renowned for being observant, something about my glower made it clear. I saw the moment when he grasped the truth about my voice.

That's when I moved. Although I grew up in a kingdom born of fire, I also knew a thing or two about water. Lastly, he'd forgotten about the vine clutched in my hand.

Coiling my leg around his, I jerked his massive frame off kilter and slipped from his arms. While I kept my balance, the prince didn't, his frame careening backward and crashing like a monolith into the creek. Moving swiftly, I snared the vine around his wrists and fastened him to a neighboring cluster of brambles.

While the prince growled and struggled with the bonds, I scrambled to Poet's dagger. Retrieving the weapon, I returned to the thrashing monster and swung one leg over his chest. Straddling the flat expanse of muscles, I watched hatred crease his features.

Even if I couldn't utter words, I still had a voice. This brutal prince had expected me to curl up like a seashell—silent and small and breakable. Except he'd forgotten that a seashell held the roar of an ocean inside it.

Temptation scorched my fingers. I tasted the glorious flavor of his blood on my tongue, from where I'd bitten him. I should kill this Royal, make him pay for what he'd done to everyone like me. I would but for one problem—the pounding of hooves from one of the main thoroughfares.

Stag hooves? Hadn't the prison guards said something about Winter traveling with such fauna?

Troops might be looking for him, or the interruption might be an ugly twist of fate. Either way, the prince and I traded one more violent gaze. A barely perceptible smirk tipped his lips sideways, and a promising gleam lit those irises. Whether I'd impressed or disgusted him, I couldn't say.

Yet why was he doing this? Why me?

The legion galloped nearer. I vaulted to my feet and skipped backward, struggling to pull my attention from the prince.

We glared and glared and glared. At last, I ripped myself from those probing eyes.

Sheathing the dagger, I raced from the scene, tearing through foliage and cursing myself for not stealing his coat and knife, if only to get warm, get better armed, and get the satisfaction of pissing him off further. Consequences be damned, a morbid part of me had liked riling that monster, seeing how far I could push him.

But no more. Trepidation licked a path up my skin, his spiteful gaze having assured me of one thing. I had sealed my fate. For whatever reason, the Prince of Winter wanted me. And he wouldn't stop looking.

Much later, I would double back and take the direction I'd chosen. Once he'd been fished from the water, cut from the bonds, and returned to Autumn's castle, I would venture back here and follow the creek. Then I would vanish, melting into a world he didn't know, could never know as well as I did.

No matter how long or far he searched, the villain prince wouldn't drag me anywhere with him. To prevent it, I would die fighting.

Even so, he'd have to catch me first.

3

Jeryn

I would catch her first. So help me.

Before she had the chance to savor her freedom, I would find her. Stalking into Autumn's castle, I cut a furious path down the wainscoted halls. Noble figures bowed and curtsied in my wake, a chorus of "Your Highness" and "Sire" swarming me from all directions. Ignoring them, I sliced my way through the masses.

I considered myself to be a patient fucking prince. Patient in the way of scientists and the slow drip of ice. The patience to test and the patience to unnerve.

But never before had my tolerance been pushed to the brink.

Fucking. Little. Beast.

The fur coat slapped my calves as I prowled toward Autumn's outmoded infirmary. Work. I needed to work. Best be quick about it before I did something rash like strangle a bystander. And I *never* did anything rash.

Our limited history had prepared me for a fight. What I hadn't expected was her stunt with that vine, nor for her to leave me soaking in an icy creek like fodder for the carnivores. I had nearly fractured my wrists trying to break free. At which point, the knights from my security detail had located me. As usual, my absence had been noticed.

My temple throbbed. She would not escape me a second time.

Nailing my features in place, I stepped into the infirmary. Courtiers, dignitaries, and commoners in various states of pain lay atop thin cots. Charred forearms. Blistered flesh. Gashes. Contusions. Stab wounds. So much for this kingdom's alleged pacifism. Dignity aside, if this nation had practiced a shred of indifference instead of leaning toward softer emotions—trifling inclinations such as tenderness—tonight's mayhem would not have transpired. The populace would have been equipped to control their disillusioned reactions once those limits had been compromised.

No matter their sovereign's transgressions, Winter would not have succumbed to pandemonium. I wouldn't have allowed it.

The castle blackout, then the subsequent riot instigated by Summer's tempestuous and bumbling excuse for a king, had left many wounded. Blood splattered the floor. A man wailed as a physician jiggled an arrow from his stomach. Were it not for this scene, I'd still be searching for that tiny fugitive.

When I got my hands on her, she would suffer. I would punish her slowly, thoroughly.

Images of mad fools howling from surgical tables occupied my head like a portfolio—an index of memories. Picking their fingernails out with tongs. Sawing off an ear. Testing droplets of an erosive liquid on their oculi and calibrating how long it took for the sockets to disintegrate. Painstaking experiments that had nonetheless yielded a stockpile of effective remedies.

She would know this anguish. In the near future, I would inflict my skills on her until she yielded. Until she became unequivocally mine.

When next we met, I would not hold back. No matter how brightly those combustible eyes glowed, no matter what volcanic expression she hurled my way, and no matter how her fucking body felt burning against mine. I would not succumb to her.

A cacophony of screams and moans engulfed the infirmary.

Shrugging off my coat, I tossed the vestment onto a stool, then rolled up my sleeves and washed my hands in a basin. Despite the numbers of patients hemorrhaging, I stalked toward a pallet where a boy whimpered under the ministrations of a healer.

Correction. An inexperienced practitioner, judging by his hesitant profile. And while patience was a strength, I drew the line at incompetence and indecision.

Approaching the juvenile's bedside, I tossed the novice an imperious look. "Move."

The man gulped, backing up as I assessed the boy's shoulder, the scalded flesh black and flaky. Expedient annoyance crept up my spine. I narrowed my eyes at the inferior idling next to me, my presence having drawn an audience of additional physicians. They had gathered to observe, to witness the genius Prince of Winter in his element.

My eyes tapered into shards. I swatted my chin toward the surplus of patients. "What the fuck are you waiting for?"

They blanched with shame, then scattered like vermin. Much better.

The boy wore the livery of a stablehand. He sobbed quietly as I knelt to inspect his arm. The sleeve would have to go, to reach the wounds adhering to the fabric. Inconveniently, this court lacked enough anesthesia to treat this number of people at once. Thus, critical procedures took priority.

I arched my gaze to the boy. "Are you brave?"

"I hope so," he sniveled.

Sufficient enough. I twisted and retrieved a pair of shears from an adjacent tray. "This will hurt," I informed him. "A lot."

The child nodded, sank his teeth into the branch I provided, and lifted his chin. As I cut into the fabric and pried it from the burns, his yellow irises gleamed in defiance of what had to be pure anguish. Fierce. Impressive. Like someone else I'd met.

A hiss pressed against my mouth. No more. She had caused me enough obsessive upheaval.

After finishing with the boy, I spent until dawn making the rounds.

One of the patients bucked and yowled as I carved through his calf. He took it worse than born souls did on my surgical table, though their mutilations were usually worse.

For fuck's sake. With exasperation flaring my nostrils, I waved a hand to an assistant. "Silence him."

After that, the wad stuffed in the patient's mouth made things easier. By morning, crimson stained my hands and soaked into my clothes.

On the way to my suite, two figures passed through a lower level. Halting at a mezzanine railing, I trained my gaze on the pair, their bodies magnetized to one another as they moved in the opposite direction below. Battered and exhausted, the man slid one possessive arm around his woman, tucking her into him.

Poet. Briar.

They did not speak yet somehow didn't need to. The jester and princess excelled in communicating with each other through mere looks, disguising their thoughts in a private manner no one could translate.

Clever. Irksome.

Not long ago, the Court Jester of Spring and Princess of Autumn had triggered a shitstorm by pledging themselves to one another. Poet had been Spring's secret weapon. With a silver tongue bred for dark ridicule and a face that would make a deity jealous, the jester had been the continent's most idolized and feared celebrity, not to mention its most desired fuck toy. Not only a performer, advisor, and whore, but an influential pain in the ass.

A treasonous one as well, with a simpleton son. Apparently, this hadn't mattered to Briar. She'd claimed the child as her own once she and Poet made their controversial affair known, then brought her new family to Autumn.

Following a succession of revels to celebrate Reaper's Fest, the insubordinate couple remained an enigma to me. I'd never understood the look between them at the public reading, nor the fervor of their dance during the night market. The intensity between them had nettled my thoughts, directing them each time to the little beast in her dungeon cell.

One level below. Alone. So fucking close.

Poet's pace slowed, his features narrowing in awareness. Devilish green irises lanced in my direction and darkened. Most victims would shrink to a pinprick from that dangerous look. They would quail while their cocks and cunts did the opposite, hardening like stone or puddling on the floor. The man knew how to target people, coerce his enemies, render them insignificant and powerless.

As did I.

Unfazed, I met his destructive glare with my own degree of contempt. Our ruse was over. The fake alliance we'd fabricated to thwart Rhys had ended. The Summer King's ruination had spared Autumn a war and Winter a headache.

Done. Finished.

Yet I had one breakable bone still to pick.

While stabbing his gaze my way, Poet tightened his hold on Briar. The fatigued princess leaned into him, unaware of the exchange. They kept going, heading to the Royal wing, likely to bathe and fuck their trauma away.

Happily ever after. Rubbish. Absurd. As if eternal bliss were truly possible.

The remaining days in Autumn came and went. The little beast had disappeared. I could not say what slithered under my skin more—that she had gotten away or escaped without a coat. Or at least a fucking pair of shoes. Madness. Foolishness. I could strangle her for both crimes.

Nonetheless, I suspected where she'd scurried off to. Her presence at the four-way creek implied only one path.

One Season.

Before leaving this formerly pious nation, I cloistered myself in a surgical room with Poet and Briar, then interrogated them while struggling to keep my voice even, to scale down the volume before it tore a hole through the castle. To that end, I omitted the episode in the forest, the better to purge information from them.

Poet and Briar had aided the beast's flight. That much had been clear when I'd registered the jester's embellished dagger in her possession. No one else had the nerve to carry a weapon that gaudy, the hilt ornamented with scarlet jewels. Not only reminiscent of the fucker's obscene wardrobe but his entire persona.

Yet. The infernal jester and princess refused to budge.

An hour later, I left Autumn with flurries racing through my bloodstream. So be it. As I'd warned them, I would hunt for the abominable beast myself. Though, logic told me this wouldn't be the last time I encountered Poet and Briar. Whatever that woman meant to them, the relentless couple planned to intercept, lest I should catch my prey.

Pity for them, they would not succeed.

I slipped into the black carriage harnessed by stags, their spiked antlers impaling the air. As the convoy sheared into motion, I reclined in my seat. Took a measured breath. Clamped my fingers around the vial hanging from my necklace. Gently, my thumb stroked the glass, a crack marring its surface.

Turbulent creature. Within seconds of our first encounter, she'd damaged the precious item. Within another second, all hell had broken loose inside me.

I should have walked away before then. I should not have stalled beside her cage, taken notice—recognized her.

We shared a history, however brief and indirect. This, she did not know.

Be that as it may, one detail didn't make sense. The woman lacked a voice, which I'd confirmed by questioning the dungeon guards, in case I had misinterpreted things in the forest. Yet I'd heard her scream. Moreover, she hadn't been mute years ago. So either I was missing a pertinent clue, or she was faking her condition.

Wheat and corn fields smothered the carriage windows. Along the forest thoroughfare, the pigmented colors of Autumn passed by in an overstimulating tableau of red and orange.

Also, gold. At the hue, my thoughts strayed to those inflammatory metallic eyes. With that exceptional hue burnishing her irises, she'd all but flung her emotions at me.

Such ferocity. So much heat.

I recalled the tattooed collar around her neck, which also hadn't been there years ago.

Who marked you?

Which peon had done that to her?

When I'd asked, the insufferable female had kept the answer to herself. From that point on, every decision I made had been linked to the fool. Isolating her in a separate cell. Searching for her in the castle during the blackout. Prowling after her when the riot had ended. Thinking about her each moment in between, tossing and turning in my sheets, festering and panting with aggravation.

Beneath my coat, red imprints encircled my wrists from where she'd tied me. A low growl climbed up my throat. I released the vial before the pressure of my fingers pulverized it.

Control. Always keep in control.

I lounged and tapped my lips. How to locate my prey? Aside from the tattoo and those eyes, I recalled the amenities of her cell, in which she'd sketched some manner of artwork into a dirt pile. That led to an image of sand impacted within her fingernails, the permanence of which pointed to one type of Summer native. One nomadic group was reputed to have that trait, a product of their lifestyle. This detail gave me enough to work with.

Time passed. When the queue of carriages crossed borders, I felt the first drop in temperature. Pine trees sprouted needle leaves. Scabrous alpine mountains loomed. A chalet castle foiled in silver glinted like a blade.

Winter.

The polar breeze blasted through my hair as I exited the carriage, the fur coat snapping against my frame. A squall thrashed about, thus limiting visibility.

Inhaling a brisk draught of air, I seized the arm of a passing soldier, frost slicing from my lips. "Get me a messenger. I have tidings for Summer."

Making a deal with Rhys was a tedious but small price to pay. When the warrior departed, I regarded the fortress chiseled into an alp of charcoal gray rock, the tips of its spires knifing into the sky.

I had two grandaunts to reunite with, subjects to lead, patients to treat, specimens to test, spies to execute. That aside, I envisioned finding the beast when she least expected it. Like an elixir, my head swam with visions of her chained, stripped, at my behest.

Whips came to mind. Her back would look gratifying after a few lashings. Perhaps forceps too. Or something longer, harder.

It might take a considerable while to trap that creature. But for her, I would wait. She might retreat to a nation of seafarers, but I hailed from a court of scholars, scientists—and hunters.

Privately, my lip curled. A hiss rolled off my tongue. "I'll catch you, Little Beast."

4

Flare

One year later

An ocean breeze sailed through my hair. The tide swabbed my bare feet, deep blue water foaming across the wet sand. Kneeling beside the peninsula's shoreline, I daydreamed while looking toward the horizon.

Kingdom of Summer.

In this land of sandstorms and tidal waves, humidity drenched people's flesh in sweat, and the briny air salted their mouths. Despite everything it had taken from me, I could think of no better place in the world.

Turning from the view, I glided a finger across the sand, my mouth lifting into a fond smile. A messenger hawk had arrived this morning with a scroll fixed in its mouth, which had contained a note from Poet and Briar inquiring about my safety and then finishing with a magical announcement. Now that Autumn had been restored, they had pledged themselves to each other, marrying on the same night they'd renewed Reaper's Fest. A year after the riot, the jester and princess had resurrected the revels, then bonded as husband and wife.

My spirits took flight. They had found lasting happiness. And someday, I would find mine.

After months of questing on foot, squatting in abandoned mills, and avoiding predators and passersby on the roads, I had crossed into Summer. Then I collapsed. More months of seafaring had followed, once I successfully abducted a boat.

From there, it had been easier to hide and finally send word to Poet and Briar. Since then, we'd been reaching out through confidential fauna messengers. Certain types of winged creatures could fly long distances between Seasons. Autumn, raptors. Summer, butterflies. Though, constant wandering meant communication with my friends was scarce.

The breeze rustled my pants and camisole. Compared to the roughspun I had spent years wearing, this material felt as soft as a cloud. Fishing for supper was effortless, but I'd swiped the garments from a market stall, as I had stolen many other things necessary for survival.

I tucked a scarf closer around my neck. Making sure the fabric concealed my collar tattoo, I glanced over my shoulder at the neighboring encampments. Moored on the beach, a cluster of boats like mine bobbed near a rocky outcropping. Sunset splashed the heavens in pink and yellow. Figures wearing caftans and jingling anklets moved across the decks, built fires in their own corners, and prepared to narrate stories.

Sand drifters. Like me.

Our kind traveled independently, aside from sharing encampments such as this one.

From one of the boat decks, an older man inclined his head in greeting, his grin theatrical. His wife waved as well, the motions exaggerated.

I furrowed my brows. Sand drifters—and most people in Summer, for that matter—didn't greet each other with this much enthusiasm.

Nevertheless, they hadn't spotted my inked neck. In all this time, I'd kept it covered since anyone who saw it would know what I was.

Shaking off the uncertainty, I returned their smiles. Trust unfurled in my chest, my hand lifting to greet them back.

Then I twisted back to the sea, closed my eyes, and listened to the lapping waves, their melody peaceful. I savored the moment, imagining a time when I had lived freely. I remembered an era from before, a drifter's life with Mama and Papa, back when we traveled in our tidefarer boat.

I could resume that life, but I had a greater purpose now. According to Poet and Briar, the villain prince was still searching for me, to no avail. I'd outsmarted him for a year. But if anyone caught sight of my tattoo, or if word of my escape reached Summer, my reported features might give me away. Thus, camouflaging myself and reaching my true destination as soon as possible was crucial.

I drew an image into the sand, running my fingers through the glittering specks. Turning sand into art had been my favorite thing to do since childhood, as if I might discover beautifully dark magic in the images. Within minutes, lyrics decorated the shore.

Seek not, find not, this Phantom Wild.
Sea paths, golden rays, to this Phantom Wild.
Light fades, mist grows, in this Phantom Wild.

It was a tune long passed through generations, the lyrics describing a secret rainforest. Everyone in The Dark Seasons knew about this hidden realm. Summer's great mystery floated somewhere uncharted in its ocean, isolated from our mainland, though no one had ever found it.

But I would. Although The Phantom Wild was an unattainable legend to the world, it was my buried treasure. The mystic forest waited to be discovered—waited for me.

Someday, I would see that legend for myself. Even if it took years, I would find that secluded world. And there, I would discover the key to helping others like me. I might not have a throne, but I did have my own special place, a realm that held the answer to my purpose, to further the crusade for born souls.

My fate had been clear from the moment I'd found a cipher inside the song. Looking closer, the lyrics formed hidden shapes—a map leading to the rainforest, replete with paths and symbols. Over the generations, no one had managed to discover this enigma. At least, as far as anybody knew.

But I had, which could only mean one thing. The Phantom Wild had summoned me, had chosen me for a special mission, and because my passion resided in aiding others who faced the same plight as myself, that had to be the reason.

The Almighty Seasons had spoken. The rainforest knew my sacred purpose and would show me the way. If I could reach that domain, I would uncover the key—the power to change Summer, as my friends were changing Autumn.

Scribing the final lyric, my finger paused. My eyes slid to the horizon, where the sun dipped behind the ocean, its slumbering descent tossing a dark shadow over the peninsula. A large wave rolled like a tube across the sea and lashed against my calves. At some point, the tide had risen and grown angry.

The landscape must be speaking to me. I took heed, tensing and flipping my gaze toward the sand drifter camp. As if they'd been staring the whole time, the couple from earlier veered their heads from where I hunched. They made a show of busying themselves on their deck, fumbling with the rigging as if about to set sail.

My eyebrows crinkled. No drifter would coast when the sea thrashed about like this. Where they'd been overly friendly before, now their jittery movements turned my stomach. Also, they maneuvered the rigging incorrectly, as though pretending.

Footfalls pounded from someplace behind me. Half a dozen boots stomped across the shore.

Terror froze my joints. My gaze widened on the couple's guilty features, and wounded fury pierced my soul. They were strangers, yet also fellow drifters.

And they'd known. Somehow, they had known to betray me.

I broke into a desperate movement. Whipping toward the drawing, I swiped my arm across the lyrics, warping the sketch to an unrecognizable blob. At the same instant, my free fingers seized the hilt of Poet's dagger tethered at my waist. Ripping out the weapon, I swerved toward the armed guards clanking my way.

"There!" one of them hollered, brandishing a curved sword. "There's the mad bitch!"

They spread out, their reptilian skin capes slapping the wind. Terror spilled down my limbs. I had expected sentinels, but no. These were knights, warriors of Summer, and far too many of them to slice through.

With a frightened growl, I lunged upright and launched toward my boat. Or rather, the boat I'd thieved from a random pier.

I made it three leagues. Hands forged of iron snared my arms, sharp outlines swarmed my vision, and the sea crashed its head into the shore. A memory flashed through my mind. A girl younger than me being caught like this, dragged away, and flung into a cell. Panic fired through my veins, and I flailed against the soldiers, roars tearing from my lungs although none of them could hear me.

I pictured a dank cell, with grime coating the walls. I remembered hunger and thirst. I remembered the darkness.

No! No, please! No, not again! I can't go back there again! Please, please, please!

Someone grabbed my dagger. Someone else rammed an elbow into my gut.

I yelped, coughed, hacked. As they lugged me across the peninsula, my thrashing heels carved through the sand, and I clung to a final glimpse of the dipping sun.

They would cage me in, lock me up, tie me down. And merciless Winter would find out. Somehow, that monster would find out.

Fear lanced through my heart. Soon, he would come for me.

5

Jeryn

I came for her. My boot heels struck the wharf as I dismounted from the great stag and thrust my gaze toward Summer's castle. The fortress stretched across a bluff, extending horizontally instead of vertically. Its towers, parapets, and colonnades spanned a cliff range, with gold banners punching the wind.

One tower in particular claimed my attention. The structure rose like an exposed target. A clean shot.

Winter knights cantered to a halt behind me. Taking my descent as permission, they disembarked from their own stags, having led the fauna from our ship upon docking. Around us, the ocean thrashed like a colossus smashing its skull into the surf. Quite the invasion of sound compared with the calculating silence of Winter.

Nicking my head sideways to loosen a kink, I pinned my gaze to the Fools Tower. Choking the reins once, I released the animal, knowing it would follow. While dissecting the edifice, I stalked forward, an order corroding on my tongue. "No one touches the prisoner but me."

My retinue would not be a problem. The instruction had been intended for Summer's warriors, to whom the order would be dispatched.

They would obey or have their intestines extracted.

As we strode toward the fortress, the knights fell quiet. Something had registered to them—a glaring, grammatical error—a half-second before the knowledge spasmed through my consciousness. They hadn't said it, but they'd heard the mistake.

My fingers stretched, preparing to squeeze something until it shattered. Prisoners. Plural. That's what I should have said.

6

Flare

Jail cells were all the same in Summer. Dark, clammy, and guarded by brutes.

Lying on my back, I rested atop a bed of moldy rushes covering the stone floor. Whereas Autumn's dungeon had provided clean cages, high windows to let in the fresh air, and edible food thanks to Poet and Briar, this place reeked of dead fish, the funk having seeped into the walls. Although King Rhys had erected this so-called "Fools Tower" only a year ago, it smelled like the slop they fed us, as if it had been festering for a thousand years, provided they fed us at all.

To distract myself from the scent of decay, I peered through the murk, staring at the lyrics scratched into the ceiling. While balancing on uneven nodules projecting from the wall and using the tip of a whelk, I'd worked in the dead of night when the guards hadn't been looking. Because they were less likely to glance up, the ceiling had been the perfect spot to engrave Summer's song.

Gazing at the lyrics, my eyes stung. I longed to dissolve into the words, into the hidden map, to disappear from this place. I yearned to break open every latch in this cell block, spring my neighbors loose, and take them with me.

Still, I refused to give the wardens my tears. They'd robbed me of enough precious things. Even our sadistic king would have to pry the sorrow from me. Not that he cared whether his captives and slaves suffered, or if he was the cause.

A week had passed since the soldiers tossed me in here, forgotten and forgettable to this kingdom. Between Summer and Autumn, dungeons had been my home since childhood. But after being dragged back to where I had originally started, they'd flung me into this newly established tower, which the Crown had built to compensate for the overflow of prisoners.

There was Lorelei, the woman split by two selves, fluctuating between a gleeful child and their scolding mother. Dante, the elder male who spoke to the ghosts of the formerly imprisoned. And Pearl, with irises like shimmering oysters and a nose as large as ore. She suffered from bouts of panic, believing hiccups meant her lungs were shrinking or the pounding of her heart meant she was dying.

Summer belittled her plight, calling it hysteria. This Season tended to call everything about us hysterical. Our homeland didn't know any better and had never tried to.

Like me, these captives had been relocated to the tower. However, we shared a history, having lived among one another for nearly ten years.

In fact, there used to be more of us. Several years before I went to Autumn, I had shared my old cell with Rune. The young man had been consumed with inventing spells to the point where he'd yank out his hair, frustrated by his failed attempts at sorcery.

Though that hadn't been the only thing engrossing him, late at night while our tower mates were asleep. I'd been nineteen and yearning for an escape, a release from the misery of this place. At my invitation, Rune had used his body to give me that relief, fucking away my virginity with one swift jab of his cock. It became a routine with us, though the sex hadn't yielded the sort of pleasure I'd heard about from other prisoners, and the aftereffects hadn't lasted long enough to provide solace. Even now in my twenty-second year of life, I'd never known the bliss others spoke of, despite seeking it with my own hand after Rune had died from an infection.

Sweat dampened my flesh, the sensation pulling me from the memory. My billowy pants and camisole stuck to my body like film. Because I hadn't changed clothes since my capture, muck stained the fabric, and the unwashed garments emitted a stale scent.

Not that it troubled me. I had plenty of other things to worry about like the hunger gnawing on my gut, the water bug scabs encrusted on my arms, and the venomous gleam in the guards' eyes.

An uncommon silence enveloped the prison. I didn't trust this sort of anticipatory quiet. The cell block seemed to hold its breath like the inside of a tomb.

Or maybe it was nothing. I'd been on edge from the moment the barred doors of my cage had swung closed. Every day since, I had expected the arrival of a certain villainous Royal.

Poet and Briar had no idea what had happened to me. I lacked parchment, a surface on which to scribble them a note, and a messenger butterfly. It would take a while before my friends suspected something, once my secret tidings stopped arriving. Until then, anything could happen.

He could happen.

I needed to escape before then. Seven days since my captivity, and my mind was still toiling for a way to break from here.

Commotion drifted from the stairway. Boots stomped along the corridor, the ruckus belonging to a large group heading in this direction, their torches flinging orange light across the cavity and illuminating the bars of a dozen cells. As they approached, their silhouettes reflected against the walls.

Rising on my elbow, I cocked my head to listen. I could tell the time based on how the darkness shifted with each hour. It was too early in the afternoon for water and gruel, much less for the guards to be in a baiting mood.

No. They were coming here for a different reason.

I lurched upright, alarm blazing a path across my flesh. The group's arrival triggered mayhem through the block, an eruption of noise shattering the silence. Manacles scraped across the ground, and my tower mates cried out.

A fleshy arm—Pyre's—popped through the shadows, his finger pointing at me. The word dropped from him like an anchor. "You."

Me.

"You. Stand."

My jaw locked. I curled my knuckles into fists.

"I ain't saying it again," Pyre warned. "Stand up or I'll make you."

Hellfire. I knew what that meant and had the proof of it across my back.

I spun toward him and crouched on all fours. If this son of a bitch wanted me to obey, he'd have to work for it, because he had evidence of me on his body too, including a few well-placed bites.

"Have it your way," he grunted while unlocking the door.

This incited more chaos. Lorelei played the child today, clapping her hands in excitement. Dante narrated the scene to his ghost. Pearl scuttled to the corner of her cell like a crab while mumbling, "Get away, get away, get away, get away, get away."

The bolt unlatched. The door groaned open.

Walking toward me, Pyre licked his chops, his teeth flashing like rotten fruit. Because these bastards were bored up here, they didn't chain me like they did the others. They liked entertaining themselves by taking wagers on how long a match against me would last. They enjoyed my temper, and I relished the chance to pound into them. Though I would lose the brawl eventually, because the men were bigger than me. Because anyone was bigger than me.

Afterward, I'd be forced to wipe my blood off the floor. But at least it would distract the wardens from taking their stresses, depressions, and resentments out on my kin.

Despite the lack of windows, the distant roar of an ocean filtered through the tower. That faint but miraculous echo clutched my heart, stalling my attack.

Pyre seized the moment, lunging and grabbing me by the ear, then hauling me off the floor. Twisting my lobe, he launched me into the bars, where my cheekbone smacked into iron, pain exploding across the side of my face. Before I could turn around and kick or scratch, he pinned my arms. The clunky weight of manacles bound me to the railing, putting me on display like a prized tuna.

Wiping his hands, Pyre exited my cage, his key twisting inside the lock.

Elated with himself, he leaned toward me, his eel breath beating against my mouth. "There we go," he taunted. "Nice and comfy. Thought you'd learn by now, but then you half-baked half-wits are too stupid for that."

While he was too stupid to stay back. My wrists might be bound, but my fingers weren't. Catching the back of his neck, I yanked the fucker forward, slamming his nose into the grille.

"Motherfuck!" Pyre howled and staggered back, calling me the usual names as he covered his snout with one hand. "Filthy fool bitch!"

With the opposite hand, he ripped out a mallet. Then he vaulted forward, raising the weapon toward where my fingers hooked around the bars.

Like a switchblade, a male hand flicked out of nowhere, the backs of his knuckles intercepting the guard. "What. Is. This?" a baritone voice murmured.

Although the words formed a question, it wasn't one. It was a demand, a dispassionate thing polished into a threat.

Foreboding soaked into my pores. I glimpsed him in a reflection, in a puddle on the ground, from a leak in the ceiling. On the water's surface, those crystal eyes sharpened on me.

The villain prince stared back, his inscrutable features peering down through the same puddle. Despite his stoic expression, those pupils glittered with long-suffering anticipation. Though unlike King Rhys, this prince didn't verbally gloat.

My head swung from the puddle, my gaze colliding with his, our eyes fusing like something about to detonate. He may have found me, but that didn't mean he'd caught me yet. To illustrate that point, a low growl skidded up my throat.

His orbs tapered, then scanned my appearance as well as the cage, appraising everything from my matted hair to the rusty chamber pot. The cold gratification he'd shown now vanished. With his hand still hovering to block the guard—a casually demeaning gesture—the prince angled his head in contemplation. Only then did he lower his fingers like a bluff, his words from moments ago lingering in the muggy air.

His inquiring silence got Pyre's attention. The guard hastened to recover from my blow to his nose. He wasn't bleeding or broken, but he was swelling up quickly. Because of that, it took a moment for him to respond.

Pyre batted his fingers my way. "As you see, Sire. It's the mad fool you requested."

"I'm aware of what it is," the prince drew out while fixating on me.

I glowered. They'd reduced me to an object. To them, my kind didn't warrant being referred to as human.

An entourage of knights formed a crescent behind the prince. The men and women carried crossbows, blades with diversely shaped edges, and baldrics loaded with throwing stars. A female knight stepped from the group, her white tresses bound and her complexion split like a half-moon, one side pale to match her hair and the other gray.

She did the rest of the talking for her sovereign. "His Highness demands to know why you're disturbing it."

"We were instructed by His Majesty to harness the prisoner for you," Pyre sputtered. "The mute bitch wasn't shackled yet." But when the prince said nothing, my nemesis gulped. "That's our duty. The mad are—"

Quicker than whiplash, the prince twisted and backhanded Pyre across the face. The guard's massive bald head whipped to the side, a crimson geyser spurting from his mouth. The smack vibrated through the hall like a wet sail hitting wood, the noise stinging my ears.

Shocked, I leaped forward as far as the bars would allow, the better to see. The prince had struck so swiftly, so impassively, not a flinch to his features. Whereas I'd put my soul into trouncing Pyre, the numb Royal had dealt with him like an afterthought.

Except he wasn't finished. With unflappable composure, the prince withdrew his knife and clicked the hilt. Instead of his scalpel, a razor flipped upright. In one smooth movement, his shadow swallowed Pyre whole. Squished against the wall, the guard howled as the prince calmly burrowed the weapon into the man's knuckles, shearing through flesh until knobs of bone materialized.

Screeches flooded the cell block. My tower mates skittered into the depths of their cages while every soldier and warden witnessed the scene. The Summer guards gnashed their teeth but knew better than to insult a future king. Meanwhile, Winter's soldiers observed Pyre's humiliation without blinking.

Horrified, I took notice of the warden's hand spurting blood. It was the same set of fingers he'd used to fling me against the grille.

Pyre hunched, gripping his shaky knuckles to staunch the flow. As much as I loathed the brute and had endured plenty of beatings courtesy of him, mercy struck my chest. I shook the bars to signal the prince, to stop the torture.

But it ended quickly. The unflappable Royal flicked his razor back into its handle slot. "You need a doctor."

His implication was clear. The prince might be that doctor, but Pyre should rely on someone else to fix him. Around us, the Winter knights fought to withhold callous mirth.

The dismissive Royal trained his eyes back on me. Earlier, Pyre had said the prince had requested me. As I'd feared, this monster must have heard about my imprisonment.

With an index finger, the prince swept aside a gnarled lock of my hair, his eyes hooking onto the symbols painted around my throat. "And who is responsible for this?"

An offhand yet intentional question. I remembered the first words he'd ever launched my way. *Who marked you?*

It would be easy to tell him. I would enjoy ratting out the culprit, if that person hadn't been punished enough. And if I believed they wouldn't seek vengeance on me later.

The reason Summer tattooed prisoners with neck collars was hardly a secret. All the same, Pyre's complexion purpled. His frantic eyes swerved to me, but when I kept my mouth shut, he pretended to misunderstand.

"The cunt deserves those markings," he grumbled around a mouthful of crimson. "Got a feral madness about her. Go for this traveling wench, and she'll chomp off your fucking thumb." When the baffled Winter clan squinted at the term *traveling wench*, Pyre clutched his oozing knuckles and explained, "She's a sand drifter."

Seething, I rammed my chains into the bars. I hated hearing those words coming from his mouth. They belonged to my family and my kin, not to this oaf.

I'd never told Poet and Briar about my history, so they couldn't have let the knowledge slip in front of the prince. Yet he regarded me without a shred of surprise.

"Indeed." His mouth ticked sideways, for my eyes only. "I am unaware of that as well."

Blood stewed my veins. Understanding dawned.

This fiend hadn't simply found out about my capture. He'd plotted it. During this year of searching, the prince must have learned about my roots, because renowned Winter supposedly knew many things. From there, he'd figured out enough details to sniff me out, likely telling Summer where I could be found.

Damn him to hell for being right. Knowing how to conceal myself amid fellow sand drifters, why would I stash myself elsewhere? Blending in with their encampments came as second nature. I'd been sure it was the last place Summer would look, with me hiding in plain sight.

What I hadn't counted on was the prince's foresight. Winter's arrival would have stirred a frenzy throughout Summer, and I'd have seen him coming. But because I wouldn't have suspected my nomadic kin, Winter must have enlisted the Summer Crown to spread the word.

By now, everyone knew Winter had King Rhys and Queen Giselle in his pocket. At the prince's bidding, my homeland had evidently incentivized sand drifters across the nation to be on the lookout for me. That fidgety couple in the peninsula had noticed my neck tattoo after all, then reported me.

My community had turned me in.

Although the prince still hadn't gotten the right answer from Pyre about my tattoo, his attention strayed. Those vicious orbs skated from my neck to my hands gripping the bars. He paused on the sight, idling way too long for my fancy.

Disgust crept across his face. Curtly, he jerked his chin at one of his knights, then at me. From there, the Royal sauntered past my cage and headed toward my tower mates.

Terror curdled my stomach. Did he mean to claim them as well? Now that he had me, why wouldn't Winter also trade for other born souls?

No. I wouldn't go. I would *not* go with this monster. And I wouldn't let him take them either. They'd done nothing to this man.

Provoke him, I thought. Get him closer, I thought.

Hurt him first. Hurt the prince.

I whisked up saliva and spat. Fluid shot from my mouth and splattered the toe of his boot, halting the Royal in his tracks.

A beat passed. Then he edged backward.

Abreast of the bars, the prince glanced sideways at me without a shred of astonishment. My fingernails and knuckles readied themselves, but then he turned fully. As he did, his hand slid my way in a stupefying brush of movement.

Tenderness?

He made contact. I paused, the skin beneath my jaw yielding to the pads of his fingers, which rested lightly against my pulse.

It was calm, regal, and almost kind when he began to squeeze. I hardly noticed until my throat shrank in his grip, snippets of air struggling to get through. I grunted and flailed, trying to wrench myself away, but he only tightened his fingers. All the while, his expression didn't change, inspecting me with a deep tilt of his head.

I rewarded him with a ferocious glare, because prey had to use their best glares against predators, in or out of this tower, in the hot or the cold, in Summer or Winter. But he merely waited as if he had all day, a purposeful sort of evil creeping to the surface, to the ice of his eyes.

I saw it. He wanted me to kneel.

The monster held on, the press of him urging me down. I resisted until my traitorous legs buckled. At which point, his fingers snapped open, releasing me to the ground, one of my knees smacking the stone and the other bending. I was quaking, kneeling, dammit.

The Summer guards cackled. The Winter knights did nothing of the sort.

Pyre spat blood while cradling his mutilated knuckles. "Anyone else from this block, then?"

By some miracle, the prince shook his head. Losing this round had at least spared my neighbors from being chosen.

Winter concentrated only on me, the tip of his boot fitting through the irons and wiping my spit across the fabric of my pants. Nudging my leg as if I were merely an insect, the prince addressed his entourage, murmuring two words he'd been waiting twelve months to say.

"This one," he confirmed before walking away.

7

Jeryn

She had it coming. After the fucking chase she had put me through, the defiant little beast had asked to be brought to heel. It required a certain patience to hurt. Any longer and my grip on that tattooed throat would have suffocated her.

Indeed. Plenty of mayhem awaited her in Winter. When I got her alone and into a lab, I'd be free to exact full retribution.

Until then, my greeting had been a preview. And a necessity. Since the woman hadn't kept her saliva to herself, I'd been obliged to retaliate. With a retinue and those pissant guards as witnesses, such defiance couldn't have gone unpunished. Our audience had anticipated nothing short of aggression from me, and I could not be seen to play favorites.

Still. It had taken a certain amount of pressure to restrict her lungs while likewise avoiding impairment.

Pacing myself, I stalked down the tower's coiling stairway, with the knights marching behind. Upon my descent, I flexed my fingers, my skin glazed in blood. Fucking imbecile. That warden should consider himself fortunate to still possess his hand after daring to touch my property. Acid sizzled on my tongue, yet I could not identify whether it had to do with the guard, the conditions in which the beast had been living, or her obstinance.

Outside the tower's ground level, a colonnade stretched toward the Royal wing's entrance. A servant waited, balancing a marble bowl. I doused my fingers in the vessel, tower scum leaching from my digits. Red water sloshed over the side and onto the tile floor.

A cloth materialized in my periphery. Wiping my hands and dispatching the textile to the servant, I strode down the walkway.

The saturated air grew thicker than a stew. Solstice, the First Knight, mopped her brow. "Curse this soggy country."

The knights were miserable, drenched in the elements. Whereas Winter's chill cut a clean, straight incision into its citizens, Summer's heat punched them in the fucking face.

At the passage's threshold, sentinels peeled open a set of double doors. I turned down my chin, brushing past them and stepping into the castle's east wing.

The knights sighed, welcoming the mist that rained from the ceiling. One wall recess displayed an hourglass tracking the time, indoor waterfalls hissed with noise, and resident macaws stabbed their beaks into their breastbones. The retinue followed me through a hall floored in glass, with dragon fish submerged beneath our feet.

One of the knights snickered. "Some of the locals walk barefoot here. Their clothing is as skimpy as scarves too."

Another reproached, "Not a stitch of lingerie beneath their silks—"

"Shut up," I murmured.

They held their tongues the rest of the way, then stationed themselves at the throne room's entrance with the Summer watchmen. A lithe female figure waited beside the arched doors, the wind buffeting her linen pants and a beaded circlet expertly threaded into her onyx hair.

Her features remained placid as I approached. "Your Highness," Queen Giselle recited.

"Your Majesty," I returned with an inclination of my head.

"How are your grandaunts?"

"They send their regards."

She wavered, choosing her next words with discretion. "And the rest of your family?"

My jaw flexed. "They are well."

The question was to be expected. Nonetheless, I did not appreciate the underlying pity in the woman's eyes. Sympathy should be reserved for the weak and fallible. My family was neither.

This fundamental point sat on the edge of my tongue. However, I suppressed the impulse. Despite her inquiry, this queen warranted respect for more than merely tolerating her windbag of a husband. Therefore, I would save my insults for the monarch who'd actually earned them. Seasons knew that temperamental shithead would leave himself open to plenty.

In any case, my family was stable. I kept them comfortable and would not have the courts believing otherwise, much less regarding my relatives with anything less than admiration. Not unless the offenders wanted their tongues sawed off with a dull knife.

"I trust you found everything in the tower to your liking," Giselle hinted. But when I let my silence speak for itself, she raised a pierced eyebrow. "I confess, your tactical instructions to alert sand drifter camps discreetly and in batches struck me. This prisoner must be of great medical value, to go to such lengths to obtain her."

Nosy woman. Powerful and capable, but nosy all the same. Having been prepared for that, I sidestepped the comment like a landmine. "Winter is an advanced nation for a reason."

Her Majesty would get no more from me. The woman was far too discerning to be trifled with. Rather like two Autumn troublemakers I had the misfortune of knowing.

Giselle contemplated the response, then tipped her head toward the doors. "You're in for a treat. He's feeling ornery today. Come see me after wasting your time."

I never wasted time. True, I should be conferring only with her. By now, everyone knew who truly ruled this court. But first, I had unfinished business with the infantile king.

My head bowed as Giselle strolled past me. Her security detail and circle of ladies vacated the sidelines to trail behind.

The doors split. "His Highness, Prince Jeryn of Winter," the sentinel announced before closing the partition and sealing me inside.

Neither of my grandaunts had exaggerated. The throne room did not have an aquarium within. Rather, it *was* an aquarium. Triangular, with transparent walls and floor-to-ceiling pools of seawater, the surface reaching an unseen terrace and illuminated from above. The tank engulfed the chamber, but it wasn't so much the size of it that made an impression.

It was the sharks.

A multitude of species infested the aquarium. The glossy figures were long and tinted blue and gray, with razor teeth and gills slicing through their skin. They swarmed the entirety of the space, casting shadows on every surface, including the Summer King himself.

The outline of a fin slashed across King Rhys's throat and vanished. He slouched in a gilded chair at the narrowest point of the room, a pair of sandals peeking from under his linen robe and an overgrown mustache tugging his face down into a mask of irritability. With such a prominent sulky exterior, it was a wonder the room did not stink of sour grapes.

The man waited for me to bow, then fought to withhold a sneer when I did no such thing. "So," Rhys began. "Based on your rather large presence, it appears our ocean didn't sink your ship."

False pleasantries with a side serving of petulance. I could think of nothing more pointless.

I stared at him. "Sometimes brute force is less effective than technique, Your Majesty."

"Is that a joke? I despise jokes."

"I do not make them. I leave that to Spring."

"One thing we still have in common, at least." The juvenile swatted his digits toward the empty seat beside him. "You see this chair? It belongs to my wife. We're quarreling, so I've uninvited her to this discussion."

"Good. That means the meeting will go smoothly."

Mistaking the comment for flattery, Rhys perked up, thus proving my point. This ignoramus provided an easy target, whereas Giselle put up a consummate fight.

My eyes ticked toward the sharks. They moved in an aimless, trancelike manner, much like born fools in a surgical lab.

"Aren't they remarkable," the monarch boasted. "Tell me. Which is the most vicious?"

"Those," I said, indicating the fish skating along the bottom of the tank, their scales a gradient of red.

The king glowered. "I mean, which of the sharks? I wasn't talking about the jester fish. Costly, flashy little blights, but…" He leered. "I use them as tank feed."

A blasphemous waste. If Rhys insisted on defying the laws of nature by fucking with a rare species, then at least use them for progressive purposes. Research them humanely instead of sacrificing the creatures purely to nurse his wounded ego.

Seasons flay me. The amount of energy people squandered on grievances and hurt feelings. Despite how little I thought of him these days, I still would have respected the king more if he'd confessed to licking his balls whenever he was feeling insignificant.

Rhys's motives had nothing to do with fattening the sharks and everything to do with the pathetic spoils of a grudge. Over a year had passed since the Reaper's Fest riot, yet he hadn't recovered from what happened with Poet and Briar.

Regardless. The black and red fish were the most vicious among the inhabitants. Herbivores, yet if threatened they used their radiant scales to restrict vision, causing victims to stagger around the ocean for hours. Plenty of time to drown or fracture one's skull against a boulder. And while being eaten alive by a shark would hurt more, ruthlessness came in many guises. The jester fish used a methodical, prolonged tactic to defend themselves, instead of a direct and quick one. That made them superior.

Hmm. Rather impractical that Rhys should keep them in a room frequented by citizens and dignitaries.

"Try again," the king bade. "Appease me and take a closer look at my extensive assortment of pets. Of all Summer's sharks, point out the fiercest."

I tapered my eyes. So be it.

Approaching the tank, I scrutinized its dwellers, reminding myself of the glass that separated us. My gaze searched for a creature striped in shades of pewter and sterling.

None to be seen. My shoulders relaxed. "It is not here."

"What isn't there?"

"A siren shark."

The king cracked out a patronizing laugh. "Don't make me doubt the expertise of Winter. You're supposed to be the homeland of reason, yet you'd expect me to offer tank space for such a boring shark? You would label it the most ferocious? I can't wait to hear why."

"Because it kills you gradually," I disclosed.

A siren shark lured its quarry. Upon which, the predator's bite produced a foaming madness shortly before death. It did not feast on human prey but rather turned the person into a fool for three days, stripping them of sanity until blessed death came knocking.

No antidote. No cure.

I did not want to talk about the fucking siren shark.

Like every social moron, the king was only asking because he found sport in quizzing Winter's heir. A prince on exhibit. Ask him anything. See how much he knew.

As for my answer, Rhys grunted in concession. "You've never been a scion of many words."

I leaned against the aquarium. "There's a distinction between many words and wise words."

"I disagree. Then again, we've hardly seen eye to eye. Not since you saw fit to side with Autumn, for fuck knows what reason. And the list keeps getting longer. You abused my tower guard, I hear. Exactly how harshly did you punish him?"

"Had you been there, I would have cut deeper."

"Then your reputation still precedes you. Despite our last encounter, I'm rankled that my son can't be like you. As we sit here, he's jamming his cock down a chamberlain's throat." Rhys swiped an oversized pepper from a side table, swallowed it whole, and continued his dissertation. "My offspring should be present to greet our esteemed guest, yet the lad has reached a self-indulgent, sex-induced age. When one has itches, they trump one's sense of duty. I don't give a shit who he fucks in his spare time, provided he doesn't abstain from stately obligations. Any advice?"

"Beat him."

"Anything I haven't tried yet?"

Withdrawing my attention from the tank, I slanted my head toward Rhys. "Let me do it."

The water's reflection trembled through the room. "Quite the iceberg, you are," the king complimented. "You exceed your family's tamer inclinations. No offense, of course."

"No offense possible." I slit my eyes. "No one surpasses my relatives."

"That smacks of devotion," he criticized. "Worse yet, affection."

It did. "We were speaking of your son."

"I suppose we were. Your grandaunts are fine queens, but you didn't inherit your disciplinary measures from those two doves. Anyway, I appreciate the offer, but taking your substantial physique into account, you'd kill my offspring. He's a fraction of your size—and who isn't, really?—not to mention, he's currently my only heir." Rhys shifted and grumbled, "I have no other spawn."

I took note of his tone. He'd made an effort to stress the point about having only one child. Though, I could not see why.

In any event, the sigh I'd been withholding tripled in density. "As much as I value non sequiturs, shall we get on with it?"

It would have been precarious to travel here solely for the little beast. In the eyes of The Dark Seasons, every nation would have viewed my behavior as circumspect, particularly as the Seasons' most impartial Royal. Yet as Giselle had implied, I'd gone to considerable trouble to snare my captive.

To prevent widespread skepticism, I had searched for the beast on the public pretense of research. I'd told everyone she had demonstrated a unique breed of madness, the likes of which I hadn't seen before. A condition I was eager to experiment on. None had debated that fictitious narrative.

But why did I really want her?

I shook off the question. Although she'd been my primary target, this trip provided an opportunity to trade per the Fools Decree amendment. This gave the impression I hadn't singled out the beast to the point of irrationality.

The king straightened on his throne. "Make your request, then."

Ludicrous man. It would not be a request.

I glided my thumbs into my belt loops. "Twenty simpletons."

"You're fucking kidding me." Officially denied the chance to have me kiss his ass, the Royal toddler spat in disappointment, "Done. I don't care which."

"Five of them, children."

Indignation creased his face. "I take that back."

"I do not."

"Think again, Winter."

"Tread carefully, Summer." My gaze minced him into cubes. "I could take a lot more from you."

The king blanched. Notwithstanding, his ruination in Autumn had placed Summer at a disadvantage. As intended, my alliance with Poet and Briar had contributed to Rhys's demise. Thus, it had set negotiating power in my favor. By gaining my help, the jester and princess had inadvertently handed me the clout to strike cutthroat deals regarding fools.

That was the first point. The second had to do with the spies Rhys had installed in every Season, to keep track of his ruling neighbors. Poet, Briar, and Avalea had exposed this crime. As it turned out, Rhys had recruited a network of scholars to keep tabs on Winter.

Prior, I'd already had my suspicions about the informants. One restless soldier had let a few criminal remarks slip among his brethren. Although he hadn't been part of the faction, he'd discovered its existence yet kept it a secret.

I hadn't been able to confirm my misgivings until Poet and Briar had propositioned me. At which point, I'd annihilated the soldier quicker than a virus.

This amounted to one indisputable fact: Summer owed Winter. Overstep in the slightest, and conflict with my nation would demolish what was left of Rhys's legacy.

The king recovered his spleen. "Of all Seasons, Winter must understand the rationale behind my actions. Now that you've had time to consider them." But when his defense failed to impress me, he bitched, "I was being pragmatic. I had to protect my kingdom!"

What this glutton meant was, he had to suck his own cock. Which had nearly cost my family their necks. Had I not intervened in time, Rhys's spies could have done irreparable damage. Though that much, he did not know.

What does Summer have on you?

Poet had dropped the question at my feet before I left Autumn. As vexing as I found him, the jester had guessed perceptively. Nevertheless, I'd prevented Summer from gaining a shred of crucial knowledge, having squashed the traitors like fleas before they had a chance to dig into my family.

My expression told Rhys how seriously I took his defense. This also made it plain that if not for his title, I'd have plucked out his solar plexus by now. At Reaper's Fest, I'd have lit that bonfire and watched with relish as he cooked like a pig. Not only for endangering my family but for employing that fucking guard who'd been handling my little beast.

"Ah," Rhys hummed with spite. "So you'll continue to snub me like they all do. You, who should have been my staunchest ally against that cunt of a princess and her slut of a jester. What did they offer you?"

This again. He'd been trying to get the details out of me ever since I stabbed him in the neck with a syringe, back when Poet and Briar revealed his duplicity to the Royals. Like a reflex, my thoughts strayed to the beast and her inflammatory golden eyes.

"Dismiss me now, but it won't last. I'm no lowly spy you can discard like rubbish," the king grated while the infernal sharks coasted in the backdrop. "We're the same creature, you and me. We have the same hatred, only with different temperatures. That's why you showed no mercy to my spies. What did you do to seek compensation? Numb their balls with a single look? Dismember their ligaments? What did it take to vanquish the opposition?"

"Ask the wolves who mauled them," I deadpanned.

That shut him up. Under the mustache, Rhys's laryngeal cartilage bobbed like a cork.

We were not the same creature. For instance, if I had set out to vanquish Autumn, I would have succeeded. Because I would have done it smartly.

The king digested my reply, then flung up his arms. "Summer doesn't trade children."

"Summer will make an exception," I instructed with velveteen malice.

Rhys's protest had nothing to do with benevolence. This court valued child simpletons for their diminutive hands, which enabled them to weave nets.

However, regional diseases thrived in this kingdom. To compensate, I had developed a painstaking method of inoculation, which Winter had offered to Summer in exchange for test subjects.

The monarch scratched the living shit out of his mustache. He could not refuse vaccines over a few striplings. "I will excuse this insolence. You're ambitious, ruthless, and hoping to set a precedent."

I raised an eyebrow. "I'm shrewd, intelligent, and immune to trivialities such as hope."

"I will require a greater number of doses."

"Not attainable."

"I warn you, Sire. I'm on the brink of fury, and I'm surrounded by sharks."

For shit's sake. Did this moron think those vaccines were easy to produce?

Someday, he would bring upon himself a painful and timely death. When that inevitability happened, Giselle should donate his brain to research. If only to display as an example of what happened when one's cerebrum shrank, due to inactivity. This, assuming I did not murder Rhys myself.

"For the customary supply, I will have twenty simpletons, five of them children," I repeated, then flicked the starving king a bone. "And ten of the mad."

"Say that again?"

"No."

A hypocritical grin lifted the king's mustache. "I believe I still like you."

I couldn't give less of a fuck. "The little beast you caged for me. Who tattooed her neck?"

The prompt brought a fatal edge to my words. Because the beast had refused to say who'd marked her, and because the guard had changed the subject, I sought an answer from someone who lacked the intellect to question my interest.

Why would the Prince of Winter care who inked a prisoner?

Rhys was too self-involved to wonder. "Don't expect me to recall minor details," he scoffed. "The fool was originally captured at a fledgling age, long before I chose her for Autumn, so hell if I remember who tattooed her." Then he gave it a second thought. "Though, a neck marking means she's deadly. I'd advise you not to get close to such an animal."

He was advising the wrong prince. I allowed that thought to show on my face.

Despite himself, the king's pupils gleamed as if he'd swallowed a mood booster. "And how do you plan to break in the prisoner?"

In the same manner I broke them all. "I'm patient."

The meeting adjourned. I would sit with Giselle later, to discuss other political matters. In the meantime, Rhys extended me an invitation to dine, then left the throne room, not noticing when his guest didn't follow.

I lingered, glancing briefly at the aquarium. Despite the sharks' vacant expressions, only an idiot would mistake them for harmless. They knew their powers, knew what their teeth could do, knew what they were capable of. And they saw me quite clearly.

I turned away, retreating to the exit as my First Knight appeared in the doorway. Solstice's white hair was tied into a bun at her crown, and her skin contrasted more intensely in this dim lighting, her face divided between a pale and gray complexion.

"All is settled, my liege," she reported. "The trade fools will be roped tomorrow night, then clamped in irons once we're aboard."

"No," I murmured. "Not the beast with the collar."

"Sire?"

"The mad female with the neck tattoo. Find out who gave her the marking, but do it quietly. Then tomorrow at midnight, bring her to me."

"Your Highness." Solstice's voice grew cautious. "Interacting with the fool is a risk. The marking means she isn't like the others."

My lips twitched. "I know."

8

Flare

I wanted my clothes back. Right fucking now!

The next eventide, sometime close to midnight, the dungeon bustled with activity. My skin beaded with sweat as some brute poked me with strange devices—pronged things and smooth things and scratchy things. One of Winter's knights held a torch aloft for him, and a fellow soldier—that woman with a half-moon countenance—stopped me from tearing into the physician. The manacles took care of the rest, the irons shackling my wrists.

The physician picked through my cropped waves, then checked my mouth and ears and eyes. Also, my neck where the symbols were painted. The Summer Crown had tattooed black sunbursts onto every prisoner, to catalog and keep us from getting far in an escape. If the markings encircled the ankles, it meant the captive was a so-called "simpleton." Around the wrists meant they were mad but harmless like my tower mates.

A painted neck meant the prisoner was a feral kind of mad, dangerous and liable to maim. The villain prince must know this, so that couldn't be the reason he kept asking about my collar.

The physician patted down my bare tits and stomach. When he shoved my thighs apart, I lunged toward him, but the chains and the female soldier kept a firm grip on me. Although I'd never been shy, I drew the line at being examined like a specimen. Giving my dignity as much consideration as he would to a rodent, the physician checked the crease between my legs, the torch flame following his movements and illuminating my cunt for the world to see.

Bile fizzled on my tongue. What was the man checking for? A magic trick? Did he suspect I was hiding a rabbit down there? Since when was having a pussy this important?

They couldn't intend for me to become a breeding experiment. This continent wanted fewer of us, not more. Summer had made sure we couldn't breed, though maybe Winter had invented nefarious ways to work around that.

Oddly, Pyre wasn't there to enjoy the show. Instead, two other guards stood nearby, the pair betting for a duel—a showdown between Winter and my naked self. One of them flaunted a sheathed dagger at his hip, the hilt's scarlet gems causing recognition to fester in my gut. The Summer troops had confiscated Poet's weapon after catching me. I'd been agonizing over what had happened to it.

A dispassionate grunt cut off my fury. The physician stood and wiped his hands. "Nothing but filth."

Curse this man. Curse him to the afterlife!

They upended a pail and splashed water over my head. I went rigid, my muscles tensing, because it was water.

Clean. Water.

Before I could shut my eyes in bliss, a pair of hands toweled me down, robbing me of the sensation. A sob coiled in my throat, the longing so great my hands soared to my face, where a few droplets remained. Suds frothed on my cheeks but popped the instant my fingers located them.

"Giving her the Royal treatment?" a Summer warden jeered from the sideline.

"His Highness wants them healthy and unsullied for transport," the physician explained. "The last thing we need is an infestation."

The villain prince. Hatred simmered through my blood.

My captors unchained and thrust me into a filmy chemise with straps as thin as weeds and a short hem barely covering my ass. The troops saw fit to honor Summer's culture of nudity beneath our clothing, but at least the garment was freshly washed and devoid of holes.

A Summer soldier joined the action and wrestled me back into a set of restraints. This time, the bindings weren't attached to the grille, nor were they irons. Awareness struck me, the material familiar. Briefly, I'd forgotten Summer's tradition of using ropes to bind their captives during transport, a practice Winter was honoring.

I hissed, declaring war as the knights fastened the cords around my ankles and snagged my wrists in front of me. The brittle restraints scratched and proved hearty. Divine Seasons, I recognized the feel of them. I knew these types of knots.

The female warrior from Winter prodded my hip with the point of a crossbow bolt. Punctuating the movement, she urged me toward the cell door. "Let's go."

Yet before she could nudge for a second time, an idea sparked. My eyes skirted to a tiny whelk on the floor—the one I'd used to write Summer's song. Feigning clumsiness, I stumbled forward and landed on my knees, then swiped the whelk from the ground. Using a deft sleight of hand, I wedged the object into the slender gap between the ropes and my wrists.

The hounds peeled me from the ground and shoved me through the door, away from the ciphered map in the ceiling. I tore my head over my shoulder, gazing toward the lyrics and their hidden image before the company yanked me from the cell block.

I made it rough for them, made them toil to get me moving, my limbs flailing like the fins of a netted fish, my teeth seeking purchase on a row of knuckles. In the end, it took every soldier on duty to drag me down the corridor.

The stairwell's fathomless pit spiraled like a conch into an abyss. My breathing grew shallow, and I ground my heels into the floor.

The white-haired knight shook me in place. "Be still, fool!"

"Or we'll take it out on your tower friends," a Summer warden gloated.

Hellfire. I went willingly, but for good measure, I shrugged his furry fucking hand from my elbow. He'd always been a wooly one, his skin germinating with shaggy thickets of hair, including his neck and back, to the point where he might be flammable. If only I'd gotten the chance to find out.

We hustled down the stairs, the stone uneven beneath the sandals they'd jammed onto my feet. A draft rushed up the corridor, surfing through my hair and making the tips dance. The ropes chafed me raw as I hobbled down the shaft, the air changing from tepid to muggy. Light bloomed at the passage's end, and that light became a gate, a giant mouth waiting to cough me out.

I reared back, my heart clattering. Frustrated, the knights hauled me forward as the gate croaked open to reveal an enclosed quad banked in torches and lined with columns.

We spilled over the threshold. Or rather, I spilled across the stone floor. The trained knights remained upright while I toppled forward and smacked the tiles. My wrists and knees smarted, but that wasn't what caused the jolt through my limbs.

It was a pair of steel-edged boots. Crossed at the ankles, they clung to a set of limbs fitted in obsidian pants.

My gaze climbed high, ascending to a set of narrow hips, to the shirt gripping every defined contour of a masculine chest, to the corrupt face angling down at me. The monster's dark silhouette leaned casually against a wall with his arms folded. Shadows clutched his frame, blotting out half of his features while the other half loomed into view.

"Stand," the prince murmured.

As usual, the command sounded polished yet lethal. Except if I hadn't made it clear by now, this monster would have to work harder with me.

I stayed put, hoping he'd abandon the wall and give my canines the opening they needed. But damn him, the prince was ten steps ahead.

Having predicted my intention, he pushed off the wall, then squatted at a distance instead of coming nearer.

No fur coat tonight. In the deep V of his shirt, his pendant swung like a severed head, the vial backdropped against a smooth plate of muscles. Limbs spread, the prince rested his forearms on his thighs, those evil hands dangling off his knees.

The posture brought the Royal's digits into stark relief. Blood stained his fingers like paint, the color reaching to his knuckles. Whatever he'd been up to today, he hadn't bothered to rinse off the evidence.

Twin pupils pierced through me. Tipping his patrician nose, my captor bore down with cold elegance. "Get. Up."

Before I could decide the most satisfying way to defy this order, the prince's eyelids hooded. Unsurprised by my refusal, he tossed the troops a flat look, clicked his head toward me, and stood.

The female knight looped her arms beneath mine and hauled me off the floor. While the prince resumed his position at the wall, a clunking noise resounded from above. Chains plummeted from the ceiling like slugs. A single manacle clamped around my wrists, layering over the rope cords.

Plucking a chalice from the concrete table, the prince watched. His lips touched the vessel and sipped. Above the rim, the shards of his eyes observed as the links hoisted my arms overhead.

High.

So high they elongated my body, forcing me to balance on my toes. The hem of my chemise lifted, barely covering the private bits, my lack of drawers about to become public knowledge yet again.

I mashed my lips together, raised my chin, and skewered him with a glare. Instead of perversion or lechery, the prince absorbed my grimace with indifference. All the same, his mouth gripped the chalice's rim with more force. He drank deeper, his throat pumping in tandem to my pulse.

Imagining the liquid slipping across his tongue, I squirmed. My resistance pulled the chain taut.

The prince's attention seized on the movement—the jutting of my hips. His crimson digits flexed around the chalice's stem. Swallowing with precision, he lowered the vessel as the knights bowed and backed out of the room.

The gate shut with a wincing noise. Then silence engulfed the quad.

Yet nothing happened. He simply waited, and the longer he did this, the greater my impulse to keep moving. That had to be what he was after. This man wanted to see me unhinged, intimidated, under his thumb.

I went still, uninterested in gratifying him, much less boosting the chemise another inch. One more twitch, and the patch of hair between my thighs would peek from the material. As it was, a current of air brushed across my breasts, the effect toughening my nipples through the fabric.

By the Seasons' grace, the whelk I'd swiped at least remained tucked between my wrists and the cords.

Our gazes crossed like murder weapons. Minutes passed. Or maybe it was seconds.

The prince's eyes faltered like a mistake, the pupils dropping to my lips. On reflex, my mouth parted. The reaction worked like an enticement—or an insult.

Shoving himself from the wall, the prince stalked my way. Long hair poured down his back, the color trapped between blue and slate, the mane tethered into a ponytail at the nape. Pacing himself like a wolf, he eviscerated the space between us while unsheathing his scalpel knife.

I tensed. My senses ran amok with fear, loathing, and something else. A strange emotion buzzed like a hornet in my navel. The instant his shadow touched my skin, the effect intensified, the threat causing my naked thighs to lock.

I held my ground as he braced the knife's tip atop my lower lip. With visible deliberation, the prince grazed the tender flesh, tracing the edges of my mouth until they trembled.

Not out of fright. No, the reaction came from someplace I couldn't name, from a horrible sort of restlessness, which increased with every skate of his weapon.

The prince spoke to my mouth. "You had a voice once."

My lips snapped shut, blocking the weapon. He hadn't bothered to examine me, so how on earth did he know that?

Taking my suspicious expression for a yes, the Royal angled his blade from my lips. "I'm a doctor," he said, by way of explanation.

Prince of Winter, genius of The Dark Seasons. Yet that couldn't be it. Not when he hadn't so much as peeked down my throat. There had to be more, another detail about my voice that gave this way. Something he wouldn't share.

Irises like glass reflected my features. What else did this fiend grasp about me?

The question must have sat on my face, because he saw through that too. "Sand drifters," he acknowledged. "Nomadic seafarers with notable traits, including sand encrusting their fingernails."

Seasons curse him. He'd noticed this.

"More than any group in Rhys and Giselle's court, such drifters live apart from the greater populace, camping in the outer reaches of Summer where few people venture." Winter cocked his head. "Where it's easy to vanish. To spend one's days drawing in the sand, perhaps."

Heat scorched me from head to toe. In addition to recognizing the sand in my nails, he remembered my sketch in Autumn's dungeon. Considering the battle I'd waged when he ordered the dirt pile swept clean, he must have reckoned it meant something to me.

That aside, it was still a marvel. To recognize any version of sentimentality or passion, this monster would need to possess a beating heart.

"I take it, there is more to your culture. But that is immaterial," the prince continued. "Ultimately, they're treasure seekers with mouths to feed and pockets to fill. That makes sand drifters susceptible to financial rewards, more so when the order comes from a Royal and the fugitive is a born fool. I suspect you will comprehend the rest."

Yes, I already had. Renewed treachery squashed my insides.

My glower drew him closer when I'd hoped it would do the opposite. His shirt chafed my bodice, inciting a maelstrom of spiteful tingles across my skin.

"Tell me," he intoned. "How did you lose your voice?"

So he knew the effect but not the cause. Again, I got the strange feeling there was more to this, some detail he wasn't saying about my lack of voice.

Regardless, I contemplated spitting in his face, but he distracted me from that impulse. "I have learned the culprit behind your tattoo. Next, I would know more."

I glimpsed those crimson-stained fingers again. Sometime between his appearance in the tower and now, the prince had found out who marked me, a gruesome hunch invading my mind about whose blood coated his digits. After how this Royal had treated Pyre in the tower, I couldn't put it past Winter to react less violently about the tattoo.

What did he do to the guard? I shuddered at the possibilities. His actions shouldn't make sense. The last thing this villain would do was punish someone for harming me. Then again, he'd stressed enough times that I was his property, and rulers didn't take kindly to their alleged possessions being vandalized. That had to be it.

I sealed my lips shut. Winter might know broad details about my life, but he didn't know the depths of them, and he never would.

My pain belonged to me. My losses were my own.

This shark had no right to them and wasn't asking because he cared to understand. Incapable of seeing me as human, I meant nothing to him. But I wouldn't become his next experiment.

When I denied him a reply, the prince lowered his timbre. "If I make an observation, you will respond." He angled his blade toward my windpipe. "Or I shall force it from you." The tip kissed the place where my voice should have been. "Nod or shake your head. Mouth the words. I don't give a fuck which. But you will obey."

My joints burned from the position, and my lips burned, and my throat burned, and everything burned in his proximity. The effects compiled on my tongue. He would keep me like this for a century if I didn't respond. But if I had to give him an answer, I would make it count.

The word fired from my mouth. "No."

A blast of sound to my ears. A silent one to him.

Still, it was an easy retort for this man to decipher, simply by reading my lips. Two letters, which ignited two conflicting reactions across his face—amazement and resentment.

Those eyes thinned with aggravation, then glittered with inspiration. "In addition to you, I have procured an assortment of mad parasites from Rhys. Why? Because the more disposable ones I add to Winter's pile, the more opportunities for testing, to treat the kingdom's real citizens. Perhaps I should have selected your tower mates while I was at it, instead of deciding against them after you spat on me. Quite clever to divert my attention, however temporary."

I barred my ivories. "I won't let you take them."

He arched a superior eyebrow. "So you're protective."

Instantly, we paused. With a few exceptions, it was rare for people to read my lips this effortlessly, and no one had ever caught on this fast. The prince appeared thunderstruck as well, yet it seemed like more than that. My reply struck this monster like a blow to the head, his features jerking as if the word had slammed into him.

As if he'd heard me.

But that couldn't be. Only I had the ability to hear myself, so I must be imagining that part. Either way, him being a scientist and a physician had likely contributed to understanding me.

And shit. By comprehending my words, he'd also stoked my defenses and exposed a vulnerability.

I snapped out of it. "I care for people. You wouldn't understand."

He recovered from the moment too, the dark blue streaks under his lower lashes crinkling. "On the contrary. I care for the right people."

Our breathing clashed, fuming with animosity.

"As accidents of the natural world, living plagues such as fools are meant for labor and research," he said. "Or—if incompetent, untamable, or unfeasible to test—they're discarded and used as decoys for hunting. Rather commonplace."

The ruler feigned contemplation. "If I don't bargain for your ilk, you'll have peace of mind. But if I do, you'll have company on the journey to Winter, which carries its own risks. Trapping allies in one place can lead to mutiny. Besides, it pleases me to see you alone. Defenseless. Isolated. It wouldn't be the first time."

I must be seeking an early grave. That explained this destructive urge to provoke him.

I replied, "Not that it lasted."

"True," the prince allowed. "But Poet and Briar are no longer around to unleash you."

"Why?" I seethed, unable to stop myself.

For the hundredth time, why me? Why single me out? Why hunt me across two nations?

Those chilling eyes flickered. "Because you broke something that meant a great deal to me."

Glancing at his tarnished vial, I scoffed. "This world took my freedom, yet a Royal can't handle a small crack in a piece of jewelry." The chain jangled as I got in his face. "Who's the weak one?"

The question chewed through his facade. Like a veil dissolving, some type of fragility rose to the surface. Although I placed him at mid-twenties, he appeared younger for an instant, the candid look there and gone before I could dive in.

The fleeting reaction drilled a hollow into me. Of all people, I understood the value of sacred keepsakes. Also, it seemed as though he was referring to more than the pendant.

But what else could I have broken that mattered to this man? And when?

The decorative chains ornamenting his boots clattered like bones, while my own chain trembled. With my body stretched, the lone manacle choked my wrists. My breasts inflated against his pecs, the span of his limbs inching my thighs apart.

Air sliced through his teeth. "You tread on thin ice."

"You're playing with fire," I threw back.

"Winter does not play." His warning cut to the quick. "It probes."

The temperature of this feud changed. My body fastened like a deadbolt. If he meant what I thought, I would attack until blood covered more than his fingers.

The prince registered my defensive stance with interest, realization glittering in his irises. "Ah. You think I would fuck you without your consent." He looked repelled. "That is the barbarian's way." Then he leaned in—so far in, too far in—and let the contradiction graze my mouth the way his weapon had. "Winter would violate you differently."

I kept vigilant, as much as possible with my arms braced to the ceiling.

"I'm not a kind man, so I wouldn't fuck that way. But providing I could stomach the task, my objective would be an alternative form of abuse," the prince explained. "First, I would make certain you wanted it."

Whereas his tone had been cold and slippery, now it leaked steam into an already-sweltering environment. A new type of heresy snaked across my knees and made a slow, infuriating track to my inner thighs.

As if I were a specimen, the point of his blade etched my heart. "All too willing, you would smother yourself against me, at which point I would subjugate you with patience."

The weapon scorched a path down my bodice, along the swell of one breast, and skidded over an erect nipple. "Thoroughly. Methodically," he muttered as the stud lifted into a rough peek.

Next, he slid the knife to my ribcage, running from left to right along each bracket. "Instead of my cock, I'd open your pussy with the hilt of my knife until you gushed like a tap, wet and quivering."

Something repulsive happened. My traitorous body morphed into someone else's—a woman I didn't recognize. Heat rose to the surface, so that pearls of sweat drizzled between my tits.

What dark magic was this? What form of Winter experiment?

The weapon sloped over my stomach and down to my navel. Scanning his descent, the prince murmured, "Then I would ply your soaked cunt with the handle, lashing in and out until hidden noises cracked from your lips like a vulgar little secret."

Because that would mean I desired him.

"Or like a cure."

Because that would mean I owed him.

For a moment, he lingered on my stomach. His brows furrowed, noticing something that darkened his features.

Moving on, he sketched my hipbone. "I would make sure you craved what you hated."

What I hated. No other emotion could better describe my feelings. Yet despite this hostility reaching a fever pitch, a molten rush flooded my bloodstream. For that, I hated myself more.

"I would make you betray yourself," the prince emphasized. "I would draw sounds from you like blood from a flesh wound."

When the scalpel knife caressed the inner ledge of my thigh, the pulse in my veins throbbed. The violent sensation pumped heat to the nexus, my pussy tightening of its own accord. To my disgust, a terrible impulse tugged my hips in an unholy direction, toward the one man who would never deserve it.

The knife climbed to the hem of my chemise, which fluttered like butterfly wings. My nemesis halted. I seethed but didn't move, since doing so would nudge the blade into my flesh.

Then he skated the knife under my skirt. Merely a centimeter, but that was plenty. My head fogged as the tip halted a scant distance from the hair covering my slit, which pounded like a muscle.

This had to be some form of manipulation or glamour. Visions of the prince's hilt fucking me laid siege to my thoughts. In response, my limbs shook like a dam about to break.

Somehow, the prince registered this effect. Like an oversight, those hellish eyes vaulted to mine, revolted fervor streaking through his pupils. He was enjoying this, and he detested this.

"That is how I would fuck you." And finally, the prince burrowed in, both of us shaking, hating. Then his voice sank to a terrible whisper. "And that's how I would become your greatest regret."

Whatever he'd been doing to me, it had transformed from hypothetical to literal. Rage kindled, combusting to the forefront and scalding every other shameless, faithless sensation in its wake. I might be shackled, but that was nothing new. Years of being confined had taught me ways to fight back.

His broad frame radiated over me as we traded bitter looks. But instead of shrinking away, I curled forward like a venomous creature and struck. With deliberate motions, I called his bluff. I rubbed every inch of my body against his, from my limbs, to my cunt, to the nipples poking through my chemise.

That did it. As if I'd pulled a trigger, the prince stiffened, his weapon arrested beneath my skirt. Relishing his confounded expression, I seized that moment and brushed my clit over the hilt. And then again.

And again. Cautious not to rub against the blade, I slid my crease back and forth along the handle while leveling him with a death glare—goading him, daring him. The maneuver issued a challenge to reach deeper, offering him permission to test me, to funnel that knife higher and see where it got him.

Try and intimidate me. Try and tame your captive. Try it hard.

And risk losing. Because who said I would regret a thing, especially if it led this man to act, to make so much of an effort, as he'd already done a dozen times. The sinuous move made it graphically clear. If I could get him to search the continent for me, to get this near to what he abhorred, to smother his fancy weapon all over my chained body, then I could manipulate him back.

In fact, I could get him to do other things. Like set me loose.

Then I'd be free to respond with all the vigor he anticipated, except my teeth would be the least of his problems. Because anything that had teeth also possessed claws and fists.

My performance worked more than I'd foreseen. The prince's hold on the weapon faltered, the reaction barely perceptible. His pupils fattened, and his eyelids turned down to half-mast, then sparkled with contempt. I saw the moment he recognized the slip, what he'd allowed to show through.

I let my thoughts burn across my face. *Your move, Highness.*

The villain prince thought he knew me, knew people like me, but it was all surface. Those crystalline eyes had been forged from a layer of ice, glacial and shallow. That's how he saw this world, whereas flames reached deeper.

    Ice might reflect fire. But fire melted it.

9

Flare

My victory didn't last. Contempt welded his features back into place. For a moment, he seemed tempted to push back, to flip the knife handle-side-up, then to angle it higher and deeper, if only to see which of us won this tug-of-war. He might do it to scare me, or to learn my breaking point, the same way I sought to provoke him.

But worse than a temper, this ruler mastered the art of restraint. I felt his grip reinforce itself. Slowly, he withdrew the knife. Without breaking my gaze, he reached up to seize the chain, his fingers straying near mine.

He shook the irons like a bell pull. At once, footsteps approached. The gate squealed open, and the same female warrior from earlier stepped over the threshold, followed by a group of other soldiers.

The prince's hiss matched his severe features. "Gag her until we get to Winter."

Then he prowled past me and vanished from the quad. The instant he disappeared, oxygen poured into my lungs, and my body cooled. Under the bonds, the hidden whelk dug into my hands. Thankfully, it stayed put.

The troop made good on their ruler's command, one of them stuffing a ball of cloth into my mouth. I growled around the bundle, then whimpered as they unlatched the manacle. My weight crumpled, and I stumbled in place, wobbling like jelly.

Snaring my arms, the unit marched me from the quad, down another flight of steps, and into an open terrace. Darkness and thickets of clouds engulfed the sky. The tower connected to a walkway leading into the castle, with its bridges, parapets, and colonnades stretching across the endless vista.

Then I heard it—the nearby snarl of a rolling sea. On a gasp, I sprang onto the nearest ledge and clutched a pillar. My neck craned, and my eyes scanned the panorama for a glimpse of the coastline below.

The white-haired knight snatched me by the hips, but my foot sole planted against her face, smothering the wench. With a grunt, she hauled me off the rim, slinging me forward each time I spun the other way.

Instead of crossing into the castle, we hunkered down another flight of cliff steps, then piled into a courtyard lush with ferns and orange lilies. A company of Winter knights hemmed in other prisoners, some born souls heckling the squad and others being harassed.

For sickening reasons having to do with the prince, Pyre was absent. Instead, one of his lackeys took up the slack, waggling his fingers in my direction and returning to the tower with a skip in his step, thrilled to be rid of me. I made it ten paces, eager to tackle that blowfish.

Tragically, a sentinel caught one of my restraints and gave a vicious yank as though the rope was a leash. "Dirty fool bitch," he spewed, boxing my ears until they rang like cymbals.

As if coming to my defense, a seaside gale lashed through the area, giving the guards and soldiers a misty smack. Despite the gag, my lips twitched in pleasure.

Over the next hours, we idled while more captives were corralled, inspected, and appraised. The second a tall shadow bled into view, I curled my knuckles into fists. The Prince of Winter appeared from an arched door abutting the courtyard. As if rehearsed, the company formed two neat rows, creating a lane for him.

My throat smarted. I still felt his fingers squeezing me there, in addition to other intimate places where his weapon had touched my flesh.

As Winter marched through the ranks, guards clamped onto the prisoners' shoulders and shoved us all to our knees. Seasons, how many times would I have to kneel for this prick?

Men and women swaddled in silver robes trailed the prince, their ruler stalking forward with purpose, unfazed by the attention, the angles of his profile so stark that my skin pebbled.

"Heads bowed!" someone barked at us. "Keep them down!"

I kept my head up, peeking through my hair. The prince stared ahead, his stride dominant. Even while aloof, there was something haughty about him, from the arrogant chin to the set of his jaw.

A few strands of his mane escaped from where he'd tied it back, the errant wisps defiantly sweeping his forehead and shoulders. He breezed past me, his fur coat swishing around his legs, which he must have retrieved after leaving the quad. Truly, how did he stand it in this heat?

Roaming peacocks flounced out of the prince's path. Alone, he mounted the stairs to a colonnade jutting from the Fools Tower, where he propped his shoulder against a column and crossed his arms. At his brisk nod, the troops got to it. They offered us dribbles of water and fish broth—meager helpings but food all the same—which I guzzled without tasting after they temporarily removed the gag.

The prince tracked every movement in the vicinity before slicing his eyes toward me. The impact sheared through my chemise, the same way his knife had glazed my flesh earlier, sharp and perilous. I weathered that enigmatic stare and blasted him with one of my own, hurling thunderbolts in his direction.

A rumbling echo stole my concentration. I twisted toward the ocean. The waves sounded restless, a great big anticipation ... of what?

While I mused over that, a chill snuck through my clothes from behind. I shuddered, imagining irises like rings of frost still fixed on me.

More time passed. At one point, the prince vanished.

A couple of hours before dawn, the knights urged us through a door, which led to a network of underground tunnels brimming with torches. The Fool Trade was ritualistic devilry, but it wasn't a parade. For that reason, ships from visiting Seasons relocated to private docks tucked away from the wharf, to complete the exchange overnight and then set sail by daybreak. The tunnels would guide us to Winter's transport and our forthcoming slaughter.

A flash of steel caught my attention. The same tower guard who sported Poet's dagger idled on the fringes while chatting with another soldier. If my arms and limbs got free, it would be easy to creep past them and swipe the weapon.

I contemplated the ropes encircling my wrists and ankles. Yes, I knew these knots. They deceived the untrained eye. Such tethers had been perfected over generations by Summer's troops, the seafaring trade, and sand drifters like Mama and Papa.

Like me.

Also, they'd restrained my ankles, wrists, and mouth. Not my fingers.

Wedging my digits into the bindings, I felt the hard outline of the whelk I'd swiped. The object was sharp, but not sharp enough to sunder thick cords. No, I had a better idea.

I'd been assigned to the same female knight, who trapped my bicep in her grip, who huffed and puffed, and who kept thrusting her gaze at everyone's restraints. Likely, Winter's culture detained people only with irons. But this court was known for its masterful ropes and impenetrable fastenings, and the ignorant troops must have counted on the lot of us being too presumably stupid, or too busy cackling or crying, or throwing fits or ranting, to unravel a kink that most Summer commoners could barely solve.

What they hadn't counted on was the daughter of sand drifters. In addition to sailing, we knew how to weave intricate nets and tie complex knots. Just as we knew how to unravel them.

My fingers strained, fiddling around until they located the whelk. Its chipped edge gave the seashell a chiseled appearance, like a cutting tool. I jiggled the prop loose, pitched it at my escort's feet, and widened my eyes. Feigning astonishment, I acted as though I'd dropped it by accident.

Releasing her hold on me, the female soldier plucked the evidence from the ground and regarded its nicked shape, ideal for shearing through rope. I ducked, pretending to submit as the wench vaulted her arm into the air, ready to strike me. Though at the last moment, she stayed the movement, her mouth compressing and her knuckles folding inward.

A frustrated scoff fled her mouth. After chucking the whelk and kicking it across the tunnel, she finally relaxed. Decoy achieved, the woman's attention turned elsewhere, and her hands fell to her sides. She wouldn't expect to catch me twice.

"Pest," she muttered to herself. "Thought that would free you?"

No, I hadn't. But then, Winter didn't know as much as it claimed to. Under the rope, my fingers caressed the knot.

10

Jeryn

Grabbing my vial pendant in a chokehold, I stalked into the apothecary. Suspended over one of the castle's indoor pools, glass walls comprised this vacant part of the medical wing. I strode without pause to a hutch displaying various bottles, including samples of universal Willow Dime—the same herb that had poisoned Princess Briar due to her allergy—as well as Spring bundleberries, Summer ferns, Autumn wheat kernels, and Winter pine.

An upper shelf held newly mixed restoratives. Among them stood a cruet filled with a clear liquid, its contents indispensable.

I should know. I'd created it.

Although I had brought my own supply, I'd recently drained my vial after meeting with Rhys in that shark-infested throne room. Replacement doses were currently unobtainable, being hefted onto Winter's ship with the rest of my belongings. I should hold off until returning aboard, yet the images of those sea creatures festered in my head. Them, and other haunting visions.

My gaze skewered past the translucent walls and into the corridors. Confirming the vicinity was deserted, I released my pendant, snatched the cruet, uncorked the top, and let a droplet fall onto my tongue. It sat there for a moment before sliding down. I swallowed and shut my eyes as the bitter taste of herbs dissolved on my palate. Instantly, the blood rushing through my veins slowed its pace, the clamminess abating as well.

One spare portion for the vial, in case I required it and couldn't locate my coffers on the ship. Then I returned the vessel to its shelf.

Hanging above a table, a paper lantern flung light across the space. The sunburst painted on its surface matched the ones Summer inked onto its prisoners. Quite a misuse of the court's reserves to brand fools on the ankles, wrists, and neck. An escapee could conceal those places beneath a pair of shoes, a set of gloves, a scarf.

Winter did not mark them that way. If that were the case, my kingdom would do so where it counted—between their brows. That way, pursuers would know where to look. Or if necessary, where to shoot.

Unsheathing the scalpel knife at my hip, I approached and traced the symbol with the blade's tip. Such thin material. Such a delicate facade. Even so, the black painted symbol blazed across the lantern like a force to be reckoned with.

The fixture caused another image to solidify in my mind. Her hands chained overhead. The way her body had strained. The extension had displayed every dip and curve, from her slender fingers, pert nipples, and taut thighs to that bobbing, tattooed throat.

Her smutty chemise had left little to the imagination. The hem had barely concealed the shadowed vent between her thighs, which had parted and quivered under the ministrations of my knife. Damp heat had emanated from her slit, the flesh bare and the temperature of her pussy scorching my knuckles.

Each time she'd swallowed, the sunbursts had shuddered. Each time that had happened, my skin had tingled with urgency.

I recalled how my knife had skated across the fabric of her clothing like a line about to be crossed. When the material had trembled, a perverse temptation had crept down my fingers. Nick her. Toss the knife. Or run the deadly point to other sensitive places that would make her shiver. Each choice had been equally tempting.

Would those hands have grappled the chains? Or would she have devoured me whole?

Potentially, the second, based on that raunchy little stunt when she'd hijacked the moment by smearing her tits and cunt against me. Then against the hilt of my knife. The slip and slide of her genitals across the handle had threatened my fucking grip on the weapon.

Telltale warmth still brimmed from the hilt, the residue of her body heat radiating against my palm. I should sanitize it. I should scrub it clean. I should come to my fucking senses. Instead, a slight floral essence wafted from the handle, an indication of how she smelled. Perhaps tasted.

My thumb stroked over the hilt before I registered my actions. Condemnation, I choked the weapon in my fingers. Another inch of pressure, and the object would crack.

She fought dirty. She knew how to fuck up her enemies.

The woman was fire. Never mind that her shallow pants and flaming irises had tested my endurance. She'd been whittling down those reserves for a while. But with all that heat rising from the beast's flesh like toxic fumes, and with the pressure of her cunt rutting against my knife, I'd scarcely retained my composure.

What. The. Fuck.

What was wrong with me?

One goddamn enigma after another. And I fucking hated enigmas.

Not least of all, her lack of voice. I had speculated whether she'd been faking this, but enough people had confirmed otherwise by now. Despite our shared history—the memory she didn't know about, from a time when she'd possessed working vocal cords—the woman had since lost her ability to speak.

And yet. Twice now, I'd understood her audibly. First, during our fight in Autumn's forest, when she had screamed. Then in the quad, when it had sounded as if she'd spoken aloud. As though every whisper, growl, octave, and flick of her cursed pink tongue were accessible like a distinct frequency, the way certain fauna transmitted noises to one another ultrasonically.

How the fuck was that possible? There had to be an explanation.

Meanwhile, she must have concluded I was simply adept at reading lips. And she would be right. Occasionally, medical practice required that skill.

On to the next matter. All this time, I hadn't taken notice of another pertinent detail until now. Only when she'd been trussed up, had I belatedly registered the slender stomach, which I'd traced with my blade. Her womb had a shrunken appearance that exceeded normal parameters. I knew what dosage had caused it, had seen it before in Autumn, when a born fool had been burned alive in the maple pasture not minutes after my arrival.

Such doses rendered prisoners infertile. Summer used this method to control its captive population.

For some reason, my knuckles curled. Although the preventatives came from Winter, an image of the beast being force-fed that treatment didn't appeal to me.

As for the tattooed collar, I'd dealt with the guard who marked her. Considering the altercation I'd interrupted in the tower, the man's punishment had been overdue. Despite the irony of all I'd done to her, witnessing his insolent hands on the beast had turned my vision red. Shaving the flesh from his knuckles had merely been a prelude. I'd given explicit orders for no one to go near my property. As a result, the guard now lacked any fingers to touch her with, much less other ligaments. I'd taken care of that shortly before polishing off the rest of him.

And while I didn't care to offend Queen Giselle by torturing one of her subjects, I hardly gave a shit what Rhys thought. The guard's wailing had been worth insulting the Crown.

The door flew open. Boot heels hammered into the room.

"Sire, there's a problem," Solstice reported.

That meant one of the captives was causing a disturbance. One rebellious little female came to mind.

I continued tracing my knife across the lantern's sunburst. "Which one of them?"

"The mute one."

Naturally. My hand stalled. I flicked my attentive gaze to the side, my silence commanding her to speak.

The First Knight's words became airborne. "She's escaped."

Two words. Only two words.

Blood rushed to my head. Escaped. Again. For a second, every sensory perception dissipated like a vapor, and every rational thought broke down like scaffolding. But before the shock could immobilize me, it gave way to logic. This time, she had no weapon, nor allies like Poet and Briar to aid her flight. Most importantly, she was restrained.

Across the lantern, I sketched my blade over the fragile outline of the sun. Envisioning the ink around her neck, I thought of her pulse beating against the place where she swallowed.

My timbre came out dispassionately. "She won't get far. Not restricted by those bindings."

A pause. "She has no bindings, Sire."

"What?"

"The mute. She removed them."

Now my head lifted, a muscle in my temple jumping. Slowly, I drew out the words. "What do you mean, she removed them?"

Briefly, Solstice went quiet. "Sire, I-I don't know," she testified. "One moment, the fool was there, and the next she wasn't. We found the ropes discarded in the tunnels."

My wrist twitched. The tip of my blade sliced through the sun.

"I assure you, Your Highness. We had Summer's army enforce the knots," Solstice hurried to explain. "They were secure, beyond anything veteran ship captains could have unraveled. I have no idea how she managed it. No one has that skill."

Incorrect. Apparently, someone did.

Slowly, now. I slowly buried the knife into my sheath and straightened. "Show me."

The tunnels began at an intersection and then spread in three directions, the arteries reeking of gutted fish and piss puddles. Solstice marched at my side while listing the details. The prisoners waited in the ship's cargo hold, the troops had swapped the ropes for irons once aboard, and whatever the fuck else she was saying. I strode ahead, unable to process more.

Summer and Winter's troops brooded in the hub. The former knights grimaced in frustration while the latter stared as if dealing with a gaggle of toddlers, each squad blaming the other for the captive's disappearance, thus achieving nothing.

I materialized from the shadows. Everyone shut up.

The units bowed and split apart. I strode toward them while swatting my hand, dismissing the genuflection. Yet another tedious waste of energy.

Stalling among the soldiers, I reached out. One of them surrendered the castoff ropes, dropping them into my palm. The cords slumped there like dead snakes. Pathetic. Pointless. That's what she'd reduced them to.

We'd always planned on switching to manacles once aboard. But given Summer's proficiency in tying knots that rivaled chains, the bonds still shouldn't have been a problem. They never had been before.

I slit my gaze. No signs that a dagger had been used. Rather, she'd loosened the ties manually. In the half-light, while unable to see what she was doing. The woman might as well have accomplished this impossible task with her eyes closed.

If I'd had the capacity, I would have grinned. Fools were rarely impressive outside of the inexplicably gifted virtuoso.

Sand drifters could dismantle knots. This, I had known. Yet against the expertise of these knights, I hadn't expected a malnourished and reckless prisoner to shed the restraints. To outwit an armed force.

"You shitheads," Indigo of Winter grunted. "You said the ropes were—"

"Our ropes weren't the issue," a Summer knight blustered. "If your first-in-command had kept her eye on the fool, this wouldn't have—"

"Silence," I enunciated.

The drawn-out murmur slithered across the tunnels. The party fell silent, eating the rest of their words.

The throb in my temple intensified. Another unprecedented side effect of this incident.

Solstice approached. "We'll alert the Crown and have the drum sounded."

I contemplated that unfavorable prospect. "That will incite unnecessary panic."

Indigo grumbled. "No drum? Your Highness, that's insanity."

Was it, now?

I tossed the ropes to the ground, useless things. Then I rounded my full height on the warrior, strolled toward him, and cracked his head against the wall.

The man growled in pain, spluttering as I calmly pressed his face against the foundation. Blood oozed from the man's ear, crimson staining his uniform.

Regardless of his combat skills, Indigo had always been outspoken. While I valued candor, I didn't tolerate it at the expense of respect. Lately, this man had been failing to hold his tongue more times than I could count. It was becoming irksome.

I cocked my head. "Do you know why I did that?"

With the knight's lips mashed between the wall and my palm, he couldn't answer. Therefore, Solstice took her cue. "Defamation," she supplied.

My first-in-command glowered at her comrade, and the retinue mirrored her expression, grimaces distorting their features. They regarded Indigo with offense not for the slight—it took more than a petulant tantrum to motivate me—but its content. In The Dark Seasons, to call anyone's sanity into question bordered on blasphemy. Addressing a Royal as such amounted to slander and prosecution.

Squashing his skull harder into the facade, I inquired, "Now when you say insanity, could it be that you're referring to me and not the prisoner?"

Pebbles dislodged from the sediment as he managed to grit out, "Of course not, Your Highness."

"Because for a moment, it sounded like you were questioning my judgment. But that couldn't be," I insisted. "No knight would make that error to my face."

These soldiers and I had built a formidable alliance. So long as they guarded Winter, its people, and the Crown, I treated them as equals. Break that pledge however, and I would respond differently.

The troops knew of my capabilities. Evidently, Indigo had forgotten. I stared. The man cleared his throat, his Adam's apple bobbing.

Much better. I released him and moved on, asking about tracks, to which a Summer knight confirmed the floors were forged of stone throughout. To the matter of fool witnesses, the ones who'd given sound answers claimed not to have seen anything.

Prongs would change their responses. As would saws and spikes.

I glided a finger along my blade hilt. "Ask them again," I instructed Indigo. "Make sure they answer."

Knowing which instruments I preferred, the man pressed a cloth to his bloody ear and bowed. "Sire."

"And Indigo?" I said, delaying the knight.

As he waited, I clarified, "Not the children."

Often, I found myself lenient toward the small ones, drawing the line and exempting them. They were necessary for growth studies, but those procedures were harmless. I had structured it that way, not condoning anything harsher.

This had been my motivation in trading for children with Rhys. Unlike every other born fool, youths endured better treatment in my court than here.

After Indigo left, a Summer knight broached, "The alarm drum would illustrate the king and queen's will, Your Highness."

"It would advertise their idiocy," I revoked. "Giselle has done nothing to earn that affront. And the last thing her deficient husband wants is another stain on his reputation."

"The mute is famished," Solstice advised the troops. "She'll be scared, sluggish, and disoriented. Her options in these passages are limited."

Disoriented, yes. Sluggish, perhaps.

Scared, debatable.

Nonetheless, I inclined my head for them to go. Summer swapped glances, deliberating amongst themselves before agreeing. They would alert Rhys if they couldn't find the captive within thirty minutes.

They disbanded. Solstice remained for my protection, which I refused with a click of my head toward the tunnel. "Just get her."

The First Knight nodded, then sprinted to join the party, her armor clanging down the west tunnel. My troops did not need to be spoon-fed instructions. Although I had given orders that no one should handle the prisoner but myself, present circumstances required me to retract that command. Technically, at least. It would appear uncharacteristic to do otherwise.

I had made certain to sound unruffled. Yet they would not find the beast. It had taken me a year, plus Summer's intervention, to corner her.

Regardless, I would not let them get to her first. So help me, they would not lay a finger on the little beast. For I intended to snatch her myself. When I'd said no one would touch that woman except me, I had not been exaggerating.

Alone, I inspected the corridors. Thinking. Assessing. My first-in-command had admitted to a mishap, that the mad female had succeeded in diverting Solstice with a chipped whelk and skulked away.

A born fool equipped to know her way around a knot. A defensive one. A protective one. Memories from the quad resurfaced. While chained like a specimen, the beast had threatened me regarding her fellow inmates.

I won't let you take them.

Seething, I spun and backtracked. The fool would not depart toward the tunnels' exit. No, she would make for the entrance. Like Poet and Briar, she would attempt to be a hero.

Chances were, the female hadn't gotten through the courtyard yet.

I emerged, prowling from the tunnels and noting the sentinels whose pace lacked distress. Either she hadn't made it past them or hadn't tried yet.

The dense area provided ample shadows amid the crawlspaces. I ignored the salutations and stalked down the connecting paths, my arms striking fronds out of the way. Yet the longer I searched, the sharper my eyes tapered.

Clouds swirled, the elements growing agitated. Although dawn would be approaching soon, an incoming storm brewed.

A warning sound pounded through the kingdom. Whereas Spring rang a tower bell, Autumn used a large horn, and Winter preferred a looming clock, this court sounded a massive drum to alert its citizens. Rigged in the patrol tower, the device inundated Summer with a percussion loud enough to raise the dead.

A steel-plated legion swarmed the castle's bridges, parapets, and colonnades. Thirty minutes must have passed. The Summer attendants had kept their word and reported the flight of a prisoner. King Rhys would turn purple over this. Spittle would fly, in which I'd be subjected to the same cumbersome bullshit I had endured in Autumn.

After traversing the courtyard, I reconsidered my efforts. I could make for the tower, after all. Or …

I thought back to this area, when the prisoners had been assembled here. I'd watched her from a distance, saw the female tilt her head as if sensing an entity. An intangible perception, probably primitive. From my position on the walkway, I'd seen her turn, wheeling toward the beach below.

I followed that trajectory. My attention fixed on a point beyond the stone ledge, a few feet down the precipice. An hourglass shadow made haste scurrying down the bluff, a rampant descent toward the shoreline.

Fuck! Tireless, troublesome creature!

It appeared, she wasn't rescuing her fellow inmates. Or she'd realized that was impossible with everyone on alert.

Tearing off my fur and flinging the vestment aside, I swung my legs over the rim. I would seize this defiant little beast by the scruff and then exercise my full, fucking patience on her.

Yes, she was fire. However, I recalled wrapping my fingers around her throat, dousing that flame before it grew strength. Because that was the thing about fire: it needed air.

II

Flare

I needed air. My throat constricted with shallow pants as I lowered myself down the cliff. Also, I needed some place to land my fucking feet. Both hung off the cliff, my legs dangling while my fingers gripped the ledge, struggling to hold my full weight.

The alarm drum pounded. I startled, my knees banging into a crusted wall of stone and my grasp threatening to slip.

Armored silhouettes with curved swords flew across the parapets. The lower town shone, its villas scattered across the range, each one connected by stairs and bridges. Candles blazed from the windows like furious pupils, their wrathful gazes searching for someone who'd gotten loose.

The Fools Tower loomed overhead, the sight blurring my vision with tears. Pearl and Lorelei and Dante were there, and no one would free them, and no one would help them, because no one *saw* them. Nobody looked at them or listened to them. It wasn't fair, and I wanted to do something, but I couldn't do anything, because I'd run out of time.

In the tunnel, I had untangled myself from the ropes. Creeping backward, I'd snatched Poet's dagger and sheath from the unsuspecting guard, then vanished. While harnessing the weapon to my waist with one of the cords, I had retraced the group's path, scurried on all fours into the courtyard, stashed myself behind the ferns, and slipped past the sentinels. I'd almost reached the stairs into the prison, vowing to my tower mates that I was coming for them. I had planned to snuff out the jail by using the ashes of Summer tinder, the same way rioters had blacked out Autumn's castle for Reaper's Fest. Then I'd intended to charge at the wardens in the dark, use their clubs to bash them unconscious, and rummage through their key rings until I found the right ones.

But the alarm drum had stopped me, forcing me back into the courtyard. There'd been so many people shouting, charging this way and that, blocking the tower's entrance.

I'd tasted the briny wind, followed the breeze, and saw him. The prince had stepped from the tunnel door, his cruel face piercing the shadows like a blade.

Another gust had rushed at me, carrying the scent of saltwater. It had been a warning or a summons or both. The Phantom Wild was calling to me, telling me it was too late to save anyone, warning me that I'd never find the true way to help born souls. Not if I didn't leave right then.

I was sorry. So very sorry. My heart cracked from being sorry.

Instead of storming the tower, I had scrambled in the opposite direction. Until now, I'd been escaping fine, navigating the bluff quickly. The problem was, I had lost my balance. The reason was, I'd seen the prince coming again.

His large shape bustled after me, illuminated by the castle torches. He must have gotten rid of the fur cloak, because his silhouette lacked prickly outlines. Stripped of that heavy mantle, he was nothing but muscle and height, every ridge of his body hewn from concrete.

The prince made the task calm, the way he descended the craggy facade. Off I ripped, tearing down the grass-tufted rocks, from one groove to the next, pebbles skipping from their perches and bouncing off my head. I fell the last six feet. My limbs buckled as I landed in a heap among the cockles, my palms sinking into the sand.

Sand. The open coastline.

Lugging myself upright, I buried my fingers in the grains, scooping them up and holding them to my face. Opening my hands, I watched them sprinkle the air and pile on my lap.

A ferocious belt of wind thrust across the beach. I whirled, following the current's trajectory while batting the hair from my face. The ocean rushed ahead, the tide eating up the shore, waves rolling across the horizon. In daylight, the water would be clear blue, the depths providing a home for starfish, and the sand would sparkle like fragments from the sun.

At least, on a bright morning, they would. Yet as twilight ascended, clouds packed the sky, and the waves turned over themselves. Both elements swirled like a brew, the prelude to a turbulent dawn.

The castle, the town, and the Royal had me cornered. All that was left was the deep. But if the undertow swallowed my weight, it would still be more pleasant than the prince ordering my painted throat on a platter.

As he scaled down the cliff, his head swung toward me. With mock excitement, I flapped my arms and waved. More to the point, Winter saw both of my middle fingers pointing upward like masts.

"Over here, motherfucker!" I called.

The prince stalled while gripping the facade, with his body twisted in my direction. It wasn't as if he could read my lips from this distance and without the aid of sunlight. Instead, I'd assumed my gesture alone would catch his attention.

Yet once again, the prince reacted as if he heard me. Not that I had time to ponder.

If an escaped prisoner was trying to avoid a shark hellbent on ensnaring her, it wouldn't make sense for that prisoner to signal his attention. Not when the prisoner had a decent chance of getting away. Flagging down the predator might hand him the advantage.

But if that shark had already spotted his quarry, and she stood exposed, waving might confuse him. He might tense, and she might take that opportunity to shock him for a second time. The bastard would expect her to race either left or right, along the shoreline. He wouldn't expect the fugitive to veer toward the ocean, and he wouldn't lay odds that she'd kick off her sandals and sprint across the sand, then plunge.

But I did. And when I did, liquid caught me in its embrace, the surf curling, the abyss urging me down. That great big force rolled, taking my body with it, my legs and arms pumping. I held my breath, which was tough considering the laughter rushing up my throat. The dumbstruck look on his face had been precious.

Now if I swam far enough, he wouldn't be able to see where I'd gone. My head breached the surface, my lips sucking air. I had traveled closer to the wharf, so I kept going, slicing through the waves toward the silhouettes of gangplanks and spars and rigging. From the gaunt to the colossal, boats and ships crowded the platforms. Some were slim, built for crossing the kingdom's rivers and the castle's interior streams. Others were long, shallow, and narrow, each fitted with a dozen oars and prows that curved like seahorse tails. The rest were larger than whales, with hulls constructed from swordfish bones.

The ships groaned under their weight. Although sentinels patrolled the docks and quays, the night watch's numbers were few. Nowhere near as many as in town, or at the castle, or in the tunnels, where they anticipated me.

Mama and Papa's tidefarer had been stolen after Summer had caught us, and wharfs commonly stored the vessels of prisoners. Usually the conveyances were auctioned off, but if unwanted—such as a boat owned by the parents of a born soul—they remained property of the monarchy, left abandoned and unused.

I pressed my palms to the ships' hulls and glided between them. A wave sent me careening toward an algae-laced pole, forcing me to dive before the water could shove me into it.

Resurfacing, I almost rammed my head into a stern, then nearly got squashed to a pulp as two boats knocked into one another. The sea pushed something at me, slamming the object against my arm, but I kept swimming. My feet kicked, the water tossing my frame about like a cork. My limbs battled against the waves and then clung to the rim of a catamaran, where I slumped to catch my breath.

Faith and strength waned. Maybe the tidefarer wasn't here. Maybe it had been moved, burned, or dismantled. Or maybe it had indeed been sold.

I went for another round, because sand drifters didn't give up easily. I guided myself here and there, here and there, here and *there*.

Nestled among the larger ships and secured to a stub, the tidefarer—our tidefarer—bobbed like a floating wagon, its shiplap painted the color of marigolds. I recognized the deck's upper cabin and the arched roof like a peddler's cart, fronted by two square sails. At the stern, a third sail fluttered, and a trapdoor would lead down to weapons, tools, and chests for storing treasures.

Ten years later, the boat was here, weathered and probably colonized by moths, but not hopeless. Summer shipwrights built the greatest water transports in The Dark Seasons.

I gripped the boat's ledge, sloshed over the side, and collapsed onto the deck. Gooseflesh popped across my arms. The wet chemise stuck to my body like paste, my nudity visible through the material, and Poet's sheathed dagger still blessedly affixed to my waist.

Hooks flanked the upper cabin's door, each one meant to hold a lantern on those calm nights when Papa would sing, and Mama would rub oil into newly woven nets. Homesickness engulfed me as I darted into the cabin, the interior's musty odor overwhelming. This room had been our home for voyages. It had been a place to narrate stories, legends, and fairytales. We'd outfitted it with stenciled trunks and decorated the floor with vivid pillows.

Mounted on the wall, I found my parents' spear. Unhooking it from the bracket, I stroked my fingers down its surface, then I curled up on the ground among the larvae-chewed bedding and hugged the weapon to my chest. I clung tightly and begged for forgiveness, because Mama and Papa were gone. They had died because of what I had done, because I'd gotten caught and thrown in a cage.

The castle drum tore me out of the trance. I abandoned the spear and scrambled from the cabin, then ducked as something sharp whizzed past my head and vanished into the night. At the wharf, a sentinel launched across the planks while nocking an arrow to his longbow.

He aimed. I moved to dodge the weapon but halted as a steel object flew in the man's direction, impaling the side of his neck. The blade drove clean through and jutted from the opposite end. Crimson sprayed from his throat and splattered the dock as he crumbled.

My eyes widened, swerving toward the figure who stood twenty paces from the dead guard. The livid prince straightened, his arm lowering from its throwing stance. Was that fury directed at me or the sentinel?

It had to be me. Not only had I gotten away, but my escape was also causing him a shitload of trouble. For certain, that lethal expression wasn't meant for the guard who'd tried to lance me through.

The prince launched in my direction. Panicking, I untethered the boat and bid the wharf farewell. My fingers tingled as I worked the rigging, my frantic heart demanding me to be swift. Mama and Papa had taught me how to navigate tidefarers, but I was a child the last time I'd done this. With haste, I fought to resurrect the knowledge and yanked on the tiller.

The sails flapped and rode the current. When I hit a point of no return, the waves sucked the boat into its grip. The tide lifted and dropped the vessel with a mad clap, and the motion repeated, then repeated again. Water doused my chemise anew, fluid lashed my cheeks, and liquid pooled on the deck.

I could let the sea take me. I could let it sink me, and I might be happy to float in that void forever, where Mama and Papa might be waiting, where nobody would find us. But I had Poet and Briar to ally with, and I had my tower mates to save someday, and I had even more born souls to defend after that, and I had my sacred rainforest to find.

In my head, I heard the song.

Seek not, find not, this Phantom Wild.
Sea paths, golden rays, to this Phantom Wild.
Light fades, mist grows, in this Phantom Wild.

It felt as if hours had passed—I'd probably grown decades older on this boat—until the sun flung golden beams across the ripples. I squeezed the tiller. The Summer lyrics churned inside me, along with flashbacks of discovering its secret. Shortly before my imprisonment as a child, I'd seen those lyrics written across a shore. A nameless somebody must have wandered by and sketched the song into the sand, maybe for fun.

I memorized the words, spent hours recreating them, then stared from different angles because something had been strange about their arrangement. Back then, I hadn't known what.

Later, I finally saw it. My gaze breached the disguise, written in the perfect way. Yes, the words made up the song, but when I looked hard enough, those words became shapes, images stringing together to create a map. The symbols included Summer's castle, its wharf, a fleet of clouds, the sea, a trio of sun rays, and a floating rainforest.

For years, I'd marveled at this discovery. When I was transferred to Autumn, I had drawn the same images in a pile of dirt on the dungeon floor. Then after I was caught again in Summer, I recreated the sketch in my tower cell.

The words rang through me now. In my mind's eye, I saw the map, the drawing, and—

I glanced skyward. As twilight gave way to dawn, faint sunrays diced through the storm, their brightness landing on the ocean's surface like a path.

Sun paths, golden rays, to this Phantom Wild.

Hope burst in my chest. I steered toward the strands of light as they skipped over the eddies, beckoning me forward.

The boat gave a jolt, tilting off course and hurtling me across the deck. My shoulder hit the bow, my molars clattering as the ocean threw a fit. I shook myself, then peeled my body off the deck, realizing the sea's outrage had nothing to do with me.

It had to do with the male hand seizing the boat's rim.

12

Jeryn

Infernal bitch. She would pay for this.

First, that sentinel had almost gutted her, a sight that had me feeling murderous, purely because he'd been targeting my property. Nothing more and no other reason.

Second, no rational being would leap into the ocean or pilot a boat during a hellish fucking tempest. The thought of her fighting this storm chilled my blood. She could break her neck. She could drown. Again, let nothing damage what was mine.

This wasn't about keeping her safe. Not a fucking chance.

I heaved myself over the side, my body slamming like a log onto the deck. Staggering to my feet, I seized the rigging for balance. From several paces away, the tiny fugitive tensed.

"Hello, Little Beast," I gritted through the tumult. "Going somewhere?"

Standing amid the chaos like an immortal, she took a precious second to scowl. My drenched shirt plastered itself to my frame, and that minuscule excuse for a dress suctioned to her body. Naked under the garment, her tits, hips, and cunt shone through the material, that threadbare layer of film serving as the only protective barrier. Sopping wet, she resembled a drenched mermaid.

The visual pissed me off. Why the fuck did I feel the urge to steady her before she slipped and fractured a ligament? This female had proven half a dozen times that she wasn't easily breakable.

The tidefarer jolted, knocking us from the bizarre trance. The woman's hand shot out, using the rigging to stabilize herself, the wind buffeting her sodden rags. In a frantic rush, she hustled to the stern and pulled on the steering rod.

Going somewhere?

She speared me with those eyes again, silently answering my question, her sneer indicating something along the lines of, *Yes, cocksucker. And so are you.*

My muscles locked. I'd been too incapacitated by the sight of her to notice one vital fact: I stood in the rod's fucking path.

The beast let go. With the force of a battering ram, the lever swung and slammed into my abdomen, launching me backward. As I crashed, another wave collided with the boat, intensifying the impact. I smashed onto the deck, a shudder vibrating up my tailbone.

Seething, I hauled my upper body off the floor, my muscles screaming with each movement. That maneuver with the lever had been a flagrant overreaction on the captive's part, this being an inconvenient time for us to flay each other. If she had sense, she would have comprehended that.

The fool grappled the apparatus, directing the boat through the maelstrom. Her gaze fluctuated between two entities—the sails and the rising sun. Whatever the fuck she was looking for, that frenetic energy needed to be contained, preferably before she capsized us.

Flattening my palms on the slippery boards, I hefted myself upright. My rumbling groan caused her to swerve in my direction. As I stumbled her way, she guessed my intention to overtake the lever, panic gripping her face.

A second later, her foot hooked beneath mine. The beast gave a harsh jerk, vaulting me backward yet again, at which point she took a flying leap toward my chest and tackled me to the floor. The planks convulsed beneath us, and the boat went rampant along with her. It shot upward, climbing a wave and plummeting into the mouth of another. A wall of ocean struck the hull, sliding us to the opposite end of the vehicle. And because she'd released the lever, the boat tipped from side to side, careening with the surf.

Fucking hell. Clearly, it did not occur to this creature that negligence would result in death.

I reached for her, but the woman saw it coming. With a glare, she cranked her arm, then slammed her knuckles into my jaw. My head rocked sideways, spots blotting my vision. She couldn't weigh more than ninety pounds soaking wet, yet that punch could have snapped my neck.

Clenching my teeth, I lunged. Heaving in her direction, I rammed into the fool, using every inch I had to roll us over. Landing on her back, the beast's slick thighs flew apart and flanked my hips, the upper half of her chemise riding high. My chest mashed into hers with the weight of an anvil, her rabid pulse thrashing against my own.

Pinning her like a moth, I snatched the female by her wrists and fixated on those gilded irises. "Cease, fool," I hissed. "Or we'll drown."

Her lips curled into a snarl. She had the nerve to glower as though I was a moron.

Fresh rancor scalded my blood. Seasons flay me, this firebrand had defied my commands more times than I could count. The second she had projected herself into this behemoth of an ocean, urgency had overcome me. The chase had continued as I'd descended from the cliff to the shore, my gaze tearing apart the coastline and my limbs prepared to dive after my quarry.

The chopping waves could have consumed her. Yet she wouldn't have escaped the tower just to sink voluntarily. A fool she may be, but she was also a sand drifter, therefore a swimmer.

Registering the wharf's proximity, I had launched into a run. Apart from the sentinel I'd killed, it hadn't been a shock to find only a small faction on patrol. Regardless of the alarm, what fool would make it that far? What escapee would take a boat? A loose prisoner would be on land, heading for shelter.

Of course, only a fool wouldn't know better than to brave a storm. I had discerned her dark silhouette on the tidefarer. By then, more bodies had charged in the wharf's direction.

That should have done it. They would have caught up. No need to have put myself in jeopardy.

Yet. Fuck.

I had stared at the black ocean. A subterranean tomb filled with sea dwellers. A tank of them. My breaths had grown shallow, and sweat had crept up the nape of my neck. To compensate, I had recalled the liquid I'd consumed in the castle infirmary, the tension draining from my pores.

Fine. I was fine.

Seconds later, I dove. Let no one … let no *fool* … prove me wrong.

The saltwater had stung my eyes and clogged my throat. But although I wasn't the most adept swimmer, I was strong. Focused. Furious. Those emotions had driven me forward, my need to capture this female eclipsing any fear of leviathans lurking in the deep. I'd kept my eyes on the fleeing conveyance, refusing to look elsewhere.

Without her noticing, the boat's tether had slipped into the ocean. At which point, I'd caught the slack and held on.

Presently, I tightened my viselike grip on her wrists, my arms still burning from the ascent to the boat's rim. The mainsail's bar swooped, beating hectically from left to right. Through the clouds, thin rays of sunlight trickled across the water.

The beast glanced toward the waves, then back to me. Either we both died in the next five minutes or lived to slay each other at a later date. Finally, this logic stretched across her face, and her joints relaxed.

Much better.

I hoisted her up. At once, the woman floundered to the steering lever, her thin arms pulling, making tenuous progress. As I strode over to help, she thrashed her hands about, signaling what to do, and we rerouted the boat.

Toward the sunrays. Not toward land.

Because there was no sign of land.

Implausible. Due to their construction, Summer conveyances could travel at fast speeds. But not that fucking fast. Yet over my shoulder, the coastline had ... vanished.

The mad woman kept checking the rays filtering through the storm. Her fanatical expression alighted, those eyes blazing with elation. Worse, the gleam on her face intensified as she directed the boat.

Suddenly, the sky burned with light and heat, the dawning sun ripping through the clouds like gauze. I twisted back around. Ahead, a new landmass appeared, a dark blot where there hadn't been one before.

The boat surged forward, pushed by another wave, driving us toward that absurd shape, which grew larger. Then bluer. Then greener. My forehead knitted, and numbness overtook my limbs.

In the water, had I been bitten by a siren shark and not registered it? Was I going mad?

Rocks broke the wave. The boat cracked open like a shell.

Instinctively, I reached for the beast. My hand shot out to grab and yank her behind me, to block her from the impact. But before my fingers could snatch the fool, she ducked her head.

Wood exploded, splintering and blasting us upward. Snatching my arm, she vaulted with me into the air. My body hit the ocean, the tide seizing my limbs and vacuuming me down. Fluid shoved me under, the depths glistening like liquified glass.

For a moment, it became quiet enough to concentrate.

Snow fell outside an infirmary window. A signet ring glinted from a trembling male hand, while the pallid fingers of a woman held it fast.

Snow fell outside a bedroom window. My grandaunts entered, knelt before my small frame, and asked if I'd like to be a king someday.

Snow fell outside a university window. The hour tolled midnight as I rolled up my sleeves and poured through the pages of an anatomy textbook.

The water heaved me up. With a great shove, it thrust me onto a coarse periphery. A surface that felt very much like sand.

13

Flare

My eyes peeled open. Water licked my chin as I lay on my back, with my head twisted to the side and fire scalding my throat. Groggy, I lugged myself halfway up. The hem of my chemise was torn, both straps frayed and blazing red cuts marring the knob of one knee.

Hellfire. My hip throbbed like a son of a bitch.

The breeze stirred, bringing with it the echo of shivering leaves. The scent of brine mingled with a strange floral whiff I didn't recognize. I slumped atop a bed of sand—brilliant, white sand that abutted a blue-green ocean tide, the color reminding me of an aquamarine.

While the lazy sea dragged back and forth across the shore, a globe of light blazed over the horizon and splashed gold onto the breakers. I wobbled to my feet and stumbled in the orb's direction. Submerged to my calves, I gawked at the sun, which glowed like a medallion, baking the world in heat and light.

I had washed up ... where?

Despite being a Summer coastline, the ocean's rumble sounded deeper, longer, and fiercer. The sights were richer in hue and exaggerated in shape, lush and overlapping. The crescent beach stretched far, a cove with no inkling of life, no footprints or docked ships. Fern trees crouched low and extended their slender necks over the jeweled water, while other foreign trees rose to a single wooded peak behind me, the thick canopy painted in too many shades of green to count, and fog coiled like a python between the treetops.

A rainforest. It was a rainforest.

I remembered. The Summer lyrics had formed a map, and that map had displayed a path within the sky's rays. I'd been escaping, then fighting the villain prince, then combating a storm. I'd seen the beams of sun and followed them while Summer's castle shrank, disappearing behind a filmy curtain. Afterward, the clouds had parted to unveil another landmass.

Seek not, find not, this Phantom Wild.

Divine Seasons! Laughter sprang from my lips. I covered my mouth and keeled over, my shoulders quaking with mirth. My giddy heels stomped the water, the disturbance scattering trumpet-nosed fish.

Quickly, my humor dissolved into relieved sobs, and I sank to my knees. Overcome, I crawled out of the ocean, slogged across the sand, and stamped my head there. I dug my nails into the ground and clung to the grainy surface, then pressed my palms against the earth like I'd imagined doing endless times. My lips brushed a kiss against the shore and muttered a prayer of gratitude.

"I'm here," I whispered. "I heard you calling, and I came, and we're together."

And I was free.

Yet my happiness died a swift death. What about the prince? Had he landed elsewhere, or had the sea taken him? I'd tried to save us both, hadn't I? Hadn't I tried? I'd grabbed his loathsome hand and thrown us into the waves, but maybe I'd flung him into the crags by accident. When the tidefarer smashed into—

The tidefarer!

I shot to my feet and whirled, my desperate gaze vaulting across the tide. Boulders jutted from the sea, and chunks of marigold-painted wood littered the shore to my right, while the rest of the slain vessel had either sunk or floated away.

With a cry, I dashed into the waves. I leaped over a stingray, its translucent body resembling a sheer scarf. After dunking my head beneath the surface, I forced my eyes open despite the sting of salt. Under and over I went, plunging and rising.

For the next hour, I salvaged what I could. Over multiple trips, I towed ashore my parents' spear, though its tip was shattered, plus rigging lines, a water net, a sand net, Poet's dagger and sheath from the ocean floor, a canteen, a front sail, part of the mainsail, and shiplap planks from the upper cabin.

My haul grew larger, which I dumped beneath a fern tree. All that had been lost flashed through my head, including the stuff I'd forgotten we owned like pails and sand hooks and stone weights for the water nets, boning and hacking knives, chests loaded with compasses, cutlery, blankets, and clothes. I hadn't recovered the boat's third sail or my parents' machete—things I needed and things that had belonged to my family.

I mourned. Sand drifters knew how to find essentials, but I couldn't locate them if the rainforest didn't want me to, if this realm had a different fate in mind.

Thirst parched my throat. Licking my cracked lips, I peered at the misty wall of trees. In the rainforest, there would be blessed springs and creeks. Not least of all, I might encounter ethereal creatures, dark treasures, and otherworldly dangers the Summer song hadn't warned me about.

But inside, I would also find the key to my fate. My purpose, my calling, my mission for born souls.

After ripping long strips of the sail cloth, I wrapped the bands around my feet. Although my toes and heels remained exposed, the cloth protected the rest of my soles.

Then I strapped a rigging cord around my waist, made a knot to secure the empty canteen and dagger, and placed one foot in front of the other. The maybe-dead prince could wait. My heart wouldn't break if the sea had taken that monster, especially not when I'd done my best to save him. I'd thrown the enemy into the waves, not at the rocks, not my fault. But if the universe had decided to play devil's advocate and spare the enemy, I couldn't best him without water.

I couldn't do anything without water. Whatever lurked inside the rainforest could be perilous, but if the song was right, deadly might turn out to be beautiful.

The mesh of shrubs looked painfully adventurous to squeeze through. Thirsty and curious, I wedged myself into the thicket. Gnarled offshoots scraped my chin and poked my ankles. The hedges ate up the sunshine, cloaking the route in darkness and crushing me so that I couldn't tell if I walked in a straight line.

I slapped my ear as something brambly skated behind my lobe. Whatever it was, it stung my flesh like a needle.

The air grew wetter, the plants tighter, the journey longer. A musty scent coated the air, making me dizzy. Creepers unfurled and reached out like fingers to snag my hair. Yelping, I jumped back and blinked through the haze.

Finally, the thicket parted. I spilled onto a path, the foul smell disappeared, and my head cleared. A dimly lit wild greeted me. Vapors slithered around the trunks while tendrils of vivid green plants glimmered among the shadows.

Then the rain fell. Washing down in droves, its arrival pulled a wondrous gasp from my lips. Smiling, I thrust my arms upward, tipping my chin and opening my mouth, the fresh, pure zest sliding across my dry tongue. My frame shook with relief, and if I started to cry, I let those tears bring me back to life.

The burning in my throat cooled. I drank and drank, then I filled my canteen.

Plucking a few leaves, I used them to scrub myself from top to bottom. I did this while laughing and weeping, the torrent leaching the sea salt from my body, soothed my cut knee, and clearing the sand from my fingernails until they gleamed white.

When the rain eased to a drizzle, I kept going. My eyes jumped from one marvel to the next. Vibrant colors glowed from every dark recess, some shades recognizable, others beyond my imagination. The flutter of goldenrod feathers. The quiver of fuzzy blossoms. Trees the likes of which I'd never seen—from sage to emerald—crocheted together and formed a dense canopy so high that my neck ached as I gaped overhead.

A melody of sounds rang from above. Cavernous warbles. The long slide of a whistle. Thuds pounded across boughs, the percussion heavy like the paws of a predator stalking its prey.

Blossoms covered a tree trunk, the bouquet spanning its height. As I padded closer, the petals flew from the bark and flapped into the air.

Butterflies! They flitted across the forest, some of their wings glowing and shifting color with each beat, from dainty pink to fiery red like stained glass. The creatures swirled around me, their sizes ranging from miniature to massive. Elated, I leaped into a dance, twirling alongside them, the jubilant butterflies fanning their wings and waltzing with me down the path.

Without warning, they broke apart and scattered. Grinning, I watched them soar.

From someplace nearby, a serpentine hiss vibrated through the air. Not long after, a low rumble skidded from another area, sounding very much like a feline's roar. The echoes caused my flesh to shiver with a nervous thrill.

"Show me your secrets," I whispered to the forest. "Let me learn. Help me find what I'm looking for."

Did this land hear me the way I heard myself? I liked to believe so.

Closing my eyes, I waited for the slightest tremble of air and deciphered its direction. Opening my eyes, I watched how this world moved, how each breeze rustled the canopy, and I ran my fingers over the offshoots, looking for breaks that would lead to a spring.

Then I squatted and pressed my palms into the earth, feeling the tremors that rose from someplace below. Setting my ear to the ground, I listened for flows and streams. The floor rumbled, though not from water. Instead, the vibrations could be roots stretching or animals prowling from a distance. Nothing more.

Of course, this rainforest would not simply hand me everything I needed. It had chosen me, beckoned me, given me the power to recognize the map inside the song. But although this place had been awaiting my arrival, it wasn't any common parcel of land like the ones I'd explored with Mama and Papa. This realm had no equal. It was the one and only rainforest in The Dark Seasons, and even with our bond, I couldn't know all the rules. The wild would show me where to discover the key, provided that I earned it.

Sitting upright, I moved to stand—then halted. Another noise cut through the foliage, the disturbance made by human limbs and a pair of boots.

I doubted anyone else had been chosen by the wild to venture here. At least, not in recent eras. Therefore, the racket could only belong to one monster.

On all fours, I scampered into the shadows and set my fingers on the dagger. The prince wouldn't stop until he got his hands on me. But I wouldn't let him claim me again.

Not if I caught him first.

14

Jeryn

She would not catch me first. If I knew one fucking thing, it was this: The little beast was alive. Not even a shipwreck would break that spirit.

And she was here. Somewhere close.

At the forest's border, I eased myself through the wall of foliage, my shoulder knocking offshoots out of the way. I'd had reservations about the hedges' penetrability, however I managed to shove myself through and emerged onto a path where the terrain expanded into a wilderness. The humidity intensified, drenching the atmosphere like a sauna. My body turned into a porous thing, with perspiration leaking from every inch of skin.

My tattered shirt and threadbare pants clung to my frame like adhesives. At least, the garments had survived the storm, including my belt, boots, and scalpel knife.

I felt around my chest for the vial, which rested near my pulse. Thanks to the stamina of Winter glass, the pendant and its contents had withstood the shipwreck. Back in Autumn's dungeon, that little beast had done the object more damage than Summer's tempest.

Reassured, I eased my grip on the pendant. If I didn't know better, I would conclude I'd walked into a mirage. Except mirages receded upon one's approach, whereas this environment became more tangible with each step.

Bloody hell. The infernal symptoms of a shipwreck assaulted me, not least of which included a depleted stomach—I'd vomited a gallon of seawater upon regaining consciousness—and a physical constitution that left me sweaty on the outside and dry on the inside.

The forest's canopy blotted out the sun. Though the darkness failed to reduce the heat, it did soothe my flesh. If I had languished unconscious on that beach for another hour, I would have roasted.

After leaning against a tree trunk and relieving my bladder of what little fluid remained inside it, I kept walking. My cranium pounded, a laceration stretched along my jaw, and welts had formed across my thighs, courtesy of the beast who'd flung that steering lever against me.

Technically, I should be worse off. A puncture wound. A severed extremity. A crushed skull. Yet improbably, I'd gotten rather fucking lucky.

My boots brushed a cluster of wet leaves, the contact cutting off my analysis. The slick underbrush glistened from a downpour that must have occurred while I'd lain comatose. Because of that fugitive, I had washed ashore on some cursed land mass.

Leaves swished in my periphery, as if something had dashed through. Awareness crawled across my shoulder blades. Without turning my head, I diced my eyes toward the commotion, to where a silhouette flashed in and out of sight.

Ah. Not a mammal or reptile. This source was human, female, and about to pay dearly for the past twenty-four hours.

Fury pulsed through my veins. Stalking sideways, I set my fingers on the scalpel knife's hilt and edged through the bushes. Pacing. Caution. Otherwise, she would hear me coming.

But when I broke into motion and lunged in the direction she'd raced, a hedge stalled my progress. My lips twitched. So the beast meant to slip around me, to initiate another cat and mouse chase. Hunting her through this forsaken climate should not trigger my pulse, yet the illicit rush of it propelled me forward like an unhealthy impulse.

Phosphorescent undergrowth shone in the dark. I tracked every shiver of leaves, each sprinting noise. Around tree trunks. Abreast of unidentified nests. My head twisted, trailing glimpses of feminine limbs and the swish of her chemise.

A mile into the hunt, I grimaced. The wall of hedges standing before me made it clear. She'd led me in a circle, to confuse my sense of direction.

The fool was toying with me. Already, she knew this terrain better than I did.

I choked the knife. My thumb traced the hilt, where multiple silts embedded into its facade. Armed with this cache of blades, I could pick which one I'd use on her.

Another tremor of vegetation resounded like a taunt. With renewed anger, I prowled ahead. Swerving into what should have been her direct path, I hissed at the empty route. After another half hour, I lost all trace of the beast.

Perhaps she had gone astray as well. Perhaps now she would take her predicament seriously.

As should I. This landscape was scarcely a playground. Developing a fetish for this chase was hardly wise while trapped in a sweltering forest teeming with fauna.

I lacked nourishment and energy. Therefore, I lacked sense.

A critical solution existed for this. The presence of greenery meant fresh drink had to be nearby, after which I'd recover the stamina to snatch that little beast once and for all.

Maintaining a hold on my weapon, I pursued an adjacent route while auditing the wild. The canopy towered one hundred feet in the air and exhibited a variety of unrecorded tree species. Or so it appeared from this vantage point, with limited visibility and nausea compromising my senses. Yet nothing about this wilderness seemed recognizable, from the leaf shapes, to the circumference of every exposed root, to the texture of each tree trunk.

An unrecognizable avian—a bird of prey?—with a long shag of plumage perched on a branch. Ants hauled a chunk of feces past my feet. Trees glinted with shades reminiscent of malachite, among countless others.

Come to think of it, color should not be this visible here. Yet its vibrancy pushed through the limited light.

Comprehension dawned. I knew what tropic environment this was—which type of fresh hell we'd landed in.

The climate. The flora and fauna. The evidence of rain.

This indicated one landscape. Over history, Summer had preserved a legend originating from some asinine song about a rainforest. Be that as it may, no one had ever set foot upon its shore. And why? Because Summer did not have rainforests.

Or rather, it was not supposed to. But how else to justify this unpopulated expanse and its sudden appearance in the ocean? Ludicrous. This may be an uncharted rainforest, but it wasn't *that* rainforest. A legendary realm that had gone uncharted for centuries wouldn't have been this easy to access—a feasibly short distance from the wharf.

There had to be an explanation. Possibly, Summer kept this wild a secret for other reasons.

In any event, Winter and Summer's fleets would find us. Giselle and Rhys's armada was more equipped than any other naval force.

The tear in my jaw throbbed. Although I'd cleaned it with saltwater earlier, it continued to ooze blood. Without a needle and thread, stitches were impossible. Moreover in this stifling climate, the likelihood of infection would increase.

Yet the corner of my lip curled. A fucking rainforest.

Despite my parched mouth, the rest of my frame dripped with perspiration. While I'd spewed ocean water from my gut, the precipitation would wring me out as my body continued its futile attempt to cool off. If confusion or dizziness arose, if my head kept hammering, or if my vision blurred …

My free hand located the vial. I thought of hallucinations, of spending my final hour in a spiral of dehydrated lunacy.

Whether or not this place experienced frequent rainfall, there must be a stable body of water nearby. Bred in a court replete with trackers, I consulted Winter's knowledge. Find a downhill slope or follow the animals. Hunters checked for sundered or distorted branches, or other signs of a trail made by fauna.

My mental faculties must be wavering on a precipice, if it had taken me this long to remember such elementary trivia. I scrubbed my eyelids to clear my vision. If it came down to it, I might have to slap the shit out of myself.

Would that beast know her way around here, through some primal instinct? Or would the raptors, reptiles, or mammals get to her first?

I hastened, stalking down the lane. The sooner I fueled myself, the sooner I would find her.

With every few steps, the mist forced me to pause and catch my breath. From somewhere in the canopy, a disconcerting hiss vibrated.

I proceeded with caution. Where fauna lived, water would flow.

Ahead, a sliver of blue sparkled through the foliage. I pushed my way into an enclosed copse of fig trees and halted before a small, glistening pool. On the opposite side, vegetation offered glimpses of an abutting shoreline, though not the cove I'd washed up on, since that expanse had been barren. At this alternate beach, detritus from the tidefarer had been lumped under a fern tree, creating a disorderly pile, as though the tide had ejected it there.

Water first. Logic second.

I located an errant stick and thrust its length into the pool. Not shallow, since the tip failed to hit the ground. Also, compared with any other water body, these eddies were cast in a strange kind of blue. I could not place the exact shade.

More hissing slithered from the treetops, their boughs shifting under the bulk of a moving creature. The sound brought serpents to mind. If the reptile kept a habitat in the trees, that meant it knew how to camouflage itself.

I considered other vital facts like prehensile tails, crushed bones, and asphyxiation. Either that, or venom.

Idling near an unknown dweller could mean death. Whereas dehydration guaranteed it.

I sank to my knees while keeping a vigilant eye on the canopy. When no other activity occurred from above, I glimpsed the water and noticed my reflection. A drop of blood swelled from the cut on my face, slid across my jaw, and plunked into the water. My weather-beaten features peered back, the sight unrecognizable—a Royal with uncertainty clouding his eyes.

I shook off the impression, then dipped a finger into the pool. The surface tensed, the ripples exerting a downward pressure. An evident misinterpretation on my part, a symptom of intense thirst. Or the product of delusional thinking.

Anything but that. Anything but forfeiting sanity.

First thing. Purify the water. Boil it with the fermented petals of a Winter violet and drink. Simple.

Not fucking simple. With what flame or saucepot? I could use saliva to enact fermentation, but I would need time. And I would need a Winter violet.

The water attached itself to my finger like a leach, the pressure so great it took effort to withdraw my hand. As if weighed down by bricks, my eyelids grew heavy.

Refusing to acknowledge such absurdity, I tested a droplet. It soaked into my tongue, fresh and pure, whereas lagoons would have contained saltwater.

I waited. No effects.

Another dose. Nothing.

I swallowed more each time, however this tentative approach would take me only so far. I formed my hands into a bowl and submerged them. The water pressure grew stronger. Toward what might be the bottom, the pool's depth appeared to be swirling.

Withdrawing my hands, I lifted them to my mouth and quenched my thirst. Liquid gushed down my throat, alleviating the bone-dry sensation. Hopefully, this would rinse my mind of delirium. Matter of fact, I could drain this pool, so great was my craving.

My hands sank back into the water, down to my elbows. I had never partaken of anything so stimulating. So ...

"Alive," I muttered.

Silence. No hissing reptile. It had left, cleared the area.

I narrowed my eyes at the whirling surface. What the fu—

The pool seized my arms and yanked me under.

15

Jeryn

The vortex swallowed me whole, plunging my weight into a roaring abyss. Water latched onto my limbs, snared around my ribs, and drove me down.

This close to the ocean, a harmless pool would be shallow. It would be salted. It would be immobile, not drowning its visitors in an undercurrent.

Beating my limbs only made me sink deeper, which made no fucking sense. I twisted against the undercurrent, the vacuum sweeping me toward its base. I narrowed my gaze, struggling to find a rift in the force. A fissure. A weak spot. My chest convulsed as I pumped, my lungs battling to keep up.

A broad tree vine appeared, plunging through the surface and smacking me across the face. I reeled back as the cord floated before my gaze. Without deliberating, I clamped my digits around the tail and felt it straining to tow me upward. Yet for some reason, my resistance gave the water strength, the pressure on me increasing.

It didn't help that my weight drove the slack down. When I dropped another three feet, the person holding the cord plummeted halfway into the tumult.

The beast's wild face and golden irises burst through the blue. Her hands gripped the cord, which had stretched to its limit, though she kept herself from going under fully. Her brows squashed together in frustration. Bubbles spilled from her lips as she said something, either a scolding or instructions.

Or perhaps a demand. *Hurry the fuck up!*

I slit my gaze. Then I rammed my heels against the water.

It didn't work. The fool's hold faltered, the whirlpool threatening to consume her.

I glanced down to see my inevitable destination. A flashing dot of light spiraled below like a distress signal. Fragments came into focus, revealing a fang-shaped pendant and a length of chain.

A sudden absence. An extraction. An irretrievable loss.

Feeling the starkness of my neck, I peered closer at the falling object. A necklace. A vial. The keepsake sank, glass glinting before the murk swallowed it whole. How ironic that it had survived the tempest only to be taken here. I would have laughed if I weren't thinking of the hands that had given me the pendant, how it used to hang off my childlike frame, how I'd slept with it, ate with it, lived with it. I would have mourned if I weren't entertaining the notion of going down with the vial, of tearing the thing from the water's grasp and then dying anyway.

Misguided, to say the least. I had to be in the grips of an illusion.

My body rose. I glanced toward the bane of my existence, who tugged me upward, the attempt successful now that I'd gone limp. When she gave a final pull, we vaulted to the surface, the brunt of it tossing my frame at her like a harpoon. Together, we hefted ourselves onto the soil and collapsed in a breathless heap.

I slumped onto my back beside her, my torso heaving and my lungs clamoring for oxygen. I patted my chest, touching wet skin and muscle but finding no vial there.

Lost. Gone.

The forest went quiet, and tree trunks vanished high into the mist. The vine rested next to me, attached to a neighboring tree. I whipped my head sideways and collided with the mad woman's gasping profile. Braced on her elbows, the beast's gaze shot to mine with a ferocity that sent a bolt of alarm across my flesh. I had been right earlier about her eyes, how they flung her emotions out to the world. I saw the hot fear.

She bounced on all fours. I shot to my feet.

The beast ripped out a familiar dagger tethered to her hip. At some point during her escape, she'd retrieved the weapon that had once belonged to Poet.

I seized my scalpel knife, flicked open the longest blade, and wielded it to block her. We halted. Our weapons braced. Suspicion climbed up my fingers, which tightened around the hilt.

I waited for an attack. She did the same.

Then my vision swam, and my joints gave. In my dazed state, the woman lowered her dagger. At which point, the world tipped on its axis. Moments later, she was leaning over me, a blurry splash of dark hair outlined by the wilderness. I saw her as if through curved glass, like an obscure specimen in a container.

Or was I the specimen this time?

Hard soil and stems dug into my spine. It seemed my prediction had come to fruition. The shipwreck, the thirst, and the near-drowning conspired to finish me off.

The fool tilted her head, benign for once in her misbegotten life. It was about fucking time, I thought as she faded from view.

16

Jeryn

Fuck. Something damp and brittle snared my wrists. When I tried to shift, an object harnessed my elbows in place, the constraint locking my wrists behind my back.

Rope. Knots.

My disoriented eyes whipped open. The metamorphosis from oblivion to consciousness stunted my vision, impairing my ability to focus during the first few seconds. Opaque blots of color oscillated before me, then solidified into a cove. Beyond a crescent of fern trees and gnarled hedges, chalk-white sand bordered a jewel-toned sea, waves smashing into the shore.

The bonds shackled my form as I lay slumped against the trunk of a tree, which extended its low, spindly neck over the beach. Predictably, my knees and ankles were bound as well.

Sunset descended, shades of orange crowding the sky. The little beast had disappeared.

To my left, a hoard of supplies had been dumped atop a sail cloth. The stockpile consisted of a canteen, that ostentatious dagger previously owned by the jester, a water net plus a strange hoop-shaped net with a chewed handle, lines of more rope, one mangled spear, another sail cloth, skeletal fragments of wood, and the figs that had been growing near the whirlpool.

The whirlpool. The place where I had swallowed freshwater in exchange for a brush with death.

Considering the setting sun's position, I must have been comatose for hours. My skull no longer pounded, but my thighs burned, and the laceration across my mandible throbbed. I assessed the damage by flexing my muscles as best I could and rolling my jaw. The gash seemed to have crusted over. No leakage. No sensation of heat. The wound might not be as bad as my dehydrated cranium had suspected. But for Winter's sake, I ached.

Slanting my head toward the waves, I stiffened. A drenched figure rose from the water like a sea witch, her dripping web of hair appearing murkier at the day's end.

She crossed the sand on bare feet. The more distance she ate up, the more of her I saw. The little beast had taken a beating from the wreck, with lacerations covering her arms and one running across her knee. Her chemise was soaked and had lost a strap, and the garment was plastered to the naked body underneath. Hollowed waist, prominent ribcage, shrunken breasts. Dusky nipples and a dark spot at the apex of her thighs. Nothing I hadn't seen before as a physician. Even so, my gaze caused the mad woman to halt, an angry flush staining her cheeks.

What? Did she think I was fond of the view? How repulsive.

Yet. A second glance at her wet breasts and pussy caused my retinas to sizzle. Some atrocious form of lightheadedness fogged my brain, to say nothing of the brief twitch in my cock.

Rage. Malice.

They had to be the culprits. For weak souls, hatred and stress manifested itself in depraved ways, including involuntary sexual frustration.

My stare progressed to her hands. Thin fingers that tied indestructible knots, steered boats through tidal waves, and pried victims from whirlpools. Hands that reached out and grabbed life by the throat. Resilient hands cast in a deep olive complexion, with a beauty mark imprinted on her thumb. Hands that fought back and survived.

Examining them for longer than necessary felt dangerous. I wrenched my gaze from the visual, only to behold another offensive sight. My scalpel knife and its sheath rested in a cord tied around her waist.

A snarl rolled up my throat. I had been so distracted by the graphic sight of this beast, I'd neglected to search for my weapon. Evidently, she'd confiscated it and then decided to make a fashion statement.

The beast noticed my reaction, her expression transforming from flushed to elated, her mouth tipping into a victorious grin. She flashed straight teeth and the site of an extracted molar, the gap visible as her lips peeled back.

Point taken. She could have used her own weapon, but in claiming mine she might as well have laid siege to my kingdom.

Slitting my eyes, I watched her flaunt the knife. Vindicated, she strode past me, her toes knocking a lump of sand across my pants.

So be it. My move would come, so long as I remained patient.

A trench cutting through the sand from the rainforest's edge hinted she must have dragged me from the whirlpool. How long had it taken her paltry muscles to accomplish that?

Depositing a net between us—this one replete with mollusks—the female dumped herself atop the sail like a makeshift blanket. While parsing through the haul, she gloated, "Your Royal Dickless isn't so Royal anymore, are you?"

"No, but Your Royal Dickless still expects you to untie him," I replied.

Her gaze snapped to mine. With her head bent, I shouldn't have been able to read her lips. That's what she was thinking.

Which meant she wasn't used to people ascertaining her audibly. Which meant my capability was rare, if not impossible.

I accepted this. I was too pissed off, too fatigued, and too shipwrecked to analyze.

She'd been taunting me, presuming I wouldn't understand her if we weren't speaking face to face. In short, she'd been trying to make me feel inadequate. But if the beast insisted on baiting a predator, she shouldn't complain if she got bitten. I would dispel any and all of her assumptions.

Right. Fucking. Now.

"Indeed, I'm proficient at reading lips," I ridiculed. "But for some confounding reason, I have the ability to detect your voice, so turning away while speaking won't help you."

Shocked indignation flashed across her face. "That can't be."

"It is," I stated. "Period."

"It's not! No one can hear me except—"

When she cut herself off, I squinted. "Except whom?" Then for the first time in my fucking life, I took a wild guess. "Except you?"

Her glower confirmed enough. It seemed we were the only two individuals capable of registering her voice.

Although I hated loose ends, this inexplicable fact wrung a smirk from my lips. "How does it feel to know you're not impenetrable?"

That did it. Snatching the hilt of my scalpel knife, she extracted it from the harness, shuffled toward me on her knees until the heat of her flesh seared mine, and traced a faint line across the gash in my jaw. "How does it feel to know you're not invincible?" she retorted.

A gritty noise pushed against my mouth. I made the most of our staring contest. Silence versus silence. Yet to my displeasure, the blast of her gaze threatened to knock me off balance, the muscles in my face loosening a fraction.

My adversary broke the contact out of dismissal rather than submission. Blocking me out, she stored the weapon, uncapped the canteen, and drank. Her throat flexed, the inked collar of sunbursts shifting in tandem, while my own throat felt dry.

Those dangerous hands went to work. She propped the mollusks beside the assortment of figs, then reached for one of the orbs.

"I would not do that if I were you," I advised.

At my prolonged drawl, she paused and gave me a scathing look. Malnourishment was the reason I'd ordered the patrol to go easy on her in the courtyard, to feed every captive a scant portion of broth during transport. Despite this logic, the thought of this female vomiting what little her system could handle had unnerved me as much as the chemise barely covering her ass.

Never mind. Back to the fucking subject.

"Eat slowly. And do not eat much," I instructed. "If you get sick or die, there will be no one to untie me. Are you following, or should I use simpler words?"

She arched her brow. Defiant. Unimpressed. That look made it clear she did not require medical advice on the subject. The beast was familiar with the concept of starvation and understood the definition of malnourishment.

Ignoring my spiteful countenance, she picked one of the bulbous figs and sniffed it carefully. Summer citizens would recognize the native fare of their kingdom, unless it originated from a presumably deserted rainforest floating in the middle of nowhere. In this place, looks could be deceiving. She knew this too, especially after the whirlpool incident.

Deeming it safe, the beast raised the fruit to her mouth, but I cut her off. "Are you aware that in Summer, the brighter the fruit, the deadlier the poison? If it is indeed poisonous?"

At my jibe, she squeezed the fig. Under that much pressure, it might detonate.

Rarely did I feel the desire to provoke. Such indulgences wasted time, whereas I preferred candor. It cut quicker, deeper, harsher. Yet I craved this creature's attention like a stimulant.

My lips quirked. "Winter has discovered many noxious plants across the Seasons. For instance, a Summer poison derived from yellow clovers, which assassins smear onto jewelry. It peels the flesh clear off."

The instant she grimaced, I made myself comfortable and lounged against the tree trunk. "Also, venom from the bite of a siren shark or a viper. I've spent years mastering the art of medicine. I've seen what the brew of nature can do to a person's eyes, mouth, blood, skin ... mind."

She just stared at me. So I fucking pushed harder. "A fruit unknown to you. Technically, you could make the prince sample it. Of course, that would mean forcing him to risk himself for you. And of course, that would turn you into the very captor you loathe." I tilted my head. "It would turn you into me."

Her nostrils curled as if she'd inhaled something rancid. Excellent. Because I had her attention, I arranged myself into an indolent slouch. "Survival or conscience. But what would a primitive thing like you know of conscience?"

Although I had instructed her to be wary of food portions, now I persisted in scaring her from eating anything at all. Not that my warning wasn't valid.

As for that last goading question, this woman saw through the test—my quest for the chink in her armor. The spot where I could probe.

Some type of daring incentive alighted her features, motivating the beast into action. Balancing the fig, she crawled toward me with the ease of a feline. Instinctive. Unpredictable. My eyes cut to her rotating hips and then returned to those irises, which shone like golden spheres in her face. I waited for the slap of her hand or some other hostile response. Possibly a mouthful of squashed fruit, which I would be sure to spit back in her mutinous face.

The mad woman approached, slinking across my limbs until our noses tapped, pausing with her thighs splitting around my waist. Droplets of seawater streaked down her neck and hit my chest. One rebellious bead dangled from a breast and splashed onto my navel, which snuck into my waistband like a trespasser.

Straightening upright, she lowered herself onto my lap. Seasons flay me, with her open limbs splayed around my hips, wet and warm on my pelvis, the effect infuriated me for reasons I couldn't begin to list. My canines ground together with enough pressure to crack enamel.

Lifting one hand, she wedged the swollen fig between our mouths. This, I had not expected. A solution. A challenge. Least of all, the sprawl of her dripping body atop mine, the proximity inundating my olfactory senses with the aromas of salt, sun rays, and wildflowers. More potent than the fruit, those fragrances saturated the air, strong enough to intensify one's craving.

My traitorous stomach writhed. I had to eat something.

Revolted, I opened my mouth at the same time she did. I bit into my side of the fruit while she bit into hers. Not succulent or saccharine, as I had expected from a common fig, but hard and crisp. Tartness slid across my tongue and quelled the gnawing in my gut.

Together, we ate and stared. I measured her movements, matched the rhythm of her lips, and kept alert for warning signs. I knew methods of taste-testing for poison. This was not one of them.

We repeated the process, biting and swallowing with our gazes fixed. But when a droplet of nectar rolled down her chin like an illegal kink, I felt a perverse need to drag my tongue over the bead and lick her clean.

Apparently, my feverish cock agreed with me. Blood rushed from my sac to the head. I blew through my nostrils until the physical violation subsided, thankfully before it progressed to a fully-fledged, hate-fueled erection. With her pussy settled in the worst possible location, she would have felt that for certain.

Equally confounding, I thought of telling her essential things. I thought of warning her there were other dangers besides poison in this rainforest. I thought of saying there were thousands of unknown hazards beyond that border. I thought of listing exposure, night crawlers, and toxic botanicals.

And what was her plan? To keep me shackled until the masses found us? On her own, did she expect to be alive by the time a fleet arrived? What did she know about rainforests? Did she understand the nuances of a leaf that killed versus a leaf that cured?

If she got injured, who would heal her?

I thought of asking these questions merely to watch the responses fly out of her mouth, to have another excuse to see her lips move. Her, a born fool. I chewed on that notion while chewing on the fig, not liking the acridness of either.

We swallowed the last of the fruit, consuming it down to the pit, which verified it wasn't an actual fig. I sensed her yearning to suck on the stone, but that would require our lips to touch. A repugnant prospect to us both, because she tossed the pit over her shoulder, and my mouth relaxed. In unison, I leaned back, and she shuffled off my lap.

The sun dissolved behind the horizon. The sky darkened to the blue shade of a bruise, and the black tide mowed over the shore.

The mad woman retreated to her makeshift blanket, steepled her legs to her chest, and wrapped both arms around her calves. She set her back to me, the motion stretching her chemise taut and delineating the slender vertebrae of her spine.

I averted my gaze. Ignoring each other for the night sounded like an ideal plan.

Though, eventually I would need to piss. And I knew what she would do about that: give even less of a shit. In which case, the only perk of this infernal humidity was that I might last a while before soiling these pants. To compensate, I would take pains to worm my way onto her precious sail cloth and soak it with urine.

The rainforest's border loomed behind us, the treetops spearing the night sky. Several minutes passed. From the corner of my eye, I took a second look, glancing at her moonlit silhouette. Precisely what was the beast's madness? The tattoo collar classified her as feral, therefore deadly. Yet despite her spitfire nature, this did not sit right with me. Summer's assessment was off the mark.

She released her upturned limbs, hunched over the sand, and drew something there. Through the darkness, I made out a rendering of waves, trees, and a crescent. A replica of this cove.

As she worked, a gleam dominated her profile, worshipful and tender. Hmm. A penchant for art, which I'd first noticed back in Autumn's dungeon. Imaginative and passionate, with a protective streak toward others. Also—

She whirled on me. "Stop doing that!"

I met her glare. "Your back was turned. You saw nothing."

"I knew what you were thinking."

"So you can read minds, beast?"

"I'm not a beast, and I'm not your prisoner!"

"Neither am I yours," I dismissed. "Tying me up doesn't make me less of a prince or you less of a fool. You think you're innocent? You think you're an authentic heroine?"

"You think you're a real leader? Some shining example of a ruler?" she threw back. "Guess what. That ship sailed with Poet and Briar."

"Meaning, you were friends with them," I sneered, more as confirmation than realization. "Indeed, they were excessively protective of you, even if they remained silent on the matter."

"That's because they're too clever for you. Brag about your intelligence all you wish, but you'll never match up to them."

"Yet unlike those two nuisances, I'm a doctor," I hissed. "I save lives."

"By stealing other lives!"

"A prince doesn't need to steal his own property. And if he's wise, he'll learn a skill or two that exceeds his throne."

When her reply escaped me, I gave her an exasperated look. To which she repeated, "What wise prince chases his quarry into the ocean?"

"A prince who knows he'll catch her."

"Your wisdom chased me to an invisible realm, and now you're trapped here, and you still haven't caught me."

"This is not an invisible rainforest," I growled. "This is nothing but an undisclosed landmass Summer has evidently kept to itself. A fool's paradise. And you're nothing but a filthy, mad plague—"

"I'm *not* a plague!"

"—who got us here by accident." I leaned forward until the bonds strained, threatening to cut off my circulation. "And you *are* a plague, which means you do not count. You're extraneous. A virus we're forced to deal with."

"The Seasons are divinities, but they don't judge me. Their courts do. Their people do. You can't say nature didn't make me. It did, like everyone else!"

"A miscalculation on its part," I dismissed.

She pointed at the sea. "I'm of Summer. I know this ocean."

"Then you should have done me a favor and drowned in it."

"Make up your mind! You wanted to catch me or wanted me to drown. Which is it?"

"You forgot about Autumn's dungeon, where I wanted you punished for the vial. Then in Summer's tower, where I wanted you to choke and kneel."

"Monster!"

"I'm not the one who's collared around the neck."

Renewed fury contracted my muscles, this time directed at the dead guard I'd whittled down to a fucking skeleton after learning he was the one who inked her.

Distracted by the memory, I missed whenever she ranted. "What did you say?"

"I said, I hate you! I hate that you chased me, I hate that you followed me, I hate that you're here. I hate everything about you!"

"That's treason."

"And I hate your people. I hate Winter and its rulers."

I drew out the words. "Think twice before speaking, Little Beast."

"Two times, I saved your worthless life."

"Extricating me from a crash and a whirlpool had nothing to do with generosity. It was instinct because at some point, you might need me to rescue you back."

"You wouldn't know how. You couldn't even save yourself in the whirlpool."

"How did you expect me to do that?"

"All you needed to do was let go and stop moving. If you had, I would have pulled you up sooner. You were flopping about like a fish, but when you stopped, the water ..." Her eyes glazed over, awareness gripping her. "The water let you go."

"It let me go," I repeated slowly.

The female scowled. "I saw it."

She made it sound as if the water had consciously made that choice. While most people in The Dark Seasons would entertain this theory, I merely rolled my eyes. "I'm heavy. I'd been struggling. When I stopped struggling, the weight eased. There's no other reason."

"You want to know if I'm right? Jump back in and see. The rainforest doesn't need to give you a reason. You have to trust it."

"If I wish to learn about something, I conduct a test. I don't evaluate deadly undercurrents by diving into their depths. Instead, I toss in something expendable." My mouth slanted. "That's what fools are for."

Coldness and apathy were acceptable. Heckling for no methodical reason was not. It wasn't the proper technique in which a physician handled a fool. So why the fuck couldn't I contain myself around her? The spitfire needed only to glare with those volcanic eyes, and I reacted. Seasons be damned, but I enjoyed her anger to the point of obsession.

Seething, she veered toward the water. In that tidefarer, she had steered with quick motions and focused on the horizon. She'd navigated from Summer with zealous determination. One might go so far as to say with knowledge and expectation.

I narrowed my eyes. "You knew."

Nothing.

"You knew this rainforest was here. You knew where to go."

Nothing.

"Tell me how," I said with fatal calm. "Tell me where we are."

I could be patient. I could.

Fucking hell. I thrust out my bound legs and kicked her drawing, my heels carving through the sketched cove and spraying granules over her limbs. The little beast blinked at what I'd done, dismay contorting her face.

With her fingers splayed, the rabid bitch slapped the rest of the drawing at me, flinging sand in my eyes. Curse her.

17

Flare

Curse him. I kept the Royal tied up, yet his presence felt like a stain on the rainforest, something to be ashamed of.

But why should I feel guilty? I couldn't trust a prince, a hater of born souls, a brutal Winter heir who'd strapped his hand around my throat. He was made of that enigma called ice, the word like a slippery thing, a surface on which I could trip and break my neck.

He would try to harm me. But while he might have had the upper hand when I'd been caged, rulers were irrelevant here. The rainforest didn't care about his lineage or authority. As for me, I had never cared.

Now we were on my turf.

I'd been dealt a blow when that varmint proved he could detect my voice in the same way I privately heard myself. For some awful reason, nature had decided to grant him the ability. But while I simply had to accept it, I wasn't about to like it.

To compensate, I did enjoy having the prince bound, as I'd enjoyed leading him astray in the forest, watching him drift in circles with a bewildered frown.

But as for my stunt with the fig, I couldn't explain that one. Although

I had sought to shut him up, to rattle the monster's nerves, I hadn't expected that eruption of heat while straddling his lap. The solid weight of his body beneath mine had caused a riot of sensations deep in the slit between my walls. My bare cunt had rested on his pants, the friction a shock to my system. The sight of his mouth glazed in nectar and the thick length of flesh between his hips had drawn unbidden dampness from me, which had threatened to leak out like evidence of a felony.

Thank Seasons, my body had spared me at the last moment, and I'd climbed off his cock before he could notice. That mistake would never happen again. I'd rather snack on shit than spread my thighs around this man for a second time.

The fitful stars blazed over the tide. Restless, I moved the supplies beneath a tree, in a shrouded thicket of frond hedges, then I used the second sail as a blanket by spreading it on the ground and wrapping half of the fabric over my body. Meanwhile, I heard the prince fussing, trying to get the sand out of his eyes since I hadn't volunteered to help. While curling up and imagining his discomfort, I smiled and drifted into slumber.

They marked me with paint. It was a molten paint, which they dabbed into my skin with a brush, its bristles made to endure the heat. The smell hit me before the burn did, but I'd been screaming for a while by then, so the first swipe of the liquid didn't make a difference.

Between cries, I squirmed against the guards, fought them so much that the markings took a long time to finish. They blamed me for that, saying, "Hold still, you tiny fucking monster!"

But I wasn't a monster. I was scared and scared and scared, because where were Mama and Papa? Would they storm the tower and come for me?

I tasted tears, a little girl crying. I remembered she was me, that I needed to protect her from the pain.

I'd gotten glimpses of the other captives, so I understood which symbolic images the guards painted around my neck. Even though I couldn't see them, I knew the markings, as I knew this Season.

My kingdom had taken me prisoner.

They tossed me into a black cell lined in bars. I raged and thrashed against the grille, my voice echoing down the tower's throat.

The guards sneered, called me a feral cunt, and gloated that I belonged to them. I shouted that they were wrong, but the oafs laughed, and I planned to bite their fingers off if they came near me again. I almost succeeded when they did, and it got me into trouble, and trouble hurt.

I imagined a safer place—a secret forest that floated in the ocean. That's where my soul and mind fled, hoping to stay there until Mama and Papa rescued me.

But they didn't come. They didn't come for me because they couldn't, because the court wouldn't let them, because they were dead, and because I was trapped.

Soon after, I lost my voice. It didn't return, but I hardly cared. I didn't need spoken words, only my teeth and my dreams to save me.

They called me a freak of nature. They said I was a fool captive, one of the mad, made of madness. But I couldn't understand why. I knew only one thing: I was twelve years old.

I jolted awake, my terrified heart clattering. The remnants of my nightmare vanished, replaced by verdant fronds swaying overhead and sunlight sparking through the canopy.

No rattling chains. No heckling sentinels.

No cage. No pain.

Instead, the lap of an ocean tide greeted me, and the distant call of a seagull brushed across the sky. I was safe. My body sagged in relief, my choppy breaths evened out, and I wiped my clammy hands dry. The nightmares didn't come each night, but they'd also never abated.

At least, this bad dream hadn't included my parents. Although the day I'd been branded was the most common one, the worst visions were of Mama and Papa trapped in their own cages where I couldn't get to them. My parents suffering, not knowing what befell their daughter, and then dying in the darkness. All because of me.

My eyes clenched shut, and I concentrated on the swaying ocean, using the gentle sound to block out the vision until it dissipated. After that, I lay there for countless minutes before sweeping aside the makeshift blanket and crawling to the enclosure's threshold.

My gaze stumbled upon a masculine form resting on his back in the sand. The prince had passed out beneath his tree. The hem of his rumpled shirt had slipped high, exposing the carved ledges of his abdomen, which rose and fell in slumber, those iron muscles expanding and contracting. A slim trail of dark hair cut through the smooth plane of skin, ran between two sloping hipbones, and disappeared into the waistband of his pants, down to where a distinct bulge outlined the length of his cock.

The same appalling sensations from when I'd straddled him returned, this time with a vengeance. My nipples toughened, and molten heat oozed from the rift in my thighs.

I shouldn't look. I didn't want to look.

Slanting my chin, I looked. With his head twisted away, that mane of blue hair shrouded his profile. Against my will, the candid sight lured me. How many citizens would donate a kidney and forsake their dignity to wake up beside him?

If they preferred monsters to saviors, that only illustrated their reprehensible taste. Admiring anything about this fiend was sacrilege.

Determined to focus on something else and prevent my damp cunt from having other ideas, I turned away. Beyond the thicket, sunlight drizzled orange and pink hues across the cove. Farther down the shore, a bright red speck fluttered through the air, then slipped behind a bush of high reeds.

Curious, I stood and padded outside. Jogging out of the prince's range, I found the creature flitting amid the stalks. Halting several paces away, I grinned in recognition at the lone butterfly and marveled at the flaming shade of its wings.

On a hunch, I twirled in place. To my delight, the motion got its attention. The enthusiastic butterfly flapped toward me and circled my head, matching my movement.

With a laugh, I raised my crooked finger like a perch. The beauty landed there, its wings pumping.

"Good morning," I confided. "Fancy seeing you again."

It had to be one of the butterflies I reveled with yesterday. In Summer, certain butterflies were robust, lived for many years, and remembered human faces. Recalling that fact, I peered closer, blessed clarity surging to the forefront. The red wings quickened my pulse. This species resembled the type who'd delivered my messages to Autumn.

I peeked around the reeds. Confirming the prince was still sleeping, I whirled toward the butterfly. "Will you help me?"

When the creature remained on my finger, I made haste. Snatching a broadleaf from a shrub, I rushed to the shoreline and squatted. After locating a seashell with a chipped edge, I scratched a missive onto the surface—a confidential message only Poet and Briar would understand.

Because the jester and princess were a miraculous pair, they had noticed parts of the map sketch when I'd been imprisoned in Autumn. But although they would never unearth the rest without my help, sending the map was out of the question, lest it should end up in the wrong hands.

I chose my words carefully and scribbled a cipher. The tidings described the route here, but not in a way others would recognize. As a master of riddles, Poet would see through the message. As a princess widely known for bookishness and reading between the lines, Briar would as well.

Rolling the leaf and securing it with a strip of seaweed, I whispered to my companion, "If you bring this to the Princess and Jester of Autumn, I'll be indebted. Will you please be one of our allies?"

The butterfly launched off my finger and seized the leaf. After circling my waist once, the creature dashed into the horizon. Water swabbed my ankles as I watched the winged being shrink to a red dot, then dissolve from sight.

As much as I needed supplies, Poet and Briar would have no means to send anything, since that feat would require a raptor too large to go unnoticed by the public. And my little messenger was strong, but not that strong. But at least the jester and princess would learn of my whereabouts. Should either of us need the other, we could call. Because now we'd know how to find one another.

18

Flare

His Royal Dickless awoke long after the butterfly had left. Protected from the sun, he reclined against the trunk and stared at the horizon as if expecting his Winter kin to bail him out of his predicament.

As for my greater role in the crusade for born souls, that key still resided somewhere in the forest. I felt this truth down to my soles, like a prophecy.

And once I found that key, I'd have to prevent my nemesis from intervening, provided the calculating monster succeeded in freeing himself. Not that it was likely. I'd seen him fidgeting, trying to unravel my knots. Good luck with that.

The prince abhorred being fed and having his wounded jaw bathed by me. Neither were my favorite hobbies, other than the part where I got to see him humiliated. I broke his fast with the scallops I'd caught, spilled water down his pipes, and wondered what it sounded like to hear a Royal choking.

He sat there, watching me swallow my own helping of water, watching me lick my lips, watching me toil in rags, and piling those details in his mind as if they belonged to him.

As if I belonged to him.

Ungrateful brute. Arming myself with the rope belt, dagger, and canteen, I quested into the forest, intending to search for a reliable water source. The prince could die of thirst or piss himself, for all I cared.

Smacking branches out of the way, I traipsed through the shadows. Claws skittered across the branches, something hissed overhead, and a feline roar pushed through the mist. Everything moved, everything thrived, everything breathed.

This place saw me and heard me. It welcomed me, except into the whirlpool where I'd lost my sense and saved the enemy.

My grin faltered as I remembered those violent eddies, and then I recalled another time, another sort of drowning—the downward pull of sand instead of liquid. That episode had taken place on a different day, with a different person. Reliving what came after and where I'd ended up because of it, I cringed.

After rescuing the worthless prince, he'd crumbled to the ground, and I'd carted his bulky dead weight, using one of the sails as a harness. It had taken a decade to reach the cove, despite the short distance and downward slope from the tree line. I'd been surprised how near the whirlpool was to the coast, reachable through a gap in the foliage.

But that old memory—of a similar day and a similar kind of drowning—had gripped me when we were snapping at each other last night. While explaining why the whirlpool had finally released him, the past had caught me by the throat.

I shook off the memories. As fog brought a sprinkle with it, another thought occurred to me. The legend said this forest was the birthplace of rain. With that in mind, the full song played in my head.

Seek not, find not, this Phantom Wild.
Sea paths, golden rays, to this Phantom Wild.
Light fades, mist grows, in this Phantom Wild.
Mist grows, droplets fall, on this Phantom Wild.
Dark woods, deep ferns, of this Phantom Wild.
Timeless rain, eternal waters, from this Phantom Wild.

Tempests swirl, pools drown, within this Phantom Wild.
Rains fade, fauna roam, through this Phantom Wild.

Apart from the song, the old tales spoke about different forms of rain including lightning, thunder, ember, celestial, and vapor rain. The day before, such fog had been followed by a safe downpour—vapor rain, based on the descriptions that had circulated over Summer's history.

I huddled beneath an awning of branches and carefully extended one upturned palm. To my relief, a soft downpour splashed from the heavens, wetting and cooling my skin. Reassured, I stepped onto the path. After unbuckling my supplies, peeling off my chemise, and hanging the garment from a low branch, I combed my locks until the matted tangles unfurled and my fingers slid through effortlessly.

As I bathed, I thought of the prince. After the whirlpool episode when he'd passed out, I had removed the dagger sheathed at his hip. He must have also lost the vial at some point, because it was gone. Stripped of his fur cloak and finery, the future king had been reduced to a mere mortal.

Heat swarmed my cheeks. By now the man had glimpsed everything under my chemise. I didn't like the weight of his stare; it made me want to smash something. Like a sin, my flesh sizzled at the memory of his eyes touching me, sliding across my form.

My disgusting reaction hardened into outrage. I cast my eyes down, gazing at the shape of my body. The tower had made a thread of me, thin and weightless.

It was his fault, King Rhys's fault, and the fault of every prejudiced soul in The Dark Seasons. Yet food wasn't the only thing the courts denied born souls.

The first time Rune had fucked me, I'd known how breeding worked. We hadn't needed to protect ourselves because I had never bled in my life, because Summer had taken care of that. On the eve of my twelfth year, Pyre had pried my mouth open and plopped three darts of liquid onto my tongue, which gave me cramps for weeks and an empty womb for a lifetime. The drug kept prisoners from breeding in cells. Moreover, it had been invented by Winter.

Standing in the rain, I hugged myself tightly. My arms and legs and hands might look meek to a prince, but they didn't act meekly. He'd do well to remember that.

The rain cleared, replaced by the echoes of scratchy caws and trembling bird whistles, and the forest glistened within its own darkness.

After throwing the chemise over my head and affixing the rope belt, I traveled down the path and gasped with delight. Plump najava berries hung in bunches from a shrub, the bright orbs shaped like bells. Inside, they would be filled with the promise of sweet juice. I'd partaken of these treasures whenever my family had made camp in outlying marshes.

Elated, I rushed toward the bush, then paused. I'd never seen najavas flourish near the coast. And as the whirlpool had taught the prince, things were not always what they seemed here.

Yet my stomach grumbled, and my mouth watered. Despite the rations I'd found, they weren't enough.

I knelt with caution, plucked one of the morsels, and pried open its womb. Nothing but familiar pulp and flesh stared back, both emitting a recognizable sugary fragrance. With a sigh, I popped the berry into my mouth. The fruit tickled my lips, the nectar riper than I remembered as I savored every bead of juice.

Eager to collect more, I picked a handful and blissfully imagined baiting the prince. Pretending he was there, I held a berry between my fingers, wiggled the fruit, and spoke to thin air. "If you want some, you'll have to ask nicely—"

The words died on my tongue, which fattened and swelled. Fear licked a path across my chest. Within seconds, my throat shrank, air fighting to squeeze through.

The berries toppled to the ground. I wheezed through my nostrils, oxygen fighting to reach my lungs. Grabbing another berry, I ripped the thing open and checked its innards. There it was, a seed nesting inside the flesh, blending in with the pulp.

Camouflaged. Because najavas didn't have seeds.

As the seconds ticked by, a dozen of them sprouted, materializing out of nowhere. Instantly, the prince's warning from the day before chewed through my head. In Summer, the brighter the fruit, the deadlier the poison.

With a cry, I hurled the bedeviled berry against the nearest tree, where it exploded into a soggy mess. Thinking better of it, I snatched a second one, then staggered to my feet and ran. My body shredded through the rainforest, the canteen and dagger rapping against my hip. Racing toward the cove, I blew through the hedges.

The villain prince observed the spectacle with a mask of boredom. The rainfall must have spat at him through the canopy, studding his clothes with droplets. Like a careless shark, he lounged as I thrashed toward the camp, dropped onto the sail blanket, and struggled to write in the sand. Except my hands shook so badly, I failed to compose a single legible word.

To which, he merely tutted. "Convulsions. Swelling."

Abandoning the sand, I attempted to respond. "I ... I can't ..."

The Royal peered closer. "Asphyxiation. Must have been venom."

"It was ... fruit," I croaked, opening my hand to show him the morsel I'd brought. "Berries."

Understanding gripped his visage as he regarded the najava. "Ah, poison. Nature defends itself with deceptions, which is one of many ways fools and normal people differ. A vigilant person is equipped with logical defenses and instincts against hazards. Though, as a presumed sand drifter, you should have known what to avoid." Sudden clarity honed his voice. "Or you were acting on impulse. You recognized the berry, therefore mistook it for edible and neglected to check the details. An exceptionally stupid fool, then."

"Hypocrite!" My fangs came out. "You should ... talk when ... you nearly ... drowned."

With an elegantly dismissive shrug, the prince said, "You will die."

I tore my dagger from the rope belt.

"You will die in pain."

Launching at him, I angled the weapon against his throat. "I'll take you ... with me."

"Is this your way of asking for assistance?"

Curse his bullshit. If I keeled over, this man would stay tethered until he turned into a skeleton. He knew as much, his nonchalance a facade meant to rankle me, because he also knew how this scenario was about to play out.

The dagger quaked in my fingers. While gasping for air, I fetishized about tracing a vein in his neck, teaching him an overdue lesson, marring him the way his cretins had marred me.

My fingers clenched the hilt. "Help."

"I don't specialize in Summer antidotes," the prince replied.

Frantically, I thought back to Autumn, when he'd treated Briar's poisoning. Although the princess hadn't told me about that event, any news about Royals traveled fast, including to jail cells. "But you know things."

The prince's irises glinted. Based on that, he might be remembering the same incident. At length, he drew out, "I might know things."

"Then ... help ... me!"

He raised a triumphant brow. "I cannot talk you through it."

Shit. I dropped the berry, scrambled behind the bastard, and cut his bindings.

19

Jeryn

The ropes dropped. I moved with efficiency, unwinding from my locked position and seizing my knife from the thicket's stockpile. Urgency had been a regular fixture in Winter's medical wing, therefore I should be used to emergencies. Yet dread coursed through my veins, a shock to the system, which had consumed me from the moment she'd sprinted out of the rainforest.

Her features twisted. Stricken. Turmoiled. Those bloated features indicated a blockage, the sight more daunting than I'd care to analyze. If I didn't school my expression, the way I had moments ago while feigning indifference, it would set her off. Already panic gripped the beast's countenance, which exacerbated her condition.

I examined the berry quickly, then scooted closer. "Look at me."

Her wild eyes stalled on mine.

"Much better," I encouraged. "Now, keep your gaze steady and listen carefully. Your airways are compromised. It is difficult, but you must quell the hysteria."

Wheezing, she nodded. Uncensored fear and trust shimmered in her eyes. This often proved the case with patients enduring physical trauma. Nonetheless, her open gaze found a crawlspace inside my chest.

The little beast spasmed, fighting to siphon oxygen into her lungs. With an outward control I didn't entirely feel, I flicked open one of the slots embedded into the scalpel hilt. A rectangular plate of steel flipped into view, the surface reflecting sunlight and enabling me to cast the brightness onto her eyes.

"Steady," I reminded her. "Eyes on me."

Angling the plate and mirroring light beneath her lower lashes, I tilted my head to inspect her dilated pupils. The orbs eclipsed her irises, the gold having vanished.

Suffused complexion. Flared nostrils. Swollen tongue.

The berry she'd swallowed had been toxic.

Because she couldn't achieve more than nodding or shaking her head, I asked a series of rapid-fire questions about what happened. While she responded, I retracted and sheathed the knife, pressed my thumb to the underside of her wrist, and assessed her pulse. Then I proceeded to the rest of her anatomy, checking her tattooed throat and windpipe.

In Summer and Winter, certain seeds released oils. If this was one such example, and if it had such an abrupt effect, she wouldn't last. At this accelerated rate, consumption would prove terminal.

Two things. Excrete the seed before it emitted too much oil. Neutralize the traces of poison already infesting the victim's system.

One, I didn't know what ingredients the rainforest contained. Two, I also didn't know how the fuck they functioned.

This environment gave me no choices but the antiquated ones. After urging the beast onto her back, I trailed my fingers over her stomach and moved upward, manipulating and pumping. Pressure, concentration, precision. With a jolt, she vomited—and a mangled seed projected from her mouth like a pellet, along with bits of mollusks and berry pulp.

I collected the seed with the pad of my index finger, grabbed a large shell from the supply pile, and shot to my feet. Stalking toward the ocean, I collected saltwater and returned to her side, where she'd resumed her upright position. After grinding the seed with a rock and mixing it with the alkaline fluid, I snatched her jaw with one hand. On reflex, she opened her mouth, and I poured the contents down her throat.

Fair enough. Saltwater tasted like shit. She gagged but kept it down.

I tossed aside the bowl and framed her face, my thumbs pausing under her eyes. "Inhale. Exhale."

Talking her through the motions and mimicking the act, we fell into a rhythm. Her respirations eased, her pupils shrank, and that burnished complexion resurfaced. Then she sucked in a resounding breath.

Internally, I shuddered. Externally, I kept my face neutral, stony, composed.

Unaffected. Unruffled.

In certain cases, grinding the source and combining it with saltwater absorbed its toxins, thus counteracting the damage. I had not tried this method before. With Winter's advanced facilities, I'd never needed to. It was hardly a guaranteed treatment, much less a reliable one, yet fuck. It had worked.

While her respirations returned to normal, she brushed her fingers over her neck. With a grunt, I batted the digits away and double checked her pulse, my hands grazing the inked collar. I instructed her to keep breathing and surveyed the rest of her vitals, then resisted the impulse to triple check them. It took longer than usual to feel satisfied with her recovery and even longer to pull away.

Once the unfathomable impact of touching the beast subsided, I retrieved the canteen and a fallen broadleaf, then watched as she drank, gargled, and wiped her mouth with the leaf. At which point, I remembered myself. Healing this woman had dominated my attention to an unbridled degree. For a moment, I'd doubted my ability to fucking think straight.

The former was common when ministering to patients. The latter was not.

Still. A physician would do this for anyone in dire need.

It. Meant. Nothing.

As she opened her mouth to express thanks, irritation replaced my concern. I took her elbow, deliberately cutting off those words. Gently, I drew the female toward me, the scent of her flesh permeating my nostrils.

Patience, I reminded myself.

And because she'd learned to distrust my intentions, her smile disintegrated. Those insolent lips parted, about to spew something defiant.

In one serpentine move, I hauled her against me. My free hand grasped her lips and squeezed until they puckered. Then a silken threat slid off my tongue. "The next time you attempt to tie me up, one of those berries will go back into your mouth." With cold civility, I gave her a harsh jerk. "Do *not* test me on this."

She smacked away my hand and wrenched out of my grasp, her features throwing unspoken vitriol at me. I considered punishing her for that, but the whiff of salt and florals assaulted my senses, perfuming the air like a hallucinogenic.

I launched to my feet, my stiff knees protesting the movement. Seasons, it felt as if my joints had aged a century.

Stalking to the water's edge, I knelt by the surf and washed my hands. The foaming ocean swabbed my knuckles. I worked quickly and kept my head bent, averting my gaze from the contemptible depths.

I would not look beyond the tide. I would not check for sea dwellers. I would not appear a coward in front of her.

Instead, I distracted myself with other thoughts. A fruit recognizable to the woman had turned out to be deceptive—a mistake anyone could have made. She had overlooked the seeds, which hadn't appeared until oxidized because even the familiar could not be counted upon here. At best, saving her had been fortuitous.

Peering at the ground, I thought of my grandaunts, who'd announced with pride at the onset of my apprenticeship, "He will be our greatest healer."

Then I thought of my grandaunts years later, trying to smile through their grief when the declaration turned out to be false. "You're doing everything you can," they had assured me.

Yet skill did not mend everything.

I grimaced at the abrasions on my wrists, the cords having rubbed them raw. The female had done an expert job of detaining me.

Would I retaliate if she crossed me again? Naturally.

Would I do a permanent job of it? By no means.

Survival didn't work that way. I may have experience in healing, but she knew Summer better than I did. We needed each other.

Too bad she had used a weapon to release me. I would have preferred her fingers instead of the dagger, so that I might see those hands work the knots, unraveling the tension in them. I went so far as to envision her digits jerking, tugging on me, her skin moving hectically against mine.

I glanced sideways. She plunged into the waves, the outline of her body spearing into the tide. I waited, scanning the surface until the object of my infatuation arched into view, her form spraying droplets into the air. As she stood mid-waist, the beast threaded her fingers through that sopping wet hair. From this distance, streams raced down her silhouette. Under the clingy chemise, her flesh would be slick to the touch, and the garment would be easy to peel off.

My fingers curled. As I veered from the sight, splashes resonated from behind, each one penetrating my spine.

I doused liquid onto my face, only to squint and curse, viciously reminded that it was saltwater. With my eyes stinging like fuck, I retreated from the waves.

By then, she had returned to the shore and set two disemboweled fish on a pair of flat stones. I took judicious note of the fare, with its green gradient of scales and long fins. The stomachs had been gutted, leaving no bones in sight.

We worked without speaking. I dug a pit while the woman arranged tinder and kindling, debris that had fallen from the trees. Leaning over, she planted a stick into a notched plank of wood, rotating the stem between her palms and pressing downward.

Speed. Friction.

I waited for her to run out of steam. Which took a considerable amount of time.

There was a puff of smoke, then nothing. Her lips pursed into a stubborn knot. Yet something about the way her brows crinkled was rather ... amusing.

Done with this unproductive display, I squatted across from her. "Let me."

"I can do it."

"Winter builds fires."

"Summer *is* fire."

"Not the same thing."

"Our kingdom created flames. From volcanoes to the ashes of Summer tinder, we're the ones who know fire best."

"Boasting is impractical, unimpressive, and won't do the job."

"Fuck you, prince. Sand drifters also cook fish this way. I've built plenty of blazes."

"That must have been a long time ago," I volleyed.

She flinched. Then she glowered, continuing to twist and grind the stick with a vengeance. Any rougher and the instrument would snap.

Yet within seconds, cinders spiraled into the air, a nest of amber and blue flames igniting into an inferno. My eyes snapped toward the female's victorious expression.

Yes, Summer was fire.

She was fire.

Her reference to Summer tinder resurrected the details of Autumn's castle blackout, when Briar had been trapped in the stronghold. Her attackers had been influenced by Rhys and supplied with the ashes of such kindling. Sprinkle any blaze with those cinders, and it could be controlled from the ashes' original source, thus enabling a person to ignite or douse multiple flames remotely from a single location. That method had snuffed every candle, hearth, and torchlight in the fortress.

By comparison, the pit's ashes were unlikely to help us here. We hardly required multiple flames unless we intended to burn down the forest.

The blaze crackled like parchment. We used sticks to secure the fish. The aroma of seared meat and sputtering grease alleviated my resentment toward her, and I gave a brisk nod of gratitude.

We drank from the canteen and savored our repast in small portions. Bland at best, yet the hot slide of food down my throat reminded me of home. Chalices topped with mulled wine, pots of steaming broth, platters heaped with game.

Nourishment revived my pragmatic side. This interlude had to end, starting with the essentials.

"Where are we?" I asked.

My dining companion wiped an arm across her mouth. "The Phantom Wild," she said with a straight face.

My eyes tapered. "Do not lie to me," I cautioned. "Ever."

"I don't lie about legends."

"Tell me where we really are."

"That *is* where we really are."

"You expect me to believe we've landed on some realm out of an infernal Summer lullaby."

"No," she sang. "I expect you to gag on your dinner."

So she would force me to squander my breath. "Did you overhear intelligence in the tower? Does Summer keep this rainforest confidential from the Seasons? Did you and your sand drifters locate it but not tell anyone? Are they here? Are you waiting for them to find us?"

"No. No. No. No. No."

Well. Although I could hear her, that word wouldn't have been difficult to read from her lips, even if the opposite were true.

I scoffed. "There's no such thing as the enigma you speak of."

"There is," she advocated, pissed off. "The song is about a hidden forest floating in the ocean, the birthplace of rain and water." She quoted, *"Tempests swirl, pools drown."*

"A coincidence."

"Bullshit. Tempests that swirl? Pools that drown? It sounds rather like the whirlpool that almost swallowed you whole, don't you think?"

I had no reply. Not yet.

The beast knelt, opting for an area that was damp from the rainfall. In the firelight, she began to draw, engraving the sand and producing strings of words. An ardent emotion radiated from her, the sight akin to rhapsody.

Finished, she sat back and gestured to a reproduction of Summer's renowned song. I recognized it from Autumn's dungeon, when she'd written sentences into that pile of dirt on her cage floor. Though at the time, I'd been more intent on ridding the unsanitary soil from her cubicle, not caring to see her languish among filth.

I processed the lyrics. Unsure why the devil it hadn't struck me until now, I deduced, "You can read and write."

She glared. "Yes. We peasants can also count on our fingertips."

"Spare me the righteous display. You're hardly the delicate type who cannot handle a simple fact. Unlike in Autumn and Winter, greater percentages of commoners in Spring and Summer are illiterate. This isn't ignorance, it's statistics. Likewise, your tongue is more elevated than most of your class."

"Disappointed you can't talk down to me?"

My combative lips crooked. "I don't need a title to do that."

The beast shook her head, dark waves sweeping her shoulders. "You're one pompous piece of shit." When I showed zero intention of defending myself, she huffed. "I see beyond the song lyrics. I see their shapes."

I squinted. "What's your point?"

"Have a look, Winter. But don't look closely. Look far."

For fuck's sake. I thought I'd left tedious riddles behind after I last saw Poet. "Do I look like a Spring artist to you?"

"You look like a shipwrecked asshole to me."

Whatever. Scientists inspected, prodded, researched. They formulated questions and employed tools to determine answers.

Look far? I could not comprehend that.

The beast got to her feet and seized my hand. Her fingers curled around mine, the contact producing a chain reaction that injected bolts of heat into every ligament I possessed. This included my cock, which had been misbehaving for far too long, the phallus twitching like a traitor.

Stumped, I let her guide me backward, away from the song. "Look," she prompted.

It took me an instant to recover from her digits strapped around my own. An enduring hand. A dangerous hand. With some difficulty, I regarded the sketch, paying particular attention to the angle from which she'd directed me.

Thinking better of it, I pried my hand from hers. "Nothing but verse and rubbish."

She scowled. "That verse and rubbish is a map."

Dubious, I took a second look. And squinted. And saw a land mass.

The mad woman hastened to the rendering and used her toes to indicate each location. "This is Summer, and there's the castle, and there's the wharf, and there's the sun. And you see here? The sun's rays? They're ciphered in the song, and they make a path—" she revolved her foot over the closing lyrics, "—to this realm."

Correct. It did resemble a map. A convincing one, sequestered in plain sight.

I moved nearer, stepping around the drawing to view it from all vantage points. Then I lowered myself beside a configuration of the castle. The letters and words, plus the spaces between them, transformed into shapes when one studied them with perception. The sketch arranged everything in such a way that it became a route from the kingdom to this deserted place.

The lines representing the sky denoted wind direction. The sun's rays indicated a direction seafarers or explorers might be able to master.

Based on the sun's position, I drew a compass in the sand. This cove faced southeast.

But what of the ambiguous distance? Despite Summer ships enabling faster travel than in any other Season, an uncharted location should have required weeks for us to reach, not the span of one fucking morning. We had to be close to the mainland.

Yet far enough that this place had gone undiscovered since the dawn of time? Preposterous.

Be that as it may, I would accept the map's existence. Faint proof, with gaps to fill.

I gave the beast a judicious glance. It would have required an acute mind to unravel this cipher. Nonetheless, the map alluded to a person having been here before. Someone had to have brought this location back to Summer's mainland.

Humoring her, I asked, "Who wrote the song?"

She blinked. "Legends don't reveal their authors unless they want to. Nature decides what it wants to share with us, as nature knows best, and we shouldn't question that. But even if it wants to unveil the scribe, legends only allow certain people to be privy to that information."

"All you had to do was say, 'I don't know.'"

Her features creased in annoyance. "For someone who grew up in an educated nation, you should have learned that nothing is simple when it comes to the almighty Seasons. Haven't you heard of The Wildflower Forest or The Lost Treehouses? Or has Winter been denied its own realms of dark magic, and the deprivation has turned your scientific court into nonbelievers?"

My eyebrows stitched together. That was a valid point. "In that case, who showed this diagram to you?"

"You prick. I figured it out by myself."

"While incarcerated."

"While caged," she corrected.

Incarcerated. Caged. Semantics.

The beast recounted how she'd found the song randomly written across a coastline when she was a child. How she had memorized the lines. How she'd discovered the map hidden within the lyrics.

I moved to the pit and added more logs, agitating the fire and setting off a combustion. "You could have used this to bargain for your freedom. Yet you told no one."

"I would never betray the rainforest's confidence," she defended. "The map is a secret, and this rainforest is sacred. It chose and summoned me to find it."

I couldn't have heard her right. "It summoned you."

"I saw its call inside the song. The rainforest revealed itself to me in those lyrics, whereas you only recognized the map because I helped you. I showed you how to look for it, and I only did so because you're here, because you wouldn't let me go like you should have."

Where to start. First, I blamed sleep deprivation for my illogical statement. If she'd wanted to bargain for her freedom in Summer, no one would have accepted her claims, much less honored a deal with her. Or in theory, power-hungry Rhys might have negotiated without intending to uphold his end of the deal. Then again, the man spent more time sucking his cock and validating his self-worth than he'd have given to any prisoner seeking an audience.

True, I could not revoke the reality of this place when elusive realms like The Wildflower Forest in Spring, The Lost Treehouses in Autumn, and The Iron Wood in Winter existed. On that account, she was right.

Yes, the Seasons had power. Most would call it magic.

But this world also believed the Seasons had a consciousness. There, I deviated from the majority. No matter what "mystical" kinship people achieved with nature, there was always a rational justification.

Even so, Flare's conviction wasn't unconventional. And even if the Seasons had a will, what made her statement ridiculous was the assumption that such a place would summon a fool. That was a fallacy. Wishful thinking at best. All because of a chance encounter with handwritten lyrics in the sand, plus a random stroke of genius.

If nature could choose anyone, it wouldn't be someone like her.

The beast lowered herself to the ground and tucked her legs beneath her. She gazed in starry-eyed wonder at the drawing, luxuriating in the sight, immersing herself in it.

Enamored. Entranced.

There was more to her story. This daydreamer was industrious and hardly unintelligent. Moreover, her anarchistic nature meant she wasn't the type to hide away on a deserted parcel of land.

She had another reason for coming here. Whatever absurd purpose that might be, she would rather slit her wrists than reveal it to the enemy.

All in good time. I was a patient man.

Also, Summer was wrong. Turbulence might accompany her madness, however feral tendencies were not the primary source. Though, the answer still evaded me. As far as my experience went, I could not assign any known condition to her.

Nevertheless, she was not free. By law of the Fools Decree, this woman belonged to me. Courtesy of the agreement I'd made with Queen Avalea—in which the Autumn ruler had begged me to save her daughter's life after being poisoned—this fiery little beast was mine.

As it should be. As the kingdoms ordained.

As I'd been bred to enforce, provided that I returned to my court. By now, Summer had sent a dispatch of my disappearance to my grandaunts. The Queens of Winter would despair of this news. Silvia and Doria would have to deliver it to the rest of our family, including …

I evicted those thoughts from my mind like tumors, then clung to reason. Summer had been on alert, the watch had seen this prisoner flee on a tidefarer, and they had witnessed me pursue her. From there, the sentinels and troops must have noted the boat's direction. Despite the likelihood of drowning, Winter and Summer would not rest until searching every billow of this ocean. Soon enough, a fleet would emancipate us from limbo.

This rainforest existed. But it was not inaccessible, much less invisible. On the contrary, it had been remarkably easy to get here.

I would return. So would she.

As long as we didn't kill each other first.

20

Flare

I might kill him first. If the rainforest didn't do it for me, I might be tempted.

Yet the poisonous berries proved he was a necessary evil. I knew the natural perils of Summer, but I didn't know this enchanted wild yet. And I didn't know how to combat illness. My survival depended on reaching a truce with him.

That's why I revealed the map's existence. Although I hadn't wanted to, I'd had no choice. Keeping this man in the dark wouldn't have helped either of us work together.

In the sweltering light, the colossus of a prince remained standing, refusing to sit beside my shadow. I gained my feet, refusing to vanish inside his.

As his eyes shifted across the map, he raised a single black brow. "You do understand, this place is deadly."

"It's legendary," I rephrased. "That comes with a price."

"Except I was never a paying patron."

I shrugged. "So leave."

Then something miraculous happened. His expression flickered, his mouth twitching in the faintest of movements. For an instant, reluctant amusement cracked through that exterior.

Was this yeti on the verge of smirking? I found myself waiting on tenterhooks, to see if I'd made a pivotal dent in his facade.

Sadly, the phenomenon lasted all of a second before his features folded into a mask. "What's the rainforest's personification?"

I wrinkled my nose. "Your clinical talk won't do us any favors."

"Is that a fact? Because what you call clinical, I call science."

"What you call science, I call spirit."

"Enough," he sighed. "I have priorities. My point is, we must gauge the characteristics of this place."

He mulled over the lyrics for extra clues. There weren't any. I could have told him this, but I had fun watching smart Winter try and fail.

Secrets were secretive. Mysteries were mysterious.

"The only way to know the rest will be to explore," I proposed.

The prince nodded. "To investigate."

"We'll scout the terrain."

"Starting with a water source."

"Then a better means of shelter."

"Hmm." Dry skepticism filled his tone. "You seem awfully confident about locating an outpost."

Whether I liked it or not, he'd grown familiar with my voice, catching on like a sail to the wind. I met his gaze, letting my silence speak for itself.

I'd found many forms of shelter with Mama and Papa. And since this rainforest had called for me, that meant I would find what I was looking for, so long as I used my wits. Also, as long as this man didn't get in my way.

The prince dissected my expression. By accident—because it must be unintentional—those black pupils sank to my mouth, causing a swarm of butterflies in my navel. Then his orbs blinked and lurched back to my eyes.

His timbre came out low. "It's settled then."

Yes. Right.

Except my mouth tingled from his gaze. Between us, I doubted anything would ever be settled.

As eventide swept over us, we preoccupied ourselves with another problem. We needed sleep. But we only had one blanket.

As the prince inspected our small enclosure, I read his mind. He would prop himself upright against the nearest covered trunk for the night.

But that wouldn't do. The man was too large, the area too compact to distance ourselves.

The blanket lay sprawled across the ground like a punishment instead of a comfort. Putting it mildly, I would rather nibble on barbed wire than lay unconscious beside this monster, but I also wasn't about to let him do me any favors.

I slipped under one side of the blanket, then spread the other end for him. "It's your choice," I mumbled before tucking myself in.

After a moment's deliberation, he expelled a resigned breath. The blanket shuffled as he reclined beside me. We made a show of arranging ourselves, if only to avoid glimpsing one another.

Though more than once, I caught him eyeing every potential weapon in the vicinity. No surprise, I'd been eyeing them too, if anything to make his sleep challenging. It would be easy to stab him, to rid this world of one more swine. Except he could have taken the same advantage and hadn't. And despite having numerous fantasies about maiming this Royal, I ultimately didn't murder unarmed people, no matter how vile they were. Otherwise, I'd be no better than him.

A few merciful inches separated us. With our backs to one another, we listened to the swaying tide. I felt grateful for the noise, which muffled our combined breathing.

Every once in a blue moon, I talked in my sleep. I'd developed this habit early as a child, but after losing my voice, the words came out undetectable unless one knew how to read my lips. Yet even with my head turned away from the prince, he would grasp whatever I said. If that happened, hopefully I wouldn't mumble anything I'd regret.

I sensed the Royal staring at the trees' canopy, thinking a million Winter thoughts. I had assumed his skin would be cold, but the villain prince emitted more warmth than I'd have wagered. More than that, a crisp aroma wafted from him. It resembled something tingly, invigorating, and masculine.

A Winter scent? I'd heard stories of needle forests and blustering winds, and although I had never inhaled those types of fragrances, I could imagine the sharp bite of them.

As the night wore on, the prince and I stayed awake until I couldn't think anymore. Yet as I drifted, I felt his weight shift and those eyes stray to me.

Plinking noises yanked me out of sleep. Bleary, I lifted my head. The makeshift blanket cocooned me, the ends tucked in although I couldn't remember having done that.

Rain drenched the cove, the onslaught slick enough that a person could slip on the noise. Lightning blasted through the heavens. Yet something about this tempest seemed different.

A male groan came from behind. I twisted, my gaze landing on the Royal who sat upright with his teeth clenched in pain. He'd rolled up his pants at some point, a cut now festering beneath the cuffs, the angry red line seeping from his lower calf.

That wound hadn't been there before. And although the fern canopy protected us from the downpour, a few drops trickled past a small gap hovering over his side of the thicket. Each time the orbs slipped through, the prince dodged them.

I whipped aside the blanket and scuttled on all fours. As I headed toward him, a splash of water nipped my shoulder. I yelped, glancing at the blood welling from that spot.

Another bolt of lightning tore through the storm. I changed directions, scurried across the sand, and halted at the enclosure's threshold. Stretching out my hand, I gasped and reared back when the water hit me. The first drips had grazed, but these other wet bastards left their marks.

This wasn't vapor rain. This was a piercing type, the droplets needle-like and falling like weapons.

Lightning rain. It breached rifts in the leaves, not slicing into the ferns themselves, nor damaging my blanket, but slipping through to strike my wrists and the limbs of my enemy.

This could be another greeting from the rainforest. This could be an initiation, to experience all the elements this realm offered. That way, I would bond more with this place, learn its secrets, and therein earn my path to the key.

In Summer's culture, we acknowledged nature's will in whichever way it required. People dove off cliffs, swam in perilous tides, and lay upon burning coals.

Ignoring the prince's shouts, I sprinted into the deluge. Racing across the cove, I opened my arms, answering the rainforest, giving myself to it. The sky bit into me, nicking my ears and elbows and thighs. It hurt but not like the ink on my neck once had, and if Summer could brand me like that, I could let this place give me other marks—let it grant me this rite of passage. I shrieked from the pangs but welcomed them as the onslaught blessed me.

By the time I reentered the thicket, my large companion glared at what I'd done to myself. Or rather, what the rainforest had done to me—how it honored me. Somehow, my clothes were intact, not a tear in them. By comparison, bloody lines covered the exposed parts, stinging and leaking. I hissed with each movement, but I also grinned because the cuts would heal. Matter of fact, the droplets no longer sliced, now that they'd landed on me, so they must only hurt on impact.

I'd forgotten about the prince whose calf had taken a hit. The split in his leg was shallow and slender, as though somebody had skimmed him with a razor.

I tugged on his weight, he thrust himself across the sand, and together we got him into a shrouded corner. The drenched shirt clutched his torso, each toned line pressing through the material.

He breathed harshly. "Cut off my sleeves."

Because the request sounded like a command, I snatched my dagger. "How about I take your arms with them?"

The prince squinted, not understanding me. "Just do as I say."

All the same, I knew what he intended. My dagger pared through the fancy material. Threads popped from the seams and bared his arms, hunks of muscle rippling into view. With every movement, those ridges flexed as if he were made of boulders instead of flesh.

My gaze lingered. Worse, my traitorous stomach flipped.

The prince caught me looking. His pupils flickered, the effect there and gone quickly.

"Not me," he rasped when I moved to dress his wound. "Divide the sleeves into strips and use them to wrap your injuries."

I stalled, confused. This man couldn't possibly care about my well-being over his own. Maybe it was because I had more cuts than he did, and as a doctor, he was being practical.

In any case, nursing myself would undo the rainforest's work. So, no.

Tuning out his grunts admonishing me to obey him, I wound the cloth around his leg. As I bent my head to the task, I felt his attention stray to my fingers, his fixation making me restless. Although I'd never been intimidated by him before, now I understood how potently he affected this continent. For such an arctic monster, this man's stare burrowed deeply.

With so little space from the rain, securing a knot became difficult. Left with no choice, I swung my leg over his lap, keeping my knees bent so that I hovered inches above his frame.

An intake of breath diced from the prince's lungs. Heat rose from his skin and brushed my inner thighs, my flesh grazing the edges of his pants, my breasts hanging inches from his pecs.

I grimaced, appalled to be this near to him. Yet that wasn't the only thing I felt. Of its own volition, my body simmered as though someone had lit a match in the humid space between us.

The prince could have shoved me away, but he must have understood the reason I'd straddled him. He went still, allowing me to work quickly. But although I avoided making contact with his bare flesh, my digits faltered against him at one point, the brush of our skin thrusting a hot buzz up my thighs.

Finished, I pulled away. While rain drummed against the treetops, droplets licked a path between my collarbones, and something candid stoked his features.

To my revulsion, the same blasted upheaval from the fig episode resurfaced. Heat seared the cleft between my thighs, agitation throbbing in the folds of my pussy. I swallowed my disgust, and he watched my throat move, his nostrils flaring.

Slowly, his eyes scanned my body, counting the slashes. Then his gaze lifted, the irises sizzling. "I need to check them."

A trade. His aid in exchange for my help. While the rainforest had done nothing I hadn't wanted, this would put us on equal footing.

Except when I gave a brisk nod of consent, he spoke in a gritty tone. "Closer."

21

Flare

Closer.

My pulse jolted in tune with the lightning. The prince glowered as if that word nauseated him. But since the feeling was mutual, we had nothing to worry about.

I could handle this. I could withstand his proximity for a moment.

On bended knees, I sidled into him, yet it wasn't enough. That much was clear from his annoyed huff. Without looking away, he set his fingers on my hips, the contact pumping me with adrenaline. Maybe this wasn't a good idea—

I gasped as he jerked me forward, my ass crashing onto his lap, the motion prying my knees apart, my steepled legs gripping his waist. Slabs of muscle radiated under me, around me, against me. Like this, he checked the cuts on my skin, scrutinizing every gash, the magnitude of his gaze funneling to the rift between my legs.

Queasiness assaulted me, born of repulsion and something else, a primal need I hadn't experienced since Rune. Except this felt harsher, fiercer.

Satisfied with his inspection, the prince craned his head. And our eyes collided. His irises flashed like quicksilver, scorn and spite clashing.

But there was more. Another impulse intruded, hectic and covetous, the combination so potent my head swam.

Shit. Oh, shit.

Everyone in The Dark Seasons feared the Prince of Winter. And just as many wanted to get fucked by him. Yet right here, I was the only thing he saw, felt, held.

Rain stabbed through crevices in the canopy, narrowly missing us and forcing our bodies to grind nearer. Unwillingly, we moved in sync. I dripped onto him, my nipples rubbed his chest, and my core fit against his.

Pull away, I told myself. Get away from him, I warned myself.

Instead, the words dropped like firebombs from my tongue. "I hate you so much."

He licked his lips, tasting my declaration. "I hate you more."

Yet the hate seemed to fuel us, feeding some twisted craving. My outtakes grew shallow and stunted. A molten sensation whittled between my thighs, the effect drastic. Without warning, the walls of my pussy clenched.

On reflex, my hips bucked an inch against the ledge of his cock, the friction streaking through my veins. The prince hissed, a curse lashing from his mouth. And on a gasp, I arched into the sharp noise. Another one of those, and I might combust.

His frame strained beneath mine, our bodies quavering like threads about to snap. The moment drew itself out, suspending us at a point of no return.

And then his cock swelled.

Long and broad, it rose into the vent of my legs. The head broadened, its solid width flush with my clit. A whine crept up my throat, the sensation so extreme that arousal poured from my crease.

The Prince of Winter pinned me in his arms. The most feared ruler on the continent had gotten his hands on me, those fingers knifing into my hips, his cock tightening.

This was wrong. So very wrong.

Yet I gyrated another inch, frustration urging me forward. In response, he gnashed his canines as if ambushed by the same vice, the same need to get rid of this feeling, to banish it from our systems.

Watching my mouth drop open, those black pupils inflated, eating up the irises. Caught up in his stare, I gave into a heinous temptation. And rolled my waist again, skating my clit against his cock.

Unleashing a pent-up noise, Winter struck. The prince shoved his forehead against mine, his mouth a hair's breadth from my own. I barely had time to absorb the sensation before he skated his incisors over my chin, down the center of my throat, and to the glen between my clavicles. Along the way, he nicked and scoured my flesh, the contact agonizing.

Then his tongue joined his mouth, the hot flat tracing my collarbones.

My head slumped back, my lips parted, and my limbs fanned apart. I would have toppled over, but he grasped me tightly, his cock getting harder. The head bloated, so that I imagined its ruddy color and the slit where cum would bead to the surface, the thought watering my mouth.

Anarchy swirled in the ravine of my thighs. Under the chemise, my bare cunt pulsated, a rush of liquid heat pouring onto his lap and seeping through the fabric of his pants.

The prince emitted a hoarse noise. Motivated by that response, I shoved my tits into him, and he reacted. Hooking his fingers onto the straps of my chemise, he peeled the material down my arms.

My breasts lifted from the bodice and into the eventide air. The points toughened into pebbles, the sensitive tips raw and aching.

An intake of breath sliced through the enclosure. "Fuck."

With my head flung backward, I couldn't see his expression. Yet I heard him, sensed him. Delirious, I envisioned those eyes piercing, the lustful weight of his gaze on my breasts.

With a hostile groan, the prince's mouth sank to the first nipple. All or nothing, he strapped his lips around the shell and sucked deeply. And all semblance of restraint fled my being.

A cry broke from my lips, somehow audible to his ears. Humming, he suctioned me into his hot mouth, then circled his tongue over the erect tip, the decadent swats throwing me into a tailspin.

I whimpered up to the trees. Over and over, this went. The prince sketched and nipped, plying me into a drenched mess, his tongue flicking until I was inconsolable.

"Yes," he encouraged against my wet nipple. "Cry for me."

I did, and I did, and I did. Spurred by my responses, he swerved to the opposite breast, his lips skewering me to pieces.

Lightning cracked. At the explosive noise, we snapped into motion.

Straddling his cock, my pussy moved in tandem to his mouth. I writhed my hips, grinding onto his distended crown, which lifted through the pants. Serrated noises cleaved from his lungs like shards of glass. Those iron muscles trapped me to him while I spread my knees, planted them on uneven ground, and hauled my waist into him.

While sucking my nipple with force, the prince's groan struck my breast. His fingers trenched into my hips and hauled me forward, rowing my body back and forth, the pace borderline violent. Shockwaves catapulted up my legs, my folds parting and soaking his lap.

And he lost it.

Releasing my nipple and seizing my ass, the villain prince hoisted me forward, thrashing my pussy against his cock and whisking his hips in unison. The chemise's hem flipped high, the brunt of his thrusts making my tits jostle.

My unruly, wet hair fell over my upturned face, and my fingers sank into his mane for leverage. Sobs tore from me, plaintive and demanding. The commotion tumbled out in short bursts. Each one incited the prince, his hands snatching me so tightly, I would bruise later.

Our bodies smashed into one another like cannonballs. Our rhythm surged from eager to frenzied. Greed shredded my thoughts to bits, drowning out the last vestiges of morality.

I flew at him. Scrambling from his arms, I whipped around and landed once more on his cock. With my back facing him, I didn't have to see, didn't have to stare. My fingers braced on his thighs as I matched the prince's frantic pace, slamming my damp hips against his, jutting my cunt into his erection, chasing this upheaval, this disorder, this pandemonium.

Grunting, he fisted my slick hair and lunged his ass. Hard and fast and rough, he charged us toward release, toward a turbulent end, the chaos escalating as quickly as it had begun. I curled my spine, my naked backside exposed under the chemise, and flayed my pussy with his length, desperate to free myself from this need, to peel it from me like a layer of flesh. As the pace increased, we belted into one another, and I didn't know anymore, and I didn't think anymore, and I didn't care anymore.

And please. And more.

Detestable pleasure spiraled between my thighs, building, mounting. With punishing shoves of his waist, the prince groaned and unleashed, pistoning to beat the climax out of me. My pussy rippled against the head of his cock, the crescendo tearing through my walls.

I came with my mouth ajar. A scream pushed against my tongue, but I refused to let it out, all the while my body convulsed on his lap.

Lightning charged through my blood, electrifying me down to the bone, the intense pleasure beyond any zenith that had come before. I pitched my backside, bucking hard and reaping the sensation to its final tremor.

The prince rammed his face into my nape and bit back a growl. His hips froze, his cock twitching through the pants, on the brink of spilling. The instant I sagged, he batted me away. Still reeling from the climax, I scurried off his lap.

With a hiss, he wrenched himself in the opposite direction and fumbled rapidly with the closures of his pants. Out of eyeshot, the prince freed his erection. Spasms racked his frame, low groans chuffed from his mouth, and his tip streamed into the sand.

After another moment, he slumped. Shifting to make sure I still couldn't see a thing, the prince bowed his head, one palm flat on the ground and the other groping his cock.

I yanked down my chemise and jerked the bodice straps in place.

My breath struggled to catch up, my heart battering into my chest.

Rain pummeled the cove. The weight of what happened drove us apart, the remnants of pleasure tingling across my skin as I tucked myself under the blanket. And although the prince kept his back to me, I imagined his calamitous features reflecting my own.

Divine Seasons. What had we just done?

22

Flare

My eyes flew open and landed on a bulky form. The unconscious prince faced me, though we'd been turned away from one another last night. Resting on his side, the Royal's substantial body loomed like a shield, those bloated muscles contorting with his intakes.

As the blanket rustled over my waist, I noticed the material covered only me, whereas the prince slept exposed with only his clothing to shield him from the elements. Had I twisted in my sleep and stolen his half of the blanket? And why did I care? He didn't deserve my concern, no matter what we'd done to each other.

No matter how intense it had felt. No matter how violently I came. No matter how I'd shaken down to the marrow.

He could have used this lapse to his advantage. I glanced at where we'd discarded our weapons, checking to make sure he hadn't pulled a fast one while I slept off the climax.

Reassured the dagger and knife were in their rightful spots, I swung my attention back to the lump beside me. Up close, he had the longest eyelashes I'd ever seen, the black threads complimenting the dark blue shade lining them. The man breathed quietly while sleeping, as if he never stopped concentrating or problem solving.

Tilting my head, I stared. And stared. And stiffened when his eyelids flapped open. Irises made of crystals ensnared me, riveted by my features before sharpening with realization.

The lightning rain. His pupils swallowing me whole. Bleeding and dripping and seething into one another's faces. My pussy writhing on his cock. Our hips crashing together.

I hate you so much.

My mouth falling open. His mouth compressing. Our bodies coming hard.

The flashback worked like a stick of dynamite. Fully awake, we jolted backward.

Within seconds, we put as much distance between us as possible, shooting from the blanket and feigning preoccupation with our supplies. They had survived the siege, whereas the prince and I had been lashed by the droplets. At least, our wounds had dried, and neither of us said a thing about the storm.

While smacking sand from my clothes, I caught the prince assessing my wounds, that explicit stare pinching my nerves. "What?"

My pulse kicked up as those cold pupils met my gaze. But if my ass, breasts, or cunt triggered him as they had last night, there was no telling.

Instead, he narrowed his eyes. "The saltwater helped. Your recuperation looks promising, but if those cuts fester or turn red, show me."

That instruction had sounded considerate. In my wavering silence, the prince must have recognized the impression he'd given and clarified, "I cannot have you decaying when I need you able-bodied."

Such a prick. Even so, my attention traveled to the dried scab on his calf. It might be healing, or I might have made it worse, since I had no experience with that sort of damage.

Jellyfish stings, coral gashes, and weaving blisters. Yes.

Razor sharp droplets of rain. No.

As I pointed, his mockery cut me off. "Your skills are adequate. I'll live beyond that. There's no need to care."

If that was how he wanted to be, then fuck him. Rather than concerning myself, I fantasized about setting fire to his scalp and serving his carcass to the nearest resident carnivore. That would solve most of my problems.

As unwilling allies, we traveled into the rainforest. The rope around my midriff anchored the dagger and canteen, and the cuts on my body had dried into scabs. The prince walked fine despite his injured calf, his leather belt securing the scalpel knife, its sheath suspended low over his rotating waist.

Threads of sunlight haloed the trees. Howls and whistles overlapped from every corner. The fauna afforded us peeks, from hummingbirds with longer wings to centipedes that stretched for miles.

Reptiles held court, their features resembling basilisks. Thick hides as black as soot, stomachs that glowed like molten rocks whenever they breathed, and tails that stretched like ropes.

"Adaptation," the prince murmured, one hand resting on his sheath.

"Diversity," I replied with a grin, the word making him frown in thought.

Endless wonders materialized through the mist, as intoxicating as the fragrance of blossoming plumerias. Along the way, we scanned the path with two sets of eyes, his of a scientist, mine of an explorer, and—

My free hand shot toward the prince, warning him to stop. But he'd already halted, also reaching out to stall me.

Because of this, our fingers brushed. The sensation crackled up my limbs like embers. In unison, we glanced down to where our digits made contact.

Not okay. Yet neither of us pulled back. Instead, his eyes trailed along an invisible object, and mine followed, latching onto the silver wire strung across the path. Our feet had paused an inch from the trap, which had to be the work of a hungry dweller. Tripping the wire would have alerted the creature of our presence.

The prince drew his fingers from mine and murmured, "I will go first."

If I didn't know him better, I would have mistaken the gesture for gallantry. Brushing off the illusion, I opened my mouth to protest.

Yet he was too fast. Methodically, the prince stepped over the wire, then twisted my way. Offering a curt nod, he extended his arm as if to steady me lest I should trip.

I gave my companion an uncertain look, then pursed my lips in sudden amusement at his austere features. I'd never beheld someone that eternally serious. Here we stood, surrounded by lush splendor, yet he acted as though we'd landed in purgatory.

Inspired, I jogged backward and hopped over the line. Alarm cramped his expression. He jolted forward as though to catch me, only to halt as I landed.

"Huh," I gloated. "So your face isn't nailed that way after all."

The prince's arm dropped. "Do not get used to it."

"Of course not. Seasons forbid, you crack a smile."

"Do you plan on risking your neck in every circumstance and with every obstruction we come across? Tell me now, so I know whether to leash you."

"I think we both know how well restraints work on me."

"They worked in the quad." His eyes raked down my curves. "As for this environment, perhaps I haven't found the right ones yet."

Why did that sound like a prediction rather than a bluff?

I stiffened, but he sauntered away before I could whip up a good retort. Ignoring the sparks across my flesh where his gaze had slid, I charged after him, miffed that he'd taken the lead.

The wilderness played a tune, birds whistling a symphony akin to pipes and flutes. My insides fluttered with delight, yearning to bond with this dream realm. How I craved its spirit and longed to become one of its forest tenants.

Wait. Did I smell mangoes?

Cocking my head, I detoured from our route. Behind me, the prince's hiss cut through the raptors' melody. "Get the fuck back here," he snarled.

Not that I listened. Whipping shrubs aside, I discovered a massive trunk attached to the deadliest looking fern tree in history, its bark riddled with thorns so large they resembled spikes, much like the ones on which King Rhys displayed the severed heads of convicts.

I peered overhead to where plump orbs dangled like ornaments from the branches. As the irritated prince reached my side, I clapped my hands, bounced on my feet, and pointed. The pickings could be mangoes, apart from the beaded texture rising from the yellowy red skin, the rind so dazzling that we saw the fruits from three stories below.

I tied the hem of my chemise between my legs. I wasn't a climber by nature, but—

"Do not think about it," the prince warned.

Naturally. I didn't *think* about it.

"Hey!" he gritted, launching forward as I scaled the first branch.

His arm swiped out to seize my ankle but missed as I scrambled up the trunk. Gripping the base of a thorn, the prince spoke through his teeth, "We don't know if they're edible."

"That's why we taste them."

"The thorns—"

"What's one more cut?"

Yep. He'd heard all of that, even though I hadn't been looking at him. And fine. I had more important things to dwell on.

Truly, I wasn't daft. After recently regretting what I'd stuffed into my mouth, I knew the risk. But if one of us didn't take the gamble, we'd starve. Sand drifters had to make this leap of faith every day.

The Royal swore under his breath, the echo louder than usual in this acoustic place. I stifled my mirth, too famished and happy to tolerate his negativity. It wasn't high so much as sharp, so I hunched and twisted around the thorns. A pointed tip scoured my toes. Gasping in pain but also chuckling, I hauled myself up and flopped one leg over a branch, marveling at the treasure before my attention diverted to a network of ropes threaded among the boughs. Cobwebs laced the cords, the lines frayed as though they might break into dust particles from the slightest touch.

Old ropes. It could be a large net to catch the fruit. Except these ropes didn't exhibit the same type of woven pattern. Instead, they stretched parallel to one another and then disappeared into the canopy.

The prince spotted the cords too. "A conveyor," he said from below.

Trepidation snatched my chest. This appeared to be some manner of pulley.

But attached to what? And created by whom?

Baffled, I shook my head. This rainforest was supposed to be deserted. And despite the familiar arrangement, the cords' brittle material was shaggy and timeworn unlike anything I'd seen before.

Relief eased my muscles. This forest was ripe with mysteries and newfangled wonders, meaning it had to be a type of natural cord, which grew on these trees, which some animal had sewn into the boughs.

While the prince contemplated, I focused on the reason I'd quested here. Yet my enthusiasm withered. The orbs had been plundered, their insides devoured by what must have been insects, save for one treat. Resigned but grateful, I plucked my only catch, then wagged it at the prince.

He rewarded me with a scowl. Then his scowl collapsed, his gaze flashing with recognition. With the sort of calm that signified restrained panic, he ordered, "Get. Down."

The Royal strode forward, about to vault up here and grab me. And that's when I heard the long hiss.

I paused, listening to the slip and slide of an animal in motion, the sounds of a predator winding itself in my direction. Slowly, my gaze scanned the trees. The noise came from everywhere, quivering across the branches and driving shivers across my flesh.

The rainforest cared about me. But that didn't mean its residents felt the same.

So when a reptilian tail lashed into view and whipped toward my skull, I ducked with a yelp. As I sank into a crouch atop the branch, the tail whisked my way again, slamming into a trunk when I scuttled out of harm's way and onto an adjacent offshoot. The wide branches anchored me as I lurched upright, wobbling and springing to another bough as the tail came back at me, aiming for my stomach but missing.

A livid noise cut from the prince's mouth. Despite his size and lack of climbing skills, he'd made it halfway up the trunk by then, with the scalpel hilt locked between his teeth.

The lithe dweller moved in a flash, its face darting from the creepers. Instead of smooth scales, barbs prickled from its body and encircled its face. Yet I recognized the type.

A boa.

It lunged, its armored body flaying like a lasso. I pitched sideways, and the boa reared, rising as tall as me. With each thwap of its tail, that far-reaching hiss slithered through the wild. The serpent lashed, and I blocked the strike with my forearm, twisting and ramming my opposite elbow into the predator.

Pissed off, the creature opened its mouth to brandish a pair of fangs. I knew a fauna display when I saw one. This was the beauty's territory, which made me the intruder.

Out of options, I cranked my arm backward as I had a dozen times with Pyre, then catapulted my fist and punched the boa in the face.

The creature lost its balance and swung over the side. Half of its body dangled there, the other half hooking onto the branch.

She wouldn't stay that way forever. Not even close.

It was fun going up, but not fun going down. The prince stalled, his visage torn between annoyed, stressed, and flabbergasted as I shimmied down the trunk.

As I caught up to him, he swore. "On my back."

I should protest. My small body could fit into narrow places, but his limbs would cover distance faster. Also, this was no time for pride. As the serpent righted itself and located us, its eyes glittered with intent.

Strapping myself around the prince like a knapsack, I held fast while he hunkered to the ground. By the forest's grace, we avoided getting impaled.

The second we hit the woodland floor, I launched off the prince. We bolted, sprinting down the aisle. My head twisted backward as our chaser shot forward, winding around boughs and snapping its fangs.

In Summer, cobras were the fast and venomous ones. Boas were supposed to be neither.

Yet this one launched like a harpoon. And if it couldn't infuse us with venom, it surely had the power to crush bones.

Shit. I'd lost the maybe-mango.

We flew through the bushes. Twigs cracked under my heels and broke skin. My short limbs struggled to keep up with the prince's tall ones, so that he clamped my fingers in his and hauled me with him.

This wouldn't work. The boa gained on us, flying in our direction through the trees.

I ripped my hand from the prince's. Remembering the wire trap from earlier, I veered off course and charged down another path, praying this would work. Chances were, the boa fancied hot blood anyway.

As if to prove me right, the serpent torpedoed my way. Ignoring the prince's roar, I double-backed and swerved past the serpent as it rocketed to the understory. Furious, it whipped around and followed. Barreling the way I'd come, I propelled down the lane, searching and spotting the silver wire.

My feet barreled past the thread, snapping it in half. I tripped over a fallen log and smacked face-first into the dirt, then flipped around as tarantulas fell like gadgets from more silver strings. Orange and black dotted the insects' fuzz, and drool leaked from their oversized fangs, likely capable of sucking blood by the tankard.

The vampiric insects intercepted the boa. They spit more intricate strands, the webs netting my predator.

Registering what they'd caught, the tarantulas changed their minds and shot back into their nests, uninterested in reptile meat. Meanwhile, the creature thrashed, getting more tangled.

Compassion tugged on me. If I freed the poor animal, it would either tear me to shreds or squeeze the air from my lungs.

I hesitated, then crawled toward the fuming reptile. It flailed about in panic, then paused, watching as I sawed at the web with my dagger, which did nothing.

Switching to my hands, I went to work untying the threads. They were strong and more intricate than most sailing knots. My fingers traced the lacework, located every complex kink, and unraveled them one by one.

At last, the web collapsed. The boa sprang forth with a hiss. I clambered backward, one hand on my weapon and the other planted on the dirt. Hunching over, I lowered my head in solidarity and maintained eye contact.

Stupefied, the boa hovered and regarded me with skeptical eyes, its vertical pupils scanning my deferential pose. My heart clattered. This might have been a stupid thing to do, but I couldn't bring myself to let a creature suffer. And I yearned to share The Phantom Wild with its dwellers, not steal it from them.

After another moment, the serpent narrowed its gaze. Then it spiraled in the opposite direction and vanished.

I slumped. Then I yelped as a pair of hands locked under my arms and yanked me off the ground. The villain prince flopped me over his shoulder like a flounder and quit the scene, his arm flexing around my ass like a steel band.

I kicked. I scratched. I pounded my fists.

The fiend shook me like a rattle. "Cease."

Reaching around, I tore open his sheath, snatched his knife, and pressed the tip against his waist. I could have used my own dagger, but stealing his felt more satisfying.

Weapon in hand, I paused a centimeter from ripping through his shirt, the action a silent war cry. Yet the man strode ahead with confidence, dismissing the jab to his side, his steps so graceful that the knife hardly moved in tandem.

I nudged him with the weapon and—

"No," he forbade.

"Yes," I snarled. Then I jabbed, nipped the material, and gasped as the flat of his hand smacked my ass, hard and stinging like hell. The sharp clap echoed through the woods, the impact jolting me.

My dagger missed its target, but my hand didn't. Outraged, I extended my arm and slapped his ass back.

For an instant, the prince stiffened. "I warn you, Little Beast," he seethed. "Behave."

Winter should know better than to order Summer around. As he kept going, I twisted and latched my teeth onto his shoulder. A hiss sliced from his mouth, his fingers snaring the roots of my hair and yanking my face from his skin. He held me like that, with my head slanted at a precarious angle, the verge of pulling a muscle if I didn't comply.

Damn him. He wasn't worth a third attempt.

After a few more steps, the prince released me, dark waves flouncing around my head. With my body dangling like a sack, I felt his muscles shift, from the plates of his shoulder blades to the carved span of his chest. The untucked shirt rode around his hips, and the wrinkled navy pants clung to his legs, the fitted cloth stretching over those taut buttocks. The ovals showed no sign that I'd made a dent, flexing instead with every step.

My pussy had been riding that strong physique to the brink last night. Vexed, I turned away before the memory got me nauseous. I couldn't afford the consequences of puking all over his clothes.

The enemy stopped. He swung me upright and let go, dumping me to the ground. As I stumbled to keep my balance, he took the opportunity to swipe his blade from my fingers, shoving it back into its encasement and then backing me toward the hedges while staring down the length of his aristocratic nose.

"Try it," he dared. "Disobey me again."

"Your rank is worthless here, *Your Highness*," I sneered. "And throwing your weight around doesn't work on me. I might be kicked to the ground, but I always get back up, and I've survived more scars than you could ever give."

At the mention of my scars, something livid flashed in his pupils. "You will not endanger yourself again. Understand?"

I frowned, stumped that he wasn't referring to my trick with his knife. No, he was referring to me gambling my safety at every turn.

Taking my silence for rebellion, the prince stalked nearer until his torso grazed my breasts. "I can restrain you for longer," he murmured. "Go ahead. Give me an excuse."

Heat simmered between us, thick and humid. With a grudge, I watched the muscles of his throat work, pumping air in and out of his lungs.

How far could I push him? What would he do to retaliate?

I stormed ahead, clearing my head of his proximity. The prince fell into step beside me as the soil transformed into a dewy carpet of grass.

Blossoms hung upside down from vines, their yellow petals drooping. That feline roar I'd once heard rumbled from a notable distance.

As I checked myself for fang wounds, he said, "The reptile did not get to you."

I blinked at his profile, which had barely looked me over. Nonetheless, this reassured me enough to dwell on other matters. "I lost the fruit."

"You could have lost a body part," he lectured.

"If I'd lost a body part, you would have sewn it back on." After a beat of silence, I glimpsed the prince's mouth tipping sideways. Fisting my hands on my hips, I marveled, "Is that a smirk?"

His lips collapsed. "Nonsense. You don't amuse me."

"Does anything?" But when he refused to reply, I sighed balefully, "The pome smelled like a mango."

"Varieties of mangoes are acidic."

"Acid is good for the soul."

"Not so good after a poisoning like yours." The prince halted in a rare slash of light and swung toward me. "Open your mouth."

I tensed. "I'm fine. My tongue and throat are still there."

"We can do this the easy way or the Winter way. Which do you prefer?"

"Which one involves my fist and your face?"

"You've been rubbing your mouth ceaselessly."

Attentiveness claimed his features. Like a reflex, I thought of his determined expression when he flushed the poison from my body, then remembered him examining my wounds last night and this morning.

My tastebuds responded, conjuring the deceptive flavor of those najava berries. Stubbornness wouldn't keep me alive. Refusing his help was just silly.

I parted my lips. My compliance allowed his fingers to ghost over my mouth, the contact gentler than I'd expected.

Then again, he'd been gentle in the tower before choking me. Yet the shivers across my body insisted this was different, and I wanted to scream because his touch shouldn't be tender. Like last night, his fingers shouldn't warm my flesh.

"Wider," he instructed, his voice uncharacteristically gruff. "Slowly."

With his thumb pushing on my lower lip and the rest of his hand braced under my chin, he tilted my head to the light. His eyes narrowed, sketching my lips and then sliding past them to seek out my tongue, where the poison had leaked.

"More," he murmured. "Let me see."

My thighs clenched, but the command found its way under the chemise anyway, his words flicking against my clit like a crooked finger. Getting ahold of myself, I unfurled the flat of my tongue. The prince's pupils fattened and sharpened at the same time. Any more of this, and that look would penetrate deeper.

But then a crease formed between his dark brows. "You lost your voice at a young age."

The question hit me like a splash of cold water. "It happened after Summer caged me. I was twelve."

Something that bordered on anger kindled in his irises. "Did your throat feel branded from the inside? Did you have a fever afterward?"

"Both. I'd been screaming until I couldn't anymore, until I killed my voice."

The anger intensified, icing his words whether or not he noticed. "Your marking caused that, not you. This kingdom uses an ink infused with ash particles of Summer tinder. When the guards painted your neck, residue seeped into your vocal cords," he explained. "It can happen. From what I see, there's tissue damage because you must have vomited some of the liquid."

I had. Pyre had smacked me over the head for that.

Loss clogged my throat. So I hadn't erased my voice. It had been Summer's doing.

In the span of an hour, the prince had volunteered to step over that wire first, to make sure it was safe, then he'd launched after me when the boa appeared, bore my weight while descending the thorned tree, and reassured me about the tattoo. He could have continued running while the viper targeted me. Instead, the prince had stormed in my direction.

The words fell from my mouth. "Thank you."

The prince gave a start, as though gratitude was foreign to him. Uncertain, he offered a brisk nod. "You're still recuperating from the poison. Your mouth will be uncomfortable today. It will pass."

An eternity went by. His breath stroked my cheeks, his body enveloping me in the scents of needle forests and blustering winds. Sweat licked down my spine and between my breasts. The slightest movement would brush my nipples across his chest, which rose and fell heavily beneath his shirt.

The moment snuck up on us like the tripwire we'd stepped over earlier. Something hidden under the surface, then suddenly there, straining tightly. If not careful, it would trap us.

Mist sprayed the trees. A breeze shook the gleaming leaves and produced a thumping noise.

The sound broke our trance. It reminded me of ropes hitting a slab, the same thought gripping the prince as well, our gazes locking in recollection. We swerved toward the canopy.

"The conveyance," he muttered.

I jerked my chin at the expanse of trees. "They would come through here."

That much, I knew for certain while remembering their direction. I had assumed the cords were natural to the rainforest, but what if that wasn't true?

We hastened toward the commotion and scanned the foliage. My fingers seized his sleeve, and I pointed to a sliver between the leaves, where a garland materialized, the current causing it to smack the branches.

I thought back to the castle blackout in Autumn, when I'd helped Briar and Poet follow the ribbon streamers installed in the ceiling. The stronghold's hallways had been as dark as a crypt, yet I'd been able to see my way through after years of living in a cage.

The prince and I trailed the cords. As lapping water struck our ears, we sped up. Hiking through a cluster of bromeliads, we climbed a small knoll.

At the crest, my breath caught. The hill led to a wide lake, along with a crumbling rocky bridge that was no longer passable, with a chunk of the platform missing. Intricate statues of fauna balancing atop one another towered on either side of the bridge. Beyond the water stood a structure covered in dripping shags of foliage, with countless levels rising into the trees, verandas and colonnades lining every story.

"The fuck?" the prince uttered next to me. "What is this?"

But he knew as well as I did. Although this ancient palace didn't exist in the written or spoken legend, anyone with eyes and a knowledge of the continent's hidden enclaves could guess.

Wonder filled my voice. "Ruins."

23

Jeryn

All I could concentrate on was her throaty sigh, which led to images of her railing my cock last night. Present sanity fled my mind, as it had less than twelve hours ago.

This woman on my lap, the hot temperature of her skin obliterating my restraint like a wrecking ball. The taste of her nipples. Her legs splayed open on my lap, her ass gyrating in my face, the trench of her pussy ramming into my cock as we rutted like animals in heat. Both of us leaking crimson from our wounds. Convulsions assaulting her body and how I'd almost fucking passed out when she climaxed onto my pants.

The despicable triumph of making her come. The aggravation because I hadn't been able to watch her while it happened.

Finally, the indefensible self-disgust. Un-fucking-forgivable.

Discovering a palatial structure at the center of a rainforest failed to overpower the memory. With supreme effort, I refocused. The fortification rose into the canopy, its uppermost level shrouded from view. Based on the deteriorating bridge and plants choking the edifice, whoever once lived here had since passed.

This abandoned structure had to be centuries old. Colonnades and verandas were commonplace in Summer's architecture, but the statues depicting a hierarchy of rainforest fauna dated this relic to an ancient era. Back then, perhaps this rainforest hadn't been a legend so much as a pitstop among the kingdom's islands, if not another official stronghold of this court.

The beast and I swapped ambitious glances. Shelter. Tools. Weapons. Many objects would have decayed or corroded by now, while others might have withstood the test of time. The ancients knew how to construct items that lasted, which justified why this building remained upright, dilapidated though it might be.

The beast stepped around me and pointed to the trees. The rope conveyor snaked through the branches, extended over the lake, and disappeared into one of the colonnades.

"They used rigging to transport resources across the forest," I murmured. "Ingenious."

"Marvelous," she said with a grin. "Except the ropes are too brittle to work. They won't hold much now."

"We will fix that."

Her head veered toward me. Those gold eyes blazed with hesitancy. I twitched, registering my reply. I had said *we*.

Venturing a dozen feet across the platform, we reached the first obstruction. Pausing at the threshold, I braced my hands on my hips and contemplated the eight-foot-wide chasm between us and the rest of the suspension.

The beast and I measured the distance, then craned our heads over the ledge. The lake glistened as clear as glass. My brow furrowed with distrust. The waters of this realm could not be vouched for.

And that was even before my eyes landed on the skeleton. Stretching along the sandy floor, the curved vertebrae of a sea dragon lay amid stalks of swaying kelp. The lattice of gills, broad skull, flared wing bones, and row of teeth revealed enough. Swimming to reach the ruins was out of the question.

Naturally, the beast had already stepped toward the banister. With a hiss, I wheeled in front of her. "No."

Her face scrunched, as if ordering her around had ever worked in my favor. "Oh, come on," she argued. "I thought you were a scientist. Sea dragons are extinct, so that beauty and the rest of its kin have been dead for a while."

"Which is sufficient enough time for them to have evolved into something else."

"Are you always this determined to expect the worst from every situation?"

"I'm determined to be logical," I ground out. "There's a distinction between vigilance and neurosis. I'm not fearful of anything."

She tilted her head, those eyes shining like brass. "I didn't say you were. But if that's true, I pity you."

Pity me? Why the fuck would she pity me?

I tore myself from her gaze. "If we find a fallen log and use one of the tidefarer sails to haul it across the platform, that might do. Or we can fill the gap with rocks, though that shall take more than a week's labor. Another possibility is to —"

A feminine silhouette flew past me and soared into the air. I whipped toward the female as she catapulted over the void, flying as though launched from a slingshot.

"Beast!" I roared, staggering at the gap's edge.

She yelped while crashing to the opposite side and landing in a bed of moss. Momentary pain cramped her features. Peeling herself upright, she panted from across the divide and tossed me a cocky smile.

I did not require a fucking mirror. I knew how low my mouth had dropped.

The audacious creature relished my astonishment, then stood and smacked clumps of dirt from her chemise. Swinging an arm toward me in invitation, she called, "See? Easy."

Recovering from the stunt, I glared at my boots. "Fuck," I muttered to myself, then charged into a run.

The bridge vanished beneath me. Mid-flight, thoughts of broken femurs, fractured kneecaps, and torn tendons passed through my mind. But while she had less weight on her, I possessed longer limbs, which shuddered as my boots smacked the ground. I stumbled forward before halting, then whirled on the female who skipped past me while patting my shoulder.

"Next time, we swim," she said.

The fuck we would. Releasing a pent-up gust of air, I gained her side as we strode past the fauna statues and climbed the steps leading to a stone door etched with a circle of droplet symbols.

The beast traced the emblems in reverence. "Rainfall."

I waited until she finished admiring the artwork. The heavy facade cracked on its hinges as I flattened my palm on the surface and pushed open the door. Instead of dust clouds, a thick wall of mist spilled from the vestibule. Cobwebs stretched like elastic from the rafters, glowing flowers sprouted from the chinks, and a birdbath—the only artifact present—stood in the room's center.

The foundation could be unstable. Our entry could disturb fragments of masonry. Objects could topple over. Predators could have built nests here.

I stepped in front of the beast, shielding her from potential threats, then reached backward for her hand. After a stunned moment, her fingers slid into mine, and my skin burned at the contact. I had reached for her without thinking, but I would not analyze the gesture. Nor why she decided to accept my offer rather than sprint through the corridors extending from every direction.

Picking around bits of rubble, I tested the floor until deeming it safe for us to walk freely. Even so, I kept a firm grip on her.

From one of a half-dozen levels overlooking the vestibule, a raptor vaulted into the air, its flapping wings reverberating. The woman startled. With an amazed chuckle, she aligned herself beside me. "We're in a treasure chest."

"We are," I agreed. "Built by whom?"

What had happened to them? Why would Summer's legend omit their existence?

Deeper into the vestibule, the echo of dripping water halted us.

The female's hand squeezed mine, and she aimed a free digit toward a passage with a downward slope. We paced in that direction. Regardless of what awaited us in these ruins, water took priority.

The tunnel burrowed underground, growing lighter rather than darker, its walls reflecting the iridescence of labradorite and germinating with foliage. The cavity dug in, arching high and wide, light brimming from an unknown source. Eventually, the channel opened to a cavern and a pool of vibrant liquid.

My companion gasped, her hand unwinding from mine. "It's a grotto."

I had read of such places. The water glinted a prismatic green, perhaps from deposits or sediments beneath the surface. Ripples trembled like veins, their reflections illuminating the scabrous enclosure.

I knelt at the rim. Sanitary. Deadly. Either possibility required a thorough check.

Yet adrenaline crept up on me without warning, sinking its talons into my nervous system. A flash of teeth and gills passed through my head, then vanished. I shook myself from the vision and flared my nostrils, making sure to exhale deeply.

If I yielded to these feelings, they would only increase. And she would see it happen.

Deprived of my vial, I lacked options. I continued to breathe, rationality cycling in my head. No need to panic. This was not the ocean, the whirlpool, or anywhere close to the beach.

At last, the sensations abated. Though, this might have been attributed to the figure in my periphery.

Having learned nothing from her near-death experiences, she pranced around the grotto and dove, plunging in headfirst before I could seize her. Shaking my head, I watched the little beast forget I existed. Her figure flew back up, dark hair spraying the vicinity with twinkling particles of water. She spritzed fluid, and her mouth parted with a laugh. For several minutes, I inspected the area while she tumbled with the agility of a mermaid, her body rippling under the surface.

A fleet of small, coiled creatures appeared from the notches and launched toward her. Cursing, I snatched the beast's arm, about to yank her out of the water.

With an excited huff, the female batted away my knuckles. "Calm down," she lectured like I was an imbecile.

My brows smacked together. "What are they?"

"Seahorses."

I hesitated before squatting and examining their tails, muzzles, and S-shaped bodies. Certainly, I knew about sharks and many ocean creatures including jester fish. Yet marine biology hadn't been my primary emphasis of study. Therefore, I hadn't come across these creatures in books.

The fool splashed, which entertained the horses. Encouraged, she arched into the water and proceeded to play with the fauna. Paddling through the grotto, she dodged their movements as they chased after her.

The muscles of my face tightened. How I loathed her carelessness. And how I envied it—that blithe and uninhibited felicity.

Done with carousing, the female scooped liquid into the crater of her palms. Resilient hands. Resourceful fingers. The view sidetracked me to the point where I neglected to intervene, to insist that I test the water before she drank from it, which couldn't be hygienic anyway with those seahorses taking up residence.

As she swallowed, my joints tensed. Agitated, I waited to see if the fluid had a contaminating effect. Yet her eyelids shut in contentment.

Following her lead, I sniffed the surface, then took a sip. Clean. Pure. As usual, not what I'd expected.

By the time I resurfaced from that thought, the beast had finished disrobing. Wadding to a shallow end, she wiggled her hips and peeled the chemise over her head, then dropped it with a loud splat. Standing only knee-deep now, her flesh glistened, beads riding across her collarbones. Pert breasts and dusky nipples that I'd briefly tasted. Rounded hips and a patch of dark hair shrouding her vagina.

Prominent ribs. Flat stomach.

Belatedly, the latter details snared my attention as they'd failed to do last night. Despite the mollusks and fish, she was hungry, a fact that did something unnerving to my system. I didn't care to see her go without food, as I hadn't cared for it in Autumn. Although Poet and Briar had been supplying the dungeon with ample fare, I'd ordered extra for the beast. No one had known this. I had threatened to sever the guards' tongues if they spoke of it. And conveniently, the beast must have assumed the provisions had come from the jester and princess.

My retinas boiled as she doused water over her hips, arms, and legs. Unconcerned. Immodest. Amid the half-light, the beast bathed herself in front of me, stroking each curve and drenching every indentation of flesh.

I knew of Summer's customs. Their endorsement of nudity. Their public baths. Winter offered as many luxurious sanitariums as Rhys and Giselle's court, however our conduct was far less exhibitionist. Though, this minor infraction paled in comparison to the anarchy we'd raised while hate-fucking each other.

The fool glanced up, sensing my attention. She scowled and lifted her chin, daring me to watch. To stare not like a scientist, but as one person to another. That searing gaze challenged me to see her that way.

If she only knew. My expression remained neutral while all hell broke loose inside me. But so long as I didn't focus on her strong fingers, I would not have a problem. By Seasons, those hands were distracting. I would not see this mad woman the way she provoked, no matter how well her body had fit to mine last night.

I was hardly reputed to be squeamish, yet inevitably I turned away, giving her privacy and consuming my own fill of the pool. As splashes resounded from her end of the cavern, I did not think about her dripping skin. I did not picture a lone bead dangling like a ripe fruit from one of her nipples. I did not envision the slickness between her thighs. While listening to the sounds of her bathing, I coped by devouring the pool's contents like a glutton, soothing my parched tongue.

Stripping off my shirt, I washed my face and torso. Not seconds later, the noises from the woman's side of the pool ceased.

My head swung her way. At once, her guilty pupils jumped from the span of my chest to my eyes. We locked gazes, the impact fizzing like a chemical reaction. Directness. Frankness. Despite the temperature of her stare and the havoc it wreaked to my dick, I appreciated the candor between us. It provided a refreshing break from the vapid females and males who burdened me with tedious sexual innuendos and pitiful contests of intellect.

We dunked our clothes and scrubbed them against the rocks to leach out the grime, including my calf bandage. The woman wrestled with a stubborn stain on her chemise. Frustrated, she puffed out her lower lip. From any other maiden, the scene would have been rather cute.

Well. What female liked to be called cute, a classification associated with pups. A word I had never uttered or assigned to anyone. Notwithstanding, the description ill-suited her. She was many things. Hotheaded. Dauntless. Fanciful. But not cute. Those golden irises and calamitous hands were hardly fucking cute.

After we laid our garments out to dry, I debated about my pants. Timidity wasn't the issue. Unlike the lighter garments, it would take longer for the article to dry.

Noticing my uncertainty, the beast smirked and crossed her arms. Another dare. The nerve of her. Then again, if this woman needed a reminder that she didn't affect me, that she didn't count, I would oblige. Now that I'd grown confident about the water, let us see who won this round.

Tossing her an impassive look, I responded in kind. A test for a test. I stood, removed my boots, unbuckled my belt, and set my hands on the waistband.

Her lips parted. Pink burst across her cheeks.

The pants fell. Instantly she whirled, pretending to scratch her arm as my phallus sprang into view. At which point, my lips quirked. Much better.

I descended, stifling a groan as the warm fluid soothed my aching joints. The beast dunked herself moments later, and a rhythmic lapping sound accompanied my breaststrokes, both noises echoing off the walls. With every sweep of water against my flesh, I sensed her furtive glances.

Unfortunately, that caused my triumph to backfire. However involuntary, the brunt of her gaze incited a hot flood to my balls. Knowing this water licked the same places across our bodies—my cock, her cunt—injected me with adrenaline.

Shit. I needed to get a hold of myself.

The tips of my hair floated on the surface like slate blue paint. My movements scattered lambent strands of light along the crusted walls. One particular streak quivered across my companion's wrists. I would have paid closer attention to that, but the seahorses vexed me, the bothersome clique following my trajectory.

The mirthful female perched on an underwater ledge and watched the scene. She compressed her mouth to keep from laughing. "Seems you've got a fan club. They like you."

"Then you entertain them," I remarked. "You're used to feral things, are you not?"

Water sprayed in my direction and smacked my profile. I jolted, wiped the droplets from my eyes, and peered at the beast as she lowered her kicking foot back into the pool.

"Oops," she chirped. "Apologies, Your Highness. How clumsy of me."

The assault achieved two things. One, unadulterated retaliation. Two, it encouraged the horses to flit around me with increasing enthusiasm, having mistaken the splash for an invitation to revel.

Refusing to engage, I slit my eyes at the creatures. "Be still."

The tone of my voice accomplished the rest. The seahorses gave up and vacated the premises. Once they'd fled, silence filled the cavern, apart from water lashing against the rocks.

The beast feigned interest in the ceiling. Obscured from the waist down, I reclined against several tiers of rock and bracketed my elbows on its grooves. "Such bravado. Yet now you avoid the sight of my body. That's out of character and Season for you."

That did it. Her gaze swatted toward me. "I'm surprised you care."

"I question everything a fool does. A second ago, you displayed the immodesty of a whore."

She raised a sarcastic eyebrow. "Tell me all about whores, if you know so much."

Frankly, she would get a more illuminating answer from Poet. I had no experience with courtesans. Nevertheless, a sudden thought lanced through my mind. The possibility set my teeth on edge, particularly when I recalled how the tower guards had handled the beast, then leered at her thighs in the courtyard.

Rage spiked my tongue. "Did any of them touch you in that tower?"

Her eyebrows crinkled. "Do I look like someone who'd have let them?"

No, she did not. My claws retracted. "Based on your countermove with my knife in the castle quad, as well as the mayhem from last night, you don't fit the description of an inexperienced female. Though dry-humping a cock and seeing it in the flesh are two different circumstances. Is that why you turned away?"

"Don't flatter yourself. I didn't want to lose my appetite. And by the way, I know what a cock looks like. Living in a cage doesn't mean I was sheltered."

Not sheltered. What the fuck did that mean?

I couldn't say what got under my skin more. Her insolence or the implication that her knowledge of sex exceeded mine.

A warning snaked from my lips. "Be careful how you respond to me. I'm keeping track of everything you say and do. Plus, every way in which I'll seek retribution once we get to Winter."

"By the time that happens, it's going to be a very long list."

"Precisely," I said, my voice husky from the bath.

The beast swung her legs in the water. "I don't know much about Winter, but I do recall there being two queens who outrank you. Who says you'd be the one calling the shots?"

"My grandaunts have other pressing matters. They rarely deal with the born. That jurisdiction falls to me."

Her scowl could have lit a furnace. "So they condone torture. The icicle doesn't fall far from the glacier."

"Do not speak ill of them," I gritted.

That gave her pause. Her eyelashes flapped as if she'd spotted a chink. Slanting her head, the beast stared for a solid thirty seconds until I shifted.

"What?" I demanded.

"They matter to you," she mused. "Everyone says the Prince of Winter has a frozen heart, yet you sound protective."

My jaw went rigid. I glanced sideways, hating to appear transparent. Nonetheless, I looped my eyes back to hers. "I am not ashamed to value my kin more than my station."

Curiosity alighted her features. Her mouth softened. "Are you supposed to be ashamed?"

I wavered. Some inconceivable force had compelled me to speak. Although I would defend my grandaunts to the death, I also didn't like this beast thinking poorly of them.

A vignette of memories flashed through my mind. "Silvia and Doria ascended the throne as a love match when I was a child, then appointed me after my parents could no longer uphold their titles." I glimpsed the beast listening intently. "My mother and father are sick."

This was no great secret. Rather, the true illness my family kept from this world had nothing to do with them.

A discomforting pang jolted through my sternum. I cleared my throat, ridding myself of the sensation. "Because of my parents' incapacity, the queens raised me. They're good women." My eyes leveled on the beast. "Do not judge what you don't know."

Sarcasm twisted her features. "Funny you should say that."

Indeed. I should have seen that coming. Although I would argue it wasn't the same thing, she wore her passions and idealisms so openly, half the time I didn't know how to respond.

Case in point, why the devil was I telling her this? Why did those metallic eyes have the power to lure such confessions out of me?

A year ago, if someone had predicted I'd be bathing with one of the mad and sharing the intimacies of my family with her, I would have laughed in the offender's face. Then I would have amputated their tongue for the insult.

All the same, a declaration crept past my mouth. "I would do anything for them, tradition and rules be damned."

"Then your heart thaws, after all," she said. "I had a family once too. I know the sound of devotion."

"Do you know the sound of a threat?" I bit out. "Don't assume you can use this against me later."

Disillusion contorted her features. "Unlike every self-serving courtier and politician on this continent, I'm not an opportunist. And unlike my king, I'm not vindictive. You mistake me for someone who sees your feelings as a weakness and a bargaining chip."

"You mistake The Dark Seasons for a place that agrees with you. In my world, family must be secondary."

"If that's true, you're rebelling."

"And blood relations aside, a Royal's duty is to put their subjects above all else."

"If that's true, you're failing."

The accusation pricked me like a needle. "On the contrary." I leaned forward, unhinging my arms from the bracket. "Thanks to the sacrifice of fools, I'm succeeding."

A rock lobbed past my head like a cannonball. The projectile grazed my cheekbone, slammed into the cavern wall, and shattered.

I glanced over my shoulder, then whipped back around. She could have split my fucking skull.

Insolent beast. For smaller crimes, I'd tortured fugitives twelve times her size.

Slowly, I rose. Again, she avoided the sight of my cock and feigned interest in the glinting water.

After exiting the pool and stepping into the pants, I slid my belt into place and dropped the shirt over my head. "I'm not an opportunist," I mimicked. "I'm not vindictive."

She bristled and spoke to the grotto. "You're heartless."

"Nonsense. If I was heartless, I would leave you here."

And then I left her there.

24

Jeryn

I stalked out of the grotto before I did something rash like prowl to her side of the pool, snatch her by the arms, haul her naked body out of the water, and fu—

A hiss sliced from my mouth. I would not go there. *Never* could I go there again.

Damnation. I should have known to take precautions. Not an opportunist? Bullshit. She had certainly seized the opportunity to lob that rock at my head. As of this moment, my fucking cranium could have been porridge on the cavern floor.

Granted, born fools had done nothing to me. No abusive memories shaped my ideologies. Instead, my mind conjured images of a striped fin and a maw of teeth.

Regardless. How I would love to make the beast pay for her insolence. The problem was, a physician did not get personal—a violation I'd been predisposed to enact since Autumn's dungeon. That, among a dozen other impulsive fuck-ups I could not justify.

I flicked those thoughts away. Done and over.

Where the hell was I?

I paused, my eyes scrolling across a series of cave tunnels. Absently, I had ventured farther beneath the ruins. My spine tightened as I regarded the configuration of illuminated labradorite cavities. Paying attention to where I was going would bloody help.

The breeze pushing through did wonders for my calf, relieving me enough that I conducted a search, heeding landmarks to retrace my steps. Pointless. Useless. The frustration amounted to a pathetic conclusion. I was lost.

Out of nowhere, a perky finger tapped my shoulder. My lips thinned. I did not, did not, did *not* turn around.

Not immediately. But when I did, my gaze landed on the beast leaning casually against the wall. "Aww," she cooed. "Need help?"

"No," I grumbled.

"So you didn't go astray? Fall between the cracks?" She gave my frame a once-over. "Not that you'd fit."

"This may come as a surprise, but when you fired that rock, you missed. My brain is intact."

"If you say so." She crooked her middle digit, in a beckoning gesture. "Want to see what else I found?"

Bragger. Sand drifter.

I made sure to walk beside the woman instead of trailing the fluttering hemline of that goddamn chemise. We ascended to the ground level, then crossed into one of the colonnade halls off the vestibule. Up a flight of crisscrossing steps, we hiked seven levels to an uppermost point and emerged onto the ruins' peak.

A cupola umbrellaed above the roof, the structure enmeshed in hibiscus flowers and ensconced in the treetops. Despite the surrounding canopy, this strategic location provided a three-hundred and sixty degree view, including panoramic fragments of the ocean and its numerous coves.

Like a watch tower, the cupola overlooked any incoming ships. Yet the platform remained shielded from intruders. Whoever built this monument had known how to stay hidden.

The beast had left the grotto to explore. She had located this perk.

I smothered my pride and gave her a quick nod. Her lips crooked, relishing the moment. Though, at least she didn't rub it in.

Over the next two hours, we investigated the ruins. The dining hall consisted of vaulted ceilings, a mammoth fireplace, a chipped stone table, and twelve chairs covered in greenery that resembled coriander leaves. Numerous sleeping quarters contained twine-constructed beds and pillows speckled with mildew. One room housed a single-tiered fountain that shifted colors for no discernible reason. Yet the water was chilled and drinkable, fresher than a glacier stream, and easily accessible compared to the grotto, which must have been a communal bathing room.

The beast discovered a cellar containing textiles—vestments, pants, shirts, and dresses tailored from silk, linen, muslin, and elements such as water itself. Boots, sandals, beads, ropes, and feather sacks appeared to be in pristine condition.

Another crypt had been used as an armory. Saws, blades, arrows, pickaxes. Their archaic shapes could have been featured in a Winter museum exhibit. Many were dull, though a whetstone would resolve that.

"Enchantment," the beast marveled, drawing her fingers over the walls, which emitted a subtle glint. "History tells us how the Summer ancients built their chambers and cellars and crypts out of a rare type of sand that hardened like stone."

I nodded while running my thumb along the curved edge of a sickle. "That allowed them to preserve objects. I have read of such practices from historic times, though I've never seen the like."

"No one living today would. Tragically, that special sand no longer exists. Over the ages, it was carried away by the wind, maybe because the wind decided it was time for other types of sand to thrive."

Unable to resist, I engrossed myself in her flushed profile and sparkling irises. Worship did attractive things to those eyes. "You believe nature has a soul."

"Everyone does." The beast glanced sideways at me, her fingers lingering on the wall. "It's not exactly a new discovery, what with Spring's

Wildflower Forest being notorious for inspiring recklessness in its visitors. Not to mention Autumn's Lost Treehouses being the birthplace of fairytales, in all their dark and alluring ways. People saying that particular enclave chooses who it welcomes past its borders, just like The Phantom Wild. Nature has spirit and a will. Isn't that why we keep faith in the Seasons? They're the deities of this world."

"Technically."

"Technically?" She swerved my way. "What do you believe then, Prince of Science?"

"I believe the Seasons have power, but they do not have a mind," I answered. "Neither a will, nor a conscience. They're an omnipotent system—a complex network of laws. That said, I'm aware my theology doesn't align with the majority."

"What about all these tales of nature welcoming only select visitors into their realms or affecting certain people in special ways?"

"Chemical, biological, and physiological reactions," I defended. "Nature isn't a fucking circus act. As for the rest, just because scientific reasons haven't been discovered yet, that hardly means they don't exist."

The beast grimaced as if she'd ingested a mouthful of excrement. "Yet you see born souls as so-called abominations."

"Apart from progressive Autumn, the bulk of this continent sees them as abominations. Whereas I see them as an epidemic. Viruses. Diseases. In my estimation, nature has agency, but it's not infallible. What almighty force would consciously create deformities on purpose?"

"Maybe the divine Seasons don't see us as deformities. Maybe they see us as they do this rainforest, its inhabitants, and the rest of the elemental world. Maybe they see us as diverse, which is how it used to be in society."

I narrowed my eyes. "I repeat. I don't believe the Seasons have a will."

Yet her speculation had not occurred to me. When one disregarded nature possessing a soul, the notion had merit. From a clinical standpoint, diversity had numerous advantages, the ability to produce medicine being one of them. However, societal diversification had not been attempted since these ancients had been alive.

The gnawing prospect refused to vacate my mind as we continued our search. We could benefit from tweezers, shears, needles, and thread. But notwithstanding the lack of surgical tools, the ruins provided other essentials.

In another chamber, decrepit columns lined one wall overlooking the wild. A hearth recessed into the opposite end must have been used for cooking, and a table fronted an adjacent facade. Small alcoves housed weathered glass jars and cracked marble pots with lids, likely for food conservation.

The conveyor hovered overhead. So this had been its destination.

Tassels of vegetation protruded from the masonry. Clusters of undergrowth sprouted between the floor cracks, flourishing without direct rays. Potential treatments. Undiscovered cures. To have a tropical climate like this one, a landscape denser than any other in this Season, the opportunities were endless.

While the beast peeked into the vessels, I knelt and swept aside a pile of dead leaves. Fungi sprouted from the surface, each cluster indistinguishable.

In one corner, the perforated leaves of a plant fanned out. I tested them with my finger, heedful of a rash. Suffering no irritation, I rubbed my thumb and forefinger over the surface, noting a chill to the touch.

The leaf's scent emitted the crispness of mint. It reminded me of pine cress, a Winter aid for respiration.

The columns provided ventilation, and the edifice filtered out the humidity, but the open prospect rendered it vulnerable to rainfall and unwelcome fauna guests. Given the lack of nests though, this wasn't a great concern. With a bit of sterilization, this space could function as a medical chamber.

The beast rubbed her arms. "It's chilly."

I rose. "It's the stone. Parts of this fortress are protected from the climate."

"No." She glanced toward a spot on the floor. "I mean, yes. But the breeze is coming from there."

Padding across the chamber, she exited the threshold. I trailed after her, rounded a hallway corner, and entered an alcove. The beast raced her palm along the wall, her fingers tracing a delineation that most could not have detected among the shadows.

After a moment, she froze. Twisting my way, she gave me a meaningful look.

Together, we gripped the crack's edge and pushed. A large panel skated across the ground, revealing a passage with steps leading to an abyss.

Gripping my scalpel knife, I descended first. The beast followed, also grasping her dagger. More mineral rocks cast over the area. But unlike the grotto, this void reeked of something putrid. And familiar.

I halted at the landing, jerking my arm behind to stop the female. Awareness crept up my nape as I stepped into a subterranean vault. My gaze scoured the region, where troughs dug into the walls, their contents providing the answer to a pertinent question.

An intake of breath sounded beside me. The woman's profile absorbed the scene, her irises flaring like torches, wonder clashing with sorrow. "What is this?"

My frown deepened. "A catacomb."

Webs encrusted the tombs, where skeletal remains lay. Chalky white skulls rested amid scapulas, clavicles, breast bones, shin bones, and fishlike scales. Tapered and rounded ears, the outlines of wings, and teeth that ranged from molars to fangs.

Humans. Faeries. Satyrs. Nymphs. Merfolk.

And more. Too many to process.

These ancients had to be the ones who'd discovered this forest. Some wore jeweled circlets, others leather vests and shingled armor. Based on the designs, they must have lived during the war between cultures, when each society except humans had either faded or killed themselves off.

Presumably, these settlers had stayed out of the historic conflict by isolating themselves here. Yet as I examined their remains, I found no evidence of accidents, starvation, or household scrimmages. So what had eventually happened to them?

My companion sucked in a breath as she caressed the cheek of a corpse. "This one was a sand drifter," she realized, admiring the frail satchel of rope tangled in the figure's digits. "Our kin are buried with these nets."

We turned to face one another. "The rainforest welcomed these people, yet none of them survived," she uttered.

"No, they did not." And from my brief inspection, I finally surmised why. "It was a virus."

Something contagious must have infested their blood. Considering our environment, this conclusion made irrefutable sense.

The beast glanced around with sympathy. "The wild decided it was their time."

Not how I would have put it, yet the distinction hardly mattered. This might be a rainforest castle, but its walls would only do so much to protect us. All the more reason to work together, to survive for as long necessary before getting the fuck out of here.

25

Jeryn

We discovered another secret before exiting the catacomb. A passage beyond intersected with other caves and crossways, including from the grotto and to the ruins' entrance, joining with the area where I'd gone astray earlier. The network reminded me of escape channels beneath every castle in The Dark Seasons, as well as the trade route in Summer, from which this little fugitive had fled.

The entrance tunnel would enable us to cross the lake, in lieu of the decrepit bridge, while some conduits echoed with ocean waves. In one cavity, we tracked the sound until emerging from a concealed threshold of rocks and vines, which deposited us at the cove where we'd made camp. We spent hours retrieving our belongings and traveling through the outlets, from the shore to our new hideaway.

The ruins offered better shelter than the cove. It was mostly dry, with access to the bathing grotto and drinking fountain. But with exposed verandas and colonnades vulnerable to roaming fauna, we would have to share a chamber.

One of the suites comprised adjoining rooms, each divided by an open doorway. Close enough to monitor one another. Far enough to stomach each other.

The beds needed to be restored first. In the meantime, we gathered clean linens from the textile cellar, fashioning them into pallets in our respective quarters.

The ashes of Summer tinder would ignite the old torches from one source, rather than us needing to build individual blazes. However, we agreed to use this tactic sparingly and only in the ruins.

Over the next week, we dusted, scrubbed, cleared debris from the most utilitarian rooms, and salvaged what we could. Next, we restored the conveyor, which ran between the wilderness and the makeshift medical chamber.

The cellar offered several articles of clothing that suited our measurements. Flowing dresses, linen nightgowns, and bandeaus paired with lightweight trousers, either cut off at the mid-thigh or cinched at the ankles, replaced the beast's chemise. Loose pants and shirts relieved me of the suffocating velvet ensemble.

However much Summer preferred nudity, a realm riddled with fatal insects was not ideal for exposure. The pants would suffice for me, but the beast collected scraps of thin material to weave into lingerie for herself. Promptly, I scratched the image of her wearing those skimpy articles from my brain, lest they should follow me to bed.

As it was, sleeping soundly became a chore. Separated by a mere twenty feet, her proximity dominated every corner of my addlepated mind. Visions of her tangled in the sheets, her mouth open and puffing air, her legs falling apart in slumber. Fucking hell.

Each morning, she caught fish and fried our meals in the dining hall fireplace.

In the medical chamber, I reorganized our supplies, making use of the alcove shelves. From the floor, I plucked samples of the ground foliage that had reminded me of pine cress.

Which led to thoughts of Winter's universities. Which led to other thoughts of a botany volume that documented antiquated plants.

At the hearth, I ground one of the leaves atop a flat expanse of rock. The mashed plant darkened and lost its pungent fragrance, as the text had instructed it would.

This felt too simple. Nonetheless, without the proper necessities, something had to give. At worst, I'd have the most hostile stomachache of my life. Possibly a fever. At least, I hoped that would be the shittiest part of it.

I grabbed my scalpel knife and extended the blade into the flames. Once the metal glowed orange, the slime went in next, close to the fire's perimeter. The mass fizzled and stank of rancid citrus, another encouraging confirmation.

After the pulp cooled, I sighed. "Motherfuck."

Then I angled the scalpel toward my bare arm and sliced.

An hour later, the little beast gawked when I passed by her in one of the corridors. Crimson-stained fingers. A bandaged gash across my bicep. Still, she did not ask what I'd done. She must have deduced I wouldn't tell her yet.

But when I did, it would hurt. Because it would be her turn.

I waited another week. Seven days in which we hunted for food, avoided carnivores, healed from our injuries, and worked on a map of the rainforest, which the woman drafted onto a wall in the vestibule.

Satisfied that my test hadn't exterminated me, I approached her one afternoon. Dangerously, she perched on the cupola's ledge, surrounded by hibiscus flowers.

Although cognizant of me leaning against the ridge beside her, she gazed in wonder at a dozing scimitar feline draped across a distant offshoot, the creature's fur a marbled mixture of red and black. Its limbs were slung over the sides, its paws dangling in the air and hiding what I imagined to be a set of claws capable of scooping out intestines with a lazy swipe.

"I've seen jaguars on other coasts, but not with saberteeth," she mused. "Those ones hang past her chin."

"Give me your arm," I commanded.

In my former life, having to say more would have been unnecessary. A glimpse would have guaranteed obedience.

This female tossed an uninvested glance toward the scalpel knife I'd withdrawn. "Has anybody ever told you that your weapon is about as polished as your bedside manners?"

I lifted an eyebrow. "Has anyone ever told you I don't give a shit?"

And for the record, my knife was not dull. This tiny minx was just trying to be snarky.

Her attention shifted from the blade to the green sludge I'd brought with me, the mixture newly ground and heated. Telling her it was a preventative earned me a hesitant look, so I took a seat beside her and explained about the treatment I'd recalled from the medical text, including details about the plant having been recorded during historic times. Although the bygone Summer remedy had gone extinct on the mainland, it had prevailed here, plausibly due to the forest's undisturbed environment.

Pulverize, heat, insert. The poultice would seep into the blood and act as a lasting barrier against infections. Not all but a moderate amount, which was better than nothing. My leg injury, those cuts from the rainfall, and that odious story about how she'd lost her voice served as a reminder. With this humidity, wounds would be susceptible to festering. As it was, we had enough worries regarding nature's influence. While I'd been inoculated from enough diseases to render me immortal, this rainforest and its fauna could transmit unforeseeable contagions.

None of which she'd be protected from. That fact thrust a bolt of alarm into my gut. What I wouldn't trade for Winter's surplus of syringes and vaccines.

"I tested it on myself," I assured her.

Bitterness flashed in those eyes. "Isn't that what so-called fools are for?"

For fuck's sake. "Do as I say."

"You tested it because I can die from it?"

"In the rare case," I confirmed. "Without it, in the likely case. By the way, one of the ancients survived whatever virus claimed their brethren."

She winced, compassion for the fallen cinching her features. But then she nodded, having drawn the same conclusion.

We hypothesized. The survivor must have composed the Summer song and brought it to the mainland. Feasibly, they'd hidden the map to commemorate this realm, paying homage while simultaneously preserving the wild's anonymity. Back then, cultures held landscapes even more sacred than today.

But to leave this realm, they must have had access to transportation. Or they'd been found—by a "chosen one" who'd been called here, according to this dreamer who believed as everyone on this continent did. Though, if I pointed out how nature would never choose a born fool, she'd merely throw my argument back in my face.

I scoffed. "Shall we cut into you, then? I have other errands."

Her eyes incinerated me. "You have less heart than a suit of armor."

"We've established that already."

Not unlike the last time she'd hurled a projectile at my head, the fool snatched a rock. My reflexes beat her to it, my palm seizing her knuckles. "Throw something at me again and I'll slit off your fingers," I said with deadly calm.

Flames rose up her neck, the hue imprinting to her forehead. "Give me back my hand."

Then I felt it. Never mind that I had initiated contact, but the sensation of my palm covering her knuckles injected heat into my bloodstream. Her bare flesh trembled beneath my own, radiating like a combustible thing.

Yet she didn't rip her fingers away. Nor did I respond immediately. Instead, we stared at one another, her breath rushing against my mouth with the intensity of a brushfire.

Seasons flay me. I prided myself on pacing, yet this delay exceeded my limits. It took far too long to react and even longer to withdraw.

Pulling myself together, I warned, "You will use those fingers to squeeze the rock for the pain. Nothing more."

With caution, I backed off. At the same time, a pent-up exhalation left her mouth, and those long eyelashes fluttered.

My other hand clamped around the scalpel knife, its tip flashing. Breaking the trance, I clicked my eyes toward her arm in a silent request.

Lifting her chin, she extended that arm. With a spare cloth, I swiped water over her bicep, which was the best I could do to sanitize it. Her arm felt like a twig, yet it flexed—hard, alert, poised for a fight. I couldn't fathom which urge was more tempting, to release this woman or grip her tighter.

"Relax," I instructed, but to which of us?

"Focus elsewhere," I tried again. "Concentrate on the jaguar or the flowers."

She did nothing of the sort. Instead, the beast watched me raise the blade, her intakes growing shallower. Because the scent of hibiscus impregnated the forest, I debated if she preferred that botanical aroma or the sweetness of mangoes.

In short, I was behaving like an amateur. Instructing myself to wake the fuck up, I angled the scalpel. "Hold still."

But as an afterthought, I added one word. "Please."

"Please?" she quoted. "Am I imagining it, or did you beseech me? I can't tell if you're in earnest or if you've been influenced by a certain court jester who knows his way around a farce."

My jaw hardened. "Never compare me to that cocky, gaudy, fucking—"

"Not a fan of Poet? That would put you in the minority."

"Trust me, I'm aware of his overhyped popularity."

The blade grazed her flesh. She gnashed her teeth.

"You'll feel a pinch," I lied. "Some discomfort."

Her eyes clenched shut, and her left hand choked the rock. Her shoulder had blossomed a sunburn, then dripped crimson once I began to cut. As the blade slid across her skin, I pressed in deeper, slicing through a layer of tissue.

The veins in her throat inflated. The vibrations of her mouth signified whimpers, though she tried to visibly conceal the pain. In truth, the female's resilience was impressive.

Many physicians sought to distract their patients during arduous procedures. I had never been among those doctors. All the same, her wincing expressions did something... unusual to me.

"So what do sand drifters do?" I inquired.

"H-huh?" she stammered.

"Tell me about your trade."

"It's not just a trade. It's a lifestyle."

"I'm listening."

She hedged. "We're voyagers. Free spirits of our Season and merchants of the sea. There are prizes that can't be found near the mainland, so we sail to the ends of Summer, to the distant wilds and outer regions, to find them."

"Prizes such as?" I prompted when she hesitated once more.

After another moment, she continued. "The plume of a ripple lark—it's a bird that lives on the water's surface. They're hard to spot at sea, but they come ashore to mate, which causes them to lose their features during the act. Salt lilies—those are flowers that float in pockets of water under the sand, and nobles like to feast on the buds. A corroded trident from a past century. Ink from a silken octopus. It's also a sand fish, so it has rich meat, but you have to dig deep to get to the dweller, and you need a sand net."

Her blood dribbled onto my fingertips. "I assume you're referring to the apparatus you rescued from the wreck. The hooped one with a handle and bristles like a comb. It has a different appearance from a common water net."

"I haven't caught anything with it yet. Not here, I mean. But maybe when I bond more with the rainforest, I'll know how."

She spoke of swamps and islands, then of her parents and life at sea. Nights on their tidefarer. Mornings catching water and sand fish. Wistfulness and devotion filled her voice.

To earn an income from traveling, sand drifters periodically returned to Summer's mainland. Having acquired rare fish and trinkets, they docked to sell their wares at the markets most frequented by nobles. Some drifters also earned commissions from the upper classes, who hired them to extract priceless artifacts.

This clarified how she'd learned to read, write, and speak with a refined tongue. Being sand drifters—therefore, of the merchant class—her parents had educated her. Moreover, treasure hunting had given this female elevated knowledge about riches.

A frown crimped my eyebrows. My mind veered back to the one memory of this woman I hadn't yet revealed.

Feigning nonchalance, I asked, "Your parents took you with them? To the markets?"

She winced. "Rarely. They said I behaved too fiery for those excursions."

"As in mercurial," I interpreted.

"Mercurial, yes. Dreamy, as well. And adventurous." She ducked her head for a moment, seeming contrite about that. "Mama said I couldn't keep calm, that I did things without thinking, or that I went wherever the tide took me. And with all the hustle, they couldn't keep a keen eye on me at the markets. Because of that, my parents fretted about me causing a scene if something riled me up. So we split up, one parent to the market and the other remaining at the boat with me. Without fail, that's how we did it until—"

She cut herself off. Those golden pupils glistened, haunted by a private recollection. Torment sat on her face like a bruise—dark, infuriating, unacceptable.

It had to be about her parents. She hadn't said what became of them after she was imprisoned, but with loss gripping her face, it wasn't difficult to guess. Yet there seemed to be more. In addition to bereavement, guilt consumed the female.

To stop those thoughts from burdening her, I pressed on. "What about other travelers? Did you grow up among them?"

"What are you playing at?" she snapped. "What are all these questions for? I told you, I'm not an experiment."

"I'm not talking to you like an experiment. I'm talking to you like a person. Isn't that what you want?"

She gave a start. As did I.

Where the devil had that come from? In Winter, I did not engage with fools, much less inquire about their lives and take interest in what they said. I simply told my assistants to strap them down.

Though if I went farther back, nor did I have prisoners relocated. I never demanded they be transferred to secluded cells where they wouldn't be disturbed, as I'd done in Autumn.

Poet and Briar had construed my actions as sinister. They had assumed I wanted to punish my quarry by locking her in solitary confinement. Except they'd been wrong.

Fewer neighboring inmates amounted to tighter security, because the sentinels wouldn't be distracted, thus they would guard the beast more safely. Keeping her separate from the other captives had also ensured a better night's sleep. It may have deprived her of company, but Poet and Briar had that covered with their frequent visits. Moreover, the relocation had granted this woman the privacy to clean and relieve herself.

If I had explained this to the jester and princess, they wouldn't have believed it. Not that I'd have wanted them to. Any conspicuous investment in my captive's comforts would not have done either of us good. Hence, I'd allowed the jester and princess to think whatever the fuck they wanted.

As to why I'd treated this woman thusly, the answer had to do with that memory she didn't know about.

Back to the task at hand, goddammit. The scalpel peeled back a flap of skin from her shoulder. At the action, she shuddered.

"Almost done," I lied.

"Bastard," she growled. "A pinch?"

"When muscles are tense, it exacerbates physical trauma. I needed you relaxed."

"Is that what you learned in Winter, back when you were a runt waiting for your horns to grow? You learned how to gut people while making them feel at home?"

"No," was all I bit out.

My voice had gone brittle. This woman didn't know the first fucking thing about my upbringing, much less what it took to heal someone. And now she was making me feel defensive. When the fuck had I ever felt defensive?

In case she detected this, I searched for something dignified to say, to cover up the mishap. "For your information, horned animals do not dwell in Winter. Our fauna have antlers and ... ears."

My patient gave me a puzzled look. "Ears."

I cleared my throat. "Paws as well. And whiskers."

Shit. I knew babbling when I heard it. The woman stared, a mirthful grin creeping across her face, the sight oddly infectious.

"What else?" she teased. "Do they have claws and talons and tails?"

This was my fault. Nonetheless, the absurdity of this conversation dragged a reluctant smirk from my face. "All of the above," I played along. "In fact, they also have muzzles and fur."

"Mmm," she replied with mock intellectualism. "How extraordinary."

"Quite."

"Except I wasn't referring to animal horns."

Then what ... oh.

I imagined the demon horns she'd been invoking, and my rueful mouth slanted farther. She folded her lips inward to keep from laughing, but her involuntary chuckles came out anyway, the sound of her laughter striking me in a disturbing place.

Abruptly, I sobered. Her own chuckles faded as she beheld something in my expression.

Unable to weather that look, I proceeded with her arm. She grunted as I lodged the mixture under her flesh and pressed the wound closed. The poultice would take effect quickly and keep the incision from putrefying. Fortunately, the preventative wasn't so deeply rooted that I needed to sear and cauterize the area.

Dressing the wound forced me to lean closer, my mouth tilting precariously near to that sunburned shoulder. Warmth brimmed from her skin, and she smelled too fucking good to tolerate. As my lips hovered, the palpitations in her neck accelerated, the visual causing my teeth to ache. I could sink my canines into her and make another mark, this one permanent.

My cock twitched. Withholding a growl, I wrapped a cloth around her arm. Drawing back, my eyes stumbled across hers, colliding with them like a pair of comets.

Who marked you? What did you do to get caged? Why did Summer brand you as a fool, when I can't discern anything foolish about you?

What are you not telling me about this forest? Why do you really want to be here?

Why can't I stop looking at you? Thinking about you? Talking with you? Wanting you?

An unforgivable question tripped off my tongue. "What is your name?"

Never once during my interactions with Poet and Briar had I interrogated them about this. While hunting my quarry, I would have demanded this only to help with the search, and only if I'd anticipated the jester and princess offering the information willingly.

If there were other reasons I hadn't wanted to know, hadn't wanted to see her as anything other than a prisoner, I wasn't about to analyze it. No matter how the prospect had enticed me, I had resisted finding out. She'd been my prey, nothing more than a target to snare.

At this juncture, I attributed my curiosity to convenience. I'd grown tired of addressing her indirectly. That was all.

Predictably, she wavered. For some reason, disappointment gnawed on my ribs, despite the fact that I'd solicited this reaction.

Yet miraculously, she answered. "Flare."

Her reply struck me between the ribs. My respiration hitched, indicating how long I'd been holding my breath.

Only when I shook off these disturbances did I register her silence, the evident refusal to ask my name in return. Yet if she ever did ask, that possibility led to another pressing question.

Would I give it to her?

26

Flare

He left the roof as swiftly as he'd arrived. Beneath the bandage, my arm throbbed. In fact, my body ached everywhere as if I'd been crudely sewn together. But I didn't mind, and it didn't matter. The rainforest would hurt and heal me as often as necessary, because that was how I would learn its ways. That was how I'd find my key.

The prince was learning too, based on the poultice he'd wedged into my arm. At least, he had kept my mind off the scalpel knife. The cut had been excruciating, yet the feeling had dulled while I reminisced about the tidefarer and my family. The prince had concentrated on his task while listening to my story, his questions distracting me from the pain.

I didn't want to think of him that way, like a healer instead of a torturer. Yet I had no clue what to make of his voice losing its cold edge or his attempt to know more about me.

I didn't want to remember his whipcord body soaking in the grotto. I didn't want to fixate on those muscled arms flexing, the lattice of his abdomen, the slopes of his hips. I didn't want to remember how my pulse had sped up or my blood had warmed. I didn't want to think about bathing naked with him or that his cock had lingered so near beneath the surface, the knowledge stoking my temperature. I didn't want to remember any of the moments since then, how close we slept to each other or that his gaze covertly followed me as often as mine trailed him. And I certainly didn't want to replay the lightning rainstorm, when our bodies had slammed against one another like a pulse.

The bandage fit snugly around my arm. For the treatment, I'd need to repay him. A trade would make us even.

I would find something fit for a doctor-prince, just as I would find my key someplace within the ruins' walls. I knew this, and felt this, and believed this. I had from the moment we stumbled upon this relic.

My eyes had been clinging to every crevice and shadow since we'd stepped inside. I'd ventured up here to search as well, before the prince had found me.

I smiled at the dozing saber-toothed feline, then tilted my head back. Closing my eyes, I inhaled the ripe perfume of florals.

"Where are you hiding?" I whispered to the key.

"What are you trying to tell me?" I whispered to the ruins.

If I kept still long enough, the walls might answer. They might whisper back, speak to me in their language, and show me the way.

Several days passed. As the sun rose, the forest resounded with noise. And as the sun peeked, the canopy buzzed with activity. And as the sun set, this world released a sleepy melody that included bird whistles and shivering leaves, like a lament and a plea and a sigh all at once.

When it was finally safe for my arm to get wet, I returned to the grotto, the pool sparkling as I stripped and dove. Warmth melted through me. I floated naked on my back, dazzled by the ripples reflected in the ceiling.

Legends were paradises and curses and wishes and horrors. They were made of miracles and monsters. The Phantom Wild allowed me to experience it all, never promising some things wouldn't hurt. Sacrifices were part of the cost, the price of exploring.

I loved this world. I adored my cuts and bare feet. What a beauty, this adventure. It was escape and exile, and that was okay for me, because I'd rather die quickly here than rot slowly inside the throat of that tower.

I'd rather be wild in a forest than go mad in a castle.

I missed Poet and Briar, and I missed Mama and Papa. But what a joy and privilege to have people worth missing, to have that kinship. My eyes stung as I let myself miss them.

The seahorses came out to play, flitting from the crevices like a brigade. Chuckling, I splashed them, and their curled tails flicked water back at me. I sank under the surface and danced with them, twirling around their shapes.

The seahorses glimmered under the surface, illuminating the abyss. They led me into a maze of underwater passages, with verdant reeds sprouting from the nooks and whiskered fish floating through the channels. I pumped my arms, sensing a gift ahead—a treasure. I'd known this feeling many times with Mama and Papa, the prediction creeping up on me. It could be the key buried under the ruins, beneath layers of stone and bedrock and liquid.

In another pool, I popped above the surface, emerging into a hollow as small as a tub. Beneath the low ceiling, broad white shrubs jutted from the walls. Their leaves resembled moth wings, delicate and filmy. I braced myself on the rocks and reached out to stroke a pad, surprised by its texture. Plucking one, I marveled at how it stretched like elastic, willowy but flexible like gauze.

A plant that felt like gauze!

Not the key. But something else I'd been looking for.

I took the souvenir with me and returned to the main grotto, hoping this flora would be an ample trade for what the prince had done to my arm. The seahorses trailed behind until I reached the shallow end, where I stopped and rose navel-deep. With a grin, I glanced back to bid them farewell.

They gave me no warning. Darting into the recesses, they simply fled.

My grin dropped, my hand suspended mid-wave as something tickled my thigh. The grotto echoed with a strange noise. A water current brushed my flesh, signaling a lithe figure behind me.

My limbs tensed. Foreboding stalked up my nape.

At a snail's pace, I turned to inspect the depth. A pointed fin cut through the eddies, and a striped blur slithered across the pool. In Summer, only lucky fish dwelled in both salt and freshwater. This predator was one of them.

My terrified mind whispered. *Get out of the pool. Now.*

Yet a person wouldn't guess how quickly the visitor moved for its size. It speared toward me, crashed through the surface, and opened its razor-sharp maw.

27

Jeryn

I'd seen a siren shark before. I had been young, a boy standing in a foreign sea, my limbs frozen in shock. Mesmerized. Terrified. The creature's skin had glinted pewter and sterling as its fins sheared through the ocean.

Time reversed. The rainforest evaporated, and a new landscape materialized, placing me on that shore. That day.

My body shrank into a child's form. I could not move, my legs paralyzed in the surf.

How did I get here? When? Why?

I snatched my vial for courage. Saltwater leaked past my lips, the brackish taste making me yearn for home.

Sleighs. Libraries. Wolves.

My fur blanket. My snowflake collection.

Mother. Father.

A desperate body splashed behind me, rushing to get near. I heard feminine panting and someone wailing my name. One of the queens. One of my grandaunts. Silvia.

She shrieked, "Jeryn!"

A knight bellowed, "The prince!"

The siren shark might have snarled, "You!"

I screamed for my parents without making a noise. My heart screamed that they weren't there. I was going to die, and they weren't there. I wanted them to slay the shark, but they weren't there. They loved me, but they weren't there.

So much hysteria on the beach. Too much.

The shark leaped, its teeth reminding me of icicles. Deadly in their clarity. Painful to behold. The sea monster lashed out, aiming for my jugular.

No. Aiming for *her*.

My vision cleared, jolting me to the present. I manifested once more in the grotto, witnessing the scene I'd stormed in on.

The siren shark charged with a screech. It whisked toward the hypnotized figure who awaited its approach, her petite limbs immobilized by the sight. Astonished. Spellbound.

I knew the feeling. I also knew wrath.

If the creature touched her, I would tear it to shreds.

I moved, cutting swiftly into the pool. As my arm slung around the woman's bare waist, memories replayed themselves like a reenactment. Years ago, one of my grandaunts had wrested me from the siren shark. Now I swerved my former captive from the attack, spinning us around so that my frame blocked her from harm, her naked spine aligning with my chest.

Shielding the female, I ripped my scalpel knife from its case and flung my free arm behind me. The blade punctured the shark's armor, a plate of scales that sprayed crimson into the air. The creature writhed in grotesque fury, its tail thwacking the pool's surface. With a shriek, it vanished into the depths, strings of blood trailing in its wake.

We stood there. Half-twisted toward the sight, we gawked over our shoulders at the water, oxygen pumping from our lungs. The monster would die soon.

As I swallowed, the acid pungency of vinegar assaulted my palate. Loathing. Disgust. Confusion. For the shark, for myself, for this woman.

And for the stinging sensation across my wrist. The quick invasion seeped into my skin like fluid ... or venom.

A sickening feeling lunged through my stomach. I dropped the knife, which hit the water's shallow end with a splash, then I shoved the woman away. She stumbled to face me, her eyes falling to where I clutched my fist. I covered it with my free hand, unwilling to look.

My throat constricted. I swiped my blade from the pool, rammed the weapon into my sheath, quit the grotto, and fled to the ruin's cupola while trapping my wrist in a vise grip.

From a distance, the scent of ocean brine suffocated me. In the vicinity, I saw nothing but rainforest ferns instead of frosted alpines. The infernal fucking flora, which confined this infernal fucking wild. Now I knew what it was like to be imprisoned, with this floating woodland caging me in.

I contemplated screaming, unsure how to achieve such a decibel anymore. I had not done so since that day. Grappling my chest, I searched for the vial but remembered I'd lost it in the whirlpool. I seized the ledge, bent over, and dry heaved into the understory.

Staggering upright, I retreated to the opposite side of the cupola, but it didn't feel right. No place in this hellhole felt right. This wasn't home, much less Winter.

Balling my hands into fists, I squeezed bones, muscles, veins, tendons. Patience, I told myself while pacing.

It would not happen to me. It would not.

"You will be fine," my grandaunts had vowed that night.

"You will be fine," Silvia had said, cradling me although I'd been thirteen, too old for that.

"You will be fine," Doria had repeated, patting my hair as I wept.

Countless times growing up, I had envisioned the opposite. The siren shark's bite turning me into a deranged being for three days. Usurping my sanity. Killing me gradually.

I had read the tomes and accounts. I had studied the imported corpse of a siren shark. I *knew*.

The venom would attack me. It would give me a fool's mind, cremating the last vestiges of intellect and rationality. I would forget logic and science. My lineage would fade. In its place, madness would surface: eating mouthfuls of sand but calling it snow, drinking from lightning rain, ranting about medicine, lapsing into a melancholy stupor.

Soon, I would become like that little beast. I might wind up choking her, as I'd attempted in the tower. Back then, it had been a bluff, however much I despised myself for having done it in the first place. This time, it might be real, an impulse I wouldn't be able to control.

I would become more brutal than before. I would go mad and hurt her.

After that, the venom would incinerate my viscera. From there, I would die.

At least my family would be spared. They wouldn't have to witness that version of me.

But who would occupy my medical den and sit on my throne? Who would replace me?

To the former, not the Court Physician's apprentice. I deplored that numbskull of a man, who exercised few aspirations in understanding basic anatomy, to the point where he couldn't tell his cock from his ass.

Clenching my eyes shut, I raised my hand. Opening my eyes, I stared. My fingers shook so violently that I mistook them for someone else's. Initially, I overlooked the details.

But then, I gave my hand a second inspection. Scratches marred the top of my wrist ... from the predator's scales. Mere scratches.

No broken flesh. No blood. No bites.

With a groan, I hung my head, dicing my quaking fingers through my hair. To have a venomous effect, a siren shark would have to sink its teeth into its prey. But it could have gotten me. From another angle, it could have happened.

The woman's feet appeared in my periphery. How long had she been standing there?

Having gotten dressed, this spy had the nerve to approach. How dare I risk myself for the likes of her? I wasn't myself around this female. I didn't conduct myself as I should.

Frigidness toward born fools came effortlessly because it was practical. Fundamental to testing for the greater good, for the health of Winter's people. Mine was an indifferent cruelty.

But not with her.

There, I had failed on every account. My malice had become personal for no reason other than her impulsions and those fucking hands. Also, the way she looked at me. Invasive. Daring. With minimal effort, this woman disrupted me, routinely pulling me into fragments.

Her arm stole out. She reached across the divide to make contact.

"Don't fucking touch me!" I growled, tearing myself away.

She wrenched her hand back, yet she didn't quail. Fleetingly, I wondered how that touch might have changed me. She might have polluted my senses with those fatal hands.

Or not. On the contrary, she might have set me aflame.

"I don't want your help," I hissed. "I don't need it."

She opened her mouth, but I cut her off. "You're nothing but a plague. Fools like you burden your families, shame your kin, ruin their livelihoods. Your minds are warped. You mutilate yourselves. You assault people. You're unnatural—and stop fucking staring at me like that! I am your sovereign, not your inferior! Do you want to know what I've done to people like you? I've shackled them to chairs. I've used them as guinea pigs."

She grimaced. Motivated by that reaction, I nodded. "I've poured untested mixtures down their throats. I've contaminated them. I've impaired their sensory perception. I've hindered their reflexes. I've amputated them while they were awake. I've administered sleeping vapors to see how it disrupted their breathing—to see if they'd wake up during surgery."

The woman's reaction blazed across her face, inflammatory thoughts teetering at the edge of her mouth, the words fixing to leap at me. In the past, I had enjoyed that. From the first moment when she'd cracked my vial, I had wanted her to pay for compromising my judgment, for branding herself into my head.

That had not changed. No, it had not.

It should not.

"You'll ask what I know about being treated like a fool. In return I would ask, what do you know about *treating* them?" I sneered. "The mad harm themselves and inflict torment on others. They roar and agonize. They attack out of nowhere, sob out of nowhere. Either they can't focus, or they finagle. They're impossible to reach.

"Do you want to know what some of the born did before we caught them? One stole a surgical probe and used it to puncture a child's eardrum. Another set a communal root cellar on fire, having claimed it housed an evil spirit. Because of that, an entire village starved for weeks until word reached us, from a peasant who arrived at the castle with frost-bitten toes.

"You'll call these abominations 'born souls' and say not all of them are unstable. Indeed, the majority are docile, unable to comprehend the most infantile thoughts and actions, nor the most appropriate ones. They need constant direction lest they should stray. They labor under the Crown's supervision. Call it slavery, but Royals shoulder the task for those who can't afford to.

"Poet and Briar may be nonconformists to this rule, but they cannot and *will not* outweigh the other leaders of this continent. I'm not like them and never will be," I spat.

Drawing a livid breath, I prowled nearer to her. "As for the mad, I've sedated them to prevent hysterics and self-mutilations. I've conversed with them, but they haven't listened. I've conducted analyses for correctives and came up empty-handed. Why did I bother? Why did I try to gainsay nature? To fix its mistake. Yet my stresses have been fruitless. All that's left is using them to develop remedies for everyone else. The end justifies the means. What else are they good for? What else are *you* good for?"

My voice hitched on that last part. An accusation to which I felt no pride.

Sunset highlighted her tattooed throat, reminding me of a vital fact. What I'd spewed was old information to her; she had already lived that reality. She'd been a captive of Summer, a pawn of Rhys, the spoils of a king's grudge. Therefore, the rant of a prince held no value to this woman.

In her silence, I heard and saw myself for the first time. Her eyes glinted like metal patina, flinging this moment back at me, explicit in its revelation. It exposed everything wrong and false about my diatribe.

About me.

Ice chipped from its foundation. It crumbled and left a vacancy behind. Something like remorse.

That was before she even spoke. "It hunted you once."

The answer to that would be a chilled breath away from other answers. Jaw tensing, I glanced away.

She got in front of me, her gaze cutting to the quick. The unspoken questions mounted.

What petrified me more? That I didn't know how to treat fools? Or that I could become one?

Who was I really trying to heal?

It didn't matter whether she'd demanded this or not. She smashed her fists into my thoughts, threw flames at me, all without uttering a sound. To achieve that, this little beast needed only to keep staring with those gilded eyes. Another minute of her presence and it would be over for me.

"Leave," I commanded.

She did not.

"I said, leave."

She did not leave.

"Go. Away."

Yet she would not let me forget this. She would force me to face it. Not because she cared or because I deserved her attention. Nowhere near that.

Fuck her. Fuck this woman for appearing in that Autumn cell, after years of struggling to purge her from my mind, after having finally reduced that brief incident to a dream.

Fuck her for tampering with my self-control, my logic, my sense.

Fuck her for breaking the vial like a traitor and tarnishing the one unblemished memory I'd had of her.

The beast shook her head. "It's a scratch. The Phantom Wild can help you fix that."

"We're stranded, beast!" I roared. "This forest cannot fix everything! I can't eke out an existence here with you. I don't have the right supplies. No advanced medicines, no actual parchment, no surgical instruments. I don't have syringes. I don't have sterilized needles or thread. I don't even have proper fucking bandages!"

A plant thwacked me in the chest. Squashed in her grip, she pressed a broadleaf into my pectoral. Absently, I took it.

Her irises were reams of sunlight. Thermal. Grating. A golden visage capable of turning me to ash.

"I told you," she murmured. "I have a name. It's Flare."

Snatching flint, rope, and her blade, she marched from the cupola.

I frowned at the plant. The drooping leaf was long and had the texture of linen. However, it stretched like gauze—like a bandage. Whereas the midrib could be an alternative for thread if I constructed a needle, perhaps from a fish bone.

Smart. Resourceful. Always.

My head whipped toward her. "Get back here!" I shouted, knowing she wouldn't listen.

28

Jeryn

I found her at our cove. On the crescent shore, she had built a fresh pit, threads of smoke lifting into the air and swirling around her. Although I had never taken mysticism seriously, with the blaze sketching her profile, she resembled a divinity. An empress of fire.

Propping myself against a fern tree, I watched her silhouette until nightfall. Hearing the shark's mercenary screech carry through the ruins, thoughts of this woman had consumed me, and I'd launched into a run. Despite the fear icing my veins, protectiveness had eclipsed terror.

I ... hated the thought of anything harming her.

Flare, she'd said. Her name was Flare.

A moniker that burned brightly. It had a temperature, like something hot and bold. One could light a match to the name and watch it ignite the world.

Pushing myself off the wall, I strode toward her—toward that name. My shadow extended over the fire as I joined Flare, seating myself adjacent to her.

While adding kindling to the heap, she said, "Campfires make it easier to tell a story."

"Mine is not a story," I said. "It is a fact."

"I hate what you've done to born souls," she muttered. "I hate you so much for that. You didn't know anything about the ones you hurt, and you don't know my tower mates. Pearl and Lorelei and Dante. You don't know what they've suffered, or what they dream of, or what they love. They have hearts and tears, but nobody asks them questions, and nobody cares about them, because the nobodies like you don't see them, because you don't understand any of us."

Moonlight lit the surf. Flames licked the air.

Flare considered me, her gaze nothing short of imposing. "But the rainforest has accepted you, and you faced a siren shark for me. Like it or not, I'll listen."

Was that the only reason she would listen? Was I entitled to any other?

Rhetorical questions. She was not sitting here to be nice. Nor was I sitting here expecting that.

True, I didn't know anything about the ones she'd spoken of. Yet I wanted to know her, more than I cared to admit.

I leaned forward, incapable of meeting her eyes, intimidated by them. Despite her past—rather, because of it—she showed more endurance than I ever had. This woman clamored, but she didn't make herself into a victim.

I weathered that gaze. "Your story is more important than mine."

"Then earn it," she answered. "Earn what I decide to tell you."

I consulted the scratches across my fingers. "I was thirteen when it happened," I murmured to the fire.

Thirteen years old. Too soon. Too much had changed that year.

Kingdom of Winter. A landscape where needle woodlands were pockmarked in snow and citizens traveled by stags, sleighs, and sleds. A court where the residents wore layers of fur and blew frost tendrils from their lips. A land where stillness and contemplation prevailed.

The sleet tundra. The monolithic alps. The glacier province.

The chalet castle looming over a frozen lake. Tapestries flossed in silver and cobalt. The scents of cooked venison from the great hall and fresh blood from the medical wing.

I had lived in the stronghold with my parents, my father the sole nephew of the Winter Queens, who had no children of their own. For my birthday, Mother and Father had given me the pendant, the vial weightless and attached to a chain.

"For me?" I had asked, gazing at my parents.

"For you," Mother whispered, her fragile smile an incision across her face.

"For our boy," Father said, his voice brittle as if crushed by forceps.

A talisman for me to keep close. A vessel in which to place something special.

Something that would keep me safe, they had said.

My mother and father had clasped hands, their signet rings pressing together. Their fingers trembled, yet I saw no other physical discomforts. It was a fine morning, the illness momentarily tamed.

"Three months earlier, chaos had infested the kingdom," I said to the flames. "An unforeseen pandemic claimed many victims."

Oddly, those in their prime were the most susceptible. Yet supplied with gifted healers, Winter had survived that epidemic, its outbreak eventually suppressed.

Though, some had languished in the aftermath. The disease had gnawed on cartilage and nerves, producing daily joint pains and shivers that racked the stoutest of frames.

The memory weighed down my tongue. "My parents had been two such victims."

I'd abhorred nature for this betrayal, blasphemed the will of the Seasons until my grandaunts intervened.

"It isn't for us to question the Seasons," Grandaunt Silvia had said.

"Nature tests us," Grandaunt Doria had added. "It has a plan."

As with the born, for example. According to my kingdom, the omnipotent Seasons had chosen people to be fools, birthed into an unnatural state for a purpose. An error to be entrusted to the monarchy. To set the example of a plagued mind—an unbalanced mind—so that everyone may know the distinction.

Fools were meant to be used. Or if uncontrollable, they would be contained like another disease.

That was what everyone had told me. But although I did not cling to superstition, I did believe in the power of illness. Like floods and avalanches, sickness was the same thing. A defect of nature.

At that age, the born had frightened me. The ones I'd seen in the dungeons and labs acted primitive or pitiful.

I had leveled my chin. If nature tested, I would test back. If a bridge between the elements and medicine existed, I would build it. I would learn to rid the world of its maladies.

To be Mother and Father's hero. To care for them and others. To undo foolishness. Or at least, learn to command it.

When I had unwrapped the vial, I'd promised Mother and Father, "I will use it to fix you."

That night, I created a make-believe draught for them, hoping to aid their sleep. But I did not enjoy pretending. What Winter citizen would?

Among the kingdom's healers and scientists, the Court Physician held the greatest office. I'd crept into the man's chambers and spent hours mixing an authentic tincture. Then I sipped the contents and writhed from an anguished stomach.

Days. Weeks. They passed.

I studied among Winter's elite. I read books to my parents.

Father and Mother could not succeed my queen grandaunts. My parents were too sick for a future reign, with no convalescence in sight. Thus, Silvia and Doria named me their heir. An unexpected birthright. A chance to have absolute power over treatments.

They set a circlet upon my head, the tapers spearing the air. News of this appointment spread through The Dark Seasons.

It was also a period of travel for my grandaunts. They left for Spring to attend the Peace Talks. Half a year after their return, the queens traveled to Summer, to meet with King Rhys and Queen Giselle. They took me along, insisting it would be a profitable experience.

I didn't want to leave Mother and Father, but I admired my grandaunts. They ruled a whole kingdom together and planned to show me how.

In Summer, I gaped in shock, overwhelmed by the sweltering heat and bright colors.

So. Much. Sun.

The climate had fried my skin, turning me into a slab of bacon. I had thought my flesh would peel off.

Presently rubbing my palms together failed to alleviate the clamminess. I nailed my gaze to the fire, lest I should meet the woman's gaze and falter. "It happened during a stroll along the coastline."

Rhys and Giselle were attending to my grandaunts, their company trailed by knights from both Seasons. As the outing required privacy from the public, a group of noble children playing on the beach were forced to relocate to a different shore. One of them had been a boy with a smug countenance. The leader of the group, I had guessed as the children departed.

At one point, I strayed to the ocean. Warm, salty, restless. Thinking to experiment with the seawater, I waded knee-deep and uncapped the vial hanging around my neck. As I bent to obtain a sample, a dorsal fin broke from the surface. In my periphery, a dark shape flashed in the waves—a large fish with pewter and sterling stripes.

Shouts erupted, the commotion deafening. I straightened, fear trapping my scream in ice.

The creature's maw split open, releasing a horrible sound. It latched onto my belt and yanked me toward the waves. Its mouth grazed my stomach, the pinprick of razor fangs about to dig in. I'd been in a daze as one of the knights skewered the siren shark, and my frantic grandaunt Silvia wrenched me from the ocean.

To the castle. To the infirmary.

The smug-looking noble boy ended up there as well, with a split lip. Though, he didn't look smug any longer. The physicians had said he'd been attacked on a neighboring shore.

It hadn't been another siren shark. Rather, I had deduced what had transpired. I knew the source of his injury, because there was more to this episode. Yet for both of our sakes, I would not impart that detail to this woman.

Later. Not yet.

Back to the story. As my paralysis wore off, I thought of the ones called born fools. I thought of my ailing parents withering before my eyes. I thought of the shark's jowls.

I wept in bed, bleating that I wanted to go home, that I was going to expire. My grandaunts had assured me that I hadn't been bitten.

But what if they couldn't see the bite? What if insanity churned in me? What if I did die?

Nightmares replaced childhood dreams. Over time, relapses ensued, the panic rising out of nowhere. I would randomly check my stomach ... and double-check it ... and triple-check it.

Months. Years. They passed.

I watched the born with more contempt and my parents with more desperation. I researched, practiced, honed my skills. I discovered a cure that mollified my parents' convulsions but not their physical torment. I treated disorders but hadn't remedied foolishness or conceived an antidote for the bite of a siren shark.

Preventions against other ailments, yes. Madness itself, no.

For instance, the clear liquid in my vial. It cured a variety of poisons and venoms, though not the one I feared.

To this day, the terror that I'd been bitten and hadn't realized it lived inside my head. Illogical. Irrational. However, the human brain was a convincing force. In sudden bouts, it dragged me under, my frantic state eclipsing reason. My mind often cycled, thus magnifying the paranoia and leading to palpitations, reducing me to a hunched figure on the floor. There, I would mutter about the shark attack, either convincing myself its teeth had penetrated me—and the effects were delayed—or reassuring myself over and over that I was fine, safe, alive.

And yes. My family knew. We kept few things from one another.

Despite my condition, they cared for me. Intolerance could be biased that way, particularly among the privileged.

But although my family tried to help, they did not know how, which caused them anguish. So rather than submit them to such distress, I chose to endure these bouts alone, barring a few episodes when they found me cowering on the ground in my suite.

To cope, I would consume the pendant's fluid. Although technically it did nothing for me, the illusion sedated my blood. In that way, the vial protected me as my parents had intended, since they lacked the strength to do so on their own.

More than anything, it gave them solace. Their peace of mind mattered most of all. I knew that if something ever happened to the vial, it would dismay them, the turmoil endangering their feeble constitutions.

Across the fire, I mustered the fortitude to meet Flare's gaze. "I do not say this to excuse myself. But you deserve to know why I lost my shit when you broke the vial."

Well. That was part of it.

But again. Later.

I would treat this moment with the care and pacing it warranted. With patience.

As she wished, I exposed my demons. "My family is my lifeline. I shall destroy anyone who endangers them." The next words sharpened like a blade. "Including your king."

What does Summer have on you?

Then I told her about Poet's parting question before I left Autumn. The spies Rhys had recruited throughout the Seasons. How I'd dealt with Winter's offenders before they had a chance to uncover sensitive information about my condition.

"If they had succeeded, I would have been branded as unstable." Before this woman, I let the confession slip from my mouth, drop by drop. "One precarious word or rumor would have marked me as a born fool."

A born fool. A mad prince.

My treasonous secret. My bigoted hypocrisy.

Over the years, the more afraid I became of myself, the more I loathed the born for reminding me of my true nature. What I had feared, I'd hated in kind.

Yet that was not all. The shrewd jester had been right about my concerns. However, Poet had been wrong about my motivation—or whatever malignant conclusion he had drawn. Fair enough.

Disemboweling my knight on the parapet in Autumn. Allying with Poet and Briar to thwart Rhys. I'd had incentives, trade negotiating power among them. Not least of all, the golden woman who'd glamoured me.

But those hadn't been my only reasons for snuffing out Summer and its spies. I had never worried for myself.

My voice hardened like steel. "As I said, no one harms my parents or my queens. If anyone touches what I treasure, they will suffer. If the court had leaked my affliction to the masses, the people would have rioted. They would have targeted my family for keeping this secret."

For my welfare and the good of our court, my grandaunts and parents had guarded this information at their own risk. Should this intelligence have fallen into the wrong hands, it would have placed my kin in danger. That had been my greatest worry.

Moreover, it would have led to the breakdown of Winter. As it nearly had in Autumn.

Even now, the threat existed. Rhys hadn't gotten wind of my secret, but he still could by alternative means. Or if not him, someone else.

Putting it mildly, my forbidden addiction to a certain female did not help matters. Though on that account, I did not give a fuck. She had always been my exception.

I finished my story, omitting that I'd lost the vial in the whirlpool. I could not go there tonight. Nor to other places having to do with our histories.

For as long as I could remember, I had made an enemy of sickness. I had been at war with it. But in doing so, I'd acted criminally. Trying to defeat illness—to cure my parents and myself—was not the same thing as trying to save lives.

All lives.

Including born souls. Like my peers, I had not taken Autumn's crusade for humanity seriously. Yet it felt wrong to me now. So crucially wrong.

This woman knew emotional and physical misery in ways I could not begin to imagine. In ways I had caused.

She had also endured nightmares. She'd had a family too. She had her affections and proclivities. She had wild and peaceful moments.

Seasons forgive me. This woman was not a damn fool.

Speaking aloud didn't atone for what I'd done to her or others. Forcing those people into labor, experimenting on them, condemning them. Expending selected individuals to treat the rest of the world.

Now it disturbed me to remember. More than that, it haunted me.

The past drained from my pores like contaminated blood. In my mind's eye, I saw every face I had tortured.

A man throwing back his head and shrieking through his broken teeth. A woman begging for mercy while I calmly strapped her limbs to the table. People screaming while I cut into their skulls. Others sedated and lost in a stupor.

I saw the tools I'd used. I saw blood splattering the floor. I saw samples of their anatomy on my shelves.

I heard them wailing. I heard them crying.

Shame. Disgust. Both emotions grabbed me by the throat.

This whole time, Flare had trained those smoldering eyes on me. I had felt the burn of her stare even when I'd averted my own. Across the flames, I weathered her judgment, submitted myself to it, and awaited the verdict.

Where she had regarded me with disdain earlier, now her pupils reflected something profound. Compassion. I had never been the recipient of such a reaction, yet I recognized it within the gilded sheen of her irises. No one communicated their emotions as potently as she did.

Unlike me, Flare's mercy proved stronger than her hate. The impact lanced through my sternum.

After a moment's thought, she leaned over and drew in the sand. Letters formed the shape of a lost vial.

Flare

A vacant space rested beside her name. An invitation not merely for a truce but something that involved multiple possibilities over time. Sincerity. Honesty. Trust. Provided that I share one final thing about myself.

The surf washed in and out. The moon poured its rays into the lacquered sea.

Her finger paused on the empty space, ready to write more letters, to inscribe me beside her. She held my gaze and waited, commanding me to make a choice.

The firelight painted her face in amber. The name Flare suited her. Finally, I met her golden eyes. "My name is Jeryn."

29

Flare

Teryn.

I repeated the moniker, and he watched me sound it out, my lips taking a while to string the letters together. He'd been given a patient name. It took its time on the tongue, whereas mine shot out like a dart and landed somewhere unexpected. Maybe that was the difference between a seafarer and a ruler, or a woman born in flames and a man born in frost. Fire moved while ice stayed still.

Although the lives of Royals were widely talked about, his name had never been mentioned in my presence. Not once in my life. The few people who'd referred to him when I was around had only used his formal title, including Poet and Briar.

I had planned to sketch the letters beside my own. But on second thought, I leaned back and gestured at the empty space.

The prince straightened as though given a pivotal task. Yet he didn't hesitate. Hunching forward, a cord of his blue mane poured over his shoulder, and the blaze sketched his profile.

Like signatures to a treaty, he scripted his name into the sand. My pulse skipped when the edge of one letter touched one of my own. I would say it hadn't been on purpose, but with this deliberate man, I doubted it.

My heart clenched for his family. I hadn't wanted to believe him, or understand him, or forgive him. But if I couldn't, what sort of person did that make me? What kind of change could I hope for in this world? Compassion was a strength, as much as any other power.

The mad prince. It made sense now.

He'd taken his fear out on born souls. The confession didn't absolve him, and I couldn't fathom anything ever would. But acknowledging it could change him.

In the face of this prince, I beheld a child afraid of sharks, of death taking his kin, of sickness taking him. People had told that boy about born souls the same way everybody told everybody about us, and that was how the boy had grown up.

I despised the man that little boy became. But now I knew why he'd transformed into a monster, and tonight he was here, and he saw me. That was something I couldn't despise.

His eyes no longer saw through me but watched my lips in anticipation, holding their reflections in pools of black as I balanced his name on my tongue.

"Jeryn," I said.

The fire sizzled. At that moment, his pupils exploded with light.

While darkness glossed the sky, we remained at the cove. Dying embers from the pit separated us as we reclined on opposite sides.

Despite what Jeryn had lain bare, a new calm settled around us. This moment should have been awkward, but something cathartic unspooled instead. Like with Poet and Briar, it happened more naturally than I would have imagined.

We had exposed ourselves to the point of ease. Except this felt different and deeper and maybe ... maybe more desirable.

I curled like a shell into the sand. "What do you miss about your home?"

Jeryn's features relaxed, the inclines smoother than before, as though bricks had fallen from his countenance. "I would rather ask you that question."

I shook my head. "We're not there yet."

Although he'd experienced enlightenment, I wasn't about to hand over my life's history at this point. He still had some unraveling to do.

The prince rolled his defined jaw, the sight more exquisite than I'd like to admit. "What would you care to know?"

"The stuff you're less likely to include first," I replied to see how much he'd learned about me.

After a moment's deliberation, the prince began. He talked about yule owls and dire wolf sleds and stag sleighs. Then he described star murals in the astronomy wing, a castle overlooking alpine mountains, and elks promenading through a place called The Iron Wood.

Points for him. These were fine choices.

On a wistful tangent, Jeryn reminisced about the richness of gravy. "Seasons, I fucking miss gravy."

Chuckling, I scooted closer to the blaze. "What does your suite look like?"

"I'll tell you, if you describe at least one particular to me," he compromised. "Consider it a trade. Your tidefarer boat, for instance. I didn't see the inside of it."

"That's because we were too busy trying to kill each other."

His eyes glittered. "Who says we've stopped?"

The husk in his voice coiled low in my stomach. Stretching that hard body across the sand, with all that hair falling like a river around his face, he resembled a lord of the sea. Though, he would probably curl his nose at the description.

The flames crackled as we stared at one another. I shook myself out of the vision, the movement knocking Jeryn from his own trance.

Registering the provocative dip in his tone, he cleared his throat. "Where did you sleep?"

"In a room below deck. My pillow was as big as me. I loved my pil-

low." I nestled deeper into the shore. "Your turn."
"My suite is furnished with mahogany wood. Everything is accented in cold shades."
I kept a straight face. "To match—"
"Do not finish that question."
"—your hair?" I baited anyway.
He gave me a stern look. "If you insist on amusing yourself, may I be excused?"
"You're actually asking my permission?"
That frown deepened in a rather endearing way. This man looked fetching whenever I got on his nerves. Pleased with myself, I asked, "What is snow like?"
Jeryn bypassed the technical things, knowing what type of details I fancied. "Sometimes the starkness can make you squint," he shared. "Other times, it's tinted blue or blackened with footprints, like it's been bruised. It can be as soft as powder or as coarse as rubble. You can make art from hard-packed snow, or it might be so light and soft that it cannot bear your weight." He held my gaze. "Always, you can draw in it."
I swirled my finger across the ground and whispered, "I was born in the sand."
"My first sight was of ice," he confided. "To this day, my family often recounts the birth."
He told me the story. Apparently, the prince had craned his small head toward the window. Instantly, his eyebrows had pressed together, his gaze assessing the frozen land beyond as if demanding an explanation for everything that existed out there.
Jeryn's features became remote. "I miss them."
I nodded. "I miss my family too."
As the sea whisked back and forth in a gentle rhythm, and the pit glowed with warmth, the prince raised himself on his elbow. "Tell me why you enjoy drawing in the sand. Tell me why you prefer it to canvas or parchment."
My finger stopped moving. "Because it's stronger than people give it credit for. Everyone adores the ocean so much that they forget what

holds it up."

I told him more about my passion, the details unfurling like a wave. All the while, he did more than absorb my answer. He listened.

By the time we returned to the ruins, it had to be midnight. Plants glowed, and damp spiderwebs glistened like ropes of diamonds. Although some areas got so dark we struggled to see our fingers in front of our faces, the moon snuck through the canopy, enameling the world in pearly light.

While I padded to my chamber, I spied on Jeryn in his adjoining room. Through the arched doorway, he rested on his back, as heavy as an anchor. From the way he'd described snow, the prince slumbered as though buried under a layer of it, his large frame going still.

I paid attention to the straight lines of his face, from the aristocratic slant of his nose to the cleft in his chin. He'd been graced with a chilling sort of beauty. Yet rainforest scars branded the prince's skin. More than anything else, I liked seeing those marks on him, proof that he was vulnerable.

I dragged my gaze from his sculpted body. It had become harder to ignore the sight. My eyes might not linger, but my mind was another story.

As I tucked myself into bed, I wondered. Did he suffer from shark nightmares anymore? My eyelids fluttered closed, the question pinching my dreams.

Hours or minutes later, I learned the answer. During the night, I lurched off the mattress, ripped from my sleep to the sound of Jeryn screaming.

30

Flare

I plowed through the haze, yanked aside my sheet, and raced toward the sound. Having abandoned his bed, Jeryn hunched on the floor of his chamber, with his back against a wall laced in begonias. Clad in only a pair of loose pants, he gripped the sides of his bent head, fingernails knifing into his hair.

It was indeed a nightmare. Some demon had slithered into his mind.

If it were me, I would have been quivering, lashing out, or rocking back and forth. But the prince stayed motionless. The naked muscles of his shoulders strained with tension, and the veins in his arms bulged like the roots of a tree.

Muffled noises grated into a pillow wedged between his upturned thighs and chest. To others, it might sound like coarse grunts. But I heard the shouts, the disorder he fought to conceal.

In my cell block, I'd never taken the suffering of my neighbors lightly. However, those bellows and sobs had never shocked me, because they'd been expected. But Jeryn's turmoil overturned every memory I'd had of him, the disturbance cracking like a shell inside my chest.

Dropping to the ground, I scrambled on all fours. The villain prince didn't see me crawling his way, yet he knew. Maybe he'd grown used to how I smelled or sounded. Either way, we moved at the same time. With his head bowed, Jeryn tossed the pillow and reached for me. A brittle sensation got stuck in my throat as I caught him, and then my feelings gave way to violence. Something had wounded him, and for the first time, I didn't like this thought.

I didn't like it at all.

In the dark, I swung one leg over his waist, climbing onto his lap just as he pulled me into him. I faced Jeryn, my thighs splitting around his waist, the short hem of my nightgown bunching high enough to reveal the profiles of my backside. His arms clamped around my middle, wrenching me closer until my breasts slammed against his bare torso, our bodies fastening together. And when my hands wove around his neck, the prince shuddered as though my touch had a devastating effect.

Heat emanated from him more than it did from me. It eclipsed the humidity tenfold, a bead of sweat leaking between my collarbones and landing on one of his own.

Amid the shadows, our limbs tangled into knots. His massive physique encased mine, and his damp forehead found solace on my shoulder.

"My grandaunts. They're old. They could be dead," he hissed, the words avalanching from his mouth as if they'd been corked for a thousand years. "My parents. They're ill and don't know where I am. They don't have me. I'm not there. I'm not there for them."

"Shh," I whispered, to no avail.

"I'm a healer," he ranted. "I heal my kingdom, but ... I'm not a healer. I've tortured people. I've maimed them," he muttered in a haunted tone. "What have I done? What the fuck have I *done*?"

I wouldn't shush him about that. He needed to say it, and I needed to hear it.

"I used them," Jeryn realized. "I used so many people to treat others. And I'm not there to change it. I'm not there to fix anything. I'm not there. Who's healing Winter? Who?"

I heard it in his voice. This wasn't just the terror of a bad dream. It was also the maelstrom of panic.

While the sun had set, Jeryn had revealed himself to me. Afterward, we'd been talking about his home, which must have triggered him, ambushing the peace we'd found. Out of nowhere, epiphanies blew through a formidable barrier and took this man captive, from his gruesome history, to every horrific deed, to his isolation from Winter. Our talk had made him think of the family he wasn't there to help, the ailments he wasn't there to fix, and the people he'd wronged.

"More prisoners will be used while I'm stuck here," Jeryn said, breaking like a wall of ice under pressure. "My family's going to die without me. They might be dead already. And I'm going to die here too. But I don't want to die here."

That last part hurt. I couldn't say why, could hardly grasp where my heart fit inside this hurt. I yearned to defend the rainforest, not a more enchanting realm to be found on this continent. But I didn't have a family anymore, whereas his living relatives waited for him.

Jeryn's kin needed their ruler. His patients and subjects depended on him, and born souls could finally benefit from his skills. If he were still in Winter, he'd have the power to help them.

During our talk, I hadn't considered that. But he had. The moment his mind had shifted, he'd gone there.

His palms burned through my nightgown, his grip crushing the material. "The siren shark," he rasped against the crook of my shoulder. "I could have been bitten. It could have ... I could be... and not know it yet. I could be dying without knowing it."

That wasn't true. He'd battled that shark and won.

For me. He'd faced that horror for me.

But maybe part of him was dying in another way. And maybe I was too. So maybe we could save each other.

Strapped in his arms and ensconced in these ruins, I couldn't draw images of comfort into the sand. Instead, I did the only other thing left and brushed my fingers through his hair, the mane slipping through my fingers like a cascade. Over and over, I combed through his roots in a tender rhythm.

The prince stiffened, his frame going taut like that of an animal, unsure what to make of this gesture. As if the touch could be a threat.

Despite his loving kin, this man had a deeper experience with pain than affection. The sort he'd kept hidden. The sort he'd inflicted. He had mentioned keeping his panics mostly to himself, wary of burdening his family too often or causing them emotional strain.

So who else had been there for him? Who had calmed the terror?

I coaxed my fingers through the layers. As I swept my hand from his jaw to the side of his mane, tucking a lock of hair behind his ear, a gasp sliced from the prince's lips.

Like I had stung him. Like this feeling hurt.

My lips swam along his ear. "Jeryn."

The whisper stroked the ledge of his skin. The prince drew in another sharp breath, as though the word had found a crawlspace, a rift to dissolve within.

Slowly—so achingly slow—he lifted his head a fraction. His open mouth dragged over my flesh, pressed to my pulse point, and stalled there.

My heart rate doubled, drumming against the place where Jeryn's lips rested, his hot breath pumping into my flesh. The spread of my legs enclosed his waist, on the brink of inching wider to accommodate more of him.

As though he sensed this impulse, a hiss diced through Jeryn's teeth. "Flare."

Not an encouragement but a warning. And yet, the cut of my name from his tongue achieved the opposite of what either of us should want. My pussy clenched, the delicate folds chafing his pants. I had taken to sleeping without the scanty drawers and briefs I'd woven. Although it was more comfortable at night, I had forgotten this precarious detail. But the rough texture of Jeryn's pants abraded my crease, the friction reminding me far too late.

We hadn't moved, yet the contact drew slickness from my walls, and the intimate lips swelled. He must feel the outline of my cunt because a severe noise rumbled from Jeryn's throat, the masculine sound haggard.

"Flare," he muttered. "Get the fuck off my lap. Now."

More than a command, it sounded like a plea. A cautionary threat meant to protect me, to keep me out of harm's way, because going farther might wound me. Because I would regret it.

And that's how I would become your greatest regret.

It didn't take a seer to predict where this would lead, the precipice we teetered upon, the rules we were in danger of shattering. We'd been in this position before, with my legs astride his body. Except during the lightning rainstorm, I'd been facing away from him, too repelled to look at his face while I came.

This time, I stared into his eyes while strapped around him. And he stared back. Which felt much worse.

This couldn't happen again. Not with an evil ruler. Not with the enemy. But was he either of those things anymore? Yes and yes. I still hated him for all the people he'd enslaved and tortured. However genuine, one conversation wouldn't change that fully.

But at this moment, did I care? The answer tightened in my slit, the private flesh of my cunt aching.

Half of me wanted to punish this prince. Half yearned to console this born soul.

I couldn't explain it, and I didn't want to explain it, and I wasn't about to explain it. With this monster, I gave up trying, because I'd rather feel, and feel more, and more.

This hadn't come out of nowhere. This disarray had been building long before the lightning tempest.

Provoked, my fingers snuck up the back of Jeryn's scalp, eager to bury themselves in his mane and pull on the roots.

In a flash, his hands seized mine. "Stop," he uttered, the entreaty too faint to have come from such a whipcord frame.

My head misted, yet I hesitated. Although I would never force anyone, the unmistakable husk in his tone betrayed him. That, and the fear. My touch scared him, but not out of disgust.

Switching directions, I swept my fingers over the crown of his head. With light motions, I draped my hands through the layers, urging him to disarm with me.

The impact ricocheted through his form, his eyes clenching shut as he committed another crime. On a groan, his mouth traced over the sunburst collar encircling my neck.

And every fiber of my being detonated.

His lips skimmed the tattoos cruelly and feverishly. Then he kissed me there, his mouth pulling my flesh between his lips. And the heat of his tongue followed, the smooth flat racing up my throat.

Oh, Seasons. He wanted me, craved me, hungered for me. And I wanted him back.

I wanted the pain of his touch, and the agony of his tongue, and the ferocity of his cock. I wanted to be taken, to be split open, to be ridden. I wanted us to wreck one another's world.

"Why you?" I begged while scraping through his hair.

Why him? Of all monsters, why this one?

Jeryn's body strained, as though tormented by the same question. Like a starving man, he plied my throat with open-mouthed kisses, his lips feeding on the sunbursts. My eyes flipped to the back of my head, my cunt melted, and my shaky fingers dashed up his scalp.

"Fuck," he seethed against the inked symbols.

The illicit sound oozed down my spine as I bowed into him, disturbing the roots and clinging for support. With every sweep of his tongue, a fractured moan dropped from my lungs. The merciless contact turned me into an explosive—a glowing ball of flame, with the power to drain the ice from this man's veins and turn him into flint.

Hellfire, that's what happened. His mouth became that flint, and my body became kindling, smoking and sizzling. Pinned against him like a spread butterfly, anticipation robbed me of oxygen.

Sultry air drenched the chamber. Glowing blossoms quivered from the bushes outside.

His face burrowed into my throat, licking and sucking the sunbursts like he wanted to consume them, to erase them. And my skin liked him so much for that. I drowned in his scent and his groans and his touch, each forbidden pass of his tongue like an apology, and I couldn't, I just couldn't.

I straightened, swooped down, and grabbed his face. Finally, I beheld the prince's expression, from the sharp irises to the inflated black pupils, from the half-mast orbs to the unhinged jaw—from loss to lust, with nothing held back.

His attention riveted on me ... saw me.

I didn't love him. Yet I understood him, and I thirsted for him, and there could be more. Little by little, there might be so much more.

I fixated on his corrupt mouth, longing to soften the contours. With a ravenous gasp, my mouth dove for his own.

The motion triggered a swift response. At the last moment, Jeryn reeled back, his palms grappling my cheeks.

"No, my little beast," the prince husked. "Far too easy."

His torso heaved against mine. Wound up like a spring, I panted into him.

His little beast. For the first time, the nickname sounded like an endearment. To that end, ambition lit his face, an impulse that urged me backward.

Far too easy.

I realized what he meant. I'd known this experience before, only this time a thrill fired through my blood.

With a hooded gaze, the enemy moved toward me. Instinctively, I skittered off his lap and launched to my feet.

Jeryn rose like a wolf on the hunt. In the shadows, the dark prince stalked my way.

As feral calls played through the rainforest, I walked backward toward the chamber's exit. In my wrinkled nightgown, I must look as rumbled as he did. Tousled blue hair fell around Jeryn's face, the snags indicating where I'd cleaved through the mess. Low slung pants skimmed his waist, his hipbones visible along with every cobbled muscle stacked across his upper body. If I peered closer, a wet mark would reveal where my pussy had drizzled onto him.

But I wouldn't peek, because I'd have to come nearer. As the prince had said, that would be too easy.

We'd begun like this. Captor and captive. Predator and prey. Tonight we would continue that way, except with another desire in mind, a different kind of chase. One that nobody was here to witness or judge or stop.

This hidden world was ours. Within it, we could be as wild as we wanted. Whoever caught the other would have their pick of the pleasure.

"I shall give you a head start," Jeryn husked.

"I don't need it," I whispered.

And his lips tilted a fraction. "Then run."

That instruction, I would heed. Twisting, I bolted from the chamber.

31

Flare

Darkness swallowed me whole, midnight lacquering the walls in black. Adrenaline propelled me down the corridors, each one draped in blossom curtains and prickly shoots. Leaves curled their fingers as if to snatch me, florals twinkled with light, and the wet air beaded down my back.

Across crumbling halls, lush verandas, and sunken chambers puddled in water, I darted through the ruins, hopping around loose bits of masonry. He had practice hunting me. The prince had learned the pressure of my exhales—their own type of sound—and grown accustomed to my shape blending in with the murk. Therefore, this monarch knew what I looked like in the dark.

Most of all, he'd learned my scent.

My pulse thudded like a drum. My lips tipped into an exhilarated grin.

In the dining hall, I slowed to a jog. A raptor took flight from one of the beams, the slap of its plumage echoing, and crickets chirped from the surrounding forest, which threaded its branches past these walls.

Our rainforest castle.

Like him, I had memorized the layout. Yet my head clouded, dazed from the havoc we'd caused each other, the sensation of his cock abrading my cunt. My senses ran amok, so that I fought to orient myself.

A pebble skittered from one direction. I whipped toward the noise, then spun the other way as a click—a blade flicking from a weapon's hilt—pierced the night from another spot. The disturbance urged me down an empty hallway, then up a stairway. As door hinges creaked, I fled down a labyrinth of passages glowing with flora.

Then I halted in realization. The noises had been intentional, meant to direct me, to steer me down an intended path. Like a creature stalking its next meal, my pursuer was trying to trap its quarry, to force me somewhere I couldn't escape.

My mouth twitched with combativeness, my thoughts cleared, and my vision sharpened. He might be a calculating prince, but I'd had more training when it came to the darkness. I could easily hunt him back.

Let the prey become the predator. Let the captive become the captor.

Let those tables turn.

Flattening myself against a wall, I skulked down the next channel. Hyperawareness chipped at my flesh, the masculine essence of needle forests and blustering winds filling my nostrils. He was close, very close, so close.

I slipped around broken pillars and shrubs that had burst through the ground. The premeditated noises from earlier ceased. Victorious, I relished the proof that he'd lost track of me. From there, I trailed his scent and the outline of his body cutting in and out of sight.

Buoyed, I made a game of circling him. Except I drew it out for too long. This became clear when I swerved around a bend—and stumbled in place.

A vast enclosure loomed before me. Bottles containing plants and liquids flashed from the recesses, including the gauzy leaves I'd excavated for him. The honed tools he'd scavenged from the armory crypt rested on a stone table, and the hearth stood empty.

I tarried at the medical chamber's threshold. Though, I wouldn't have come here on purpose, nor ushered him like some enabler. At some point, I had unknowingly forfeited my advantage, and he'd reclaimed his.

With a frustrated grunt, I padded backward while staring at the chamber. One step, then two steps, yet I knew.

It was too late.

My feet skated across the uneven floor. Facing the interior, I retreated another yard, then bumped into a solid form.

I tensed, a gasp catching in my throat. A slab of muscles aligned with my back, his chest contorting from each breath. Heat prickled down my spine, the temperature seeping through the nightgown. My limbs locked, a feeble defense even though he didn't touch me, keeping his evil hands to himself.

Regardless, he hardly needed to do more. Already, the walls of my pussy tightened.

Jeryn's head bent over my shoulder, his jaw slanted toward my profile, and his rasping voice struck the ledge of my ear. "Poor little beast. It appears you've gone astray."

My words shook. "You cheated."

"No," he hissed. "I strategized."

Dammit, he was right. He'd waited me out, knowing I would grow impulsive. To catch me, all he'd needed to do was be patient.

He murmured against my earlobe, "I have obsessed over every facet of your body until each scent, sound, and movement branded itself into my head. I have spent every waking hour committing you to memory. That's how I hunt what I want." A silken noise oozed from him. "Though, to be fair, I would call this a draw. You gave chase longer than I had predicted. For your cunning and insolence, I have a mind to make you suffer."

My eyelids fluttered, and my skull grew heavy. Unable to help myself, I lolled my head, bracing it atop the hard plank of his shoulder as his teeth nicked my lobe. For the thousandth time, I shouldn't want this. This chamber should trigger nine years of torment, rousing every demon to the surface. Instead, my soul rebelled to an intimate and frightening degree.

The truth softened his words. He hadn't driven me here to awaken trauma. The healer in him had brought me here to overturn the effect, to mend what had come before.

"Tell me," he whispered into my neck. "Have you ever been examined?"

The question electrified my skin. I nodded, but my gulp signaled it hadn't been enjoyable. More than once, I'd endured painful inspections, one of them shortly before Jeryn had me chained to the ceiling.

The prince noted the tension in my joints, a deadly noise slicing from his tongue. "Who was it? Give me names."

I shook my head. His method of punishment would make me no better than the people who'd hurt every imprisoned soul on this continent. I fought back, but I didn't torture or murder. Neither would I let him do so on my behalf. I was better than that, better than every tyrant in The Dark Seasons.

Besides, Jeryn couldn't get to my tormentors from here. And I didn't want to think about those days.

I wanted *here* and *now* and *this*.

Jeryn translated my silence. "So be it." Releasing another breath, his chiseled torso pitched against mine. "Then permit me to correct my mistakes. Allow me to treat you." The next word poured down my skin, gritty and imploring. "Please."

Permit him. Allow him.

Please.

My exhalations turned choppy. I had barely finished nodding, my mouth falling open as his mouth dove in and gripped the crook of my neck. With a hot tug, Jeryn sucked on the tender flesh, pulling whimpers from my lungs.

I coiled into him, my ass curling against the high ledge of his cock. Taking my reaction as permission, a gravelly noise skidded from Jeryn's mouth, then he seized my hips and walked us forward.

Together, we crossed the chamber. On the way, Jeryn reached out and snatched something from a wall hook, then stalled us at the room's midpoint, beneath the overhead pulley.

He released my neck. "Will you trust me?"

Again, I nodded. "Yes."

This man had opened himself like a wound, exposing his demons to my judgment. Finally, I would trust him. By now, I knew.

He would not harm me. Not anymore.

From behind, Jeryn unspooled two cords of rope, looped them over the pulley, and let the items drop. The prince guided my arms upward, then tied the slack around my wrists, binding me in the same position from Summer's castle.

I chuffed air like a pump as he secured the bindings, neither too tight nor too loose. My body stretched comfortably instead of being forced taut, as it had been in the quad. Also, my feet remained flat on the ground rather than extended on my tiptoes.

"Command it, and I shall stop," he intoned. "Are we in agreement?"

"Silly prince," I whispered. "I can release myself."

A cool and corrupt breath stroked my cheekbone. "I know."

He'd never said anything about needing to untie me. This prince knew I could untether myself if I wanted to. Doing so would be my choice.

Yet I didn't resist.

My consent wrought an indulgent noise from Jeryn, who reached in front of me and dragged the backs of his knuckles down the center of my body, between my erect breasts, down my stomach, and under the nightgown. A whimper rolled from my lips when his fingers combed through the sprigs of hair shrouding my pussy, then cupped the damp swells.

"Fuck," he hummed. "So slick."

My head slumped against his rampant heartbeat. A firm set of fingers etched my folds, those doctor's hands tracing with concentration. Fluid seeped from me and leaked onto Jeryn's digits, his index finger skimming the crease, passing back and forth with precision. My flesh crackled, and my lips parted, the teasing motions wringing a cry from my throat.

Jeryn groaned, hearing every fractured sound. The thought had me pressing into him, swiveling my ass harder into his broad cock, the rounded head jutting through his pants. The prince shuddered, sank his incisors into the side of my throat, and bent a finger between my soaked walls.

My muscles quivered around that digit, then sealed around him to the knuckle. I whined and bucked against his hand, desperate for *higher* and *deeper*, my hips rolling toward his upright finger once, twice. Our pants resonated in the chamber, then another digit pitched between my folds, prying me apart.

With deliberate motions, Jeryn began a steady pump. This doctor worked into me, siphoning in and out, stroking compact areas I'd never felt before, the tips of his fingers reaching places I hadn't known existed.

He crooned into my throat, his lips sketching my collar tattoo. Then a third finger slipped inside me, his hand hitting a barrier that flung embers through my veins. All the while, his wrist ground sinuously against my clit, inflating the stud. For mercy's sake, I hadn't predicted he could do this, hadn't imagined he could wring these feelings from me.

This much pleasure. These many sounds.

I hadn't turned to glimpse him. Yet I heard everything my moans did to this man, coarse noises grating from him and hitting the edge of my throat.

Famished, Jeryn's mouth opened and closed on my skin, kissing the delicate curve of my neck as if it were my mouth. For the second time, his tongue flexed and lapped over the ink markings, swabbing as if to wipe them away.

Or to ingest them. To take my place.

Divine Seasons. What was happening to us?

My head spun from the tug of his mouth, the liquid thrust of his fingers, and the arousal pooling from my cunt. Then without warning, Jeryn peeled his lips away. Muttering a curse, he slid his fingers out of me, the loss so acute that I grunted in protest.

Get back here, dammit.

The prince stalked around my body and faced me. Shadows slashed through his features, those irises piercing through the murk. His expression bordered on merciless, the harsh lines of his face riveted by the sight before him. I hadn't known coldness could be this enticing, this profound, this smoldering.

That look was mine. Tonight, it belonged to me.

Despite the bindings, I wasn't the captive in this scenario. From the entranced way he looked at me, I never had been.

Power shot through me. In this moment, I could request anything from him, and he would offer it freely. I might be tethered and on display, but I had this man ensnared.

My very own villain prince.

Perspiration glazed his torso, the muscles of his abdomen contracting as he prowled my way. The moment my breasts grazed his bare chest, our breathing staggered.

With effort, Jeryn unpinned his gaze from mine and traced the pads of his fingers over my body, trailing the same path his knife had in the castle, except softer and safer. What he'd called an examination became an exploration, and what had been atonement became admiration.

Him, an observer. Me, a wanderer.

Like this, he touched me in a way I had always wanted to be touched—with unbridled worship.

His fingers drew across my collarbones, then over one puckered nipple through my nightgown. From there, down my ribcage to my hips, and the outer edge of my thigh. My blood raced, his path leaving a brushfire in its wake.

"Your temperature is elevated," Jeryn observed. "Otherwise, everything is in working order." Pausing for effect, his baritone narrowed to a sliver of noise. "Thus far."

Those ruthless fingers stalked beneath the hem of my nightgown, riding up my inner thighs and pausing inches shy of my aching pussy. Aggravated, I groaned and nudged my waist toward that teasing hand.

Jeryn's nostrils flared, but he spoke calmly. "The last time I had you like this, do you know what I really wanted to do?"

Yes. I knew because a horrible part of me had wanted the same thing. I licked my lips, the motion triggering Jeryn's attention. His eyes raked to my mouth, his pupils eclipsing those irises.

I saw his intentions. As much as my villain prince fancied answers, he also fancied actions.

My pulse slammed into his. I let the request fall from my lips. "Demonstrate."

Those orbs glinted. His free arm jerked, and something flashed in my periphery, though I couldn't look away from him. Not until the scalpel knife materialized. I sucked in a breath, then released it as his gaze returned to mine, reminding me that nothing he did would hurt.

Not in a bad way. Nervous energy replaced fear as his fingers choked the hilt. With a deft click of his thumb, a slender blade flipped upright. "How many nightgowns do you possess?"

"Plenty," I assured him, because the ruins had preserved the wardrobes of multiple females.

The prince approved of that answer. "Good." Then the fabric ripped in a single tear as he ran the blade down the middle. My nightgown split and flared around me, my tits and stomach and limbs pushing into view.

Humid air caressed my nipples and the patch between my thighs, the sensation wondrously erotic. The material hung in two panels from my shoulders. Jeryn left the straps alone, his features tightening as he beheld every curve of my body.

"Much better," he said. "Now spread them."

Arousal puddled in my cunt. I delayed for a moment, enjoying how it affected him, the ledge of his jaw ticking. Another minute, and he would use that marvelous word again.

Please.

Yet he wouldn't be the only one. Taking pity on us both, I widened my stance, exceeding his wishes and exposing my sleek folds. In this balmy room, the nub of my clit swelled.

"Fucking hell," Jeryn swore. "Perfection."

Yes. That.

Let him realize everything he'd been wrong about.

Excitement fizzed in my stomach, another boost of power surging through me like thunder. He'd seen me naked enough times, and I'd felt those eyes on me countless other times too, but never like this. And I liked the difference, and I wanted more of it, and I needed that now.

The knife flicked back into its hilt. Jeryn shoved the weapon into the sheath at his waist.

And then he sank to the floor. And I swallowed a hot gale of air.

On bended knee, Jeryn hooked my right thigh over his shoulder. This close to my spread pussy, his eyelids grew heavy, his gaze absorbing every pink and pliant inch.

After a moment, his head craned. Jerking a few errant locks of blue from his forehead, Jeryn bonded his gaze to mine, his features stripped to the bone.

That candid stare breached a corner of my heart, a terrifying emotion sneaking through. This sort of cruelty should be threatening, yet it wasn't. Although I knew my worth and didn't need his appraisal, that didn't stop my soul from bursting.

This future king had begged. And now I'd gotten him to kneel.

Lowered before me, Winter's ruler waited like a subject. And although I should have felt validated, greater need washed through me.

I wanted him to get up and put us on equal footing. I wanted my hands in his hair, my fingers caressing the blades of his cheekbones, and my touch thawing the ice of his eyes. I wanted us melting together.

The request teetered on my lips, then dissolved as the heat of his breath brushed my clit. A gasp trembled from me, the vibration traveling to my knees, so that Jeryn felt my response.

A deep hum scrolled from his mouth. Securing my thigh to his shoulder, his fingers tightened, fastening me in place. When I made no protest, the prince took that as encouragement. His rapt attention quested from my face to my spread cunt.

And then he dipped his head.

His profile vanished into the gulf of my legs, that blue mane grazing my skin. From this angle, I beheld only the crown of his hair. Yet oh, how I felt his nearness, how he panted against my intimate flesh.

With agonizing slowness, the vile man drew out the moment to the point of excruciating. Then at last, a groan ripped from his lungs. And the wet flat of his tongue flexed against me, dragging along my crease in a single, prolonged lick.

Every word I'd ever known, every feeling I'd ever felt, and every thought I'd ever had dissipated like mist. My fingers seized the overhead ropes. My mouth dropped open on a cry. I stared, watching Jeryn's bowed head, my body trembling as his tongue swept across the slit of my pussy, laving the folds and gliding up to the distended flesh poking from the hair.

The pointed tip of his tongue sketched the tip of my clit before rowing backward and repeating the motion. Another whine curled from me, spurring on the prince who lightly stroked the length of my cunt, mopping up the slickness. An appreciative moan sliced from Jeryn's chest as he tasted, swabbing me back and forth, back and forth, back and forth, until I became delirious.

Embers vaulted up my spine. Despite not being a virgin, I'd never known such anguish, hadn't envisioned the heights my body could reach.

The prince traced the oval center, exploring my shape, circling and spreading my arousal. My muscles quivered, but I held still. He liked this because it enabled him to explore thoroughly, and forcing myself not to move also magnified the intensity.

At the same time, resisting the urge to gyrate my hips became another form of distress, equally blissful and terrible. I watched the prince's head sway, each motion punctuated by a flick of his tongue. Moans skittered from me, hinting to Jeryn the impact he was having. This man was an expert in physical tension, skilled in the innermost workings of the body. He followed the signs, hunted for them.

Indulging my desire, he scrolled his tongue around the rim of my entrance. Glimpsing me one more time, he praised, "Keep your pussy open for me."

Then his tongue slipped between my soaked folds. And the world capsized. Snapping into an arch, I threw my head toward the ceiling.

"Ah!" I keened into the rafters, into the rainforest, into the sky.

Jeryn growled, the texture of his voice hitting my flesh. My walls parted and suctioned around him, my pussy throbbing, dripping down his throat. In a steady rhythm, he probed his tongue in and out, swallowing every drop that seeped from me.

The frayed nightgown hung from my shoulders, and my hair hung in the air, and I hung suspended. Ecstasy fired through my veins. Something tight and hot coiled in the juncture of my thighs, worsening as Jeryn beat his tongue firmly into my core.

Unable to help myself, I swatted my waist toward his mouth. Like a ferocious tide, the tempo sped up as he reached farther, deeper, higher. I rocked my hips, whisking my pussy against his face.

Jeryn snatched my ass for leverage and matched my movements. Together, we flung my cunt and his mouth together. Shocks of pleasure blasted up my limbs. Shadows clutched the ceiling, and the cords nipped at my wrists.

But Jeryn wasn't finished. He made that clear as he reeled his tongue from between the flanks of my pussy. I whined, displeased by the loss. With menacing amusement, he kissed my crease once, then licked his way to my clit.

Sighing against the peg of skin, Jeryn latched on, strapping his lips around the bud. At the first warm lash, I splintered apart, my body hurling farther back. Every sensation I'd ever known rushed to that spot, joining a thousand other foreign sensations. The point of his tongue swirled around my clit, his pace unbearable, unrelenting.

My thighs fell wider, and my weeping got harsher. By now, shouts tumbled from the pit of my stomach. I sobbed freely under the grasp of his mouth, his tongue flicking over the crest, patting that spot until my thoughts drowned. Only this existed, only the clench of his lips, only the flex of that tongue.

Jeryn alternated between licking the peak and sketching its shape. Lost in a glorious haze, I swung my body toward him, pleading for more, demanding it.

On another ragged growl, the prince linked his arm under my other leg and hoisted it from the ground. Looping it over his opposite shoulder, he splayed me as far as I could go. Palming my ass to keep me elevated without the cords biting into my skin, Jeryn pinned me to him and renewed his attack.

Snatching my clit, he gave a hard suck. Equally covetous, the pressure of his mouth threw me into a rage. I hollered, loving that Jeryn heard the noise.

On and on, he rowed that tongue against my inflated flesh, causing it to rise and swell more. For minutes or years on end, I cried and cried, my body desperate for a release that remained out of reach.

I chased it, chased every swat of his tongue. Shameless, I pressed my thighs into his shoulders and used the momentum to gallop against his face, my tits bouncing, my knees steepling. My joints burned with exertion, and I burned like a torch, and my heart burned like a star.

Maybe the rainforest had glamoured us, or maybe it had willed us to this moment, had chosen us to mate like wild creatures. Or maybe we liked each other better now. And maybe it was something more than that.

Releasing my clit, Jeryn lurched his tongue between my walls again. Using my ass to lunge me forward, he pitched deeper, harder, longer. I charged at him, spreading myself and riding his mouth.

"Yes," I entreated. "Jeryn!"

As his name emptied from my lungs, the prince lost control. A mercenary groan wracked his frame, and he hauled me into him, lurching his tongue fully into my pussy, fucking me with his mouth, wetting me to the brink.

I drenched his lips, my walls fluttering, the wave cresting. His own growls filled my ears, and his hands spanned my backside, and my limbs straddled his shoulders, and my cunt smothered his palate. Even then, it wasn't enough, might never be enough.

I swiveled my waist, fantasizing that his tongue was his cock, only longer and harder. The head would strike a narrow spot that made me soar. The base would widen my opening. My body would flood him to the seat.

Jeryn's mouth pistoned as though he knew my thoughts. Motivated, he struck into me faster and wetter and firmer. All the while, he held me close, bolstered me midair.

Squeezing the cords, I bobbed on his tongue, syncing myself to his movements. Like this, we became one force of pleasure. Like a tsunami, the release built, escalating higher and quicker.

And more violent. With my head lolling backward, I pounded my hips with his tongue, frantic to reach that precipice, the pinnacle I'd never achieved before this.

"Now," I implored. "Make me come."

A dark and cruel hiss. Jeryn withdrew his tongue and cinched around my clit, hauling on the bud and simultaneously licking the tip. He held back nothing, his mouth fucking me so deftly, so tirelessly, as though I were indestructible.

I'd once condemned him for assuming me to be as breakable as a seashell. Not anymore. Now he heard the ocean's roar inside me, felt it building on my lips, ready to crash through this room.

I spiraled out of time, out of place, out of mind. Bolts of lightning jolted through me, wet heat engulfed me, and his hands anchored me.

My head fell forward, needing to see him, needing that contact before it was too late, before I was too far gone. I had to believe this was real, that we'd breached enemy lines and discovered something better and stronger.

Jeryn must have registered the motion, because his gaze leaped toward mine. Kneeling and sucking me into a stupor, those flashing pupils grabbed my own and stayed there. With his mouth pinned around to my pussy, he sucked my clit and dabbed the peak over and over. Every part of him clung to me—hands and eyes and lips.

He let himself be seen, a coldhearted prince drained of hate and worshiping a born soul.

My mouth fell ajar. I stilled, then shattered into pieces. My pussy spasmed, the muscles contorting against his lips, a rush of liquid streaming from my opening to soak Jeryn's tongue. Hot, black pleasure sluiced through my limbs. The great rupture tore through my body, rushing from my cleft to the edges of my being.

At first, nothing came out. Then all at once, everything came out.

I combusted, flames erupting, the climax vaulting from the depths of my throat. I came with a tremulous roar, the noise somehow penetrating Jeryn's ears. He heard and felt and saw the rapture break through me. Pupils expansive and glassy, he seized me tighter, and he pumped his tongue while I rode out the tumult.

I came for what seemed like hours, came so intensely my throat went raw. For a moment, I thought I might faint. Yet an eternity later, the pleasure ebbed, and I sagged against him.

Humming his approval, Jeryn released my pussy and licked his lips. "Such a sweet little beast," he indulged.

Unhooking my legs and draping them over his waist, he rose while hefting me against the wall of his chest, where I slumped like putty. Gentler than I'd expected, he banded one arm under my backside and untied me with the other hand.

My arms flopped, aching but not chafed. Winded, I shivered from the aftershocks and predicted his next move. He would return us to our chambers and leave me to my bed.

As Jeryn stepped toward the threshold, I grabbed his bicep. "Stay," I whispered. "Stay here with me."

He frowned in stupefaction, as if the request was foreign, his reaction pinching another unknown place inside me. This man might have a bond with his family, but he didn't know intimacy. At least, not this kind.

I didn't either. The plea tasted strange on my tongue. What he'd done to me, no other man ever had. I felt this truth in more ways than one. I'd had caring parents, and I took Rune for a brief lover, but I'd been confined for years until landing on this island. Living in a prison, I'd never experienced a connection like this. No one had awakened such feelings in me before.

I gave Jeryn a look, telling him I felt as lost as he did. He took a moment to absorb that, then carried me to an open-air window ledge overlooking the forest. Swinging one leg across the rim, Jeryn sat astride the sill and propped me closer, where we strove to recover our breathing. My thighs straddled his hips, and my clit skidded over his broad cock, which stood high through his pants. I nestled into the prince's frame, my pulse teeming with his.

I wanted to ruin this man, to taste him the way he'd tasted me, to dominate his moans, to claim them. I wanted to fuck his body until the sun rose and we saw each other in the light. I wanted us to share ourselves with each other.

Also, I yearned for my hands on him. Just as I craved his mouth on mine.

Slanting my gaze to his, I found a pair of Winter eyes devouring me. My heart fluttered as I reached up to sketch his jaw, cup his face, and warm his skin. I braced his profile, ready to usher his lips to my own, to rock my tongue with his, to consume his voice.

Kiss me.

Jeryn saw the move coming like a surprise attack. For some reason, my intentions fractured the spell, some form of dismay lancing through his features. Pulling away, he caught my fingers.

My brows crinkled in disappointment. "Why?"

The roughness in his tone opened a wound. "Because I cannot fucking take it."

This man didn't say things casually. What came out of his mouth was always intentional.

He couldn't handle my touch? He couldn't take kissing me?

I swallowed my confusion, not wanting to spoil this moment. Letting the questions go for now, I basked in the atmosphere, the echoes of the rainforest, the thud of Jeryn's heart, and his arms encasing me. Finally, contentment rippled through my stomach, and my lips tilted into an exhausted grin. My eyelids drooped, the darkness pouring in.

Hours later, we awakened together. Slumped against the recessed wall framing the window, his chin rested atop my head. My cheek nuzzled into his torso, his strong arms locked around my waist, and my legs were spread over his lap.

Jeryn made a rumbling sound, his sleepy groan setting my blood to boiling. My eyes fanned open. Dawn streaked the forest and medical chamber in gold, a rare sight in the morning. Unseen creatures buzzed, and blossoms drenched the air in fragrance.

The prince held me so tightly, it would take a crowbar to pry my body from his. Enjoying the phenomenon, I sighed and curled into his frame.

And then he froze. And so did I.

Wrapped up together, we remembered. As I glanced up at him, the prince looked down at me, and finally we saw one another in the light. We remembered what he did to me, how it had felt and sounded.

Disgust had plagued me after we'd unleashed during the lightning rain. But repulsion wasn't the problem anymore. This time guilt squeezed my ribs instead.

Sprawled naked atop his torso, I licked my lips. "It was—"

"—a mistake," he finished.

32

Flare

Was it?

The transcendent way his mouth had made me feel shouldn't have been a mistake. Yet as dawn spilled through the rainforest, remorse wrung me out like a cloth. That, and a strange loss.

Whereas my regret had everything to do with this man's heinous past, Jeryn weathered my gaze with a repentant one of his own. Not because he'd touched a born soul—we had dismantled that barrier—but because of other reasons that stacked like bricks on his face.

He was a ruler. I was a fugitive.

He came from Winter. I came from Summer.

Nothing this prince did was spontaneous. He possessed a will of iron and a calculating mind. Every step he took was on purpose.

Panicking, seeking comfort in my arms, dragging his mouth across my neck. Like the night of the lightning rain, none that had been planned, yet he hadn't stopped himself. Stalking me through these ruins, kneeling at my feet, and licking me into a frenzy had been deliberate.

But when Jeryn's eyes dropped to my mouth, heat passed through them along with caution. I understood why, yet there seemed to be more he wasn't telling me.

My limbs flanked his waist, the pome of his cock hot against my pussy, while the shredded nightgown hung off my shoulders. With our lips swollen and hair disheveled, we had made a mess of one another. And if we weren't careful, it would happen again.

Crawling up his chest, I planted my hands on the wall, on either side of his head. "So we agree."

A jagged breath pushed from his chest. "We agree."

Then and there, the clamshell of my heart closed. The rainforest had embraced us, had led us to this point. I wanted this to mean something beyond a mere tryst, and I wanted to savor the beauty of last night. But I couldn't.

The prince thought me resilient. The rainforest had granted me the vitality to face all threats. So why did this choice feel painful? Why did my chest clench as much as my conscience? Only last night, I'd been sure nothing he did would ever hurt.

I was wrong.

Our silence formed a new blockade, hardened into a new shield, rose like a new wall. Yet it took a long time for the villain prince to release his grip on me, and it took a long time for me to climb off his lap, and it took even longer for us to let go.

Days passed, then weeks followed. We kept ourselves busy, diving headfirst into tasks. Not that it often worked, the tension thickening like sap.

Only with the passage of time did we find ourselves arguing, bantering, and talking more comfortably. In between quarrels, we lapsed into conversations. In a series of moments, we discovered each other.

We mapped the rainforest. The underground ruin caves led to different parts of the island, though we couldn't rely on them to reach every terrain. Over time, we recognized forks in the paths, danger zones, and fauna territories. Then came the day when we journeyed without having to follow our map.

Slowly, I befriended the wild's fauna. Hummingbirds roosted on my shoulders. Seahorses swam with me in the grotto. Vipers slinked from the crevices, curious as I tiptoed nearer, too fascinated for Jeryn's liking, who shoved himself between us until I hopped around him to greet the creatures. From a serpent with pearlescent skin to a horned viper, the animals slithered around me with animated hisses, then twined themselves along my arms like bangles while I laughed.

One afternoon, a boa with a barbed face approached. I recognized her as the one I'd battled and released from the tarantula webs. The female skated out of the shadows, her movements hesitant.

I recalled her bafflement when I'd freed her from the webs. Maybe she sensed a kindred spirit. The rainforest seemed to think we should meet, so I trusted its judgment. And what a pretty enchantress!

As we studied one another, a second figure prowled from a shrub. The red and black feline with saberteeth stalked forward, her shoulders revolving sinuously. When an intrigued purr rippled from the animal's throat, I knelt and tentatively scratched behind her ear, which prompted the female to bump my leg, the motion bringing a smile to my lips.

Minutes later, I found myself galloping on the jaguar's back with the boa draped over my shoulders. The feline unleashed a roar, the serpent vibrated its forked tongue, and I howled, celebrating what the rainforest had always known, that we were all creatures of nature.

They returned me to the ruins, the jaguar leaping over the bridge gap to the opposite side. Jeryn stalled his movements, gawking from the entrance steps where he'd been whetting one of his scalpel blades. As we trotted his way, the shocked prince rose to his feet. He took in my skimpy camisole, which was sewn to a pair of tiny shorts, the boa strung like a deadly necklace around my throat, and the jaguar balancing me like a steed.

Me and my fauna pack.

"Seasons forbid," Jeryn uttered. "You fucking reckless woman."

Something more than alarm filled his tone. Deep and resonant, it sounded very much like esteem.

As more weeks floated by, I searched the ruins for my key, reciting the Summer song for clues, checking cracks in its walls, wading through shallow pools in sunken chambers, and breaking open dusty compartments. I also used my nets to catch fish, some of my excursions turning up treasures from our wreckage, including my parents' machete lodged beneath a boulder. Elated, I jumped up and down, then gyrated in circles around Jeryn.

The prince might have dipped his head and grinned. A little.

And despite the memory of his mouth on my flesh, a routine developed, and a friendship kindled.

Jeryn spent time creating restoratives. One day, I watched him from around a corner. I'd been avoiding peeking into his medical chamber, the place where my legs had splayed around his head. Today though, the sound of him working lured me.

The prince stored plant samples into jars and pots. He itemized the collection, seemed satisfied by the assembly, and held a petal to the dim light.

I knew this sort of passion, felt it whenever I drew in the sand.

Then I recalled the mangoes I'd tried to harvest during our first hike together. Not only might it taste delicious, but Jeryn could have some medical use for it.

I crept away, leaving him to his work. Harnessing one of a dozen satchels I'd found in the textile cellar, I ventured from the ruins and located the thorn tree, my mouth watering at the ripe new crop of orbs hanging from the canopy.

Because the boa and I had developed a fellowship, I didn't worry about an attack this time. Instead, I used the trunk spikes as footholds and eased myself around their tips. After collecting enough mangoes to fill my bag, I descended the trunk, nearly reaching the bottom when my foot slipped. A yelp lurched from my mouth as I smacked to the ground, most of the fruits scattering across the understory.

When I shifted to get up, sharp jolts tore through my side. I wailed while forcing myself to stand and toil back to the ruins via the cave tunnels, one of which ended at the main steps. It took I-don't-know-how-long to climb them, and I kept hunching over, pausing to lean against the railing, with only a few mangoes left in my satchel because it had hurt too much to gather the rest. Once I got to the threshold, I buckled against the door frame, the rainforest spinning in my vision.

As if sensing a problem, the prince materialized at the threshold. Taking one look at my clammy features, he strode forward.

"Fuck," Jeryn hissed, catching me before I fell. "Turbulent woman. Glutton for disaster. Reprehensible bane of my—"

"Okay," I griped. "The rainforest and I are kindred. It would never scathe me for good unless I deserved it, dishonored it, or stopped trusting it. Where's your sense of adventure?"

"On the fucking ground, where it belongs." Jeryn fingers roamed over my abdomen, his touch rousing a horrible and all-too-familiar vision of me arching toward him while my cunt drenched his tongue.

"You cracked a rib," he gritted out.

Hellfire. That would make it hard to fish, hike, and complete a thousand other tasks.

I threw a fit to keep the prince from carrying me. Instead, I leaned my body into his as he took the bag from my shoulder and supported my weight inside.

Even with all the ingredients he'd amassed, Jeryn could do nothing for my rib. He tucked me into my bed, and I cursed life itself. Though, I didn't mind the prince doctoring my injury and hovering over me, nor the blue slide of his hair across my mouth. If it weren't for the nastiest hurt in the world, I would have paid more attention to the sensations.

"Don't fucking do that again," Jeryn warned, then caught the urgency in his tone and steeled his voice. "We don't have enough supplies for mishaps."

True. Regardless of what the ancients had left behind, we weren't living like Royals. Still, that wasn't the only reason his words had shook with worry, though we pretended not to hear it.

Each rain blessed me as I offered myself to the initiations. Vapor rain was safe, whereas lightning rain pierced flesh, and thunder rain produced a bruising shower that pounded its fists down on us. Meanwhile, celestial rain shimmered like falling stars, which didn't last long and happened only at night. Lastly, storms at dawn scalded like acid—ember rain, according to the legend.

Turned out, breaking my rib wasn't the last time Jeryn got upset when I threw myself into danger's path. The prince applied an ointment to my ember rain blisters, though the pain lasted hours.

We concluded the droplets affected humans and the fauna, but not the landscape or inanimate objects. Ultimately, only creatures were at the sky's mercy.

After experiencing my rites of passage, I avoided all but the celestial and vapor rains. Gradually, the prince and I learned when to trust the sky and when to escape it.

The echo of flowing water led us to an oasis where waterfalls cascaded down hilly brackets and splashed into a turquoise pond. After smelling and touching and tasting the water, we reckoned it swimmable.

On the bank, I sketched Papa's lopsided grin, Mama's peaceful stare, Poet's wicked eyes, Briar's freckled profile, and Jeryn's cold stare. A melody played in my ears, my throat humming as I finished. When a breeze tossed sand from a distant area into the air, I danced inside the funnel, revolving my wrists, swaying my hips beneath a strappy dress, and kicking my legs—and stumbling.

Backdropped by the cascades, Jeryn watched me. His eyes kindled like timbers, the impact both a thrill and a threat.

It took forever for him to shatter the distance between us. His tall body sauntered forward with stealth and loomed before me, his open shirt flapping in the wind, almost but not quite caressing my bodice. It was the *almost* that probed the slit between my thighs, where his mouth had spread me open.

My tongue peeked out. I licked bits of salted gold from my lips, a wet trail that his gaze followed.

A teardrop of sweat glided down his temple. His mouth opened, primed to speak.

I braced myself, my pulse thudding and need coiling in the nexus of my thighs. No matter how much time passed, my urges only became more dire. Especially when I stashed myself in hidden parts of the ruins and fingered my pussy. While plying the tender walls, stroking my clit until it swelled, and pumping my fingers, I would imagine his face and body and lips until my walls contracted, and I came into my fist, with his name ripping from my lips.

The evidence must have shone on my face because Jeryn's pupils darkened, seconds before he tore his gaze away and strode past me.

Every night as he slept in the connecting room, a mere twenty feet from me, I thought about filling his bed, how it might feel to slip under sheets that smelled of him, with his body heat wrapping like arms around me, my curves resting against his weight. To sleep beside a man who cared for me, wanted me. I imagined hearing the deep rumble of his chest, with my head tucked there, safe and sound and sated.

I pictured him fucking me in that bed, his hips snapping, his cock grinding me into the mattress. And every night, I muffled my whimpers. And whenever this happened, I heard his own bed creek as if he were changing position, or trying to stop himself from getting up, from getting closer to the sounds I made.

Then came the day when I stumbled upon him in a cave pool beneath the ruins, bathing with his back turned.

Oxygen leached from my chest. Jeryn stood knee-deep, the taut outline of his ass consuming my view. Wet and smooth and tight, with divots in the sides, those buttocks flexed while Jeryn scrubbed his fingers through his hair.

As every ridge contracted across his body, I gripped the wall to keep from slipping. Then I scuttled farther back into the corner, unable to peel my eyes away.

In Summer, citizens grew up exposing their bodies, the same way Spring did. Albeit, that sinful court treated nudity like a game. And in my kingdom, it was a matter of practicality.

Strip or suffer heat stroke. Plain and simple.

Not plain with this man. And definitely not simple.

Jeryn had the mind of a scientist and the body of a warrior. Toiling here made up for the lack of swordplay, this new life and its endless chores inflating his physique even more, from the trunk of his spine, to the taper of his waist, to the firm swell of that ass.

I'd never seen Jeryn fully naked. Even now, the sight of his cock remained a mystery. But I imagined its size and shape—the slit across his crown, the weight of his sac—just as I'd fantasized about every hot and ruddy inch whenever I stroked myself in private.

A heady groan of satisfaction rolled from Jeryn's throat, similar to when he'd pitched his tongue inside me. The ripples lapped at his legs. His muscles flexed as he lathered his chest, and his mane brushed the ridges of his back.

If I peeled off my clothes and joined him, what would he do? If I seized his cock in my fist, would this Royal protest or let me pump him into a helpless growl, his climax drizzling down my fingers?

I yearned for the answers. And I dreaded them.

With a slight twist of Jeryn's body, the faintest silhouette of his cock rose, the round head flushing wide and dark from between his hips. No more than a curve was visible, yet my body reacted like a hurricane, swift and destructive. Slickness warmed my pussy, and a whine got stuck in my throat.

Jeryn paused. One second. Only one second. Then he resumed

bathing, his fingers carving a harsh path through his damp hair.

I expelled a breath, my cheeks on fire, my nipples pebbling, and my cunt on the brink of spilling. He could have caught me. Somehow, Jeryn could discern the noises I made, and I could only be thankful he hadn't this time.

Surely, he had no idea I was there.

33

Jeryn

I knew she was there. If the scents of salt, sun rays, and wildflowers hadn't given Flare away, the tempo of her breathing did. Stunted. Shallow. The beastly little minx sounded as if her lungs had collapsed.

Fuck me to hell. I wanted to grab her.

My insubordinate cock agreed, hardening like a cursed pipe, as though welded that way. The stem lifted painfully, the crest's circumference expanded, and my foreskin darkened.

Condemnation, but I needed to rid myself of this incessant thing. If she didn't leave in ten seconds, cum would bead from the cleft, and a growl would carve a path up my throat.

Arrested in the water, I locked my muscles, wrestling to keep still. I could wait her out. I could be patient. I could be. But if I turned and met her gaze, it would be over. She had witnessed too much already. One more exhibition, plus one more look, and I would have no barrier left. The sight of her would bury me under its weight, and I would willingly suffocate.

If semen didn't spill from my phallus first, blood would ooze from my pours. I fixated on the glistening water and endured the anguish as heat rushed from my sac to the tip. After what happened in the medical chamber, the little beast had claimed all the power, the ability to rip me open.

 Her flesh materializing from the ripped nightgown. Her body arching toward me.

 Those hands braced overhead. Those cries lurching from her mouth, inexplicably loud in my ears.

 Flare's thighs astride my mouth. Her pussy convulsing and wetting my tongue. The beast's glorious face lost in rapture. I had never witnessed anything more exquisite.

 After I had tasted Flare's body, she had wanted me to kiss her. An entreaty which I had rejected, telling her I couldn't take it. Her mouth would have destroyed me.

 My molars compressed hard enough to shatter a bone. With supreme effort, I resumed bathing. Except the chore became laborious, as if I were moving through tar. Those combustible eyes made contact without trying, the heat of her attention burning my veins. Any longer, and I'd turn to give her the uncensored look she wanted.

 If that happened, it wouldn't end there. Putting it mildly, the sensation of her eyes on my bare cock would have the opposite effect. I would snatch Flare from her hiding spot and fuck her into the nearest wall until she was convulsing.

 This avid gaze of hers might fucking kill me.

 At last, her breathing faded. Next, the brushfire of her stare vanished. Then the familiar fragrance evaporated like an illusion. As if cognizant of my thoughts, she had fled.

 I should have been relieved, yet my head fell forward. My eyes cinched shut, her absence creating worse chaos—an exponential loss. One that exceeded my longing for Winter and everything I'd left behind.

 Fuck. I sloshed from the water, but instead of prowling after her, I threw on my clothes and cut in the opposite direction. More distance. I required more distance, lest I should change my mind, catch the little beast, and destroy us both.

I shoved past the old stone doors, slammed down the ruin steps, and struck into the wild. The aftermath of what happened propelled me forward as I took refuge in the vegetation, stalking into the tangle of trees.

Perhaps she had realized her error. Perhaps the notion of spying on her former oppressor had disgusted Flare. Perhaps she'd had time to remember that.

I hoped she did. It would be best.

Charging through the understory, I traveled from one spot to another, my calloused soles resistant to the hard soil. Since I'd forgotten my satchel, I gathered what specimens my hands could carry. My fingers tore stems by their roots, dirt spitting from the ground as I pulled.

Tugged. Yanked.

This pitiful attempt at productivity failed to placate my body. My cock stiffened like a piece of iron, making it difficult to navigate the rainforest on solid limbs. Dispatching the bundles onto the forest floor, I slouched against a tree while visions of Flare infiltrated my head.

Long before she'd craved me, I had coveted her. The addiction had begun within moments of that dungeon in Autumn. Or perhaps before then, back when she hadn't known I existed.

For all my attempts to hide these impulses, I had succumbed eons prior to her own descent. This woman had ruined me from the start. Her eyes had been the first culprits, stinging me with their light. After that, those enduring hands had pushed me to the edge.

Inevitably came the nights I had lost control with her. First, the lightning rainstorm. Then I'd awakened in a debilitating fit of anxiety, and Flare had come to me. The moment her hands had landed on my flesh, I'd lost all fucking sense.

Flare in my arms, comforting me. My panicked state running the gamut from ramblings to a forbidden embrace that broke my restraint and unleashed my tongue.

Presently, my cock strained. The head bloated, the distended length widened, and the entire goddamn ligament shoved against my pants. I picked open the clasps, my dick springing from the flaps and stretching against my abdomen. The stifling air coated my aching flesh, the glaze consuming my attention.

The sight brought more figments into stark relief. Illusions of her arousal slickening my cock, her desire seeping down my skin.

The roof of my crown darkened. Fluid pressed through the incision across the top.

I strapped my fingers around the base and dealt with the frustration. Helpless. Bewitched. Hissing, I siphoned my hand up and down, from the seat to the tip, each motion punctuated by my stifled groans. The commotion pressed against my teeth, but I held back. In this forsaken forest, who knew what would happen if the noises became airborne. The wilderness might carry them off to wherever Flare had gone. Comically, avians might imitate the fucking sounds to her.

Not going to happen. I clamped my mouth shut, squeezed the radius of my cock, pumped the skin with measured strokes. Moisture permeated the air, lubricating me down to my testicles, which hung heavily.

Blood surged across my fingers and inundated the glans of my cock. Chuffing oxygen, I recalled every second with Flare. Her hips grinding into my lap during the lightning rainstorm, her pussy saturating the fabric of my pants. Then my teeth on her salted throat on the night I'd panicked, my mouth sucking on her pulse point, my tongue laving her collar tattoo.

I had wanted to rinse the inked sunbursts clean. I had sought to purge her of those infernal symbols.

And later. How I'd sank to my knees, prostrating myself and lapping at the soaked crease of her thighs. Her response, pure and pleasured. Her orgasms and the sweet taste of her cunt. I had been the one plying Flare, but she'd been the one to finish me off.

I had lied. Blatantly. Flagrantly. It hadn't been a mistake.

Embers scorched a path from my balls to the line of my crown. Fluid rose, prompting a muffled growl. Swiping my thumb over the drops, I smeared myself and lunged my hips faster.

It would be easy to shut my eyes. I could pretend she was here, watching me. To that end, I could delude myself. Instead, I fixated on my dick and let it serve as a reminder. I would only ever indulge alone and had no right to more.

Flare deserved an actual prince. Not a cruel one. Not a mad one. She hadn't been timid when I licked her pussy, and she hadn't moved as though pleasure was utterly foreign to her.

Thoughts of Flare mindless, sweating, and crying out beneath the rhythmic thrusts of a lover caused my retinas to burn. Envious growls launched up my throat. My erection broadened, deepening to an angry reddish shade, and veins inflated from the skin.

A single word leaped to the forefront. *Mine.*

I gripped my cock harder, flung my hips faster. Wrathful, I vaulted my ass forward, jutting my cock into my fist.

I envisioned skewering that lover with a pronged blade and shearing them in half. I fantasized about Flare reaching for me instead. Her head slumped back, her mouth open, sounds only I could hear pouring from her lips. I imagined her arching in my medical chamber, with her limbs splayed around my flexing waist, sharing a new type of madness with me.

Fluid rushed up the length my cock and pushed into the head. My sac heated. My vertebrae tingled. I slung my dick until the pressure hit its breaking point and then tensed, my body so tight it might crack in half. Then I licked my lips, tasting the residue of her climax. Then I replayed the cacophony of her orgasm. Then I recalled those hands on me, that mouth yearning for my own.

With a violent shudder, my cock spasmed. I mashed my lips, blocking out the ragged groans that tore from my chest. I came hard and long, oblivion wracking me to the bone. Hot jets of cum spurted down my knuckles as I bobbed my hand, drawing out the final drops.

Not mine. She would never be mine.

My greatest error? Her name on my lips.

"Flare," I rasped into the forest.

Instead of mending the chasm between us, time enhanced it. I could be standing a thousand leagues from Flare, and she would still dominate my thoughts. I could be standing even farther away, and my cock would still twitch at the briefest thought of her. To cope, we relied on buffers.

Work. Progress. Industry.

Cloistered in the medical chamber, I struggled to keep my mind off Flare's thighs straddling my head and her cries of pleasure. An impending migraine brewed as I surveyed the botanicals and other natural resources I'd been cultivating. The blue fig I'd eaten with Flare—back when she'd restrained me on the beach—alleviated pain when combined with the juice of a chameleon leaf.

The mangoes also obtained by Flare—when she had cracked her ribs—decreased fever and nausea if boiled into a tea.

The sour-sweet flesh of recognizable guavas assisted with digestion.

The pulp of plantain stems treated abrasions.

The leaves I'd discovered on that first day exploring the ruins did well for infections.

Yet other cures had to exist, advantageous against sicknesses in The Dark Seasons. Though, such restoratives would never circulate if I remained here.

Prior to the night I had panicked, the reality of this place had already been haunting me. My disappearance could have had drastic effects on my parents. Either they believed me dead, or they were dead themselves.

The plausibility blunted my concentration. I strode to the opposite wall that had once housed a series of windows but now only brandished columns. Overlooking the rainforest, I gripped the pillars on either side, fighting to steady my respirations.

They were alive. They must be.

As were my grandaunts. Though, Silvia and Doria must have been forced to consider a new successor by now. I detested that notion, however imperative. I would not desert Winter without vetting my substitute. I wouldn't leave the court vulnerable to an alternate heir—a sloppy ruler like Rhys, who exercised about as much restraint as a brutish lion and might disregard the people's welfare.

The prospect set my jaw. Naturally, my grandaunts would not appoint someone like that. I'd do well not to underestimate their judgment.

Nonetheless. How quickly the mind overtook rationality. How powerfully the amygdala seized control of one's faculties. If I dwelled, I would resort to hysteria. If the rainforest were compassionate, it would provide me with an ingredient for sedation.

Anything to keep from reaching for the safety of Flare's arms again.

After the siren shark, I avoided the grotto. Although I did not say why I'd chosen an alternative cave pool in which to wash, I insisted Flare do the same. Because this woman was not obtuse, she guessed why and made no argument. Not even when I kept watch as she bathed.

While disrobing one morning, her shoulder strap dropped low. Like a tease, the material flashed the arc of a nipple, reawakening the memory of that disk quivering between my lips.

I swerved away, my life dependent on this motion. Narrowing my eyes, I scanned the pool's depth, searching for a striped dorsal fin despite this being a different water source. No matter what, the creature would not get near her.

The whole time, my pulse hammered. But I could not say whether the palpitations escalated because of the shark, the flash of naked limbs in my periphery, or the deafening sound of Flare splashing naked into the deep.

When Flare rode that jaguar across the bridge to the ruins, the sight had drained my lungs. Fear came first. Protectiveness next, until I witnessed how the animal moved loyally beneath her.

Then came another extraordinary reaction. Deference. Mounted on the feline, with a viper around her throat like a necklace, she transformed into a ruler of this wild.

A queen of her own making.

So perhaps ... perhaps this place had indeed chosen her. Or perhaps she was a greater force than even she gave herself credit for, beyond whatever the forest dictated.

When Flare had fractured her rib, I checked on her more than necessary, monitoring her as she slept.

Staring. Watching.

Purely to make sure. No other reason.

Though, keeping my impulses platonic became increasingly difficult. With regular nourishment, Flare's body filled out, endowing her with wider curves. Tits that pumped with each breath. A shapely ass that bent over. Hips that swayed from side to side as she danced in a sandstorm, a performance that incited predatory instincts, the need to pursue her.

No matter how I sought to purge these cravings from my system, they persisted. The antidote for such a chronic condition didn't fucking exist. At the very least, something to dilute my sex drive would have been welcome.

Weeks became a month, then another month, then another. These clustered feelings pulled on my chest like stitches, tight and straining to break free. I tried organizing them, then refuting them.

I fucking tried.

Yet her impassioned words uprooted me, her musings and opinions no longer irrelevant or infuriating. At some point before the siren shark's attack, I had ceased talking with Flare merely out of obligation. On the contrary, I'd met her halfway, wanting to hear her thoughts. Somewhere along the way, ours had become a partnership.

Then it became something else. Except I had no right to need her, obsess over her, want her. Much less to have her.

That was the mistake. Not touching or tasting Flare, but believing I had earned that privilege.

The second she'd broken my vial, I had despised Flare. I'd loathed her for destroying that which was precious to me. And thus, for betraying the one memory I still kept from her.

Then in Summer's tower, I had wrapped my hand around her neck. How I wanted to mutilate myself for those crimes. How I longed to pare the cartilage from my bones, torture myself the way I would torture anyone who laid a finger on her.

No. I had not earned Flare's affection. No monster ever could.

We stumbled across a jungle in the south. A break in the canopy allowed light to flood the ground, burying the environment in dense plant life, the route barely passable.

Undeterred by the labyrinth of greenery, Flare played a game of hide-and-seek with her fauna pack, including the reptile and—for fuck's sake—the saber-toothed jaguar. As they slipped through cavities of foliage, the beast's eyes sparkled, her laughter chiming through the brush. Her joy was a vibrant thing, penetrating the shadows, impervious to them.

I stared. This was how Flare looked when she was happy.

No one had found us. We hadn't been rescued. Despite that ... when I looked at her now ... when I saw and thought of nobody but this woman ... I hardly gave a fuck. In moments like this, I viewed this realm through her eyes.

Beauty. Freedom. Sanctuary.

Regardless, losing sight of each other in the forest was a constant gamble. To calm myself, I inspected a hedge of prickled vines. When I got too close, one of the threads snatched my hands. The confounded thing tightened with each of my attempts to move, thus stifling my circulation. Superb. It figured I would tread cautiously and then encounter a nefarious plant, whereas the little beast pranced about yet remained unscathed.

Soon after, the object of my envy and desire popped from the shrubbery. Registering my predicament, she used her dagger to extract me from the snare. When her digits traced the welts around my wrists, the blood rushed back in.

"See?" Flare beamed. "The rainforest can trap or heal."

Seasons flay me. The sight of those hands grabbing things, claiming them, healing them. By some miracle, I refused to yield, to let my baser instincts take over.

But I wanted to. And I wanted to. And I fucking wanted to.

More than that, a new ambition veered my thoughts into uncharted terrain. I would like to do something nice for her.

My fingers stole out and tucked a wavy lock behind Flare's ear. To my satisfaction, a shiver passed through her.

The words dropped from my mouth. "Have dinner with me."

34

Flare

What ... did he say?

My fingers rested on his wrist, and his digits lingered in my hair, neither of us moving. As we finally rose in unison, Jeryn stepped into me, and I inched nearer. We hadn't idled this closely in months, not since that pivotal night in the medical chamber.

The gap of his open shirt revealed too much skin and not enough. Restlessness crept across my fingers, the urge to touch him instinctive, as it had been for a long time.

Surrounded by a thicket of foliage and baking in the sunlight, I beheld his stricken features. The villain prince had spoken without thinking. I enjoyed what that did to his expression, impulsiveness looking rather fetching on him.

His invitation pulsed through my chest. "You want me to have dinner with you?"

The villain prince rubbed the back of his neck, discomfort stringing across his features. "Yes," he said. "If you're hungry."

Amusement lifted the corners of my mouth. "We have dinner together every night."

"Right. Correct." He grimaced at himself, growing more tongue-tied by the second. "I meant ..."

"You meant ...," I drew out.

The tormented prince cleared his throat, then thrust a hand through all that hair. "I thought ... that is to say ... I would very much like to ..."

It was naughty, but I couldn't help myself. Mashing my lips together, I kept deliberately quiet and watched this future king fumble, relishing the phenomenon for all it was worth.

Giving up, Jeryn swore under his breath. "I'd be honored if you would ... accompany me for something more ... ceremonial."

"Ceremonial," I repeated, a grin threatening to burst from my face.

Scientific Jeryn would have said *unconventional*. Royal Jeryn would have said *stately*.

This Jeryn had searched for a word that mattered to me, one I'd appreciate.

My flesh warmed, his effort driving me to take pity. Trying to be helpful, I ventured, "Are you asking me on a date?"

His eyes tapered as though the concept was beneath us, as though it didn't measure up to whatever this was. "An engagement," he proposed. "An intimate meal."

Of course, not a courtship. Nothing fancy or formal. I smiled openly, because his suggestion sounded far better.

Misinterpreting my silence, Jeryn hastened to add, "I thought it would be nice." Then his speech slowed. "We could do with something ... nice."

Yes, we could.

The reply rested softly on my tongue. "I'd like that."

That night, I tossed the fifth outfit to the floor. Standing in the textile cellar, surrounded by dresses that cascaded like water and pants as light as petals, I could not pick a thing to wear.

The ancients had tailored their wardrobes with extravagant fabrics spun from all sorts of elements and forgotten materials. Everything felt airy, trimmed in precious lace or exquisite needlepoint, with no beading or gems to weigh them down. Flowing and layered, every option seemed to either swim or float through the air.

While I'd never been the recipient of such clothes, sand drifting for treasures had taught me plenty about finery. I used to dream of wearing something fancy—something pretty. Our kin made do with practical garments for expeditions, and although we were part of the merchant class, few of us could afford the luxuries we excavated.

Chests crowded the cellar, their lids open like gaping mouths. Despite my longing to try on every stitch after a lifetime of fantasies, I'd been limiting my choices to the essentials, not daring to drape myself in anything precious.

I tarried, nervousness and indecision stalling my movements. How I wished Poet were here to help me. During his visits to my cell, that jester had shown up looking equally disheveled and impeccable, his presence turning every head in his sphere. The man oozed dark sex appeal and dressed to slay every room he stepped into, even if filled with hundreds of people. It didn't take a connoisseur, much less a free citizen, to see that.

As for Briar, her elegant and tidy wardrobe had a fierceness to it—confident and regal. Yearning gripped my throat. I'd sent that messenger butterfly ages ago but hadn't yet received a reply. In any case, if the princess were here, along with the ladies who'd embraced her on Reaper's Fest, they would also know which garment to choose.

Instead, I had made a mess of the cellar. Fisting my hands, I strode to the final chest and carefully picked through a stack of opulent choices.

Then my fingers halted, a gasp tumbling from my lips. At the bottom of the pile rested a masterpiece. Unspooling the outfit from its confines, I marveled at the sumptuous vision. It was the most beautiful fabric I'd ever seen.

Mama and Papa used to say that when a treasure was special, I would know.

They were right. A thrill swirled in my chest. I stripped naked, shook out the fabric, and held it up to my frame.

We'd agreed to meet a while ago, but it had taken a century to untangle the knots in my hair. As eventide approached, I rushed into the vestibule where Jeryn waited with his back facing me. Except I dashed too quickly and slid sideways from the corridor. Staggering, I grabbed my skirt at the last moment, saved myself from going down, and jumped back into the hallway before the prince could witness a crash landing.

Plastering my back to the wall, I clutched my stomach and got a hold of myself. Then I wheeled and peeked around the corner. The sight eased my jitters and had me pressing a fist to my mouth, to contain my mirth.

Jeryn bowed his head, braced one hand on his waist, and used the other to tap a wrapped object against his thigh. With a muffled oath, he surged into motion, pacing the chamber's length like a tiger. All the while, he fussed with the item in his hands, crushing and releasing it.

Any more of this, and he would wear out the stone floor. But then he started mouthing to himself, as though rehearsing a speech.

The hushed makings of a chuckle tripped through the room. At once, the prince swung toward the disturbance, and I realized the noise had come from me.

Why should I expect anything else? This man heard me when no one else did.

Across the vast space, his eyes found mine. From mounted wall brackets, torch flames licked the air. He must have ignited them with Summer tinder, although we'd agreed not to do this often, apart from whenever we needed additional light while working.

Orange hues brushed his face. As he wheeled my way, I stepped from the corridor.

And Jeryn froze. Mid-turn, the villain prince halted, the parcel dropping from his fingers and hitting the floor. Whatever he'd been about to say died on his lips, shock transforming his features as he watched me come forward.

That dark gaze devoured me whole, shedding any remaining shyness from me. I glided toward him, feeling powerful and magical and beautiful.

A red skirt—dyed in the same ethereal shade as my butterfly companion—fell to my ankles, multiple layers whispering against the floor. The matching cropped bodice clung to my breasts and left my midriff bare, while the straps hooked around my shoulders, bracing slightly off the edges. I'd picked a hibiscus flower of the same color to tuck behind my ear, and slender sandals twined around my feet, the deep olive straps blending with my skin.

Also, the sheath holding my dagger rested in a thin band, which encircled my thigh. The slit in my skirt revealed this too.

A barely perceptible "Fuck" drifted from Jeryn's throat. He raked his gaze over me, those pupils reflecting every torch flame. The unbridled look melted through my garments, ratcheted my heartbeat, and struck between my thighs.

I admired him in kind. The villain prince had chosen ebony linen, the shirt and pants fitted without being constrictive. A deep V accentuated his collarbones and the shadows of his pecs, he had rolled the sleeves up his forearms, and a pair of narrow boots that had once belonged to an ancient resident climbed up his limbs.

Breaking from his stupor, Jeryn stalked my way. We paused in the room's center, this terrain unfamiliar for both of us.

The speechless prince stood there. "You look ..."

Yet he trailed off, unable to finish. My spine tingled, feeling the brush of every compliment that never made it to his lips. "I'm late."

"I don't care," he uttered. "I would have waited far longer."

The reply brimmed like kindling in my navel. Despite his pacing from earlier, I believed him.

At length, the prince spun toward the item he'd dropped. Swiping it from the floor, he glimpsed the object with hesitation, then returned to me. "For you."

He seemed plagued while extending the parcel. Stunned, I accepted the item wrapped in broadleaves and tied with a cord of rope.

My confusion triggered Jeryn. "It is a gift," he explained, his tone uneasy.

I nodded to reassure him. "I know. It's just that …" Swallowing, I met his eyes. "I haven't been given a present in a long time." After a beat of silence in which Jeryn's features pulled taut, I wondered, "But why?"

This man planned things. Yet my birthday wasn't for another several months, nor did I have an achievement to celebrate.

"I do not have a reason." He gestured to the package. "I came across this plant and thought of you."

Fighting to contain a smile, I worked the bow loose, giving Jeryn a shrewd mock-glare at the knot he'd attempted, apparently to test my skills.

"Nice try," I snarked while picking apart the cord.

The corner of his mouth ticked up. However, he remained agitated as the broadleaves flapped apart to reveal a corked bottle filled with glistening gold fluid.

At my inquiring look, Jeryn hastened to speak. "It's a preservative. An oil extracted from an herb. To protect the weaving in your nets."

Amazed, I peered at the liquid. I'd been mourning the lack of plant oils here, often used to keep sand and fishing nets intact, and had mentioned it to Jeryn—only once, months ago.

Yet he'd remembered.

When I made no reply, the prince's features twisted. "It's practical," he emphasized in a rush. "It will give your hands a rest and keep them from chafing. I see how often you maintain those nets, and—fucking hell." He carded a hand through his mane. "This was unimaginative and a stupid idea. I should have made you hand salve instead. Something scented with plumeria—"

I launched at him and flung my arms around his shoulders. Jeryn went still, his own arms extending and hovering. A second later, he enfolded me in his strong embrace, my toes inching off the floor.

I twisted my head and spoke into his hair, "Thank you."

Presents had been rare in my life, as it seemed gratitude had been rare in his. As I pulled away, relief and a tinge of pride flickered across his face, shortly before he smoothed out that expression.

Jeryn gestured toward one of the hallways. He lifted his free hand, setting it abreast of my lower back and ushering me without touching. "Come."

Except I stayed put as he strode toward the wrong corridor. Registering that I hadn't moved, he turned and raised an eyebrow.

"The dining hall is that way," I said, indicating a different passage.

In the dimly lit chamber, the villain prince's irises glittered. "We are not going to the dining hall."

Without another word, he offered his hand. Drawn to that mystery, I set my free fingers in his.

Jeryn's hand folded around mine. The contact threw flecks of heat up my arms, the rush going to my head. As though experiencing the same jolt, the prince's grip on me tightened.

He strode ahead, guiding me through the ruins and into one of the caves. Behind him, I clutched the bottle of oil in one grip and fought to collect myself. How could holding this man's hand yield the same profound emotions he'd wrought in his medical chamber, when I rode his tongue? The effects teetered between scary and invigorating, like holding a shooting star, a burning thing. More than that, it felt safe.

At one point, I stuffed the bottle in my skirt pocket and reached out to touch Jeryn's hair, but then I pulled back at the final moment. If I made contact, we might never leave this tunnel.

We navigated through the passage—which he'd also illuminated with torches—and crossed a vast distance before emerging aboveground. Stepping from an archway nestled within a knoll, Jeryn led me into the eventide.

I sucked in a gust of air. We stood at the threshold of an unfamiliar cove. It was smaller than the others, with frothy white sand curling around a glossy bay. Ferns swayed in the breeze, boulders laced in blossoms rose from the depths, and a thousand stars swam on the water's tranquil surface.

Jeryn released my hands and watched as I floated ahead, a mesmerized gasp slipping from my lips. "Divine Seasons," I said, twisting this way and that. "I would have remembered us finding this place."

"We didn't," his baritone voice replied. "I did."

I veered his way, a breeze sweeping through my locks. It was impossible to miss those irises gleaming with satisfaction. I might be a sand drifter, but he came from a land of hunters, and he'd chased me across two kingdoms. Of course, I wasn't the only one who could find hidden things.

Jeryn's confidence wavered. "Do ... you like it?"

A grin split my face as I marveled at the scene. "It's breathtaking."

Then I noticed a stump tucked beneath the awning of a tree, the drooping branches and their willowy foliage forming a curtain. Two stools abutted the stump, where a candle gleamed, likely kindled by Summer tinder. Plates, cutlery, a pair of chalices, and a covered trencher graced the makeshift table.

A lump budded in my throat. I peeked at Jeryn hovering nearby, then swerved back to the ambience. He must have brought items from the ruins, which must have taken half the day.

No one had done something like this for me before. I'd never sat at a fancy table in my life.

Jeryn's shadow loomed at my back. "It's not as elegant as I would have liked."

I whirled toward him. "I love it."

His mouth slanted in pleasure. For such a ruthless man, this prince had been bred with courtly manners. He took the bottle of oil he'd made for me and set it on a bed of grass, then offered me a chair, where a lightweight blanket rested over the back.

The meal included salted trout, which he must have grilled from our stash, along with citrus and figs like the one we'd eaten after washing up here, and nectar that smelled of crushed grapes.

I gave Jeryn an impressed look. "You cooked."

"I've watched you," he confessed, lowering himself to the opposite seat and draping a hand over the chalice's stem. "Though, I cannot say it will taste as good."

The point was, he'd tried. I bit into the fish, the sea's essence and a tangy flavor melting on my tongue. A moan dripped from my mouth, and juices from the fish leaked down my chin.

I swabbed my tongue across my lips to collect the residue. In unison, a finger stole out. We paused, our gazes fusing. Jeryn had leaned over to wipe the juice from my chin, the contact electrifying me from head to toe. The prince's pupils darkened, his stare opening me wider beneath the skirt, the hard press of my chair clashing with the gentle motions of the starry sea.

As if drugged, we edged back to our seats. Despite that one perilous moment, the conversation flowed like water. Hours could have passed without us noticing, the subjects ranging from tasks that needed attention at the ruins to memories of our kingdoms and tidbits about our families.

Temptation drew my gaze to the water. "It looks as if the celestials plummeted from the sky."

"I'm certain you'll find out the moment you dive in," Jeryn predicted while lounging like a merman.

That he read into my words and expressions used to threaten me. Now it only sent pleasant shivers across my skin.

The balmy night air, decadent food, and enchanted bay transported us to an easy place. Jeryn's features relaxed, and I nestled into the chair, the mood animated. As time passed, my tongue loosened, and I realized something.

This was more than nice. It was fun.

Swallowing his last helping of the fish, Jeryn hummed in appreciation, the masculine sound stirring my knees like broth. "It is not gravy or stew," he granted. "Yet I can't complain."

Prompted, I reminisced about treats from the mainland that I missed. "Sea bass."

Catching on, Jeryn tilted his head. "Roasted game."

"Passionfruit."

"Cranberries."

Then our gazes locked. At the same time, we groaned, "Pastries."

And those groans melted into chuckles. Creases formed on either side of Jeryn's mouth, his grin leisurely.

Which people had been privy to this side of him? I doubted many, yet instead of feeling victorious, envy prickled my scalp. This Royal must have been surrounded by men and women, admirers who'd wanted more than his approval.

I sobered for one reason, while Jeryn sobered for another. "When was the last time you tasted one?" he said in a low, guilty tone.

One what? A pastry?

The stars grew sharper while floating atop the sea. A chilling breeze sailed through the foliage curtain and made the candle wick tremble. The flower tickled my ear, and my hair hung a bit longer, yet it failed to conceal my collar tattoo.

At the question, I glanced toward the ocean. "Before they took me."

Poet and Briar had delivered pear tarts to my Autumn cell, but I'd never been able to savor those treats, because I'd been too famished to gobble them slowly. If I ever tasted their actual sweetness, I couldn't recall. Experiencing such thorough pleasure hadn't really happened since my imprisonment.

Jeryn's fist rested on the table between us, his knuckles straining. I glanced from his hand to a set of pupils lit with fury. That, and guilt.

The truth wedged itself between us. Still, it wasn't too late to close that gap. I'd put off one detail about The Phantom Wild for too long.

I scooted forward. "I need to tell you something."

Candlelight cast across Jeryn's face. He stared back without skepticism, encouraging me to forge ahead.

At last, I felt more than a truce. Now I felt trust.

And so, I told him about my fated purpose. How the rainforest had called out not merely to offer me sanctuary, but to provide a key—a greater purpose in helping the unfairly condemned in this kingdom. Somewhere in the ruins resided the answer to that mission, the steps I must take.

In the beginning, Jeryn hadn't believed the rainforest had chosen me. I'd known why, figuring he doubted a so-called "born fool" would ever be summoned by nature.

But now, I felt him listening and absorbing. Where once he would have spit on my passions, now this prince contemplated everything I told him. He asked questions, and I gave answers, and we shared possibilities. He took what I said seriously, his logical mind contributing to theories. Whereas I searched for answers based on sensation, Jeryn rationalized how there might be hidden relics in the ruins, which could provide artifacts worthy of research, remnants of the past that would somehow advance the crusade for born souls.

We debated at length before he reclined in his chair, a thought furrowing his brow. "What do you think this purpose will involve? What actions will you take?"

I blinked. "The rainforest will tell me."

"I'm not asking what the rainforest thinks you can achieve. I'm asking what you think you can achieve." He leveled his gaze with mine. "Of what quest do you believe yourself capable? On which of your skills will this mission rely?"

My tongue stalled. This man wasn't being condescending. Rather, he was earnestly trying to help me figure this out. But I'd only ever assumed the rainforest would decide which abilities I needed for this pursuit. My fate would choose which skills mattered the most.

When I told him this, Jeryn threaded his fingers. "Seafaring. Exploring. Your expertise in locating precious items, which certainly helped you uncover the map. What about those talents?"

I wavered in confusion. "The rainforest selected me to read the map. The rest is ultimately a means to find my key."

"Meaning your self-made abilities are irrelevant compared to what nature designates for you? That discovering the map had only to do with fate instead of any personal skill?" His head flopped to the side. "You're selling yourself short, Flare."

My gaze scrunched like a wad of paper. "I trust this forest."

"You should also trust yourself. Your strengths don't begin and end in this realm."

I didn't know what to say to that. But while his words simmered in my head, Jeryn added, "Be that as it may, when you locate this key, that leaves the matter of how to use it. Regardless of its identity, it will most certainly require departing from this realm. You cannot affect a continent while in isolation. Yet you also can't leave as a fugitive without plotting how to avoid getting caught again."

I cocked my head. "Will you try and stop me?"

"Chain you? String you up?" His voice turned rough. "I've done so before."

He wasn't talking about the castle quad but a different place, a closer one where he'd also had me arching with ecstasy, the molten recollection pouring down my skin.

Nonetheless, I held that gaze. "I'm done being someone's prisoner."

"I said nothing about that. But restraining you would keep you safe. At least, until we have a sound plan that guarantees your head remains attached to your neck."

When Jeryn said things like that, it was hard to keep still, to keep myself from tracing the shape of that vicious mouth. "I've been contemplating that. But I need to find the key first, which might reveal the solution."

Jeryn tapped his finger against the stem of his chalice. "Doubtless, Winter and Summer are searching for us."

"They won't succeed. This rainforest is invisible to them."

"Humor me. If they manage to get around that barrier, that means time is of the essence. Your key must be found sooner rather than later."

"In which case, this sand drifter will need the help of someone from a land of hunters and engineers and inventors. To discover more of the ruins, I could use his support."

Jeryn's features gripped mine. "You have it."

Not until he spoke those words had I realized how badly I'd wanted to hear them. Relieved, I admired the stars hanging over the sea. "It's beautiful here."

"It is." A deep and penetrating pause followed. "So beautiful."

That husky timbre caressed my skin. Mist showered from the

heavens, and celestial rain suddenly fell from the clouds, the droplets shimmering like constellations. I rubbed my arms absently, and Jeryn responded by rising. Unfolding the blanket from the back of my chair, he draped it over my shoulders.

Nestling into the fabric, I stared as he returned to his seat. I wanted to save people, while doctors like him wanted to take care of them. Though, only recently did he extend that desire to all citizens.

Jeryn's eyes skirted toward my collar peeking from under the blanket, and his jaw clenched. "No one deserves those markings. Least of all, you."

I swallowed. "In blessed moments, I forget about them. But whenever I remember, it's like the ink is sizzling, branding me all over again."

No matter how far I went, I would never be rid of this harness around my throat. I had told Jeryn many things, but the memory of being caught as a child—what happened that day, what I'd done to earn my tattoo—squatted in my gut.

I couldn't think about it. Not yet.

The villain prince also hadn't asked, seeming to understand I needed time. Whereas I got the feeling he withheld a secret of his own.

Who marked you?

He'd already found out. All the same, I whispered, "It was Pyre."

"I know." Wrath contorted Jeryn's face. "That's why I dismembered him."

My chest hitched. I'd figured as much. That accounted for Jeryn's bloodstained fingers in the quad and why I hadn't spotted Pyre on the night I escaped. However, knowing the truth and hearing it spoken were two different experiences.

The prince's eyes flashed like torture devices. "I showed him no mercy."

That malevolent look reminded me of his roots. I would be unwise to assume that side of him didn't still exist, in all its methodical cruelty.

He sat there, the pose casual despite the fatal edge to his voice. "Except I would do worse now. If anyone came near you, I would prolong their punishment for years." He drew out the words like a series of cuts. "I would kill them patiently."

Celestial rain pattered the trees and plinked into the sea.

There was a time when I would have been disgusted by his brutality. Now too many other emotions pulled me in too many directions.

Everything he'd done to me. Everything he'd done *for* me.

All of it roused a question. To get the answer, I shrugged the blanket from my shoulders and pushed back my chair. My skirt brushed the sand as I moved toward the villain prince, then it rode high as I made the next move. Before he could say another word or push me away, I swung one limb over Jeryn's lap and straddled him.

35

Jeryn

Damn her.

First, I had lost my grip on Flare's gift when she'd walked into the vestibule wearing that fucking outfit. Seasons, the little beast had conspired to annihilate me. Depleted lungs. Aching cock. Erratic pulse. I'd scarcely had the brains to count above the number five, much less to utter a syllable.

Second, my inability to concentrate or articulate myself every time she smiled or laughed. The prepubescent grin that kept cracking from my lips, because her joy was infectious. The pride of showing Flare this place after discovering it, of witnessing her pleasure, of sharing a table and a meal together. The urgency to touch her. At one point, I had reached out, wanting to adjust the flower in Flare's hair when she hadn't been looking, only to pull back at the last moment.

Third, the sight of her feasting. With each voracious bite, she had licked her fingers clean, that curling tongue hypnotizing the everlasting shit out of me.

Condemnation, I had barely kept a steady hold on my chalice. This had been the case until she'd imparted the details of her search for a hidden key, an unknown mission regarding born souls. Then and there, my focus had solidified. And therein came the fourth nail in my coffin.

She trusted me.

Flare had been withholding this information. But finally, she'd confided in me.

And now with me thoroughly disarmed, the little beast committed the final critical act. She draped her body atop mine, her warm thighs splitting around my waist, the position rucking up that infernal skirt. Like a snare, her knees steepled, caging me in.

Slick heat brimmed under her skirt. The dainty fabric of her drawers chafed my pants. Fuck, the material was so finely spun it delineated the shape of her pussy.

My cock had already grown rebellious. Although I'd been rock hard since the vestibule, my erection sprang higher, the crown pushing into Flare's navel. For devil's sake, I had chopped humans to pieces without batting an eyelash. Yet this female's ass resting on my pelvis whittled me down, as though I were a pathetic juvenile receiving his first lap dance.

However, that did not render me speechless. Rather, it was her face. The softest expression I had ever known stared down, followed by the softest touch. Slanting her head, Flare drizzled her fingers down my profile.

Sense deserted me. Pain cramped my features, the sensation threatening to seal my eyes shut. Her coaxing touches had always hurt.

That beating organ in my chest accelerated. Too much and not enough.

"What are we?" she wondered.

A surplus of confounding emotions shone in her countenance. Fragile edges. Breakable feelings. I could not fathom these reactions, where they came from, or how to manage them. The only ones I recognized were desire and fear.

What were we? Allies? Friends? Lovers? Where did enemies fit in?

My degenerate hands seized the bottom of my chair, lest I should grab Flare's hips. Out of options, I asked, "In what capacity?"

Her mouth thinned. "You're stalling."

"I do not stall. I don't even waste time ripping off the bandage. Rather, I cut to the quick. At which point, my replies are rarely what others want to hear."

"Tell me what you feel for me. I can handle it, same as I've always handled you."

Her weight. Her curves. Her scent.

No fucking way could I answer this question reasonably. Not in this precarious position. And not with my aforementioned desires and fears stuffed in my mouth.

The rainfall intensified from a steady shower to a thick downpour. The deluge cascaded outside this enclosure. It slapped the ocean, where the tide had risen, starry sheets of water agitating the shoreline.

Like a repeat offender, Flare shimmied closer. Her irises melted, those eyelids fanning when the stub of her clit abraded the stem of my cock.

"I know you have feelings for me in *that capacity*," she said, then flattened a dangerous palm against my pectoral, where my pulse went rampant. "But is there more?"

She hovered, her features caught between two inclinations. Daring. Yearning. That last one, I would have trouble demolishing. I'd rather ingest arsenic than wound this little beast.

Yet somehow, I would overcome the sight of her. To fucking prove it, I arched an eyebrow. "I could make the same statement. You're as wet as that ocean."

A fetching shade of red suffused her cheeks. By now, she must have registered the dampness seeping from her lingerie into my pants. How intensely could I make her flush? As pink as her pussy had been when my tongue had spread it wide?

Tempted to experiment with her complexion, I added, "Your temperature rises when you're aroused."

She ran a digit across the smudge of blue beneath my lower lashes. "And your eyes change color."

"Your exhalations thicken, as they had when you watched me bathe."

Contrition deepened Flare's skin. "You've watched me too."

I had. On many occasions. Similar to castle life, privacy was a luxury here. We had writhed in the other's presence while sick and groomed in plain sight of one another. I had raved twice in her presence. Most pertinent of all, I had lost control during the lightning rainstorm and in the medical chamber where I'd fucked her with my mouth. At this juncture, we had seen a great deal of each other.

Be that as it may, the impetuous female curled into my torso. Thus, she reminded me of one remaining appendage she hadn't yet observed.

I slit my eyes. Usually, a mere look from me had warriors pissing themselves. But such attempts were futile here. Watching me fight to maintain composure entertained the beast, her fingers making a cataclysmic trek from my jaw to my abdomen, the effect toughening my dick.

"Do you have a remedy for that?" she asked.

"I should be so lucky," I husked.

"Does it hurt?"

"No comment."

"What makes it happen?"

"You cannot be serious."

Her teasing features contorted into a scowl. Marvelous. I had vexed her. That, I could live with. Whatever was happening between us could not be categorized, but anger toward one another... That, we had down to a science.

"I was asking about the medical reason," Flare clarified. "I know plenty about the graphic one."

My brows rammed together. The question came out like a statement. "You're not a virgin."

"I'm twenty-two years old," she reminded me, as if that justified everything.

Except she'd been imprisoned since childhood. So who the fuck had introduced her to sex?

Her expression implied she had as much experience as I did. Or rather, she assumed she had as much experience. However, my retinas were too busy detonating to conceal a forsaken thing. Notwithstanding how I'd eaten Flare alive in the chamber, experience did not stare back at her.

Flare stilled in disbelief. "You're ... you haven't ..."

"I've been busy," I snarled, dismissing the matter. "Did they hurt you?"

The little beast gave a start. "I answered that already."

Yes. When we had discovered the grotto, she'd confirmed no one had ravished her.

Nevertheless, I repeated myself. "Did. They. Hurt. You?"

"No," she upheld. "He didn't."

"He," I repeated, the pronoun drawing out my fangs.

Flare shrugged. "I don't have a preference. Everyone is comely to me, so long as their soul is beautiful. But yes, it was a man. We shared a cell for a while."

We had the same penchant. My limited history aside, I had no type. Intelligence attracted me, among other unique facets belonging purely to this woman.

Relief that she hadn't been violated eased the death grip on my chair, another brutal inclination taking its place. As they had when I'd pumped my cock in the forest, images blackened the edges of my vision. Flare writhing beneath a male. Encouraging it. Enjoying it. Prior to the medical chamber, someone else had made her climax, presumably more than once.

Mine.

Again, the offensive word inserted itself into my brain.

Mine.

As though I were the least bit entitled.

Mine.

At Flare's gasp, I registered my hands groping her hips. The unspoken word must have also surfaced on my face like a blemish.

In the candlelight, her pupils kindled. "You're jealous," she realized with too much enthusiasm.

"I am not jealous," I growled. "I'm livid and plotting to commit a dozen counts of murder upon my return to Summer's mainland."

Rather than repulse Flare, this confession only brightened her features. "Why?"

I sidestepped the question. "Did he taste you?"

"No."

"Did he make you come?"

"I don't know."

Considering Flare was no longer chaste, I had supreme difficulty believing she couldn't tell the difference between an orgasm and a one-sided ejaculation. "Did it feel the same as it did on the night you dry-humped my cock? And in the medical chamber, did it feel the same as my mouth?"

She glimpsed my lips. "Nothing has ever felt like your mouth."

The answer breathed life into my veins. My expression must have revealed as much, because she resurrected her earlier question. "So is there more?"

What are we? Is there more?

Dangerously, I shook my head. "Be careful what you ask for."

"If you're trying to intimidate me, you picked the wrong woman."

"Indeed. I believe that's how our relationship began."

"Does that mean I won't get an answer?"

"Impertinent, vexing questions," I gritted, detesting what I was about to say. "Do you want me to desire you? Or do you want to be desired by anyone?"

Flare grimaced. "That's a mean question."

"I'm a mean person."

"Not to me."

In other words, she would not let that happen. In other words, neither would I.

This resilient female would not allow anyone to treat her abysmally. Moreover, I would rather slit my throat before reverting to my malignant self where she was concerned. Everyone else was expendable, but this woman...

This woman. My exception to every vicious rule.

"I'll amend," I conceded. "It's a pertinent question. We're stranded."

"What does that have to do with anything?" she demanded.

Exasperation and vulnerability twisted her features. Seasons flay me, but I loathed the sight of her trembling mouth. I despised myself more for causing it.

Regardless, I pried the facts from my throat. "Your options are limited here. I'm going to question whether it's my desire you seek, or if I'm merely a substitute."

She glowered. "Because it would be so easy for me to do that to somebody. Is that it?"

"I did not say that. I know you wouldn't use a person."

"Then you should also know I don't want just anybody!" Flare argued, punctuating the words by slamming her palms against my chest. "If that were true, and if I didn't have any dignity, I would have fucked the hilt of your knife while you had me chained."

I jerked her into me. "Are you saying I was the only one impacted by hate-fueled attraction back then?"

"Oh, I felt that. I just wasn't about to surrender to it. But we've changed."

"Yes. The lightning rain forced us into closer proximity, and the contact segued to lust and a round of hate-fucking. Then I broke down in the ruins, and my panic inspired your pity, which incited more lust and even more chaos."

"You stubborn man! Always overanalyzing!" She fisted our hands together and pressed them to my heart. "This isn't something you can define, categorize, and store on a shelf."

Rain struck the canopy. That turbulent hand seared into my flesh, the contact ambushing me. Another inch, and her touch would sink into the black hole of my chest.

Before she could do increasing damage, I released her digits. "We're marooned. You have no other options for a lover."

"That goes for you as well," she pointed out.

I would not answer that. To do so would amount to my downfall.

To be honest with myself would produce a terrifying possibility. Had I been occupying my throne, swarmed by a kingdom's worth of courtiers, there would still be no other options but her.

"Flare," I gusted out. "You don't want me. Not in that way." With effort, I finished, "And I cannot want you."

She flinched as if I'd jabbed her with a needle. "Because you think I'm a so-called 'lowly fool.'"

"Don't say that. My hate came from fear, because I was a coward. Now my resistance is for a different reason."

She waited for more. I veered my gaze past the curtain of foliage, to where the starlit ocean thrashed against the shore. "I'm unskilled in expressing sentiments."

"Then learn how," Flare commanded.

The fire in her voice yanked my eyes back to her. "In the daylight, you're industrious."

She blinked. Her mouth tipped, as though on the verge of a chuckle. "I'm what?"

An embarrassed muscle rolled across my jaw. I sounded like a fucking technician. And an idiot. Furthermore, a paltry excuse for a wordsmith. That arrogant shithead who called himself Poet was a man of verse, whereas I was a man of facts. I did not possess the jester's silver tongue.

Witnessing my humiliation, Flare swallowed her mirth. "Go on," she implored. "Please."

And fuck. Whenever she gave me that look, I collapsed like a deck of cards.

"In the daylight, you're bold." I feasted my eyes on that scorching red dress. "By the firelight, you're brilliant. Always, you're enduring." Finally, my hand rubbed one of the hibiscus petals tucked behind her ear. "You have the skill to unhinge me. Your impact is significant." Wincing, I let go of the blossom. "And I ... cannot comprehend ... that I merit your attention."

The torrent fell around us. The ocean lashed against the bay.

Yet Flare's tender voice drowned out the elements. "Was it a mistake?"

I recalled what we'd said in the medical chamber, after I sank to my knees for her. "I don't know."

"You're lying."

"Is that what you think?"

"Look around you!" She threw her hands toward the ambience. "This place, this dinner, this night. You didn't do this because it was a mistake. You're not jealous about my lost virginity because it was a mistake. You're not listing my lack of options and your lack of right because it was a mistake. What you're doing is denying the truth!"

Muttering an oath, I fastened onto her hips and pushed her backward.

"Jeryn—" Flare's hand dove under her skirt, whipped out her dagger from the cord harnessed around her thigh, and slammed it into the makeshift table. The tip impaled a fraction of space between my spread fingers, where I'd grabbed the surface, intending to rise. Scalding me with her gaze, she finished, "—you're not going anywhere."

"No," I clipped. "Unfortunately, I'm not."

Not on this island. No matter what plans we made, departure wasn't currently an option.

The implication sliced from my tongue. Flare's eyebrows crinkled with rage. If actions had not discouraged her, the candor of Winter had.

Irritation, remorse, and fifty-five other catastrophic emotions laid siege to my body. I wanted her to lance me through with her weapon. I wanted her to punish me, torture me for that response. But my court was nothing, if not tactical.

I leaned forward, my breath cutting against hers. "I admire you for all the reasons I'd specified. I respect what I was too bigoted to appreciate before. But this dinner was my way of atoning for past transgressions while also granting us a reprieve from chronic stress. However, make no mistake. I don't want to court you. I don't want to coddle you. And I don't want to romance you."

Then I rubbed salt into the wound. "I want to fuck you."

Flare went rigid. Even so, her pupils dilated. She sat there, beautiful and unattainable.

Not for me. Not mine.

So be it. "Let us be honest about what this really is," I continued. "You're here. I'm here. We have our appetites. That's why I rutted with you during the lightning rain. That's why I knelt and tasted your cunt in the medical chamber. That's why I'm planning to make you come again. And when I do, trust me: You will know. Because your climax shall be deeper than this ocean, harder than the tide, and longer than my fucking patience. But it will not have anything to do with passion."

Revolted with myself, I diced her so-called truth to pieces. "*That* is what I feel for you."

Fucking now. If I didn't get out of this fucking chair now, I would lose the battle.

Taking advantage of her shock, I snatched Flare by the waist and deposited her on the opposite seat. Vaulting from my chair, I charged from the alcove. The downpour soaked my frame as I stalked to the ocean's edge, my vision blurring and my head about to spontaneously combust.

Yet I knew. Retreat wouldn't work. I could travel a thousand miles from here, and I would never be far enough. I would never stop feeling the brushfire of her presence.

Under the deluge, I stalled at the surf's edge. The water sliced over my boots. Bracing my hands on my hips, I stood there.

One. Two. Three.

I turned. There she came, charging toward me like a firebolt in that fucking gorgeous dress, with that fucking gorgeous glare. Flare's wet hair was plastered to her cheeks, the flower in her hair sagged, and her eyes blazed.

She looked freshly inflamed. Or freshly fucked.

Rough. Fast. Angry.

No. I could not escape her. In fact, nostalgia struck me as she stormed my way. How long had it been since we last feuded? We were overdue for an altercation.

"Jeryn!" she grated, getting in my face. "Talk to me!"

"We talked," I shouted through the tempest. "You were there."

"Admit you're lying! Admit there's more!"

"I can't!"

"Why?"

"Because—"

"Why?"

"Because I'm obsessed!" I bellowed, the rain and ocean rioting around us. "I'm obsessed with everything about you! How your hands are strong one minute and gentle the next. How they grip a weapon one moment, then brush the hair of your enemy in the same breadth. How the sunlight clings to your skin, your lips pinch when you're about to argue with me, your mouth lifts into a smile when you sleep. How you've endured hell for most of your life but look at this world as if it's made of a thousand colors others can't see. I'm obsessed with you when I shouldn't be—because of everything I've told you! I'm nothing but ice! And you're ..."

I gave the fuck up, the confession ripping from my throat. "You're the fucking sun."

Flare paused. Her features slackened, yet her eyes did something more damning. They shimmered like crushed gold.

Droplets sat on her eyelashes and drenched her gown. My shirt adhered to my chest. We stared at each other, soaked and raw from screaming.

"You're trapped here with a monster," I reminded her, my voice as gruff as limestone. "You see beauty in darkness. But here, darkness is your only option."

In any other circumstance, Flare would never choose me. How could she after everything I had done?

And that's how I would become your greatest regret.

I had said as much to bait her. Little had I known how correct I would become.

She did not deserve such a fate. She should not have to regret anything.

Least of all me.

I moved to walk away, to vacate the premises before she opened her cursed mouth. Otherwise, I would change my mind and start this mayhem all over again. But before I could stride in the opposite direction—to who the fuck knew where—the scalpel knife at my hip disappeared.

Like a pickpocket, Flare confiscated the only thing that would get me to launch at her. She bolted, taking my weapon hostage and racing with it to the ocean. On a hiss, I shot after her.

Wading through the surf, Flare extended her arm, fixing to toss it. Patience be damned. I sheared through the waves and snatched her wrist. Knee-deep, I whipped the woman around, cinched my free arm around her waist, and crushed her wet fucking body against mine. The tide crashed into us, rivulets of water spilling from my frame onto hers.

With a jolting motion, Flare tried to jerk away. Yet I squeezed until she grunted and surrendered the blade.

I released her wrist and caught the scalpel by the hilt. My free arm remained banded around her, squashing her body against me. We panted into one another. Her irises fired, then sank to my mouth and lurched back up. That small act had my cock jumping, rising to the point of agony.

I'd hauled Flare clear off the sandy floor. Her stomach pumped, slamming against my own.

A plea lit her countenance. A quieter flame.

Fuck me to hell. My mouth tilted closer to hers, my lower lip abutting her own. She inched nearer, curling herself into me.

Anarchy flooded my veins. With a gnash of my teeth, I let her go. She stumbled in place, a wave smacking her stunned profile. Wet and too tempting to withstand, she watched me with fury and need stringing across her face.

This vision, I had no right to. The obscene, monstrous, desperate ways in which I wanted to defile her would end us both.

Unwilling to trust myself, I sheathed the blade and bade a retreat. Stalking toward the beach, I did my best to shake off the residue of Flare's sopping body. But I could not ignore the heat of her words.

In my periphery, I caught sight of her mouth moving. Deliberately.

Violently. She knew I would see the accusation. More than that, she knew I would hear it.

"You're right," she dared. "You are a coward."

Fucking. Little. Beast.

With a growl, I pivoted the fuck around and shot back to her.

36

Flare

Like a battle and a victory, the villain prince strode across the sand with his features twisted, all brutal beauty and violent surrender. Every intention cluttered his face, as though we were about to commit a hundred counts of treason.

Jeryn's long limbs smashed through the waves. As he strode forward, his hand ripped out the scalpel knife and flicked open one of the blades.

Anticipation and triumph blasted through me. Butterflies broke from the cage of my stomach.

I could stand there and wait. Like captured prey, I could freeze up.

Instead, I whipped out my dagger and bolted toward him. Like adversaries racing into warfare, we shot toward one another, smashing through the high tide. I rammed into Jeryn at the same time he barreled into me.

With a snarl, the prince used his free hand to seize the back of my neck. "You fucking saboteur."

Then he hauled my mouth to his. And my heart exploded like dynamite.

As our lips slammed together, a volcanic sound blasted from my throat. Jeryn's mouth crushed against mine, his wet lips clamping, slanting us at a livid angle. A howl got stuck in my throat as I thrashed my mouth against his, the collision instinctive, as volatile as the waves.

Those ruthless lips wasted no time. Slicing his tongue across the seam of my mouth, Jeryn pried me open and drove inside with precision. I needed no coaxing. My own tongue dove for his, coldness and heat clashing.

The impact buckled my limbs and wracked his frame. Together, we shuddered into the kiss. Because oh fuck, we were kissing.

We were *kissing*.

Neither tender, nor exploratory, we threw ourselves into the tempest. With a destructive rhythm, Jeryn flexed his tongue into mine, whisking against every sensitive inch. I keened and rode that tongue, falling into cadence with him, the tempo ferocious.

Somewhere in this world, walls shattered, towers fell, and the rafters of a fortress collapsed. Someplace on this continent, hurricanes cracked mighty ships in half, sinking them to the bottom of an ocean. Somewhere, opposing forces raised weapons and unleashed bloodshed.

And nearby, the rainforest watched us. And around us, the water flailed.

This was how it felt to surrender and conquer. This was how it felt to kiss a villain.

Jeryn banded his arm around my middle, his digits choking the knife hilt. His unhampered palm rushed to my ass, spanned one cheek, and hoisted me into him. My feet left the ground, hovering inches off the ocean floor. The muscles of his arm bulged as he braced me, bearing my frame as though I weighed no more than a plume.

Still holding my dagger, I flung my free arm around the ramps of his shoulders. My fingers launched into his hair and groped the roots, pulling hard and harsh.

The prince seethed. His lips quaked against mine, and that greedy hand snatched my ass firmer, the reaction fueling me like timbers. He liked it rough.

Oh, but I knew rough, as I knew soft. I thrived off that jagged noise, as I thrived off gentler ones, and I could handle both.

We brandished weapons in one hand and clung with the other. With every thrust of our tongues, this kiss felt like fucking, and the fucking felt like fighting. Jeryn split my lips wide and pitched his tongue deeply, the force of it sizzling through my veins.

He groaned, the sound rippling through me and dropping between my thighs. He'd been right before. I'd grown wetter than the sea.

Our sodden clothes rustled together, thin and constrictive. I had loved this dress before, but now I hated it, as I hated Jeryn's shirt and pants. And the feeling intensified when the long ridge of his cock pushed into my clit.

Uttering an irate sound, Jeryn's fist surged to my scalp. Suffocating the knife hilt, he jammed his wrist against my head and fastened me to him, the better to lash his tongue with mine. He angled the blade's edge away from my skull, his towering frame resistant against the waves. And although I trusted him not to nick my skin, the ever-present risk sent a buzz through my system.

Then I knew. Whatever happened next wouldn't be safe or sweet. It had never been that way between us.

No, this would be daring and drastic. This would be beautifully feral. This wild night would be real and nowhere near a mistake.

Yet if we held tight, we'd make it through the tumult.

Jeryn kissed with every muscle, every bone in his body, and every ounce of blood. Trapping my head in place and locking his other hand to my ass, he ground his mouth into mine. As his kiss shoved into me, I shoved back. Each of us sought to dominate the other like a power play, all teeth and nails. The strong motions of his jaw loosened my own, and the deft whips of his tongue stoked my insides.

My body erupted. I pooled against him like candle wax and kissed him the fuck back.

Under the eventide sky and above the depths, I drowned in a new sort of darkness. One where the light shone clearer and brighter.

I wanted us stressed but determined. I wanted us to struggle and survive through it. I wanted us to deserve this, to revel in this, to steal this for all it was worth.

We inched back for an instant, merely long enough to swap positions, angling our heads in a different direction before raging back into the kiss. Fed up with everything we'd done and said, we shut one another up. With a deprived groan, Jeryn's hot mouth seized mine as though he'd been holding out for years, as though his patience had finally been tested to its limit.

I nicked his lower lip and skated my teeth across the line of flesh. Jeryn hissed with satisfaction, then skewered his incisors into the crook of my mouth. Shivers plied me from head to toe, and a needy whine curled from my throat.

His lips were sharp but smooth, holding the flavors of dark wine and darker blood. At some point, I must have drawn crimson, and he'd done the same, because I tasted droplets of our combined blood, as though we'd been kissing with fangs.

The tide slapped against us, and stars chipped into the sky, and celestial rain doused the remains of our clothes. All the while, we kissed frantically, his bloody tongue swiping with mine.

Each fit and tug of our mouths slickened my pussy until I couldn't tell the saltwater from my desire. The arm I'd slung over his shoulder quivered. How I managed to keep a hold of my dagger, I would never know. The rest of me had succumbed ages ago.

Yet it wasn't enough. I told Jeryn as much by whimpering into the kiss. Or maybe it came out as a grunt.

The prince obliged. With his other arm, he locked my ass in place and hefted me fully off the floor. Waves belted against us, adding to the momentum as I hooked my legs around his waist.

Splayed against him, I linked my ankles above his ass. Using the leverage, I burrowed down on Jeryn and snatched his mouth. He growled, lancing his tongue past my open lips, the pace carnal.

My spine crackled like kindling. A splintered moan skittered up my throat and filled the hot cave of Jeryn's mouth. He swallowed the sound without mercy, then strapped his lips around my tongue and sucked hard.

Chaos ensued. At the pressure of his mouth, my body liquified, and I turned into the ocean—a force of nature.

The moment he freed my tongue, I pleaded something dire. I had no idea what. Yet Jeryn responded with urgency, both of us vaulting backward and severing the kiss.

Heaving for air, we absorbed the effects from our swollen mouths, to the glaze in our eyes, to the disarray of our wet hair. This kiss hadn't sought a reconciliation. Rather, it had waged a passionate war.

This happened. We'd never be able to take it back.

We watched each other for a second, only a second, just a cursed second. Then I moved first, racing my dagger up his torso and shearing the shirt open, the clasps popping. The panels flapped apart, the expanse of his torso consuming my view. Rainfall scraped down his pecs, raced between his sloped hipbones, and vanished into the waistband. A grid of muscles contorted across his abdomen, a hot flush tinting his ivory skin, mine for the taking.

My eyes burned, spurring Jeryn to action. The instant his shirt flared apart, another tearing sound hit my ears. My skirt already possessed a slit, but his knife did extra damage, slicing the ancient fabric up to my waist. Shredded like a curtain, the skirt parted and fell around my limbs, enabling me to move without hindrance.

Except this prince wasn't done. Those eyes gripped mine, his pupils black and flashing with intent. With a fitful glare that had nothing to do with me and everything to do with that dainty barrier covering my pussy, Jeryn looped one digit around the gusset of my drawers. Fixing them in place, he flicked his fingers, the knife paring through the fabric.

I gasped as the material flopped apart. Mist hit my folds, the patch of hair glistening for his gaze.

Jeryn muttered under his breath, "Much better."

Then he cut more. The knife cleaved through the sides until the drawers fluttered from my body and hit the ocean. Waves caught the material and flung it out to the celestial sea, where it disappeared.

With the skirt open and my cunt bared, that left my bodice. Not giving Jeryn time to destroy the rest of the dress, I grabbed the edge and whipped it over my head. My breasts heaved into the night air, my nipples dark and puckering, the points aching.

The prince's irises glittered at the sight, then rose to my face. "You slay me."

I felt that confession in every place that mattered. My head and heart and body blazed to life, so that I went up in flames.

Jamming my dagger into the sheath at my thigh, I clasped his face and hauled his mouth back to mine. Jeryn crooned, punching my tongue with his own. My nipples swept against his chest, and his cock stretched higher, and our drenched skin seared into one another.

How I wanted his mouth to travel, to lick every inch of me. How I longed to blow open those pants and seal my folds around his cock. How I yearned to ride him in the midst of this turbulent, starlit sea.

But first, my parched tongue had other cravings. I squirmed until Jeryn caught on. With a hoarse groan, he pried his mouth from mine.

Before he could react, I scrambled from his grasp, my feet hitting the sandy bottom. Stealing his knife with one hand and planting my free palm against his chest, I steered him farther into the deep. Pushing him back to a cliffside fringed in leaves, I gave a shove.

Jeryn's back struck the stone, a masculine grunt skidding from his throat. Foliage shrouded the rough surface, offering him a cushion amid the chinks. As for the rest of it, this man could handle pain.

And good. Because he would need that perseverance for what came next. Holding his gaze, I pinned him against the rock and angled the weapon's tip at his throat. With our open mouths grazing and my tits squashed into plates of his torso, I traced the bulge in his throat. As we panted, the knife skimmed down to the ravine in his collarbones, then between his pecs.

Jeryn's eyes gleamed. He enjoyed the severity of it, the knowledge that I could make him bleed at any moment.

And truly, those orbs had never been clearer. Only this man could appear lucid, even while lost in a heady stupor.

My lips curled into a fiendish smile against his mouth. I leaned in, my bent elbow stabbing into the stone beside his head. Using the knife to caress his flesh, I ghosted around one perfect nipple, which hardened into a peek.

From there, I circled the crest, then dragged the knife's point across his pounding heart. If I cut there, would I discover skin or cement? Months ago, my answer would have been different.

Jeryn peered hotly, intently. Pressing the blade's tip into his flesh scoured him, a teardrop of crimson bloating to the surface. Lowering my head, I draped my tongue over the bead, lapping up the blood while a hum rumbled from his frame.

Instead of briny, the morsel tasted crisp. Swallowing, I coasted the weapon lower, to the bunched muscles of his abdomen. The descent was a bumpy one, the contours hard until smoothing out once more as I teased the weapon over the ledge of one hipbone—then pressed a little deeper. When a thin line of red appeared, Jeryn's teeth flashed. His mouth sought my own, but I veered out of reach, relishing his frustrated growl.

To make matters worse, I flitted my tongue vertically over his lips. This incited another coarse noise, his reaction drawing more arousal in the rift of my limbs.

As my weapon slid past those hipbones, things got more invigorating. Slanting the knife, I paused over the waistband and gave him a scorching look of inquiry.

Jeryn's inhales grew shallower. "Third switch on the hilt."

My thumb pressed the handle. The blade retracted while another flicked upright. Polished and curved, it would sunder greater obstacles.

The prince's exhales quickened. He expected me to stay upright and on my feet.

I pulverized those assumptions to smithereens. In one fluid motion, I flipped his weapon in my fingers and plummeted to my knees.

Jeryn's face slackened. His intake of breath sliced through the air, the sound tickling my ears. Despite the fervor around us, that noise eclipsed every crash of the tide against the breakers.

He gazed down at me, his features bewitched. And maybe a bit daunted, fearing how much he could withstand. Also doubtful I'd be merciful. Yet he remained fastened to the cliffside, obeying my unspoken command.

Don't move, Your Highness.

His eyelids hooded, irises glinting under a half-mast gaze. Ever the purposeful villain, he reached overhead and twined his wrists around a pair of vines, then grabbed the cords.

Good man. Disciplined man.

My stare praised him for that move. Power stoked my blood, because it also meant he couldn't trust himself to stay composed without restraints. Winter expected me to smash through those defenses, aware that dealing with Summer required stamina.

With me, this man had high expectations. With me, his patience would be exhausted.

Jeryn could have insisted I didn't have to do this. But he knew, and I knew. I'd never been subservient, never been fragile, and never did anything I didn't want to. I wasn't kneeling to pay him back for the medical chamber, nor was I doing this simply to please him.

I was doing it for me. Because I craved it.

This Royal went pliant, placing himself at my behest despite the risk of breaking down. That alone set my soul on fire.

Although the surf whipped about, this recess provided shelter from the ocean. The starlit eddies were calmer here, enabling me to stoop without getting slapped by waves. Water sloshed over my thighs, painting me in the constellations that swam on its surface, as though they'd landed there. The sand sank under my weight, and salt-spray misted the hulls of my breasts.

As I licked my lips, Jeryn's cock lifted, the shape and size of him straining through the pants. His pupils expanded like bottomless wells, my reflection filling them, as though I were floating inside them.

Floating. Not sinking.

I liked being there. I longed to be everywhere on him, to imprint myself on his flesh so he would never forget this.

The slab of his chest hitched, the muscles contracting like marble. On display, this glorious monster belonged to me.

First, I sampled the blood from his hipbone, sweeping my tongue across the incline. His nostrils flared as he watched me lick the crimson from his skin. The saltwater must sting him, but he showed no sign of caring. Rather, a different kind of suffering consumed his expression.

My eager fingers burned as I raised the knife to the closures of his pants. Glimpsing Jeryn's rapt features, I snipped open the clasps, the blade's edge plucking at each one. More sharp intakes followed from above, each one stoking my confidence.

The flaps opened, and his cock sprang free, and my body burst into flames. My imagination had been generous. Yet nothing compared to this authentic vision.

That long, hard, wet cock thickened under my gaze. Tall and firm, its height was greater than I'd pictured, the column ruddy and the crown even darker. A tight slit cut across the peak, where a pearl of liquid rose. The whole gorgeous thing looked sinful, from the feverish hue, to the distended veins, to the heavy sac between his thighs.

Thirst overwhelmed my senses. His cock could fill me to the brim. Soon enough, it would. And it wouldn't end until the tide ebbed. But first, I descended into a forbidden, real-life fantasy where an evil prince succumbed to my touch.

A delirious combination of fury and excitement whetted my appetite. If he wouldn't admit there was more, I'd get him to shout it. I would get him to bellow this truth until it became so loud, it drowned out the ocean.

Jeryn clenched the vines, forcing himself to remain still. Those eyes clung to my features, absorbing my reaction. Pinned against the cliff, he drew oxygen into his lungs and waited for my appraisal.

Craning my neck and meeting his eyes, I fanned out my skirt to show him what I thought of his cock. Braced with my thighs wide, I exposed myself. From the intimate swatch of hair, my clit jutted forward, and the pleat of my body leaked.

A choked noise ripped from Jeryn's throat, the vines pulling taut.

He liked what he saw.

Pleased, I skated his blade over the head of his cock. While I drew the point faintly along the slit, the bridge of his length twitched, and more liquid beaded to the surface. Like this, I sketched his flesh, tracing him lightly from the roof to the base, the way I would draw a symbol in the sand.

Jeryn's mouth opened. Even then, he didn't move.

At last, I withdrew the weapon. Boosting myself, I wedged the hilt between his teeth and nodded my encouragement as he clamped on, trapping the knife between his ivories. This way, he would have something to bite down on.

Then I dipped my head and followed the weapon's previous trail. Only this time, I did so with my lips.

After being denied his taste for too long, I hunkered to the shore and grabbed the taut muscles of his ass. Then I draped my tongue against the seat of his cock and gave him a single, unbroken lick.

Jeryn's body tensed. A frayed noise shook from his chest.

"Oh fuck," he grated around the handle.

From the sac to the crown, I drizzled the point of my tongue across his flesh. Then I passed over the slit, collecting his arousal, the essence dissolving on my palate.

Still, he did not move.

Never had I done this with a man. Yet with this Royal, the impulses came as naturally as breathing. As a wanderer, I knew how to search and find. I would locate every devastating sound he was capable of making.

With an eager sigh, I lapped back and forth over the head, each swipe pulling on his voice. Moans skewered from him, the baritone deeper and richer and harsher. Emboldened, I swirled my tongue around the pome and swabbed more cum from the line in his cock.

The length stiffened further, elevating to his hips. I dashed my tongue up and down the column, flicking his sac and gliding back to the top. Over and over, I did this, sampling every broad inch.

Until it wasn't enough. And so I strapped my lips around the crown and sucked.

Despite the hilt jammed into his mouth, Jeryn's hiss cut through the tempest. The vines snapped as he braced against them and watched me through a mess of slate blue hair.

Spurred on by his gaze, I sealed my mouth around the stem and bowed my head toward the base. His flesh filled my mouth, and I rolled my lips back up, then down again. Uninterested in pacing or prolonging the sensations, I bobbed into it, siphoning his bare cock.

Jeryn's growls quickened. His joints shook, and his skin warmed against my tongue, pellets of arousal dripping down my tongue. He held fast while I pumped, tugging and dragging on him.

I sighed around the crown, the reverberation causing him to buck once, the vibration rushing across his flesh. All the while, my clit throbbed. By some miracle, I felt what he felt, the onslaught agonizing.

One free hand dove between my thighs. The instant it did, Jeryn hummed.

He gazed in rapture, his cock widening in my mouth. Cinched around him, I flexed my tongue repeatedly across his slit and continued rowing my head. Matching that rhythm, I spread my folds and pitched my fingers high, probing with slick motions.

Overwhelmed by the wet friction and the heat of his cock, I curled my toes into the sand. I yanked his ass closer and hauled him deeper, draining him of every noise in existence.

And finally, my teeth nicked his skin. And then he moved.

His spine arched into the cliff, he flung his head back, and another word launched from his chest. With the knife blocking his voice, only pieces of the word came out audibly.

Yet I heard him. And my heart leaped into the ether.

Withdrawing from my pussy, I clutched his backside and sucked him into me. My elated cry rushed across his skin, urging him to say it again.

Jeryn hollered in tempo to my mouth, but the word got lost. And although I wanted him to spill all that pleasure down my throat, I also longed to hear that word, and I yearned for even more. Always so much more.

Jeryn spit out the knife, setting the word loose. "Flare!" he bellowed into the sky.

Puckering my lips, I gave another healthy tug. And another. And another. The villain prince continued to shout as I yanked those violent sounds to the forefront.

And the world went wild. And we went wild alongside it.

37

Flare

Releasing his cock, I burdened him with another lick and spoke against the crown, "Even your pleasure tastes cruel." And he moved again. Ripping his arms from the vines, Jeryn vaulted off the facade, snatched his weapon from the sea, and rammed it into the sheath. Then he grabbed my arms and hoisted me off the ocean floor before I could finish him off.

I moved in sync, stringing my legs around his waist as he crushed me against him, my thighs flanking his cock. The rigid muscles of his body welded me to him, all that skin and sinew flush against my own. His pale complexion flexed in stark contrast to my olive one, a combination lovely to behold. Yet he was darkness, and I was lightness, and we balanced one another.

Despite his bulk, never once had I felt small while encased in his grasp. Whenever this man held me, he made me feel larger than life. And even more than the rainforest, I sensed our fate. We'd been destined for this moment.

You're the fucking sun.

Yes. That was it.

I'm nothing but ice.

Except I'd grown to like ice.

Jeryn's arm linked beneath my ass, while the other hand cupped the back of my head, securing me to his frame. Our mouths panted against one another. I splayed my fingers across the bracket of his jaw and rushed my lips over his.

"Let me feel what ice is like." Tilting my head, I nipped his earlobe. "Smooth." Then I licked the cleft of his chin. "Solid." And I quested my mouth down the side of his throat, to where his vocal cords rested. "Sharp."

The prince shuddered, his fingers digging into my scalp and backside. I dined on his neck, sucking on his pulse until it sped up.

Muttering a primitive sound, Jeryn clamped the sides of my face and jerked my face up to his. Our wet hair tangled, the strands plastering to our profiles. Those eyes froze on me, brilliant and stinging. He could pierce an enemy through with those orbs.

As a fiend, he used to glare for hateful reasons. Now that expression reflected different emotions, a blend of aggression and ardency. Glaring hotly at me, Jeryn's pupils fattened, threatening to eclipse the crystal of his irises.

He took his turn, assaulting my ear and scraping his teeth over the rim. Blood rushed through my limbs and oozed from my core. Tucking his brutal mouth behind the shell, the prince dabbed his tongue into the crevice, ecstasy pouring through me like black silk.

Smooth.

But not tender. No, the swipe of his tongue was assertive.

Next, he drew my earlobe between those teeth and wrapped his mouth around the slender flesh. With a croon, Jeryn's lips strapped on and sucked. An influx of shivers plunged down my spine, only these chills were dense.

Solid.

The prince released my lobe. He sliced his incisors down the center of my throat, then across my collarbones, then down the knob of my shoulder. The trail left flurries in its wake, bliss and frustration scattering to the edges of my being. Gasps tumbled from my mouth, and my fingernails bit into his skull, and my cunt gyrated against his cock.

Sharp.

Seething, Jeryn withdrew. His ravenous face leveled with mine, fixing on my features for a moment. Then he steered my head back, urging me into an arch. This pushed my breasts into his torso and my stomach into his ribs. As the tide whipped against the shore, I suspended myself above the tumult, my hair dangling like seaweed.

For leverage, my fingers latched onto the nape of his neck. Though, I wouldn't slip or fall. Not with him there.

Even if I did, I knew how to swim. And I knew how to survive the drop.

With my body extended and on wet display, the prince paused. Hyperawareness sensed his eyes roving across every inch, his stare sinking to the marrow of my bones.

The moment lasted an instant before the prince's mouth lowered. Heat enveloped my nipple as his lips closed around the bud, the peak of his tongue licking me raw. I reeled farther back, a cry launching from my lungs. My lips parted, hanging ajar as more whines dashed into the air.

Jeryn groaned around the nipple and seized it harder, toughening it into a rock. Then he unleashed, kissing my breast the way he'd kissed my mouth. Disjointed moans streamed from my throat, each one splintering into the night.

My pussy leaked onto his cock, which rose from the loose panels of his pants. The waistband slumped, his ass materializing from the fabric. I knew because my heels were digging into the tight swells, shoving the garment farther down.

Jeryn made an icy noise. As if drained of air, he abandoned the nipple, cupped the opposite breast, and husked into the other disk. The pleasure chipped me to pieces, my whimpers growing choppy.

This man laid siege to my body as though intending to hoard every inch. Such an entitled prince. Such a manipulative man. Yet if he stopped, I would declare war.

Finally, his mouth relaxed from around the nipple. Inching back, he muttered against the peak, "I'm going to fuck you until we break."

His promise fired through my veins. I'd been prepared for that since this night began—and even before then, from the moment he reached for me in a panic. What's more, the prince's vow caused my stomach to flip, anticipation tingling my spine. That, and pride.

This ruler had the world at his feet, but no one had ever warmed his bed. His whole life, he hadn't requested a lover, hadn't summoned a courtesan to his suite, hadn't taken a partner.

Yet of all the people who worshiped and feared him, Winter wanted me. He had knelt to taste me, then restrained himself to be tasted back, and now he gazed at my features as though his life depended on it. More than lust, passion stared back.

This, I understood. Sick with desire, fed up with waiting, he didn't care to be patient any longer, and I didn't want to deny what I needed, and we didn't bother regretting this.

It wouldn't be gentle or slow. It would be chaotic. It would deplete us.

I would let this villain fuck me in the darkness. And I would fuck him back until the rising sun blasted us with light.

I nodded and spread my legs around his hips. My ankles linked above his ass, the ovals fully visible over the waistline. I'd thrust the pants as far as they would go without sliding down, the better to admire the firm divots and profile of his backside. The silhouette was as taut as the rest of him, including the high column of his erection.

It stood firm and flushed. The cap was broad, the width so thick my hand would struggle to encase him.

Astride his waist, I wiggled closer. My damp thighs fanned outward, my pussy bracing against the hard stem. I lifted myself, ready to span around his cock, to capture the tip between my legs.

To help him.

But the villain prince uttered an offended noise. "I'm a virgin," he hissed. "Not a saint." He palmed my ass and jerked me into him, his heavy cock primed at my entrance. "I'm also a doctor." His mouth sliced a path across mine. "I know where the fuck to go."

In trying to assist, I may as well have called him an amateur. Nonetheless, I purred, "Prove it."

At the challenge, Jeryn's expression turned critical. The sight entrapped me, so that I didn't notice his hips swing back until the last instant. Then his waist lashed upward. And in one fluid motion, the hot length of his cock thrust between my folds.

I died a thousand deaths. A cry broke from my lungs. On impact, my frame jolted and hunched into him.

A groan quaked from Jeryn's throat, the seismic noise traveling across his body. From the crown to the sac, every inch of his cock filled me to the brink, slick yet hard as metal. Its girth opened my pussy, splaying my limbs farther, my knees hiking at a greater angle.

Hell. Fire.

Our slack mouths hung open, our exhalations dashing against one another. Shackled like this, we peered at each other, overwhelmed by the sensation of his cock poised inside me. This instant when fantasy became reality.

The prince's shape alone caused my lashes to flutter, the barest motion, the briefest friction sending a quick lurch of heat to the cleft of my thighs. In reflex, my cunt gripped him tighter. And in response, an aggrieved noise churned from Jeryn's mouth.

Suspended, we fought to recover ourselves, the last few seconds threatening to drain us. However, we'd never been a delicate pair. We knew agony, and even though this was unlike anything I'd felt before, it didn't take long for me to adapt. Nor him.

Swapping one more dark look, we flung ourselves into one another. Jeryn trapped my ass and slung his cock wholly out of me, then pitched back into my slit.

Then again. And again. And hellfire, again.

The buildup over and done with, the prince swiped his hips, his ass jutting between my thighs and splitting them apart. Heat shot through my blood. Pained whines fled my tongue, each one in tempo to the lashes of his cock.

Keeping his gaze on me, Jeryn's features narrowed, furious concentration stringing across his features. With precision, he fixated on my reactions, using them to guide him. He angled his crown and pistoned, his buttocks working into me, the strength of his cock inciting mayhem.

Helpless, I let my forehead drop against his own. This close, our pupils fastened, challenging one another, demanding to see who outlasted the other. As though we were still adversaries, we pressed into each other while his hips struck between my thighs.

Stunned noises rushed into the air between us. Quickly, the muscles of my body expanded to accommodate his width, sealing around his flesh and sucking him deeply. Repeatedly, tirelessly, I crushed his roots in my fingers and rode his waist.

Our gazes tipped downward. Together, we watched our drenched bodies slapping, my cunt astride his cock, his crown pumping into my crease, his sac hitting my skin, and how my arousal smeared him.

Driven by the sight, Jeryn accentuated his movements, slinging his cock harder, faster. My whimpers launched into the heavens. The world blackened at the edges, all but the pulse of the whipping waves. I became nothing but sound and sensation. Because of that, I became everything.

I'd only ever been taken in the dark. But tonight, constellations swam in the ocean, illuminating the eventide so that I saw everything. I beheld what it looked like when someone pleasured me, what the grind of his waist did to my own, and how a deep flush burned across my skin.

My breasts jostled, my hips linked with his, and my body vaulted upward. The rhythmic snatch of Jeryn's waist soaked me anew, my pussy widening for him, gripping and releasing his erection. We viewed all of this.

Then we watched as I charged into motion with him. Invigorated, I hefted myself up and down, matching his cadence. Linking my calves firmer around his ass and hooking my fingers to his nape, I used the momentum to bounce atop his cock. I raised and lowered myself in succession, my folds cinching Jeryn to the seat.

His eyes flashed, those controlled features slipping as I exaggerated the motions. I wanted to see his breakdown, to cause his downfall, to breach the final barrier.

In tandem, Jeryn whisked his body into mine, possessive and punishing. I attacked in kind, synching my body with his, waists slamming, hips beating.

Time and space vanished. Summer and Winter ceased to exist.

Our groans grew heavier and hotter and harsher. As one, we turned into wild creatures living in a wild land, each of us competing to overcome the other, to claim the other. We fucked the same way we'd shouted and crossed blades—hard and rough and livid.

But no longer hateful. Not that. Never again.

Fire licked up my spine. My cries multiplied and grew sharper, while Jeryn's growls became huskier, angrier.

An eternity passed, with neither of us lagging. Every second provoked us more and more and more. Like a drifter and a pursuer, we sought one another's weak spots and our hidden spots.

Never mind how the prince managed to bolster my weight for this long. The stamina of his cock was nothing short of excruciating. With measured jabs, the brunt of Jeryn's waist pitched me high.

I swiveled my hips, my pussy and his cock crashing together. With rivulets streaming down my skin, I galloped on him, rowing back and forth. The pleasure crested, nirvana approaching. I keened, racing after that crescendo, fearing its end.

I screamed into the sea, "More!"

"How much more?" Jeryn gritted, then flung his cock deeper. "This much?"

He siphoned higher, the tip of his cock striking a tight place that split me in half. My thighs flayed wider, and my cunt opened wider, and my mouth fell wider. "Oh!"

"Louder," he hissed. "Louder, my little beast."

That, I could do. With him, I could make noise that shot across continents.

I let loose in every way. Barreling forth, I bucked my hips into his, shoving his cock deeper and higher, my walls flooding Jeryn.

His head craned back, the better to see my expression while our hips smashed into one another. The prince's growls overlapped with my moans. Seizing my waist, he bobbed me above his standing cock, the head parting my walls on each descent, inciting a flurry of prickles down my skin.

We could die from this. The pleasure was so intense, we might burst and scatter across the sea. Yet I didn't stop, wouldn't stop, couldn't stop.

Don't you dare stop.

Though, I couldn't tell if I was warning myself or commanding him. Either way, it didn't matter, because nothing else mattered right then. And maybe nothing else ever would outside this ocean or beyond this rainforest.

But to make sure, I thrust down on Jeryn's cock and vented against his mouth, "Was it a mistake?"

He rasped, the response strangled.

I flexed my pussy, seizing around him. "Was it?"

Again Jeryn hissed, the reply getting lost in his throat.

Yearning to dislodge the answer, I rushed my waist into his. The bud of my clit slid against the stem of his erection as I wrapped myself around him, locking him down. Yet this man didn't seek escape. Instead, he looped one palm over my shoulder and hauled his cock upward, plying my folds with quick jabs.

I shouted, my head tipping back. Then the rest of me tipped back from the onslaught, my fingers fisting the roots of his hair for balance. Anchored, I held on for fate's sake.

Wave after wave drove across the shore. New stars floated before my eyes, these ones brighter and fiercer.

Bowing backward, I sprinted my hips with Jeryn's. He braced me, both hands ensnaring my shoulders, the position granting him deeper access. Just so, he threw his waist forward, fucking deftly into me, each pass synching with my plaintive cries.

I clamped onto his length, my muscles contracting around him, the pleasure mounting. Our sodden hips surged into swifter motion, hammering together. My moans scattered across the cove, and Jeryn's growls escalated into bellows, his baritone losing control along with the rest of him.

I could sink into that sound, plunge into the darkness. Based on the disorder coming from the prince's mouth, he would plummet with me.

The intimate flesh of my cunt constricted. Pleasure coiled there, the pressure building as this prince fucked me so good, so long, so much. Any moment, I might pass out.

He'd been right. This man knew where the fuck to go.

I clung to him and shouted, my thighs shaking, my hips racing to that precipice. Jeryn met that vigor with his own. He put his entire frame into it, his cock lashing, prying me open, drenching me.

His muscles quaked with the effort, that toned body flexing. The moment his cock pulsated, I straightened and aligned myself with him, unwilling to look away, to miss the sight of him coming.

His features remained fixed on me. And I realized. He was holding back, urging me to climax first.

But no. We would do this as equals.

With a hectic moan, I framed his ass and circled my waist, my pussy cinching his cock in a vise grip. Jeryn understood. Then he whipped into me at a breakneck pace, hitting a rapturous spot, tormenting me at a brutal angle.

As we watched each other, the tension spiraled, spiraled, spiraled. Then we paused. Then we collided. The pleasure unraveled in furious waves, an influx of heat releasing through my blood, from the peak of my clit to my deepest core.

A long suffering cry tore from me. At the same time, Jeryn's features twisted with agony as he roared. I crushed my open mouth against his, the better to feel the tremors of his mouth, the better to taste his breath as he came.

My pussy convulsed around Jeryn's cock, which spasmed and released a stream of hot fluid. Our private muscles clenched one another, and our limbs fused, and our doused bodies shook. We came loudly and endlessly and primally.

The aftershocks went on until the rain stopped and the tide ebbed.

Only then did I crumple into Jeryn's arms, boneless and woozy. My lungs and heart struggled to calm down, warm eddies swimming through me.

His own pulse pounded like a fist. With his cock still hard and hot inside me, the prince anchored one arm under my backside and dove his free fingers into my hair, cradling me to him as we fought to calm ourselves.

At last, I lifted my gaze. A pair of black pupils stared back, their gleam intentional.

"Again," he growled.

My insides somersaulted. Although this wasn't my first time, I hadn't been prepared. Divine Seasons, I would never have been prepared for anything like this.

I relished the shape and size of his cock pelting between my folds, his body fitting so well to my own. Tilting my head, I slid a lock of hair behind Jeryn's ear and repeated, "Was it a mistake?"

Then and now. Was it?

Jeryn tightened his hold on me. Finally, the walls toppled. "No."

I closed my eyes, storing the word in a crevice of my heart. "Then tell me how you feel about me."

After a spell, I opened my eyes to find Jeryn shaking his head. "I do not know how."

My heart winced. He didn't know how to express anything like this, anything beyond his experience. Aside from familial affection, he'd only know cruelty and coldness. But no passion or desire.

Yet despite the angry sex, this had meant more.

My breathless lips parted. I opened my mouth to say as much when Jeryn stiffened. "What the fuck?"

With our clothes shredded and our bodies still attached, the prince tapered his gaze on something in the distance. Flummoxed, I twisted in that direction.

Through the mist, a small ship was moored to one of the adjoining coves, the quarter deck visible from here. But although cliffs and trees blocked the vessel's figurehead, I spotted the most important part.

Flapping from the mizzen mast was a bronze flag, the cloth lacking an emblem to identify itself.

Not that it needed to. This also explained why Jeryn hadn't sounded alarmed, because he'd drawn the same conclusion.

The unmarked flag meant this ship had come in secret. And the brown color meant only one Season.

"Autumn," I whispered.

38

Jeryn

With Flare's cunt still encasing my cock, I scarcely had time to process this turn of events. Not three seconds into the aftershocks, I might have called the view a hallucination wrought from making her come. Perhaps the vision of her glowing eyes, flushed cheeks, and moaning mouth had intoxicated me. Merely looking at her was enough to inebriate my system, to say nothing of bringing her to orgasm.

Except where my body had been spilling into Flare moments ago, clarity returned. It slapped me across the face as my little beast squirmed in my arms. Despite my desire to grip her tighter, to fuck her in a dozen various ways, the other half of my reflexes did as she bade and released her.

The soaked muscles of Flare's pussy slipped from around my dick, the hasty movements causing me to groan. Painful. Mournful. At the disruptive noise, she halted. Eyes shimmering, she grabbed my face and dropped a quick kiss on my lips, denying me the chance to snatch her mouth and reciprocate. A disgruntled growl scrolled from my throat, to which she chuckled.

Swinging her head toward the ship and then back to me, Flare patted my shoulders, urging me to make haste. She scrambled down my torso like a crustacean, her feet hitting the surf, seawater splashing around her ankles. Yet it was the vision of her dusky nipples and glistening vagina that triggered the lucid side of my brain.

I broke from my stupor. We launched into motion.

The slit in her skirt left no part of Flare's anatomy to the imagination. As for the bodice, the ocean had swallowed it whole like a delicacy. Under no circumstances would anyone be permitted to see her disrobed.

This visual was mine.

Although Flare had sliced open the clasps of my shirt, it was better than nothing. After sealing the flaps of my pants, I peeled off the sopping garment and tossed it her way.

Flare caught the fabric and threw her arms into the oversized sleeves. Because she'd severed the closures, the resourceful female used her dagger to slice horizontal incisions down the center, enabling her to tie the front shut. Then she rolled the cuffs up her forearms, the hem hanging to her knees.

However, the skirt was a lost cause. With the slit ascending to her waist and displaying every glorious attribute between her hips, Flare hopped out of the garment, letting it puddle to the sand. At which point, my lungs drained.

Her, in my wet shirt. Her, with that mussed hair. Her, newly fucked.

This view. Also mine.

Frantic, the gorgeous little beast draped her skirt across the chair where we'd feasted. Together, we raced from the cove and through the caves.

This could be a trap. It could be an ambush. Except such logic did not add up. Summer and Winter would charge into the forest, intent on locating me and apprehending Flare. Neither court would need to disguise itself.

Even if that were the case, neither court would know what appropriate—and effective—disguise to wear. Nor would they present themselves as Autumn. This much at least, I had concluded upon sighting the ship. Otherwise, I'd have thrown Flare over my shoulder and vacated the cove at the first hint of danger.

The occupants of that ship were clear. The reality hit me slowly, then expediently.

Regardless, I would not take chances where Flare was concerned. I seized the beast's fingers and maneuvered ahead of her, with the knife harnessed to my hip.

Returning to the ruins, we sprinted up the stairs. Across the halls. Past the vestibule. Through the stone doors. At the landing, we stalled in our tracks.

Two figures stood on the bridge, on the fortress's end. With their backs turned, they marveled at the ancient platform and the leviathan skeleton resting on the lake floor. The man towered behind the woman, with his arms secured around her middle.

The tall male with a dark shag of hair wore what could only be described as insolent attire. Snug boots with intricate pleating, lightweight pants dyed in demon-black, and a shirt of the same shade, fitted to accentuate his muscled physique. At least, he'd been wise to forgo the customary leathers and heavily accessorized trimmings, but while the closed footwear and breathable textiles made sense, his choice of color would do him no favors in the sun tomorrow. Not that he would ever give a fashionable shit.

The slender female attached to him was outfitted in a khaki linen jumpsuit. A herringbone pattern accented the bodice and ran down the sides of her pants, and long sleeves protected the woman's arms. As always, understated elegance combined with practicality.

A stack of mismatched bracelets encircled the man's wrist. The scarlet ribbon in particular caught my eye, which matched the one ornamenting the woman's hand beneath her cinched wrist sleeves. I'd seen this pair wearing such cords on prior occasions.

Two other facets identified them. Red hair plaited into a loose braid. Two verdant irises that gleamed like mischief itself when the couple twisted our way.

Having heard the doors creek open, they stared. Amazement. Astonishment. Both reactions carved into their features, one face as sharp as a thorn, the other cut like a diamond.

Briar. Poet.

Princess. Jester.

At my side, Flare sucked in a breath. In unison, a similar noise ejected from Briar. The little beast leaped down the steps, the hem of my shirt flapping around her naked limbs. At the same time, Briar launched into a run.

The women vaulted toward each other. With joyous cries—one audible to the world, the other not—they crashed together. Flinging their arms around one another, the females clutched and rocked from side to side, their bodies shaking with elation and relief.

From behind the spectacle, Poet observed with a tilt to his lips. Amusement brightened the jester's eyes, the lashes lined in black kohl.

My woman was the first to pull away. She cradled Briar's face and planted a sequence of kisses on the princess's freckled cheeks. In turn, the princess unleashed a teary laugh and inched back to comb through Flare's hair.

"Finally," Briar exclaimed. "Did you miss us?"

"Come now, my wifely thorn," Poet's satin voice interrupted as he sauntered toward them. "Don't you know? Everyone misses us."

Predictable. Pompous.

That shirt hung open to his navel, revealing a sculpted torso. Once a vain fucker, always a vain fucker. Beyond that, the word *wifely* elicited a memory.

My gaze clicked once more toward the scarlet ribbons. The ends of Briar's ribbon hung longer, evidence that it had once belonged to Poet. Whereas the tips of his own bracelet dangled shorter, proving it had previously graced the princess's arm.

They had swapped. The sight, along with Poet's endearment, reminded me of news that had traveled across the continent before I'd traveled to Summer. Poet and Briar had gotten married in private, then celebrated later with their family and the kingdom.

"Well?" The jester opened his arms to Flare. "What are you waiting for, sweeting?"

As Flare whirled to embrace Poet, a barbaric noise sliced across my tongue, too low for them to hear. Nonetheless, the little beast skipped backward and shook her head, delivering the same question I'd been thinking.

She uttered a word that came out inaudible to them. A one-syllable inquiry the jester and princess could nonetheless read. "How?"

How were they here? How had they found us?

Yet the beast seemed expectant, hardly surprised when Briar grinned. "We had help," she explained, indicating a red butterfly perched on the bridge's rim.

The creature had been stationed there, but now it sprang into the air and landed on Flare's crooked finger. Another member of her fauna pack, I concluded.

Delighted, the beast stroked the butterfly's wings. "Thank you, my friend."

Thank you. As in, the creature had done her a favor.

My eyes narrowed. Every Season had its fauna messengers. Summer relied on the generosity of butterflies, among certain marine species.

At some point while here, Flare had contacted Poet and Briar. Given how long it would have taken for the fauna to reach Autumn, then for the jester and princess to act, Flare's missive must have been dispatched prior to ... everything that had happened.

The butterfly flapped into the trees, its red wings vanishing into the thicket. It must have led our guests here. Across the sea, through the rainforest, into the cave tunnels, and to the ruins.

My attention slid back to Flare. She hadn't told me about her missive to Poet and Briar. Not that I could blame her. Only recently had Flare trusted me enough to reveal her belief about finding a key in this realm, an indication of her purpose for born souls.

But while I understood her reasoning, I stalked down the steps at a languid pace, my voice wry. "You have explaining to do, Little Beast."

The levity from seconds ago died. The trio spun my way, only one of them looking pleased. Flare's teeth flashed into a brilliant smile, her eyes sparkling like melted suns.

As for the revolutionaries beside her, I encountered a different reaction.

Briar's eyes widened. Her hand flew to one of those projectiles she favored as weapons—thorn quills, one of which materialized from a hidden location amid her clothing.

Poet's orbs flashed with rancor. With a lethal hiss, he maneuvered in front of the women, ignoring Flare's protest. In a series of rapid-fire movements, the staff I hadn't noticed until now cut across his fingers, the murder weapon flipping in a sequence meant to eradicate its opponent.

Then the staff froze, its tip aimed at my cranium, though I did not flinch. Notwithstanding his protective instincts regarding Flare—the only tolerable characteristic about him—did I still hate this parasite?

"What have we here?" the jester drawled. "'Tis an unwelcome bystander."

Yes. I fucking did.

"Jeryn of Winter," he mused with fatal calm. "The prince who's so fucking smart, it's made him fucking stupid."

"Poet," I greeted with mock civility. "It's unfortunate to see you again."

"Likewise." He raised an eyebrow. "I take it, cruelty is still your specialty."

A verse. Two minutes. The bastard had been here only two minutes, and already his tongue had taken to spewing frivolous shit.

As for cruelty, I gave him a flat look. "Fortunately for you, I have no current interest in causing pain."

Poet appraised my sun-bleached pants. "Then you should have worn something else." Nudging the fabric, he murmured in a tone equal parts seductive and deadly, "Of course, I could change this color to red. It would be a pleasure."

With the staff poised in his grip, his muscles flexed like rocks. Moreover, the jester's wrathful expression made it plain. If the rod didn't crack open my head, the dagger stashed in his boot would impale my stomach.

I had fought at this man's side during Autumn's castle blackout. I knew his skills, from a mastery of artifice and sin to a capacity for violence.

This threat, I had anticipated. I gave the pair a deadpan look that illustrated a crucial fact: I hadn't reached for my scalpel knife.

At length, my unwillingness to brace the weapon tethered to my hip registered on them. That, and my state of undress, which mirrored Flare's.

Momentary confusion wrestled across their features. Only then did they notice pivotal details. My torn shirt haphazardly concealing Flare's nudity. The rumpled brown waves sweeping her shoulders, as though she'd walked through a tornado. Her naked legs, my low slung pants and exposed torso, the bite marks on our skin, the red stains where I'd sucked on Flare's throat.

To the outside observer, we'd either been fucking or fighting. Though, whether it had been consensual or involuntary was the next unanswered question for this couple. And since they'd witnessed how I had treated Flare in Autumn, the jester and princess drew a false but fair conclusion.

Fuck.

With a furious growl, the jester charged.

I had known he could move fast, yet I hadn't given the man sufficient credit. He launched with the speed and strength of a panther. But before I could block his staff with my fist, Flare got there first. And before I could shove her out of harm's way, lest the staff should clip her by accident, her fingers seized the weapon mid-strike.

The jester's rod halted inches from my skull. The force of Flare's grip jolted Poet in place. Despite her size, she was strong. And despite the velocity of his attack, the man had registered her intervention in time, his serpentine reflexes stalling at the same moment.

Flare rushed between us. Holding up her palms, she blocked Poet and Briar from me, urging back the jester's weapon, albeit marginally.

"Don't!" she rushed out, although they couldn't understand her verbally. "It's alright. He's my ..."

My inhalations seized up. What would she say?

Yet she didn't need to articulate a thing. Although the jester and princess failed to comprehend her words, Flare's gesture and its implication penetrated. We watched them connect the pieces, from our disheveled state to the absence of clothing.

Poet came from the promiscuous court of Spring and had a profligate history. Neither of these applied to Briar, however she was married to this man, and they were rarely seen with their hands off each other. Of all couples, these exemplars knew sex when they saw it. Albeit belatedly, they also knew when the desire was reciprocated.

They also knew Flare. The sated blush painting her face spoke volumes.

As for me, whatever evidence stretched across my visage as they caught me gazing at Flare altered their stances. Their heads flipped between us, surveying with fresh eyes. Old wounds. New wounds. A scar had formed on my bicep, courtesy of an unclassified spider as massive as a fucking horse. Flare had a similar blemish on her lower back, in addition to scars made by talons and tusks.

The astute jester and princess also knew survival when they saw it.

Poet's features sharpened. "Wicked hell."

Disbelief pinched Briar's countenance. "It cannot be." She veered toward Flare, checking the woman from head to toe for injuries or signs of duress. "You and him. On purpose?"

Flare peeked at me. I hardly gave a shit what the jester and princess thought, but the unfathomable look on the beast's face escalated my blood pressure. Minutes ago, she'd been coming around my cock. To say the least, we hadn't been afforded time to figure out where we went from here.

Yet those eyes gleamed. Willing. Voluntary. She twisted toward Briar and nodded with a small smile.

A typhoon of air emptied from my lungs. I wanted to snatch her. I wanted her back in that ocean. I wanted to kiss the living fuck out of her. Yet I had no right to feel that craving.

Worse, Poet noticed my reaction. Having worn a mask for most of his life, this man missed nothing. No detail was safe from him.

I scowled, for all the good it did. The jester picked apart my features, searching for a trick but finding none. That led to an alternative interpretation, with Poet narrowing his gaze, an inspired glint reaching his eyes.

Shit. I had liked this man better when he'd been seething.

After a moment, Briar relented. Poet followed suit and disarmed his staff.

Still, they did so with reluctance. Although they trusted Flare's word and would not second guess her choices, the couple remained vigilant toward me.

I expected nothing less. For all they knew, I had been exiled for months. But for all they knew, I also hadn't changed.

"Well." Briar cupped her hands in front of her, then elbowed Poet. "What's this? My husband being uncharacteristically quiet?"

"'Tis rare, but it happens," Poet remarked while scrutinizing me. "I must have misplaced my tongue somewhere between the *wicked* and the *hell*."

"Good," I grunted. "Leave it there."

His feigned grin tightened like a noose. "Give me time, sweeting."

The fuck, I would. My glare only motivated his infernal mouth to slant, not quite amiable, but no longer mercenary. Taking hostile pleasure in my annoyance, he tsked. "Think carefully, Prince of Pestilence. Show me your weak spot, and I'll discover a shiny new toy."

Footfalls resounded from the ruins' east wing. I whipped toward the disturbance, my fingers landing on the knife hilt and then ceasing. My brows stapled together as an athletic figure strode from the foliage, a sleeveless bronze vest exposing a fleet of raptor tattoos that climbed one muscular arm. No armor. No cloak. Yet he possessed the vigilant gait of a warrior.

The glowing vegetation sketched the man's angular visage in subtle light. It was enough. His presence returned me once more to Autumn's castle blackout.

Twilit blue irises. Ashy blond hair that radiated in the dark. Twin broadswords as long as wingspans, which he braced in his grip.

Surly but chivalrous. Ethical. Principled. And intuitive to the point of absurd.

Aire.

Moving like the wind itself—forceful, intrinsic—Autumn's First Knight halted beside the lake, inclining his head to the jester and princess. "This outpost is clear." His attention strayed to the ancient building, reverence claiming his features. "Long have these walls been silent."

"And yet they are occupied," I stated.

The man swerved. Disapproval clashed with discipline as he registered my presence. "Your Highness." He lowered his head, then did a double take when he noticed Flare.

More to the point, the knight comprehended how little she wore. I would have snapped his neck then and there, but for the swift manner in which he glanced away, the gesture courteous rather than amorous.

"Er ... hello ... I'm ..." Aire cleared his throat, then muttered to himself. "Seasons, does no one in this clan stay dressed for long?"

"You say that like it's a bad thing," Poet remarked.

Briar flushed, testifying to the number of times this warrior had encountered the jester and princess in compromising positions.

The virtuous knight grumbled. He opened his mouth to reply but froze. Nothing about the atmosphere had changed. Nonetheless, his demeanor tensed, some form of instinct or perception tensed his jaw.

This would have been the moment to withdraw my knife. Same for the rest of this group, each of us armed with our choice of weapons.

But rather than charge, Aire did the opposite. With a perceptive grunt, the soldier jammed his broadswords into the crossed sheaths at his back and stalked past us. In unison, we turned to watch as he ambushed a cluster of shrubs germinating beneath the fauna statues. There, he thrust one fist into a hedge, gave forceful tug, and yanked a smaller form from its confines.

An indignant feminine shriek echoed through the rainforest. With one arm, the knight seized the intruder by the back of her hood and hauled her a foot off the ground. Under the cloak, the female squirmed, flailed her limbs, and threw punches in Aire's general direction.

Flare gasped. My gaze tapered.

A girl.

Ample curves filled out the vestment, pants, and tunic. Despite the abundance of her figure, plus indications that she would grow tall someday, she could not be more than a juvenile's age. A younger sister, perhaps.

Although the mantle shielded her features, the female's voice rang through clearly the moment she opened her mouth. "Get your mangy fucking paws off me, knight!" she growled while slapping Aire's forearms.

Offended by her vocabulary but evidently accustomed to it, the soldier huffed. "It appears we have a stowaway."

Without ceremony, he released the female. She stumbled into the middle of our group but fumbled to keep the hood over her head, the motions panicked. As her fingers wrestled with the fabric, I caught sight of the girl's arms. Some manner of vine-like pattern marked her flesh, neither scars nor ink. Rather, it appeared to be a type of skin condition.

The girl pushed down her sleeves. She had to be roasting in that cloak, yet she tucked the edges around her face and turned up her chin. This hinted at more of the same pattern across her chin, though in this light and with the hood blocking my view, I deciphered little else.

Poet groaned. "Fuck."

Aire's gaze skimmed the female from head to toe, checking for injuries despite the cloak. Satisfied that she'd gotten here in one piece, he moved on. "Brazen creature," he sighed with displeasure. "If it isn't the infamous Someone."

"I told you," she barked at him. "I'm not a 'brazen' anything, and I'm not called Someone anymore. My name is—"

"Aspen!" Briar reprimanded with a mixture of horror and anger. "What on earth—"

"I'm fine. I'm half-aquatic fae, so getting here was easy."

Not about to swallow such bullshit, Briar crossed her arms as though they were used to the girl delivering chronic fibs. "I'd love to know how you accomplish that."

"I swam?" Aspen replied hopefully. "I can hold my breath underwater for days at a time, so I just needed to grab the ship's, uh, rudder thingy and let the vessel pull me."

"A brazen one and a liar," Aire accused while looming over her.

The girl wheeled on him and stabbed a finger into his chest. "I'm no liar, you dickhead."

When everyone remained quiet, she hedged. "Fine. It was a wee bit tight in the cargo hold, but I managed."

"Clearly," Poet remarked with a dark twist to his lips. "Couldn't stay away from my wife and me, could you? Most people have this problem."

Humble as ever. Yet there was no masking the displeasure in Poet's tone.

"Okay, look." Aspen raised her defensive palms. "I wasn't planning on following you."

"Another lie," the First Knight grunted.

The female scowled at him. "Did your sixth sense tell you that?"

Aire's forehead crimped, straining against something. Following a moment of unease, he clipped, "Any honest person would have no trouble detecting falsehoods."

Umbrage peppered her voice. "My decision was last minute."

"That is not the point. It's dangerous here!"

"Oh, cut the shit. It's dangerous everywhere, so you can stop doing that."

"Doing what?" Aire galled through his teeth, exasperated.

From a harness at her hip, Aspen whipped out a short axe and pointed the blade at him. "I've had enough of you playing the holier-than-thou bodyguard. I can take care of myself. Go work off your hero complex on someone else."

"You are not a trained fighter."

"Oh, my mistake. I guess this axe is just for show."

The stowaway shoved past Aire, leaving him to stare after her with a slack jaw. After a beat, the warrior veered his gaze to the jester and princess. With a lash of his arm, he gestured at the empty spot where Aspen had been standing, as if to say, *Can you believe her?*

So. Not a younger sister.

Her weapon struck my memory. The girl had made a brief appearance during the Reaper's Fest riot. She'd thrown her axe across the town square and pinned King Rhys to the fire stake like a pig.

Pointed looks from Poet and Briar drew the girl near. While Aire stalked off to patrol the bridge, the trio murmured to one another, their measured voices indicating this girl was part of their clan and had earned the right to be treated as an equal player. Nevertheless, this didn't change the fact that she'd inserted herself into something confidential and perilous. The stowaway looked sheepish, although that feisty lift to her shoulders persisted.

Flare and I exchanged a fleeting glance. The impact scorched my flesh, the private moment squeezing into the space between us. My fingers extended toward hers, eager to touch, to grab, to—

The huddle split. Our trance broke.

With one more glance beneath her lashes, Flare peeled herself from my gaze and padded toward Aspen. Gently. Slowly. With the hem of my shirt fluttering around her limbs, Flare scooped up the girl's hands, the flesh engraved with a pattern of foliage.

Flare gave her a vivid smile and mouthed a declaration. To which, the stowaway blinked, not comprehending a word.

"Flare said you're a daughter of the trees," I explained.

The jester and princess vaulted their gazes my way. Against their will, I had impressed them. While I should not give a shit, my chest experienced a boost of pride.

Yes, I knew this woman well. Indeed, I understood her perfectly. Let them see this.

Aspen's attention detoured over Flare's shoulder and landed on me. Her eyes expanded, then sought refuge in Flare's features, a timid grin sliding across her mouth and revealing a beauty mark hidden under the mantle.

Flare twisted to the jester and princess, her eyes glistening as she pronounced the next two words slowly. "You came."

Because that had been easy to read, Her Highness snatched up Flare's fingers. "You untied me from the bonfire. You saved my life," she stressed. "Of course, we came."

In the background, Aire gained Poet and Briar's side. Where there had been two yesterday, tonight there were six.

My little beast spoke, the word easy to read and meant for everyone. "Welcome."

39

Jeryn

In the dining hall, plants snaked through the gaping windows. Wedges of melon, plates of snapper filets, and pitchers of water occupied the table. Flames crackled from the seven-foot-tall fireplace because, despite the heat, we needed the light.

Poet and Briar sat across from us, their presence surreal. They'd set out for Summer under the cover of night, while the Autumn Court slept. Only Queen Avalea, that minstrel friend named Eliot, and Briar's three ladies had known the reason, though they hadn't been privy to the rainforest's location. The jester, princess, and First Knight had kept that secret between them, intending to quest here first, to confirm Flare's wellbeing and make certain I hadn't chained her like an animal.

Witness accounts had spread across the Seasons. The Prince of Winter had chased a prisoner of the Fools Tower into a turbulent sea. As predicted, Winter and Summer had been searching ever since. Naturally after receiving Flare's message, Poet and Briar had worried about what I'd do to her.

The group still regarded me with apprehension. They respected Flare's choice, but that did not mean they agreed with it. In opposition to the merciful ethos of Autumn, I wouldn't be surprised if they wished for me to remain exiled. This clan had no love for a ruler known to experiment on his captives.

In any event, the Autumn clan had protested the trio venturing here without backup, yet they'd remained behind for vital reasons. Her Majesty had a nation to lead, the others would tamp down any speculation about where the jester and princess had gone, and everyone needed to look after Poet and Briar's son, Nicu. As a born soul, the child required a great deal of care. For that, his parents only trusted their allies, who'd become well-versed in the boy's condition.

Aire had basic training in sea navigation. But the soldier's connection to the elements had been the true advantage. Coupled with the butterfly who'd led them across the sea and Flare's coded instructions, the group had managed to find us. While the butterfly had somehow known to fly to these ruins, Aire's sensory perception—whatever the hell that meant—had done the rest.

A fanciful explanation. At least, to the latter. That I accepted Aire's uncanny abilities rather than seek logical details suggested my intellect was lagging. Considering the explosion of heat that had blown the roof off my skull while fucking Flare, I wasn't thinking straight.

Instead of joining us, Aire and Aspen stood guard near the floor-to-ceiling windows.

Poet lounged in his chair with exaggerated elegance. He draped an arm across the back of Briar's seat, his glossy black fingernails toying with the end of her braid.

Flare and I had led our group on a tour from the vestibule, across verandas and colonnades, and up to the cupola roof. Along the way, we'd guided them through the medical chamber, the fountain room, the sleeping quarters, the textile cellar, the armory crypt, and the grotto with its caves.

Alongside Poet's dubious frown, Briar scrutinized my countenance. Like a proper princess and a devoted friend, her composure teetered between decorum and destruction.

Their expressions make it clear. *If you hurt her, your ass is ours.*

I inclined my head. *She would get to me first.*

Seeing as I'd rip to pieces anyone who touched Flare, I appreciated the threat. However, they should not underestimate her own skills.

The couple read my expression, my declaration satisfying them. At which point, I realized they'd been testing me.

Having abandoned footwear, the stone floor cooled everyone's bare feet. My little beast rested sideways in her chair and propped her legs atop my thighs. Possessively, I clamped one palm high over her limb, my blood heating from the gooseflesh that sprinted up her skin. A few more inches, and my fingers would reach her sweet cunt. But although my fingers twitched, I forced myself to behave.

We'd changed into appropriate attire. I had donned a shirt and Flare a short dress with fringes trailing across the hem, and she'd piled her dark waves loosely at the crown of her head. To be frank, I wanted to ruin her efforts, undo that hairstyle, shred those garments. If no one else were here, she would have been sprawled across the table by now, and I would have been scissoring those thighs apart while ripping more sounds from the back of her throat.

Seated opposite me, Poet's features reflected dark amusement. Skilled in the art of debauchery, this scoundrel had gauged my thoughts.

Whatever. As if he wasn't itching to get Briar alone, to take advantage of the sweltering atmosphere and do damage to the princess's genteel sensibilities. With how often they fondled one another, those two wouldn't last more than five minutes after this roundtable convened. And that calculation was me being ambitious.

Enjoying my annoyance, Poet got more comfortable and carded his fingers deeper into Briar's plaited hair. "This humidity looks good on you," he murmured to her, then jutted his chin toward Flare. "And you."

Then he regarded me. "But not you." Then swiftly, the prick reconsidered. "Though, it's refreshing to see you without the pelt of an endangered species draped across your shoulders."

I gave him an astringent look. "It had been peaceful until you got here."

"Do I get a coin for every time you commit perjury?"

"Only if I get to stuff each coin down your throat until you lose the ability to converse."

"You underestimate how much experience I have swallowing."

Briar dropped her face into her palms. From another corner, Aspen's snort traveled across the room. Standing at his post, Aire said nothing, but one didn't need a microscope to see his capillaries were bursting. As for my little beast, she folded her mirthful lips together.

The continent knew of the jester's unconditional fidelity to his wife. However, The Dark Seasons also knew of Poet's extensive history prior to meeting Briar. Our lack of clothing aside, this whorish expert deduced what had occurred before Autumn docked ashore.

No. Flare and I had not been peaceful in the slightest.

"Indeed. We were fucking when you arrived," I confirmed flatly. "End of discussion."

"Popped your frozen cherry, did she?" Because Spring and Summer's cultures spoke without censure, the motherfucker regarded Flare. "I hope the sex lasted longer than his replies."

I would boil him alive someday. "It certainly lasted longer than your train of thought."

"Be careful what you imply. Twisting words is my job."

"Last I heard, a jester's job was to tell a superficial joke."

"Jokes keep us warm."

"Furs keep us warmer."

"Gentlemen," Briar interrupted, lifting her regal head from her palms. "We didn't travel all this way to do battle."

Flare flapped her fingers toward Aire and Aspen, silently implying, *Tell that to them.*

The four of us twisted toward the knight and stowaway patrolling the area from opposite ends. Aire kept stealing glances Aspen's way, his profile discomforted but attentive whenever she got too close to something remotely unsafe. An uneven stone. A shadow shaped like an insect. Yet he never cautioned her, likely because she wouldn't take the chivalry well.

Briar caught onto Flare's meaning and sighed. "Protective instincts. Guarding people is second nature for Aire, whereas Aspen constantly seeks to validate her independence. It's admirable, though sometimes I worry they try too hard." She gave me a concerned look. "In this climate, what else should we be concerned about, other than predators and the elements?"

"I'll administer something to prevent infection for each of you," I said. "It's not a vaccine, but it's the best I can do. In any case, I do not prognosticate prematurely."

"Glad to hear it." Poet's voice thinned to a razor's edge. "Though on behalf of many, I'd be happier to believe it."

Across my lap, Flare's limbs stiffened. There it was. After learning my family was doing well—I'd interrogated the jester and princess within moments of entering the ruins—and being updated on the current state of each Season, this discourse was overdue.

The beast and I had tackled many things in private, but not yet the subject of my intentions toward born souls. How I would move forward and what I would do. Had we been given more time alone, this would have been our next conversation.

I rubbed Flare's thigh and spoke to our guests. "You're expecting a proclamation."

"We're expecting a confirmation," Poet solicited. "For a start, enlighten us. How did this—" he swung a finger between me and Flare, "—phenomenon happen?"

Because this clan had brought supplies, Flare took up a quill and paper, courtesy of the princess. That made it easier for her to communicate.

Offering an abridged version of what had transpired after Flare escaped, we described our time in the rainforest, from the moment we'd crashed here to the instant we spotted their ship. We also clarified how Flare could hear her own voice and that I possessed the same inexplicable skill. As to the reason for this, no one had a solid theory. Though, neither did they dwell for long, especially considering Aire's unaccountable intuition.

In any case, Flare and I omitted the obvious. No need to inform this lot of how thoroughly and deeply I'd buried my cock inside her minutes prior to their arrival, to the point where I still felt her pussy clutching me.

It took a while for our audience to resurface from the tale, including the discovery that they sat amidst The Phantom Wild. By this point, Aire and Aspen had approached, the knight taking a seat beside Briar and the girl hopping onto the tabletop. The clan had been gazing in fascination at our surroundings, but now they marveled at the forest anew.

"So the legend is true," Aire mused.

Briar grinned at Flare. "In the dungeon. You were drawing this landscape."

"An image hidden within verse," Poet intoned.

Flare beamed. After the women exchanged smiles, the princess folded her hands atop the table. "Flare has vouched for you. So educate us, Winter. What is your position these days?"

I switched my attention to Flare's expectant face. "It does not align with Winter's regarding born souls." Then I transferred my gaze to the group. "That said, it's complicated."

"What is it with Royals and the word 'complicated'?" Aspen huffed. "If there's a job to do, then do it."

"Leadership does not work that way," Aire defended. "Navigating politics and society requires delicacy."

"Politics, society, *and* delicacy can kiss my ass."

The puritan knight grimaced. "Someone should chop off your vulgar tongue."

The girl produced her axe and flipped it between her digits. "And what appendage do I get to take from you?"

As if he'd never spent time in Poet's raunchy company, the soldier went crimson.

Briar shook her head. "We don't have the luxury of disregarding certain structures and traditions just yet. However biased, disdainful, and ignorant some of those mindsets have become over history, avoiding carnage is paramount."

To stress the point, I splayed my free fingers on the table. "It's complicated because Autumn is the only court that doesn't view any of its citizens as abnormal."

"Because if they weren't normal, they wouldn't exist," Poet bit out.

"An oversimplification, sadly."

"Nay, a fact. You get off on facts, do you not? Allow me to provide you with more. Confinement nor brutality have helped. Science has not educated on this front. Nothing you've done has aided those whom you call 'fools.' Nature doesn't make mistakes; however, humans do so with aplomb. For bigotry and violence come in many guises, as do goodness and innocence. Nature distinguishes us all, not merely some of us. Thus, our job is not to exclude ignorantly."

"It's to unite sagely," Briar finished.

I leaned back in my chair. "If I'd been given a chance to finish, you might have heard me agree with you."

The table fell quiet. This clan stood divided between those who looked at the matter viscerally. Flare, Poet, Aspen. Whereas the rest of us viewed this conflict through a pragmatic lens. Me, Briar, Aire.

Or perhaps the knight straddled that line. As did the princess, who exchanged meaningful looks with the jester. It did not take a mind reader to know they were thinking of their son—Nicu—who lived and breathed at the center of their consciousness. That accounted for Poet's impassioned outburst. He was a skillful player, but for all his manipulative cunning and talent for deception, the man was also a father.

I clarified, "By oversimplification, I'm not referring to myself. I'm illustrating how others will view the matter. Your campaign benefits from prudence as well as spirit. But to sway Winter, one methodology is more viable than the other."

A sheet of parchment slid in my periphery. My head veered toward Flare's handwriting across the paper. *If you could return today, would you?*

Everyone craned their heads to read her question, then awaited my response.

I kept my face neutral. Because I knew Flare better than anyone here. I did not like where this line of questioning would lead.

Before I could formulate a response, Flare withdrew her limbs from my lap and straightened. *You should leave*, she wrote.

Indeed. I had seen that coming. Just as I saw her features struggling to remain intact, which wasn't like her. Flare did not conceal her emotions. On the contrary, she flung them at the world.

Yet the only facet giving her away were those golden eyes, which shimmered with pain. The sight churned my stomach. I knew what she meant. With Autumn's ship docked here, I had a chance to return, to incite widespread change.

And she was right. But for one problem.

I twisted in my chair to face her. The word dropped from my mouth like a stone. "No."

Thunderstruck expressions surrounded us. They had not expected that from me. Regardless of my stance on the matter, an opportunity to go home had crashed onto my lap, yet I wasn't taking it.

Flare's tattooed throat bobbed. Her quill scribbled across the parchment. *We talked about this.*

"We did *not* talk about this," I spat.

"If you stay, there will still be labs and dungeons and towers," she rattled off, dismissing the paper entirely. "Innocent people will still be traded, locked in chains, marked with collars. If you go back to Winter, would you do something to stop that?"

Goddamn her. Since the shark attack, I had been questioning the treatment of born souls.

Had my court made the most of learning? Or had my people restricted it? What constituted madness? Some exhibited it more than others, but were the Seasons handling those complexities competently? Doing all they could to comprehend and classify them?

No, I had not expected to stay here indefinitely. Yes, I had been deliberating how to act on this subject.

Nonetheless, most of my time—seconds, minutes, hours, days, weeks, months—I had only been thinking of Flare. Her plans. Her freedom. Everything beyond this woman had become secondary.

Flare gave our visitors an apologetic look and scripted an abbreviated version of her argument. By the time she finished, I recuperated my voice. "I would take the steps, as Autumn has done. But no court can change the world swiftly."

My little beast compressed her lips and penned another response, for the benefit of everyone in attendance. *Then you should start now, while Poet and Briar are here with available transport. You should go where you can make a difference.*

"You're saying I make no difference here," I accused. "What about your quest? The key to your part in this crusade?"

Briar's head flew from me to Flare. "What key?"

I'll find it on my own, she wrote. *Like I found this realm.*

Hours ago, we'd been making those plans together. Hours ago, she'd gotten me to serve my feelings on a platter. Hours ago, I'd been fucking her like an addict, both of us succumbing to this chemical reaction.

Now she was pushing me away.

Flare held my gaze, her chin trembling. As I opened my mouth to raise hell, she turned to the group and wrote, *When I'm ready, may I call on you?*

"We're a clan," Briar said quietly. "You can always do that."

Aire inclined his head. "You have my word as well."

I'll need transport to Summer's mainland—

I hissed, "Flare."

—where I can steal a boat. That is, if I haven't already built one myself.

She scripted the rest at lightning speed. Her fated quest. The evasive key to fulfilling her role in this campaign, in liberating the born souls of Summer. How the answer resided in these ruins. That once she found it, she would need to leave this realm, to enact her purpose.

With the same expediency, I lost my shit. Internally, I wracked my brain for an alternative. One that didn't involve me getting on that fucking conveyance. Not yet.

Winter and Summer were hunting for us. If they found Flare and me together, they would arrest her.

With the iron grip I had on Rhys, he would not lift a finger to my beast. Regardless of the mayhem she'd caused, the king would be an idiot to override my authority. And even if he did, the man would fail as he had in numerous other pursuits. Ultimately, I could bend Summer to my will.

But I could not bend Winter.

The court would expect its prince to treat Flare as I'd always treated born souls. To do otherwise would rouse speculation. Provided I found a way around that obstacle, citizens would resent Flare for shipwrecking their future king. They would retaliate, which meant not taking the risk to begin with. Although I would mutilate anyone who came near Flare, consequences be damned, the only way to protect her from my kingdom was to keep her away from it.

Poet and Briar could give Flare sanctuary, if she were willing to leave with them. But she'd made her feelings plain. While I could fling her over my shoulder and dump her on Autumn's ship, I had stolen enough of her choices. All the Seasons had.

While Flare had more to offer than simply what the rainforest dictated, she needed to figure that out for herself. Finding a purpose in this crusade was her decision, her ambition, her right. I would not take that choice from her. But until the day Flare located that key and set forth on that mission ...

"You cannot live here alone," I seethed, cutting off the questions and answers jumping between all participants.

Flare's quill scratched across the leaflet at lightning speed. *I have my fauna pack. I'll survive.*

"I did not say *survive*."

She slapped her palm down, splattering ink across the paper's surface. Flipping over the page, she wrote, *I've forgiven you once. But if you sacrifice the fates of more people just to keep me company, I won't forgive you again!*

My fist rammed into the table. "This isn't about keeping you company! This is about more!"

Oxygen vacated the room. Aspen had leaped off the furnishing. Aire's palm extended in front of her, as if to block the stowaway from getting caught in the crossfire of shouting. Briar's compassionate gaze strayed between me and Flare. And Poet ...

The jester reclined in his chair, with one arm resting over the princess's seat. The other hand was draped over his mouth in contemplation. From above his knuckles, the man's probing eyes absorbed the scene.

Flare's orbs glistened. My objections wounded her. I could handle anything—except that.

If she asked, I would renounce my crown for this woman. Whatever it took to stay by her side. However many throats I had to slit. Whichever sacrifices I needed to make. But more than that, I would do as she wished.

And she was right. I thought of my family, my kingdom. As a ruler, I would also do this for them.

My insides buckled. Decision made, I leveled my gaze on the clan. "Winter will join your enterprise. I offer my allegiance to your cause."

Silence. Obviously.

For the second—or perhaps third or fourth—time, these insurgents regarded me as if I'd peeled off my face and revealed someone different underneath.

All except Flare. Beside me, I felt the intensity of her gaze.

After a flabbergasted moment, Poet spoke to Briar. "Sweet Thorn, reply on my behalf. I do believe Winter has rendered me speechless."

I reined in my irritation. "Is that humanly possible for anybody to achieve?"

"What about Winter's experimentation?" Briar asked. "Your medical testing?"

"In the future, I will devise a plan to extinguish and supersede those practices."

"It cannot be as elementary as that."

"It is not."

The health of this continent relied on Winter's advancements. No society would sacrifice that benefit so easily, no matter what anyone thought of equality.

"In my court, humane methods of research will be complicated," I affirmed.

"I know about treatments. I was raised by a healer," Poet replied. "Humaneness isn't complicated, Winter."

I inclined my head. "And yet."

Because the jester wasn't naive, he capitulated and packed his own experiences into one word. "Alas."

Precisely. Humaneness was not complicated. Getting my court to redefine and accept new practices was. To say nothing of redefining humanity, which necessitated both kingdoms' cooperation.

Winter's knowledge and Autumn's empathy.

Winter's science and Autumn's sensitivity.

As for when to leave, I would not compromise. "I will go, but only when the opportunity is right. My return must overcome multiple impediments. Chiefly, I must ensure my arrival under no circumstances endangers Flare. And I must preserve the trust of my subjects without inciting suspicions about where my allegiance lies. Royals can't take a shit without the court knowing the number of minutes we spend squatting. The concept of privacy is nonexistent, and I haven't begun to reflect on how I'll convince my queens of this venture. Therefore, planning takes time. Patience."

"Aye," Poet murmured. "Success takes even longer."

"Until then, I have a proposal."

Sarcasm flickered in those obscenely green oculi. "Should we be worried? The last time we negotiated with you, a knight lost one of his organs."

"I'll revise. This is not a deal, it's a tactic. Autumn has taken the first step. Winter will take the second. In the interim, we must anticipate the opposition."

Poet's timbre hardened into granite. "Rhys."

"But we dealt with him," Briar contended. "He's a ruined monarch."

"More to the point, my wife brought the cocksucker to his knees."

"Let us keep it that way," I pressed. "My meeting with him left much to be desired."

I recapped the conference in Rhys's throne room. With his role reduced, the monarch had time to kill and ample hours in which to stew, a fact that could backfire once he finished licking his scrotum. Poet had all but mutilated the sovereign, Briar had humiliated him, Giselle had made his crimes public, and the Seasons had rejected him. Strip a person of everything, and all they had left were suicidal tendencies.

Poet tilted his head, unkempt layers of dark hair falling around his face. "The only thing more dangerous than a confident king with everything to lose, is a broken king with nothing to lose."

"Unstable rulers go down quickly, but they do not stay down forever," I forecasted. "He will revisit his vendetta."

"Don't fucking do that," the jester growled, noticing the wince in Briar's features and reading into its meaning. Clasping the side of her face, he urged, "This doesn't mean you failed. On the contrary, Sweet Thorn. You walked through fire on Reaper's Fest, inspired your subjects to stop the riot, reunited the nation, changed the fate of born souls, restored the court's relationship with Spring, got Summer to kneel, and crushed his influence in Autumn like a fucking insect. None of that has changed, least of all your triumph."

A small grin lifted Briar's lips. "Our triumph."

Poet smirked. "I do enjoy getting some credit. It gives me an excuse to brag. In any case, if the shithead doesn't know how to stay down when it comes to the rest of this continent, we'll remind him."

Flare wrote on her leaflet. *All of us will.*

At which point, the tenacious princess nodded and leveled her chin. "Rhys will need an arsenal to exact retribution."

"His Majesty may yet acquire such an advantage," Aire predicted.

"Or someone else on his behalf," Aspen added. "He's done it before, but that doesn't mean he ran out of minions. People like using other people."

Especially if you get them angry enough, Flare testified.

My palms beaded with perspiration. "Which brings this discussion to what Rhys has on me."

Gasping, Flare abandoned the quill and set her hand on my arm.

At her touch, waves of heat rolled through my bloodstream. Until now, I had confessed this only to her. The gamble was extreme, but it had to be done.

Poet furrowed his brows, accurately recalling our talk in Autumn when he'd asked that precarious question. *What does Summer have on you?*

My hesitation motivated Briar. "Whatever secrets you keep, we can't guard them without knowing what they are."

I pinned my gaze on Flare, who nodded in encouragement. The confession sat on my tongue, then took a nosedive off the edge. "I am a born soul."

All semblance of noise fled the room. No one spoke. No one breathed. While focusing on Flare, it came out in fragments, from the virus that stole my parent's health, to the siren shark, to my condition.

Fear. Panic. Irrationality.

Terrified fits that sent me to the floor. Hunching over and venting to myself.

By the end of it, Briar's hand covered her mouth. Poet's lips had parted, shock numbing his tongue. Aire gaped, and Aspen peeked beneath her hood.

Flames from the hearth tossed an orange glow through the room. The meal sat untouched.

The princess swerved her gaze from me to the woman at my side. "Flare?"

In that tentative voice, the meaning was clear. I was a born soul, but what about Flare? Despite Summer branding her with a so-called "feral madness," I'd long since dismissed that notion. Yet I also hadn't perceived her actual condition, and based on Poet and Briar's demeanors, they had trouble defining it as well.

Then again, having such a condition wasn't the same as wearing a bandage. Unless the person displayed their behavior openly, as the jester and princess's son did, everything was otherwise locked inside, where people couldn't see it.

Pain, torment, and guilt flashed through Flare's eyes. I had witnessed this happen on numerous occasions, starting with the day I'd cut into her arm, and we spoke about her past. There was more to the tale, details that plagued her, and I fucking hated seeing her deal with that. I wanted Flare to open up, but she hadn't yet. Even now, she was not ready.

That much was evident when she swallowed and turned away. Briar and Poet watched Flare, seeming to draw the same conclusion. They cared, but they would not pry.

Instead, the princess offered Flare an understanding smile, then redirected her attention to me. "Your Highness. You have our support."

"And our silence," Poet assured me.

I frowned. So easily?

Their expressions spoke for themselves. They would not discount the horrors I had committed, but they would grant me leave to atone for them. Of all people, this group knew firsthand the gravity of such knowledge.

Poet and Briar, as parents of a born soul. Aire and Aspen, who appeared to harbor their own unspoken connections to the subject.

Their response disarmed me, anxiety draining from my veins. Grateful. Humbled. At length, I cleared my throat. "If Rhys learns of this, he'll use it to harm my family, discredit the monarchy, and dismantle Winter. With my court in disarray, he could then seize the opportunity to go after Autumn."

"There was a time when we believed he wouldn't incite a war." Aire's gaze strayed to the abutting rainforest. "But if Winter suffered a breakdown in leadership, if civil unrest the likes of Reaper's Fest were to occur there, and if Summer became unhinged with little left to risk, carnage across the continent would be likelier."

Poet nodded grimly. "And bloodier."

Flare needed time to find her key, assuming it existed here. I needed time to plot my return to Winter, including all contingencies. This clan needed time to establish a Seasonal alliance without causing an uproar. We also needed time to find out what Rhys would do next, to predict his moves and set up countermoves. The king needed time to either find out my secret or go on a delusional rampage once learning of Winter's reformation and Autumn's evident influence.

Who succeeded first remained to be seen. Thus, my idea. During the meeting with Rhys, he'd made a defensive comment that had stuck with me.

I have no other spawn.

Not that anyone would give a shit if Rhys was concealing illegitimate heirs. Certainly not enough for me to quote him. Although Summer's queen didn't deserve an adulterous husband, she barely tolerated the man, and technically infidelity wasn't a ruinous crime in the eyes of their subjects.

Yet the thought prompted me to consider what else the king kept secret. This notion, I brought up to the group, which inspired a debate. A man with a penchant for spying was a man who believed every leader was like him. Dishonest. Traitorous. In his mind, all sovereigns had skeletons to bury. Hence, whatever he was hiding could be an effective weapon.

Flare took up the pen, knowing what I would suggest. *He spied on everyone else once.*

Briar's features alighted. "So we spy on him back."

"Correct," I said. "With a notable player."

Poet's trickster gaze sharpened. And as the only Summer citizen present, Flare's pupils blazed.

"Giselle," they said in unison.

Yes. The queen would comply. Her spouse had done enough damage to their nation, and she would not tolerate another downfall purely because Rhys didn't know when to quit. And although her stance on born souls remained the same, Giselle would hardly sanction a needless war.

We strategized. Poet and Briar had experience in court manipulation. They would appeal to Giselle, petitioning for Her Majesty to monitor her husband as a precaution, for stability's sake. In fact, quite possibly the woman was already doing that.

In which case, the jester and princess would request to be informed. With the Reaper's Fest riot still fresh in everyone's consciousness, the queen would honor this obligation. All the while, Poet and Briar would leave me and Flare out of the equation. No one outside of these ruins could know our whereabouts.

The clever pair had already scheduled a conference with Giselle, on the pretense of maintaining civil relations. In case they were spotted at sea by Summer's armada while enroute to the rainforest, they'd needed an excuse.

On the way back to Autumn, they would meet with the queen and set our plan into motion. Meanwhile, Flare beseeched Aire to check on her tower mates. Despite everyone's protests, Aspen volunteered to sleuth among the guards. Apparently, the stowaway had a gruesome history of getting around troops. One that had involved the forced assassination and beheading of a knight, at the behest of Autumn's Masters Guild.

Needless to say, a feud began in which Aire threatened to string Aspen by her ankles if it meant keeping her out of harm's way. And although they valued her skills, Poet and Briar concurred due to the girl's age and lack of formal training. To which, Aspen stormed to the opposite end of the chamber and resumed her patrol.

Hours passed. Shadows shifted across the walls, indicating somewhere close to midnight. When Briar yawned, Poet slid an arm around her shoulders.

I experienced a prickle of envy over their union. Choosing a mate of an unmatched rank or Season was prohibited. Only this couple had ever challenged that edict. None could impugn Poet's magnetism and Briar's tenacity. The jester declared himself without censure, while the princess exemplified a supreme force of will. As a Royal, she negotiated that fine line of being a radical and a ruler. They complemented one another, doing so freely, because fuck the naysayers.

My eyes clicked over to Flare, who peeked back from between her dark lashes. It had been too long since I feasted on the sight of her. Pinpricks of light flickered in her pupils, every look a blow to the chest. Her gaze shoved me back to the ocean, to the memory of her naked legs around me, my cock fucking the tight cleft of her body, and her moans firing into the sky.

Holding her. Pleasuring her.

Rarely did I venture that near to the tide. Yet at that moment, I hadn't once thought of the siren shark.

Silhouettes shifted in our periphery. We glanced toward Poet and Briar, who watched us. Once not long ago, these two had found themselves at odds, their relationship all kinds of forbidden. They had experienced forced proximity, in addition to forced separation. Their affair had once been a secret, so they understood the emotional endurance it required.

Except their marriage was permanent. What Flare and I had was fleeting. This roundtable had reminded us of that.

Winter. Summer.

Eventually, we would leave this wild. Me, back to my court. Her, on a mission in this kingdom. We might be allied with the same clan, but we weren't headed in the same direction.

Her gaze met mine—and she rose. The sudden movement scraped the chair legs across the floor. All heads swiveled her way as she quit the hall, muttering something about preparing rooms for everyone. Though from that angle, they wouldn't have been able to read her lips.

Her absence dug a hole in my chest. I launched from my seat, intent on charging after her.

"Stay," Briar intervened, peeling herself from Poet's arms. "I will go."

After gliding her palm across the jester's shoulders, she gathered the writing instruments from the table and rushed after Flare. At once, Aspen wavered from her spot, then trotted in the princess's wake.

The makings of another hiss cleaved up my throat. I did not like this arrangement. Flare's torn expression had cut to the quick, and I wanted to be the one going after her.

Locking my jaw, I stalked to the windows overlooking the tropic forest. Bracing one hand on my hip, I glared at the tangle of trees. The other hand pressed hard into the adjoining wall, the only thing keeping me from launching after Flare. It did not matter where she went; every molecule in my body felt her presence in these ruins.

Poet materialized to my left, a single lazy shoulder propping against the dilapidated casing. Aire flanked the opposite side, setting his foot atop a stone bench, firelight sketching his bird-of-prey tattoos.

For a while, we watched The Phantom Wild.

At length, I brooded. "Out with it."

As anticipated, Poet had more shit to say. His perceptive tone lowered. "So how much time do you really need?"

Fuck him. Fuck this jester and his shrewdness.

As for the knight who possessed his own ludicrous abilities, the man's blue irises drew a similar conclusion.

I had claimed that planning a return to Winter would take time. I just hadn't been truthful about the amount.

To make matters worse, a question chewed through my restraint. The last thing I wanted was advice from this man. Yet Winter understood the value of credibility, an advantage of which Poet had in spades.

Clearing my throat, I spoke around the rubble in my mouth. "When did you know?" At the jester's confounded look, I flitted my eyes toward the door through which the princess had disappeared.

He arched an eyebrow. "Are you asking when I fell in love with Briar?"

An aggravated noise skidded from my chest. "Give me concrete facts. Not a maudlin verse."

Instead of relishing this moment, Poet stared. There had been a time when he would have skewered me for getting near Flare. To say nothing of what his dagger would have done if I'd stood within a ten-mile radius of Briar.

This bastard excelled in peeling back one's secrets, having mastered the intricacies of deception. He grasped when someone was in earnest and when they wore a disguise.

If I wasn't being genuine, this jester would know. Somehow, the soldier to my right would as well.

Poet made his choice. Facing the vista, his eyes flashed with memories. "She enticed me the moment I spied on her during a welcome feast in Spring, as she stood amid public displays of fuckery with her head aloft, despite the fear she tried to conceal. She ruined me in a hall of mirrors when we sparred, her tongue as sharp as my own. She claimed me when she met my son. She seduced me in a garden maze where she danced, then in her Royal suite when I sank to my knees for her, and then in a library where we fantasized together. She broke me in a bell tower, after a shitstorm roundtable. She owned me when we committed treason, rescued my son, and got thrown in jail. She destroyed me on Lark's Night, when we fucked until dawn, and she got me to shout until my lungs gave out."

His words turned to silk. "I didn't fall in love with Briar in a single moment. I fell hard over a thousand moments."

He had one job. Facts without prose.

Then again, Flare was a romantic. She would admire his speech.

I wavered, feeling incompetent and hating to show it. "I was looking for a definitive moment of epiphany."

Poet's lips twitched. "I know."

Aire scrubbed the back of his mottled neck. Noble. Straitlaced. I could guess which explicit part of Poet's recitation had affected the knight's complexion.

The amused jester knew this too. "Never fear. Your turn will come."

Aire grunted. "If it does, I shall not be vocal about the effects."

Poet swung his gaze toward me and mouthed, *Liar.*

Despite myself, my lips ticked sideways. Like Poet, this much I had learned. No one knew a damn thing until it happened to them.

Avians cawed, and mammals roared. Even at this late hour, a sauna would have been more comfortable.

The mood blackened as my thoughts returned to Poet's earlier point. I spoke through my teeth. "I will not leave her."

Not yet. I just ... would not.

Conflicted, Aire observed me with a mixture of reproach and respect. "Few rulers choose devotion over duty. You are among them."

I sliced my head toward him. "I gather you have some practice with that."

"It is a simple truth, not based on firsthand experience. I'm not a monarch. And I have no devotions that surpass duty."

"None despite your unearthly intuitions?" the jester countered.

The knight's attention flickered toward the door where the women had exited, then he directed his gaze back to the forest. "My senses provide a service to others. Not to myself."

My frown deepened. Regardless of what I believed about premonitions, he looked as if a bad omen weighed down his thoughts. But although the man had more to say, he remained quiet.

Poet contemplated his friend with a perceptive expression, then let the matter drop. Instead, he leaned deeper into the casing. "Heed this, Winter. Don't think any of us will stop watching you. If you fuck up with Flare, I'll shear the flesh from your bones. That is, after she and Briar are done with you."

"Warning noted," I stated. "And accepted."

His probing features slanted my way. "You've changed, sweeting."

"Is that a compliment?" I wondered.

"Nay." His mouth quirked. "'Tis an alliance."

40

Flare

The silk shawl rippled through my hands like a watercolor. Blues and greens swam across the ancient fabric and poured through my fingers. A treasure, easy to hold and just as easy to release.

Bolts of cloth and open chests crowded the textile cellar. Because the rainforest found its way into everything, blossoms snaked through the jagged crevices. Petals illuminated the space, along with the torch I'd ignited.

I should have been gathering preserved blankets and pillowcases. Instead, my fingers unfolded the shawl and pictured an ocean wave unfurling. I envisioned two bodies lost in that sea, lost in each other. Their bodies joined at the waists, the male's hips lunging between the woman's spread thighs.

My eyes closed. And I remembered.

Mere hours before, when the lashing waves had surrounded us. My limbs tied around Jeryn's wet muscles. His pants low and his cock pivoting into me. Divine Seasons, how violently the villain prince had claimed me, and how wildly I'd claimed him back.

In our shared cell, sex with Rune had been a distraction. In this rainforest, I could barely name what had happened with Jeryn, because no description felt large enough, wide enough, or deep enough.

I'm going to fuck you until we break.

My skin heated as if I'd been dipped in a cauldron. Yearning gripped my chest, my stomach, my throat.

In the dining hall, I had told him to leave The Phantom Wild. That had been my wish, the rightness and wrongness of it clashing on my tongue, so soon after mating amidst a star-filled ocean. I had meant every word and hated it at the same time.

… until we break.

He'd kept his promise. From the moment his mouth had slammed against mine, too many emotions had been severing me in half.

I folded the shawl and placed it back into the chest. As I rose, his scent wafted from my skin as if he'd seeped into me. Unable to stop myself, I inhaled the back of my wrist, drawing needle forests and blustering winds into my lungs.

His home, which I would never see. His court, which would take him from me.

A shadow materialized. A slender hand glided into view, a leaflet of parchment tucked in a set of groomed digits.

"You forgot this," Briar said from beside me.

Turning, I accepted the sheet with a tired smile. The princess stared, empathy painting her freckled features. A plait of red hair blazed from her head, and the scarlet ribbon hugged her wrist, proving she needed no other embellishments to set this continent on fire.

We hadn't known each other for long, yet we'd saved one another's lives, and a true kinship had formed. I had missed her dearly, and she'd come here for me, and that bond had tightened. I loved her, as I loved Poet.

As I reached out to cup her face, Briar's gray eyes softened, expressing the same emotion. In fascination, she took in the sumptuous gowns and swimming garments, amusement filling her voice. "It's a wonder we managed to tear Poet from this chamber during the tour.

Though, it won't be long before he returns."

We chuckled. Then her attention traveled to the blossoms coiling through the cellar, the petals glowing like jewels. Shaking her head in awe, the princess swept her gaze to me and beamed. "You found what you were looking for."

Not quite yet. I had found the rainforest, a fauna pack, and a clan of friends. And I had found more in the prince. But I hadn't yet unearthed the key to my purpose, still hidden somewhere among these walls.

I thought back to what Jeryn had said at the cove, when I confided in him. What did I suppose my mission would be? What part of me would serve that purpose? And why couldn't I answer that without the rainforest's help?

Meaning your self-made abilities are irrelevant compared to what nature designates for you? That discovering the map had only to do with fate instead of any personal skill?

You're selling yourself short, Flare.

I hadn't known how to respond to that. I'd only ever assumed the forest would dictate everything. Yet the unsettling questions had been burrowing deeper, forming a gaping hole of uncertainty in my head.

Nonetheless, my spirits lifted. Briar had remembered what she'd said in Autumn's dungeon, when we first met.

I hope you find what you're looking for.

While explaining my quest to the clan, I'd told them about being summoned to the rainforest through the song lyrics and its hidden map. Because I had called to the jester and princess, The Phantom Wild had allowed them passage as well. No one had seen them come, and no one would see them go.

I took up the leaflet and quill. *But truly, this forest found me.*

Briar smiled. "Then it chose wisely."

"Why?" interrupted a feminine voice.

Aspen stepped from the cellar stairs, her hood draped around her face. Dropping onto a humped chest, she cocked her head. "Why did this place choose you? Why you, over anyone else? What makes you more special than other people?"

Briar's expression sobered. She opened her mouth to reproach the girl, but I set my palm on the princess's shoulder, quieting her.

For a moment, bafflement lurched in my gut. I peered at the girl, who held her breath in anticipation. She had a snarky tongue, which I liked. Although her appearance with the First Knight had startled me, the rainforest surely had approved of their presence, and I'd been delighted to meet them.

Honesty had radiated from the soldier. Because of that and his otherworldly bond with the elements, I felt an immediate kinship with him. Besides, Poet and Briar trusted the knight, and they'd needed the backup, and he would not betray them.

Neither would this girl. This mystery female, who had vine patterns twining across her skin, as though she were made of trees. I'd seen glimpses here and there from under her sleeve.

She wasn't asking this question to be mean. She was asking to understand.

This returned me once more to Jeryn's questions. What did I think the quest would be? Which part of me was suited to the mission? Without the key's help, I still didn't know how to respond.

But I did understand the ultimate goal.

Flattening the parchment against a wall, I scripted my reply. *If I'd been given a choice, I would have asked the rainforest to give sanctuary to my tower mates instead of me. And if I were selfish, I would keep this land to myself, hide away, and do nothing. Fated I may be, but this quest isn't about me. It's about born souls.*

Aspen stood and inched nearer to read the page. She pursed her mouth in contemplation, then shrugged. "Well okay, then."

We exchanged grins. My mouth flashed teeth, and her lips curled, a beauty mark tucked above her upper lip.

An investigative expression crossed the girl's face. "So you're a sand drifter, right? And you uncovered these ruins? The tales say drifters know how to discover relics and things. In that case, how do you track down something that ... that doesn't want to be found?"

Briar tilted her head. "Such as?"

"Nothing specific." Aspen shrugged. "Just curious."

She wasn't just curious, but the princess and I didn't probe. We respected a person's sacred yearnings and knew the value of protecting one's secrets, much like those exquisite physical traits she kept hidden.

Pensive, I thought about her question and wrote, *You go where people don't think to look. Or sometimes where they don't dare to search. And you follow your heartbeat.*

From under the hood, the girl's eyebrows seemed to crinkle, but she accepted that answer. Then her attention strayed to the trove of patterns and fabrics.

Intrigued, she strutted to a case of bangles. "So where else has your heartbeat led you?" Picking one of the bracelets from the pile, she swung it like a hoop. "Bet he's got long hair and a face that could cut glass."

She'd only been teasing. But the instant my throat bobbed, Aspen ceased toying with the bauble. Her head panned to Briar, who studied me gingerly. Because they had witnessed the quarrel between me and Jeryn, they wavered, uncertain if I wanted to talk about my connection to the prince.

My quill shook across the parchment, the question meant for Briar. *When did you know?*

The princess's eyes gleamed. Her freckles darkened along with her blush, but she did nothing to contain the smile stretching across her face. Passion filled her voice like an ocean—deep and eternal—as her gaze became remote, diving into unseen memories.

"I desired Poet when I first saw him dance." A rueful chuckle slipped from her mouth. "Though, I would have never admitted it. But that desire only grew with every moment in his presence—an orchid garden, a hidden cottage, a night when we crossed paths in the kitchen, when I nearly succumbed to that yearning."

For a moment, she whispered to herself more than to anyone else. "If he'd struck that water glass from my hand and hauled me forward, I wouldn't have stopped him."

Briar flushed anew, remembering Aspen's presence. "I admired Poet when I met his son. I melted for him when we first kissed in the mud."

"I'm sorry," Aspen interrupted, raising her hand. "Did you say, in the mud?"

After we finished chuckling, Briar marveled, "I yearned for Poet every second after that, whenever he shocked me, inspired me, empowered me, seduced me, provoked me, infuriated me, touched me. I fell in love when I hurt him. I fell in love when I lost him. I fell in love when we were in jail. I fell in love when we were free again. I fell in love more than once, repeatedly, constantly." She traced her ribbon bracelet, her irises swirling with heat and devotion. "And one night in a forest, that love became unbreakable."

From the depth of her voice alone, I knew what had happened. It was the same turbulent thing that had erupted between me and Jeryn in the ocean. I wondered if Briar would have conveyed more about that night with Poet, had Aspen not been listening.

The princess turned to me. "You will have that too. If you don't already."

The truth stung my throat. I couldn't write this down, couldn't make it permanent.

But it came out anyway. "It will end."

If my voice were audible to them, they would have heard it splinter. Jeryn would leave when he was prepared. This would end, and we would go our separate ways, doing what we could for this world.

The knowledge lanced through me like a spike. It had been easier when we'd been resisting our attraction and our feelings. It had been easier to hate him, easier to feel hostile pain. But after what happened in that celestial ocean, this type of hurt was far worse.

Although I'd spoken the words, Briar's features twisted, and Aspen stepped closer. Either they had managed to read my lips, or they simply related to loss and heartbreak and things that couldn't be, no matter how much we wanted them.

Briar ducked her head, prompting me to look at her. In those earnest features, I beheld not just a leader who reigned, but a woman who cared. "My father once told me that we can't help who enters our hearts. To deny that would be to deny our truest self. However, I didn't understand what he meant until Poet." Thoughts of the jester stoked her irises like kindling. "It can be infuriating, terrifying, and agonizing at times." Then her mouth tipped into a smile, and every scorching emotion in existence fueled her words. "But it also yields the most profound emotions you'll ever know."

And I was happy for her. But the tiny dent in my own heart didn't promise the same fate. After the lightning rainstorm, we'd been disgusted with ourselves. After the medical chamber, we felt guilty. But in the raging sea, we surrendered. The prince and I gave in to something transcendent. By clawing at each other, we clawed our way through scorn and lust, breaching another barrier.

Months ago, I had wanted to drown that man. But now my longings were scattered all over this rainforest, cast in too many directions to forge one path. I didn't love him. Yet I burned like a flame, and I ached like a flesh wound.

The feelings roped around my stomach, even as I shook my head and wrote, *He's leaving*.

"He is not gone yet," the princess reminded me. "I know what it feels like to have limited time—an hourglass draining, with no means to stop it. But it's worth taking advantage of that time. To seize it with both hands." Her expression lightened. "And who knows? Perhaps it will last longer than either of you expect."

Not everyone is Poet of Spring and Briar of Autumn, I scripted.

"They shouldn't be," she affirmed. "Every passion is different. That makes this world diverse." She took my free hand in hers. "And that's what we're fighting for."

The knot in my stomach loosened. The mood lifted, with Aspen parading around the room, nonchalantly gliding her fingers over the robes, nightgowns, dresses, and trousers. "I mean, with all the fuck-me looks passing between you two, it seems like you're having a ton of fun with each other. Secluded in this hot forest with a gorgeous prince who looks like that? Why stop now?"

I penned a response and held up the paper. *He's cold, actually.*

"Even better," the girl replied, batting her lashes in exaggeration. "You get to thaw him."

I laughed. This girl could cut down a warrior one moment, then banter or flirt the next, her boldness infused with a dose of feminine moxie. Someday, she would sashay through a room with the same finesse she used in wielding that axe.

All the same, Briar groaned. "Your mother shall have my head."

Aspen's shoulders hunched. "My mother won't notice," she mumbled, then sought to rectify the comment when we frowned at her. "Oh, she's a good person. But she's not ... she's unwell."

"You know, you can tell us," Briar coaxed, indicating they'd had this conversation before.

But Aspen waved her hand. "Anyway, you're one to talk, Highness. You and the jester only need to glance at one another, and the room becomes a smut scene."

The princess cleared her throat. "Poet has been teaching you too many phrases."

"The hell, he has. I don't need a man to teach me anything." With pride, she jabbed a thumb at her mouth. "This tongue is all mine."

"And with the number of fibs you tell, it's going to get you into trouble someday."

The girl patted the axe squatting on her hip. "That's what this is for." Her eyes wandered toward a blushing pink bustier attached to a crimped skirt, which dangled from a rack. "That sure is pretty."

We followed her gaze toward the dress. I beamed, set down the writing materials, and pranced to the garment. Plucking it from the collection, I held it aloft and shook the hanger in invitation.

"Yes," Briar exclaimed. "Tailored to your measurements, it would look lovely on you."

We guessed, at least. It was hard to tell with the girl concealed.

Temptation lit Aspen's eyes. Yet the moment was fleeting. We might as well have bade the girl to approach a booby trap. The confidence we'd witnessed moments ago deflated, shyness causing her to retreat a step.

"I don't think so," she muttered, fidgeting with her hood. "I'd much rather see that armory crypt again. Any chance we can revisit it before that surly knight gets there and hogs up the goods?"

I set down the dress and retrieved my writing instruments. *You have a kinship with weapons.*

"I like seeing how weapons are made," she answered. "I forged my axe myself."

"Aspen, you never told us that." Briar smiled and gestured to the weapon. "It's extraordinary. Are you telling me we have a prodigy in our midst?"

The girl's posture straightened. "Prodigies are under ten, but I'm thirteen." She patted one curvy hip. "It'll be more obvious soon. I've filled out nicely already."

"Indeed, you have. For the longest time, Poet and I thought you were a bit younger, but over the last few months, that assumption changed. You're growing taller every day." The corners of Briar's mouth lifted. "Nonetheless, it's a remarkable age to perfect such craftsmanship."

From inside the hood, Aspen's skin appeared to flush. "Which is why I'd rather try on weapons than dresses."

"Or you can do both," the princess improvised, sensing the girl's interest as much as I did.

I set down the paper and quill, then padded toward Aspen. She flinched but didn't pull back when I traced a finger along her knuckles, each one strewn with a pattern akin to wood grain, entwined with leaves and brambles and petals. It resembled ink, yet it wasn't. The enigma sank deeper, trenching through her as if she'd inherited it from the land.

"You wear nature on your skin," I whispered. "How lucky to be blessed with this gift."

Despite my moving lips, Aspen somehow understood the compliment. In the future, her body would grow more enhanced, accompanied by the promise of a smoky voice, if I detected her vocal cords right. She would be stunning, with her ample form covered in foliage. By then, hopefully this girl wouldn't hide.

Beneath that hood, two hazel irises glinted. A tail of crimped hair flopped down her chest. If she pulled back the vestment, I had the feeling she would take our breaths away.

Aspen hedged, her attention flitting to the array of clothing. "Is that what boys like? Or ... men? Do they want beauty?"

Briar strode forward. "They want strength. They want intelligence."

I collected my writing tools and wrote, *Beauty is merely a first impression. Passion comes from someplace deeper, and it lasts longer.*

Aspen made a valiant effort to conceal her enthusiasm. "Fine, but maybe ..." She motioned toward a silver dress. "Maybe that one."

The polished material flashed like the edge of her axe. At her age, it would need to be altered, but the girl refused. "Nah. I'll grow into it later."

Yes, she would.

Briar clapped her hands once and feigned an industrious expression. "Now then. As it is, my three ladies are going to flay me for not bringing any souvenirs back from this cellar. But we had best make haste before my fashion-victim husband gets here and claims everything for himself."

Earlier that night, I had climaxed in the arms of a villain prince. This clan had weathered a long journey and an arduous roundtable.

We should be exhausted. Yet we spent the next hour exploring the textile cellar. Under her vestment, Aspen shimmied into the oversized dress, then discovered a plume among the jewels—something she could use to embellish a hat back home. The three of us tried on clothes, dressing one another and filling the cellar with laughter.

We traveled down the corridor with our chosen booty when a draft rustled Aspen's cloak, and muffled male voices drifted from an area Jeryn and I hadn't yet shown our guests.

Setting down the sacks of clothing we'd filled, the females trailed me toward the noise. The alcove's rolling door stood open. Descending the steps, we found the men tarrying with torchlights in their fists, the flames tossing orange across the catacomb.

The knight, jester, and prince wheeled our way as we entered. The prince's face cut straight to mine. He took a step toward me, then halted as if about to step on glass. He wanted to stride my way, to see if I was okay, the impulse written all over him. But he wasn't sure if I wanted that.

I did. My body wanted it so much, the craving itched across my flesh, and my feet pricked with the urge to jump on him. I longed for whatever this miraculous thing was, as much as I feared losing it. But if I gave this man leave to come near me, I might not recover when it ended.

Briar's gaze jumped across the sunken crypt. "This was never part of the legend."

Aspen gave a dazed whistle. "Not something you see every day."

"Aire was having a moment," Poet explained, sauntering to his wife, taking her hand, and guiding her deeper. "One of his senses got a second wind."

"Since then, he's been muttering nonsense," Jeryn groused, reluctantly prying his gaze from mine.

The knight glanced about, his handsome features introspective. "There was a quarrel in this room between family members." His eyes flashed. "Another time, a forbidden tryst between lovers."

Poet described how Aire had been analyzing every room they'd passed on the way here. The knight had philosophized about who'd lived in which chamber, what they had been feeling or experiencing in a given moment, and what had occurred in different rooms. A debate between warriors. Children playing and climbing trees. Residents building these walls and hunting in packs. Aire didn't know all the details, but he felt the essence of them, as if the former dwellers had left their fingerprints behind.

Only one person in this room scoffed at the notion. But Jeryn withheld further judgment and said, "I believe they were eradicated by—"

"A virus," Aire finished. "They were slain by a virus."

Jeryn's eyebrows pinched together. He crossed his arms like a stubborn scientist. "Lucky guess."

We glanced about, paying homage to the fallen. Carefully, we disbanded and ambled through the tomb, identifying more ancients.

One of them lured me nearer. Because we had been here only once, the prince and I hadn't noticed half of the people resting throughout the space.

In one of the compartments lay a skeleton wearing a topaz belt. I waved Jeryn over and pointed. "This one," I said when he approached.

His concentrated gaze narrowed, seeing what I did. "A born soul."

Before historical propaganda about born souls had spread, some of them had been highly ranked for their extraordinary minds. Those who were, had been given these precious belts. At least, in Summer that had been the case.

"They're not the only one," Poet murmured, looming beside another cell where a small body donned the same grand accessory.

Our clan scouted through the hollow, torchlights rippling across the crusted walls. We found more born souls among the humans, faeries, nymphs, and other figures. Jeryn searched for signs of enslavement but found none. Although this wasn't a surprise given our continental history, it did confirm the tales. Before born souls were persecuted, everyone lived freely. This catacomb proved they'd done so in peace, without a hierarchy.

"They resided here as equals," Aire reminisced. "I sense as much."

My lips peeled into a wistful smile. "And look what they made."

After Jeryn translated my words, Poet intoned, "A castle that has withstood centuries in a rainforest."

"And functioned soundly," Jeryn appraised. "It is a valid point. These ruins were built to last, despite environmental hazards."

"So this society got along fine," Aspen concluded.

"More than that," Poet said. "They thrived."

"The Seasons could not refute such evidence," Briar insisted. "Poet and I have gained headway making the same case with The Lost Treehouses." The princess spun my way, reading my thoughts. "This could be what you've been looking for."

My heart clattered. The key to my purpose. I had found it.

41

Flare

But no, that couldn't be it. Although this discovery felt promising, there was a problem.

My shoulders collapsed. Racing to get my quill and paper from where I'd left them by the door, I penned two words. *We can't.*

When everyone balked at me, I shook my head and kept writing. *We can't let the continent know about the ruins.*

"Why not?" Aspen galled.

But after a second of contemplation, Poet's gaze flickered. He knew what I would say. "Fucking Rhys," he hissed.

Jeryn had caught on as well, his features sharpening. "He would demolish these ruins. He would destroy this proof before it had a chance to circulate."

Briar's chin set. "Giselle could oppose him. She's one half of Summer."

"We cannot take that gamble. The odds are slim that we can protect the ruins."

The prince might as well have read my mind. The risk couldn't be taken if we only had one shot, and that shot would be taken in the dark.

Giselle might spurn her husband, but that didn't mean she disagreed with his intolerance.

She would leash the king to avoid war. But she wouldn't stop him from decimating the ruins, if it meant the continent kept its so-called property. Even if her heart had softened a fraction, the queen would fear the consequences of a liberated society. The breakdown of her nation.

No, we had to preserve this fortress and its history. Which meant our clan had unearthed proof we couldn't use.

But there had to be another way, a different key. Maybe it was connected. Maybe I was supposed to bring this knowledge back in another form, without telling people about this rainforest's location, without revealing the map or the ruins.

And if there was, I would find it.

For a precious week, we lived in a dreamscape. Jeryn and I introduced our clan to the forest's magic, including its treasures and dangers and rainfall, the better for everyone to protect themselves. I also presented my fauna pack to them, thrilled when the animals pranced around Aspen's legs and made her chuckle, the spectacle tipping Aire's mouth into a fond smile.

We combat-trained throughout the ruins, using every level as a mock battleground. Poet switched between his staff and a set of daggers, his sculpted chest dripping, his body twisting and spinning as if he was made of liquid. Briar challenged him by throwing a series of thorn quills, the couple's movements syncing. Their eyes magnetized to each other, the fight akin to a mating dance, the princess's gaze on her husband's elastic muscles, his eyes fixating on every part of her. I predicted their clothes wouldn't stay on for very long after practice.

Aire flew through the ruins with his broadswords, his body moving like a gale. He crossed blades with Jeryn, who brandished one of the ancient swords from the armory crypt. Both men stood as shirtless as

Poet, the vision stunning as the jester cut into the fray, skewering his staff between the two fighters. Skin and sinew glistened with sweat, the alpha energy palpable.

Aspen had traveled to another level, to throw her axe at targets. She'd left the moment Aire had stripped off his vest and fretted over the girl staying out of harm's way. To which she had flipped her middle digit and sashayed in the opposite direction, a blush nonetheless tinting her fingers.

I waited for my turn. Gulping water from a canteen, Briar panted beside me and feasted on the jester, while my gaze clung to Jeryn's marble torso, the contours hard and smooth. His movements were more systematic than the other two, aloof and direct and cutthroat.

That body had been inside me. Those hips had snapped with abandon between my thighs.

I clenched my thighs, then got sick of waiting. I needed to move, to stab something, to throw a punch. Leaping between the men took them off guard. Instead of using Poet's old dagger—it gratified him to discover I still had it—I switched to my parents' machete, which I'd polished after retrieving it from the underwater boulder.

Ducking beneath Aire's broadsword, I twisted and used my weapon to block Poet's staff. Then I swerved the other way and threw my fist toward Jeryn's jaw.

Because I'd learned plenty from my brawls against the tower guards, and the prince had witnessed one of those matches, he saw this maneuver coming and blocked the move with his bent forearm. We paused, our gazes colliding. I felt that look down to my core, which had grown wet from watching him wield that knife in nothing but loose pants, his mane affixed into a bun at his nape.

Our companions dissolved into the background. Aire strode off while muttering something indecipherable. Poet and Briar disappeared, likely to have their way with each other.

Jeryn and I careened forward. My weapon crossed with his, our exhalations ramming together. His eyes dropped to my mouth, and mine did the same.

I realized the group had left us alone on purpose. And this was real. This marvel between us was so very real, and there was no going back.

Exhilarated, I called him out. "Stop holding back."

Jeryn blinked. He hadn't been going easy on me, because he knew what I could handle. Yet those pupils blackened, because he also knew one other thing as I broke our stance and sidled away. I hadn't only been talking about the training.

We swam in a jeweled pond. Or rather, four of us swam. Jeryn and Aspen elected to watch, one wary of siren sharks and the other picking at the ground.

Outfitted in a skimpy one-piece garment meant for bathing, Briar rendered Poet speechless. The dark green material gleamed like an emerald, and the low V dipping down the front offered scallop-edged hints of her breasts.

I wore nothing, my unshod heels kicking up sand as I dove naked into the waves. At my exposure, Jeryn's jaw tightened, mayhem storming in his pupils. His mercenary gaze checked Poet and Aire's reactions. But hailing from Spring, with a sexual history that outdid every citizen on the continent, and having eyes only for the princess, Poet wasn't fazed in the slightest. In fact, he would have stripped as well, were it not for the youth in our midst.

Aire averted his eyes out of discretion, his discomfort having less to do with Jeryn's scowl and more to do with Autumn propriety. Instead, the knight monitored Aspen as she roamed the shore gathering cockles. Ever the watchful soldier, her safety remained his priority.

Maybe this penchant had to do with the little brother Aire had lost—a born soul who died at a young age, a tragedy the soldier had confided about during one of our fireside meals. Maybe Aspen reminded Aire of that boy. Or she reminded him of Poet and Briar's son, Nicu, whom the knight also guarded in Autumn. Either way, he'd taken to looking out for Aspen, regardless of how often she tried to dissuade him.

Unable to rip his gaze away, the jester prowled his wife through the water while she chuckled. At the chase's end, Briar wrapped herself around his toned body, and he gripped the back of her head, their mouths clutching in a heated kiss.

My eyes stole toward Jeryn, who swerved his gaze from my own. We hadn't touched since the ocean, much less allowed ourselves to occupy the same space alone, avoiding the subject of where to go from here.

Until him, I had never feared the unknown. Yet the memories of every moan and shudder kept me awake at night, as I stroked the cleft of my body and pictured his face. Each time, I wedged a fist into my mouth. Crying out against my knuckles muffled the commotion, the noises detectable only this man could hear, the short distance between our chambers a punishment and an enticement.

Our clan plotted, envisioning a future continent with all Seasons united. Over firelit talks, the princess would recline her back against the jester's chest, his arms linking around her middle and his chin resting on her shoulder. Aire would sit opposite them, and Aspen would perch on low branches or window seats. As for me and Jeryn, we took up chairs opposite from one another—whether to keep our distance or soak up unhampered views of each other, I couldn't say.

I ventured to the fountain room at dawn, eager to dip my toes into the stream—only to stall in my tracks.

Briar's naked spine jutted against the central column while Poet stood between her spread legs. Naked and drenched beneath the shower, the pair rocked into one another, the jester's bare ass pitching leisurely into the vent of his wife's thighs. While the fountain poured streams down their entwined limbs, they panted and feasted their gazes on one another.

For an instant, I marveled. Briar's freckled breasts rubbed into Poet's rippling chest, and his irises flashed like crushed bits of jade.

With a low growl, he seized the back of her head and pumped slowly, sinuously. Their open mouths grazed, and their eyes clung, and private groans echoed through the space.

That's what it looked like to mate while in love. That's how it looked when two people knew one another's bodies, as they knew one another's souls.

That was passion. That was eternal.

It looked so beautiful. *They* looked so beautiful.

After a spellbound second, I whirled behind the threshold. In the corridor, I flattened myself against the wall, astonishment stapling my feet to the floor. Liquid moans drizzled into the atmosphere, in cadence to their deep lovemaking.

"Poet," Briar whimpered. "I love you."

"I love you more," Poet hissed. "And I'm going to fuck you that way."

Guilt pinched my throat for stumbling in on them. Yet a tender smile curved my lips, their passion filling me with light. If only two people could grace this wild with their happiness, I felt glad it was them.

Poet and Briar had earned the freedom to consummate in every corner of this continent. And I hoped they would.

As their moans grew louder, thoughts of Jeryn holding me, kissing me, fucking me, tugged a wistful sigh from my throat. Thankfully, my friends couldn't hear it.

But the man standing in the shadows did. My gaze staggered across Jeryn idling halfway down the hall, those eyes piercing through me. He must have come up here to quench his thirst, the fountain being our main drinking source.

The prince's orbs simmered with awareness. He heard them too. The sensuous noises caused him to tense, his fingers seizing the flagon he'd brought with him.

While Poet's groans and Briar's cries shook through the ruins, the prince and I watched each other in the half-light. While they celebrated their bond, we remembered the night when lightning rain had fallen, when he'd knelt before me, and when we let loose in a thrashing sea.

We sucked in forbidden gusts of air. The crux of my legs warmed, and his nostrils flared, yearning gripping us by the throats.

But swiftly, Jeryn's features creased. Then he turned, his tall form dissolving into the passage, the vision blurring as my eyes stung.

The breathtaking sounds continued, resonating from that breathtaking couple. Like a balm, it eased the longing. And so I smiled through unshed tears, then left my favorite couple to their pleasure.

We danced in a lush copse where raptors whistled a tune. It was the type of sultry but energetic music that thrived in Summer's culture, meant for people to lash their hips and spin in complex patterns. Partners gyrated in a fast tempo while pressed against one another. To heart pounding rhythms, citizens would dance to break a sweat.

In this rainforest, the elements replaced instruments. This sacred copse emitted its own percussion and acoustics, like drums pounding while birds of prey added their own song, and vibrating twigs replicated guitar strings.

Poet had been the one to find this place. And despite having no Summer roots, the jester was a paragon of movement. He knew the steps, as he knew the dances of all Seasons, keeping up with me as we joined hands.

We twisted one another into a dizzying pattern, our arms whipping about like fluid. Jubilant, I ducked and spun around Poet while our hips matched the pace.

Aire bowed like a gentleman and offered Aspen his hand. Although I couldn't see her expression under the hood, I sensed the corner of her lips tilting. Naturally, their dance was innocent, using measured steps one would find in a ballroom. Still, the interaction was endearing.

Briar and Jeryn indulged in a similar formal dance. However, their heads routinely craned toward me and Poet.

The princess basked in the sight of her husband, who donned a sheer vest, his torso rippling under the mesh. Whereas his wife had chosen a gown of bronze and scarlet, which fell to the floor like water and revealed a plunging back. I had overheard Poet growl seductive notes into Briar's ear when she'd first stepped into view.

As for the prince, he watched me with an intensity that burned my flesh. Trussed up in a short dress woven of ivory and gold, my body glowed like a candle. But it was his sizzling gaze—not the dancing—that had me sweating.

Without warning, things got sneaky. Like matchmakers, Poet and Briar circled past one another and switched partners. With seamless motions, the jester slid my hand into Jeryn's while the princess did the same to the prince. Forcing us together, the clever pair wrapped their arms around one another and continued dancing through the enclosure, as if this had been choreographed.

The prince and I halted. In the glowing light, our gazes fused.

From a few feet away, I heard Poet murmuring against his wife's mouth, "She likes to lead."

"So do I," Briar flirted before the couple got lost in one another.

The heat of Jeryn's body simmered against mine. Our breathless pants mingled. And yet self-consciousness gripped his features.

"I don't know how ...," he began.

I heard the rest of his confession. He didn't know the steps to this type of dance.

My mouth lifted into a grin. Proving the jester right, I took Jeryn's hands and guided them to my waist. *Follow me*, my expression said.

And the look on his face declared, *Anywhere*. And I lost the ability to exhale.

Sinuously, I whipped my hips from side to side, demonstrating the tempo. Gradually and patiently, he mirrored the cadence until we moved like water.

Then we were dancing. Then everything sped up.

My arms journeyed up his chest, and my fingers swam in the blue strands of his mane, and his fingers dug into my flesh. Our foreheads landed together. Damp air thickened between us, the music growing heavier, its thump resounding.

I pivoted, whisking our joined hands overhead, then whirling beneath them. My body spiraled around his, my feet kicking with the rhythm. Aligning my back with his, I ground my ass into Jeryn's, tremors wracking his frame.

In a sudden motion, he whirled, his torso abutting my spine. We swayed, the prince's chin hovering over my shoulder, his arms enfolding me. Those hard fingers splayed over my hips, searing through my flouncy linen dress.

When his mouth brushed my jaw, I gasped and rotated. Resuming our original dance, I clutched his nape and revolved my body with his.

The mesmerized prince made good on his vow. He followed me wherever I went.

The time came to say farewell. Armed with our plans and promises to reunite, we said a temporary goodbye while the stars animated the sky.

At the shoreline, Briar and I gripped one another tightly. I hadn't told her what I'd seen in the fountain room, although I knew this pair well now. Once rumored to be a prickly Royal, the princess had changed. If I admitted to having walked in on the scene, Briar would blush and chuckle sheepishly. Whereas Poet would make a sinful remark, devilish amusement glittering in his eyes.

Nonetheless, that memory belonged to her and Poet, likely among numerous others. For I was certain they'd found plenty of nooks in this forest, in which to make each other shout.

"Soon," the princess whispered into my hair.

"Soon," I pledged over her shoulder, although she couldn't hear me.

We would see one another again soon. Along with the plans we'd made, the jester and princess had sworn to negotiate for my tower mates when they arrived in Summer's mainland. They would bargain to get Pearl and Lorelei and Dante out of Rhys's clutches, then into the safety of Autumn.

They had also agreed to monitor the wellbeing of Jeryn's family remotely. While the Queens of Winter and his parents couldn't be told of his whereabouts, much less that Poet and Briar had seen us, they would at least make sure his kin were alright. Also, they would send us tidings on the states of our kingdoms.

"Come here, sweeting," Poet said, sauntering our way and opening his arms.

I strapped myself around the jester and gave him a mighty hug. As we broke apart, I plucked a leaflet and quill from my pocket, then wrote, *Behave yourself.*

His lips slanted. "I make no guarantees."

As the rest of our clan gathered by the tide, Aire read my words and grumbled. His bronze cloak flapped in the wind, and the breeze combed through his hair as he regarded Poet. "Since when would you ever behave yourself in any situation?"

"I wouldn't. Not unless it impressed my equal," Poet murmured, tucking his wife into his side. "I'm at her service."

Aspen mock-huffed. "I cannot with this man." She tilted her gaze to Briar. "You're one lucky bitch, you know that?"

"I remind her every day," Poet said fiendishly. "And on every surface."

"Whatever it takes, do not let him elaborate," Jeryn commanded with a stony expression.

As the prince strode toward the gangplank, Poet leaned into me. "He looks at you when he thinks you're not aware."

The words clutched my heart. I scribbled, *You notice that?*

"Sweeting, everyone does."

So did I. Constantly, I felt Jeryn's eyes on me.

"Perish the thought of me encouraging you with that one," the jester continued. "However, he's not the same bastard we met in Autumn." Intrigued, he arched an eyebrow. "You possess magic."

A lump budded in my throat. I gestured between us to illustrate my words, then scripted, *We all do.*

Poet raised my knuckles and kissed them. "Make him grovel for a little longer. It'll do the man good." Lowering my hand, he smirked.

"As for the rest: Let's stir shit up, shall we?"

Before our kin left, we stood at the edge of the ocean and watched the moon blaze through the darkness. We would stand like this again someday, united with the rest of the clan. Briar's ladies, her minstrel friend, and her mother.

Jeryn and I stared as Autumn's ship cut through the sea. When the vessel dissolved into the horizon, all went silent. And we were alone again.

42

Jeryn

We gave each other a wide berth while harvesting flora that yielded a topical application for burns. Squatting beside the cluster of stems, I brooded in silence. In my periphery, Flare wrenched the same specimens by the roots and jammed them into her satchel.

Typically, I preferred routine. Presently, it unnerved the shit out of me.

It had been like this for days since the clan left. Uncertain. Unresolved. We had decided, and our paths would eventually diverge, yet the question of what happened until then remained.

The air shifted. We paused and slanted our heads as clouds piled overhead, replacing the meager lacings of blue sky that strained through the canopy. Out of nowhere, insects and avians scattered.

Flare and I followed suit, racing across the dirt and hunkering beneath a copse of ferns. An instant later, the firmament boomed, and the downpour began.

Thunder rain. Its impact assaulted the vegetation, striking with enough force to knock a person to the floor. Blows to the head could result in concussions. I'd suspected as much since our initial encounter with this deluge, back when Flare had exposed herself to every type of onslaught before I could stop her. Believing it to be part of the rainforest's initiation—in accordance with Summer's culture of answering nature's will—she'd been determined to subject herself. With this particular tempest, she had dislocated her shoulder and cursed me to hell as I'd reset it.

As the torrent punched the ground in frustrated sheets, Flare's elbow bumped into my waist. She did not have enough space.

I shifted, placing myself at the edge of our shelter, which provided her with ample room to hide. Partial exposure left me vulnerable, a lone droplet hammering against my knuckles. I hissed and shook out my wrist.

A belt of wind drove through the forest. The clouds were moving swiftly. Perhaps ten minutes of this and we could separate.

Flare's body heat brushed my back. Depleted of patience, I counted. When I finished, the weather cleared.

On reflex, we checked on each other. Neither of us suffered from contusions other than the mark on my hand. That nuisance had already formed into a purple bruise.

Satisfied, we drifted apart. As the hours passed, I caught myself glancing over my shoulder. Flare's legs kicked through the underbrush, her movements producing a swishing sound that matched the sway of her hips, the plants caressing her thighs like fingers.

Enough. For fuck's sake.

I turned away, stalking farther from her. Memories of my cock lunging into Flare, fucking her upright in the ocean until cries poured from her mouth, lingered like the traces of a forbidden stimulant.

I crouched low, jammed samples into my bag, and flinched in surprise. A spindly tendril of green had snatched my wrist. Evidently, I'd wandered a considerable distance off course and ended up in the jungle, where these shrubs had grabbed me once before. While Flare and her fauna pack had played hide-and-seek, the vines had cinched harder each time I'd moved. That had been when I asked Flare to have dinner with me.

I rotated my wrist, exercising cautious motions that kept the plant's grip from intensifying. At length, I disentangled myself from the stranglehold. Quite the formidable hazard, these shrubs' method of defense, which required prudent maneuvering, to avoid getting stuck. Otherwise, this trap would be a danger to one's circulation, among other potential consequences.

I studied the hedges, some of them matching my height and others surpassing it. What had Flare said during our early days? Look farther. Not closer. Although this rule did not always apply, things weren't always as they seemed in this rainforest.

I stepped back and angled my head, imagining how she might view this convolution of foliage. From a distance, something about the pattern struck me. In other parts of this environment, chameleon flowers disguised themselves in plain sight like Flare's map.

The afternoon light waned. My vision would soon be impaired.

I observed at length, noting a concealed break in the hedges. Raising my palms, I approached, expecting to feel the first stab of the wall. Instead, my hands bypassed the shrubs, their density an illusion.

Inching my way through, I stepped into a camouflaged passage. Withdrawing my knife, I progressed through the channel. As the minutes passed, the sound of boiling liquid amplified.

Through a tunnel of offshoots, I strode into an enclosure. Steam rose from a round depression of water. The liquid glowed, its color reminiscent of lapis lazuli, and bubbles shot to the surface from below.

I went through the scrupulous motions of testing the pool, including sticking a branch into its depth to see if it charred the wood, then consuming small bits in stages. The scent, clarity, temperature, and taste appeared to be safe.

By the time I ruled out possible threats, dusk had fallen. Flare would notice my absence. With the sky and moon shrouded, we'd have to navigate back to the ruins by memory.

I rubbed my thumb over the opposite hand, where the raindrop had struck me. Absently, I glanced down. The bruise had smeared, its discoloration having rinsed off after coming in contact with my finger, which was damp from inspecting the bubbling water.

My eyes narrowed. I rubbed my skin again, erasing the mark, although the ache itself persisted. Nonetheless, a theory presented itself and stunted my breathing. Quickly, I stalked back the way I'd come, making a swift trip of it.

Flare had kept to the same vicinity. I found her sitting on the dry soil and admiring the day's end, with her head craned to the forest canopy. Any other companion might have glared and asked me where the hell I'd disappeared to.

She twisted and blinked at my outstretched hand. "Come with me," I murmured.

No protests about missing the sunset. No warnings about the dark paths we'd have to travel through later.

Not that we hadn't grown used to it, but we'd ventured farther from the ruins than usual at this hour. Ever dauntless, Flare set her fingers in mine, the touch producing a blast of heat through my veins.

Fuck almighty. This woman.

Encasing her fingers in mine, I led us to the jungle. As we got closer to our destination, my blood stirred at the prospect of her reaction and what the pool might do for her.

Once we arrived, Flare's lips parted. Her gilded eyes landed on the water and its churning surface, the incandescence resistant to the darkness. I suspected some manner of fluorescing mineral was present, whereas she would expect enchantment like most people.

"I think it's a wellspring," I said. "Healing waters. The spring is hot, conducive to muscle relaxation. But that's not all."

We deposited our satchels, weapons, and belts. The clothes stayed on, though I reached behind and whipped off my shirt, and Flare wore nothing but a slinky linen dress that flounced around her ass. We submerged ourselves. I groaned, the heat washing over my joints while Flare dunked her head, resurfacing on a laugh.

Yet quickly, her mirth deteriorated. It had to be the expression on my face, which had to do with the sight of her neck.

"What?" she asked.

Speechless, I snatched my shirt from the rim. Holding her gaze, I brushed the cloth across her throat and held it aloft, exhibiting it in the water's glow. Traces of paint smeared the fabric.

Flare's eyes widened. After a shocked moment, those irises glistened with comprehension. Then disbelief. Then wonder. A gasp dropped from her lips, and a tearful smile lifted her features.

My lungs failed to function. I had always known she was exquisite. Those metallic eyes. Those enduring hands. But this vision of her was devastating. Freedom made her more stunning than she'd ever been.

Without a word, I offered Flare the material. She took it, her movements eager as she doused the shirt and washed away the sunbursts. The tattoos drizzled, black ink streaking down her body and melting into the spring.

I had not seen her cry before. And while I'd never put stock in miracles, the sight of her joyful tears knocked the fucking wind from me. Seasons flay me, but this moment might turn me into a believer.

With a grin, Flare handed back the shirt. I accepted the garment, crushed it in my fist, and tossed it aside, the wet material striking the ledge. My fingers itched to cup her face. Fuck, I wanted to do a lot more than that.

Underwater, my arms snaked around Flare's waist and tightened, hoisting her against my frame. Like this, she hooked her fingers over my shoulders, and her forehead settled against mine, our noses tapping.

Flare's soaked dress abraded the muscles of my torso. Her nipples toughened, the points scraping my pectorals. Beads drizzled down our chins as we tilted our heads, my exhalations rushing against hers.

My tongue flicked one of her tears and tasted salt. Simple. Pivotal. Then my mouth dragged to hers, our lips resting against one another.

The brink of a kiss. The threshold of more.

I uttered a gruff noise against her lips. "Flare."

"Jeryn," she replied.

Our names filled the enclosure, a latch breaking open after being sealed for too long. I had fucking missed this—touching her, talking with her.

With a shitload of discipline, I marshaled my thoughts. "That night at the ocean. I meant what I'd said." I welded my eyes shut. "I do not deserve you."

Abruptly, she pinched my chin, urging my eyes to open. "Yet you still had me that night. As I had you."

A muscle throbbed in my jaw. "I traded for you. I took you captive."

"But you wouldn't now." Flare sketched a finger across my lower lip. "Besides, nobody owns me anymore."

"And if I have my vicious way, no one ever shall. Yet we are worlds apart."

She nodded. "And in our own world."

I groaned. "You've fucked up my life."

"That makes us even."

"I'm sorry," I hissed, the words slicing from my gut. "I'm so sorry, Flare."

Although I would not ask forgiveness, her bare throat bobbed. "I forgive you, if you forgive yourself. If this has to end someday, let's use the time we have left."

"That will lead to pain. I won't do that to you."

"It's my choice. And with the pain, it will yield something else." Her other palm cradled my jaw. "Something beautiful."

I leaned into her touch, a strange sound creeping out of me, brittle and destitute. "What if I can't do this justice? What if I fail you?"

"Let's find out." She dipped her finger between my aching teeth. "Make love to me."

43

Jeryn

Make love to her. As though I knew how. As though I would succeed. She whispered with conviction, knowing what she deserved and somehow believing me capable of giving it to her.

I had fucked Flare before, but I had not done this. The request dismantled every bit of knowledge I had ever cultivated. Not for the first time, I found myself on the precipice of uneven terrain. Once more with my little beast, I didn't know how to accomplish something.

My muscles tensed. Fuck, I was … nervous.

Yet like a thousand times before, her touch persuaded me to try. What she wanted, I would seek out. Anything she wanted, I would give. Disappointing this woman was not an option.

The vivid blue water glittered. Bubbles rushed to the surface, foaming against her skin.

Recalling every time Flare had brushed through my hair, caressed my jaw, and glazed her mouth over mine, I used those memories as guides. Easing my grip on her waist, I dragged my thumbs over her hipbones.

Flare's eyelids fluttered, restoring my confidence. With each respiration, our wet bodies siphoned together. Her breasts inflated into my chest, the contact agitating my blood.

Skimming my palms under the dress, I raised the material, peeling it up her body. The slow progression compromised our breathing. By the time she extended her arms, and I whisked the sodden garment over her head, our exhales were in tatters.

Her cinched nipples peaked above the water's surface, the sweet thatch of her pussy nudged my cock, and her naked throat glistened. The makings of a growl stoked low in my throat. Tacking my gaze to hers, I seized her waist and walked us backward.

Her fingers fell to the front clasps of my pants. My dick shoved against the garment, my sac throbbing. While sweeping her mouth over mine, Flare picked open the closures and spread the flaps.

My ruddy cock lifted from the material, the torrid water licking my flesh. Flare whimpered as she strapped her digits around the base, encasing me in her grip and rolling up and down. Everlasting shit. The tip grew so broad that I hissed into her lips, making them quirk.

Wanting to feast on that grin, I sauntered forward. Water sloshed over the rim as Flare's ass hit the edge. A puff of air vacated her lips, and she let go of my distended cock. With my frame pressing Flare into the spring, I released her waist and pushed the pants down. She watched, her gaze bright as I stepped out of the garment and flung it to who-the-fuck-knew-where.

With a sigh, the beast captured me, her arms linking around my shoulders. She could not see my cock, as I could not see her cunt. Yet beneath the depth, we felt both.

Rubbing. Tormenting.

I'd grown as firm as iron, and she had become as drenched as the sea. We flattened ourselves together, the better to feel it, to know it. Despite the times I had made her come, some manner of clothing had always stayed on, wedged between our skin, separating us. Tonight, we shed those obstructions.

Wholly naked. Skin on skin.

I relished the stimulation, the profound sensation of her body heating my own. Then I sought more. Summoning additional patience, I let my fingers roam.

Beneath the spring, the pads of my digits traced her outer thighs. Flare shivered, her hands diving into my hair. Encouraged, I ghosted my touch to the ovals of her ass, spanning and kneading the swells. Such an expansive shape for such a tiny figure. She carried it magnificently.

I hummed, learning what my hands did to the beast, committing to memory how she flushed while being idolized.

Taking the afforded time, I slid my palms up the ladder of her vertebrae, then down again. Circling to her pussy, I rasped, "Spread them."

Nodding, Flare split her limbs. With an appreciative groan, I crooked my digits and rowed an index finger along the crevice, which leaked onto my skin. Her head flung back, and her mouth opened, a frail moan filtering into the canopy.

Hard as a rock, I ascended to the peg of skin rising from her center, the clit swollen and delicate. My thumb patted the flesh, the pressure light and coaxing as more whines fell from the pit of Flare's throat.

That glorious, unmarked throat.

Uttering a hoarse noise, I tucked my head into the corner of her neck. My mouth plied her with open kisses, my tongue swiping over where the tattoo collar had disappeared. And Flare dissolved, sagging in my arms.

While I devoured her pulse point, my fingers wandered. Combing through the hair of her pussy. Traveling across her stomach. Climbing her sternum. While sucking on her neck, I pinched her nipples and stroked her tits, then ran my hands along her arms.

Fern trees slumped overhead, their branches hanging like tassels. Steam from this bath coiled into the air, eventide having descended fully.

I lapped my tongue, kissing her throat the way I kissed her mouth. My lips folded over her skin and tugged. Meanwhile, I edged my fingers along her wrists and the curve of her waist.

She liked this. Her thighs inched wider, demonstrating as much.

My little beast enjoyed being sampled like a vixen, catered to like an empress. Further proof of this oozed from her cleft and smeared the ledge of my cock.

The gap of her legs bade me entrance, my hips slipping between them. Yet I needed her wetter. As I had often taught myself, I could do better.

So much better.

I tracked every sigh like a hunter, tested every inch of flesh like an experimenter. With a subtle growl, I dragged my mouth down her throat. There, I skated my incisors across her clavicles.

Flare bowed into me, her grip on my scalp tightening. "Oh," she whined.

"Like this?" I crooned against her. "Is this good?"

She nodded. And so I rode my teeth across her collarbones, then licked into the basin. "And this?"

In response, her fingernails bit into my skull, and my mouth slanted. "Tell me," I demanded. "Show me."

As I lifted my head, Flare dropped her disoriented gaze to mine. She clung to me, the confession tremulous on her tongue. "I don't... I don't know everything I like." Her hands fell to my cheekbones. "Only the things I've felt with you."

My retinas burned. From his grave, I would raise the man who'd fucked her while caged, then snap each of his bones for failing to please her, for seeking only his release and disregarding her need for respite. If the effects had not lasted, he hadn't been doing it right.

But I fucking would. Seething internally, I gave a languid jut of my cock against her soft pussy. The brunt caused her mouth to fall open.

I spoke into her lips, quoting her earlier suggestion. "Let us find out."

The front of her body had been tended to. That left the rest.

I wheeled her around. Filaments of mist writhed into the air, and the water rippled with our movements. Anticipation magnified her exhalations, her chest pitching into the spring's rim.

First, I nibbled on her ear while skating my palms down her arms.

"Teach me when you enjoy it." Lifting those arms up and behind, I threaded her fingers over my nape. "And say it."

Again, she bobbed her head. There was a time when Flare had questioned how I understood what she said, even with her face turned away. By now, she knew.

I heard everything.

My thumbs kneaded her shoulders, loosening the kinks. Pressure. Anatomy. Pacing. These things, I knew well.

Flare sighed as I massaged her deeply, the back of her scalp lulling onto my shoulder. Grinning to myself, I rolled my knuckles down to the scapulas, then to her tailbone.

The head of my cock broadened. Her relaxed moans did this, as did the sweep of her ass into my pelvis.

"That," she heaved. "I like that."

Good. So very good.

I flexed my fingers against her until she became boneless. Stroking her hips. Stroking the pleat of her cunt. Stroking the top of her clit. Stroking the backs of her knees. I ministered to every contour.

"There," she encouraged. "I like it there."

How I favored instruction. How I appreciated candor.

Flare was wrong. She knew a lot about what she liked.

Doctors preferred using tools, but without any at my disposal, I sought an alternative. Reaching overhead, I picked a leaf with a slender, white tip that contrasted marvelously with her complexion.

I rushed its point across her mouth, along her jaw, down the profile of her body. Flare gave a surprised gasp. Intrigue filled the sound, the stimulation plying her with goosebumps.

Tilting my head, I glimpsed her eyelids falling shut. She bent into me, her buttocks rocking against my dick. I sucked in air but resisted the urge to thrust. The leaf quivered over her waist, over the split of her buttocks, and under the water.

Chuffing into her ear, I inquired, "This?"

Tucking the stem between her thighs, I caressed the lips of her pussy. To which, Flare mewled, "Yes."

The entreaty sent a bolt of heat to my cock. I swabbed her with the stem, its plumelike tip etching the folds, sketching the shape of her clitoris until I imagined it swollen.

She would be dilated. She would be dripping and hollow.

Abrasive moans spilled from her lungs. Her wild pulse rammed into my own.

Reaching in front of her, I gripped the spring's ledge with one hand, desperate to restrain myself. To prolong this. To savor this. But for good measure, I sank my mouth into her shoulder and sucked, wringing another yelp from Flare.

With my free hand, I brushed her cunt raw. As I did, she swiveled her waist, riding the leaf until she was shaking.

The momentum never altered. It remained gradual. With each leisurely pass, Flare's temperature escalated.

Intoxicated, I listened as her moans shredded into the night. The sounds increased, and her joints quaked, the impending climax wracking her body. Like a cord pulled taut, my little beast strained herself into the motions, bucking her lips while I caressed her pussy with the stalk.

She stalled. Then she broke into a fit of convulsions, her slit pouring onto the leaf while she came.

I heard and felt her pleasure down to the bone. My cock doubled in size, along with that pounding vital organ in my chest.

"That's it," I praised against the side of her throat. "Just like that."

No sooner did Flare collapse, than I snatched her chin and twisted her lips up to mine. "Now give me one more."

She would come again. Longer this time.

Breathless, Flare crushed her lips to my own. I fused us together, latching our mouths and pumping us into a lengthy kiss. Prying the seam wide, I flexed my tongue with hers, feeding on the remnants of her orgasm.

One of her palms abandoned my scalp to rest on my profile. Groaning, I put all my strength into the kiss, spearing my tongue. I could take her in a thousand ways, with a million tools, and it would never suffice.

Even now, it did not. Winter hadn't finished with Summer yet. It could not, should not, would fucking *not* end with a leaf. She wanted her villain prince to make love to her, and I meant to exceed that request. Indeed, I would make her rapture my life's work.

With my lips clamped to Flare's, I chucked aside the stem and licked into the heat of her. My palms cupped her tits, the nipples ruching. Flare keened into my mouth, her pleasure vibrating down my throat.

Pinning her to the spring, I nudged my waist into the split of her thighs. With eager motions, Flare scissored her limbs farther and arched her ass. A jagged sound fled my lungs, my hands seizing her hips and positioning her.

My heart hammered into my chest. Volatile sex, we had perfected. This was something else.

Terrifying. Alluring.

I peeled my mouth from Flare's and urged her forward, bending her at a slight angle. Hunching over, I nestled my hips, the pome of my cock primed at her entrance. Fucking hell, the folds of her pussy emitted warmth and wetness, still glossy from the aftermath of her first climax.

My mind ceased to exist. In its place, something visceral, instinctive, and evocative took over.

Setting my hands on her hips, I angled Flare's entrance. Then in a single, fitful, prolonged slide, my cock pitched between her folds. One inch, then another, then another. At which point, I lost the ability to keep track.

We gasped. And gasped. And fucking gasped.

My cock opened Flare, her spread pussy clamping around my length, slathering my flesh in her arousal. Pivoting higher, I accessed a narrow point that turned her gasp into a cry.

Hitting that place, I groaned. I had missed this so fucking much.

Encased in the hot grip of her cunt, I swung my hips back, exiting her to the tip and then pistoning again. The friction wrung me out, depleting me of air, sweat bridging across my skin.

With slow lunges, I severed her thighs apart and struck that tapered place inside her. Repeatedly. Softly. Using my knees, I applied all the leverage I had into every languid pump.

Flare tightened around me, spilled around me. Pleas tumbled from her mouth, each one cracking on a moan.

"More," she beseeched.

And so I went deeper, sinking my dick to the brim. She bucked her ass, whisking it against me, joining the rhythm. Together, we rocked back and forth, achieving a new depth.

A growl skidded from my tongue. "Watch your world," I encouraged. "Watch this forest as it watches you."

Flare stared ahead to where the trees towered, their leaves phosphorescent. Predatory noises roared from a remote place. Condensation laminated the grass and slickened our bodies, which enhanced the motions. With her muscles relaxed, I siphoned even deeper, my cock fluid inside her.

I groaned, my head fogging as she squeezed me to the sac. My beast fixated on the wild and sobbed aloud. For my ears only, the octave increased with each patient lash of my cock.

Eddies fluxed across the spring. Suds launched to the surface.

My body mirrored the needs of her own, Flare's ass swiveling with mine. Rather than increase momentum, our hips locked, grinding steadily, leisurely.

I could stay like this forever. I could drown in her wet body. I could sink with her and never resurface.

Let her pleasure fill the recesses. Let her voice dominate this land.

Anguished cries pulled from Flare's mouth. Her pussy grabbed my cock, tiny spasms fluttering around me. A prelude to her next orgasm.

Blood flooded my testicles. Delirium consumed my head.

The bath's temperature made everything looser, sleeker. It intensified the depth of Flare's body. With our flesh doused, we moved with ease, perspiration beading across our skin.

My mouth fell open, pressure building on the roof of my dick. Fuck, how she drenched me. But how much wetter could I make her?

With renewed ambition, I put my entire frame into the task. I hefted myself into her cunt, my thrusts lethargic yet penetrating.

Flare threw her head back and sobbed harder. I felt the throb of her vocal cords, which matched the throb between her walls. I chased those noises, pursued them. But however I relished being privy to the sounds, a greater desire eclipsed that privilege. More than hearing Flare reach nirvana, I wanted her to shout so loudly the world would listen.

"Set your voice free," I urged into her hair. "Make yourself holler."

Flare gyrated her hips, thumping her core into my lap, her moans accumulating. A profusion of fluid heat gushed down my column, wrenching heavy groans from me. One would think we were depriving one another instead of the opposite.

Not to be outdone, she rounded her hips, pliable and wanting. The flanks of her pussy drenched me to the brim, her cleft and my cock working together, fucking into one another.

Her thighs quivered. Her body jolted in tempo to the motions, her fingers scrambling to grab something, anything.

People held hands while making love, did they not? I moved on reflex, out of sheer need, and extended my fingers. Over the surrounding grass, Flare grabbed them and laced our digits into fists. The gesture tugged on a dormant part of me, driving it to the surface.

We clenched, held fast. The veins in my wrists rose, strained.

I bowed my head into her shoulder, summoning every ounce of willpower to keep my thrusts even. The muscles of my abdomen crunched with each measured pass. Flare angled her head toward me, kissed my temple, then broke away on a moan.

Time disappeared. We maintained a silken pace, our waists moving in sync, Flare's buttocks rolling, her cunt pumping down on my cock. Rather than making love to my little beast, the tides turned. Now we made love as equals.

And like equals, we acted in tandem.

Flare twisted. "I need to see your face."

"As I need to watch you," I agreed.

Ravenous, we pried ourselves apart. I whipped my cock from inside her, and she gave a needy whimper as I spun her to face me. Those irises sizzled, pouring light all over me, the brightest fucking thing in this forest.

Tacking her to the spring's edge, I cupped Flare's profile in one hand and hooked the other leg over my waist, bracketing her in place. She steepled that limb high and grasped my ass, urging me to fuck back into her.

Clutching Flare's cheek and thigh, I whipped my cock. She jostled upward, her mouth parting on a moan. My mouth braced the side of her throat. My growl struck her neck, the noise followed by another as I rekindled our rhythm.

Flare cried out and dug her fingers into my buttocks, the commotion punctuated by each slow beat of my pelvis.

"More," I husked into her skin.

And she lowered her pussy farther around me.

"More," she begged.

And I made love deeper into her.

"More," I hummed.

And she spread herself wider.

Howls clawed through me. Fuck drowning or sinking. I would expire like this—would die shouting with her.

Lifting my head, I snatched her breathless mouth. Flare whined into my lips, her tongue yielding with mine. The kiss tested my limits more than anything else, its delicacy cracking through layers of ice.

I fucked her as a shattered prince. She made love as a free woman.

"You're mine now," she sighed.

"And you were made for me," I swore.

In hate. In fear. In lust.

From the beginning, I had belonged to her. More than a throne, a kingdom, or a court, she commanded my every move I made.

Flare dug her fingers into my ass, hauling me deeper. She hoisted her other leg over my waist, driving me harder.

Vivid water illuminated her slack features. Yet I needed to view the rest of her, to witness as much as possible. The better to adjust and accentuate my efforts.

I lifted Flare from the spring and curled her backward. Guided by the motion, she reclined across the grass, sprawling herself for my gaze. Only her petite calves floated in the pool, framing my hips.

There she was. My little beast.

Flare's short waves spilled across the green. Dusky nipples. Scarred stomach. Glistening thighs. Out of the water, blue droplets held their pigment and glazed her body like a gem.

A rarity.

And that lovely pussy, which clung to my cock. That pert clit, which swelled from her crease. Such a superb vision.

She waited for me, her eyes gleaming with too many unidentified emotions to withstand. Soft ones. Bright ones. I could not name them, but I experienced the brunt of their impact.

My equilibrium faltered. My heart ceased.

Standing over Flare, I shook my head in mystification. Grabbing her knees as if to steady my balance, I asked, "What is this look on your face?"

In Winter, citizens sneered at inexperience. They scorned one's lack of knowledge, fluency, literacy.

Flare's pupils glistened. "I think it's the same thing staring back at me. Something I've never felt until now." She smiled and covered my hands with hers. "I think it's passion."

What remained of my composure bled into the spring, purged like the ink that had entrapped her for nearly a decade. Without another word, I spread Flare's knees and probed her with my cock. Flare's skin pinkened, she slumped into the grass like a nymph, and her mouth hung ajar.

Everything came out. Moans. Cries. I jolted my hips forward, filling her pussy, thrusting to the hilt.

Suspended, I gave myself over to this. My gaze burned into hers, each of us watching the other.

My dick pumped farther, deeper, higher. Her core opened wider, wetter, warmer.

With prolonged movements, our waists rocked. I slid my palms to her hips and lifted them off the grass, altering the slope of my cock. This also changed the decibel of Flare's moans, the noises compounding.

My stem broadened. The crown tapped that sweet spot within her, the angle of my body gliding freely.

Groans scraped from my throat. The pressure augmented, threatening to break me in half.

Make love to me.

I blew through my lips and used every joint, muscling into Flare, determined to satisfy her request. She snared my arms and arched into the air, her knees bending around my tireless waist, a scream wobbling on the tip of her tongue.

On the precipice, Flare cried out, "I'm going to come."

"Then do it slowly," I panted.

The rest came out hard, deliberate, authoritative. I'd spoken like a king. That's how her pleasure made me feel. And no matter how this woman owned me, this rule I would not compromise on.

Her first.

Flare's body trembled over the grass. Her pussy quavered, the supple walls clamping onto me, soaking my cock.

Finally, I surged forth. Velocity took over, my hips lunging, fanning out her things. While others made love only one way, we would do this in a thousand other ways.

Flare's thighs clenched, trapping my hips. Her fingernails cut into my biceps. Like that, she pitched off the grass.

Then she unleashed into the canopy. With a holler, my little beast flung her orgasm into the air, the sound expansive. She came long and hard, and fuck yes. So very slow.

The nexus of her thighs convulsed. Her cunt pooled like a river down my cock.

I pumped, drawing out the sounds, encouraging them. As her wet flesh contorted around me, my groans stalled, a new noise pressing through my lungs. Heat rushed to my head, blood ruptured up my cock, and my lips unhinged.

I bellowed just as slowly, emptying into her, spilling my release.

We stared. And came. And came. Our moans tangled, then faded into the darkness.

Out of breath, out of mind, I hefted Flare off the grass. Then I yanked her into a hug.

44

Flare

The wellspring pulsed with heat, tendrils of mist swaying around us as I curled into Jeryn's hard body. His grip secured me to him, his warm cock firm inside me, our bodies intimately attached. Hooking my limbs around the prince, I hugged him back, packing everything I felt into the embrace.

Nothing and no one felt like this. Not even the rainforest's call.

My head banked up to meet his eyes, the dark orbs flashing. He cradled my cheeks, his thumbs brushing the water from my lashes and then moving to my mouth. Those fingers traveled across my lips before descending to my neck.

My bare neck.

Remembering the tower cell where he'd choked me, I compared that memory with this newfound contact, the miracle of living without a collar and the sensation of someone touching me there, reverently and gently. Smiling, I flung my head back. Thrusting my face toward the treetops, I let this enemy-turned-lover explore my throat, then I swallowed a lump and tasted freedom.

Riveted, the villain prince spanned my ass with one palm and caressed my skin with the other. Luxuriating in the moment, I reunited with his gaze. My mouth lifted into a smile, begging and inviting, and he groaned with relish. Jeryn's lips rocked into mine, his tongue stroking with my own, and we held ourselves suspended, our eyes clinging.

We watched ourselves kiss.

The darkness of his pupils reignited the flame. We hadn't known how to make love until tonight, but we'd caught on quickly. And oh, divine Seasons, I needed to breathe.

Pulling back, I gulped the humidity into my lungs. "You're a quick learner."

Jeryn had been on the verge of taking my mouth again, but his swollen lips twitched. "You're an excellent tutor."

I liked this naughty side of him. Or rather, as naughty as this man could get. I liked even more that he reserved it for me alone.

Tucking a lock of hair behind his ear, I whispered, "Hello, Your Highness."

"No," he hissed, his free digits spanning my jaw. "Only Jeryn."

"Is that all I should call you? Not fair."

"Call me anything." He kissed beneath my ear. "Villain." Then my shoulder. "Monster." Then the top of one breast. "Lover." Then his mouth found my heart. "Except leave the title out of it. You are not my subject."

"Then what am I?" I implored.

The prince's head rose, those irises clear and sharp. "You are everything I want and nothing I deserve." He leaned in, the words rushing against my lips. "You are my purpose."

I set a hand to his chest, stopping him. "Does this mean you agree? Will you have Summer until the day we say goodbye? Do you wish to savor the time we have?"

"Fuck, yes," he swore.

Happiness crackled through me like embers. Because the climaxes made me feel greedy, I allowed him a quick kiss, my tongue tingling as he stroked into me. Then I swung my head back, elated by his protesting grunt and feigning coyness. "And what about 'Doctor Jeryn'?

Can I call you that?"

"Mischievous beast," he growled. "You trifle with me."

"Mmm-hmm. It's a habit I'm unlikely to break."

"Call me doctor, physician, healer. Whatever the fuck you want." He jerked me into him. "Now enough. I will have you again."

His mouth dove for mine. Chortling, I veered away, enjoying his displeasure. Sex hadn't done much to satiate this man. Not that I would complain about another round, but my pussy was sore, and his cock couldn't possibly still be ...

Oh. The long ridge between my legs proved otherwise.

Still, an impulse overtook me. We knew this rainforest, from each shadow to every fauna call. We'd learned to find our way in the darkness. Besides, who said we would ever stop this game of chase?

Fancying the sight of him riled up, I tipped my sly head. "If you want me again—"

Without finishing, I scrambled from Jeryn's body, too slippery for him to react quickly enough. Hopping out of the water, I tore into my dress, and snatched my rope belt and machete. Then I jogged backward and raised my arms. "You'll have to catch me."

Jeryn's eyes bloated. He launched from the spring. "Flare. Wait."

I sloshed out of reach, puddles splattering all over the place as I sprinted from the enclosure. While knotting the cord around my waist, I catapulted back the way we'd come, realizing too late that I'd forgotten to grab my satchel full of the plants we'd gathered.

Jeryn hollered my name. Chuckling over whatever he called out, I hurried down the path, knowing he would come after me. If need be, I would sense my way through the jungle and see through the wild's bountiful dark, with its roaming predators and patches of color. That's how I would lead him on a merry hunt.

We had this entire rainforest in which to mate and revel and live out loud.

His voice speared into the night from someplace behind. I dashed around prickly bends and passed under arches braided with stalks of green. Twisting over my shoulder once, I checked to see if he'd gained on me.

A creeper snatched my wrist, yanking and making me stumble. In seconds, the cord slithered around my arm, then scaled up to my elbow. I tried to leap back, but the vine tightened, insisting I stay put.

Suddenly, my pulse sped up. I had been playing, toying with the prince. But my grin collapsed, because this part wasn't funny.

I twisted in distress, hoping to untangle myself with the opposite fingers, but the vine latched onto that hand too. Meanwhile, another one strung itself around my ankles like a manacle, trapping me against the hedge. I jerked my feet and wrenched my elbows, crying out as the bonds cinched harder, forcing me in place. The spindly cords weren't sharp but deceptively soft, like the feathers of a peacock.

I remembered what had happened the last time Jeryn handled one of these vines. We hadn't returned since, so I'd forgotten what these jungle plants did, how they defended themselves, how their grip intensified the more a person struggled.

The whirlpool had the same effect. As did a certain pit of sand I'd once encountered, long before Summer had imprisoned me.

I glanced around, realizing I'd gone the wrong way, diverting from the path Jeryn had originally taken me. I hated myself for this, for not looking where I'd been going.

"Flare!" Jeryn hollered.

I opened my mouth to yell, but one of the vines slung around my neck. The contact seized my lungs, terror stalling my voice. If I shuffled, used the plants to make a racket and signal where I was, the vegetation would burrow deeper, snaring around my body like chains. The vines would tighten, grab my windpipe, and suffocate me.

Please, not my throat. Not that. Not again.

Tingles ricocheted across my fingers, the cords preventing my blood from flowing. My knees buckled, my body toppling sideways into the webbed wall. A family of shoots trussed me up like a fish in a net, shackling me like a prisoner. They would give me welts, scars maybe, and a new collar.

Bugs screeched, the trees bristled, and it was so dark. My name bellowed from Jeryn's mouth, tearing across the distance, but I couldn't scream. I tried anyway, wheezing into the mist, thinking of a thousand sand dunes I had dug myself out of, the places I'd explored with Mama and Papa, the times they had warned me of dangers and the times I ignored them. I had survived each mishap, albeit scratched up and bloodied and beaming at the majesty of nature.

Only once, had I regretted it. And I'd destroyed my parents because of that. I had condemned them to a prison, and it was my fault, my fault, my fault. I had doomed their lives, lost them forever, and then lost myself inside a cage.

Even now, I hadn't learned. I still leaped into this world with open arms, despite what it did to my family, despite languishing for years in that cage. Summer called me feral and mad. And they were right, weren't they? That had to be the reason I forsook all I'd held dear, for the sake of a whim. Just like now.

My hands and feet went numb, as if they'd been cleaved off. I wondered if my head would be next as it dropped forward, my eyelids growing heavy. I could fall asleep here, woozy and stuck in this new cage with the vines, until they mummified me up to my lips.

Lips. Teeth.

Oh. My teeth.

My mouth dragged toward one of my trapped wrists. I would have to bite through the knots, and since I knew how to undo such snares, I understood what places to seek out. With my mind frothing like bubbles, I squinted at the enmeshed stems and searched for their centers, the kinks holding them together, the places to gnaw on.

My lips found the right strings and chomped, a cool syrup oozing down my tongue. The vine shuddered, and I wobbled, and an invisible wind blustered through me from the inside. I bit again, and again, and again. Then I swung my chin in the other direction, chewing some more, snapping the threads. My throat filled with air as it got free, and my arms flopped to my sides as the bonds fell, a queer sensation prickling my lips and fingers.

That left only my legs. I blinked down at them, marveling at how strange they looked wrapped up. The cords twined to my calves and scuttled higher, covering every inch of my skin, swaddling me the way spiders did to their prey.

One false move, and the vines would whip me back into place, then drag me into their web. I inched my hand down to the machete, drawing it from the rope belt, and bent my quaking knees, sinking as far as I could without disturbing the foliage. I found more knots and flicked my weapon, slicing through them.

But the prickles got worse, spreading to my toes. It felt like the opposite of warmth, the reverse of heat.

What was happening to me? Why were my teeth clacking?

I licked my lips, tasting more syrup. The cords fell away, the forest spun, and I crashed to the dirt floor. Footfalls pounded toward me, arriving as I hit the ground. Crystal and slate blue blurred together, such a regal combination. I had been poisoned by fruit, and he'd survived a siren shark attack. Although the latter had never penetrated the prince's blood, we knew how it felt to have our bodies violated by this dark, wild, lovely place.

I figured it was my turn once again. Mama used to say everything in fairytales happened in groups of three. Maybe in legends too.

At least the vines hadn't scarred my neck. That made me happy.

As the prince manifested above me, I grinned. "Jeryn-n-n, I esc-c-caped. I s-s-saved myself."

45

Jeryn

She lay in a pile on the ground, with the vines scattered around her like severed arteries. The sight dug a trench in my stomach. I tossed our satchels aside and plummeted next to her.

"Flare," I said.

"Flare?" I hissed.

"Flare!" I growled.

Beaming up at me, she uttered something indecipherable, her words slurring and her teeth chattering. Her head slumped as if she'd been drugged. She passed out, the deep olive leaching from her complexion, the skin glazed in a frosted pallor. It resembled the sort of cold I hadn't encountered in months.

Numb. Chilled.

After getting caught in the web of vines, she must have fought against them, thus exacerbating the problem. The plants had cut off her circulation, which accounted for the rawness around her wrists and ankles. And based on the mottled skin, Flare's neck had been assaulted as well, which must have terrified her. Still, the discoloration was fading quickly and would leave no scars.

With the machete, she had clearly liberated herself from the snares. Indeed, she saved herself.

Then she had damned herself, these vines somehow causing a decrease in body temperature and a loss of consciousness. But if that were the case, I'd have experienced those symptoms in the past, back when my own wrist had been trapped.

I went to work. She needed me to be calm, brisk, precise. My little beast needed me to be right.

Clasping Flare's face, I tipped it toward a beam of forest light. I checked her pupils as best as I could, those gilded eyes having lost their luster. Bereft of heat, fury, spirit.

Fuck. My pulse rate tripled. I checked her heartbeat, which had waned.

Flare's hands started to bloat, a cast of pale blue creeping across them. From there, the color swiftly progressed to her lips, as if her blood had turned to ice.

No. No!

Not her. Never her!

My finger skated across her mouth. Frantically pulling away, I held my digits aloft and rubbed the pads together, a cool fluid coating my skin.

Swearing under my breath, I peered at one of the limp vines. Leakage dripped from its stub, the edge crusted as if someone had bitten into it.

Flare and her incisors. From circulation to contamination. One that mimicked hypothermia.

My hands tore through the satchels. Pointless, I remembered a second later. We hadn't gathered anything to treat this.

I scooped Flare against my torso and wrenched her off the ground, packing her tightly into my arms. Gradual body heat was paramount, but by the time the embrace should have had an effect, the symptoms hadn't abated. That fucking blue tinge still assaulted her flesh.

Disregarding the bags and hauling Flare from the dirt, I crushed her against my chest and vaulted into a run. Speeding her to the wellspring, I wavered for a crucial moment. I might not be thinking straight. Thermal water could shock a hypothermic body and seize the heart.

It could in Winter or any other Season. But in this rainforest? In this wellspring?

I waded into the water with Flare. Splashing liquid over her welts dissolved them, but that was all. When I submerged us, the temperature did nothing to warm her.

"Flare," I urged.

In that name, I professed too much, admitted too many things. Like an avalanche, the words poured out.

"Don't do this to me," I warned, rubbing Flare's arms to imbue her with body heat. "Don't test me this way." But when that didn't suffice, I coaxed desperately, "The forest needs you, remember? Don't abandon it. And what of the key? Who else will carry out your mission?"

Her lips parted but emitted no sound. I spoke quicker while dousing fluid over every inch of her flesh. "Flare ... please," I stressed, my throat congesting. "Don't fucking leave me."

That rebellious mouth hung open, depriving me of a response. Nothing in my medical chamber would solve this. When it came to venom and poison, the rainforest knew how to mask itself, and developing treatments in that regard had been elusive. Aside from that berry incident with Flare, other redresses had slipped from my grasp, lost to me.

Slipped. Lost.

My free fingers sought the hollow of my chest. Winter wore the perils of ice on its shoulders. Within certain forests, one might encounter a poison derived from a translucent nut. Eating it produced a rapid, frost-bitten state. I had devised an antidote that worked against multiple poisonous and venomous infestations, including that one. I knew the remedy's bitter, herbal taste well. I'd administered it to myself countless times over the years, although I hadn't needed it. Not for that reason.

I'd been taking it to calm myself, to ward off the contrived portents of madness. Until arriving here, I'd been wearing that restorative around my neck.

The vial and its contents, sunken at the bottom of a whirlpool. Engulfed in what might be a sandy floor.

Seething, I launched from the wellspring with Flare clutched in my arms. On the way back down the path, I swiped her sand net from the discarded satchel. Thankfully, she often insisted on traveling with that net.

Drenched and out of my fucking mind with fear, I cut my way out of the jungle and shot through the rainforest. Yet within seconds, my limbs hesitated on the safest direction. I knew how such ailments affected their victims. Charging to the ruins where she'd be protected required a longer trip, which would deplete Flare of critical time.

The echo of rushing water reached my ears. My gaze cut south toward a clearing where waterfalls poured over rocky projections and converged in a pond. As opaque steam clouds launched from the surface, I remembered this place. We'd been here before, when Flare slayed me by dancing in a small funnel of sand.

Two options broke me in half. To squander precious minutes racing to the ruins. Or to preserve those minutes and trust this realm, as Flare would say.

With haste, I lay her gently on the bank. I moved quickly, peeling off the sodden clothes and grimacing because I lacked a blanket in which to bundle her.

I could not leave my beast here alone. But if I didn't, she would not survive.

A purr rumbled from behind. Knife in hand, I whipped toward the disturbance. The jaguar from Flare's pack approached, its marbled fur saturated in red and black. I stiffened, ready to block Flare from the creature but halted at the tender noises coming from its throat. Something protective kindled in the feline's eyes as she came nearer, her expression cautious on me.

I stared, calculated, assessed. The animal wanted to help.

Carefully, I watched. Prepared to attack, I observed as the sabertooth padded over to Flare, slumped to the bank, and curled beside her limp form, the fur certain to keep her comfortable.

So be it. Cupping Flare's frigid cheek, I leaned down and whispered against her mouth, "Wait for me, sweet beast."

Tearing to my feet, I snatched her sand net and raced from the waterfalls. From the ruin caves, the route to the whirlpool would be direct, but it would also be longer. If I could squeeze or climb my way past the boulders separating this side of the island from where we'd originally set up camp, I would reach my destination faster.

I broke through the forest and catapulted onto the southwest cove. Waves smashed into the cluster of rocks, breaking apart with a shout, spraying my face and torso. In this setting, navigating the crags would be destructive. But at high tide, swimming around it was out of the question.

Affixing the sand net's handle to my belt, I contemplated the slick, uneven surfaces that could shred me to ribbons. My size. My unshod feet. The fact that I couldn't see a fucking thing, forcing me to feel my way through.

Madness. Foolishness.

Flare. Cold. Dying.

In seconds, I reached the boulders. My palm skimmed the partition for an opening, only to locate a channel too narrow for a damn eel to slip through. I would gut myself open on the jagged facade or get consumed by the tide.

Flare.

I dropped to the ground and crawled into the artery. Let this ocean try and rip me apart.

My limbs raked through drenched clumps of sand, the ocean plowed into my frame, and saltwater doused my eyes. Gritting my teeth, I whisked my face sideways, avoiding another onslaught. I dragged myself to the right, then left as the enclosure swallowed me, its razor-sharp walls chafing on all sides. A wave shoved itself down my ear canal and flooded my throat until I vomited, and something carved into my lower back.

The conduit expanded. Finally, I sucked in a mouthful of air and spilled onto the southeast shore. Blood from a wound I couldn't see painted the sand red.

Staggering upright, I shot back into the forest, offshoots scraping me raw like the edges of a thousand swords. It would have been unfeasible to forget this place, even if I hadn't chronicled the terrain with Flare. The pool swirled near the rainforest border, abreast of the cove.

I heard the eddying water before I found it. Pausing at the maw of the abyss, I felt the surface towing me into the memory.

The seething tug of the water. The absence of breath. The vial, stolen from me.

Was there a bottom? Unknown.

Might the vial be down there? Hopefully.

Could Winter innovation have produced such a durable piece? Potentially.

I'd told Flare about the pendant's contents. She knew it had been lost, but I hadn't mentioned the source. She might have assumed it happened during the shipwreck. A fortunate thing, for if I'd told her after we became friends, the reckless female would have plunged into the depths and attempted to retrieve the necklace. In her efforts, she might have gotten sucked under.

In all this time, I hadn't endeavored to recover the vial. Afraid to try. Afraid to fail. Afraid to succeed. To rely on that liquid again.

That wasn't all. I glared at the vortex, my nostrils flaring with shallow exhales, panic crawling under my skin. Siren sharks could make a home down there.

Flare's eyes. Flare's smile.

I fisted the net, filled my lungs with oxygen, and dove in. The whirlpool clamped on, yanking me down its throat, the water circuiting and swallowing me whole.

Rotating, I opened my eyes. Phosphorescent light from above illuminated the void. Pumping my arms increased the pool's hold, plunging me into its bowels.

I remembered this. As I thrashed and encouraged the water, its grip drew on my weight, wheeling me in.

My ribcage ached. My limbs smarted.

More. Then farther.

At this subterranean level, I could no longer see a fucking thing. Reaching out, I grappled for a foundation. At length, my fingers shaved the liquid and hit sand. I leveled my palms and felt around, letting the whirlpool tow me along the floor. Its speed helped to scout the area quickly.

Yet nothing. Everywhere, nothing.

The sand net, then. Which I had no idea how the fuck to use.

Withdrawing the handle from my belt, I took an educated guess and thrust the bristling apparatus against the ground, sweeping in a side-to-side motion. The longer I combed the bottom, the deeper the net burrowed. But each time it snatched something, the entity turned out to be a stone or reed stalk.

Careening back and forth, I kicked to ensure the pool kept me down. My chest burned, and my throat compressed. The water was choking me, the passing seconds tenderizing my flesh for the inevitable shark attack.

The net jerked and tightened like a fist, hooking itself to an object. I felt around the mesh with my free hand, my fingers making contact with a piece of glass, its fang shape affixed to a chain.

Yanking up the net, I caught the item. All the while, her words cycled in my mind.

All you needed to do was let go and stop moving ... when you stopped, the water let you go.

Seizing the vessel, I let my body slump and felt the whirlpool's hold loosen.

Overhead, swirls of black, blue, and green rippled from beyond the surface.

Yet I would freeze this world to see gold.

46

Flare

I would burn this world to see crystal. One more time to see those eyes, to feel them piercing me like crushed ice.

Or no, I wouldn't burn this world for that, because it would be selfish. But I would forsake every sunset and sunrise. I would dwell in darkness for another chance to savor his face, hear his voice, and wrap my body around his.

At least we'd made it real. At least, for a moment.

I should be afraid, yet relief washed away the fear. Before sinking into this void, I'd been shivering, a terrible sensation biting my flesh. So much cold was drowning me, pulling me down.

But now the deep held me fast, nestling me into its embrace. At some point, I must have broken the surface. I sighed, expecting to feel the afterlife, someplace lush and vibrant and warm. Heat soaked into my pores at last, and blades of grass tickled my toes. Yet it seemed so real.

The whoosh of tumbling water brushed my ears. The scents of blustering winds and needle forests coaxed my senses. Then a set of knuckles traced my neck. The place where I used to wear a collar but didn't anymore.

My eyes tore open—and found what I'd been searching for.

Two flashing irises stared down at me, so dazzling it hurt to look at them, so clear I might have been peering into glass. Dark blue lined his lower lashes, which widened as I stirred, relief and something bottomless consuming those orbs.

My villain prince.

We lay on the ground, with his large frame cocooning mine. I'd been curling into him, a blanket covering my naked flesh and his body heat radiating into me. His free arm clasped my waist, holding me tightly. He fastened me to him as though I might disappear, as though he would keep me from vanishing or sinking or drowning by strength and force of will.

My fingers shook as they stole out to etch his jawline, unhinging it from its locked position. At the touch, a ragged breath tore from him. He seized my palm and suspended it against the side of his face.

"Flare," he rasped.

My lips lifted into a contented smile. "Jeryn."

But instead of replying, the prince's head dropped forward, and he buckled. Tremors wracked the muscles of his bare torso, as if a thousand rocks were tumbling from his back.

Confusion and concern urged me to shift, to splay my fingers over his cheek. "Jeryn?"

But he shook his head, then flipped his gaze back to mine, at a loss for words.

A dawning sky swam overhead, a honey color filling the heavens as I rested on a green bank. Beyond, an oasis of waterfalls smashed into a turquoise pond and spritzed the air. We'd been here before, when I had sketched in the soil and danced in a sandstorm.

But the last thing I recalled, we had been making love in a wellspring, and then I dashed into a maze of vines, and then ...

I remembered. The gripping vines. The tendrils shackling me. The vicious cold. I'd collapsed right before Jeryn's face had swum above me.

And I knew. Death had tried to haul me down like quicksand, ripping me from this rainforest, from my purpose, from my friends.

From him.

Grief and gratitude clotted my lungs. My eyes stung, and a dry sob squeezed from my throat. "You saved me," I choked out.

Jeryn seized my face. "No," he hissed, pressing his forehead to mine. "You saved yourself. Then you saved me."

I'd seen many expressions on this man's face. Frigid brutality. Cold indifference. Callous superiority. Hate and lust. Remorse and shame and trauma and panic. Intrigue and fondness. Passion and desire.

But I'd never seen this look. Raw and petrified, unbridled and unconditional. His features spasmed, on the brink of collapse, an uncharted emotion smashing through that facade.

"You saved me," he repeated, the next words tearing from the pit of his stomach. "But I almost lost you."

Another sob dropped from my mouth as I kissed the crook of his mouth. "But you didn't."

"But I almost did."

"But you didn't." My lips veered to his jaw. "I'm here." Then to his cleft chin. "I'm here." Then the ramp of one cheekbone. "I'm here, Jeryn."

I sketched his mouth, the contact tremulous. His eyebrows pinched in agony, then relaxed as I planted kisses on every crease, every trench across his countenance. Angling my head, I sketched the underside of his jaw where it met his throat, tasting the low rumble of a groan.

The cords of his muscles unwound. His fingers dove into my hair and gripped my scalp for dear life.

As the cascades tumbled down rocky brackets, our intakes shifted from unsteady to solid. Jeryn hovered, his hair falling around us. I laved his neck, then up to the ridge beneath his earlobe, to show him I was here, to assure us both.

I was here, breathing, and alive. And so was he.

With each taste of him, liquid heat poured to the center of my body, a delicate throb building. Whimpers dripped from my tongue. My ministrations quickened, desperation building, a celebratory rapture.

For an instant, Jeryn hesitated. The doctor in him thought we should slow down, that I needed rest. Any moment, he would insist upon it.

But I'd been sleeping for long enough, and since when had nature ever kept me down for long? More dreams wouldn't soothe me. No, I wanted the verve of life and its untamed rapture.

The prince must have sensed this. At last, he hummed, his head lolling forward in supplication. He shared in this rejoicing, this wild need to revel in our survival.

What he felt, I felt.

What he realized, I realized.

I didn't need him strictly to stay alive or satisfy a craving. I simply needed his presence, his arms, his mouth, his words.

My hands raced down his pecs and abs, the contours hitching under my fingertips as I lightly scraped down to the ramps of his hipbones, where a trickle of dark hair led to his waistband.

I sketched the rim, the motions gentle. The prince's high cock shoved against his pants, and a rumbling noise grated from his chest. "Flare."

Yes. Me. Only me.

"I never," Jeryn husked. "I never fucking knew ..."

Never knew it could be like this. Neither had I. He was the last person I'd imagined wanting and the last person I could let go of.

This villain was mine. And I was his.

I steepled one leg. The edge of the blanket slumped over my upper thigh, and the gap opened for him. Jeryn must have felt the heat brimming from my crease because he groaned once more and lowered himself closer, giving himself over to me.

I feasted on his shoulder, biting tenderly. I switched to the opposite side and skated my mouth up his collarbone.

A chain hung from around his neck, an empty vial dangling from the end. While I'd been dreaming and dying, the prince must have found it at last. The fang-shaped memento had lasted all this time, without a chink or scratch, except for the one I'd made long ago.

Plucking it between my digits, I rubbed my thumb over the crack.

Then I raised the pendant to my lips and gave it a soft kiss.

Jeryn. Snapped.

With a growl, he clamped onto the back of my head and hauled my mouth to his. Our lips collided, tongues hurling into each other. I whined, scratching my fingers through his hair and heaving him into me.

He lunged, veering over me fully, his waist splitting my thighs apart. The magnificent weight of his body wrenched me backward and ground my spine into the grass. Snaring my wrists, Jeryn rammed them overhead, stamping my hands to the bank.

Bowing over me, he crushed our mouths together, splaying my lips wide and rocking into them. My head flaked into stardust, and my body blazed like starlight. I vaulted into the kiss, our tongues dashing.

His cock pulsed, thick and heavy against my aching cunt. My inner folds slickened, arousal pouring onto his pants.

Gritting out another noise, Jeryn drove the blanket down and flung it aside. I lay sprawled under him, naked and vibrating with need. My nipples hardened into points, and my body inflated with each anticipatory exhalation.

Jeryn drank in the sight. Irises like crystals, like glass, like ice. They engulfed me, then disappeared behind his swollen pupils.

From hate-lust beneath a lightning rainstorm, to a darkly sensuous night in his medical den, to the passionate surrender in the ocean, to our bittersweet union in the wellspring, every time had been unique. A dangerous but intimate path we'd needed to take, to arrive in this moment. For all the chasms we'd crossed, this was unlike anything that came before and anything that would come after.

The backs of my eyes burned, threatening to spill.

Jeryn kissed my lashes. "Do not," he pleaded, sensing the tumult. "Please do not."

"Then take them," I implored. "Take them away."

Until every teardrop had drained from my soul.

On a guttural rasp, the vanquished prince heaved me back to him and crushed his lips to mine again, driving his tongue with my own. I arched my breasts, my nipples abrading his torso, the traction stunning. Moaning into the kiss, I caught and sucked on the flat of his tongue, loosening a hiss from him.

Prying his mouth from mine, Jeryn worshiped the rest of me. Stamping my hands into the grass, he sucked on my throat, nipped at my pulse point, and licked down the gulp between my breasts. Dragging his mouth over one swell, he gripped the crest between his teeth and drew on it while swabbing his tongue over the peak.

A shriek got stuck in my mouth, pleasure sizzling between my thighs. With every tug of his mouth, the noise rose closer to the surface until it catapulted into the trees. Jeryn hummed his approval around a mouthful, then swept to the opposite nipple, circling the bud and sucking it raw.

Every stunted noise in existence wrung from my lips. I needed him everywhere, filling me to the brim, as deeply as he could reach.

Jeryn raked his mouth down my stomach, then grabbed my knees and yanked them apart. My pussy splayed out for him, pink and soaked. Those eyes glinted, his angular features taut. His beauty had always been on the merciless side.

Lifting my legs and latching them over his shoulders, Jeryn plied my skin with kisses. His mouth traveled from the indentation of my foot, to my ankles, to my calves. He dabbed his tongue behind my knee and over the caps. This man wouldn't stop until he'd left imprints of himself on every inch.

But there was more. The touches and kisses were attentive, healing. Winter gave more than he took, because this world had already stolen so much from me.

Curse him. If he wanted to stop me from crying, this wasn't the way. Yet I couldn't stop this man, wouldn't stop him. My eyes clung to the sight, my chest constricting as he ran his mouth up my inner thighs. This vision of unbridled devotion wetted me anew.

At last, he released my legs and thumbed my folds, tracing the oval opening with concentrated urgency. My mouth fell open on a cry. Tilting his head, Jeryn watched the wetness seep from my cunt, liquid dousing his fingers. Helpless, I bent off of the grass as he traced me. Then I rolled my hips, coating his hand, the motion saying please, please, please.

"There we go," he murmured. "Show me where you need me."

"Inside me," I chanted between gasps. "Get inside me."

Crooning, Jeryn plunged his head between my thighs and stroked his tongue up the pleat. The cries kept coming, kept emptying. I snared fistfuls of his hair and rode his mouth, his tongue licking and probing my walls.

My hips vaulted as Jeryn strapped his mouth around my clit and sucked. Uttering a famished noise, he swerved his tongue over the crest, hardening the knob of flesh until my body shook.

But not enough. This wasn't only about me. It was about us.

I made a plaintive noise and batted at his shoulders until Jeryn released my clit. My fingernails stabbed into his flesh, pulling on him.

Come here. Come to me. Come with me.

As he crawled up the center of my body, Jeryn's hand lowered. Deftly, he picked open the closures of his pants, his gaze fusing with mine. I reached out to help, undoing the clasps, then kicking the material down his legs with my heels.

His cock jutted free, its girth ruddy and swollen, cum rising from the line at his crown. Staring at me, Jeryn shuffled the pants from his limbs. His naked body covered mine, my knees pitching high around his backside.

So much weight loomed above me, so much hardness. I'd never seen a glacier, but I imagined his complexion looked the same. Despite the sun, this trait hadn't changed.

Hellfire. Jeryn.

He anchored himself upright, the better for us to witness each other's undoing while waterfalls crashed into the neighboring pool. Muscle on muscle, bone on bone. My legs coiled around his waist, my fingers about to scar his back until it bled.

The prow of his cock braced against my pussy. We panted into one another's mouths, wincing at the teasing pleasure. I bucked into Jeryn's waist, imploring, pleading, demanding.

His eyes hooded. Deliberately, he nudged the inflated tip into the opening, accentuating the motion with a velvety request. "Tell me."

"Fuck me," I entreated, my words crackling like flames. "Let me fuck you back."

"Seasons, Flare." Falling victim to my plea, the prince grabbed my thigh and looped it higher, then swung his cock forward an inch. "What else?"

I mewled, "Lose control with me."

Another groan. Another inch.

"What else?" he prompted. "Tell me what else."

"Break down with me. Fall with me."

He pivoted deeper, the width of his crown spreading my pussy. Although we kept our attention linked, I glimpsed his broad flesh sinking into me. The crest had vanished, and the stem darkened, the sight robbing me of breath, the contact staggering.

My eyes lifted to his. I gripped his face and drew my tongue across his lower lip. "Make us come."

His features tightened, but his eyes gleamed. With a hiss, Jeryn slung his hips between my thighs, his cock flexing halfway into me.

Unable to stand it, I met him the rest of the way. Grasping his waist, I raised my hips and gave a shove, using the momentum to flip him over. On a husky grunt, Jeryn hit the grass while I swung my leg over his hips and landed astride him. Sitting upright, I straddled his body, all that strength and sinew expanding beneath me. I lowered my pussy fully onto his cock, engulfing him to the sac.

A noise ruptured from Jeryn's mouth. He bowed into me and cut his fingers into my hips. "Fuck," he seethed.

That word, coupled with his voice, charged through me. Awe and adoration electrified my veins. That, and an arduous sort of power. Not because I dominated him but because we shared that domination, equally given and taken.

My cry mingled with his groan. I shook above him, and he shook underneath me, my cunt grabbing him to the hilt. Divine Seasons, this feeling never wilted, this desire never waned. Rather, it kept growing, unfurling across every edge of my being.

I dug my fingernails into Jeryn's chest, threatening to break skin. I knew how he liked to mix pain with ecstasy, as he knew I loved to marry tenderness with ferocity, lightness with darkness. We knew each other by now.

"Look at me," my prince uttered. "Keep looking at me."

I did. "Keep looking back."

"I'll never stop. Wherever I look, you will be the only vision that consumes me."

Because he saw me. And he heard me. And he knew me. Because he was different, and I was different, and we'd never be the same again.

Our bodies vibrated like wires. It took a while to recover.

Jeryn caressed my knees, my thighs, my waist, my breasts. Watching me, he thumbed my nipples and savored how my eyelashes fluttered.

Desire bloomed across my flesh. His body spanned the ground, the tide of his blue hair shored on the grass. I splayed over him, the muscles of his stomach clenching under my gaping thighs. My gaze riveted on the place where my pussy grabbed his cock, enchanted by the sight to the point where a low growl crawled up his throat.

My arousal oozed down the prince's flesh. Another rumble scrolled from his chest as he felt my insides grasp him to the base.

Then I unraveled like the sea, like a tail of flame. Bracing my palms on his chest, I swayed my waist. This lodged him higher, deeper.

Jeryn's mouth unhinged, baring his teeth. And that was how I rode him, jutting my hips, stroking his cock. Each teasing swat pulled a groan from his lungs and threw me into a stupor.

Never did our gazes waver. Jeryn's sharp eyes locked with mine, the wells deep and dark but open. So wide open for me, my reflection filling his pupils the same way he filled mine. In this secluded realm, nothing else existed. If we stood on opposite ends of a crowded room, it would be the same. And if we lived oceans and mountains and forests apart, he would still encompass me. I would still feel him, hear him, see him. Just as he would feel me.

My throat was clogged with too many emotions to endure. I channeled them into my movements, the force enhancing every sinuous circle of my hips. Poised above him, my thighs spread wider, sealed his cock in the cleft of my body, rowing my pussy over him.

Jeryn's pupils bloated, his pulse point drumming against his neck. The vision ignited sparks down my spine, my walls dripping down his length, the connection astounding, how we rubbed together. I was so wet, and he was so hard, and we worked in tandem.

Pressing firmer onto Jeryn's chest, I swiped my waist and brushed my fingers over his nipples. Tremors tracked down his frame, black pupils eclipsed his irises, and a hiss slipped from his tongue. Those reactions incited a delighted frenzy, power and ardor fueling me to exaggerate the movements, my curves grinding.

His palms slid to my ass, encouraging my thrusts. He lay there as I took him, as I indulged myself, as I pushed us closer to the brink. Anchoring me to him, boosting me above him, Jeryn gave me dominion over this, for as long as I needed. I fucked him, and I fucked myself, and I made love to us.

"Bewitching," he urged. "You look so fucking glorious when you ride me. So gorgeous when you pleasure yourself. So stunning when you take my cock inside you. It's excruciating. It's paradise."

Actions rather than endearments or comely words had always been his nature. Yet at his speech, blood rushed up my thighs. I sped up, galloping on him, sucking his girth into me. Exquisite tension swirled in the spot where our bodies clamped together. Moans poured from me, my body undulating like a wave, building and heightening. But not yet reaching.

Mist beaded across the sculpted plank of his torso, mingling with sweat gliding down the side of his throat. Cravings parched my tongue, so that my head dove, my mouth catching his neck like a prize in my net. He tensed and then slumped, his head flinging backward as my lips devoured his skin, my tongue tracing a vein and drawing in its thudding pulse. At the peak of his throat, the round part that bobbed whenever he swallowed, I latched on. And under his jaw, I licked while a rough sound tore out of him.

His grip tightened on my backside, burning me to the core. I marveled and ached for more of the forbidden, more of this felicity.

How could this feel primal and precious all at once? How could anything feel this elemental, like we'd been fated for this?

I chased my hips, chased his cock, chased the answers. Pleasure splintered from my mouth, one after the other, each noise falling into a collision with his sharp grunts. I relished the erotic sight of this future monarch, with sunburns and scars on his flesh, dewdrops on his temples, and his mouth unhinged.

He may have given himself over, offered his body so that I might find euphoria in the aftermath of terror. But I wasn't the only one who'd survived this rainforest. We had done that together, and we would do this together as well.

I bent farther over Jeryn. My fingers sought his own, our digits threading and balling into fists on either side of his head, like a knot of our own making. Using this leverage, I lurched backward and forward with abandon, yanking shouts from the prince, which tangled with my sobs.

Skin slapped against skin. Hands squeezed together atop the grass.

How Jeryn managed to remain stable, merely watching and gripping and encouraging, I couldn't fathom. Whereas I thrashed and writhed, he now recognized my torment, answered my call, and broke into motion.

Strength and stamina detonated beneath me. Releasing my fingers and bracing my buttocks once again, his hips launched upward, the head of his cock striking deeper, higher. It pitched to a narrow place that jolted me upward, moans scattering from my lips.

At the rhythmic friction, his cock thickened, and my pussy melted. Our eyes narrowed as we hauled ourselves into one another, the brimming ledge of his erection pumping and retreating, each pitch of our waists accompanied by unrelenting growls and plaintive cries. His ass propelled off the grass, the pace flinging my thighs apart. Like this, I took every concentrated snap of his hips, welcoming the profusion of heat unspooling inside me.

The dawning sun beat down on us. We worked for this, worked for each other. Like the times before, this would be earned and would be remembered long after we howled into the sky.

Elation gripped my heart, need poured from my cunt, and I climbed higher. Moans skittered from my lungs. Jeryn felt that ripple inside me, his muscles shuddering in response.

On a rasp, he seized my ass harder and heaved me into him, tugging my pussy over and over on his lap. For a moment, I went limp and let him steer me, enjoying the force of his hands, the magnitude of it. My body arched, my head flinging backward, my hair falling across my face.

"Oh!" I wailed. "Oh, Seasons!"

"Give me noise," he gritted out. "Give me every noise."

Yes. I transformed into the cascades, racing freely and wildly, coursing at full speed to a precipice, about to plunge headfirst over the promontory and split into a million glittering pieces. My voice followed suit, unleashing into this jungle, delivering sounds only this prince and the rainforest could hear, because only they understood. I made noise by movement, with my mind and my heart.

Bolstering himself on the bracket of one arm, the prince raised his upper body and sloped his cock higher still. The position changed the angle of our fucking, the head striking just so. I shouted with this man, my breasts bouncing into the air and my hips dashing into his.

Jeryn fought to keep his head up, determined not to let go, to keep himself from buckling. His cock expanded, thicker and hotter. It siphoned into me, fucked with such vigor that I strapped my fingers around his shoulders, the better to take it. My pussy constricted, small tremors cresting.

My villain prince hissed, "You have slayed me."

And I could not stay away from those lips any longer. Not after that.

Down into his arms, I landed. My knees pitched around his tireless hips, my nipples rushed against his pecs, and my fingers hooked over his shoulders. Our mouths crashed together, rocking and panting.

I curled into him, and he palmed my ass and jerked me forward, and forward, and forward. His tongue whisked my own, the echoes of lovemaking trapped between our lips. And like this, we discovered a momentum and a deep, sacred spot.

This meant more than kinship. It meant something beyond desire. I cared for him, and I trusted him. I liked his eyes on me, his arms around me, his breath in my hair. I had felt this bond only once before, with my mother and father. Yet this boosted my heart to another level, the epiphany claiming my soul.

"Do you feel it?" I whispered, slinging my hips faster.

"Fuck, yes," he groaned, pumping deeper. "I feel it."

I could have hollered. Hate had separated kingdoms. But this enduring feeling could unite them.

I bounded on his cock, and he opened my cunt, our waists in sync. Jeryn veered his swollen lips from mine, then mashed his face against my own. I relished the sharpness of his groans, and I replied with heated gasps that fell against his mouth.

My flesh seared. My pussy tensed around his cock, the crescendo so near, driving us ahead.

Seeing my eyebrows crimp, Jeryn put everything into the motions of his hips, fucking into me with his entire frame. Glazed in sweat, I strung my arms around his shoulders and leaped into him, my walls squeezing to the hilt.

Three words floated across my tongue, so often used by lovers. But Jeryn got there first with a declaration of his own.

"You own me," he said against my mouth. "You rule me."

The world exploded. Flames burst inside me like an inferno, my pussy seizing up and then erupting, hot pleasure spilling down my limbs. Oblivion rushed from my core, to my knees, to my lips. My mouth unhinged, and I bellowed into his lips, and he stalled at the same time before shattering.

A roar barreled from his chest, his muscles quaking. Warm liquid streamed from his cock while I convulsed around him. As one, we came hard and long. I clawed through his hair, and he bowed his head into my neck, both of us clasping, riding out this wave. Unending battle cries wrenched from my being, and Jeryn emptied his lungs against my throat, his pulse ramming into mine.

We fixed in place and crested to the hard root of our pleasure. It coursed from the center of us, sluicing through my limbs, glowing in my blood, from that place where his cock pulsed inside me.

Slowly, patiently, we rocked our hips, soaking up every last ripple of pleasure. My breasts heaved into his torso, my inner walls drenched and clutching him. Wheezes tumbled from my tongue, and Jeryn swallowed for air while keeping his hold on me.

Finally, we floated back down to earth. Jeryn rolled on top, his body burrowed within mine and my limbs flanking his waist, refusing to let him go. The hairs along my legs tickled his, my feet resting on the backs of his knees. I sighed up to the sky, my fingers swimming in his hair.

Jeryn balanced himself on his forearms, wary of crushing me. He swept the hair from my face, the better to see my expression. Our eyes fastened as he descended to claim my mouth. He sketched my lips with his own, and I slanted my head, our mouths folding languidly. And it happened again, and again, and again.

Our lips layered and tugged. With each pass, each new tilt, we kept our eyes open and watched one another. Exhausted and sated, we panted into the next kiss, and the next, and the next.

I could keep him inside me for eternity. Maybe that was possible if we got ambitious enough.

Jeryn's lips crooked against mine. That scant inch told me he knew my thoughts.

Soberly, he framed my face in his palms and continued flicking his tongue between my lips, matching the restless tempo of our hips, which still lolled together. The taste of salt and frost made my head spin.

The waterfalls misted us. The ferns trembled. While coming, I'd forgotten where we were, and I continued to forget, and I made sure Jeryn forgot with me.

We kissed the past away. And as we did, the sun rose.

47

Flare

I stirred in his strong arms, drowsy from slumber. As my eyelashes fanned open, early morning clung to the waterfall crags, and I caught him staring down at me with a fond expression. We'd been lounging naked at the bank all day, pausing only to eat and drink and touch, with the canopy of trees shielding us from the sun.

My fauna pack lounged atop one of the brackets beside the cascades. The jaguar lapped at her paw, the butterfly perched on a boulder, and the boa tucked herself into a shaded bush sprouting from the rocks. According to Jeryn, the feline had guarded me while I'd been unconscious and Jeryn had rushed to find his vial. She had left after the prince returned but came back at some point while he and I were sleeping. This time, my other two kindreds had accompanied her.

Jeryn's body temperature eased the aches in my muscles. Though, I wasn't the only one caught in an afterglow. The prince's features were relaxed, his complexion refreshed from all we had done, how long and loud we'd pinnacled.

A masculine hum resounded from his body as I curled into his side. He braced one hand behind his head and cradled my scalp with the other, his hands toying with my hair. Tucking my cheek into his chest, I slung one leg over his waist and drizzled my fingers across the cobbled surface of his abdomen.

Jeryn's timbre roughened, his cock already half-hard. "You tread a fine line."

To our senses alone, my laugh came out husky. I craned my head toward him, balanced my chin on his torso, and drummed my digits against his muscles. "When has that warning ever worked on me?"

He let out a rare but faint huff of mirth. "True."

"You know, this is the first time we've gotten to do this."

"Do what?"

"Savor the aftermath."

He hesitated. "Could you get used to it?"

I pretended to give it some thought, then chuckled when he nudged my side as if offended. "When you delay like that, it torments me."

"Does it?" I teased, crawling higher up his body. "Tell me more."

"Bewitched. Smitten. Obsessed," he listed while nibbling on my neck. "Do not pretend you don't know this."

I bit back a giddy smile, then shrugged. "I might get used to it."

Pleasure spread across his face. I liked seeing Winter this way, casual and carefree. It would shock the world.

Sprawled across the grass, with all that marvelous flesh on display, the sight caused my heart to skip. Long layers fell around Jeryn's face as he pulled away from my throat and mouthed, *How are you?*

I glanced at the sparkling cascades. "Thirsty."

The prince rose, not bothering with clothes, which allowed me to admire the taut motions of his ass. Minutes later, he returned with our canteen, which he'd brought from the ruins—along with other supplies including food and a blanket—while I rested. After everything that had happened, I'd simply wanted to stay here by the waterfalls, soaking in the peaceful atmosphere.

While I sat up with my breasts hanging freely and the blanket puddling around my waist, I guzzled from the vessel. By then, my fauna pack had come nearer, to check on my wellbeing.

As I drank and greeted my friends, Jeryn unpacked a bottle of plumeria salve he'd made for me. Concoction in hand, he strode my way but frowned at the boa, jaguar, and butterfly settled against me.

"Off," he ordered.

The animals hissed and growled and flapped wings. But at my gentle whisper, they returned to their spot by the waterfall.

Motioning for me to sit up, Jeryn lowered himself to the ground and rubbed the balm across my neck. I sighed, inhaling the floral essence.

The prince had told me the story, what happened after I had bitten through the vines, how they'd poisoned me, and how Jeryn had found me. The whirlpool had taken his necklace months ago, yet he'd jumped back in and found it with the help of my sand net. Afterward, he had fed me the last of the vial's liquid, not knowing if the antidote would work or if I'd keep swelling and turning to ice.

I moaned as his hands kneaded the floral ointment into my shoulders. "Your fingers."

"What about them?" he asked.

"The way they sink into me, reaching so deeply. Prince Jeryn, the Cruel Healer. Yet your touch isn't cruel, it's lavish."

"I don't know whether to thank you or bid you're welcome," he remarked in amusement.

I laughed. "Both."

Jeryn had the walk and talk of a Royal, but he also wasn't the fur-cloaked monster I'd first met. The Phantom Wild had cut and bruised and hardened every ridge more than it already had been. Also, it had softened other places and brought a new clarity to his eyes.

I could draw his likeness into the earth. But to get those features right, I'd need something with a finer point, like a feather quill.

While he tended to my back, I drew across a patch of soil as if it were sand, forming symbols into the bank. A tidefarer, a rainforest, a hidden palace.

"You're good," Jeryn murmured over my shoulder. "Images that speak without words. If they were aware of it, monarchs would summon you across the Seasons to demonstrate such a spectacle."

I imagined my sand art reaching the hearts and minds of this continent. The possibility fluttered in my stomach. The thought of being heard ... the chance to have a voice ... to bond with so many others ...

Your strengths don't begin and end in this realm.

As they often did, Jeryn's words from our dinner on the beach returned, including his declarations about my mission. If the rainforest weren't able to tell me which of my skills could help born souls, would I be able to figure it out myself?

What did I have to share with this world?

Twisting my head Jeryn's way, I wondered, "What about the people? How would they react?"

"That would be for you to discover," Jeryn answered. "But whatever you made them feel, they would not forget it."

"Would you?"

Those eyes darkened. "I will never forget anything you've made me feel."

Setting aside the ointment, Jeryn wiped his hands and wheeled me toward him. We reclined in the grass and lay on our sides, facing one another. I drew the blanket over our waists, barely enough to cover his beautiful ass and my hips.

Like this, we stared at one another. The waterfalls threw mist into the air and filled this haven with secretive noises.

"When the poison seeped into me, I thought of Winter frost," I said. "Does the cold sting like that? Is it so intense that it burns? Is there no sun?"

"There is—"

"It didn't sound so when you described it. How can such an icy place have star murals, sleighs drawn by stags, dire wolf sleds, and yule owls?"

"Flare—"

"And you talked about elks in a forest called The Iron Wood. And you mentioned gravy. Is it warm? How do the animals not freeze?"

A wry look crossed his face. "May I talk?"

"What?" I asked innocently. "I'm not stopping you."

He threw back his head and burst out laughing. The baritone sound heated my flesh, so that I longed to drag my tongue across his mouth and learn what his mirth tasted like.

Recovering, Jeryn twined a wavy lock of my hair around his finger and admired how it sprang back into place, reshaping itself. "Winter has as many havens as it does perils, just as each court possesses its own courtesies and malevolence."

That didn't excuse the dungeons, towers, or oubliettes, the places where they dumped people like Pearl and Lorelei and Dante and Rune.

I scooted closer, the movement prompting him to wind an arm around me. "You once held me in contempt for being mad, yet your feelings changed." I seared my gaze into his. "So has your definition of madness changed too?"

Jeryn glimpsed my neck and then dragged his eyes to mine. "Flare, I—"

"Because who says the free citizens of The Dark Seasons aren't just as mad? Is it normal to scorn and enslave the way they have? The way *you* have? Was it normal for Pyre or the rest of the tower guards to enjoy tormenting prisoners? Is King Rhys sane after everything he's done to born souls? To Poet, Briar, and their son?"

"Flare. You know I don't feel that way anymore."

Air gusted from my lungs. Jeryn had joined the clan. Of course, he didn't feel the way he used to.

"It's just …" I touched my neck. "Being trapped by the vines, so soon after ridding myself of that collar. I hate to think of others suffering like me when they don't deserve it."

"Do you trust me?" When I nodded, he gathered me to him. "Then tell me. What did you do?"

What did I do to get caught? What did I do to condemn myself and my parents? What brought me to the tower? Why had Summer painted a collar around my neck?

He'd told me about his past, but I hadn't shared mine. I hadn't been ready. Now I wanted nothing more than for him to know me entirely.

Safe in his arms, I told him about growing up as a drifter. How I would climb the mast of our tidefarer to stroke the clouds. How I'd once slammed an iron pail across a shark's face because it wanted to steal my favorite sand net. How I had danced on hot coals and through sandstorms.

I described Papa, who threaded his hair into tight braids across his head, wore a looped ring in his eyebrow, and was short and plump. He was all hugs and booming laughter, with a voice as deep as a boar's.

I described Mama, the tall and tranquil one of our family, who narrated folktales every night when I didn't want to sleep.

They called me their flaming girl, the greatest treasure they'd discovered together. Though sometimes I burned too hotly. That's what they used to say whenever I raged or did something without thinking.

When this happened, Mama would caress my hands and whisper for me to be calm and careful. I tried, yet I often got upset about unkind words or hurtful actions from strangers.

While passing through a canal thoroughfare, another sand drifter had once called Mama a harsh name, so I smashed the handle of the man's oar against his boat. And in a swamp, I splashed a bucket of sludge at a swindler for cheating my parents out of coins. These things, I did before Mama and Papa could stop me.

And I did one other thing too.

Because of my turbulent whims, Mama and Papa didn't bring me to the markets with them. Instead, one of them would always stay behind with me. But one day, we docked ashore by the castle, with a heavy trunk of wares to sell, too weighty for a person to cart alone. Even though it had built-in wheels, the chest would need both Mama and Papa to transport it. They'd had to leave me there, making me promise to stay put in the tidefarer while they set off for the lower town.

Mama had whispered, "Be soft and be good. No wandering or engaging with strangers. Remember."

"I will," I had vowed. "I'll remember."

Our tidefarer was moored out of sight, surrounded by trees. I'd been ensconced in the boat and gazing at the beach when a group of children appeared. Despite their fancy clothes, they seemed to love the shore as much as I did, because they played in the sand, throwing damp balls at each other and giggling.

Children like me, I had thought! They weren't sand drifters, because they looked too regal for that. I guessed they were nobles, but I didn't care, because that didn't make us different. Not if we all loved the shore.

What could happen?

I sprinted out of the tidefarer. When I approached them beside a grove, they stopped chortling and gaped with wide eyes. I didn't know what to do or say, and I hadn't thought to bring my sand net to impress them.

One of the girls ran her gaze over my clothes and exclaimed that I was a sand drifter. Then a boy prompted me, asking if I had treasure on my boat. Nodding, I dashed aboard and returned with a clear seashell, as translucent as a piece of glass, a rare find that my parents had forgotten to take with them.

The boy snatched it from me, and the children gathered around to peer at the charm, but they grew uneasy when the male packed my shell into his pocket. I reached for it, but he wouldn't give it back, and the fire in me simmered. That shell belonged to my family.

"Want it back?" the noble boy asked.

I didn't trust the question, so I stood there, anger creeping up on me as the sun hit my back. Its bright glare made the children squint, like they couldn't see me well. And maybe they truly couldn't, because none of them defended or helped me.

If I wanted the shell back, I had to take it back. That's what the noble said, right before he wadded up a clump of wet sand and lobbed it my way like a grenade.

The ball smacked my shoulder and broke apart, spraying into a million flecks. I froze in surprise, long enough that another ball launched and shattered against my neck, the impact pulling tears from my eyes. That he turned this beautiful setting into a backdrop for cruelty set the fire roaring. I cannoned after the spoiled brat, dodging the sandy balls he pitched at me. He had no right to the seashell and no right to violate the beach.

A moment later, I landed on top of him, and I was punching his noble face into the coast, blood spraying from a gash on his lip. But that wasn't the problem. The problem was, we'd rolled across the ground—and the ground was sinking. It grabbed and sucked us down. At first, it was enchanting, so I let the bloody boy go and gawked at the spectacle.

It was a new discovery, the quicksand. I'd only ever heard of its existence.

One of the children screeched. A girl seized her skirt and bolted into the trees, with the rest of them following her.

Because I wasn't moving, the quicksand didn't consume me as fast as it did the boy, who screamed and thrashed. Reflexively, I snatched onto a tree root and managed to haul myself out of the mess, then I crawled to the edge and watched the boy flounder and spit curses at me. It would serve this boy right if the sand took him, so I stared until he was up to his neck and had begun to whimper.

The fear in his eyes stabbed my conscience, made me feel wrong about scaring him, even though there wasn't any real danger. It was only sand, and I was going to pull him out anyway, because he was just a boy. A fiendish boy but also a child like me.

All the same, he deserved for the beach to give him a scolding first. He pleaded that he was sorry and to please help him. Desperate, he swore to give my shell back.

Since I had already been fixing to save him, I stretched out my hand. The noble had lunged for it, and our fingers grazed when a pair of gloved fingers hauled me upright. Knights swarmed us in a commotion of steel and shouts, with the other children on their heels. Then the boy was being rescued, his mouth bleeding from where I'd attacked him. Crimson oozed from his hip as well, because the seashell had shattered in his pocket, crushed to pieces when I'd tackled him.

I mourned those shards. I hadn't kept my promise to Mama and Papa like I was supposed to, and now a treasure was destroyed, and the boy's lips gushed from a split. I hadn't meant to do wrong, but it was an accident, and everything was all right now.

Yet the children shrieked that I'd come out of nowhere and pounced on their friend. All the while, the boy said nothing about it. Not about taking my shell or baiting me, because he was too busy coughing up grains. His clique accused me of booting him into the quicksand, that I'd been pushing him into it and going down with him like a mad girl.

"Like a mad girl," they cried. "A mad girl, a mad girl!"

I rushed at them, screaming that it was a lie. Appalled, the Summer knights yanked me back, and I heard the boy tell them in a small, shaken voice that I'd been about to let him drown. Over and over, he repeated that I meant to let him drown, sounding like he really believed it.

I wouldn't have. I'd have given him a beating, and I might have chipped a tooth, but I wouldn't have done worse. I had just wanted my shell back.

The knights dragged me across the shore. The more I hollered—"I'm not mad! I'm not mad! Mama! Papa! I'm not maaaaaad!"—the tighter their hold on me became.

As the knights stole me away, the last sight I took with me was of the beach—of my footprints in the sand.

Later, Pyre gloated and told me they'd caught my parents too. Mama and Papa had been tossed into a dungeon for concealing me from the Crown, while I was sent to a different cell.

And maybe Summer was right. Maybe I was mad, because why had I gotten so angry and attacked that boy over a seashell? Why else would Mama and Papa have kept me away from the markets so often?

Over time, I started to believe what everyone said about me. I was dangerous. Not to kind people but surely to evil or harmful beings, especially if they threatened what I cared about.

Only the rainforest had seen something good in me, something worth summoning. And that became my only light in the darkness.

Fury contorted Jeryn's features as I finished the tale. "Anyone who ever hurt you, I will massacre them when I return to Winter. Let that be my first task." He seized my cheeks, thumbs stroking my skin. "You're safe now. You're free."

A lump clotted my throat. "Don't hurt anyone for me. Violence is the reason I got myself locked up in the first place. I want no more of it."

In place of rage, a haunted look strained his face. I wondered if the quicksand story reminded him of the whirlpool, until he uttered as if to confirm, "The boy had a split lip."

I flinched. "I didn't mean it."

"And bloody pants."

"From the seashell."

Jeryn grimaced as if he'd anticipated this answer. He scraped his fingers through his hair, his next words sounding like a confession. "I was there."

I couldn't have heard him right. But when I said nothing, his eyes lifted to mine, and he repeated in a strained tone, "I was there."

"No," I balked. "I would have remembered a young man with blue hair."

"I was close by. On the same beach. It was the day of the siren shark."

Oh. *Oh.*

Yes, that day. He and his grandaunts had been touring the coastline with the Summer Crowns, and there had been knights escorting the Royals, and because those Royals wanted to be private, a group of children had been forced to migrate elsewhere.

Jeryn reminded me, "The boy with the split lip. I saw him earlier that day, on the beach with the other children." The distant memory played before his eyes, his voice narrowing to a knife's edge. "At one point during the stroll, I succumbed to curiosity. While my grandaunts were indisposed, I slipped from my security detail and followed the children to a neighboring shore. I arrived as the soldiers were dragging you away."

The muscles of his throat bobbed. "I saw the guards hurting you. I saw the look on your face." His eyelids clenched shut. "I have seen that moment ever since. You were a vision so unfamiliar to me. Wild. Golden. Ethereal. You were the most beautiful creature I'd ever seen. The urgency to save you had gripped me, yet I was a mere boy, unsure of what to do. Before I could race to your aid, the guards had clamped you in irons, and the noble youths were screaming about madness.

"The term stalled my tracks and scared me. I started to question if you were safe or deadly, because I hadn't known better. Instead, I returned in a daze to my side of the beach, my mind overpowered by you. I fought to distract myself by stumbling into the water, thinking to collect a sample for my vial, and hadn't noticed the shark's approach."

In a timbre scraped raw, Jeryn admitted the rest. When his grandaunts took him to the infirmary after the shark attack, the noble boy was admitted soon after. The physicians had whispered that he'd been assailed by a mad girl near the ocean.

The same day. The same hour.

The soldiers had been dragging me to danger. Meanwhile, the prince's grandaunts had been dragging him to safety.

"Your screams were the first sounds I ever heard from you," Jeryn rasped. "In Autumn's dungeon, I did not merely notice you. I recognized you."

Tears clung to my lashes. When we met on that fateful night, he'd already seen me before.

And he'd heard me. In Summer's castle when Jeryn had me chained in the quad, he commented on my voice, declaring how I had possessed one in the past. To that, I'd been stumped, questioning how he could have drawn that conclusion without knowing a thing about my life, much less without examining me. And I hadn't believed his excuse of simply being a doctor.

So this was it. He'd known me for years, long before I knew him.

Jeryn's repentant gaze searched mine. I witnessed the self-loathing across his face. If he hadn't been there, those children wouldn't have traveled to another part of the shore, and they wouldn't have seen me, and I wouldn't have gotten into trouble. If he had rushed to my side and defended me, the guards and children would have thought twice about discounting a testimonial from the Prince of Winter.

If and if and *if*.

But instead of dwelling on that misfortune, I cupped his jaw. "It wasn't your fault."

"I saw you being hauled away," he snarled. "I saw you and did nothing."

"Just because you were on that beach doesn't mean you sent me to the tower."

"Ignorance sent you there. Royals like me kept you there."

"Then in Autumn, why did you …"

"Why did I treat you that way? Because I spent years trying to forget your existence, desperate to evict the memory of you from my mind, out of fear and guilt. Although you captivated me at first sight, I quickly second guessed that feeling, long enough to stay my actions.

"For a while after, I regretted that. But over time, the more I grew to fear what this continent deems as foolishness, the more loathed it. Out of misguided self-preservation, I convinced myself you were mad after all, and I should move on." His fingers tightened on my hip. "Then Autumn happened. When I saw you behind those bars, you consumed me once more."

He admitted the rest. Ordering my dirt sketch swept away hadn't been intended as punishment. Rather, Jeryn had wanted my cage cleaned, unaware of what the pile meant to me.

But when I broke the vial and marred something precious to him—a gift from his parents—I shattered his first image of me as a tyrannized girl.

"If fear hadn't fueled my disdain, perhaps I wouldn't have overreacted about the vial," Jeryn admitted. "I was embittered and sought to punish you for the disillusionment, to further convince myself you were mad and did not matter. You were right to cast me as a villain. Cruel. Cold. I relied on those traits to deal with you, even while I obsessed about you every waking moment."

Having me isolated in a separate cell, not to torment me but to give me peace and quiet. Seeking me out during the Reaper's Fest riot, not to trap me but to make sure I was unharmed. Jeryn had found himself acting out of protectiveness instead of viciousness.

I brushed my mouth against his. "Now we know."

"Now we do," he murmured.

The waterfall spilled down mantels of rock. At some point, my fauna pack had departed into the rainforest. They must have known Jeryn and I needed this time alone.

"Flare," the prince hissed, clasping my cheeks. "You said it wasn't my fault when I didn't help you. Now I'm telling you, what happened to you and your parents also wasn't your fault."

Pain lanced through me, grief and guilt wringing tears to my eyes. My voice crumbled to pieces as I palmed my face and hunched over, letting Jeryn fasten me to him while my body jolted from weeping, the cries heavy and endless.

"I have nightmares about being caged," I sobbed. "Though, it's only happened once here, back on our first night. But the worst nightmares are of Mama and Papa suffering. I got them into trouble. They died because of me."

"No," Jeryn intoned. "They died because of prison." When my tears ebbed, he lifted my face to his. "It was not your doing."

"Pyre said I had a feral madness. Everyone said it too."

"Anyone can be susceptible to anger. You were an excitable, imaginative child with a temper and an impulsive streak. That's why your parents kept you from markets; rightly so, they didn't want anyone to misconstrue your behavior. As for that noble boy, he was in shock. The other children shouted in his defense, purely out of hysterics, and those fucking knights overreacted. But you are not feral. This would have been evident if The Dark Seasons had educated itself correctly about the distinctions. Instead, we've all been learning in the fucking wrong way."

Jeryn traced my skin with his thumbs. "Flare, you have lived through something horrific, and it has scarred you. Captivity and bigotry taught you to believe something that wasn't true, and confinement among baiting guards reinforced that." His eyes bore into mine. "You are not mad. And you must forgive yourself. Your parents would want that for you. They'd want you to live without regret."

Hope eased the knots in my chest. His words washed through me like an ocean wave, rinsing away the ashes. Finally talking about it with someone—with him—poured warmth inside me, where there had always been bleakness.

Leaning over, I drew in the soil, the motions luring me, soothing my thoughts. Onto the earth, I sketched a seashell, whole and unbroken.

Then I turned in Jeryn's arms. "One more thing."

Jeryn hauled me against him. "Anything."

"No more secrets."

He ran his fingers down my arm. "No more confessions."

"And be with me. Not just until we say goodbye but after. If we part ways, we do it with a plan to meet again, to stay together no matter the distance or time."

"You don't need to propose this." His gaze burned into mine. "After almost losing you, I won't let you go again."

Flipping me onto my back, Jeryn dipped his head to my throat. "To the ends of the earth, I will meet you. Until the end of time, I'll wait."

Tingles spread along my flesh. I wound my legs around his waist, chuckling tearily as he growled into my neck like a hungry creature.

"Forgive me," he intoned ruefully against my skin. "I could not wait to taste you again."

The admission stalled my humor. A stampede of wild animals sprang loose in my chest while he tucked into my throat.

"Couldn't wait?" I repeated.

"Could not wait," he said.

Another pause. I might have teased Jeryn about his lack of patience. Instead, a grin stretched across my face. "That means you love me."

48

Jeryn

At first, I did not respond. Could not.

The emotion seemed disproportionate to the upheaval inside me. The word was too small, the pronunciation too slippery. It didn't sound deep enough, much less stretch far enough, lasting only a short while on the tongue.

Looming between her thighs, I raised myself above Flare and gazed down. Searching. Sensing. A spectrum of color draped itself across her body, and those sunlit irises rested on me. The sight inundated my being with insurmountable sensations, too overwhelming to compartmentalize.

A puncture. A squeeze. A softening.

My lungs. My stomach. My heart.

As children, we had suffered. Summer had taken everything from Flare, including her family and the chance to discover herself. The only thing left had been the rainforest, a realm that gave her a purpose. A way to cope through years of captivity, to define herself even though there was more to her, if she would only see it.

While I had spent my life terrified that I'd go mad from a siren shark attack. A bite that almost happened, but never actually had.

Flare wasn't a born soul. But I could not say the same about myself.

Nonetheless, the shark had not made me cruel, and neither had my bouts of panic. True, they had created fear. But *I* had made myself cruel. In my ignorance, I had made the choice to be brutal.

That was the true definition of foolishness.

Yet she accepted me. Yet she forgave me. Yet she wanted me.

Flare lay naked beneath my form. Beautiful. Boundless. Flay me to hell and back, I could not take it.

If I loved her, then I would fucking love her.

Bracketing myself over Flare, I swung my waist, the probe of my cock urging a moan from her tongue. While spreading my little beast open, I hissed, "Every thought I've ever had."

She arched into me and sighed, "Everything I've ever felt."

My hips rolled between her thighs, and my black heart fell from my mouth. "You have disrupted it all."

Time slowed and accelerated, illogical as it seemed. The days ebbed, yet the weeks passed quicker. I didn't give a shit about making sense of this.

We lived inside a globe, a speck in the ocean. Feral. Riveting. It grew familiar until we knew this realm as we did our Seasons.

With the aid of fauna messengers including Flare's butterfly and Autumn raptors, we maintained routine contact with Poet and Briar. My grandaunts had been blessed with stout constitutions. Health-wise, they fared well, if not emotionally aggrieved. Whereas my parents remained feeble, oftentimes medicated against pain.

The queens had not informed Mother and Father of my disappearance, not wishing to cause them agony. Instead, Silvia and Doria had told them I'd gone on an extended tour through The Dark Seasons, out of political necessity. Under their orders, the court maintained this fabrication, preventing public discourse from reaching my parents' ears.

Meanwhile, Summer was stewing in its shit. Poet and Briar had met with Queen Giselle and traded for Flare's cell mates, then ferried them to Autumn. The jester and princess had also succeeded in swaying Her Majesty to monitor her fuckwit of a husband.

Rhys's spite had been festering like an abscess. Lately, he'd been growing quiet, which meant he was amassing secrets, possibly mobilizing new allies, zealots and extremists who refused to believe he could do wrong.

These missives provoked me and Flare in two conflicting ways. Motivation to act. Dread to separate. We made plans while clasping tighter at night, my cock slinging deeper into Flare, her pussy clutching me harder.

We had made a vow, regardless of time and distance. Once Flare had unearthed her purpose and I returned to Winter, we would keep knowledge of this rainforest hidden, protected from Rhys's interference. The Phantom Wild would be our meeting place. Someday, it could become something more for the benefit of this continent; the possibilities would remain open. Until then, we continued searching for the answer to Flare's mission—how to spread the word about this ancient society without exposing the rainforest.

Flare mastered the craft of sand art by using drawing tools. Stems, branches, leaves, conches, quills. And those strong, enduring hands.

Six months passed. With Flare's experience in seafaring and my origins in a Season known for advanced engineering, we set out to construct a small boat. The replica of her family's tidefarer would serve Flare when her time came.

Thus far, the execution of this vessel had involved numerous failures and redesigns. Although we possessed some requisite technical skills, neither of us were shipwrights.

Flare was persistent. I was patient.

We lay in a dozen different positions at night. In my bed or hers. On the sand or beside the waves. Under the constellations, beneath the forest canopy, doused by the rain. I would scoop her against me, or she would splay herself on my chest and pass out. Her spine would curl into my chest, my arm would fit around her waist, and our limbs would tangle like cords.

I would watch her sleep. Then I would awaken to find her eyes sparkling on me.

We stood beneath the prismatic fountain as though it were a shower, my fingers scrubbing through her hair. We bathed in safe waters, washing and fucking.

I returned with her to the cascades and admired my little beast diving into the pond, the rope of her spine and her lovely ass disappearing under the surface. As she swam, beams of sunlight caressed her thighs.

I still avoided the grotto, where the siren shark had found us. Other waters grew more tolerable, including the sea. Though, the apprehension never left completely.

But this pool contained no predators, hazards, or tricks. Stripping myself bare, I waded in after her. Enjoying the heat of her gaze as she fixated on my dick, I pursued my little beast, chasing her through the depths. The feigned hunt made her chuckle and hurl chunks of water my way until I caught her with a growl.

With her legs twining around my waist and that reckless mouth seizing mine, nothing could have prepared me for the eruption of heat. I attempted to walk it off, carrying her with me. Yet the water failed to subdue my aching cock as I floated us across the pond, aimless and meandering.

As if aware of my problem, Flare toyed with the roots of my hair and nipped my nose. Unaccustomed to playing, I wrinkled my nostrils. Yet I allowed her to do as she pleased, so long as those hands kept touching me.

Later, I flicked my tongue across her teeth while slinging my hips into the V of her thighs. And after multiple orgasms, Flare flipped us over and shoved me down, her hard nipples scraping my pectorals.

"I want to know what else we can do with each other," she purred. Seasons flay me. We made sure to find out.

Flare and I spent each dawn fucking like wild creatures, my hips pounding and our screams blasting through the forest. We spent every dusk having sex until I lost my voice from roaring, and Flare's body went up in flames.

It was never enough. I could not stop touching this woman, could not stop eliciting responses from her. Alternately, I had worried about our vitals exploding and then ceased giving a shit. Flare could withstand any force. As for myself, my lungs and heart could rupture, and it would be worth it.

I took my little beast on whatever surface had not yet been consecrated. I hunted her through the ruins, through the cave tunnels, through the forest, through the rain, through the fucking dark. She stalked me in kind, with the victor claiming the other on the spot. While I sought to make Flare come from numerous positions, she annihilated my self-control with minimal effort. A smile, a touch, a laugh was enough to destroy me, to say nothing of her pleasured cries.

On the ruins' bridge, beside the towering fauna statues, I issued a command. "Turn around," I gritted. "Hands on the ledge."

Defiant, Flare waited me out by strip-teasing. Only when the dress had finally come off, sufficiently riling me up to the point of where I practically foamed at the mouth, did she comply. Swinging her ass toward me, she linked her fingers over the bridge railing and bent forward. My fingers were the first culprits, hooking into the cleft of her body while she cried out and soaked my knuckles. Next, I fitted my cock to her, slinging in and out, my groans converging with her sobs. The more noise she made, the longer I fucked her, the more places I reached.

Being an explorer and experimenter had its perks. On that same bridge, adrenaline consumed us. With Flare's permission, my cock eased from her pussy and edged into her backside. Using a balm, the tip of my cock widened her tight passage with each concentrated thrust. All the while, my thumb pressed into her clit, the stimulation relaxing her muscles.

Flare's pain became her pleasure, a reward that had my dick standing higher. I beat my hips, deepening the orifice. The result produced goosebumps down her back and pulled an inconsolable moan from Flare's mouth, the sound of which pitched my eyes to the back of my skull. Her ass rode my cock, her anus sealing around me until we lost all presence of mind.

In my medical chamber, she would feign illness, playing the coy patient and distracting me from work. At which point, I would use a number of convenient tools on Flare.

Many were smooth. Others were not.

Other days and nights, we writhed atop piles of linen, in carpets of moss, next to the tide. Sprawled inside her largest sand drawing—a depiction of the continent—I threw my cock into Flare, her cunt wetting me to the base and her elated moans compounding in my ears. Then I clasped her to me and nibbled on her throat while she laughed.

I knew nothing of courtship or romance. But I did know how to hold my little beast through a nightmare, heal her injuries, listen to her words, fuck, kiss, talk, and remember. That, I could do.

No description measured up to what this felt like. The effervescence of her climax. The building delirium of mine. The uncoordinated release that racked my frame, launching shouts from my mouth.

Friction. Pacing. Cadence.

All three had us shaking for air. We exhausted ourselves, then started over again. And in that time, six months became one year.

49

Jeryn

Standing at the mouth of the dining hall fireplace, I glared at the iron cauldron hanging over a flame. Petals and leaves swam in the concoction. Flare had expressed her love for their flavors, but although they smelled fragrant individually, blending them had been an unwise idea. Scents akin to overripe raisins and distilled vinegar clashed, which could not bode well for the taste.

If I had stuck to making her favorite hand salve, this morning would have been fruitful. But no, I'd insisted on trying something new, without guaranteed success. The woman sleeping in my bed tended to have this impulsive effect on me.

While Flare loved delicacies, we'd tasted nearly every option available to us here. Picturing her excited face after sipping a customized blend, my logic had gone rogue. Yet for all my knowledge, I was shit at this. Ladling a spoonful, I waited for the fluid to cool. Sampling this atrocity would tell me more.

In the interim, I scowled. Years of medical training. Transplanting organs, eliminating pathogens, treating illnesses, creating remedies. If I could do that, I could fucking make tea.

The weight of someone's presence warmed my naked spine. Two slender arms flanked my waist from behind and crossed over my abdomen. Her wildflower scent drugged my senses, mingling with the aroma of Winter. The tempting little beast must be wearing one of my shirts. And likely nothing else.

The knowledge worked on me like an intoxicant, the buzz fueling straight to my cock. Despite how I'd exhausted her last night, she had not overslept.

Flare spoke against the gap between my shoulder blades. "You didn't wake me."

"Because if I had, I would not have left our bed," I supplied. "Not for a very long time."

"That doesn't sound like a problem."

"I wore you out last night. You needed your rest." My lips tilted. "Doctor's orders."

"Cruel man."

"Insatiable enchantress. And yes, to the cruel part."

Flare smiled against my skin, producing a ripple effect down my vertebrae. "Good morning."

"Good morning," I returned, taking her hand and massaging it.

We stood listening to the cauldron gurgle. Finally, she inquired, "What is that? It smells foul."

"An experiment," I lied to save face. "For ... vitamin supplementation."

Prolonged silence. Shit, she'd heard something in my voice.

"Was it for me?" she asked softly.

With anyone else, I would have said no. With anyone else, I would have sounded convincing.

Her head swung toward the dining table, where I'd laid out priceless plates, her beloved figs along with an assortment of berries and melon wedges, and stone chalices for the tea. Breakfast was her favorite meal of the day, and I had meant for this to be a commemorative one.

She swerved back to me and brushed her mouth over my bicep. "Will you let me try it?"

I winced, then ladled a spoonful and tested the fluid. The taste confused my palate, too sweet and too acidic. "I don't think—"

But before I could dissuade her, she plucked the spoon—"Flare," I growled—and presumably brought it to her mouth. With my back to her and one arm still wrapped around me, I pinched the bridge of my nose and waited.

She sampled the disaster, her breasts jiggling as she coughed in mirthful surprise. "That's ... um, delicious."

Twisting slightly in her direction, I arched an eyebrow. "Try again."

Faking it would not get past me. Because she'd learned this long ago, Flare broke into chagrined laughter, and my mouth slanted with humor.

The flames crackled, echoing through the dining hall with its restored table and chairs, newly swept floor, a display of ancient serving ware that Flare had discovered in an old hutch, and an urn of hibiscus flowers situated atop the mantel. A year later, this woman had transformed the ruins into more than a hideaway.

So much more. So much better.

Flare's fingernails burrowed into my abs. "Happy anniversary."

I skated my fingers over hers. "Is that what this is?"

I felt her nodding and smiling into me, a combination impossible to resist. "Well then." I retrieved the lid with a cloth and covered the cauldron, then turned to face her. "Let's have an anniversary."

I gave myself three seconds to fetishize her just-fucked hair, golden eyes, and my shirt hanging inches past her hips. Rumpled. Edible. I grabbed the backs of her thighs and hoisted her off the ground. Beaming, Flare connected her forehead with my own as I walked us to the table. She made a noise of delight as I set her atop the surface, stood between her open legs, and picked a fig from the bowl.

Sketching the fruit across her mouth, I deepened my voice. "Open."

Flare scooted closer, the tail of my shirt riding up to her buttocks, the heat of her cunt rubbing against my pants. "Or what?"

"Or I'll repeat myself more clearly," I deadpanned.

My oversized shirt sleeves hung low as she wrapped her arms around my bare shoulders, the delectable seam of her lips splitting for me and biting into the bulb. I watched her chew, the sight doing critical things to my pulse. "The Prince of Winter, forced to repeat himself?" she quipped after swallowing. "What a scandal."

"A transgression indeed," I concurred with a tilted head.

Flare stole the rest of the fig and urged it against my own mouth. "In that case, I might as well keep provoking you."

I bore my gaze into hers. "Who says you ever stopped?"

Then I sank my incisors into the orb, consumed it in one gulp, and relished her dilated pupils. Disheveled, flushed from sleep, and half naked, we proceeded to feed each other. Taking turns, each of us selected from the arrangement of fruits and watched the other consume them to the final droplet of nectar. I lapped the remnants from beneath her jaw while she chuckled, then sucked on that spot until she gasped.

In turn, Flare drew her tongue over my fingers to mop up the juice, producing a jagged noise from me. Between bites and taunting maneuvers, we spoke of random things or lapsed into comfortable silence. Familiar. Intimate.

Pressing her to me, I sneaked my palms under the shirt and ran them over the tops of her ass. "What else are you hungry for?"

A blush stained her cheeks. "The one thing I can never get enough of."

The hiss I'd been withholding sliced from my throat. "Fuck the food."

My arm whipped across the table. Dishes and their contents flew off the edge, ceramic, silver, and stone crashing to the floor. Flare yelped, her irises gleaming. She liked disorder, preferring to call it "beautiful chaos," especially when inciting it from me. Only this woman held such power.

My little beast. My beautiful chaos.

Seizing her face, I braced her head, giving my tongue the leverage to lick the rebellious mirth from her lips. Fuck it. Fuck everything but this. My mouth gripped her own, my tongue spearing against Flare's.

Her elated chuckle disintegrated into a whimper, the noise activating every carnal impulse I possessed. Cupping her ass with my free hand, I hauled her against me. My cock thickened, rising against the flap of my pants and caressing her clit. Seasons flay me.

Flare kissed back, lashing her tongue with mine and scraping the ridges of my back. She tasted of figs and fire. Sweet. Scorching. My mouth loathed to remain still, breaking from her swollen lips and charging down her throat.

The momentum kicked her body backward. I roped my arm around Flare's waist to protect her from hitting the tabletop, and she flung out her hand to brace herself. Hooking her thighs to my hips, she bowed at a steep angle, granting me unhampered access to her pulse.

I could swallow that pounding button. I could devour her heartbeat.

"Jeryn ... ahh," Flare moaned as I glided my teeth up her ear. "You know ... 'Fuck the food' isn't exactly ... healthy for a doctor to say." She flung her head farther back. "What happened to ... all those lectures ... about nourishment?"

"I'll nourish you," I professed into her skin.

"And eating properly?"

"I'll eat you."

So help me, I would splay her out like a banquet. I would dine on every inch of flesh. I would feast on her wet pussy until she came across this table. I would make a fucking meal out of her. And in doing so, she would consume me whole.

"Eating me might hurt," Flare cautioned, breathless.

I launched upright, pulled her flush against my chest, and thumbed her chin. "I will never hurt you." My lips quirked. "Unless you want me to."

"Mmm. I might like a side of pain with my climax. Though the pleasure might be so good, it'll become agonizing."

"I'm a physician. I'll lick your wounds."

"Now that you mention it, I do feel some curious tingles. Maybe I need to be checked, to make sure I have the strength to handle you."

Oh, she could fucking handle me more than anyone on this continent. Nevertheless, my mouth ticked sideways. Doctor-patient kink. We'd done this before, except presently I had none of my tools within arm's reach.

"Sensible," I agreed, stalking my mouth over hers. "You are due for a general exam."

Technically, I had conducted one of these on her already. Or rather, several of them purely for my peace of mind. This forest would not harm my little beast, or I would pull every tree from its roots. In any case, those sessions had been in earnest, not out of foreplay.

I braced one of her feet on the table's edge, the position exposing the glistening seam of her labia. Fucking hell.

My fingertips skidded across her toes. "Phalanges," I murmured as though checking off a list.

Flare panted as I traced along her shin. "Tibia," I continued.

My scalpel knife was the only medical apparatus currently in my possession. I withdrew the weapon, flicked out a pronged lever, and used it to sketch the knee of her dangling limb. "Patella." She yipped as I lightly tapped the flat against that spot, her leg kicking upward in response. "Reflexes."

From there, I skimmed up her thigh. "Femur."

The lever grazed from her hips to her stomach. Then across the center of her chest. "Sternum." Then to her hands, where I kissed her fingers. "Phalanges again."

Pausing for effect, I ducked the tool between her legs, the edge brushing through the curls of her pussy. "Pelvis," I groaned, observing her slit getting wetter. "Slick and flushed."

"Is that good?" Flare husked.

With a jerk of my wrist, I closed the instrument and chucked it aside. "Very good."

She keened as I reclined her backward and splayed her limbs wide. Her heels rested on the ledge, all of her spread out for me. A study in eroticism and stimulation. "Relax," I said while picking open the closures of her shirt. "Ease your muscles for me."

On another moan, she went slack. Her tits spilled from the neckline, the nipples ruching, followed by curves and hips. The sight of Flare's parted mouth, beauty-marked by a single fleck of sand in the crook of her lips, robbed me of breath. She fucking suffocated me without so much as brushing my throat.

On a groan, I dove in. Hunching over her, I devoured each place I'd examined. Kissing, sucking, biting. She shook across the table, her whines cementing into cries when I stretched fully onto the table, whipped her upright above me, sat her on my face, and dipped between her thighs.

Holding her legs astride my head, I plied the tip of my tongue up her cunt and ended at her clit. Repeatedly, I laved her until she was drenching my mouth. Then I latched onto the sensitive crest of skin and sucked like a deprived creature.

Flare crushed my hair in her fists and writhed above the table, the volume of her sobs escalating. Sucking her clit raw, I eased my tongue back to her crease and pumped my tongue between her flanks, soaking her thoroughly.

Yes, I could make it hurt if she wanted. Yes, she could take it.

No, I would not survive this.

"Divine Seasons!" Flare shrieked, her body tensing like a coil. "I can't."

You will.

I doubled my efforts, applying all my reserves to the act. My tongue pistoned and drank her arousal, then returned to her clit and patted the delicate flesh until her joints ruptured.

She came with a cry hard enough to split granite. I groaned against her pussy, the flesh quivering like a leaf against my lips. Only when she slumped did I start again.

No sooner did I release her clitoris than we launched off the table. I vaulted upright, yanked the oversized shirt from Flare's body, and tore her off the table.

Hoisting her off the ground and striding from the dining hall, I made quick work of the distance. Crossing hallways and up stairways, I growled into Flare's chortling mouth. While carrying her through the ruins, I kissed her to within an inch of our lives.

With the flat of my palm, I rammed open the ancient door to our suite. We still shared adjoining quarters, though now we occupied the same bed, alternating between rooms.

In Flare's chamber, I dropped her onto the mattress so hard she bounced. As she crawled backward, I crawled forward, the bed creaking. I knocked pillows out of the way, and she wrestled with my pants, shoving them from my frame.

We'd had each other up against every surface. The walls. The floor. The furnishings. To say nothing of the locations in and out of the ruins.

Today, I did not give a shit about variety. I wanted her only in this bed.

Heat and sweat filled the room. Sheer drapes billowed from the posts.

Flare spread herself again, the span of my hips shearing her limbs apart. I snatched her wrists, tacked them overhead, and sought her mouth again. Flare moaned into the kiss, our tongues thrashing.

Yet a smaller noise also squeezed past her lungs, the sound watery. Like she might weep.

I lurched back, but she shook her head before I could ask. "You didn't hurt me. I just ..." Her gaze crumbled. "I don't want this to end."

Fuck. The entreaty stabbed me through the ribcage.

The tidefarer we'd finally built had completed numerous successful trips around the island. Transport would be ready whenever Flare was. Likewise, I had plotted my return to Winter, with every detail in order.

After Flare set out on her boat, I would sail to the mainland with the jester and princess, where they would deposit me at the docks. There, I would pretend to have been rescued by anonymous seafarers after having been stranded on a remote peninsula.

Flare would embark on her mission through Summer. I would return to Winter.

Even so, it would not end after parting ways. Despite the distance, we would send secret letters and return to each other, reuniting here whenever we could. That was the plan.

Yet. The key to her quest still evaded her, regardless of how vastly she'd been searching.

Until then, I wasn't going anywhere. Neither was she.

I hissed into her mouth. "It won't end." Flare released a pleasured noise as I snapped my hips, the head of my dick nocking at her warm cleft. "We're not leaving this room until I've fucked every sigh, moan, and cry from your mouth."

"Then make it last," she urged, whining as I flexed my waist and pitched my cock.

Tight heat sealed me to the balls. My growl tangled with her moan, our bodies quaking from the impact. I had breached her pussy before she'd finished that sentence.

Thus, I slammed into her again. And again. And fucking again.

I hammered my ass, the brunt of my cock jostling Flare across the mattress. Her tits swayed, and she bowed into me, her knees lifting toward my biceps and engulfing me deeper.

The motion nudged a softer sound from her. There was the first sigh.

Motivated by that, I rolled my erection out of her and whipped into those soaked folds once more, hitting a narrow place that she particularly enjoyed. This pulled a pliant noise from Flare. There was the first moan.

Crushing her to me, I snapped my hips, filling her cunt to the brink. To which, she exhaled fire against my skin. There was the first cry.

And more came. And more.

Releasing her wrists, I clamped onto her buttocks. Fastening her to the bed, I struck in and out. Hard. Slow. Our groans collided, the octaves heightening. The stem of my cock broadened, her desire coated me to the sac, and our hips locked.

Fucking became lovemaking.

Lovemaking became fucking.

With her, there was no difference. I felt it all.

Circulation. Palpitations. Vertigo.

This madness. This normalcy.

Flare wiggled her hips and twisted. I reeled my dick from her body as she flipped onto her stomach and grappled the mattress's edge. With a growl, I snared her hips and hefted them upright, angling her body and rising on my knees. Then I lunged into her again.

She chanted and belted her waist backward, meeting my thrusts halfway. I fucked into her at a new slant, the rhythm vigorous. She arched. Balanced vertically, I lashed forward and savored the view of her backside bobbing, the split of her limbs taking my erection. Heat emanated from her sweet cunt, ripping an inarticulate noise from my mouth. Torturous. Exquisite. She bent lower, rooting my cock deeper, her pussy encapsulating me.

I hunched, Flare twisted her head over her shoulder to catch my mouth. Our tongues met, the steam of her lips yielding under my own.

"Please," Flare implored.

"Please, what?" I panted.

"Please don't stop." She kissed me and whispered, "Never stop."

Not from a thousand miles. No fucking way would I stop anything with her.

I charged after those sighs, moans, cries. Yet I needed to see her features when she came around me. Reciprocating that desire, Flare shimmied forward, breaking us apart.

I whisked Flare onto her back again, and she slammed me against her, threading her legs over my shoulders. My body fell into hers, flush and dripping with sweat. And fuck, I ground my dick inside her, the powerful motions splaying her thighs wide. Heaving for oxygen, we perfected a strenuous and concentrated tempo.

Perspiration drizzled between her breasts. My abs burned while working into her. By Seasons, I would make sure she found elation first.

Flare's cries accelerated. I fused her mouth with my own, tasting every quiver of her tongue. Her waist seized up, because she was going to come.

Right. Fucking. Now.

I slowed my cock, plaguing her until the final shout cracked from her lungs. Her pussy rippled and clenched around me, launching another groan from my throat. I met my little beast halfway, my waist stalling. For a second, my vision went black. Then my bellow smashed through the room, cum spilling from my crown and into Flare's convulsing body. But when my eyelids flashed apart, black turned to gold.

I fell into the color. I fell so fucking hard.

We crashed to the bed, my pulse slamming into her own. Condemnation, she would kill me someday.

Flare linked herself around my body, her tits brushing my damp skin. With my forehead pinned to hers, I fisted her dark brown waves, which had grown a few inches, though she usually preferred to keep it shoulder-length.

While our lungs recovered, we listened to the forest. Reptiles. Mammals. Sometimes I forgot other sounds existed besides these— the wild fauna and my little beast. Occasionally, it proved difficult to recall the noises of Winter.

The crunch of snow. Dire wolves howling from the pines.

I knew them. But I could not replay them.

Flare's breathing changed. I lifted my head and surveyed her flushed smile. She never hid her expressions. From the beginning, that alone had fascinated me as much as it had unnerved me. Now I couldn't get enough of those candid looks, her brilliant grin reactivating my sex drive.

"Tell me what you're gushing about," I said.

She tilted her head. "How do you know I'm gushing about anything?"

"Your exhales last longer whenever you're daydreaming."

She traced my jaw, then jutted her chin toward the surrounded drapes. "Actually, I wanted to thank you for the curtains."

I had found sheer fabric in the textile cellar, the material functioning well for our bed. The mesh was light and airy, screening insects from us at night. Practical but attractive. For this anniversary, I'd thought she would like them and had installed the curtains while she slept this morning.

My mouth crooked. "Never thank me."

Flare owned me nothing, whereas I would indulge her for as long as I drew oxygen. She knew this but refused to listen.

Case in point, she nipped my lower lip. "That will only make me show gratitude more enthusiastically."

I quirked a brow. "Is that so?"

"Mmm-hmm." Her fingers coasted down my navel, the descent causing my muscles to jump, my spent cock twitching with just as much subtlety. "Rules are meant to be broken."

My voice turned to gravel. "And how would you break mine?"

Leaning up, she swept her lips over mine. "I already have."

That, she had. For this reason, I kept my little beast in bed for the next three hours, fucking us into exhaustion. After the fifth orgasm, I ceased only because my cock would fall off if I didn't calm the bloody hell down.

However, Flare had other ideas. She sprawled on top of me, her legs fencing my hips. "What next?"

With a half-chuckle, half-groan, I sampled her neck while she brushed through my mane. "Patience," I murmured, ravenous against her throat. "Remember. We still have time."

All at once, Flare gasped. She went still and repeated to herself, "Time."

Leaning back, I furrowed my brow while she directed her gaze toward the marks we'd scratched onto the opposite wall. A makeshift calendar tracked the days, weeks, and months. It was one of her drawings, similar to the sketches she composed in the sand.

Realization set her irises aflame. Her features veered back to me. "I found the key."

50

Flare

We emerged from the cave tunnel and onto the northwest cove, an area we journeyed to occasionally for gathering firewood. The aquamarine sea glittered, the low tide trailing its fingers over the frothy sand. Threading my fingers with Jeryn's, I dragged him to the shore, then hunched to the ground.

My prince wore only his pants, the material buffeting his long limbs as he squatted beside me. The breeze winnowed against my linen shorts and smocked camisole while I raced my fingers through the sand. Having practiced this art piece, it didn't take long to create.

Twelve months. Three hundred and sixty-five days. One year ago today, we washed ashore. Since then, a thousand hopes, a thousand emotions, and a thousand experiences. Those, and a single desire. The man I'd wanted nothing to do with became the man I wanted to share everything with.

We had learned each other's fears and wishes. I knew what provoked him, and he knew what comforted me. We had learned one another's favorites—colors and food and fauna. I knew his passions, as he knew mine.

And finally, I understood The Phantom Wild's reason for calling me.

Kneeling before the sea, I sketched a vial pendant. Inside the pendant, I added intertwining symbols, including a fur cloak, his scalpel knife, the siren shark that haunted him, and the rainforest flora he'd turned into medicines.

Finished, I gestured toward the artwork with a flourish. "Happy anniversary." Swallowing, I said, "Now your vial is mended."

Jeryn blinked at the drawing. For a while, he didn't respond, staring as though unsure what to do with this gesture.

I hesitated, my heart crumbling to powder. Did he not like it?

But then his chest hitched, and I realized. Other than his necklace, sentimental gestures had been scarce in his life. He didn't know how to process his gratitude.

Shaking his head, Jeryn muttered something. Then he grabbed my face and crushed his mouth to mine. I smiled into his lips, gasping as he inched back and murmured, "Thank you."

My soul flapped its wings. Giving him another quick kiss, I pulled back and pointed. "This is my gift to you. But it's also the key."

Jeryn frowned, then his features smoothed out in understanding. "Sand art."

I nodded. "What you felt just now ... from seeing this ... that's the key."

His mention of time had made me think of the calendar I had drawn in our suite, and that had made me think of my sand art, and that had made me think of the piece I'd been planning to sketch for our anniversary. I had meant for it to be a present, but now it became more, because the sand art had also made me think of emotions, memories, and stories.

Tales. Verse. Lyrics.

The places where experiences and lives were chronicled and interpreted. Like the ancient Summer song with its secret map—buried treasure waiting to be discovered. Like the epic story that described the Seasons' history, which Poet and Briar had translated to one another during a public reading for Reaper's Fest, a recollection that Jeryn had shared with me. And like every tale that existed in The Dark Seasons, from the ones passed down to the ones newly created.

I thought of each way Jeryn and I had broken through barriers of communication. Words. Sentences.

Then I thought of Aire's words in the ruins, when he'd sensed past events within its walls.

There was a quarrel in this room between family members.

Another time, a forbidden tryst between lovers.

I thought of Jeryn's reaction when I first confided in him, when he asked what I believed my mission would be, and when he questioned why I relied on the rainforest more than myself to dictate my purpose.

Lastly, I thought of what he said about my art after we made love beside the waterfalls.

Whatever you made them feel, they would not forget it.

They wouldn't forget it because people didn't forget the things that changed them. In all its glorious and diverse forms, art stirred the soul and reinvented kingdoms. My sand drawings were the key. The rainforest had summoned me not to find the answer among its ruins. It brought me here to find the key within myself.

I'd been relying on this realm to designate my worth and steer my destiny, instead of looking inside. But Jeryn had been right. My fate wasn't about what this world had planned for me. No, it was about how I could contribute to this world on my own.

If I took the stories from this place—from my time with a prince, a year in which we'd learned differently about each other, in which we felt something wholly new toward one another—I could bring them back to Summer through my art. Just as truth lived in books and paintings and music and poetry, I could depict our tale, and the tales of those who'd once dwelled here, who lay in the catacombs but whose essences still filled the ruins' halls. I could draw the scenes that Aire had sensed. I could show how an ancient society—which had included born souls— had thrived. And I could do that without revealing the ruins' existence. Even more, I could share how enemies might overcome their hatred long enough to find love.

The legend of this place had existed within a song. Whoever left this rainforest ages ago had hinted its existence through lyrics.

Seek not, find not, this Phantom Wild.

I would bring more of this realm back through images in the sand, across all shores in Summer, for everyone who came to view them. If I did this, maybe the art could inspire my homeland. Maybe people would think differently about born souls.

I had a voice. This was my key.

I told this to Jeryn. Though from his expression, he'd known where I was going with this.

We stared at each other. Hope and amazement clashed with sorrow and longing as our gazes clung. If I'd found my key, that meant it would soon be time to leave. But it wouldn't be forever. We had made that vow to each other.

So although my heart throbbed painfully, I crawled across the sand. Growling, he tugged me onto his lap, and our mouths locked, the kiss steady like the ocean.

The deep flex of his tongue poured heat down my skin. Pulling back, a wistful grin slanted across my face, and Jeryn's eyes darkened with a promise. After making love all morning, he'd said we still had time. And we did. We had today, tonight, and tomorrow. And maybe a little longer, enough to squeeze out a few more droplets of happiness.

We stayed like this, clasping until Jeryn combed back my hair. "Let's build a fire at home. I'll strip you down in front of it and make you come again."

Home. He'd said home.

I nodded, my throat swelling. Every time we left the ruins, we carried our weapons—his knife and my machete, which I'd taken to using more than Poet's dagger. Not only did the blade remind me of my parents, but it was easier to hack through vegetation. After venturing back to the ruins and retrieving two oversized slings that I'd woven, we returned to the cove and set about collecting kindling, since we were running low and the trees here shed their trunks more than anywhere else. Plus, the timbers were drier.

We packed our wood into the slings and set them on the ground, then took a walk by the water, my fingers entwining with Jeryn's. At one point, his arms snaked possessively around me from behind, and he buried his face in the side of my neck, making me chuckle. Like this, it was difficult for us to walk, our limbs stumbling through the tide.

"You're a villain," I teased.

"Correction," he replied into my throat. "I'm your villain."

I opened my mouth to answer when two things happened. The sky rumbled, signaling thunder rain. It wasn't unusual, yet for some reason, foreboding crawled like a spider down my flesh. Next, a red flash darted from the forest's border.

Jeryn trailed my gaze toward the butterfly flapping wildly in our direction. My little companion had been acting as our messenger between Summer and Autumn, though we hadn't been expecting her yet.

The prince and I hastened toward the creature. I crooked my finger for the female to land upon, her wings fluttering rapidly.

"What is it, my friend?" I asked. "What's the matter?"

Jeryn hissed, bothered by something else I couldn't sense. "Flare," he warned, drawing out my name in a low baritone.

Glancing the wild's edge, I scanned the mesh of leaves, searching beyond its depths. Then I felt it—a presence. More than that, an intrusion. The offshoots rustled and shuddered.

Snarling, the prince snatched my waist. He whipped me behind him and ripped out his scalpel knife. We halted, arrested inside a shocked second, then two seconds, then three.

A gust swirled through the foliage. Then an athletic form cut through the underbrush, his movements familiar. Ashen blond hair and blue eyes materialized, along with the flash of two broadswords.

"Aire!" I exclaimed in confusion while scrambling from behind Jeryn.

"What the fuck?" the prince muttered, disarming his weapon.

The knight's bulk shoved through the bushes. Striding into view, he stalled, relief and urgency contorting his face. "Your Highness. Flare. We—"

"I said, what the fuck?" Jeryn seethed. "I almost impaled you."

The butterfly landed on my shoulder as I rushed to the warrior's side. "What—"

Aire held up his hand. "I cannot explain." He flung his chin toward the southeast. "We docked a skiff on the other side, but it's not a story for now. We must leave. Now." A grave look dimmed his features. "They're coming."

"Who?" I shook my head. "Leave where?"

Despite the lack of quill and parchment, my gesture and confused features communicated enough. Grasping my meaning, Aire opened his mouth, but I swerved toward Jeryn, too agitated to remain still.

Except my bafflement was cut off by the haunted expression carving through his face. The prince's eyes flashed as he stared into the distance, his features blanching as if he'd just encountered a ghost.

Following his gaze, I saw it. Blasting through a curtain of fog, the massive Winter ships smashed through the ocean like bulldozers.

51

Flare

When I was little, I used to imagine ships were wooden whales, gentle giants who ruled the sea. These vessels appeared small from afar, but their sails told me better. From here, I made out the swollen bellies of their hulls and the spearing bowsprits. These were no gentle giants on a peaceful expedition. These were monsters beating aside the waves, their silver figureheads aiming for the shore.

Then a second armada followed, this one hailing from Summer, their golden masts lancing into the sky. I stumbled backward, the scent of brine stinging my nostrils. It couldn't be real. I had to wake myself up from this nightmare. Now.

Except Jeryn and Aire saw the ships too. But how? How was this happening? The rainforest couldn't have summoned this legion as it had me.

A shrill noise gutted the sky, the ships' horns tolling. The cacophony scattered a flock of macaws from the ferns, because they saw the enemy as well.

Soldiers clamored, hollering and pounding across the decks. They were too far away to see our shapes, but if the naval vessels were real, they would anchor soon.

I thought of their mainstays smacking the ocean floor, the iron weights breaking off a hunk of coral and crushing kelp. Skiffs would paddle the rest of the way, drive across the sand, and make track marks in the cove.

The butterfly launched off my shoulder and flapped into the trees. I charged toward the sea, to defend this land. An arm clamped around my waist and heaved me back.

Furious, I swung my fist at Jeryn, but he caught my knuckles. "Flare," he cautioned.

His complexion hadn't regained its color. From the sight, a new thought seized me. If we weren't dreaming, Winter was coming to get him.

His pupils darkened. I stared at those black pits, his gaze confirming there were too many of them to fight. And if they were searching for him, that meant they were also looking for me.

Protectiveness sharpened those eyes, which clicked over my shoulder to the forest. He calculated, then his gaze snapped to me. He nodded, and I nodded back. Then his hand seized mine, and I strapped my fingers with his.

And we ran.

Veering around, we bolted into the rainforest with Aire bringing up the rear. Ferns rattled as we catapulted through the thicket, the trees patrolled by birds of prey, hundreds of caws scratching my ears. Jeryn and I had hewn a wider path through here ages ago, but the rainforest was immortal and unpredictable. No matter how much we knew of it, The Phantom Wild knew more. It grew itself back, clogging the spaces quickly, with new surprises burgeoning out of nowhere.

We ducked under creepers and sprinted around trunks. But shit. We'd left our wood slings behind for the convoy to see. With that evidence in sight, there was no telling whether they'd comb the beach first or brave the wild straightaway.

How had they known where to look? How could the rainforest have let them in?

The Phantom Wild was sacred. They didn't deserve this privilege.

Although I no longer wore a collar tattoo, my flesh sizzled where the sunbursts used to be. A growl rolled up my throat. Like hell would I let Summer or Winter take me again.

Bromeliads flashed in the darkness. An insect flew into my clothes and pricked my side with its stinger. Our race kicked up an ugly, rotten stench from the undergrowth, its rancidness clashing with overripe floral whiffs.

I inhaled dampness and sweat. More than that, I felt the dip in heat and shift in the fog, pushed by an incoming force. Jeryn and I stopped. As did Aire, who'd sensed the change in his own unearthly way.

We couldn't see or hear beyond the canopy, but the hairs on my arms rose.

Jeryn halted next to a compact batch of shrubs and flung aside the branches. "Inside."

I released his fingers and snatched the knight's arm, tugging him toward the enclosure. At first, Aire protested, his call-of-duty instincts resisting. But after checking the terrain again, he hunkered behind me. After scanning the environment, the prince crashed through, his body alongside Aire's walling me in like a barricade.

Thunder rain fell, the droplets slamming into the ground. We huddled there, with Jeryn's arm reaching behind to shield me, while I swiveled my face into the ravine of his shoulder blades and breathed him in.

He said something over the deluge, and Aire said something back, their voices getting louder and faster. Yet I heard them in only snippets, the story patching together.

In low tones, the details flew out of Aire's mouth. "We arrived from Autumn for a meeting with Giselle. This morning, a tower guard noticed your drawing on the cell's ceiling. They questioned everyone, asking what it was."

Poet, Briar, and Aire had traveled to Summer for a conference with the queen. While there, they'd sought an update about Rhys, but although they hadn't gained new information, word about the map had reached Giselle while the clan had been present. Such a simple thing. The guards had never looked at the ceiling, not once when I was there, because they'd had lots of practice looking without seeing. Our cage wasn't worth inspecting.

Yet this time had been different. But because the jester and princess had already given my tower mates sanctuary in Autumn, Lorelei, Dante, and Pearl weren't the ones to expose me during the interrogation. Instead, one of the other prisoners had. Because of my penchant for sleep talking, they'd noticed my mouth moving one night and made the connection.

Few people could read my lips. Still every soul in that cell block had learned to see in the dark, to understand how my lips moved. In fact, I had spent time helping them, teaching them to understand me. Although I'd been closest to my tower mates, I'd lived on-and-off with the others for almost ten years. With nothing but time on our hands, they had learned to communicate with me. But none of them had ever told me I talked in my sleep about the song.

"The wardens threatened them for details, then had the map copied," Aire whispered while glaring through the foliage. "Autumn's ship was a risk, so we took a skiff before the fleet set out."

Jeryn grunted. "A remarkable coincidence that Winter happened to be in attendance."

"No, Sire. Your Queens had grown desperate. With Giselle and Rhys's approval, Winter recently ordered a fleet to be permanently stationed in Summer, lest your whereabouts should be discovered. In any case, our clan disbanded to find you upon docking."

"Where are they?" I whispered. "Poet and Briar?"

Jeryn translated my question. To which, Aire consulted the forest, his attention riveted, scanning the atmosphere for a sign. His jaw tensed in frustration, his grip tightening on the broadswords. "I do not know."

I deflated. The absence of Autumn's ship would have been noticed on the mainland. Its presence here would have identified the clan. Taking a skiff from the wharf stood to reason. Likely, they had docked somewhere hidden, which meant searching for me and Jeryn had taken a while.

Splitting up made sense, and it was no wonder the instinctual knight had located us first, alongside my butterfly companion. But now our friends were alone in the wild, where predators roamed and thunder rain punched craters into the earth.

If Summer or Winter caught them, what excuse would the jester and princess give? They were clever. Yet fear for their safety thrashed inside my chest.

The troops couldn't find our friends. The troops couldn't find the ruins either.

Our fortress. Our home.

The ancients, whose existence needed to be preserved for this campaign. If Summer stumbled upon and reported the rainforest's castle, Rhys would demolish it.

How had my homeland deciphered the hidden map? The prisoners had explained what the sketch represented, but it would have taken a chosen one to see through the lyrics. Or at least, to enable others to see them.

Jeryn squeezed my fingers, aware of my thoughts. He would say a talented Summer captain or cartographer could have decoded the map, along with the help of a Winter genius. But what about my calling? Unless the forest had a purpose for bringing these ships here.

Aire cocked his head, then stretched his gaze over his shoulder. He must have felt my questions, attuning himself to my dismay. "Sand drifters read the map."

My features crumpled. Of course, the Crown would have employed my kind to interpret the lyrics. If our culture could navigate the crevices of this kingdom and find priceless treasures, drifters had the best chance of understanding my sketch.

Still, I was the chosen one, not them. The rainforest had bestowed me with the ability to see the map.

Aire's irises glinted. "You did not fail this wild."

Mist filled my eyes. This man read emotions the same way he read nature. What a beautiful gift—and what a haunting burden.

Then again, this land had called me to find the key within myself. Yet maybe it didn't have a connection only to me, but to everyone. Because we were all part of this world, all part of nature, all linked to one another, our paths converging and diverging. Every sacred realm in The Dark Seasons had its pull, and the difference resided in *how* it welcomed each of us, and what happened when we arrived. Maybe we were all chosen ones, and maybe the outcome was a mixture of destiny and choice. Not one or the other.

And that was okay.

Jeryn stayed quiet. I peered at the honed shadows of his profile, which I doubted even Aire could penetrate. But if a person close to this prince knew where to look, they'd find a crawlspace, the fissure where he concealed his thoughts. He was considering the knights who'd disembarked from the ships, the torrent presently ambushing them. Fated or not, if they expected to march through here without a problem, they had a vicious surprise coming.

The rain became a drizzle and then dissipated. In its place, bushes shivered, remote voices filtered through the understory, and steel rang. They'd made it inside.

"Your Highness, this is ludicrous," Aire growled at Jeryn.

"Quiet," the prince clipped. "I'm thinking."

"Concealment should not have been the plan. At least, not for you."

"I know."

"You could have provided a distraction."

"I know."

"If you wanted Flare to get away without them giving chase, you should have stayed behind to deter them."

"I know," Jeryn stated while peering into the trees.

On the shore, when Aire had stressed that we needed to leave, he'd meant him and me. True, Jeryn's presence would have distracted the fleet. Yet I recognized the harsh set of his features, that concentrated dip in his brows. To stop them from finding me, Jeryn would have cut through this army with his bare hands. Although he knew I could blend into this forest without his help, his first impulse had been to remain by my side.

More than that, my prince had another reason—a motive he kept to himself. And there was no way I'd have left him behind in that cove anyway.

Footfalls trampled into the rainforest, the sounds carrying through the storm. More than a dozen soldiers groaned and grunted, the rain having pummeled them like hammers.

"Stay close," one hollered.

"A torch!" another called. "We need light!"

"Fuck the light," someone else grumbled. "Do you want to get us mauled?"

"Mind this path. Something's getting close."

Something. Not somebody.

They spoke loudly, shouting the words "Prince" and "Prisoner." That kind of racket would draw the faunas' attention. And if they disturbed that nest in the creepers, they'd be pincushions in no time.

The troop made it another three paces. Then a woman barked, "Don't, you idiot. We don't know—"

A man bellowed, his pained shrieks ripping through the forest. I knew that torture. One of them had gotten thirsty and taken a gulp from a stream that burned its victim's tongue off. Jeryn and I had discovered this waterway over the past year and avoided it. The soldier groaned and hacked as if half of his mouth had been melted off, the grisly scene preoccupying the troops.

Aire launched forward. "Now."

"Wait," I cautioned, snatching his arm and pointing to an overhead bough.

"Patience," Jeryn murmured, having recognized the same thing. His gaze was also fixated on the spot I'd indicated, where a barbed tail slithered along the branch, its source getting nearer to the voices.

The boa from my fauna pack. After bonding with the creature, I'd learned about her powers. With a strike to the nape, the serpent's quarry would die in agony, with blood spurting from every nook and cranny of their skin. Despite my kinship with the animal, she had the ability to condemn her targets to a hellish death. Or if not, this legion would harm her.

Terror clenched my throat. Frantic, I scrambled for a way to distract her, to keep the female out of harm's way without alerting the troops to our presence. But the snake hissed, already noticing me hiding like prey and sensing why.

No sooner did the burned soldier go silent than another knight screamed. And then many knights screamed.

"Get it!" a voice raked. "Slaughter the fucker!"

No! Not her!

I vaulted past Aire and Jeryn, only for the prince to snatch me back. His palm clamped over my mouth while I thrashed, but his cool voice stroked my ear. "Look."

And I looked. And I saw the boa shooting past the soldiers, her movements too rapid to follow, fluidly dodging the army's attack. As she sank her fangs into a warrior, a feline roared through the wild. From the undergrowth, a jaguar leaped on the springs of her paws, her saberteeth and claws bared while other predators stampeded into the scene, including anacondas and leopards and reptiles with tusks. Among them, my fauna pack laid siege, defended their home, and protected me as one of their own.

Voices howled. Flesh and ligaments tore. Blood ran like a river.

Man-made weapons struggled against the onslaught. To say nothing of the flora, brambles spearing legs, creepers snaring waists so tightly they threatened to sever each armored body, stinging tree sap tacking men and women to the trunks, and bottomless streams that only appeared shallow before they sucked victims into an abyss. Against the predators' speed and strength, the knights toiled in a battle with nature.

"Seasons almighty," Aire breathed.

"I can't!" I wailed, flailing as Jeryn dragged me out of the shrubs, away from my pack. "I can't! I won't leave them!"

"Trust what you see, Flare," he growled. "Give this wild credit."

Aire nodded his agreement before launching ahead. I stalled, because the rainforest was eternal, and it had lasted for centuries without me, through eons of elemental disasters. A few soldiers wouldn't overpower this realm.

Jeryn was right, and Aire sensed this truth, so I had to keep faith. My pack would be safe. If I didn't believe that, my heart would crumble to dust.

We quit the gruesome spectacle, our feet flying, gaining distance. Or so we thought until Aire swerved to avoid a leopard with glowing spots, the creature bounding inches from him, forcing the knight through a beam of canopy light.

"The shadow," a man yelled. "There!"

"It's another creature!" another bellowed.

It wasn't. But if they mistook us for the fauna, so much the better. Still, one of them hollered, "Seize the monster!"

Damnation. I veered toward Aire while ripping the machete from my rope belt, then skidded in place when a small object whizzed past us and blasted the first assailant off his feet. I squinted, making out the shape of a dart as another one fired through the foliage.

Or not a dart. The object was quill shaped like a thorn.

My eyes widened. Briar.

Relief flooded my being as a flash of red hair dashed into the scene. Clad in a dark jumpsuit and with a braid crowning her hair, the princess catapulted into view. With pinched features, she narrowed her gaze, fighting to see through the murk. Then she flung another thorn quill across the divide, using the forest's glow to guide her aim, as I'd once instructed during her visit. The weapon hit its mark, knocking down a female warrior.

The thorn quills disintegrated seconds after impact, some newfound form of design that I hadn't seen from her before. This would prevent the troops from identifying Briar's signature weapon.

Awe stretched across my face. Stumbling to a halt, Briar exchanged nods with Aire, then sought my gaze.

"Flare," she gasped.

"Briar," I called.

In the dark, we lunged for each other, clasping in a quick hug. The cacophony of bloodshed consumed the wild. Human shadows collided with fauna outlines, and knights jabbed their swords, combatting the predators and each other. Confusion ensued, with the soldiers unable to tell comrades from animals, trees from giants, plants from weapons.

This lush, dark rainforest disoriented them. The fray spread like a rushing tide.

Jeryn's silhouette rammed into someone. He lashed his knife, and the attacker hunched, fluid spraying from their throat.

Another knight surged toward him. I growled and flew in their direction, swiping my machete across the soldier's legs before he planted a weapon in the prince's back. Then another blade hurled toward me, and Jeryn belted out a murderous growl, flinging me behind him and slicing through the person's stomach.

A flash of steel arched our way—and split under the force of a staff. A whipcord form blew from the shrubs, a pair of arms windmilling the rod and cracking the enemy's skull.

Poet.

The jester hissed, his green eyes flaring, visible for an instant. He slipped into the shadows again, twisting and spinning while bodies toppled around him.

Aire moved like a tornado. Briar's thorn quills intercepted flying stars from the Winter soldiers. Jeryn's deadly precision took his opponents down too fast for them to register the attack, his aim focused on arteries and vital organs. And I moved like a member of the fauna, quick and sure.

A woman shouted. Glancing back, I spotted a flash of white hair and split complexion of pale and gray, like that of a half-moon. Upon hearing the female, Jeryn faltered. In the castle, that knight had worked under his command, and she'd been the one monitoring me shortly before I'd escaped.

The female gained on my jaguar, who tore into one of her brethren. Darting the animal's way, I snatched a vine from a branch and threw myself to the ground. Sliding on my hip between the feline and the woman, I flung out my leg to trip her. The Winter bitch landed face-first, a crossbow slipping from her fingers and her armored shoulder popping like a bubble.

I snared the vine around her limbs and yanked it in place. With the knot wound so tightly, she wasn't going anywhere. For all this knight knew, a log had felled her, and an errant creeper had done the rest.

Pitching to my feet, I whirled and caught up to our clan, who'd stopped to search for me. "Sorry!" I said while jetting past everyone.

We cut a retreat, the troops having misidentified us as creatures. The echoes of pandemonium faded once we reached one of the underground caves, which deposited us at the ruins. We had sworn not to lead anyone here, but for some reason Jeryn had forced us in this direction.

Barreling up the front steps and staggering to a halt inside the vestibule, Aire bent forward to catch his breath. "They do not suspect us. The legend and its fauna will dissuade them."

Regardless, Poet hauled Briar against him and spat, "Jeryn, what the fuck?"

"We can't stay here," the princess agreed. "The ruins—"

I shook my head at them, indicating that we weren't actually staying here. Then I looked up at Jeryn, who clasped my face and raked his eyes over me, checking for wounds. His expression confirmed this hadn't been impulsive, because he rarely did anything that way.

With reluctance, he released me and snapped to everyone, "Wait here."

Then he strode down one of the halls. Unable to stay still, I raced after him, hastening up a stairway and into our adjoining chambers. In the doorway, I watched Jeryn shove every stitch of my clothing into our satchels, then add my sheathed dagger and my collection of nets to the pile.

Hitching the straps over his shoulder, the prince stalked back to me and took my hand. Without a word, he led us down the steps. In the medical chamber, he collected bundles of herbs and florals, shoving them into the bags as well, along with our old canteen filled with water and fruits from the dining hall. After that, we reunited with the clan.

Poet, Briar, and Aire took one look at the satchels. A conclusion pulled their features taut, but only the princess let her emotions betray her. She peeked my way, compassion glossing her gray eyes.

Trepidation sank to the pit of my stomach. We vacated the ruins, fled down another tunnel, and emerged at the southeast cove where Jeryn and I had moored our newly constructed tidefarer. Next to that, bobbed the skiff our clan had used to sail here.

All seemed peaceful except for the swaying waves. I couldn't say the same for my insides, which twisted into knots.

After exchanging words with the jester and princess, Aire inclined his head. "Make haste," he advised before striding to the skiff.

My brow furrowed as the knight sailed on his own, shrinking to a dot on the horizon. "Where is he going?"

"To the wharf," Poet answered, guessing my question more than reading it. "He'll make certain it's vacated by the time we get there."

But why hadn't Poet and Briar gone with Aire? Jeryn and I would be fine on the tidefarer. If we caught a current, we could journey farther east with our pursuers none the wiser.

And then...

Then what? We had no plan for this. Leaving wasn't supposed to happen this way.

Grief clogged my throat. This couldn't be the end. We hadn't had a chance to say farewell to the rainforest or my pack.

"Take this," Jeryn instructed, handing the satchels to Poet and Briar.

The pair tossed us grave looks before carrying the items to the tidewater. Far too late, the harrowing thought occurred to me. Jeryn had packed my clothing and weapon—but not his. I'd missed a detail, something he wasn't spitting out.

Jeryn stared past me, to where Poet and Briar had boarded the tidefarer. His eyes sent a message across the divide, and I sensed them receiving it. The jester and princess busied themselves, loading the deck and pretending not to witness this moment between us.

"Jeryn—," I began.

"Come," he said.

I accepted his hand, letting him guide me to the sea's edge, where the tide brushed the shore. All I could think was, he'd cut me off. He rarely did that.

Something was wrong.

My feet stalled, the sand scratching my feet. Jeryn had erased me from our home, packing items only I would need. All along, the prince had intended to get here before they did, to make sure I had what I needed for travel.

But what about him? Where were his possessions?

Jeryn stood beside me, watching the ocean sparkle, and I cursed his silence. I stared at him, ready to shout. But then he turned my way, expecting this reaction, because he knew that I knew.

He wasn't coming with me.

52

Flare

He wasn't coming, but he also wasn't staying. My villain prince was going back to Winter as planned.

Only much sooner. And without any intention of coming back.

We wouldn't get to say a peaceful goodbye. We wouldn't have another day here.

I jumped on him, except not with open arms. I pounded my fists into his chest while shouting, "No" and "No" and "No!"

I wanted to knock him down and drag him onto the tidefarer, take him prisoner like he once took me. Weeping and raging, I put my whole body into it. Punching Jeryn felt like punching a cliff, but I didn't care, and yet I never cared more. Worse, he didn't fight back, which made me angrier.

"No!" I cried. "No, not like this! It's not supposed to happen like this!"

Every muscle in his face twisted, a thousand terrible emotions threatening to smash through. He clasped my waist, holding me as I attacked him. "It must," he said. "You have to leave me here."

My face crumbled. I sagged, my mouth landing against his neck, with his vial pendant wedged between us. "I won't."

"You will."

"I won't!"

"Flare." Jeryn pried himself away and grabbed my shoulders. "Listen to me."

"We'll keep hiding until they're gone."

"So long as there's a chance either of us are here, they'll tear through this realm."

That killed whatever else I'd been about to yell. We had vowed to stay together no matter the time or distance, no matter if I sailed these seas and he sat on his throne. My prince and I had sworn to bridge that forbidden chasm. All this time, we'd been thinking and plotting and preparing. And if the Seasons ripped us apart like this, we wouldn't have the chance to enact those plans.

But if he left with me now, only for us to separate calmly later, there would be no one here to distract the troops. Finding him and apprehending me was their goal. If Jeryn remained, he would satisfy one agenda and stifle the other. This would also provide a more believable return for him, and it would give him an opportunity to protect the rainforest from further conquest.

My eyes burned. I saw every cut and scar on his face, including the ones that had disappeared. I saw tenderness and sacrifice reflected in his eyes. I should have expected this, should have known what he'd choose and why.

Anguish cracked me in half. "Jeryn," I begged. "Please."

Please don't do this. Please don't let me go. Please don't break my heart.

His forehead fell against mine. "You will do as I say and get in that fucking boat. You'll be careful, and you'll disappear so that Summer won't find you." His voice lowered to a tormented whisper. "So that I won't find you."

So he wouldn't find me. Lest Jeryn should grow desperate and commit himself to another cat and mouse chase, I had to make sure he would lose.

"Do not let yourself get caught again," he hissed. "This is my command."

"Bullshit," I gritted through my tears. "You don't rule me."

"And I never have." His eyes flashed. "Yet it was worth a try."

"We can escape together. We can find a way. We just need a moment."

Jeryn's chest collapsed as if my pleas had crashed there like bricks. "Flare."

Shackle him, my heart wailed.

Release him, my head implored.

Wildly, I shook my head. But seconds later, the resistance deflated as his thumb traced my wet cheek. "I would tear this continent in half to get to you. I would surrender my crown. I would live and die anywhere, to stay by your side. But from Winter, I will bleed myself dry protecting you. I'll tighten Rhys's leash, divert my court, stop anyone from searching."

I choked out, "But you're my home."

The truth struck my chest like a javelin. We'd built a home here, but more than the rainforest, this man was my home. My sanctuary and my refuge and my safe haven. And from the way he shuddered, I had become his home too.

A furious sob broke from my lips. "Hellfire, Jeryn. Don't ask this of me."

"Royals don't ask." He took my hand and pressed it to his chest. "And my little beast does not wither."

No. I didn't. Not unless I let these monsters win.

They had taken my parents and my freedom. Now they sought to take my prince.

But if this world dared to come between us, we would fight back. Even if it meant facing that battle from opposite sides of this world.

The mystical elements of this realm wouldn't deter Summer from swarming it. Nature was formidable in every Season, so the legend wouldn't intimidate King Rhys. Instead, he'd be salivating to get his greedy hands on this place, if only to destroy the ruins and any proof that an equal society had lived here.

If the ancient palace wanted to be found, it would be. Just like this realm had been discovered. Or if it wished to remain hidden, it would make sure of that too.

But that didn't mean we should step aside and do nothing.

I spoke quickly. "If they didn't see us, and if they think the attack was only from the fauna, and if they don't find the ruins ..." Fire raced across my tongue. "Convince them this realm is riddled with plague. Make them fear this rainforest."

Those observant eyes sharpened. "Viruses."

Yes. Like the one that claimed the ancients. In the eyes of The Dark Seasons, only a scientist would know how to survive that. Even better, only the most advanced scientist, from the most advanced nation. Jeryn could paint a horrific picture of sickness. If there was one thing Summer feared besides the wrath of Winter, it was contagion.

With a firsthand account from the Prince of Winter, no one would brave coming here. Certainly not His Majesty. That would keep the ruins protected from Rhys.

Jeryn agreed. Yet a hundred logistics, a hundred obstacles, and a hundred contingency plans sat on his face. "This will delay us. To meet here in the future, we would need to be sure, to have a guarantee that returning undetected is safe, which shall take time." His throat contorted. "A long time."

My heart sank like a pebble to the bottom of the sea. Jeryn had described often enough the life of a Royal, in which he'd have twelve times as many people watching him after this. Upon his return, the court would be focused on every move he made, and his security detail would increase tenfold. For all his tactical genius, this man would be guarded like a priceless object, to the point where he'd have no means to avoid detection.

We had expected to send one another secret messages. But with him guarded more intently, a reunion or any contact would have to wait for longer than either of us could predict.

Jeryn caressed the side of my face. "Until then, you have your key now."

My true voice. The way I spoke through my art. Only hours ago, I'd figured out just how much of myself I had to offer this world. That my voice, my destiny, and my strengths didn't come from the rainforest. They came from me.

This prince had reminded me that I had a choice in my fate.

"Tell me I will see you again," I choked out.

His voice turned as solid as iron. "I will come to you. I will always come."

A sob dropped from my mouth. He would come. But not soon. Not even close. That part, he didn't say.

All the same, he snatched my cheeks. "Know this. I would chase you to the ends of the ocean, to the bottom of the fucking sea. I would mutilate anyone who stopped me." His fingers knifed into my hair. "So help me, I would freeze this world for you."

"And so help me, I wouldn't want you to do that. If you're going to act for my sake, then heal this world instead."

"Selfless little beast," he murmured. "So be it."

"Good." Folding my hands over his, I gave him the dirtiest look I could muster. "Because I will hunt you down if you don't."

"That isn't a threat," he countered. "It's a temptation."

Tears puddled in my eyes. This morning after fucking the day away, and he'd said we still had time.

Suddenly, one year felt like one second. It had gone by too fast. We wouldn't find out how it felt to have more time. We would lose those dusks and dawns. We would forsake every sunset and sunrise. We could sacrifice every lost kiss and touch. We would surrender the life we'd barely gotten to taste.

Poet and Briar had earned their happy ending. They were blessed, and I couldn't be more elated for them. Yet I envied their bond. When the prince and I next saw one another, it could be months or years. From then on, our reunions would be sporadic and risky. They would always be fleeting.

What we shared would remain unknown, never existing for the world to see. Our language was fire and ice, it was ferocious and enduring—a language of survival. It was a rainforest, something that remained elusive and isolated.

Like our shared ability to hear my voice. Like Aire's sensory powers. Like Aspen's beautiful markings. Like Poet and Briar's unbreakable union.

If magic existed in nature, it must exist in humans and fauna too. If nothing else, Jeryn and I would always share this private link.

Let this go, my blood said.

Hold on tight, my heart said.

I surprised Jeryn—the last surprise—and slipped off his necklace. Crouching to the ground, I packed the vial with sand, sealed the vessel, and rose to loop the strap back over his head.

"To heal you when you need it," I said, the words splintering on my tongue.

He clasped the pendant, his features constricting. "I have nothing to trade."

"Yes, you do." I framed the hard ridge of his jaw. "You've already given it to me."

His name, his kiss, his body. He'd given me his thoughts, his fears, his doubts, his regrets, his shame, his desires. In those ways, this cold prince had given me his heart.

Jeryn's gaze clung to mine. Those irises grew tender in a way I'd once thought impossible. He soaked in the view as though he were staring into the sun.

The muscles in his face cinched, and heat swirled in his pupils. "I belong to you." Seizing the back of my head, my villain prince swooped down and hissed against my mouth, "Everywhere you are, I shall be yours."

His mouth grabbed my own, ripping open my lips and pulling a grieving noise from me. I flung my arms around him and sobbed into the kiss. My mouth latched on, catching the desperate flex of his tongue, angling my head and fitting my own tongue to his.

Groaning, Jeryn locked my scalp in place with one hand and gripped my ass with the other. His strong arms banded me to him, enabling his mouth to reach deeper, to locate the depths of my soul.

I kissed him because I wanted him. I kissed him because I needed him.

I kissed him because I loved him.

I loved this villain prince more than any legend or wish I'd ever had. I told him with my moan, the clench of my lips, the way my tongue roped around his. I let him feel it in the quiver of my mouth, the nip of my teeth.

I kissed him for the year we'd shared. I kissed him for someday.

Jeryn's body hitched. His ferocious mouth crushed mine harder, hotter. He hoisted me into him, my tears leaking into the place where our lips fused and rocked.

Just one more time. Just one more minute.

Would I remember the shape of this kiss? Would I remember the last gasp of it?

Yes and yes. I felt in us science and spirit, caution and curiosity, sanity and wildness. There was sense and madness everywhere, like love and hate. We'd been lucky to explore both. Whatever came next, our story had happened. And maybe what we'd had here, and who we became together, was the greatest sort of revolution. If we were possible, maybe other things were possible. Like the jester and princess, stories such as ours could move kingdoms.

With an agonized groan, Jeryn thrust his lips from mine. *Now*, he mouthed through his teeth. *Leave now.*

Yes. Now. If I didn't, I'd break my promise and make him break his. I'd split and scatter into a million glittering flecks.

With a pained cry, I whispered against his mouth, "I love you."

Then I turned and ran. Saltwater scorched my eyes, yet somehow I kept moving.

Poet and Briar waited by the tidefarer, empathy consuming their features. They understood this pain all too well.

As I reached them, the jester quietly extended his hand, and I took it. I knew what would happen next. Once the sun had set, we would dock at the wharf where I'd originally escaped. Under the cloak of night, we would say goodbye from there, with Poet and Briar returning to their ship alongside Aire.

The tidefarer would be mine. I didn't know where I would go first. But as a sand drifter, I'd let the waves show me the way, because there were so many places, so much of Summer to see. And so much of my voice to offer.

Poet shoved the tidefarer from the shore and leaped inside. I hunched over the rim and snatched up a fistful of gold, then rose to my feet. The vessel sliced through the sea, and the clearest jeweled blue rippled under us.

The trees swayed. From the bushes, my fauna pack crept into view, having followed my scent. Relief washed through me because they'd survived and come to bid me farewell. I bowed my head in gratitude, and my trembling lips blew the animals a kiss, swearing to return someday.

Ahead of them, a shadow loomed on the cove. I warned myself not to look, but I did. My villain prince stood there. He watched me, and I watched him, and the smaller he got, the more my heart grew.

No longer did I see his face, but his shape remained. And I loved that shape. I loved it so much.

I grinned through my tears. Spreading my fingers, I let the wind take the sand, sprinkling it over the water and setting it free. Then I turned to face the sun.

53

Jeryn

I turned to face the sun. But not the same one. Not anymore. Beyond the medical den's open mullioned doors, the castle terrace extended toward a vista of alpine mountains capped in snow. The afternoon sun was a gray bruise in the sky, dull and murky compared to the burning firmament I'd grown used to.

A shaft of pale light hit my profile. The wind pierced my skin, its chill cutting across the tight ledge of my jaw. Winter did that to people, polished the essential parts. I appreciated how it numbed the soul, the blast of cold enabling me to function.

I rounded back to the table, my boots striking the tile floor. The sterilized room peered blankly at me. Shelves of manuscripts, scrolls, diagrams. Instruments with smooth and serrated edges. Curettes, extractors, tubes, shears, lancets, surgical knives. Blue cupboards of flasks, beakers, jars. Tinctures and elixirs.

This den was the only place that made current sense to me. Everywhere else in this fortress, I hadn't gotten used to the surplus of luxuries. Glass windows. Polished furnishings. Baths and servants at my disposal. Meals consisting of game and wine. The wardrobe of velvet and leather. People bowing and curtsying the instant I strode into a room. Overwhelming.

On the surface before me stood a row of bottles, each labeled by my hand. Specimens of a legend and a kingdom. Plants of the rainforest, as well as the woodlands looming outside this stronghold.

My fur coat was draped over a chair. A draft rustled the prickly collar.

I flattened my palms on the table and stared at the vessels. Transporting my remedies from the ruins, plus samples of the rainforest's flora, had offered advanced remedies. Yet I scowled. I had been at this for ages, trying to find the correct blend of Summer and Winter that would yield new treatments. Personal restoratives of a family nature, in addition to humanely tested remedies, compared with the toxic mixtures and sharp methods of experimentation mounted on the wall.

I might not succeed. Even assuming I did, this feat could take decades at minimum.

So be it. I'd been bred for that.

A knock caused the door to wince. My eyes sliced toward the entrance. Fucking incompetence. I had given instructions not to be disturbed. It appeared I would have to illustrate my wishes more tangibly.

Well. Few knew whether to translate my silence as "Yes" or "No," much less "Come in" or "Get the fuck out." That had not changed, with only a rare mastering the skill. This included my first-in-command, my family, the jester and princess, and ...

Fuck. I scrubbed Flare's face and the last three words she'd whispered from my mind. For her sake, I would not risk going there. If I did, the memories would incapacitate me.

Despite not receiving an answer, Indigo entered. The sight of that perpetual nuisance stiffened my joints. I'd been having doubts about his fealty since before my exile in Summer, a state of affairs that hadn't changed.

The warrior's silver cloak swept the floor as he bowed. "Your Highness."

"I'm indisposed," I clipped, giving him a pointed look that caused his posture to waver.

"Yes, Sire," he replied with uncertainty. "However, the Queens request an audience."

Ah. I straightened and relented with a brisk nod.

Yet the knight dallied, his mouth compressing as if he'd been holding that insufferable trap shut since he and the convoy had stumbled upon me in the rainforest. I had returned to them once Flare had vanished out of sight with Poet and Briar. Thereupon, I had made sure to deter the legion from discovering the ruins. The fake camp I'd set up near the shore had achieved that.

Indigo had been the one to unspool the vine from around Solstice's limbs. With pride, I could presume who'd used those knots to detain my First Knight. In any case, only one-quarter of the troops had survived the rainforest, its predators, and the wounds our clan had inflicted in the dark.

Presently, the soldier lingered but said nothing. My eyes thinned, and I lifted a brow in cold inquiry.

His bravado faltered. So much for verbalizing himself. But for treasonous reasons, I deemed it unwise to encourage this one. For a long time now, my intuition had been detecting the reek and prowl of an imposter.

Like a hotshot, Indigo flexed his shoulders. Indeed, here it came.

"You were gathering wood, Sire," he testified.

It took a moment to comprehend this. He meant the lumber Flare and I had been collecting at the cove. Prior to the chase, we'd abandoned those timbers.

To this, I said nothing but waited for more.

Not for long. "There were two slings."

And I had two arms. Though, pointing that out would sound defensive.

On to the next query. My silence prompted the knight to grow a pair of testicles. "It seems uncommon that you would leave them there."

Correct. "Uncommon" was putting it mildly—a deliberate choice of word, often tossed casually around like daggers during roundtables between adversaries.

How uncommon to make that decision.

What an uncommon train of thought.

Anyone trying to survive wouldn't abandon supplies, especially not a methodical man like the Winter Prince. Meaning that if I'd been gathering wood when the armada had appeared, I must have seen the ships. Yet I hadn't remained to greet my rescue until later, in a different location.

Meaning I had vanished. Possibly in a hurry. Shortly before my brethren had been shredded by unseen forces, which they'd assumed were purely fauna.

I stared, denying this bullshitter my response. To do otherwise would require bending to his will.

I could remind him of what had happened to the last soldier who'd broken my trust. Though, doubtless Indigo remembered that disembowelment. He had witnessed that incident in Autumn, when I'd gutted one of his fellow soldiers in the presence of Poet and Briar. And while the troops had trusted my judgment, understanding the knight to be some form of traitor to the Crown, Indigo had nonetheless been casting me cursory glances ever since.

I would deliberate whether Rhys had recruited this warrior as a spy, but no. The Summer King's informants had been scholars. By contrast, Indigo's attitude could be a result of my falsified allegiance with Poet and Briar, which had been out of character for me. I had made the public excuse that I'd suspected Rhys of duplicity and therefore worked alongside Autumn to expose the king. While the explanation had satisfied my court, this soldier's wariness hadn't gotten past me.

Unlike Rhys's spies, Indigo didn't require the influence of Summer to motivate him. Nor did he know about my condition, because the spies hadn't gotten that far into their investigations. Instead, the knight's misgivings were rooted in something else, feasibly having to do with Flare.

With deadly calm, I selected one of the bottles and parsed its contents, holding it up and speaking in a detached voice. "I heard a disturbance in the wild and assumed some of the troops had crossed into the forest ahead of the rest. Naturally, I pursued this possibility." With supreme focus, I set down the vessel. "I understand why you're smarting that my Summer captive got away from us both—"

"I'm not smarting," the obstinate knight protested.

Cooly, I lifted my eyebrows. At which point, the man sealed his mouth shut. Cutting off Winter's prince was tantamount to civil disobedience. He might as well be asking me to extract his balls with a set of pliers.

Because he stayed quiet for a minimum of ten seconds, I trampled over the silence. "Needless to say, wood was hardly on my mind."

Once more, Indigo recovered. This time, he had the guts to grow confident. Therefore, insolent.

His eyes flickered. "Pray, was anything else on your mind, Sire?"

Two words. "The forest."

The deadly realm with its perilous rainfall and carnivorous fauna. This fact insinuated I'd been too preoccupied to acknowledge anything but the dangers my visitors had placed themselves among. Logically, I had meant to warn them. At which point, I'd gotten caught up in the presumed fauna ambush.

Indigo had anticipated a guiltier answer. However, the reply made sense, as had my numerous other explanations regarding the past year. Details about my survival to the convoy, to the nobles, to my family.

What. When. Why.

I had weathered Winter's inquiries and responded with dismissals, abbreviated versions, half-truths. While I detested removing Flare from the equation, as if she had lasted only a short while with me, my accounts had satisfied the court.

I thought of my fierce little beast. The image froze in my mind, every facet of her preserved under a layer of ice. If anyone tried to breach it, they would find themselves stripped of their flesh and missing several pertinent organs.

I respected my knights. My whole life, I'd treated them as my equals. But I had limits. Where the safety of Flare, my family, and my kingdom were concerned, let no one test me. Most of all, anyone who meant my woman harm would die graphically. And slowly, for I was known to be a patient executioner.

My expression mirrored the man's shrewdness—then exceeded it a thousandfold, cautioning the knight to remember his place. Underestimating the Prince of Winter was a fatal error. One more slip of the tongue would smack of treason and condemn him to a prolonged death sentence.

Go ahead, I silently provoked. Question the prince.

Indigo flinched and retreated a step. Much better.

But just in case. My fingers fell to the scalpel knife at my hip, and my voice sharpened like steel—refined, polished, lethal. "Is there anything else?"

"No." Indigo cleared his throat. "Nothing, Sire."

I cocked my head. "One might think you actually mean to keep the queens waiting." When the man blanched, registering that he'd neglected his sovereigns, I murmured, "Dismissed."

Spite lurked at the fine edges of his countenance. With a bow, the motherfucker grunted, "Your Highness."

Your Highness. That form of address, I had yet to reacquaint myself with. It compromised my equilibrium, as it had within seconds of my rescue, when I'd found myself surrounded by men and women-at-arms, the troops sinking to their knees and chanting.

My name. My title.

Long live ... somebody.

Indigo stalked away. After everything that had happened regarding that incompetent pissant of a monarch, Rhys, this knight wasn't my first enemy. Nor would he be the last.

Be that as it may, the shithead would not speak out again. To this court, I was too smart, too merciless to challenge unless he wanted to donate his liver to research. Moreover, Indigo valued his rank above all ambitions. It outweighed his aversion toward born souls or the unlikely notion of his sovereign protecting one.

Someone called my name. I blinked, my head snapping toward

where my grandaunts stood at the suite's threshold, with their arms entwined and their gazes clinging to me. Silvia, the sentimental. Doria, the steadfast. They had sprinted down the steps in cloaks of amethyst and sapphire when I'd returned, then wept and flung their arms around me before I'd properly dismounted from my horse and planted myself on the ground.

The blanket of snow under my boots. The woodland scents of pine, cedar, and smoke. The arctic temperature biting into my flesh.

The culture shock had rendered me useless. I'd slumped into Silvia and Doria, my face burying in the tufts of their white curls.

I had anticipated my arrival, expecting to make straight for my parents' chambers. Instead, I had procrastinated like a fucking coward, unable to carry myself there. For hours that day, I'd shut myself up with the queens in their antechamber until they urged me, saying it would be fine.

At last, I had reinforced my spine and summoned the courage to navigate the halls. Approach the Royal Suite. Dismiss the guards. Knock, step inside, close the door.

Since then, months had passed. Still, Silvia's tear ducts filled behind the rims of her spectacles whenever she saw me, as though I might vanish again.

Guilt assailed me. Yet I would do it again. For Flare.

I stepped away from the table and inclined my head. "My Queens."

"Jeryn," Silvia gushed.

"Come," Doria beckoned, motioning toward the terrace.

The women strolled outside. Behind them, I shrugged into my coat and followed, the fur slapping my calves and the chain accents of my steel-tipped boots rattling like bones. I stepped up to the railing, where the chalet castle pitched over the vista, the stone sills and overhangs dripping with icicles. Ahead, I peered at the panorama of coniferous trees. Snow powdered the needle leaves, the trunks' widths could house villages, and owls kept vigil somewhere in the branches.

No ocean surf. No buzzing mist.

This land was quiet. A whisper might cause an avalanche.

Each morning, I awoke in priceless bedding, expecting the opulence of my suite to look different. Warmer. Brighter. I expected a female body to stir naked beside me. I often caught myself leaning in for a kiss, reaching for those enduring hands, eager to flip her over, spread her thighs around my hips, and fuck her until she felt nothing but my hard cock and earth-shattering bliss.

I cleared my throat, pulling myself together as Silvia and Doria gained my side. The women flanked me like bookends. So they meant business.

Doria spoke first. She gestured behind her toward the medical den. "You spend a great deal of time there."

"I always have," I deflected while studying the view.

"Not to this extent. The people wish to see you."

"They have seen me."

In my periphery, the queens pruned their lips. My reply was not untrue. The people had seen me that first evening, after I'd reunited with my grandaunts. Emerging onto the castle's deck, I had stood before the masses, and the kingdom had cried out. The court had chanted my name, the mayhem flooding my eardrums.

In my suite that night, I had bent over a plant pot and tossed up my meal. I'd gone from being cloistered to this. Escorts, callers, well-wishers.

Swamped. Constantly.

A feast with the courtiers. A meeting with the queens and our council. Another meeting with the Court Physician. An inspection of the castle's infirmaries, medical halls, laboratories, dispensaries, apothecaries, clinics. An update on new research practices, most of which involved practices that curdled my fucking stomach, which I planned to shut down and supplant.

All in due course. Proceeding tactfully was paramount.

Another feast. Another meeting. A queue of hunters and university students, the line stretching around the castle, my subjects eager to welcome their prince home.

Finally, a visit to another part of the castle. One that my grandaunts must have heard of by now. While that trip had been overdue, it had also been a risk. To prevent widespread talk, I'd needed to make the effort look like an afterthought rather than a priority.

Be that as it may, the citizenry wanted to see me as often as my family did. It was not a request.

Doria spoke with concern. "You seem unhappy."

"Lady Noelle shall be arriving in a fortnight. She and her kin are to be esteemed guests," Silvia hinted. "You remember her, don't you? The pretty one from the glacier province?"

"Her brother will be attending as well," Doria added, prompted by my silence.

Either the sister or brother would have sufficed, if that arrangement were my desire. Yet only one preference dominated my mind, body, soul. One person.

The queens had hoped this news would alter my mood. I cast them a sidelong glance that declared otherwise, to which they exchanged fretful looks.

Doria broached, "We heard you've been visiting the fools quarter of the dungeon."

"What else did your spies tell you?" I wondered.

"That you're inspecting their living conditions—a transaction you didn't discuss with us. Among other courses of action."

That was true. To the former, I did not wish to implicate my grand-aunts should people draw an unwelcome conclusion about my visit to the dungeon, however well I'd paced myself.

The latter invoked my dealings with Summer. To avoid suspicion, Poet, Briar, and Aire had remained on the mainland when I'd arrived. With their ship docked the whole time, no one had suspected them of a thing. Not even Summer's oafish king or its astute queen.

Poet and Briar had assured me that Flare had set off on her tidefarer without incident. The news had buckled my limbs.

Several days later, the jester, princess, and knight had departed for Autumn while I met with a groveling but petulant Rhys and his better half, Giselle. Thereupon, I instigated the plan Flare and I had forged before parting ways.

To keep Summer's nose out of The Phantom Wild, I had cited unknown diseases lurking in the forest, the contagions likely unresponsive to vaccination. Considering my warnings and experience as a castaway—not to mention an authority on illness—the report had shaken Summer. The court now believed its rainforest to be contaminated and wanted nothing to do with that realm. Not even seafarers and sand drifters would venture there.

Rhys had asked how Summer could atone for my so-called traumatic misfortune. In an alternate reality, lobotomizing the cocksucker would have been refreshing. In this reality, such a crime would complicate Season relations. Not that Summer stood a chance of winning a war against Winter. But neither was that the point.

As compensation, we'd come to a documented agreement regarding The Phantom Wild. Summer had declared the rainforest neutral continental territory and placed it under Winter's jurisdiction. I had requested sovereignty under the guise of medical research. Coming from me, it was a sound reason that everyone understood.

This ensured the rainforest would remain uninhabited, its history preserved. Having the ruins under Winter's protection meant Rhys could not touch it, which would enable our clan to supply details of the ancients after all. How they had built a castle and created a diverse community, which had lived in peace and prosperity until their untimely demise. Prior to the invasion, had I thought of negotiating the realm from Summer, it would have given Flare and me a chance to expand our plan.

Nonetheless, we would add this to our list of assets. Once the time was optimal to use this wildcard, our clan would act. But not yet.

As for reuniting with Flare in the rainforest, I could not say when I'd see her again. She had her mission now. Moreover, for Winter to take its eyes off my every move would require an insufferable amount of patience.

But before then, the chasm of Flare's absence might be the end of me. My chest constricted, the knowledge calcifying.

As to my dungeon visit, Silvia misconstrued the reason. "You needn't be worried about any fools escaping. The mad woman was an isolated incident in Summer."

Do not call her that.

I contained the growl that clawed up my throat. My family didn't know any better than I once had.

With my hair tied at the nape, the crisp air bit into my jaw. I would not allow these women to think harshly of my spirited little beast. If I could not impart the truth, I would at least circulate her bravery. "Before the woman died, she saved my life. I would have drowned were it not for her."

That quieted them. I had told my queens this upon returning, but I would remind everyone until Flare was immortalized in a way she deserved.

I'd informed the court that she had vanished within the first few weeks of isolation, likely having been killed either from a carnivorous predator or one of the viruses that infested the forest. An assessment that stood to reason, since few in the Seasons expected a so-called "fool" to be smart enough to survive. Against every impulse I possessed, I had made sure to sound dismissive while recounting the story, indifference another bloody prerequisite of this farce.

And her name was Flare. Not "the mad woman."

"You appointed me to oversee the treatment of born sou—" I set my teeth and corrected, "—born fools."

"Ah. We did," Doria recalled, elbowing her wife.

"Oh, yes," Silvia agreed. "Our memories are ..."

"Stubborn?" I suggested fondly.

They chuckled. Light snow fell, its descent reminiscent of rainfall. Farther off, dire wolves hunted in packs, and elks guarded The Iron Wood.

Fear gnawed on my bones. Where was she? Was she happy? To prevent myself from caving beneath the weight of those questions, I must keep busy.

I regarded my queens with deference. "Do you have faith in me?"

"Eternally," Doria affirmed. "But we worry about you."

"It's what grandaunts do," Silvia quipped, setting her fingers on my forearm.

At length, Doria contemplated my features. "You are much changed."

Poet had echoed that in the ruins. My blood's temperature agreed. "I have an agenda."

"Then speak your mind."

"That shall take a while."

"For you, we're never in a rush," Doria replied.

I exhaled. They'd tended to me as a child when my mother and father had taken ill. They had appointed me as their successor. They'd reassured me after the siren shark attack. Always, these women had placed their confidence in me, even back when they shouldn't have, when being a healer had rendered me a monster.

"I have ideas for Winter," I said. "I will tell you, but I have a meeting to initiate first."

Doria's fingers twitched on my sleeve. Silvia's eyes trembled. I hadn't been home for long and knew what they feared, because I feared it too—that a conference meant I would be traveling. That something would happen, and I would not return.

Except I had no intention. For if I ever left these borders, I would only be tempted to find Flare, to embark on another obsessed chase for my little beast, hunting for her until my feet bled.

And if I succeeded, I would never leave my woman.

Only one thing guaranteed I wouldn't succumb to this. Flare was free. That liberty would not last if I abandoned this life, no matter how much I craved her.

"I'm not going anywhere," I assured Silvia and Doria. "Rather, someone is coming here."

"Who?" Silvia asked.

The one couple I needed on my side. To enact a plot that had been outlined in the ruins, in a dining hall with five other inhabitants.

Social and medical reform was a momentous undertaking, a gamble that would involve not only the queens and myself, but our reluctant council and a host of enemies. To make a solid case to Winter, I needed an irrefutable strategy and more than facts or figures.

No. This degree of treason required allies.

Winter needed Autumn.

54

Jeryn

Three days later, the terrace's double doors swept open. Only this time, a different pair of visitors stepped onto the platform.

Solstice halted at the threshold, made the proper announcements, and moved aside. The two figures materialized, a drizzle of snow falling around them.

Poet's raven jacket clutched his athletic frame, with a matching scarf trimmed in wide ruffles flouncing from the high collar. His fitted black leather pants, sterling-embellished boots with heels, and leather gloves stitched in a motley pattern of black and sterling completed the outfit.

A red crown of braids encircled Briar's head, and a charcoal fur mantle hugged her frame, with gray suede gloves encasing her fingers. From her earlobes, platinum stars dangled.

My hand grasped the railing so hard, the cement might crack. Yet I remained still, fighting to keep my gaze austere despite the palpitations.

The princess folded both hands in front of her, then dipped her head like a genteel Royal, the embodiment of sobriety and refinement.

"Your Highness."

Beside her, the jester perfected the same role. He arched an eyebrow—a painted blade sliced through the left orb—before inclining his head. "Winter."

Well played. I gave them a curt nod. "Autumn."

Behind them, Solstice vanished. At my instruction, the First Knight would take up residence at the medical den's entrance. Far enough from this terrace not to overhear anything, but near enough that this meeting wouldn't seem circumspect.

The doors sealed shut. The facade dropped.

Briar's stately expression collapsed as she rushed to my side, with Poet close on her trail. Shifting from ceremonial to informal, the princess seized my hands without warning, the gesture of familiarity taking me off guard.

"Jeryn," she whispered, puffs of frost falling from her mouth.

"Briar," I replied, then nodded to her husband. "Poet."

The jester stood behind his princess, with one hand braced on her hip. Not ten seconds in, patience fled me. Regardless of my exterior, they saw past the veneer, to where hysteria lurked. Another fucking second of waiting, and the terrace ledge would need repairs.

"We have not heard anything," the princess supplied.

It was all I could to keep the anguish from cleaving through my visage. I had expected this blow, yet Flare's optimism had rubbed off on me. I'd hoped my little beast had sent them a missive, something they could pass on to me. But indeed, the danger was too great, even in the safe keeping of a fauna messenger.

Poet and Briar had presumed I wouldn't possess more information about Flare. It was even riskier to send me tidings directly.

The princess gave my digits an encouraging squeeze. "She must be safe then."

By one account, this was true. If Flare had been recaptured in Summer, we would have heard about it.

Yet. Typhoons. Leviathans. Rapists. Anything else could happen.

No. If she were hurt, I would feel it.

Briar released me and inched backward, tucking herself into Poet's chest.

The perceptive jester spoke next, his voice low. "And how are you, sweeting?"

Only this once would I condone the endearment. Since returning, no one had asked me that question. Not in that way. More than my kin, these two had witnessed how Flare and I had lived in that rainforest.

The jester waited alongside Briar. Concern. Empathy. They watched me as though consoling a friend.

Is that what we were? Friends?

The notion chipped another fragment of ice from my chest. Briar had once been banished from Autumn; she and Poet had been forced apart. As a Royal, Her Highness had also been bred to keep certain public emotions in check. As a darling to the same Crown that would have sooner clamped his son in irons, Poet had worn a mask in the Spring Court for years.

Indeed. They knew how the fuck I was really doing.

My suite. My bed.

The throne room. The banquet hall.

Escorts. Advisors. Chancellors. Nobles.

I'd never felt less alone. Nor lonelier.

I diced my gaze toward the alpine mountain vista, where the peaks bit into the hemisphere like fangs. "That is irrelevant."

"You miss her," Briar interpreted gently, the truth suffocating. But when I kept my gaze averted, she set her palm on my fur-clad arm. "You will find each other again."

"And if it is not safe?"

A humorless chuckle escaped the princess. "I ask myself that every day, with my husband and our son."

"My wife isn't the only one." Poet leaned one hip against the rim and regarded me with a slanted gaze, his features brought into stark relief against the chilled panorama. "Alas, sweeting. You'll never stop asking that question, no matter if you're standing a thousand miles apart or in the same room."

I cast them a furtive glance. Amid the gray sky, Poet's green, kohl-lined eyes stood out like a sinful defiance. And how the fuck he'd managed to stride across an ice-laced terrace in those heeled boots without slipping on his ass, I had no clue. The motherfucker made it seem effortless. On that score, no one in Winter could get away with wearing such an ensemble.

Poet would turn every head tonight at the welcome feast. I'd seen him eviscerate Autumn's chaste sense of propriety merely by stalking into a room. With that face and voice, he was a walking aphrodisiac, smirking and flaunting his tongue as if he'd invented sex. Case in point, that mussed, fuck-me hair routinely looked as if his wife spent the majority of her nights yanking on the roots.

On that score, the jester would disappoint each noble and dignitary in attendance. As much as people lusted for him, the man had eyes only for one woman.

The freckles dotting Briar's countenance were more pronounced in this climate. Her plaited tresses burned through the frigid setting, and her poise balanced out Poet's fiendish appearance.

They made a striking pair. Never once did this power couple take for granted the luxury of being together. Nor did they remain ignorant of the constant threats they continued to face.

With renewed ambition, I revisited the other reason we'd convened here. The plans we had made in the rainforest. Our intentions for Autumn and Winter, the merging of our courts for the same crusade.

In The Phantom Wild, we had plotted. Now we would act. To get my little beast back someday, this must be the path.

Poet wrapped his arms around Briar from behind. We stood at the terrace edge, assessing the vista. A blustering wind slapped the fur coat against my limbs and shook the chains of my boots.

Nestled into the alpines, candlelight flickered from countless windows throughout Winter's universities and museums. It wasn't a lower town so much as a small city.

I regarded the view while addressing my allies. "For all Winter's knowledge, we have been educated singularly. Flare's false imprisonment and the incarceration of any born soul, among countless other errors in judgment, prove as much. It will take time and science but also testimony. To start, tell me what's happened since the Reaper's Fest riot. Tell me how you convinced your people in the long-term. Tell me what I don't know, then share these facts with my queens and our court. Help me to convince them."

Medical remedies only did so much, providing advantages and disadvantages. Ultimately, they couldn't be solely relied upon.

Unlike Winter, the Kingdom of Autumn had been learning differently. Avalea, Briar, and Poet's court taught born souls practical skills, valued and enhanced their inherent abilities, and treated them by mindful means as well as medical.

Poet and Briar's son, for instance. Nicu's affliction had to do with an impaired sense of direction, lacking comprehension of space, distance, and location. He could not tell the difference between north and south, the distinction between a kitchen and a bedchamber.

I recalled additional symptoms, though his parents had never volunteered further information. Back when I'd cured Briar from the Willow Dime poisoning, I hadn't bothered to ask questions, much less cared. Not that the princess or jester would have provided details about their son to the enemy. Regardless of our alliance against Rhys, we hadn't been on trusted terms.

"A family's knowledge would assist," I said. "Give Winter the information we haven't considered. I'll do what I must to prove alternative ways of treating mental conditions. This is to say, the ones that actually require assistance. This, we must also learn to decipher correctly, in addition to identifying conditions with accuracy."

Poet rubbed his absurdly sculpted jawline. "Winter needs Autumn's advice. You do realize I won't let you live this down."

Over-confident motherfucker. I gritted out, "You do realize we're standing within twenty feet of a lab equipped with sharp tools. I have a set of pinchers with your name on them."

"Evidently, you've never seen my pleasure toy collection."

"We accept your invitation," Briar said, amused by our mutual antagonism. "Every step forward is a step closer to Flare's return."

The jester's lips crooked. "Wine, first. Felony, second."

"And soon enough when it's safe, Flare will tell you where she is," Briar avowed. "In her own way, she will find you."

Her name burrowed into my skin. My baritone came out like a devoted hiss. "Not if I find her first."

Our initial roundtable with Silvia, Doria, and the council didn't go well. The meeting incited political upheaval, as well as a few tedious hissy fits from the advisors, chancellors, treasurers, chief physicians, and military leaders. Voices drifted from the throne room and into the halls, which filtered through the court, which led to gossip.

Had the prince gone mad in that rainforest?

Everyone speculated. They stared and whispered. They beseeched the queens behind my back and questioned my ability to rule.

I did my fucking job and proved them wrong. On a routine basis, I debated with my grandaunts and the council. I cut down the advisors' theories with utilitarian facts and a surplus of icy stares that dared them to contradict me.

With the jester and princess as allies, wit and wisdom became its own power, sentiment and science aligning like weapons. This consisted of rebuttals and examples from Autumn, my experience in Summer, innovative ways to improve the kingdom and its treatment of born souls, and the reasons for its importance. To my intrigue, Poet and Briar had perfected a secret method of communication involving hand gestures, proving industrious during these sessions.

After they returned to Autumn, we continued our correspondence, which included Queen Avalea. I copied Winter documents procured from universities and medical halls, then had the scrolls delivered to Autumn: decrees, regulations, historical cases, technical assessments, and alternatives for integration. Many of them were solid, to which Briar replied by underlining passages, utilizing her talent for finding loopholes. Poet added his own brand of cunning to the missives, citing ironies and contradictions to the Seasons' beliefs.

We proposed incentives to expand Autumn's cause and sway Winter. A critical hindrance was medicine. Among numerous other cures, the former contents of my vial had been developed through experiments on born souls. Heinous as they were, Winter's methods had resuscitated Flare.

It had saved her life. I would not have changed that.

As to future creations—that, I would change. The restoratives I'd created in the rainforest, along with new remedies including botanical specimens from the wild, would hopefully assist. After presenting these options to the queens, I listed solutions for replacing experimentation, including a novel form of treatment: physicians of the mind.

Moreover, we could study volunteers afflicted with various conditions, both mental and physical. The trials would be conducted with the subjects' permission, and only providing they were fully capable of giving such consent. This allotted willing participants a chance to have their health assessed and treated at no cost to themselves. Rather, they were compensated with currency or other advantages.

Physicians listened with a vested interest. They could not deny the benefits, especially the bonus of unique ingredients.

A bargaining chip. A case that validated my sanity.

Relieved, my grandaunts granted me leave to shift Winter's practices. To extract some born souls from confinement, on an individual basis.

Moderately. Slowly.

Weeks turned into months. Months turned into a year.

Rumors traveled from beyond Winter's borders—talks of mysterious drawings appearing on Summer's beaches. Intricate sketches on different shores materialized at random, the renderings created inconspicuously overnight.

Lovers on the shore, in the sea, in a wellspring, beside a waterfall, in a bed.

Guards in a tower. The faces of a hundred citizens. Depictions of a rainforest. Flora and fauna. Ruins with ancient chambers.

Renderings of moments Flare and I had shared, anonymously depicted. Reenactments of the memories Aire had sensed during the clan's visit.

A society where born souls lived freely. A community that had thrived.

This offered a connection between the ruins and its history, without revealing its existence. This was her key. One of her own making.

No one knew where the next drawing would turn up. Each sketch was created in an honest but complicated form, illustrating the lightness and darkness of this continent. It appealed to the Seasons' attachment to stories, verses, and legends passed across generations, with the creator using images to convey unspoken words.

Fool. Human.

Trapped. Free.

Hate. Love.

Reports said the artwork left onlookers breathless, baffled, troubled, furious, shamed, awed. Sometimes people cried. Sometimes they kicked the sand, destroying the sketches.

It could be a sand artisan. Or perhaps a sand drifter. Someone whose work campaigned for change, questioning the definition of humanity.

A signature. A message. A dare.

Winter and Autumn couldn't strike Summer where it most mattered. It had to be a person from the Season itself. A woman who knew its landscape, spoke its language, was fluent in its heat.

While reading the report in my suite, my mouth lifted. "Much better, Little Beast."

Two more years passed. In that time, I expanded Winter's scholarship. I eradicated the kingdom's experimentation practices on born souls. Using Autumn's model of integration, some of them lived and worked among their neighbors. Others did not.

Some Winter citizens accepted this. Others did not.

A noble tried to poison my grandaunts and learned the extent of my patience when I got him into my medical den. A hunter set a knife to my throat while I slept, but Solstice intercepted the man.

More such assassination attempts followed. Still, Winter began to change, as did Summer. My efforts paired with Flare's inspired a shift in the people.

Both courts eased their laws. Gradually, my nation set some prisoners free. Despite Rhys's tantrums, Giselle gave the same orders in Summer.

According to the queen, her husband had gone from stewing to simmering the pot. However, she had no idea with whom he'd aligned himself. Nor did our clan. That unnerving mystery had yet to be revealed.

Not wanting to be left behind, Spring followed suit in releasing select captives and slaves. Briar's ladies and her friend Eliot served as ambassadors there, which made communication go smoother.

Some liberated individuals required guidance from Autumn and Winter, which we provided. It was not an immediate revolution, but the change was considerable. It needed to be slow, to prevent as many riots, rampages, protests, and skirmishes as possible.

Indeed, those happened. We'd have been unwise not to expect it. But after the Reaper's Fest riot, our clan was more prepared.

Although the trade amendment still existed in the Fools Decree, we would eventually get to that document. Perhaps not this year or the next, but in due time.

Inspired by my actions, my grandaunts' perspectives about humanity changed, yet they faced scrutiny. Often, it tempted them to forsake the cause. Each time, I convinced them not to.

Then one day, the decisions fell solely to me.

Silvia went first, in her sleep. Doria, one month later.

Honoring their wishes, Winter buried its queens in the ice sculpture park where they had met. I hadn't gotten to tell them. On many occasions, I'd wanted to, but there had never been the right moment, never a safe one until recently when it was too late.

Instead, I spoke to their graves. In a low tone, I spoke her name, the word an ember on my tongue—hot and painful. But somehow, I knew they'd heard it.

The kingdom mourned. Then it crowned me.

The court celebrated. Then it made its expectations known.

Yet at twenty-seven years old, I showed no interest in women or men. I refused to marry, which led to inevitable whining among the council.

Regardless, only one woman existed for me.

Three years since I last saw her, touched her, tasted her. The day after my coronation, I knelt in the snow, to write something there. Something that Flare might sense, wherever she was. Something that called out to her. However, I knew.

I fucking knew. I could do much better than this.

When Mother and Father sent for me, I entered the room and sank to my knees before them. They looked older than they should have. Settled in their chairs beside a fire and with furs draped across their laps, their bodies appeared as frail as twigs.

As the nearby flames crackled, my parents clasped their hands with mine. Our three signet rings glinted in the morning light.

"Son," my father said, his blue hair threaded with strands of silver.

"Father," I replied. "Mother."

My mother grinned, her eyes the mirror image of my own. "My Jeryn."

The words ended on a hacking cough. Gingerly, my father patted her fingers while I rushed to hand Mother a steaming cup of herbal tea, the drink soothing her throat.

Always ill. Never cured.

Nevertheless, they were lucid and mostly happy. And they knew me. They knew what I'd been yearning to say, the truth I loathed to conceal. As they glanced at my vial of sand, then at me, they understood.

"You're in love," Mother whispered. "And you're waiting for her."

Not a day had passed that I hadn't yearned for my little beast. Not a night that I hadn't reached for her in my empty bed. Not a second when her parting words hadn't replayed in my head and lacerated my chest.

I love you.

In dreams, I saw her. Those burnished eyes. Her face flushed, the blood rushing to her cheeks as I stroked my cock deeply into her. Her vivid gaze worshiping a place that we'd once called home.

And fuck. Her hands.

Mother caressed my jaw. Before I could make a reply, Father prompted, "Then stop waiting."

Hope infused my blood. Winter was reinventing itself. As such, my kingdom knew I'd evolved as well.

Summer was shifting too. Because of her.

Flare had become a legend. Although her drawings didn't move everyone, because no person could accomplish that feat alone, she elicited reactions from this continent.

A conversation. A shift.

A sand artist whom none had ever seen. People tried to decode her travel patterns, to gauge which coast she would visit next, but failed because they lacked patience. Because they did not observe.

Because they had not lived and survived with her.

I consulted the locations where Flare's renderings had been discovered, as well as the dates when they appeared. The days and times were unpredictable and seemed random to most, but not to someone familiar with her wandering nature. I consulted atlases, researched Summer's shores, recalled what she'd told me about the culture of sand drifters.

I dove into my own memories of her. I might be wrong, but I had chased this woman once before. I could do so again.

On the pretense of business, I sent a dispatch to a coastline several days north of Summer's castle. Timing was crucial. The missive must be left shortly before she got there. The messenger's task was to find the appropriate shore and write a note by torchlight, scripting into the midnight sand.

I handed over a sealed note containing a cipher—my own pathetic excuse for a drawing, which indicated a place, day, and time. That, and two words camouflaged in the design.

A call. A plea.

If she wanted to. If she wanted me.

55

Flare

I wanted him. Always, I felt his mouth on mine, his arms around me, his breath caressing my skin.

Standing at the ocean's edge, I watched the sway lap over the bank, mellow waves brushing the sand. My lips tilted up. In the past three years, I had seen countless seas and rivers and islands, but this peninsula was among the most peaceful bodies of water I'd ever beheld.

Usually, I launched myself into the abyss. I would skip through the waves, swim with stingrays, dodge jellyfish, and ride marlins. I would dance naked under the sun and bathe amid mangroves. I would leap and dive headfirst.

Tonight, I stood still and admired the view. The salty breeze winnowed through my sarong and illuminated the whorls—newly inked and metallic—climbing up my bare calves. Celestials glittered, dotting the black sea with specks of light. In this ambience, I remembered the last time I stood on another beach, at another time, with someone who'd branded himself into my heart. Closing my eyes, I felt his mark on me like a special type of ink. But instead of crying, I grinned.

No other landscape compared to an ocean at midnight, perfect for secrets. Tethered near a cluster of high grasses, my tidefarer awaited me. Because this beach wouldn't stay empty once the sun rose, I needed to leave my signature and depart soon.

Gazing at the waves, I contemplated what to draw, what symbols to leave behind. Yet nothing came to me. Instead, my mind drifted to the memories that had arisen only moments ago, including all the things that had happened since the rainforest. Since my villain prince.

Flashbacks of the last few years replayed in my head …

On the boat with Poet and Briar, I spent my first hours—and after him, and after us—wanting it all back. The Phantom Wild had disappeared by then. From there, only water surrounded us, a sparkling world beneath a scalding sky. But that wasn't enough, because the ocean wasn't my home. I'd left my home behind, given up what had been mine—ours.

And maybe the rainforest was calling me to return, and maybe it wasn't too late, so I changed my mind and dove over the side. My body crashed through the surface, the aquamarine sea drowning out Poet's bellow and Briar's shout and the new storm that had arrived without warning. I swam, not caring about the nearby presence of a predator in the depths, a swordlike nose cutting past me.

Instantly, a mesh of rope had ensnared my waist. The jester fished me out of the abyss and dragged my weight aboard. And in their arms, soaked and sobbing, I let Poet and Briar embrace me.

That's when I felt it in my bones, in my throat, in my stomach. I felt an ache, an understanding. I'd hurled my body into the sea and lost my way. I'd been leaving my freedom behind without giving thought to my promise and what Jeryn had said. In one heartbroken moment, I had forgotten about the voice I could share beyond the horizon. Instead, I'd leaped into the arms of a wild ocean, with its sharks and sea monsters, desperate for reunion and willing to risk myself.

Because of that, I thought about living that one glorious year with a prince. And I realized there was a little madness there. It thrashed and thrived inside me, like it did in everyone else in this world.

Because love was madness. In this way—and many different ways—maybe everyone was a born soul.

In hindsight, I guessed it was a dangerous thing to do, to fly into that tempest, to need a person that much. To love him that much. But that feeling could also empower. My soul, filled with Jeryn, would give me strength no matter how far I traveled.

My memories were safe. So I had everything I needed.

The truth grew roots inside me, because I was somebody in this world. I'd always been and always would be. I was loved and gave love, had been cursed and blessed, by people and a legend and myself. In the rainforest and apart from it, I was somebody.

The jester, princess, and I met with Aire at a remote part of the wharf, near the abandoned boats where I'd first escaped. Under the blanket of night, we said our goodbyes and made a pledge. It wouldn't end there. We would reunite again, because that's what families did.

I sailed on, venturing to my purpose, my mission in Summer. I explored forgotten lagoons, mythical reefs, and sunken ships. I caught treasures and found prizes such as jeweled pods. When I braved markets with a hooded head—peddling my wares enabled me to survive—news circulated about The Phantom Wild, the Prince of Winter's rescue, and his survival despite the fatal illnesses that infested the rainforest. Jeryn had done his part, and people cringed while speaking of our home. Coming from the Winter Prince, medical genius of this continent, his description of viruses amounted to scripture.

Even sand drifters refused to quest near the rainforest. And no one ever mentioned the ruins, knowledge of its existence remaining unknown.

Camping apart from the masses protected me. Though, sometimes I had to lodge in less secluded places, needing to refresh my supplies. One evening, I rested not far from a bustling village. There, I heard from other passing drifters about Jeryn publicly aligning himself with Poet and Briar. And my hopes took flight.

That night, I created my first sketch. Up until then, I'd needed time to reacquaint myself with Summer, to hear what the people were saying and learn how to respond. From there, I practiced my artwork, drafting as musicians and novelists and painters did.

Squatting in the sand, I drew the Fools Tower. From dusk till dawn, I depicted the prison's height, its walls, and its spire. The images came to life, yet they didn't make me bitter. Instead, my blood tingled with power.

Inside the shape, I wrote a word. Then I left the drawing there, and as my boat bobbed toward the next distant land, I watched a child skip from the road and onto the shore. She spotted what I'd done and called out to her parents, a pair in peasant garb emerging behind her, maybe on a morning walk. They joined her by the sketch and stared.

My heart soared. I wondered if they would bring other people to see it, long after I had left. And so I did this again and again.

Wherever I went, wherever I landed, I inlaid my visions into the coasts. I drew a chain of rope, a misty forest, a droplet of rain, a community dwelling in a wild castle, a society where all manner of people lived without slaves, without hatred, without suffering. Within those drawings, I communicated unwritten words about truth and lies, captives and captors, enemies and allies, nature and humans.

While I couldn't tell the story of every born soul, because our fates and demons and passions were all unique, I could be a spark. If one person's tale could inspire people to hear more tales from others, maybe countless lives and mindsets would change. And if a cold prince could learn to love instead of hate, and if a fiery captive could learn to forgive and love that prince back, maybe many other hearts could change.

Long ago, the world had painted me. And now I painted the world.

Although I ached to send a message to the man I loved, I resisted that heartache by focusing on my art. The more of Summer I experienced, the more shapes I created. And the more shapes I created, the more I reclaimed myself. And the more I reclaimed myself, the more I owned myself, the more I found myself.

Over time, I composed thousands of messages in the shadows. Never once did I need light. Because I knew how to see in the dark.

Three years later, I'd found my voice. Turning away from the sea, I strolled along the tide, where the water met the sand. Always, I walked on the edge of things. As the water swabbed my ankles, I scanned the coastline for the right spot to leave my next signature.

The sarong whispered against my thighs. Beaded bracelets hugged my wrists, each one attached to a ring encircling my middle finger, the ornaments jingling with my movements. The melody sounded like a song.

Humming to myself, I skimmed the bank. Then I stopped. Everything in me stopped.

My limbs stalled, and my thoughts vanished like smoke. The only thing that kept moving was my heartbeat, which drummed against my chest.

Several paces away, a sketch burrowed into the sand. One that I hadn't drawn.

Located a safe enough distance from the ocean ensured the drawing wouldn't be rinsed before dawn, as if the maker had known this was my method. As if the source had intended for their creation to be found.

In all this time, I'd kept my traveling pattern erratic, lest Summer's Crown or curious spectators should try to catch me. I had earned followers and admirers. But I'd also amassed my share of foes, those who despised the content of my artwork. Either someone was emulating me, or someone had been expecting me.

I yanked the machete from a harness across my back and padded cautiously to the drawing. As the image of a familiar place became clear, my gaze seized on the camouflaged symbols indicating a date and two words hidden within.

Rule me.

The weapon toppled from my fingers. A whimper fell from my lips.

Knees buckling, I dropped to the sand, my eyes clinging to the message. With shaky fingers, I etched every line of the rainforest. Tears heated the backs of my eyes, because I understood this call. I knew what this meant and who it came from.

Staring at the plea, I melted into a weepy chuckle. He'd made his offer and left the choice to me. And now I knew what I would draw in the sand—a reply, because I had a message for him too.

Except not here. No, I'd sketch my response elsewhere.

Leaves shivered, the sound traveling a great distance to reach me from a sacred realm. Like a fated calling, the noise seemed to ask, *Are you ready?*

Wiping my eyes, I rose to my feet. "Yes."

Hellfire. Finally, I was ready.

56

Jeryn

I paced like a lion in my suite, then paced the throne room, then paced the medical den, then paced the castle deck while Mother and Father observed me in amusement, then paced before a roundtable of council members—who had no idea what the fuck kept me on edge—until they complained of neck spasms from having to swerve their heads back and forth.

Far too fucking long passed before the courier returned. He had completed the task, albeit without glimpsing her, while I'd expected as much. That little beast wouldn't be caught if she did not wish to be.

Weeks later, I sailed to The Phantom Wild, pretending to commence a research expedition regarding the landscape's viruses. I traveled alone, with the exception of Solstice—my First-in-Command knew nothing of my intentions but wouldn't report a word about me disembarking from the ship without backup—and a discreet sand drifter who cared about riches more than secrets, and who feared my retribution enough to keep his mouth shut.

Wary of exposure to illness, the captain docked only long enough for me to set foot on land. Good. I would have cut him with a look if he'd shown the slightest interest.

Dropping a sack of coins in his palm, I stalked from the vessel and waited until he and my First Knight shrank into the horizon, with orders to return in a week. Although Solstice hadn't liked following this order, I'd proven well enough that I could live here without incident. Also, issuing unbreakable commands was the perk of being a king.

Regardless of what happened next, I had a place to sleep and had learned how to survive in this environment. And for Flare, I would wait infinitely longer, should the need arise.

Patience.

I strode across the shore. No crown. No fur cloak. Only unembellished clothing, along with a scalpel knife and a necklace.

The wind buffeted my open shirt. The tide struck my heels.

My pulse rammed into my ribs. If she'd seen my message, she might be here.

With my breath suspended, I gripped my satchel of necessities and stalked toward the cove where we'd said goodbye. The ocean rocked under an orange sky. The sun ducked into the water, and the restless sea rushed back and forth.

Pulse clattering, I scanned the perimeter. Yet only a vacant coastline greeted me.

Nothing more. She had not come.

My heart shattered, crackling like glass. And well, it wouldn't be the first time she'd broken something that belonged to me. The only difference was that everything I had, she now owned. I'd made that clear in the message.

Which she must have seen. Which she had not reciprocated.

The choice had been hers to make. And hers alone.

I turned to leave at the same time a low roar alerted me, followed by a hiss. My eyes trailed the noises and landed on an unlikely trio of fauna lounging at the tree line, where the beach met the forest. The saber-toothed jaguar reclined across the sand, the boa coiled like barbed rope around a low branch, and the red butterfly squatted on a bush, each pack member regarding me intently.

"We meet again," I said. "Been watching over this realm, have you?"

Naturally, they didn't respond. After a moment's consideration, I squatted and pulled open the satchel. "Come here. I may have brought a delicacy from Winter for each of you."

I glanced up, expecting the creatures to approach. After a few seconds, I halted my movements and frowned. The pack had not budged.

Then again …

Rising with the bag, I noticed what I hadn't before. A slender rope was knotted to the same bush on which the butterfly perched. My eyes followed the cord running through the sand and ending at a tidefarer boat that floated over the sea. High reeds blocked the vessel from sight, which explained why I hadn't registered it, nor had the man who'd piloted me here.

She knew how to hide. And for all my logic, I should have deduced the obvious. The fauna weren't here by chance.

No. They were guarding the boat.

My head snapped from the vehicle to every corner of the shore. In a daze, I stalked toward the conveyance and stalled halfway. A string of letters materialized in my periphery, pulling my gaze down. To the sand. The words.

Catch me.

Potentially, a tease. Likely, a dare.

I left the cove and loyal fauna behind, a premonition urging me into the rainforest, my pace quickening. Sweeping aside ferns with one arm, I disappeared into the wild. The shadows cloaked my figure, and the sweltering heat soaked my shirt. A viper slinked across the branches. Bromeliads burst with color and perfumed the air. Simians howled from the canopy.

The mist thickened, vapor rain approaching. I smashed through the foliage and into one of the hidden cave tunnels. Emerging before the ruins, I charged up the front steps and slammed through the doors.

Across the humid vestibule. Down the cobwebbed halls.

Taking two steps at a time, I barreled up to the cupola. Emerging on the platform, I stumbled in place, the scene threatening to send me to my fucking knees. Seasons flay me, that was even before the aromas of salt, sun rays, and wildflowers flooded my senses.

Among garlands of hibiscus flowers, Flare turned from the vista at the same time I skidded to a halt. Across the divide, we stared while beams of light peeked through the canopy, creating a spotlight between us.

Fuck me to heaven. I drowned in the vision of deep olive skin and dark waves that brushed her shoulders. Like a sea queen, she wore a flowing skirt and an oversized shirt tethered at the waist, with her feet unshod. Reckless. Beautiful. I shook my head, my throat tight and my tear ducts doing things I hadn't allowed them to do my whole life. Not until this moment.

Because she had made a choice. And she came back to me.

57

Flare

I came back to him.

Across the sea, I hurried back. Across a thousand miles, I rushed back.

There he stood, filling the cupola's doorway. Crystalline eyes riveted on me, long hair dashed around his features from the breeze, and his open shirt revealed smooth muscles—but for several old scars from our time here—and the vial of sand hanging around his neck.

My eyes glistened. My heart burst.

He dropped the satchel he'd been holding. I dropped the hibiscus flowers I'd been picking.

With a cry, I sprinted across the stones. On a growl, Jeryn charged. Launching his way, my bare feet threw flecks of dust into the air. Vaulting toward me, his strong body got larger, closer.

Divine Seasons. I was on him first, flinging myself into his arms. My body crashed into his, the collision wild and desperate and everything that mattered. A tormented noise ripped from Jeryn's lungs. His hands snatched my hips and tore me off the ground, my legs hooking around his waist as he rammed me against him.

Balancing my ass with one powerful arm, Jeryn grabbed the back of my head, his gaze taking a precious moment to soak me in. Then with a snarl, his lips dove for mine. In a single move, he lunged my head forward, his lips seizing my own and breaking them open.

A fractured sound cracked from my throat as I clutched his face. Our mouths locked, fitting as they used to, as they always had. With our lips crushed, we threw ourselves into the kiss, the force of it encompassing every minute, hour, day, week, month, and year apart. And oh, this felt the new and old, different and the same.

So much had changed. Yet nothing had changed.

My nostrils inhaled needle forests and blustering winds. His touch ignited my soul. So achingly familiar, so eternally missed.

Jeryn.

The hard line of his jaw shoved forward, splitting my lips and pouring lava through my veins. In a rampant tempo, he flexed that hot tongue inside me, infusing my blood with pleasure and yearning. My cry melted into a moan, and I opened wider for him, our tongues writhing.

He still tasted of dark wine, still hissed in that same cutting way. Only now, the sound lasted longer, reached deeper. Rhythmically, he skewered my tongue with his, flexing into me until my thighs sizzled and my limbs turned to batter.

We should talk. We should slow down.

But when had we ever done anything in the expected order? And when had I ever cared about expectations?

I clasped him tighter between my legs, my breasts heaving into his torso, the sensations heady and surreal. Elated tears burned the rims of my eyes. Pained whimpers cluttered my tongue, which quaked against his own.

Our mouths clamped, the kiss shaking, tongues tangling. I weaved myself around him, welding my body to his, knotting us together. Never again, after this. Let no kingdom come between this ever again.

We lurched back only long enough to draw a sliver of breath. Then we switched angles and flew back into each other. A territorial noise grated from Jeryn's lungs, and I smiled into the kiss, my delirious moans alternating with sobbing laughter.

On a rasp, Jeryn pried his mouth from mine. "Flare."

"Jeryn," I wept and chuckled.

He shook his head in disbelief. His thumbs stroked my cheeks, my eyelashes, my swollen lips. "I didn't know if ..."

If he'd redeemed himself. If he was worthy of me.

I sank my hands into his hair, the blue mane spilling between my fingers. Tilting my head, I gave him a watery grin, because this Royal shouldn't have doubted.

"Silly man," I said.

Happiness and desire flooded my being. That, and one other emotion. A feeling that belonged only to him, an enduring bond that hadn't been severed and never would be.

Jeryn dropped his head to mine and braced me into his chest. "My little beast."

"My villain king," I whispered.

That's what he'd become. A king of Winter. Yet he was still the man who'd claimed my heart in this wild, still Jeryn, still mine.

The king swooped down, his mouth aiming for me. In a sudden mood to play, I reeled back and nipped his lower lip. The movement jutted our waists together, his heavy cock flush against the cleft of my thighs. Wetness seeped from my crease, and a throb spread to my clit.

We panted into one another. Between the gaping shirt, his muscles hitched, and his pulse drummed into my own. Our fingernails curved, biting into one another's flesh.

The king bared his teeth. "Say it," he begged.

My mouth curled. "Work for it."

Taking advantage of Jeryn's surprise, I wiggled from his arms. Shimmying to the ground and hopping out of reach, I sidled past him. He needed only a moment for understanding to dawn, a famished light honing his irises.

This, we'd always done well. As slow as a wolf, the king turned on his heel. Those predatory eyes targeted me as I sashayed backward and crooked my finger.

"Come and get what you want," I taunted.

From then to now, this hunt had never ended. He'd chased me across nations, and I had chased him back across the sea. Until the last sunset, this would be our own kind of sacred hunt.

The king prowled my way, possessiveness stretching his features taut. The blades of his cheekbones sharpened. Those clear eyes fixed on me.

For my viewing pleasure, Jeryn stripped out of his shirt. His sculpted abdomen and whipcord arms contorting with his movements, the sexy vision parching my tongue.

Matching his gesture, I plucked the waistband of my skirt, the material trembling down my legs and puddling to the floor.

Jeryn swore under his breath, his black pupils flashing like knives. I wore nothing beneath the skirt. Metallic whorls of ink danced up my calves. At the crux of my thighs, my slit glistened, the folds shaven clean, as Summer women sometimes preferred. Because he'd never seen my pussy this bare, I relished his furious reaction. Those eyes reflected mayhem, devotion, and worship.

His gaze conveyed a dozen things. That I'd stolen his breath. That I was protected. That I was his.

That he was mine.

At a leisurely pace, the king's lips tipped into a cold grin. "Run."

With a giddy shriek, I flipped around and raced past the cupola. Bypassing the stairwell facade, my toes slapped the parapet as I bled into the shadows. Heart clattering, breathing shallow, I darted through swatches of darkness.

Plumerias glinted. The sultry air glossed my skin in sweat.

How I'd missed this. The wild. The chase. Him, coming after me, seeking me, ravenous for me.

Run from me, Little Beast.

Catch me, Villain King.

Because the ruins' highest level extended from one end of the palace to the other, there were plenty of crevices in which to get lost, to stash myself. Through drooping tails of foliage, I rounded a pillar. Colorful sprays of flora illuminated the space, gold and emerald and ruby dappling my flesh.

At the sound of footfalls, I whirled to evade his approach. At another bend, his silhouette appeared, forcing me to whip around and sprint in the opposite direction.

I could have jetted down the stairs, into one of the corridors. Yet there was time for that later. From this day forward, we would have so much time.

Plastering myself behind a column, I stalled. Nervousness wrangled a smile across my lips. My chest heaved with antsy breaths, the sounds audible to him, regardless of the fauna calls pushing through the trees.

Rapt with anticipation, I twisted and peeked. He stepped into view like a specter. Loose pants gripped his waist, the V of his hips a primal temptation.

Those lucid eyes probed the expanse. And they landed on me.

I bounded from my hiding spot, letting my expression speak for itself. He may have spotted his quarry, but she'd spotted him first.

The king's mouth twitched, the faintest hint of amusement. As he stalked forward, I backed away with a naughty, joyful, beaming smile.

Despite the dark lust carving across his face, Jeryn's eyes gleamed. "Going somewhere?" he wondered, his gaze raking down my frame while unbuckling the clasps of his pants. "Think again."

"It's a big forest," I reminded him. "Plenty of areas to escape to."

"Good. Because when I catch you, I'm going to make you come for years on end. In every corner, on every surface, in every chamber, and in every fucking pool of water."

My knees quivered. "Only if I let you catch me."

Skirting the column, I untethered the knot of my shirt and let the hem tremble down my hips. Then I picked open the first closure, then the second, then the third. My breasts lifted from the material, the dusky points of my nipples hard and tight.

"Fuck," Jeryn hissed again. "Come here."

That baritone voice penetrated me to the marrow. Deep as a chasm, sharp as a blade, icy as Winter itself. Arousal puddled in the seam of my legs, my wet cunt pulsating.

Instead of obeying his request, I edged along the rim on jellied legs, expecting him to follow. Then I yelped. Jeryn's arm punched through the mist, snatched my waist, and yanked me forward. I flew across the stones, my breasts jostling as the king slammed me against him.

"Gotcha," he rasped, flanking my hips and steering me backward across the roof.

"Wrong," I vowed against his feverish mouth, my hand cupping the bulge of his thick cock. "I've got you."

A choppy breath fled his throat. "You've always had me. From that first moment on Summer's coast, you were the most stunning creature I'd ever seen. In Autumn, you became more so." Through the pants, his solid length warmed my hand. "Alluring. Intimidating." He jerked me into him, rough but reverent. "That's when you became the strongest creature I had ever seen. I could not think straight. With you, I have never been able to think straight."

My heart leaped into the sky. On a covetous growl, I snared his waistband and tugged the king firmer against me. Our mouths smashed together, clinging and rocking into one another.

As our tongues fought, we erupted into motion. Stumbling with me across the platform, Jeryn peeled the gaping shirt from my shoulders. His lips fastened to mine, his tongue flicking deftly, electrifying my skin.

I whined into his mouth, the sound brushing against his groan. My hands snaked under the open waistband, dove into the heat of his body, and found his cock primed for me, the stem hard and hot. Molten noises skidded from his mouth as I palmed the weight of his sac, draped my fingers up the veins, and thumbed the wide crest. A bead of cum rose against my digit, intensifying the pounding between my thighs.

Jeryn pinned my frame to the nearest pillar and kissed me deeper, graver, needier. Together, we shoved the pants down his limbs. The bridge of his cock rose, flushed and flared at the head, the vision wrestling an appreciative sound from me. I wanted him inside my body, thrusting eternally, climaxing forever, filling that hole, the empty space no one else could reach.

My dominant hand siphoned up to his ruddy crown and down to the seat, and his mouth clamped onto mine. We traveled naked across the level, back to the cupola. Along the way, we attacked one another, taking turns to pin the other against the next available surface.

He nailed me to a wall, gasps jumping from my mouth on impact. Scooping one breast in his palm, Jeryn gusted his lips over my nipple and spoke against the sensitive peek. "I need to know if these perfect tits taste as I remember."

His voracious mouth latched onto the bud, stretching it between his teeth and sucking. Embers blazed where he devoured me. I clawed through his hair, shoved my aching breasts firmer into his mouth, and chanted a million entreaties.

Spurred by my response, the king dragged his lips to the other breast and vanquished the last vestiges of my balance. My joints gave, but he bolstered my weight as he licked the shell, kissed my breasts, and groaned with satisfaction.

Then we were off again, steering one another across the ruins. My tongue sketched the cleft in his chin, his fingers traced my slick cunt, my teeth skated across his jaw, and his lips consumed the ledge of my ear. By the time we reached the cupola, he'd turned me into the sun—burning, flaming so hot and bright I could scorch the world.

At the top of this forest, I shoved Jeryn down onto the ledge. Overlooking the wild and the distant roaring sea, I climbed atop his lap.

At the same time, Jeryn snatched my hips, split them wide, and hauled me into his frame. My pussy bucked into his cock, the friction heavenly. I whimpered, my clit bracing his crown, sparks dashing across my skin.

Desire leaked from my body, coating the top of his erection, mingling with the fluid rising from the line of his tip. Restless, I strapped my arms around his shoulders and poised my entrance above the head.

Eyes glazed, Jeryn palmed my ass in one hand and clasped the back of my scalp with the other. "Only you. There has only ever been you."

He didn't mean strictly in the rainforest. My patient villain king had waited for me, as I'd waited for him. Three years, but not a second longer.

My eyes stung as much as his did, that single tear like a loose chip of ice. I flicked my tongue over his lashes, and his eyes darkened, the deep wells of his pupils pulling me in.

His cock twitched against my slit. My crease dripped down his flesh.

Jeryn pitted his fingers into my ass and held me firm. "Show mercy, Little Beast." He nudged his cock. "Say it."

I pressed my lips against his. "I love you."

A hiss cut through him. Then he swept his waist upward. With one steady pump, the broad head splayed my cunt.

My mouth fell open, remembering this, missing this. My thighs shook around him, my knees bending on the ledge.

With another measured piston of his hips, his cock plied me deeper, reaching higher. A moan quavered from my lips. I matched the movement, giving in kind, swatting my waist and lodging him farther between my folds.

"Say it," I echoed, gliding my teeth along his throat.

Jeryn fisted my hair. With slow, agonizing juts of his cock, he opened my pussy wider. "Your strength." His waist circled, making my eyelids flutter. "Your fearlessness." Fixing my hips to his, the king slid out and swung back in. "Your selflessness."

He contorted his buttocks, the motions rendering me delirious with want. "Your words. Your voice." Because he could hear me. Because he was the only one who'd ever truly heard me. "All of you." My arousal smeared Jeryn to the base, pouring freely now and urging another groan from him. "I fucking love every piece of you."

Then he lunged upward, his cock pitching to the hilt. I arched, a cry vaulting from me. Seasons, yes.

We didn't wait, because we had done enough of that. We charged into each other, moving in desperate sync. Ushering my gaze down to his, Jeryn launched his hips, and I bore my pussy down on him, our waists beating, our faces pressed.

"I have thought of this," he grunted. "I have wanted this every second since you left."

"I did too," I whispered. "I touched myself every night, made myself come to memories of you."

The king rasped and hurled his cock into me, keeping pace with my swinging waist. The points of my breasts rubbed his pecs, which rose and fell in rapid succession. I hunched into him, lost in a stupor, lost in his arms, lost in this forest. And there, I found my treasure.

My love. My home.

With sweat drizzling down my spine and my hair in disarray, I unraveled like a loose knot, my stomach waving, grinding on his lap. I savored the feeling, his cock expanding, the prow splitting me open. I bobbed up and down, flinging my hips into him, moans shooting from my mouth, loving how he watched me, his gaze piercing.

With our bodies attached, mist poured onto us. We made love and fucked until everything beyond faded. I feasted on the sight of him, how the sharp inclines of his face tightened with each measured pass of his cock, my pussy sealing around the rigid flesh, his control slipping with every whip of my ass.

Heat swirled in the place where we pumped into one another. The volcanic noises I made grew louder, longer, faster. Jeryn's cock hardened more, spreading my walls, the traction building.

He saw it happening, felt the combustion approaching. I wept, because it was too good, too soon. Yet Jeryn only magnified the torture by accentuating his movements and grabbing me tighter, tacking me to him so that I felt every puncture of his cock.

"You're going to come," he hissed. "You're going to do that now."

"Fuck," I sobbed. "Please."

Please not yet. I wanted more, everything, always.

But before I could delay, my senses climbed that zenith. My cunt tensed and then burst into the ether. Eddies of heat scattered, my pussy convulsing and draining down his cock.

Jeryn made a serpentine noise. His waist didn't let up, siphoning in and out while I broke apart around his thrusts. I shouted from the pit of my lungs, the tumult blasting like dynamite, like a roaring ocean, like a heartbeat.

Linked around Jeryn's powerful bulk, filled to the brim with him, I writhed like a bonfire. I came for him, for myself, for us. Then I collapsed, the climax flowing through my veins, stirring my body to life instead of exhausting me.

The king held me fast, his gaze intent as I rode out the crescendo. And still, his waist kept thrusting, his cock stroking my walls and reigniting me. Not seconds into this bliss, he riled up my senses again.

Unable to keep still, I arched my waist and released Jeryn's length. Elated by his protesting grunt, I unwound my legs from his waist, scrambled off his lap, and reached for him. My villain king catapulted off the ledge, knowing what I sought.

Spinning me toward the vista and nipping the side of my throat, he murmured, "Eyes on the wild, my beast."

My pulse clamored as he ran his palms up my biceps and lifted them. Twining my arms over his shoulders, Jeryn threaded my fingers atop the nape of his neck. Flush against his torso, I felt his heart galloping, his cock lifting against my ass, the flesh glazed in my climax.

Securing me to him, Jeryn glided his knuckles down my side. My eyelids hooded at the sensuous maneuver, then my head rested on his collarbone as he sank his fingers between my thighs. Oxygen caved from my lungs as he felt the shape of my pussy, the soaked groove, and the ruched flesh of my clit.

Muttering an oath, he swirled the liquid over my bare folds. The gesture stoked my cries, his name dangling off the tip of my tongue. I squirmed, then sighed when he pulled away, ghosted his hand down my inner thigh and hooked beneath my leg. Raising it off the ground, Jeryn fanned my limb outward and planted my foot on the rim.

On instinct, my other leg extended, splaying me fully. Humming, the king banded one arm around my midriff, joined his free fingers with mine at his nape—and lashed his cock into me.

Like a rope pulled taut, I snapped. My spine arched into Jeryn's muscles, a moan clotting my throat. The position changed the angle of his flesh, the crown striking high and narrow.

From behind, Jeryn resumed his pace. He threw his pelvis into me, the width of his erection hitting that dazzling spot, the place where my screams resided. In tempo to his body, I jostled upward, taking his thrusts, my pussy drenching him.

I matched his cadence, using the ledge for momentum and rolling my backside.

Jeryn panted into my neck, his breath fraying at the seams. "Kiss me," he demanded. "Kiss me, Flare."

Twisting my head, I captured his mouth with my own. I swallowed his groans, sweeping my tongue over his and licking every sound. Avid, Jeryn burrowed his lips as if I might disappear.

Our mouths braced, moans colliding there. He pounded into me, and I pounded back. The brunt of our movements grew rougher, faster, headier. Ardency had us clasping one another, an attempt to fuse ourselves together, forming something unbreachable.

Jeryn flexed his tongue and pitched his cock, the motions far from composed. I cried out and reeled my cunt, sucking him deeper. My fingers met with his over the back of his neck, and his other arm pressed me close.

"I would kill for you," he swore, thrashing his waist into my ass. "I will live for you."

Venting for air, I pleaded, "No. You will live *with* me."

For a third time, we moved in unison. Jeryn released me and slung his cock from between my thighs. Vacating the ledge, I whirled on him, and we flung ourselves into each other.

The king hoisted my leg over his hip and fastened me there. I grabbed his ass in one hand and seizing his profile with the other. His free digits carved into my hair and hauled our foreheads together.

This was my favorite way to fuck him. Standing tall, face to face, equal in every way.

Dark blue lined those frosted eyes, the orbs catching me in their grip. I rubbed my nose with his, prompting a hiss and an instinctual flick of his waist. Rocked to the core, I cried out again as Jeryn hauled his cock between my folds.

My pussy grabbed his solid flesh as it pumped. Like this, his tip struck a place that wrenched a holler from me.

"Jeryn!" I encouraged. "Oh, Seasons. Right there."

"Where, my beast?" He exaggerated his movements, snapping his hips and splitting me open for him. "There?"

"Yeah," I said, nodding vehemently.

Fuck me there. Love me there.

Flush with each other, we stared and vaulted in place, mist and sweat raining down our skin. Anguished sounds fell off my tongue, in tune with our movements. Jeryn throttled his waist between my legs, his fingers bracketing my thigh, my knee steepling over his lurching ass.

We shouted into one another. The noises merged into a single one, loud enough to fell the trees, powerful enough to stir the ocean. It went on and on, my body sealed to his, rubbing and shaking and gyrating.

The weight of his sac hung heavily, the sensation enticing as the wide head of his cock stuck in and out. His tempo stretched me, filled me, fueled me. My pussy clutched his girth, the length toughening, the abrasion turning me into a firecracker. Any moment, I would ignite, blast into the canopy, and explode into a thousand flecks of light.

Jeryn's gaze moored itself to my own, eyes flashing, the slopes of his face tightening. I knew that look. I loved that look. Those eyes like glass, so clear on me, easy to see through. They revealed everything, including the heat pressing against the edges of his being.

I'd seen him come infinite times, knew the harsh slant of his features meant he was close. Blood mottled his glistening chest, the size of his cock broadened, and his muscles shuddered. The impending release gushed to the crown of his body, his vigorous cock soaked by me. His fingers burrowed deeper into my backside and scalp, and his tongue pressed against the wall of his teeth to restrain a bellow.

He was suffering, holding back, waiting for me. The knowledge kindled me anew.

Releasing his ass, I slid my hand up the side of his frame, tracing every toned muscle. My palms skimmed his lunging waist, the track of his spine, the hewn surface of his abs, the plates of his chest. Jeryn's gaze flickered, awe and chaos churning there.

My hands alone did this to him, I realized. Maybe they always had.

My free fingers cradled the ledge of his jaw, my thumb stroking his profile. With the other hand, I continued my ascent, gliding and sketching over his biceps, his pecs, drawing a path to his heart.

When my palm landed there, Jeryn's pulse went wild. It slammed into my hand as though trying to break through and reach me.

Leaning down, I brushed my lips over that spot and kissed. A stricken noise blew from his lungs. I gasped as Jeryn caught my chin and hefted my gaze back to his. The pupils blackened to a point where I saw my reflection, my golden irises dominating his vision.

Then I gasped again as Jeryn's mouth shoved into mine. His tongue pried open my lips and drove inside, stoking me with feverish laps. A moan split from my throat, his kiss in tune with the sinuous thud of his hips.

He worked his cock, fucking me beautifully. Keening with bliss, I clamped around him, my pussy fluttering. Once more, the heat built in the nexus of my legs, every stroke of Jeryn's waist edging us to the brink.

On a hiss, he quickened his pace and wrenched his mouth away, the better to watch my response. I mewled from the short, shallow juts of his hips. The muscles of his abdomen clenched, the flat of his stomach grazing my aching clit.

I met his enthusiasm, matched his fervor with swats of my waist, my cunt rippling around him. Jeryn's mouth hung ajar, his breath thick and hot. Yearning to disarm him completely, I withdrew from his jaw and dove my fingers between us, the place where our bodies locked. Coating my fingers in slickness and traces of cum, I quested my hand to his lips.

While splaying a set of fingers over his heart, I trailed the opposite digits across his slack mouth, charting its shape and then dipping inside. A feral noise cleaved from Jeryn's chest. His lips closed around me, devouring my fingers and tasting us.

Tasting the flavor of our lovemaking.

My turn. I pulled away from his mouth and sucked the same fingers, my head swimming as our combined arousal seeped into my tongue.

Then our lips slammed back together. I seized his face while he squeezed my thigh and cupped the back of my head. We flew at one another, fast and deep and loud.

Pleasure spiraled at the crux of my legs, stalled at the precipice, and dropped off that cliff. Not into oblivion. But into eternity. My pussy convulsed, and his cock spasmed, and a prolonged scream tore from my body.

Jeryn hollered my name, his body shattering. Liquid heat streamed from the crown and spilled into me. I clutched his jaw, coming for a second time, coming with my villain king, watching the rapture tear his features to shreds.

We shouted and clung and didn't let go. Never would we let go again.

With my cunt still pulsating, I sagged into Jeryn, and he slumped against me. We staggered, his arm shooting up to a low hanging branch and steadying us. Our eyes met, and I chuckled in breathless exhaustion while a grin dabbed at the corner of his mouth.

Struggling to recover, Jeryn sobered first, the candidness of his gaze quieting me. Our hands roamed, unable to stop touching, needing to prove this was real. Looping beneath my other thigh, he hoisted me off the ground and strapped those steel arms across my back, his cock still inside me. Linking my ankles over his ass, I wrapped myself around his frame, hugging him back.

For a long time, we stayed like that, inhaling and exhaling. I clasped him tighter, and he gathered me closer, his fingers skating up and down my spine, my hands lost in his damp hair.

Separated by kingdoms, I'd spent three years dreaming of this moment, hoping for this moment, fighting for this moment. All this time, it had only ever been this man. And his earlier declaration had made it clear—the feeling had stayed mutual.

Jeryn pulled back and nuzzled my face until I chuckled again. At the sound, he descended deeper into the crook of my throat, humming and biting and enjoying how I squirmed, because he knew my ticklish spots.

Inching back again, he brushed the tousled hair from my forehead, then carried me from the cupola. The kisses and touches continued as Jeryn traveled into the heart of the ruins, then into the cave tunnels, where the grotto waited.

The surface gleamed, strands of light dancing across the walls. Aside from that one shark attack, none of its kin had appeared during the time we'd been living here. Yet Jeryn froze on the threshold, his eyes searching the depth for a shark. I saw it then, how his panic hadn't lessened over the years.

Predatory waters might always be a source for him, but the fear dwindled as I caressed his cheek and whispered. Because if he would be my safety, I would be his.

We didn't have to go in, I told him. We had other cave pools to choose from.

Still, my touch eased the trenches in his visage. Focusing on me, Jeryn made his decision and waded into the pool, not wanting to be ruled by his past at every turn. Slowly, his intakes evened out, and while this respite might not last, it worked on him for now.

He'd chosen to bring us here, turning what had once been horrifying into something better. That was promising. As for the rest, we would live through it minute by minute, day by day. Together.

Although I hated to detach from him, Jeryn slid his cock from between my walls. He bathed me, and I splashed water down his torso, then we submerged ourselves.

Jeryn pinned my slick flesh to his and dove that evil mouth beneath my jaw. "I'm going to fuck you again," he swore into my throat.

I whimpered and curled into him. "Here."

"Soon," he agreed in a husky timbre.

But first, we told each other everything. Despite his craving, Jeryn resisted with only a minor growl. I slipped behind him, my breasts resting against his shoulders as he reclined into me and hooked my legs over his stomach.

The last three years unfolded in whispers, interrupted by kisses and Jeryn's mouth searing a path across the whorls on my calves. He liked the markings, inked symbols of my own choosing.

From somewhere above, I heard the ocean run its wet fingers over the sand. Despite other elusive places such as The Wildflower Forest and The Lost Treehouses, people still questioned the details about this realm.

How had it remained uncharted for centuries? How had a born soul been the first one to see the map hidden within that legendary song?

Maybe because nature didn't discriminate between born souls or anyone else, because it was diverse in its flora and fauna, as varied as the people who lived on this continent. And maybe the elements had cloaked the forest through a trick of sunlight.

I would say the forest chose its visitors for a sacred plan. My villain king would say no such thing. And that was okay.

The reason all these mystical places existed across the Seasons could be science or faith, happenstance or destiny. Though for once, I wondered if it might be both. Logic and madness. Explicable and magical. Yet always wild, such as humanity itself.

We talked about this until my hand got sneaky. Reaching in front and sliding down his granite chest, I snaked my fingers around his cock, which lifted beneath the water.

A hiss diced between Jeryn's teeth. "Fucking little beast."

I purred into his ear. "Where should we mate in this grotto?"

"Wherever you want. I'm at your disposal."

"Oh, I'm never disposing of you. I'm keeping my king."

"Much better, because I'm not letting you go again. As I said, I plan to make you come in every part of the forest."

The question crept from a crevice inside me, a place that still worried this would end. "Only in this forest?"

Taking the hint, Jeryn moved without hesitation. My hand fell from his cock as he straightened, twisted, and hefted me in front of him.

Planting me on his lap, he framed my cheeks. "Come with me," he said. "Come to Winter."

I blinked, my heart skipping a beat. I had expected us to meet here, in the ruins on a lasting basis. A safe haven where no one could judge or condemn us.

Yet Jeryn's face reflected a greater ambition. One replete with determination and devotion.

I knew this man better than to assume. He didn't mean to divert my mission or change my purpose. He would never ask that of me. Yet this went beyond a compromise. It was a risk and a chance and a dare. It offered more than a secluded realm. This promised everything, from danger to happiness.

Mistaking my silence, he rushed ahead. "I don't mean ... I would never ask ..."

My eyes prickled as I set my fingers on his mouth. "I know what you meant."

Relief cemented his voice. "Let Winter be your home, as Summer has become mine."

"Split our time."

"Yes," he urged. "But not apart."

Not apart. Together.

I would travel through Summer, and he would rule his nation, and we would meet every month, alternating between my Season and his. Although Jeryn had claimed I'd vanished in the rainforest and likely perished from predators or an illness, that tale would be easy to reverse, thus painting me in an impressive light regarding my resourcefulness and survival skills. He vowed to keep me safe in Winter, which would be possible now that our kingdoms were shifting, the people changing. I would stay in his court for however long I wished, whenever I wished.

We would show the world that even hate could turn into love. This would be our key. Our new mission.

After three years, we'd earned this.

First, we would spend time here, reuniting with the rainforest and each other. Then we would set out for a world of needle forests and blustering winds.

"Winter is yours." Jeryn's throat constricted. "If you'll have me."

Through my tears, I grinned and knotted myself around him. "I warn you, I might set your kingdom on fire."

"I'm counting on it." My villain king hauled me forward, his thick crown poised at my entrance. "And if you'd like, we can stop somewhere on the way."

I sighed in pleasure, lowering myself on his cock, my pussy taking him deeply. "Where?"

As Jeryn rocked me on top of him, his lips quirked. "Where we began."

58

Jeryn

Two weeks later, Flare nestled into my chest as we sat in a private courtyard with our clan. Distant maple trees rose into the sky, and copper foxes skulked across the pasture. My little beast marveled, pointing at every detail with excitement. Each time she did this, someone in the group explained what she was seeing.

I would have assisted, but the sight of her awed face and the gold dress hugging her curves distracted me. I tilted my head, watching those eyes glow in wonder at the colorful leaves, the harvest fields, the library-style castle, everything. We'd been in Autumn for three days, yet her amazement had not waned.

Wrapping my arms tighter around Flare's waist, my mouth tipped sideways. Then my grin flattened into a glower when I noticed Poet from across the blaze. Lined in smudges of kohl, his green eyes glinted with amusement. The fucker enjoyed my besotted expression and was deciding how best to antagonize me about it.

His wife rested in the same position as Flare. Wearing a cerulean gown with a short standing collar across the back of her neck, Briar lounged into the jester's torso, her husband's muscles visible beneath a fitted jacket.

Briar's ladies—Cadence, Posy, and Vale—engrossed themselves in conversation with Flare, who wrote her responses down for them. The women talked over each other, eager to hear about our year in the rainforest. More than once, they murmured suggestive comments that included terms such as *survival smut* and *jungle porn*, then gestured at me when they thought I wasn't paying attention. Whatever else they said made Flare chuckle, because she'd never been shy.

Eliot joined us. Flames illuminated the minstrel's scruff jaw, the blond bun tethering his hair, and the lute tattoo extending down the side of his throat. He indulged Flare's music requests, a stringed tune from his instrument filling the air.

As for my unexpected metamorphosis, it had taken a while for the minstrel and ladies to believe it. Flare's presence, as well as Poet and Briar's endorsement, had swayed them more than I had. Despite my attempts at congeniality, their expressions had made it clear: I knew shit about how to be friendly. Only after watching me with Flare had they accepted my change of heart.

Aire returned from patrolling the vicinity. Despite this courtyard being restricted to Royals, one could not be too careful. My arrival with Flare had caused a stir, whispers among this court flowing like wine, which would only increase in Winter.

Briar and Poet had arranged a celebratory gathering, replete with candlelight and sumptuous fare. But first, essential matters needed discussing. After several days of rest, it was time. Yet another reason for this location, away from witnesses.

A curvaceous figure entered the courtyard, her red hair arranged atop her head. Everyone rose, curtsied, and bowed. Queen Avalea glided our way with a convivial smile, her body swathed in a violet gown.

Reaching out, she grasped Flare's hands. "You make a welcome addition to this band."

Flare bobbed her head, then used her leaflet and quill to write, *Thank you, Your Majesty.*

Before taking her seat, the queen scrutinized me and whispered,

"Spend your life deserving her. That's an order."

The inclination of my head satisfied Avalea, who settled beside the princess and jester. Then a final shadow entered the courtyard, the hooded female causing Aire to frown in trepidation, as he sometimes did in her presence.

Ever the gentleman, he pulled out a chair for Aspen. She faltered, the skin of her neck flushing under the mantle before she lifted her chin and sidled past him, which made the knight sigh as he reclaimed his seat.

"Behold, the comic relief has arrived," Aspen declared while perching on Cadence's chair arm. "In case anyone missed the town crier's announcement, I've inherited Poet's vocation, minus the orgies and kink fests. I'll be training with him as the next jester celebrity, with a talent for livening up treasonous roundtables."

Poet's nefarious grin belonged in an erotic novel. "Careful, sweeting. I'm a hard act to follow."

"How hard?" Cadence wondered, then shrugged innocently when Briar pruned her lips. "What? I'm just saying."

"Well, don't," the princess scolded, albeit good-naturedly. "You have enough consorts to keep you entertained."

"A lady can never have enough," Cadence boasted. "Credit my Spring origins, but I'm enjoying not having to choose. Multiple love affairs are fun. Anyway, I was only teasing."

"I mean, your husband also left himself open for that one," Posy chuckled.

"I never leave myself open for anything," Poet remarked. "For I'm always intentional."

Ugh. Seasons forbid.

In any event, the stowaway wasn't serious. Her lies had increased in frequency over the years, especially when the fraudulence discomforted Aire, who valued honesty as if it were scripture. At seventeen, not only had Aspen grown as tall and voluptuous as Her Majesty, but the female's tongue had gotten even snarkier.

Safety aside, another unspoken quandary dismayed the knight.

His brows crimped as he watched Aspen, hunting for something he couldn't locate.

The conference proceeded. To start, we still lacked intelligence about Rhys's plans and conspirators. Considering how much time had gone by, and accounting for the skills of every member present, this should not have been the case. Yet even Queen Giselle hadn't uncovered anything, despite having the misfortune of sharing the man's bed.

Poet consulted a chalice of merlot, which he circled lazily. "That motherfucker can't be working alone."

"With the right manipulation, he needs only to light a match," Briar contributed, her expression daunted. "Reaper's Fest proved that."

"One of the Seasons' elites?" Cadence wondered while twirling a lock of dark green hair around her finger. "It's not like he hasn't gone there before."

"That's too simple." Eliot set down his lute, propped his elbows atop his knees, and counted off his fingers. "He already went after the crafters of Autumn, the scholars of Winter, and the performers of Spring."

"Then he got greedy and broadened his reach," Posy said while balancing Vale's limbs on her thighs. "The general public came afterward."

"Commoners and courtiers," Vale summarized. "What better group to incite for a riot?"

"Okay, so who's left?" Aspen wondered.

"This is where you jump in, handsome," Cadence prompted Aire. "Aren't the elements sending you any of those creepy signals?"

The knight had been contemplating something in the atmosphere. "My abilities are not without their limits."

Flare cocked her head toward the flames, then her wide eyes swerved my way. Our thoughts converged, drawing the same conclusion.

We spoke in unison. "Defenders."

Every head swung toward us. From their perspectives, Flare had mouthed the word, reacting too viscerally to write it down for the group. Nonetheless, my voice and her slow pronunciation made it clear.

Flare had spent almost a decade under lock and key, whereas I merely needed to remember Indigo. To this day, the knight overstepped and underestimated, thinking I didn't notice him auditing my every move. Dismissing the soldier would have been circumspect. Instead, I kept him close.

Knights, soldiers, guards. This stood to reason. Rhys had recruited spies, then used his influence to mobilize citizens. Now he would go after the defense, enlisting trained fighters from within every border.

A chunky ring glinted from Poet's finger as he tapped the stem of his chalice. "A Seasonal army."

Vigilance creased Queen Avalea's features. "Do you have evidence?"

"No," I replied. "But we shall."

"To amass a Seasonal army without the courts knowing would require years of effort," Briar deliberated. "That would explain why it's taken us this long to discover anything."

"An underground operation," the jester surmised. "In the meantime, he'll wait until we believe we've won. 'Tis likely when the fucker will strike—once peace is within our grasp."

"Would he risk waiting that amount of time?" Posy doubted. "An intermission would give the Seasons an extended window for change."

Flare took up her leaflet and quill, holding up the paper for everyone to see. *Not that amount of change.*

"Not to that extreme," I agreed. "Laws have loosened, practices have been altered, and a percentage of captives have been liberated. But freedom in totality will take longer."

A generation. Perhaps multiple generations.

Between medical, educational, and social reform over the recent years—four thus far, if we counted from our initial meeting in the rainforest—we had made tremendous headway. But not yet on the scale we intended. To say nothing of how the populace treated liberated born souls like lepers and death targets. At least, in Spring and Winter, where progress was still vulnerable.

Avalea's gaze slid across each face. "Provided this is Rhys's true course of action, we must be certain."

"We'll continue spying," Briar petitioned. "But we do it through his budding army."

"Whoever they are," Poet said. "Wherever they are."

For however long it took. Which could be a decades-long investment. The king's endeavor would likely require even more years than had already passed, so whoever took on such reconnaissance would have an abiding commitment ahead.

One voice murmured through the grim silence. "I will do it."

We glanced at Aire's taut features as he stared into the fire. Being the First Knight made him the ideal candidate. As an informant, he would blend in with the troops. Avalea gave her approval, followed by Briar and Poet.

Aspen's attention jumped from him to the queen. "What about me? How do I help?"

"By staying out of it," the knight snapped.

Although the hood concealed the female's expression, there was no mistaking the offense in her smoky voice. "I'm a fighter too."

"But not an advanced warrior," Aire corrected.

Offended, Aspen rose from her perch beside Cadence. "Give me a target."

The knight raised his brows, as if daring her to say that again, to command him as if he were of a lower rank. "Excuse me?"

"Give. Me. A. Target."

Aire wavered, then mellowed his tone. "You have already proven your worth, Aspen. That's not what this is about."

She bristled. "And I don't need your supernatural intuition doing me favors."

The knight's jaw locked while searching her face for a second time. His expression struggled with something, as if pushing against a blockade. "This is not intuition, it's common sense. You're too inexperienced."

"Don't treat me like a rookie."

"And don't undermine my rank."

"Just because you lead an army doesn't mean you can order everyone else around."

"Why do you constantly fight me about this?" he grated in exasperation. "I took a vow to serve this nation. It's my duty to safeguard this clan. I'm protecting you!"

Aspen swerved and flung her axe toward a lowermost branch. Her weapon hacked through the ligament, which crashed to the floor. Focused. Capable. She'd barely had time to register her target before aiming.

Eliot whistled. Flare and the other women grinned in admiration. Lounging like a panther, Poet raised an eyebrow.

Validated, Aspen swerved toward the knight. "Can an advanced warrior do *that*?"

Everyone watched as Aire reclined on impact, as if the blow had struck him instead of the branch. The pair fell into a staring contest. Until suddenly, the knight's mouth clicked upward in bemused resignation.

"Brazen creature," he relented.

Aspen gave a start, taking that response as an acknowledgement. After another moment, her voice turned saucy. "Why, thank you."

The group broke into chuckles, though Aire ruefully shook his head. "Nonetheless, I must take this path alone."

"I agree," Avalea said. "I'm sorry, Aspen."

Each of us concurred. She was no longer a child, had gained experience by playing an involuntary assassin for the Masters, and brandished her axe like an extension of herself. Thus, Aspen's ambition wasn't unwarranted. But while the female had excellent skills in sleuthing and had begun training with the troops, she wasn't a veteran soldier. This level of risk necessitated only the most qualified participants.

Aspen flinched, but lifted her chin with dignity. "Raincheck, then."

The First Knight hesitated, yet a faint grin tilted his mouth. "Brazen *and* headstrong."

Nonetheless, he didn't succumb to her request. And I suspected she would have argued for a guarantee, had the man's smile not disarmed her.

A sheet of paper materialized in my periphery. Although Flare could have spoken the words to me and not been overheard, her handwriting stretched across the surface, indicating she didn't want to get everyone's attention.

Aire has a premonition about Aspen.

My countenance tapered. After taking a second look at the individuals in question, I recalled the talk between me, the jester, and the knight in the rainforest four years ago. At one point, Aire had glanced at the door where Aspen had disappeared, then he'd made a comment.

My senses provide a service to others. Not to myself.

I glanced down at Flare, who had twisted to meet my gaze. She shared Aire's intuitive nature, though on a different level, so something in his demeanor must have struck her.

Duty aside, this explained Aire's vigilance toward the girl over the years. I didn't exactly subscribe to omens, but I understood how others reacted to them. Possibly, the knight weathered some type of superstition regarding the female.

Whatever his precognition, it could be innocent. Or it could not be.

It could have something to do with the group. Or it could only be about her fate.

If the honest knight anticipated this would affect the clan negatively, he would speak up. Otherwise, it wasn't our place to investigate this theory. Not unless we saw a clearer reason to probe.

Borrowing the quill, I wrote my reply. *We'll wait and see.*

To which, Flare nodded after reading the words.

The clan scheduled another conference to address details of this new phase in our plan. Once that was settled, Cadence vacated her chair with Posy and Vale, the trio venturing to the banquet table. The meeting having adjourned, Eliot joined the women.

Avalea left to retrieve a young boy who bounded from the Royal wing's exit. Dark, shaggy hair that swept his shoulders. Defined cheekbones. Wide-set, green eyes that leaped from his face. Vocal cords that chimed like a silver bell. The youth sprinted across the bricks and followed a garland installed from the door to our fire pit.

Nicu. Poet and Briar's son.

At the age of ten, the boy required color-coded ribbons to aid his sense of direction. With practice, the need had lessened, though the jester and princess suspected this would never fully abate.

Their son crashed into Flare, who welcomed his hug. "Sun empress," he greeted. "Your eyes have lit a fire."

"And yours have given it warmth," she gushed, having discovered Nicu's inherent skill for reading her lips.

The boy launched my way, expecting the same treatment. "Frost king!"

"No," I said, the word stalling him from coming near.

Poet rolled his eyes as if I were useless. While children did not intimidate me, I'd hardly ever claimed to be a doting individual.

Not that it ultimately dissuaded Nicu, who pasted himself to my side anyway. "Do you have a fallen star for me?"

"He means a snowflake," Flare explained for my benefit.

While no one else heard her, they grasped the nature of our exchange. Frowning, I glanced at the princess for aid, who pantomimed and encouraged me to hug him back.

Awkwardly, I patted the boy's shoulder. "Er, there there."

Poet pointed toward his son and disclosed to Briar, "He did not get his taste in kings from me."

Stimulated by everyone's presence, Nicu unpeeled himself from my arm and shouted, "Party!"

"Ah," the jester gloated. "Now *that*, he got from me."

The boy raced to Aire. "Come spin, but leave your wings here."

Apparently *spin* meant dancing, and *wings* referred to Aire's broadswords. Unsheathing his weapons, the knight set them beside the pit. "At your service, my liege."

As Nicu yanked on his sleeve and dragged him away, Avalea sighed. "Nicu shall miss him."

Aspen's head veered between the queen and knight. "Miss him?"

"When Aire's gone," Briar clarified with a wistful expression. "Gathering intel on Rhys's budding army means traveling for a long time." She twisted toward her husband. "We must do something special to bid him farewell. Once the time comes."

"Aye." Poet grinned like the devil. "Aire loves being the center of attention." He jutted his chin at me. "Much like Mr. Personality over there."

Flare's shoulders shook with mirth. My gaze skewered the jester, but Aspen's voice cut off my chance to retaliate.

"For how long?" she asked.

"Months," Poet guessed. "Years."

"It's too soon to tell," Avalea informed.

Aspen went still, her expression impossible to gauge beneath the hood.

The queen abandoned her seat and approached the group as they formed a circle dance. The jester purred something into his wife's ear and pulled her into the fray. At the last minute, Briar snatched Flare's arm and hauled her with them.

Twisting over her shoulder, my little beast gazed at me with bright eyes. "Come," she said.

"Soon," I rasped.

I wanted to watch her first. Happy. Free. Like this, I could stare at my woman for eternity.

As Flare melted into the revels, the corner of my mouth lifted, then dropped as Aspen approached her axe, its blade still affixed to the branch. Witnessing Aire grin at something the ladies said, Aspen ripped her weapon free and charged through an abutting gate.

But while the girl's sporadic departures were common, Flare spotted her leaving. She caught my eye, worry creasing her face and resurrecting our earlier exchange. Silently, we communicated. It didn't hurt to know more.

I nodded to Flare and strode in the female's wake. Halfway down a neighboring lawn, I located her retreating form. "Stowaway."

With a sigh, she wheeled around. "Assassin. Stowaway," she listed. "It's my fault, I know. I used to make everyone call me Someone. Naturally, people got creative after that. But I do have a fucking name."

"Aspen."

"Thank you."

"Aspen."

"What?"

"Dry your eyes," I advised.

A discerning pause. Her defensive voice wobbled. "I'm not crying."

"Clearly," I stated dispassionately. "Otherwise, the salt from your tears would leach into your skin. Which would hurt."

Yet another pause, confirming my speculation. Not only that, but she had forgotten to include "Brazen Creature" among her assigned monikers. Though, I doubted this had been accidental.

This route led in two directions. One, toward additional courtyards. Two, past the barbican, then down the brick road carving through the maple pasture, lower town, and harvest fields before bleeding into the beech forest. Though, I could not say which path she would choose.

Aspen kicked her toe against the ground and feigned nonchalance. "So what's the cost for medical advice?"

I would not be a competent doctor if I didn't know where this was going. Stepping forward, I instructed, "Show me."

Aspen wavered, then rolled up her sleeve and held it aloft for my examination. The lacy pattern reminiscent of wood grain, plant vines, and blossoms scrolled across her skin. Similar to tattoos yet textured in certain places like scars. It looked as though she'd been born from roots instead of a human womb.

Questions were essential. No, they did not hurt. No, they did not impair the girl's movements or give her adverse symptoms. Yes, the pattern covered the rest of her. And yes, she'd been born this way.

Following my inquisition, Aspen pulled back and shoved down her sleeve. She lifted her chin despite the split in her voice, like a twig about to break. "Can you fix it?"

The wellspring in The Phantom Wild might erase the markings, as it had from Flare's throat. However, that body of water presently resided too far away. And that was not the point.

I'd never been a coddling man and would not start now. But I could offer reassurance. "I cannot fix something that is not a problem."

She deflated. Hazel eyes flickered beneath the hood, gazing to where the open gate revealed the knight. Ducking her head, Aspen adjusted her cloak, smoothing out the wrinkles as if cognizant of its drab brown color and humble stitching.

"Must be nice to be a courtier," she said. "To have attributes."

Aspen lacked nobility. Yet she possessed the latter—curvy, tall, feisty—irrespective of what she thought about the pattern entrenched in her flesh.

Be that as it may, physical traits were irrelevant to Aire. He had never given Aspen's skin a second glance, much less any part of her anatomy. He was not a satanic being who preyed on innocents.

Strictly, he did not see Aspen that way. No honorable man would with a young girl. And although pity took me by surprise—doubtless an influence of Flare—I would not endorse Aspen's hopes. Regardless of the knight's upcoming quest, Aspen's seventeen years to Aire's twenty-seven made this an impossible discussion.

Rejected. Resigned.

That was how this female sounded. Whether toward her condition, the view, or both, it was hard to say.

The wind buffeted a tail of crimped hair that dangled from her hood. She spoke while staring into the courtyard. "What does it take to prove you don't need something?"

I squinted. "Tell me why you're asking."

"No reason."

"There is always a reason."

"Are you calling me a liar?"

"Why would I do that?" I deadpanned. "You have a name."

Under the cloak, her pupils flickered to me and gleamed. Walking backward, she shrugged one shoulder. "Much obliged, Winter King."

So indeed, she was leaving the premises. "You need a carriage."

"Actually, I've never needed much." Sauntering away and raising both arms in a what-can-I say gesture, she bullshitted, "I'm secretly a vampire who shapeshifts into a bat. No one will bother me in my dark form. How else do you think I completed missions for the Masters?"

"Rather tough to carry an axe that way."

"The axe shifts too," she called over her shoulder, not missing a beat.

I watched Aspen vanish down the lawn. She was hiding something. But whether it was related to Aire's undisclosed sensory perception wasn't clear.

Boots cut through the grass, the swagger familiar. I restrained a hiss as Poet materialized, his hands buried in the pockets of his leather pants.

Halting at my side, the jester's silken voice inquired, "Are you thinking what I'm thinking?"

I scoffed. "Is it possible for us to share the same thought?"

Considering Aspen's penchant for disappearing acts, Poet must have noted her absence.

Staring into the distance, he murmured, "Everyone has their secrets."

And not every secret was nefarious. Likely, Aire had foreseen some manner of doomed fate for the girl. All the more reason for him to look out for her.

Though, Poet grasped something else about Aspen. "Broken hearts. Faults and fools."

"It is a crush," I dismissed. "She will recover."

"Did you, sweeting?"

"Fuck off. What I feel toward Flare is not a passing fancy."

"In which case, anything's possible."

I grunted. Fair enough.

Candles pulsed from the castle, with its brown masonry and shutters. For several minutes, Poet and I studied the landscape beyond. The Wandering Fields shivered, their pathways capable of leading intruders astray for an eternity, swallowing them whole until delirium and death came knocking. An effective yet macabre form of natural defense, especially for Autumn.

"Anything is possible," Poet repeated. "Including whatever else you think Rhys is hiding."

I almost respected the man's shrewdness. Because we consulted each other before anyone else, I had spoken to Flare about this first. As for the clan at-large, I'd been pacing myself, waiting to be certain. Yet I had forgotten not to discount this jester and his resourceful wife. Likely, Briar suspected the truth behind my silence as well.

Not for the first time, I thought back to that day in Summer, when I'd met with Rhys in his throne room, and he'd emphasized a point that shouldn't have needed emphasizing.

I have no other spawn.

In the rainforest, I'd neglected to share this comment with the clan because I hadn't taken it seriously. The recollection had only prompted me to vocalize the broader notion of Rhys's penchant for keeping secrets. But lately, I'd been thinking better of this.

"An heir," I said.

Poet's head whipped in my direction. "You mean, his son."

Shaking my head, I drew out, "Not that one."

A beat of silence followed. "That's … not what Briar and I saw coming. You're saying he has an illegitimate kid."

"I'm not saying. I'm speculating." I turned to face him, my fur collar scraping against my jaw. "If so, he doesn't want the world to know about them. The enigma is why."

It could be fear of his wife's retribution, because perhaps Giselle didn't know about the man's infidelity. It could also be his pride for maintaining an untainted dynasty.

Except I knew about guarding familial secrets. As did Poet, who'd hidden Nicu from the Spring Crown for years.

Following my recap of Rhys's comment, Poet debated. "'Tis a matter not handled lightly."

Indeed. Of all people, the jester understood the vulnerability of this subject. As far as we knew, the king's mystery offspring had done nothing wrong and hardly deserved to pay for their father's crimes.

Still, this could be an advantage. Or it could be a lost cause.

Time would tell. For tonight, we let it go.

Poet glanced in the courtyard's direction. "Before I snatch my wife, drag her to the nearest corrupt spot, and fuck her senseless, allow me this." He gave me a sidelong look. "You deserve Flare."

I still loathed this pain in the ass. Yet the words closed their perceptive fingers around my chest. The place where all things related to Flare existed, a gear that needed only to be twisted for the rest of me to respond automatically.

The jester relished my speechlessness and smirked. "I always get the last word, sweeting."

Before I could retort, he sauntered back to the courtyard. Trailing him, I watched the scene unfold.

Briar's ladies gyrated against the minstrel. Avalea spun with Nicu and Aire. Occasionally, the knight craned his head to search for a member who wasn't there, his brows furrowing.

Poet snuck up behind Briar and spun her to face him. She chuckled as he pressed his forehead to hers and brandished a wicked grin, steering the princess backward until they slipped around a corner, likely to Briar's private grounds where the fucking would commence.

Later, I would confide in Flare about Aspen and Aire. Just as we would talk about many things we'd need to prepare ourselves for.

Until then, the rest of this night was about us. No one else.

Sensing these thoughts, my little beast agreed with me while twirling like a flame and catching the heat in my gaze. Jutting her hips, she crooked a beckoning finger and lured me with those golden eyes. I stalked after her, pursued her, chased her. When I seized Flare's ass and jerked her into me, she gasped with laughter.

We swayed, not caring who saw us. Her warmth melted through me, her pussy covertly rubbing against my cock in a destructive way.

Skimming her palms up my torso, Flare spoke against my lips. "What are you thinking?"

"That I love you," I murmured. "That I must have you."

She nipped my jaw and teased, "Only if you ask nicely."

"I shall never be nice," I hissed, digging my possessive fingers into her flesh.

Flare sashayed while guiding me toward the door leading into the Royal wing, where we shared a suite and a very large bed. "Except to me."

I followed her steps, because I would follow her anywhere. "Except to you."

Always, my exception. Always, my undoing.

And tonight, I would fuck her amid the fire.

59

Flare

Tonight, he fucked me amid the ice. In a Royal suite of mahogany wood and navy drapes, a fire roared within a stone hearth. Before those crackling flames, two bodies rocked together, my shadow blending with his, our silhouettes rolling like waves.

A fur blanket slumped around my hips as I straddled the king's lap, arched toward a ceiling of intricate beams, and lost my breath from the sensation of his mouth on my skin. Jeryn bowed his head between my breasts, kissing the place where my heart beat, a hot exhale and a cold hiss rushing against that sacred spot.

It belonged to him. Just as the deep pulse drumming from his own chest belonged to me.

With a final snap of his waist, Jeryn's cock wrung a cry from me. With a last rippling clench, my soaked cunt drew a groan from him.

We shuddered against one another, coming slow and long.

Afterward, I sank into his frame, and he nestled me close as we stared into the fire, basking in the rapturous aftermath. Jeryn nuzzled my throat, making me chortle and shove him down, the better to see this private spectacle. Sprawled on the rug, with his arms crossed behind his head, he admired me looming over him.

Naked and astride Jeryn's cock, I traced the side of his face. My villain king. Mine forever, until the last sun set.

Outside, flurries drizzled from the sky like fallen stars. The blustering wind howled, along with a resident dire wolf. The day had only begun, dawn barely rising over mountains fringed in needle forests.

The world outdoors called to me. Jeryn quirked an amused brow, knowing what would happen. I hadn't been able to keep still from the moment we'd arrived in Winter, in a carriage pulled by towering stags. He'd loved watching me marvel at every drop of snow, every pine tree, every warm drink, every furry creature, every wing of the castle. He had shown me endless places in this Season, and there was so much more to discover.

As he expected, I hopped off his lap. The furs slipped from my body as I whipped around, hastened past intricately cut glass doors, and raced from our suite. My bare feet sprinted across the terrace overlooking alpines, redwood timbers, and a frozen lake. Wild snowfall dashed around my face, the cold stinging yet invigorating.

Puffs of frost blasted from my lips. Not bothering with any of the extravagant robes or coats Jeryn had gifted me—blue velvet and purple silk and gray cashmere—I flung my arms overhead, shut my eyes, and welcomed this new tempest.

Heat brimmed down my back. A handsome shadow loomed from behind as Jeryn approached. Waiting until I'd had my fill of the snowstorm, he swaddled a fuzzy cloak around my shoulders, the hem brushing my ankles, then rubbed my arms.

Shivering, I leaned into him, and he strapped his arms around my middle. This was freedom and happiness and love.

Jeryn's voice filled my ear. "Tell me what you would like to see today."

"Everything," I whispered.

"Ambitious. Adventurous. It's a good thing I have patience." The sated husk in his tone curled my toes. "I'm at your command, Little Beast."

I laced my fingers with his. "I warn you. I'm rather daring. We might end up somewhere dangerous."

"So be it. We'll survive."

Yes, we would.

Jeryn had gradually introduced me to his kingdom, starting with all the landscapes I yearned to see. Always attentive to how I felt, what I needed. Always protective to the point of terrifying his subjects. This hadn't changed about him, because only I saw the softer parts.

For now, we played roles. I was his Royal guest, the Summer drifter who had crashed on an island with him and saved his life more than once. Miraculously, I'd turned up alive despite Jeryn's previously staged theory that I had died once we'd lost track of each other in The Phantom Wild.

My survival skills impressed Winter, especially since I hadn't succumbed to any of the rainforest contagions Jeryn had listed to the world. He wasn't the only one who had lived there for a year, without getting struck by a virus. To this, Winter credited our resourcefulness and cited pure luck graced by the Seasons. And well, they weren't wrong.

As for what became of my tattoo collar, we told everyone the truth. The rainforest had washed it from me.

This still didn't mean anyone wanted to go near the so-called contaminated forest. We would make sure to keep it that way. At least, until the time came to reveal more.

Jeryn and I had our plan. We would let the court grow used to me, the way Autumn had slowly gotten used to Briar, Poet, and Nicu. I proved what they'd finally been learning, how this world needed to understand more about madness and the nature of born souls.

I had my demons like everyone else. But I wasn't what Summer had painted me to be. Winter was realizing that too.

Although many in this court looked at me with suspicion or bitterness, some were intrigued. Maybe there would always be enemies. Such was the life of a ruler and a rebel.

Yet it was worth the risk.

Meanwhile, Jeryn and I kept our bond a secret. Hidden in plain sight, like the rainforest. A private passage between my suite and his made that possible.

Soon, we would stand before this court and share our union. Once it was safe, we would shout it to the world, with our clan beside us.

Whatever lay ahead, we would endure. If we could survive a dark rainforest forged of legend—our second home, where my fauna pack dwelled—and if we could overcome our pasts, we could overcome anything.

Ahead, candlelight sparkled from a city of museums and universities and chalets. The air carried the scents of woodsmoke and *him*. Excitement fluttered through me as I craned my head, searching for a glimpse of a snowy wolf or the infamous Iron Wood hidden in the alpines.

In a few days, our clan would be traveling here, our plans against Rhys and the threat of invisible enemies growing more perilous by the day. Yet regardless of the distance between Autumn and Winter, unity blossomed with each battle fought and won. With them, I felt the makings of a stronger bond, not merely friends but a family.

Jeryn kissed my shoulder. "You shall freeze."

"Don't you know?" I teased. "I'm fire."

A delighted yelp launched from my mouth as he whipped me around. Those crystal eyes glittered, and his lips parted as if what he saw robbed him of breath.

"And you have melted me," he swore.

No one had ever looked—*looked*—at me that way. Like a woman and a goddess. Like a lifeline. Like a human being. Like anyone else on this continent, yet like no one else in this universe. My heart kindled as though he'd lit a match.

I laughed as he snatched my thighs and hauled me off the terrace floor. Based on the low growl slicing from his tongue, I knew what this man wanted. Divine Seasons, we never got enough of each other.

With my legs knotted around Jeryn's waist, I stroked the harsh angles of his face. "But we're not done yet."

"Indeed," he hissed against my smiling mouth. "We shall never be done."

As the snow fell, my villain king snatched my lips with his. Then he carried me back inside, back to the pile of furs, and back to the flames.

60

Aspen

Six months later

At parties, something always broke. Whether a pricey glass or a fancy vase, the casualty inevitably went down, spilling glass or ceramic shards across the floor. But other things could shatter too. Things people couldn't see, because they didn't look closely enough.

My fingers clutched the gate bars. Between the intricate ironwork, I peeked into the maple pasture, where our band hosted a farewell revel.

Eliot played his lute, his eyes gleaming at a nobleman with dark skin and gray hair, who stared back with a smitten expression. After a slow burn courtship, the pair had been going hot and heavy ever since.

Meanwhile, the ladies threw back their heads and laughed.

Queen Avalea and Nicu ignited a lantern, letting it soar into the clouds.

In the shadows, Poet whispered dirty talk against Briar's mouth, something pornographic based on how she curled into him.

Jeryn pinned Flare against a tree while she playfully dodged his kisses, making the king work for his snack.

Beneath an arbor, courtiers flocked around a knight, each of them wishing him well on the confidential Autumn mission to which he'd been assigned. At one point, the soldier grinned politely at something a lady said, his gesture staining her cheeks a fresh ballerina pink, the exchange containing enough sweetness to rot a person's teeth. Such a perfect damsel, with a perfect hourglass figure and perfectly manicured fingers. Just like the rest of them.

It wasn't the first time he'd attracted a fan club. Neither would it be the last. All of them would still be here when he returned from his crusade.

Poet had said it could take months. He'd also said it could be years.

My eyes stung, but I sucked it up. Like the Winter King had once guessed, tears hurt when they struck my flesh.

At that moment, Aire's head lifted. For an entire thirty seconds, his eyes—the blue of a midnight sky—searched the pasture.

I clenched the bars, the husk inside my chest throbbing. I pretended that gaze sought a girl who wore a hood, that he could see through any barrier and find her, that she occupied a tiny corner of his mind.

Wishful thinking. Pipe dreams.

His gaze flickered in concern, failed to locate me, and returned to his audience.

My chest splintered like wood chips. Again, something always broke at these shindigs, but it wasn't always the stuff others noticed.

Smoothing out the secondhand gown I'd saved up for, I released the bars. I'd been invited, had gotten dressed up for the occasion, but honesty? Because sure, I could be honest sometimes, I didn't feel like tossing back shots of hard cider and getting shitfaced tonight. I'd only embarrass myself in front of him, and if my sloppy tongue went rogue, I might admit something I shouldn't.

Below my sleeves, I glimpsed the wood grain and leaf pattern disfiguring my hands. Swallowing the lump in my throat, I arranged the cloak and shielded my features. Through the lower town and past The Wandering Fields, I trekked into the beech forest. In that amount of time, I broke a record and managed not to cry. Yay for me.

My mangled heart was another matter. At this rate, I'd need a hammer and a few nails to repair the damage.

Not three seconds into the woods, a voice cut through the night. "Do they suspect anything?"

I halted on the leaf-strewn avenue and ground my teeth. The asshole had arrived earlier than expected.

At his question, guilt and fury punctured my chest. I couldn't do this anymore.

"Go fuck yourself, Majesty," I grunted, moving to leave but yelping in pain when King Rhys seized my bicep and crushed it in his fist.

Wraithlike, the man popped from the shadows, his long-ass mustache blending like soot with his black robe. "Mutation," he sneered. "You forget yourself. I'm a king, your superior, and I know where you live. I know where your mother sleeps, should you fail to cooperate. So let's try this again. Do they suspect anything?"

I bit my tongue hard, leashing the words. But when I thought of Mother resting defenselessly at home, my voice forced its way through. "They don't know about him."

Him. That was all I'd gotten out of this dickhead, which was a lot more than I'd wagered. Why King Rhys kept an illegitimate heir a secret couldn't be the spoils of a one-night stand. In Autumn, that would be a scandal. But in every other nation, this douchebag could denounce a bastard son.

So yep. Whomever Rhys had messed around with behind his wife's back, the consequences had a sharper edge. Something shady as hell.

In any case, I was being only half-honest, since I couldn't guarantee the clan didn't know anything about the chink in Rhys's armor. Poet might have already guessed. Briar too. They were the hardest to trick. Except Jeryn was the smartest, Flare the most imaginative, and Aire … he was the most intuitive.

Any of them could find out. At any time.

Whereas His Royal Dipshit had only pulled this skeleton from his closet because he didn't think anyone would believe me if I publicized the news. And with my mother's life in his grip, I wasn't about to try.

Turned out, my axe stunt on Reaper's Fest hadn't been forgotten, when my weapon had pinned Rhys to the pyre. If I hadn't possessed the skills he'd needed, this man would have committed his ten-thousandth war crime and already had me decapitated for humiliating him.

His eyes squinted like the pits of a spoiled fruit. "What else?"

Shit. Under his scrutiny, betrayal tasted like piss in my mouth. "They know about the Seasonal army."

The king grated. "Then steer them in a different direction."

I hate you. And I hate this. And I never asked for this. And I want out. I won't let you hurt them. So help me, I'll hack off your nuts with my axe first.

True. I was a first-rate liar. Even I bought that empty threat, at least for a second.

It hadn't started out this way. I'd teamed up with the clan, then Rhys had cornered me six months ago by angling a blade at my mother's heart while she'd been sleeping. Proving how easily he could get into our home without me realizing it, he'd dropped an ultimatum at my feet.

The problem was, deceiving the cleverest band of revolutionaries on the continent for much longer was going to be impossible. The only reason I had managed thus far was because I'd gotten lucky.

But luck eventually ran out. It always did.

Rhys cocked his inflated head. "Is there a problem?" And when I refused to answer, enlightenment glossed his pupils like slime. "Ah. The knight in shining armor."

I made the mistake of stiffening. To which, he sneered. "You care about those filthy rebels, but him in particular. Foolish girl. He's a grown man, a decade past your age, and a soldier of noble birth with a court full of admirers. In short, he's out of your league. And what are you?" Rhys spat, chiding me for having the audacity to fantasize. "A penniless peasant with a heathen mother who should be in chains and a deformity too grotesque to show the world."

My chin wobbled. Someday, I would be older. But as for the rest, Rhys's snub burrowed in like the markings covering me from head to toe.

Yet if he wanted to rub salt into the wound, he could waste his precious time. Although that gash had widened into a crater over the years, I refused to be easy pickings.

Eyes watering, I raised my head beneath the hood.

Rhys tsked. "Pathetic little pauper. He will never look at you in any other way. The only thing you're good for, is what I say you're good for. Liar. Cheater. Killer. That's what you are."

Correction. That's who the Masters groomed me to be. What's more, this lazy-ass tyrant was now taking the credit, capitalizing on the fruits of dead people's labor.

Pitting Rhys with my best eat-shit-and-die glare, I taunted, "Must be one hell of a scary prince you've created, for you to be this spooked about his existence. One would think he's got power over you."

Something unprecedented flashed in the king's eyes. Something like fear ... and shame.

Recovering from the sucker punch, Rhys gripped me hard enough to bruise. I gnashed my lips, repressing a cry as he leaned in. "However long it takes," he threatened, his charbroiled breath hitting my ear. "Get it done."

Then he slithered into the bushes, where his cult waited with a set of horses. Mist choked the trees, their golden leaves trembling.

That dickhead may have me temporarily under his thumb, but it wouldn't last. It might take years, but I'd find a way to outsmart him one day. I'd beat this wanker of a king at his own game. Whatever I had to do, I'd protect my mother and the clan. Even if it meant keeping my enemy close, duping the people I cared about, and losing their trust.

I thought of my friends, who had embraced me, who'd been nice to me, who welcomed me into their circle. Like a masochist, I pictured their disgust if they ever found out. The expression on Aire's face if he learned the truth.

Liar. Cheater. Killer.

Rhys hadn't been wrong. But with all the names I had ever carried on my shoulders, he'd forgotten one.

Traitor.

Aire and Aspen's spicy story is next in book 5.

Want steamy NSFW character art of Poet and Briar's reunion scene from Burn?

Sign up for my newsletter
to unlock an exclusive digital download,
for 18+ subscribers' eyes only:
https://nataliajaster.com/newsletter

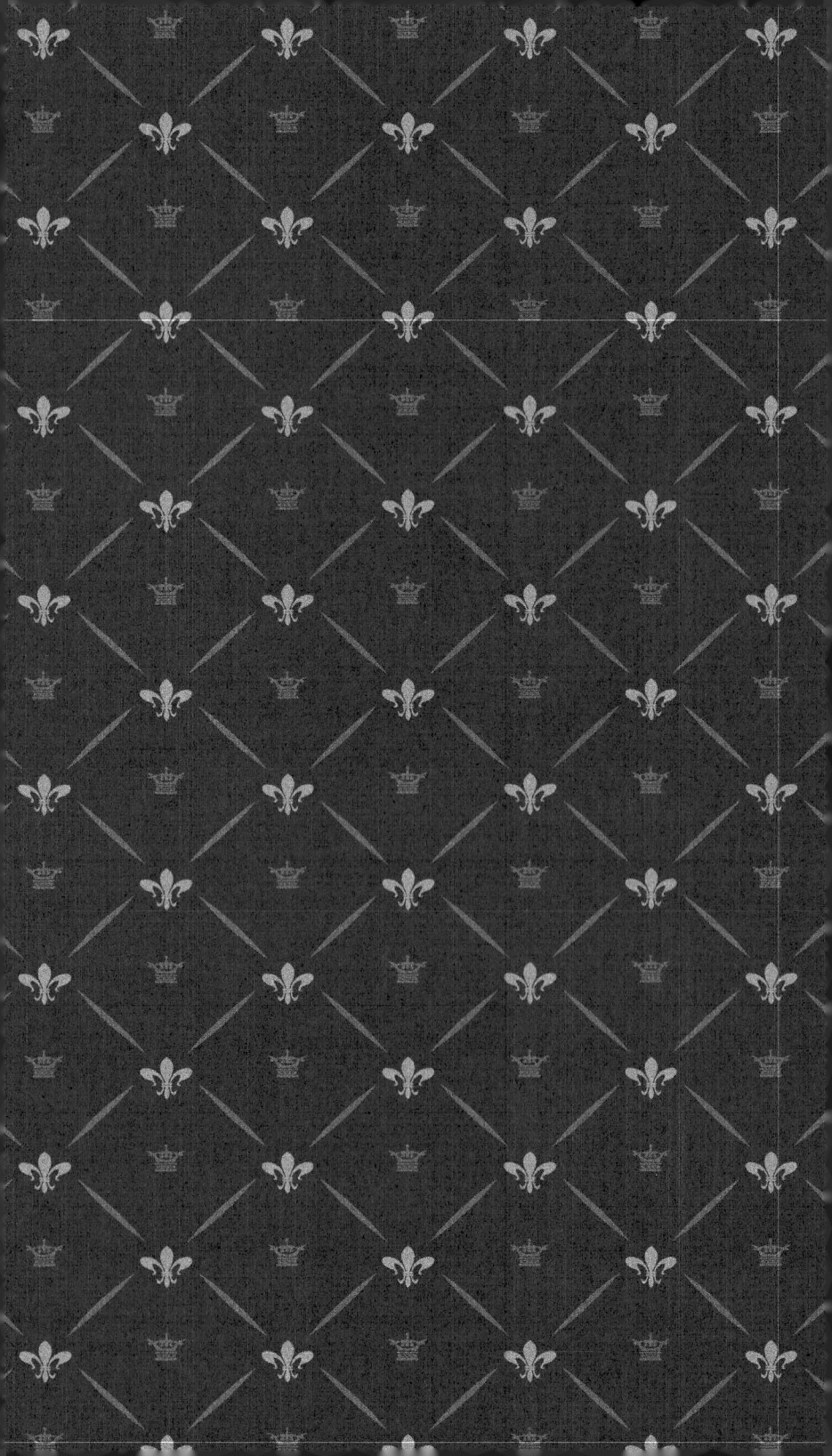

Author's Note

Wicked hell! Are your hearts still intact? You're not alone, sweetings. Mine went through the ringer with this one, but the journey was worth it.

Without a doubt, this was among the hardest stories I've ever worked on. I say this with every book, but I feel it acutely here. If anything, it was certainly the most challenging of the series thus far.

Poet and Briar were a tough act to follow, especially because they had three books in which to captivate you. Whereas Jeryn and Flare had one chance to make you fall in love with them. Hence, I knew this was going to be an immersive deep dive. I hope they stole your hearts as much as they did mine.

Despite this being the second edition of a romantasy I wrote years ago, rekindling Jeryn & Flare's story and evolving it into something darker, spicier, and more complex was a major feat. Exciting. Terrifying. Intimidating. All of it.

Jeryn's character pushed my boundaries. Although he said and did things that made me uncomfortable, it was essential for two reasons. One, it kept his character authentic. Two, it exposed the full scope of this world. And because his love for Flare dismantles his hate, it shows how even a villainous soul can change.

Flare's ethereal nature is a striking contrast to Jeryn. I love when opposites attract, and she balances him with her kindness, imagination, and spirit.

What has blossomed between them is an enemies-to-lovers passion I'll never forget. Through all the rage, tension, heartbreak, heat, and happiness, these two have discovered an unbreakable bond. One that will help to move kingdoms.

And how about our fierce clan of revolutionaries! Naturally, Poet insisted on being mentioned, as well as his sweet thorn, Briar. It was sheer bliss reuniting with this power couple, as well as the rest of the ensemble. Rest assured, they'll play key roles in the last two books. You haven't seen the last of them, sweetings.

Aire and Aspen are up next!

Grumpy-sunshine. Forced proximity. She falls first, he falls harder.

For age-gap reasons, and because Foolish Kingdoms is a saga that will span nearly two decades by the end, their story will have a BIG time jump. Get ready because we're returning to Autumn, then finally to Winter in book six.

Aire and Aspen's scorching hot story is coming in *Lie* (Foolish Kingdoms #5).

Make sure to follow me on Amazon for release alerts.

And if you've come this far in the series, thank you so much. Blood, sweat, and tears went into every book. And I cannot wait to do it again, to continue this crusade with you, and to fight beside our fearless couples.

XO,
Natalia

Acknowledgments

Thank you to the court of beta and sensitivity readers, who generously offered such incredible feedback for this story, plus some wickedly enjoyable (and naughty) reactions. You guys pushed my skills and helped to make this a better story.

My wholehearted gratitude to Michelle for your beta prowess and eternal friendship.

To Kat from "Kat's Corner, Proofreading, Editing & PA Services" for your proofreading magic and all the real-time comments that made me grin like a fool.

To my family, for your support and patience.

To Roman, my soul mate and silver-tongued troublemaker.

Always, to the Dark Revelers hype team. And to everyone who has read, loved, and shared The Dark Seasons universe with this bookish world.

You are kindred. You are Royals.

About Natalia

Natalia Jaster is a fantasy romance author who routinely swoons for the villain.

She lives in a dark forest, where she writes steamy New Adult tales about rakish jesters, immortal deities, and vicious fae. Wicked heroes are her weakness, and rebellious heroines are her best friends.

When she's not writing, you'll probably find her perched atop a castle tower, guzzling caramel apple tea, and counting the stars.

Come Say Hi!

Bookbub: www.bookbub.com/authors/natalia-jaster

Facebook: www.facebook.com/NataliaJasterAuthor

Instagram: www.instagram.com/nataliajaster

TikTok: www.tiktok.com/@nataliajasterauthor

Website: www.nataliajaster.com

See the boards for Natalia's novels on
Pinterest: www.pinterest.com/andshewaits

Printed in Great Britain
by Amazon